**SELECTED AND CONDENSED
BY READER'S DIGEST**

THE READER'S DIGEST ASSOCIATION LIMITED, LONDON

CONTENTS

Acclaimed crime writer Robert Crais brings the streets of Los Angeles to life in this taut thriller about ex-con Max Holman. He's a bank robber who is determined to go straight, but on the day of his release, after ten hard years in prison, everything starts to go wrong when the son he barely knows is murdered. It seems like a random crime, but when the victim is a cop—especially a cop with a criminal for a father—the motives are never simple.

THE TWO MINUTE RULE

ROBERT CRAIS

In 1774 one of Captain Cook's ships returned from the South Seas with a small bird on board that was destined to become extinct. Centuries later, the bird is the obsession of a wealthy collector who asks London-based natural history expert John Fitzgerald to help him track it down. Fitz's quest becomes a fascinating journey into the personal life of an 18th-century British naturalist, whose secret love affair almost cost him his fame and fortune. A debut novel of rare originality and emotional power.

THE CONJUROR'S BIRD

MARTIN DAVIES

BENEATH THE SNOW

CAROLINE CARVER

307

The icy, empty expanse of the Alaskan wilderness provides a stunning backdrop for this novel by rising star Caroline Carver. When brilliant research scientist Lisa McCall goes missing in a snowstorm near the small settlement of Lake's Edge, her sister Abby flies out from England to find her. One look at Lisa's ransacked cabin is enough to tell Abby that her sister is in terrible trouble. Risking her own life she sets out to find her before someone else does . . .

In the tradition of Sebastian Junger's *The Perfect Storm* comes a new, riveting account of underwater adventure from journalist Robert Kurson. When divers John Chatterton and Richie Kohler came across the twisted wreckage of a WW2 German U-boat off the New Jersey coast in 1991, they knew it posed a tantalising puzzle—especially since no official record of any such sub existed. Risking their lives, they returned again and again to the site in an attempt to solve the mystery. A true story that reads like a thriller.

SHADOW DIVERS

ROBERT KURSON

453

the two minute rule

Robert Crais

When four Los Angeles policemen are gunned down in a seemingly motiveless attack, a lot of people want answers. No one more so than Max Holman, whose son Richard was one of the officers.

So why is it so difficult for the grieving Holman to get information . . . and why are the police being so cagey?

Prologue

Marchenko and Parsons circled the bank for sixteen minutes, huffing Krylon Royal Blue Metallic to regulate the crystal as they worked up their nut. Marchenko believed Royal Blue Metallic gave them an edge in the bank, made them fierce and wild-eyed, Royal Blue being a warrior's colour; Parsons just enjoyed the spacey out-of-body buzz.

Marchenko suddenly slapped the dash, his wide Ukrainian face purple and furious, and Parsons knew they were on.

Marchenko screamed, 'Let's get this bitch *DONE*!'

Parsons jerked the bolt on his MP5 rifle as Marchenko swerved their stolen Corolla towards the parking lot. Parsons set the safety, careful not to place his finger near the trigger. It was important not to fire until Marchenko gave the word, Marchenko being the leader of their little operation, which was fine by Parsons. Marchenko had made them both millionaires.

At 3:07 p.m. they turned into the parking lot and parked near the door. They pulled on black ski masks, as they had twelve times before, then pushed out of the car, the two of them looking like black bears. They were both decked out in matching black fatigues, boots and gloves, and load-bearing gear strapped over the armoured vests they had bought on eBay. With so many extra magazines for their rifles and Glock pistols bristling from their vests, their bodies looked swollen. Parsons carried a large nylon bag for the money.

Broad daylight, as obvious as two flies in a bowl of milk, Marchenko and Parsons sauntered into the bank like WWF wrestlers entering the ring.

The first couple of times, Parsons had worried that they would be caught, but this was their thirteenth armed bank robbery, and robbing banks had turned out to be the easiest money either of them had ever made.

When they went in, a woman in a suit was on her way out. She blinked at their black commando gear, then saw their guns and tried to reverse.

Marchenko kicked her legs from under her and pushed her to the floor. He raised his rifle and shouted, 'This is a robbery! We *own* this bank!'

That being Parsons's cue, he raked the ceiling with two bursts from his rifle that knocked loose ceiling tiles and shattered three rows of lights. Debris and ricochets spattered the walls and pinged off desks. Spent casings streamed from his rifle, tinkling like silverware at a feast. The noise was so loud that Parsons never heard the tellers scream.

Their thirteenth bank robbery had begun. The clock was running.

LYNN PHELPS, the third woman waiting in line for a teller, dropped to the floor. She grabbed the legs of the woman standing behind her, pulled her down, then checked the time. Her Seiko digital showed 3:09 exactly. Time would be critical.

Mrs Phelps was a retired sheriff's deputy from Riverside, California. She had moved to Culver City with her new husband, a retired Los Angeles police officer, and had been a customer at this branch for only eight days. She knew these two bank robbers were not professionals by the way they wasted time waving their guns. Professionals would have immediately grabbed the managers and had the tellers dump their drawers. Professionals would have been paying attention to the clock.

Lynn Phelps checked the time again: 3:10. One minute had passed, and these two idiots were still waving their guns. Amateurs.

MARCHENKO SHOVED a short Latin man into a counter laden with deposit slips, and screamed, 'Get your ass DOWN!'

Marchenko hit the guy with his rifle, knocking him to the floor. Then he spun away, his eyes bulging out of the ski mask. 'Everybody stay on the floor. Anyone gives us any shit you better kiss your ass goodbye.'

Parsons's job was easy. He kept an eye on everyone, and kept an eye on the door. If new people walked in, he grabbed them and shoved them down. And he shook down the tellers while Marchenko went for the key.

Banks kept their cash in two places: the teller drawers and the cash locker in the vault. The cash locker was locked, but the manager had the key.

While Marchenko got the customers on the floor, Parsons whipped out his nylon bag. There were four tellers, all young Asian women, and at a desk behind them an older fat broad who was probably the manager. Another banker sat at one of the two desks on the public side of the tellers.

Parsons stalked over to the tellers, waving his gun. 'Stand away from the counter! *Step back, goddammit!*'

Behind him, Marchenko had pulled the desk clerk to his feet, screaming, 'Which one of you has the key? Goddammit, who's the manager?'

The woman at the desk behind the tellers stepped forward, identifying herself as the manager. 'You can have the money. We're not going to resist.'

Marchenko shoved the one he had down, then stalked round the pass-through behind the tellers.

While Marchenko took care of his end, Parsons ordered the tellers to step forward to their stations and warned them not to trip the alarm beneath the counter. He told them to dump their drawers on their desks, leave out the dye packs, and put their cash into the bag.

While they were bagging the cash, a man with short grey hair entered the bank. Parsons saw him only because he noticed one of the tellers looking. When Parsons glanced over, the man was already turning to leave.

The rifle jerked up and three rounds ripped out with a short sharp *brrp*. The man windmilled and fell. Parsons glanced at the people on the floor to make sure no one was trying to get up, then turned back to the tellers.

The last teller had put her money into his bag when Marchenko returned from the vault. His bag bulged. The real money was always in the vault.

Parsons said, 'We cool?'

Marchenko smiled behind his mask. 'We're golden.'

He came out from behind the counter. Parsons zipped up his bag. If a dye pack exploded the money would be ruined, but the nylon bag would protect him from the indelible ink. The dye packs were sometimes on timers, and sometimes on proximity fuses that were triggered when you left the bank. If a pack exploded, the cops would be looking for anyone wearing indelible coloured ink.

Turning for the door, Marchenko shouted his signature farewell. 'Don't get up, don't look up. If you look up, I'm gonna be the last thing you see.'

LYNN PHELPS checked her watch as the robbers stepped out of the door. It was 3:22—thirteen minutes since the two bozos had entered the bank. Professional bank robbers knew that the Two Minute Rule was sacrosanct. If you hit a bank, you had two minutes to make your robbery and get away. That was the minimum time it took for a bank employee to trigger a silent alarm, for that alarm to register at the bank's security firm and for the police to respond. Every extra second increased the odds of being caught. A professional would leave a bank after two minutes whether he had the money or not. Lynn Phelps knew that. Sooner or later these guys would get bagged.

Lynn Phelps stayed on the floor and waited. She did not know for certain what was lined up outside, but she had a good idea.

As PARSONS BACKED out of the bank, he bumped into Marchenko, who had stopped only a few feet from the door when the amplified voice echoed across the parking lot.

'Police! Do not move. Stand absolutely still.'

Parsons absorbed the scene in a heartbeat: two nondescript sedans were parked across the lot; a black and white police car was blocking the drive; on the street behind it was a beat-up van. Men in plainclothes were set up behind the vehicles, aiming pistols, shotguns and rifles. Two uniformed officers were at either end of their radio car.

Parsons said, 'Wow.' He did not feel afraid or any great surprise, though his heart was pounding.

Marchenko raised his rifle and opened fire. The movement of Marchenko's gun was like the OK sign. Parsons opened up, too. He felt light punches in his stomach, chest and left thigh. He dumped his magazine and jammed in another. He swung towards the black and white, rattled off bullets, then swung back towards the sedans as Marchenko fell, dropping like a puppet with cut strings.

Parsons saw that one of the men behind the sedans had a rifle like his own. As he lined up, bullets snapped through his vest and staggered him. The world was suddenly grey and hazy, and his head buzzed with a feeling far different to the Royal Blue Metallic. He sat down hard on his ass. He slumped back, but did not feel his head strike the concrete.

Shapes and shadows floated above him, but he did not know what they were, and did not care. His last thoughts were of the money, all those perfect green dollars they had stolen and stashed. It was waiting for them.

Then Parsons went into cardiac arrest, his breathing stopped, and his dreams of the money vanished on the hot, bright street in Los Angeles. Long past their two minutes, Parsons and Marchenko had run out of time.

86 days later
1

'Y ou're not too old. Forty-eight isn't old. You got a world of time to make a life for yourself.'

Holman didn't answer. He was trying to pack. His possessions were spread out on the bed: four white T-shirts, three briefs, four pairs of white socks, two short-sleeved shirts (one beige, one plaid), one pair of khaki pants, plus the clothes he had been wearing when he was arrested for bank robbery ten years, three months and four days ago.

'Max, you listening?'

'I gotta pack. Lemme ask you something—you think I should keep my old stuff, from before? I don't know as I'll ever get into those pants.'

Wally Figg, who ran the Community Correctional Center, kind of a halfway house for federal prisoners, picked up the cream-coloured slacks and held them next to Holman. Wally admired the material. 'That's a nice cut, man. What is it, Italian?'

'Armani.'

Wally nodded, 'I'd keep'm. Be a shame to lose something this nice.'

'I got four inches more in the waist now than back then.'

Back in the day, Holman had lived large. He stole cars, hijacked trucks and robbed banks. Fat with fast cash, he hoovered up crystal meth for breakfast and bourbon for lunch, so jittery from dope and hung over from booze he rarely bothered to eat. He had gained weight in prison.

Wally refolded the slacks. 'You'll get yourself in shape again. Give yourself something to shoot for, gettin' back in these pants.'

Holman tossed them to Wally. 'Better to leave the past behind.'

Wally looked sadly at Holman. 'You know we can't accept anything from the residents. I'll pass'm along to one of the other guys, you want.'

'Whatever.'

Max Holman's suitcase was an Albertson's grocery bag. Technically, he was still incarcerated, but in another hour he would be a free man. Being released from federal custody happened in stages. They started you off with six months in an Intensive Confinement Center, where you got field trips

into the outside world, counselling, that kind of thing, after which you graduated to a Community Correctional Center, where they let you live and
work in a community with real civilians. Holman had spent the past three
months at the CCC in Venice, California. Today he would be released from
full-time federal custody into what was known as 'supervised release'.

Wally said, 'Well, OK, I'm gonna go get the papers together. I'm proud
of you, Max. This is a big day. I'm really happy for you.'

Holman layered his clothes in the bag. With the help of his Bureau of
Prisons transition supervisor, Gail Manelli, he had secured a room in a resident motel and a job; the room would cost sixty dollars a week, the job
would pay a $172.50 after taxes. A big day.

Wally clapped him on the back. 'I'll be in the office whenever you're
ready to go. Hey, you know what?'

Wally slipped a business card from his pocket and gave it to Holman.
The card showed a picture of an antique timepiece. *Salvador Jimenez,
repairs, fine watches bought and sold, Culver City, California.*

Wally explained 'My wife's cousin. He fixes watches. I figured maybe
you havin' a job and all, you'd want to get your old man's watch fixed. You
want to see Sally, you lemme know, I'll make sure he gives you a price.'

Holman slipped the card into his pocket. He wore a cheap Timex with an
expandable band that hadn't worked in twenty years. He used to wear an
$18,000 Patek Phillippe he stole from a car fence who had tried to short
him on a stolen Carrera. Holman choked the man until he passed out. But
that was then. Now, Holman wore the Timex even though its hands were
frozen. The Timex had belonged to his father.

'Thanks, Wally, thanks a lot. I was going to do that. This will help.'

Wally left as Holman returned to his packing. He had the clothes, the
$312 that he had earned during his incarceration, and his father's watch. He
did not have a car or a driver's licence or friends or family to pick him up on
his release. Wally was going to give him a ride to his motel. After that, he
would be on his own.

Holman went to his bureau for the picture of his son. It showed a gap-
toothed kid with a buzz cut, dark skin and serious eyes. Donna had sent
Holman the picture during his second year of incarceration, a guilty spasm
because she wouldn't bring the boy to visit his father in prison, wouldn't let
him speak to Holman on the phone, and wouldn't pass on his letters, such
as they were. Holman no longer blamed her for that. She had done all right

by the boy with no help from him. His son had made something of himself and Holman was proud of that.

He placed the picture in the bag, then sat on the bed. It was a big day, but the weight of it left him feeling heavy. He was going to get settled in his new room, check in with his release supervisor, then try to find Donna. It had been two years since her last note, not that she had written much, but the five letters he had written to her since had all been returned, *no longer at this address*. Holman figured she had got married. He didn't blame her for that, either. They had never married, but they did have the boy together and that had to be worth something, even if she hated him. Holman wanted to apologise and let her know he had changed. If she had a new life, well, he wanted to wish her well with it, and then he wanted to get on with his.

Holman was still sitting on the bed when Wally came back.

'Max?' Wally stood in the door like he was scared to come in. His face was pale and he kept wetting his lips.

Holman said, 'What's wrong? Wally, you having a heart attack, what?'

Wally closed the door. He glanced at a little notepad like something was on it he didn't have right. He was visibly shaken.

'Wally, what?'

'You have a son, right? Richie?'

'Yeah, that's right.'

'What's his full name?'

'Richard Dale Holman.' Holman stood up. He didn't like the way Wally was fidgeting. 'You know I have a boy. You've seen his picture.'

'He's a kid.'

'He'd be twenty-three now. Why you want to know about this?'

'Max, listen, is he a police officer? Here in LA?'

'That's right.'

Wally came over and touched Holman's arm. 'It's bad, Max. I have some bad news and I want you to get ready for it.'

Wally searched Holman's eyes as if he wanted a sign, so Holman nodded. 'OK, Wally. What?'

'He was killed last night. I'm sorry, man. I'm really, really sorry.'

Holman heard the words; he saw the pain in Wally's eyes and felt the concern in his touch, but Wally and the room and the world left Holman behind like one car pulling away from another on a flat desert highway, Wally hitting the gas, Holman hitting the brakes and watching the world race away.

Then he caught up and fought down an empty, terrible ache.

'What happened?'

'I don't know, Max. There was a call from the Bureau of Prisons when I went for your papers. They didn't have much to say. They wasn't even sure it was you or if you were still here.'

Holman sat down again and Wally sat beside him. Holman had wanted to look up his son after he spoke with Donna. He hadn't seen the boy since he was thirteen, two months before Holman was pinched in the bank, running alongside the car as Holman drove away from Donna's. Holman had shown up out of the blue, so stoned he couldn't remember why his face was bruised, then suddenly he was driving away again and the boy was running along-side the car, his eyes wet and bulging, screaming that Holman was a loser. Holman still dreamed about it. Now he was left with the sense that every-thing he had been moving to for the past ten years had drifted to a stop.

Wally said, 'You want to cry, it's OK.'

Holman didn't cry. He wanted to know who did it.

Dear Max,

I am writing because I want you to know that Richard has made something of himself despite your bad blood. Richard has joined the police department. This past Sunday he graduated at the police academy by Dodger Stadium and it was really something. The mayor spoke and helicopters flew so low. Richard is now a police officer. He is strong and good and not like you. I am so proud of him. He looked so handsome. I think this is his way of proving there is no truth to that old saying 'like father, like son'.

Donna

This was the last letter Holman received, back when he was at Lompoc. Holman remembered getting to the part where she wrote there was no truth about being like father like son, and he hadn't felt embarrassment or shame; he'd felt relief. He remembered thinking, *Thank God, thank God.*

He wrote back, but the letters were returned. He wrote to his son care of the LA Police Department, just a short note to congratulate the boy, but never received an answer. He didn't know if Richie received the letter. He didn't want to force himself on the boy. He had not written again.

'What should I do? Is there someone I'm supposed to see? Something I'm supposed to do?'

Holman had served a total of nine months juvenile time before he was seventeen years old. His first adult time came when he was eighteen—six months for grand theft auto. This was followed by sixteen months of state time for burglary, then three years for a stacked count of robbery and breaking and entering. Altogether, Holman had spent a third of his adult life in state and federal facilities. He was used to people telling him what to do.

Wally said, 'You go on with what you were doing, I guess.'

'What about the arrangements?'

'I don't know. I guess the police do that.'

Holman tried to imagine what responsible people did at times like this, but he had no experience. His mother had died when he was young and his father had died when Holman was serving the first burglary stretch. He had nothing to do with burying them.

'You want to see one of the counsellors? We could get someone in here.'

'I don't need a counsellor, Wally. I want to know what happened. You can't just tell a man his boy was killed and let it go with that. Jesus, Donna must be devastated. I'd better talk to her.'

'OK. Can I help with that?'

Holman had no idea where Donna was. 'I don't know. The police gotta know how to reach her. If they called me they would've called her.'

'Let me see what I can find out. I told Gail I'd get back to her after I saw you. She was the one got the call from the police.'

Gail Manelli, Holman's Bureau of Prisons release supervisor, was a businesslike young woman with no sense of humour, but he liked her.

'OK, Wally,' Holman said. 'Sure.'

Wally spoke with Gail, who told them Holman could obtain additional information from Richie's commander at the Devonshire Station up in Chatsworth. Twenty minutes later, Wally drove Holman out of Venice and into the San Fernando Valley. The trip took almost thirty minutes. They parked outside a building that looked more like a modern suburban library than a police station.

They identified themselves at the reception desk and asked for Captain Levy. Levy, Gail said, had been Richard's commanding officer.

A uniformed officer about Holman's age came out. Levy was a short, compact guy who looked like an ageing gymnast, with silvery hair and stars on his shoulders.

The officer looked at Wally. 'Mr Holman?'

'No, I'm Walter Figg, with the CCC.'

'I'm Holman.'

'Chip Levy. I was Richard's commander. If you'll come with me I'll tell you what I can.'

He shook Holman's hand, and it was then Holman noticed he was wearing a black armband. So were the two officers seated behind the desk.

Wally waited in the reception area. Holman followed Levy along a hall and into an interview room. Another uniformed officer was already waiting inside. He stood when they entered.

Levy said, 'This is Dale Clark. Dale, this is Richard's father.'

Clark took Holman's hand in a firm grip. 'I was Richard's shift supervisor. He was an outstanding young man. The best.'

Holman muttered a thanks. It occurred to him that these men had known and worked with his son, while he knew absolutely nothing about the boy.

Levy asked him to take a seat at the table. 'Can we get you some coffee?'

'No, I'm good.'

Levy settled across from him and folded his hands together on the table. Clark took a seat to the side on Holman's left.

Levy said, 'OK. I'm sorry you had to find out the way you did—through the Bureau of Prisons—but we didn't know about you.'

'What does that mean?'

'You weren't listed in the officer's personnel file. Where it says "father", Richard had written "unknown".'

'If you didn't know I existed, how did you find me?'

'Richard's wife.'

Holman took it in. Richie was married, and Donna hadn't told him.

Clark must have been able to read him because he said, 'You've had no recent contact with your son?'

'I was hoping to get back in touch now that I'm out.'

'You could've called him from the correction centre, couldn't you?' said Levy. 'They give you guys plenty of freedom.'

'I didn't want to call while I was still in custody. If he wanted to get together I didn't want to have to ask permission. I wanted him to see me free with the prison behind me.'

Levy seemed embarrassed, so Holman pushed ahead with his questions.

'Can you tell me how Richie's mother is doing? Is she OK?'

Clark answered. 'We notified Richard's wife. Our first responsibility was her, you understand? If she notified his mother or anyone else she didn't tell us; that was up to her. It was Richard's wife who told us about you. She wasn't sure where you were housed, so we contacted the Bureau of Prisons.'

Levy took over. 'We'll bring you up-to-date with what we know. It isn't much. Robbery–Homicide is handling the case out of Parker Center. All we know is that Richard was one of four officers murdered early this morning. We believe the killings were some sort of ambush.'

Clark said, 'Approximately one fifty is when it happened.'

Levy continued. 'Two of the officers were on duty and two were off— Richard was not on duty. They were taking a break together. They were out of their cars, their weapons were holstered, and none of them radioed that a crime was in progress or a situation was developing. We believe the weapon or weapons used were shotguns.'

'Jesus.'

'This happened a few hours ago. The task force has just been formed and detectives are working to figure out what happened. We'll keep you informed on the developments, but right now we just don't know.'

Holman shifted in his chair. 'Do you have a suspect?'

'Not at this time.'

'So someone just shot him, like when he was looking the other way? In the back? I'm just trying to, I don't know, picture it, I guess.'

'We don't know any more, Mr Holman. I know you have questions. Believe me, we have questions, too. We're still trying to sort it out.'

'Did he suffer?'

Levy hesitated. 'I drove down to the crime scene this morning when I got the call. Richard was one of my guys. Not the other three, but Richard was one of us here at Devonshire so I had to go see. I don't know, Mr Holman— I want to tell you he didn't, but I don't know.'

Holman watched Levy, and appreciated the man's honesty.

'I should know about the burial. Is there anything I need to do?'

Clark said, 'The department will take care of that with his widow. We don't know when his body will be released from the coroner.'

'All right, I understand. Could I have her number? I'd like to talk to her.'

Levy laced his fingers on the table. 'I can't give you her number. If you give us your information, we'll pass it on to her and tell her you'd like to speak with her. That way, if she wants to contact you, it's her choice.'

Holman looked at the floor. 'OK. I understand.'

He couldn't remember the number at the motel where he would be living. Levy walked him out to the reception area where Wally gave them the number, and Levy promised to call when they knew something more.

When Levy was heading back inside, Holman stopped him. 'Captain? Was my son a good officer?'

Levy nodded. 'Yes, sir. Yes, he was. He was a fine young man.'

HOLMAN'S NEW HOME was a three-storey building one block off Washington Boulevard in Culver City, sandwiched between a car repair service and a convenience store. The Pacific Gardens Motel Apartments had been on a list of housing suggestions that Gail Manelli had provided. It was clean, cheap and located on a no-transfer bus route Holman could use to get to his job.

Wally pulled up outside the front entrance. They had stopped by the CCC so Holman could sign his papers and pick up his things. Holman was now officially on supervised release. He was free.

Wally said, 'This isn't any way to start, man, not your first day back with news like this. Listen to me—if you want a few more days at the house you can stay. We can talk this out. You can see one of the counsellors.'

Holman picked up his bag and opened the door. 'I'll get settled, then call Gail. I still want to get to the DMV today. I want to get a car as soon as I can.'

'Just remember you have people pulling for you. Not everyone would've went down the way you went down, and that shows you got a strong natural character.' Wally put out his hand. 'You're a good man, Max. I'm a call away, twenty-four-seven.'

'Thanks, bro.' Holman climbed out and waved as Wally drove away.

THE MANAGER of the Pacific Gardens Motel was an elderly black man named Perry Wilkes. He owned the building, lived in the only ground-floor apartment and manned a desk that filled a cramped corner of the entry hall.

Holman had arranged for one of the eight studio apartments available at the Pacific Gardens. He had already filled out the rental agreement, and paid his rent two weeks in advance along with a $100 cleaning fee and a six-dollar key deposit. When Holman first looked at the place, Perry had lectured him on noise, late-night doings, smoking pot or cigars in the rooms, and making sure his rent was paid on time.

Now Perry took a set of keys from his centre drawer and handed them to Holman. 'This is for two-oh-six, right at the top in front here.'

Holman went up to his room. It was a simple studio with dingy yellow walls, a shopworn bed and two stuffed chairs covered in a threadbare floral print. He had a private bath and what Perry called a kitchenette, which was a single-burner hot plate on top of a half-size refrigerator. Holman put his bag of clothes at the foot of the bed, then opened the refrigerator. It was empty but clean. The bathroom was clean, too. He cupped his hand under the tap and drank, then looked at himself in the mirror. He had worked up a couple of mushy bags under his eyes and crow's-feet at the corners. His short hair was dusty with grey. He felt like a mummy rising from the dead.

Holman rinsed his face in the cool water, but realised too late that he had no towels, so he wiped away the water with his hands. He left the bathroom, sat on the edge of his bed and dug through his wallet for phone numbers, then he called Gail Manelli.

'It's Holman. I'm in the room.'

'Max. I am so sorry to hear about your son. How are you doing?'

'I'm dealing. It's not like we were close.'

'He was still your son.'

A silence developed because Holman didn't know what to say. Finally he said, 'I just have to keep my eye on the ball.'

'That's right. You've come a long way and now is no time to backslide. Have you spoken to Tony yet?'

Tony was Holman's new boss, Tony Gilbert, at the Harding Sign Company. Holman had been a part-time employee for the past eight weeks, training for a full-time position that he would begin tomorrow.

'No, not yet. I just got up to the room. Wally took me up to Chatsworth.'

'I know. I just spoke with him. Were the officers able to tell you anything?'

'They didn't know anything.'

'I've been listening to the news. It's just terrible, Max. I'm so sorry.'

Holman glanced around his new room, but saw he had no television or radio. 'I'll have to check it out.'

'Now, if you need a day or two off because of this, I can arrange it.'

'I'd rather jump on the job. I think getting busy would be good.'

'If you change your mind, just let me know.'

'Listen, I want to get to the DMV. It's getting late and I'm not sure of the bus route. I gotta get the licence so I can start driving again.'

'All right, Max. I'm sorry you had to start with this terrible news.'

'Thanks, Gail. Me, too.'

When Gail hung up, Holman picked up his bag of clothes and fished out the picture of his son. He stared at Richie's face, set the picture on the little table between the two chairs, then went downstairs to find Perry at his desk.

'Listen, I need some towels up there.'

'You look in the closet? Up on the shelf?'

'No, I didn't think to look in there. I'll check it out. I'd like a television, too. Can you help me with that?'

'Might have one if I can find it. Cost you an extra eight dollars a month, plus another sixty security deposit.'

'OK, hook me up. I'll give it back to you when I get one of my own.'

Holman went next door to the convenience store for a *Times*. He bought a carton of chocolate milk to go with the paper and read the newspaper's story about the murders while standing on the sidewalk.

Sergeant Mike Fowler, a twenty-six-year veteran, had been the senior officer at the scene. He was survived by a wife and four children. Officers Patrick Mellon and Charles Ash had eight and six years on the job, respectively. Mellon left a wife and two small children; Ash was unmarried. Holman studied their pictures. Fowler had a thin face and papery skin. Mellon was a dark man with heavy features. Ash had chipmunk cheeks, wispy blond hair and nervous eyes. The last of the officers pictured was Richie. He had Holman's lean face and thin mouth and the same hardened expression Holman had seen on jailbirds whose ragged lives had left them burnt at the edges. Holman suddenly felt angry and responsible. He folded the page to hide his son's face, then continued reading.

The article described the crime scene much as Levy had. The officers had been parked in the LA River channel beneath the Fourth Street bridge, and apparently had been ambushed. Levy had said that all four officers had holstered weapons, but the paper reported that Officer Mellon's weapon had been drawn, though not fired. A police spokesman confirmed that Sergeant Fowler had radioed to announce he was taking a coffee break, but was not heard from again. The article gave no information about the number of shots fired, but Holman guessed that at least two shooters were involved. It would be difficult for one man to take out four trained officers so quickly that they didn't have time to return fire or take cover.

Holman wondered why the officers were under the bridge, then he read that a police spokesman had denied that an open six-pack of beer had been found on one of the police cars. Holman concluded that they had been down there drinking. Back in the day, he had ridden motorcycles down in the river bed, hanging out with dope addicts. The concrete channel was off limits to the public, so he had climbed the fence or broken through gates with bolt-cutters. Holman thought the police might have had a pass key, but he wondered why they had gone to so much trouble just for a quiet place to drink.

Holman finished the article, then tore out Richie's picture. He put it in his wallet and walked back upstairs to his room.

He sat by his phone again, thinking, then finally dialled information.

'City and state, please?'

'Ah, Los Angeles. That's in California.'

'Listing?'

'Donna Banik, B-A-N-I-K.'

'Sorry, sir. I don't show anyone by that name.'

If Donna had married and taken another name, he didn't know. If she had moved to another city, he didn't know that, either.

'Let me try someone else. How about Richard Holman?'

'Sorry, sir.'

'OK, thanks.' Holman put down the phone.

He took out his wallet again. His remaining savings of $300 were tucked in the billfold. He fished through the bills and found the corner of the envelope he had torn from Donna's last letter. It was the address where he had written to her only to have his letters returned. He studied it, then slipped it back between the bills and left his room.

Perry nodded at him when he reached the bottom of the stairs.

'Perry, listen, I need to get over to the DMV and I'm running way late. You got a car I could borrow?'

The old man's smile faded to a frown. 'You don't even have a licence.'

'I know, but I'm running late. You know what those lines are like.'

'Have you gone stupid already? What would you do if you got stopped? What you think Gail's gonna say?'

'I won't get stopped and I won't say you loaned me a car.'

'I don't loan shit to anyone.'

Holman watched Perry frowning, and knew he was considering it.

'I just need something for a few hours. Just to get over to the DMV. Once I start my job tomorrow it'll be hard to get away. You know that.'

'I did you a favour like this, it couldn't get back to Gail.'

'Come on, man, look at me.' Holman spread his hands.

Perry opened the centre drawer. 'I got an old beater I'll let you use, a Mercury. It ain't pretty, but it'll run. Cost is twenty a day, and you gotta bring it back full. And if you don't bring it back, I'll say you stole it.'

Holman passed over the first twenty.

PERRY'S MERCURY blew smoke from bad rings and had a nasty case of engine knock, so Holman spent most of the drive worried that some enterprising cop might tag him for a smog violation.

Donna's address led to a pink stucco garden apartment in Jefferson Park. It was an ugly two-storey building with a skin bleached and blistered by unrelenting sun. Holman had imagined that Donna would live in a nicer place. She had complained of being short of cash from time to time, but she had held steady employment as a private nurse. Holman wondered if Richie had helped his mother move to a better area when he got on with the cops.

Donna had lived in apartment number 108. Holman stood outside with a nervous fire flickering in his stomach, telling himself he was just going to knock and ask the new tenants if they knew Donna's current address. It was hard to stop feeling like a criminal, but finally he knocked on the jamb. The door opened and a balding man peered out. He held tight to the door, ready to push it closed.

'You caught me working, man. What's up?'

Holman slipped his hands into his pockets to make himself less threatening. 'I'm trying to find an old friend, Donna Banik. She used to live here.'

The man relaxed and opened the door wider. 'Sorry. Can't help you.'

'She lived here about two years ago, dark hair, about this tall.'

'I've been here, what, four or five months? I don't know who had it before me, let alone two years ago.'

Holman had a thought. 'Does the manager live here in the building?'

'Yeah, right there in number one hundred. Mrs Bartello.'

'OK. Thanks.'

Holman went back along the sidewalk to number 100 and knocked.

Mrs Bartello was a sturdy woman who wore her grey hair pulled back tight and a shapeless house dress. She opened her door wide and stared out through the screen. Holman introduced himself and explained he was trying to find the former tenant of apartment 108, Donna Banik.

'Donna and I, we were married once, a long time ago. I've been away and we lost track.' Holman figured that was the easiest explanation.

Mrs Bartello's expression softened, and she opened the screen. 'Oh my gosh, you must be Richard's father, *that* Mr Holman?'

'Yes, that's right.' Holman wondered if maybe she had seen the news about Richie's death, but then he understood that she hadn't.

'Richard is such a wonderful boy. He would visit her all the time. He looks so handsome in his uniform.'

'Yes, ma'am, thanks. Can you tell me where Donna is living now?'

Mrs Bartello opened the screen wider, her eyes bunching with sorrow. 'I'm sorry. You don't know. I'm sorry. Donna passed away.'

Holman felt himself slow as if he had been drugged; as if his heart and breath and blood were winding down like a phonograph record when you pull the plug. 'What happened?'

'It was those cars. They drive so fast on the freeways. She was on her way home one night. That was almost two years ago now. The way it was explained to me several cars lost control, and one of them was Donna's.'

Holman said, 'I need to find Richie. You know where I can find him?'

'Well, no, I just saw him when he came to visit.'

Holman suddenly wanted to tell her that Richie was dead, too; he thought it would be the kind thing to do, but he didn't have the strength. Then another thought occurred to him. 'Where was she buried?'

'That was over in Baldwin Hills. The Baldwin Haven Cemetery. That was the last time I saw Richard, you know.'

'Did many people attend?'

Mrs Bartello gave a sad shrug. 'No, not so many.'

2

Holman rose early the next morning and went down to the convenience store before Perry was at his desk. He bought a *Times*, a pint of chocolate milk and a six-pack of miniature doughnuts, and brought them back to his room to eat while he read the paper. The investigation into the murders was still front-page news, though today it was below the fold. The chief of police had announced that unnamed witnesses had come forward and detectives were narrowing a field of suspects. The city was offering a $50,000 reward for the arrest and conviction of the shooter.

Holman went downstairs and was waiting in the lobby when Perry showed up. Holman said, 'I need that car again.'

'You got another twenty?'

Holman held up the bill and Perry scooped it away.

'I need the TV.'

'It's in storage. I'll get it this morning.'

Holman picked up Perry's Mercury and headed south to City of Industry. Taking the bus would have been smarter, but Holman had a lot of ground to cover. He never exceeded the speed limit and was wary of other drivers.

He arrived at work ten minutes early and parked on the far side of the building because he didn't want his boss, Tony Gilbert, to see him driving. Gilbert would know that he did not yet have his licence.

Holman worked for the Harding Sign Company in a plant that printed art for billboards. During the past two months, he had trained part-time as a trimmer in the printing plant. His job was to load huge rolls of fabric into the printer, make sure the fabric fed square, then make sure the automatic trimmers at the end of the process made a clean cut. Holman had learned the job in about two minutes, but he was lucky to have the gig and knew it.

He clocked in, then looked up Gilbert, who was going over the day's schedule with the printer operators. Gilbert was a short, thick man with a bald crown who swaggered when he walked.

Gilbert said, 'So, you're officially a free man. Congratulations.'

Holman thanked him, but let their conversation die. Throughout the morning he kept an eye on the clock as he worked, anxious for the free hour he would have at lunch. At 11.10 he took a break. When he was standing at the urinal another inmate hire named Marc Lee Pitchess took the next stall. Holman didn't like Pitchess.

'Ten years is a long time,' Pitchess said. 'Welcome back.'

'You been seeing me five days a week the past two months. I haven't been anywhere.' Holman finished and stepped back from the urinal.

Pitchess was staring ahead at the wall. 'You feel the need, I can hook you up, your basic pharmaceuticals, sleep aids, blow, X, oxy, whatever.'

Holman walked out and looked up Gilbert again.

Gilbert said, 'How's it going, your first day?'

'Doin' fine. Listen, I want to ask you, I need to get to the DMV to take the test and after work is too late. Could you cut me an extra hour at lunch?'

'Don't they open on Saturday morning?'

'You have to make an appointment and they're booked three weeks. I'd really like to get this done, Tony.'

Gilbert didn't appreciate being asked, Holman could tell, but he went along. 'OK, but I want you back by two. That should be plenty of time.'

'Sure, Tony. Thanks.'

When Gilbert turned away and steamed off across the floor, Holman walked back to the office and punched out, even though it wasn't yet noon.

HOLMAN BOUGHT a small bunch of red roses from a Latin cat with a big plastic bucket full of flowers at the bottom of the freeway exit ramp. He felt guilty because he hadn't thought to bring flowers before seeing the cat with his bucket, even more guilty because Donna was gone and Richie hadn't thought enough of him to let him know.

Baldwin Haven Cemetery covered the wide face of a rolling hillside just off the 405 in Ladera Heights. Holman turned through the gates and pulled up alongside the main office. He took the flowers inside with him. The office was a large room divided by a counter. When he entered, an older woman with grey hair glanced up from a desk behind the counter.

Holman said, 'I need to find someone's grave.'

She came to the counter. 'Yes, sir. Could I have the party's name?'

'Donna Banik. B-A-N-I-K. She was buried here about two years ago.'

The woman went to a shelf and took down a heavy ledger. She flipped the pages, mumbling the name, Banik, Banik, Banik . . . She finally found the entry, wrote something on a slip of paper, then came out from behind the counter and led Holman to a table with a map on it.

'Here, I can show you how to find the site.' She checked the coordinates written on the slip, then pointed on the map to a tiny rectangle in a uniform rank and file of tiny rectangles. 'She's here on the south face. We're here, so turn right out of the parking lot and follow the road to this fork, then veer left. She's right in front of the mausoleum here, third row from the street, sixth marker from the end. If you need any help, just let me know.'

Holman climbed back into the Mercury and followed the directions to Donna's grave. He found a small bronze plaque set into the earth bearing her name and the years of her birth and death. On the plaque was a simple legend: *Beloved Mother*.

Holman laid the roses on the grass. He had rehearsed what he wanted to tell her when he got out a thousand times, but now she was dead and it was too late. He told her anyway, staring down at the roses and the plaque.

'I was a rotten prick. I was all those things you ever called me and worse. You had no idea how rotten I really was. I used to thank God you didn't know, but now I'm ashamed. If you had known you would've given up on me, and you might've married some decent guy. I wish you had known. Not for me, but for you. So you wouldn't have wasted your life.'

Holman returned to his car and drove back to the office. The woman was showing the map of the grounds to a middle-aged couple when Holman walked in. After a few minutes, the woman left the couple and came over.

'Did you find it OK?'

'Yeah, thanks, you made it real easy. Listen, I want to ask you something. Do you remember who made the arrangements?'

'For her burial? You want to know who paid for the burial?'

'Yes, ma'am. She and I used to be together, but we hadn't seen each other in a long time. I didn't even know she had passed until yesterday, and, well, it's not right that I didn't share the expenses. If you can give me a phone number or an address, I'd like to offer to help out on the costs.'

The woman went back to her desk and searched until she found the slip with the plot numbers. 'That was Banik, right?'

'Yes, ma'am.'

'I have to find the records. Can you leave a phone number?'

Holman wrote Perry's number on her notepad.

She said, 'This is very generous. I'm sure her family will be glad to hear from you.'

'Yes, ma'am. I hope so.'

Holman went out to his car and drove back towards the City of Industry. With the time and the traffic he figured he would get back to work before two o'clock, but then he turned on the radio. The station had broken into their regular programming with news that a suspect had been named in the murders of the four officers, and a warrant had been issued for his arrest.

Holman turned up the volume and forgot about work. He immediately began looking for a phone.

He drove until he spotted a sports bar with its front door wedged open. He jockeyed the Mercury into a red zone, got out of the car, then hesitated in the door, taking the measure of the place until he saw a television. A young bartender with sharp sideburns worked a half-dozen alkies sipping their lunch. The television was showing ESPN but no one was looking at it.

Holman went to the bar. 'You mind if we get the local news?'

The bartender glanced over. 'Whatever. Can I get you something?'

'Club soda, I guess. How about that news?'

The bartender brimmed the glass, then set it on the bar before changing the channel, and there it was, several high-ranking LA Police Department suits holding a press conference.

The bartender said, 'This about those cops who were killed?'

'Yeah, they know who did it. Let's listen.'

The bartender turned up the sound. An assistant chief named Donnelly was recounting the crime. Pictures of the murdered officers flashed on the screen as Donnelly identified them. Then another picture appeared.

Donnelly said, 'We have issued a warrant for the arrest of this man, Warren Alberto Juarez, for the murder of these officers. Mr Juarez is a resident of Eagle Rock. He has extensive criminal history including assault, robbery, possession of a concealed weapon and known gang associations.'

Holman stared at the face on the screen. Warren Alberto Juarez had a thick moustache and hair slicked tight like a skullcap. He was making his eyes sleepy to look tough for the booking photo.

Holman nodded at the bartender. 'How much for the soda?'

'Two.'

'You got a payphone?'

'Back by the bathrooms.'

Holman put two dollars on the bar, then followed the bartender's finger towards the phone. When he reached it he dug out his list for Levy's number up at the Devonshire Station.

When Levy came on, Holman said, 'I heard on the news.'

'Then you know what I know. Parker Center called less than an hour ago.'

'Do they have him yet?'

'Mr Holman, they just issued the warrant. They'll notify me as soon as an arrest is made.'

Holman took a couple of deep breaths and forced himself to relax. 'All right, I understand that. Do they know why it happened?'

'The word I have so far is it was a personal vendetta between Juarez and Sergeant Fowler. Fowler arrested Juarez's younger brother last year, and apparently the brother was killed in prison.'

'How was Richie involved with Juarez?'

'He wasn't.'

'Wait—this asshole killed all four of these people just to get Fowler?'

'Mr Holman, listen, I know you want this to make sense. I would like this to make sense, too, but sometimes they don't. Richard had nothing to do with the Juarez arrest. So far as I know neither did Mellon and Ash. Maybe we'll know more later and this will make sense.'

'They know who was with him?'

'It's my understanding that he acted alone.'

Holman felt his voice shake. '*One guy*, and he shotguns four men just to get one of them? This doesn't make sense.'

'I know it doesn't. I'm sorry.'

'They're sure it was Juarez?'

'They are positive. They matched fingerprints found on shell casings at the scene with Mr Juarez. My understanding is they also have witnesses who heard Juarez make numerous threats and placed him at the scene earlier that night. They attempted to arrest Juarez at his home earlier today, but he had already fled. Listen, I have other calls . . .'

Holman thanked him, then called Gail Manelli. 'Hey, it's Holman. Remember you said if I needed a few days you'd square it with Gilbert?'

'Do you need some time off?'

'Yes. There's a lot to deal with, Gail. More than I thought. Can you square a few days with Gilbert? That guy has been good to me with the job—'

'I'll call him right now, Max—I'm sure he'll understand. Now listen, would you like to see a counsellor?'

'I'm doing fine, Gail. I don't need a counsellor. Thanks for squaring up the job for me. Tell Gilbert I'll call him in a few days.'

'I will, Max. I know you're hurting, but the most important thing you can do right now is take care of yourself. Your son would want that.'

'Thanks, Gail. I'll see you.'

Holman put down the phone. Gail had her ideas about what was important, but Holman had his. The criminal world was a world he knew. And knew how to use.

CRIMINALS DID NOT have friends. They had suppliers, fences, dealers, collaborators and bosses, any of whom they might rat out and none of whom could be trusted. Most everyone Holman met on the yard during his ten years at Lompoc had been arrested and convicted because they had been fingered by someone they knew and trusted. Police work only went so far; Holman wanted to find someone who would rat out Warren Juarez.

That afternoon, Gary 'L'Chee' Mareno said, 'You just gotta be the dumbest gringo ever.'

'Tell me you love me, bro.'

'Here's what I'm tellin' you, Holman: why didn't you run? I been waiting ten years to ask that.'

'Didn't have to wait ten years, Chee. You coulda come see me in Lompoc.'

'That's why they caught you, thinkin' like that! Me, I woulda jetted outta that bank straight to Zacatecas like a chilli pepper up my ass. C'mere, ese. Give a brother some love.'

Chee came round the counter at his body shop in East LA. He wrapped Holman in a tight hug, it being ten years since they had seen each other— since the day Chee had waited outside the bank for Holman as the police and FBI arrived, whereupon—by prior agreement—Chee had driven away.

Holman first met Chee when they were serving stints at the California Youth Authority, both fourteen years old—Holman for a string of shoplifting and burglary arrests, Chee on his second auto theft conviction. Chee, small but fearless, was being pounded by three bloods on the yard when Holman, large for his size even then, wailed in and beat the bloods down. Chee couldn't do enough for him after that. Chee was a fifth-generation White Fence home boy, nephew to the infamous Chihuahua Brothers, two miniature Guatemalans who macheted their way to the top of the LA stolen car market in the seventies. Back in the day, Holman had fed Porsches and Corvettes to Chee when he was sober enough to steal them, which wasn't so often towards the end, and Chee had driven on a few of the bank jobs; done it, Holman knew, only for the rush of living crazy with his buddy.

Now, Chee stepped back, his eyes serious. 'It's good to see you, bro. C'mon back here; we'll get away from this noise.'

Chee led Holman behind the counter into a small office. In the day, these same offices had been the centre of a chop shop Chee managed for his uncles, breaking down stolen cars into their component parts. Now, Chee ran a mostly legitimate body shop employing his sons and nephews.

Holman made a show of looking around the office. 'Looks different.'

'*Is* different, homes. My daughter works here three days a week. She don't wanna see titty pictures on the walls. You want a beer?'

'I'm sober.'

'No shit? Well, good, man, that's real good. Goddamn, we're gettin' old.'

Chee laughed as he dropped into his chair. When he laughed, his leathery skin accordioned with acne craters and tattoos from his gang days. He was still White Fence, a certified veterano, but out of the street life. Chee's face grew sad, staring at nothing until he finally looked at Holman.

'You need some money? I'll front you, homes. You don't even have to pay me back. I mean it.'

'I want a home boy named Warren Alberto Juarez.'

Chee swivelled in his chair to pull a thick phone book from the clutter. He flipped a few pages, circled a name, then pushed the book across his desk. 'Here you go. Knock yourself out.'

Holman glanced at the page. Warren A. Juarez. An address in Eagle Rock. A phone number. When Holman looked up, Chee was staring like Holman was stupid.

'Homes, that why you came down here, cash in on the reward? You think he's hidin' in a closet down here? Ese, *please*.'

'You know where he went?'

'Why you think I'd know something like that?'

'You're Little Chee. You always knew things.'

'Those days are gone, bro. I am Mister Mareno. Look around. I ain't in the life any more. I pay taxes. I got haemorrhoids.'

'You're still White Fence.'

'To the death and beyond, and I'll tell you—if I knew where the home boy was I'd nail that fifty myself. He ain't White Fence; he's Frogtown, from up by the river, and he ain't nothing to me 'cept a pain in the ass. Half my boys called in sick today, wantin' that money. My work schedule's blown. Forget that reward, Holman. I tol' you, I'll give you money, you want it.'

'I'm not looking for a loan.'

'Then what?'

'One of the officers he killed was my son. Richie grew up to be a police-man, you imagine? My little boy.'

Chee's eyes went round like saucers. He had met the boy a few times, the first when Richie was three. Holman had convinced Donna to let him take the boy to the Santa Monica pier for the Ferris wheel. Holman and Chee had hooked up, but Holman had left Richie with Chee's girlfriend so he and Chee could steal a Corvette from the parking lot. Real Father of the Year stuff.

'Ese. Ese, I'm sorry.'

'The police say Juarez killed him. Some bullshit about Juarez's brother.'

'I don't know anything about that, man. Whatever, that's Frogtown, ese.'

'Whatever, I want to find him. I want to find whoever helped him, too.'

Latin gangs derived their names from their neighbourhoods: Happy Valley Gang, Garrity Lomas. Frogtown drew its name from the old days of the LA River, where neighbourhood homies fell asleep to croaking bullfrogs before the city lined the river with concrete and the frogs died. Juarez being a member of the Frogtown gang wasn't lost on Holman. The officers had been murdered in the river.

Chee eyed Holman. 'You gonna kill him? That what you wanna do?'

Holman wasn't sure what he would do. 'He was my boy. Someone kills your boy you can't just sit.'

'You're not a killer, Holman. Tough, yeah, but a man would do murder? I never seen that in you, homes. You gonna kill this boy, then ride the murder bus back to prison, thinking you done the right thing?'

'What would you do?'

'Cut off the boy's head, hang it from my rearview, and ride straight down Garrity Boulevard. You gonna do something like that? Could you?'

'No.'

'Then let the police do their business. They lost four of their own. They're gonna take lives findin' this boy.'

Holman knew Chee was right, but tried to put his need into words.

'The officers, they have to fill out this next-of-kin form at the police. Where they have a place for the father, Richie wrote unknown. He was so ashamed of me he didn't even claim me. I can't have that, Chee. I'm his father. I can't leave this to someone else. They're saying Juarez did this thing by himself. C'mon, Chee, how'd some home boy get good enough to take out four armed officers all by himself, so fast they didn't shoot back?'

Chee shrugged. 'A lot of homies are coming back from Iraq, bro. If the boy tooled up overseas, he might know exactly how to do what he did.'

'Then I want to know that. I need to understand how this happened. I'm not racing the cops. I just want this bastard found.'

'Well, you're gonna have a lot of help. Over there outside his house in Eagle Rock, it looks like a cop convention. My wife and daughter drove by there at lunch time just to see. His wife's gone into hiding herself. The address I gave you, that place is empty right now.'

'Where'd his wife go?'

'How can I know something like that, Holman? That boy ain't White Fence. He's in with that Frogtown crew.'

'Little Chee?'

Witnesses at two of the bank jobs had seen Holman get into cars driven by another man. After Holman's arrest, the FBI had pressured him to name his accomplice. They had asked, but Holman had held fast.

Holman said, 'After my arrest—how much sleep did you lose, worrying I was going to rat you out?'

Chee's eyes grew vague. 'Not one night. Not a single night, homes.'

'Because why?'

'Because I knew you were solid. You were my brother.'

'Has that fact changed or is it the same?'

'The same. We're the same.'

'Help me, Little Chee. Where can I find the girl?'

Holman knew Chee didn't like it, but Chee did not hesitate. He picked up his phone. 'Get yourself some coffee, homes. I gotta make some calls.'

An hour later, Holman walked out, but Chee didn't walk with him. Ten years later, some things were the same, but others were different.

HOLMAN DECIDED to drive past Juarez's house first to see the cop convention. Three news vans and an LAPD black and white were parked in front of a tiny bungalow. Transmission dishes swayed over the vans like spindly palms, with the uniformed officers and news people chatting together on the sidewalk. Holman knew Juarez would never return here, even if the officers were gone. A small crowd of neighbourhood civilians gawked from across the street, and the line of cars edging past the house made Holman feel like he was passing a traffic fatality. No wonder Juarez's wife had split.

Holman kept driving.

Chee had learned that Maria Juarez had relocated to her cousin's house in Silver Lake. Holman figured the police knew her location, probably had even helped her move to protect her from the media; if she had gone into hiding on her own they would have declared her a fugitive and issued a warrant.

The address Chee provided led to a small clapboard box crouched behind a row of spotty cypress trees on a hill lined with broken sidewalks. Holman parked at the kerb two blocks uphill, then tried to figure out what to do. The door was closed and the shades were drawn, but it was that way for most of the houses. Holman wondered if Juarez was in the house. It occurred to him that the police might be watching it. He examined the neighbouring cars and houses, but saw nothing suspicious. He got out of his car and walked to the house. He knocked.

A young woman threw open the door right away. She couldn't have been more than twenty-one. She was butt-ugly, with a flat nose, big teeth and black hair greased flat into squiggly sideburns.

She said, 'Is he all right?' She thought he was a cop.

Holman said, 'Maria Juarez?'

'Tell me he is all right. Did you find him? Tell me he is not dead.'

She had just told Holman everything he needed to know. Juarez wasn't here. The police had been here earlier, and she had cooperated with them.

Holman smiled. 'I need to ask a few questions. May I come in?'

She moved back out of the door and Holman went in. A TV was showing Telemundo. He could see through the dining room and kitchen to a back door, which was closed. A central hall opened off the living room and probably lead to a bathroom and a couple of bedrooms.

Holman said, 'Is anyone else here?'

Her eyes flickered with suspicion. 'My aunt. She is in the bed.'

He took her arm, bringing her towards the hall. 'Let's take a look.'

'Who are you? Are you the police?'

Holman knew a lot of these home girls would kill you as quick as any veterano, so he gripped her arm tight. 'I just want to see if Warren is here.'

'You know he isn't here. Who are you? You are not one of the detectives.'

He brought her back along the hall, glancing in the bathroom first, then the front bedroom. An old lady wrapped in shawls and blankets was sitting up in bed. Holman gave her an apologetic smile, then pulled Maria out to the second bedroom, closing the old lady's door behind them.

Maria said, 'Don't go in there. My baby. She is sleeping.'

Holman held Maria in front of him and cracked open the door. The room was dim. He made out a small figure in an adult's bed, a little girl of maybe three or four. Holman stood listening, knowing that Juarez might be hiding under the bed or in the closet, but not wanting to wake the little girl. He heard the buzz of a child's gentle snore. Something in her innocent pose made Holman think of Richie at that age. He tried to remember if he had ever seen Richie asleep, but couldn't.

Holman closed the door, and brought Maria into the living room.

She said, 'You weren't here with the policemen—who are you?'

'My name is Holman. You know that name?'

'Get out of this house. I don't know where he is. I already tol' them. I want to know who are you? You don't show me your badge.'

Holman forced her down onto the couch. He leaned over her and pointed at his face. 'Look at this face. Did you see this face on the news?'

She was crying. She didn't understand what he was saying, and she was scared. Holman realised this but was unable to stop himself.

'My name is Holman. One of the officers, his name was Holman, too. Your husband murdered my son. Do you understand that?'

'No!'

'Where is he?'

'I don't know.'

'Did he go to Mexico? I heard he went under the fence.'

'He did not do this. I showed them. He was with us.'

'Where is he? Tell me who's hiding him.' Holman grabbed her throat. His hand encircled her from ear to ear as if acting with a will of its own. He had no sense of what he was doing or why.

But then she made a choking gurgle and Holman saw himself in the moment. He released her and stepped back, his face burning with shame.

The little girl said, 'Mommy?' She stood in the hall.

Maria said, 'It's OK, my love. Go back to bed. I'll be with you soon.'

The little girl returned to her room.

Holman said, 'Listen, I'm sorry. I'm upset. He killed my son.'

She shook her head. 'It was her birthday, the day before yesterday. He was with us for her birthday. He wasn't killing no policemen.'

'Her birthday? The little girl?'

'I can prove it. I showed them the tape. Warren was with us.'

Holman tried to understand what she was saying. 'I don't know what you're telling me. You had a party for the little girl? You had guests?'

She waved towards the television. 'Warren brought us one of these video cameras. It's at my house. We took videos of her blowing out the candles and playing with us, the day before yesterday.'

'That doesn't prove anything.'

'You don't understand. That show was on, that one with the comedian? Warren put her on his back so she could ride him like a donkey and he was going around the living room in front of the TV. You could see the show when Warren was here. That *proves* he was with us.'

Holman had no idea what show she was talking about.

'Those officers were murdered at one thirty in the morning.'

'Yes! The show starts at one.'

'You were having a party for your kid in the middle of the night? C'mon.'

'Warren has the warrants. He has to be careful when he comes by.'

She seemed to believe what she was saying, and it would be easy enough to check. If her videotape showed a television show on the tube, all you had to do was call the TV station and ask what time the show had aired.

'OK. Lemme see it. Show me.'

'The police took it. They said it was evidence.'

Holman worked through what she was telling him. The police took the tape, but clearly hadn't believed it cleared Warren of the crime—they had issued the warrant. Still, Holman thought she was being sincere.

The little girl was back in the hall.

Maria said, 'I'm sorry your son was killed, but it was not Warren. I know what is in your heart now. If you kill him, that will be in your heart, too.'

Holman pulled his eyes from the little girl. 'I'm sorry about what I did.'

He went out of the front door. The sun was blinding after being in the dim house. He walked back to Perry's car, feeling like a boat without a rudder.

Holman put the key in the lock, then was suddenly hit from behind so hard he lost his breath. He smashed into the side of the car as his feet were kicked from beneath him and they rode him down hard onto the street.

When Holman looked up, a red-haired guy in sunglasses and plain-clothes held up a badge. 'You're under arrest.'

Holman closed his eyes as their handcuffs shut on his wrists.

3

It was four plainclothes officers who hooked him up, but only two of them brought him to Parker Center, the red-haired officer, whose name was Vukovich, and a Latin officer named Fuentes. Holman had been arrested by the Los Angeles Police Department on five separate occasions as an adult, and in every case except his last (when he was arrested by an FBI agent named Katherine Pollard) he had been processed through one of

LAPD's nineteen divisional police stations. When they brought him to Parker Center, Holman knew he was in deep shit.

Parker was a tall white and glass building that housed the LAPD's chief and the chief's assistants, and the elite Robbery–Homicide Division, a command division overseeing Homicide Special, Robbery Special and Rape Special. Each of the nineteen divisions had homicide, robbery and sex crimes detectives, but they worked only in their respective divisions; Robbery–Homicide detectives worked on cases that spanned the city.

Vukovich and Fuentes walked Holman into an interview room on the third floor and questioned him for more than an hour, after which another set of detectives took over. Holman knew the drill. The cops asked the same questions over and over, and if your answers changed they knew you were lying. Holman told them the truth about everything except Chee. When Vukovich asked how he knew Maria Juarez was with her cousins, Holman told them he heard it in a bar, some Frogtown paco bragging that he screwed Maria in Junior High, him and sixty-two other guys, and spouting that the cops Warren killed had probably been bagging the little slut, too.

Eight forty that night, Holman was still in the room, having been questioned on and off for more than six hours without being booked. Eight forty-one, the door opened again and Vukovich entered with someone new.

The new man studied Holman for a moment, then put out his hand. Holman thought he looked familiar.

'Mr Holman, I'm Walt Random. I'm sorry about your son.'

Random wore a long-sleeved white shirt and tie without a jacket. A gold detective's shield was clipped to his belt. Random took a seat opposite Holman as Vukovich leaned against the wall.

Holman said, 'Am I being charged with anything?'

'Has Detective Vukovich explained why we pulled you in?'

'No.'

Holman suddenly realised why Random looked familiar. He had been part of the press conference that Holman had seen on TV in the bar.

Random said, 'When the officers ran your vehicle they found thirty-two unpaid parking violations and another nine outstanding traffic violations.'

Holman said, 'Jesus.'

Vukovich smiled. 'Yeah, and you didn't match the DMV description we got of the vehicle's owner, you not being a sixty-four-year-old black male.'

Random said, 'We spoke with Mr Wilkes. You're in the clear so far as the car, even though you've been driving it without a licence. So forget the car and let's get back to Ms Juarez. Why did you go see her?'

The same question he had been asked three dozen times.

Holman gave them the same answer. 'I was looking for her husband.'

'What do you know about her husband?'

'I saw you on TV. You're looking for him.'

'But why were *you* looking for him?'

'He killed my son.'

'How'd you find your way to Ms Juarez?'

'Their address was in the phone book. I went to their house but the place was crawling with people. I started hitting the bars in their neighbourhood and found some people who knew them, and pretty soon I ended up in Silver Lake and met this guy said he knew her. He told me she was staying with her cousins, and that's where I found her.'

Random nodded. 'He knew her address?'

'Information operator gave me the address. The guy I met, he just told me who she was staying with.'

Random smiled, still staring at him. 'Which bar was this?'

'I don't know the name of the place, but it's on Sunset a couple of blocks west of Silver Lake Boulevard. I'm pretty sure it had a Mexican name.'

Holman had driven past earlier. Sunset was lined with Mexican places.

'Uh-huh, so you could take us there?'

'Oh, yeah, absolutely. I told Detective Vukovich three or four hours ago I could take you there.'

'And this man you met, if you saw him again, could you point him out?'

'Absolutely. Without a doubt. If he's still there after all this time.'

Vukovich, smiling again, said, 'Hey, you busting my balls or what?'

Random ignored Vukovich's comment. 'So tell me, did Maria Juarez tell you anything that would help us find her husband?'

Holman suddenly found himself liking Random. He liked the man's intensity and his desire to find Warren Juarez. 'No, sir.'

'Did she tell you why he killed the officers? Or any details of the crime?'

'She said he didn't do it. Told me he was with them when the murders were committed. They have a little girl. She said it was the little girl's birthday and they made a video that proved Warren was with them at the time of the murders. She said she gave it to you guys.'

Random said, 'What were you planning to do when you left her?'

'Same thing I was doing before. Talk to people to see if I could pick up something else. But then I met Mr Vukovich.'

Vukovich laughed and changed his position against the wall.

Holman said, 'They really have a tape?'

'She gave us a tape, but there are questions about when it was made.'

Vukovich added, 'They didn't have to make their video at one o'clock on Tuesday night. We believe they recorded the talk show, then played it back on their VCR. You watch her video, you're seeing a recording of a recording. We believe they made their tape after the murders to use as an alibi.'

Holman frowned. He understood how such a tape could be produced, but he had left Maria with the sense that she was telling the truth. 'One more thing. Richie's commander told me this was a personal beef between Juarez and one of the other officers, Fowler. Is that what it was?'

'That's right. It started a little over a year ago. Fowler and his trainee stopped a kid for a traffic violation. That was Jaime Juarez, Warren's younger brother. Juarez grew belligerent. Fowler pulled him out of the car and found a few crack rocks in his pockets. Juarez claimed Fowler planted the stuff, but he got hit for three years in the State. Second month in, a fight broke out and Jaime was killed. Warren blamed Fowler. Went all over the east side saying he was going to do Fowler for killing the kid.'

Holman took it in. 'Have you named any other suspects?'

'There are no other suspects. Juarez acted alone.'

'That doesn't make sense, Juarez doing this by himself. How did he know they were down there? How'd he find them? How does one street dick take four armed police officers and none of them even get off a shot?'

Random pursed his lips. 'He approached from the east using the bridge supports for cover. He was thirty feet away when he started shooting. He used an autoloading shotgun. Two of the officers were shot in the back, indicating they never knew it was coming. The third officer was likely seated on the hood of his car. He jumped off, turned, and took his shot head on. The fourth officer managed to draw his sidearm, but was dead before he could return fire. Don't ask me which was your son, Mr Holman. I won't tell you.'

Holman felt cold. His breaths were short.

Random checked his watch. 'We know there was only one shooter because all the shell casings came from the same gun. It was Juarez. This video was just a halfassed attempt to cover his ass. As for you, you're free to go.'

Holman stood, but he still had questions.

'Where are you in finding the guy? You have a line on him or what?'

'We already have him. At six twenty this evening, Warren Alberto Juarez was found dead of a self-inflicted gunshot wound. Same shotgun he used to murder your son. Still had it in his hands.'

Random extended his hand once more. Holman felt numb with the news, but took the hand automatically.

'I'm sorry, Mr Holman. I'm truly sorry that four officers were lost like this. It's a goddamned shame.'

'Then why in hell did you ask me if his wife knew where he was?'

'To see if she lied to me. You know how it works.'

Holman found himself getting angry, but fought it down.

Random opened the door. 'Let's make sure we're clear on this—don't go back to Ms Juarez. Her husband might be dead, but she is still the subject of an active investigation.'

'You think she was involved in the killings?'

'She helped him try to get away with it. Whether or not she knew before the fact is still to be determined. Don't get involved in this again. We're giving you a break because you lost your son, but that consideration ends now. If we bring you back to this room, Holman, I'll charge you and see that you're prosecuted. Do we understand each other?'

Holman nodded.

Vukovich peeled himself from the wall, and gently slapped Holman on the back. 'C'mon, bud. I'll take you back to your car.'

AS THEY DROVE to Holman's car, Vukovich said, 'Maybe I should take you home instead of letting you drive. You don't even have a licence.'

'First thing I hear when I get my release is that Richie was killed. I had more on my mind than the DMV.'

'Get it done. I'm not just being an asshole. You get stopped, you're just going to end up in trouble.'

'Tomorrow. First thing.'

Holman made it back to the motel without being stopped and left Perry's car in the alley. Perry was waiting when Holman entered the lobby, leaning back behind his desk with his arms folded and his face pinched.

Perry said, 'You know how much I hadda pay in back fines?'

'You should've told me I was driving around in a wanted vehicle. You rented me a piece of shit that could've put me back into prison.'

'I didn't know about those tickets! Guys like you get'm driving around and don't even tell me. Now I'm stuck with the bill—two thousand, four hundred, eighteen dollars!'

'You should've told them to keep it.'

'They were gonna boot it and hit me for the tow and the impound. I hadda go all the way downtown in rush hour to fork over that dough.'

Holman knew that Perry was dying to hit him for a reimbursement but was worried about the repercussions. If it got back to Gail Manelli, she would know that Perry was renting his vehicle to unlicensed drivers. Then he would lose out on the tenants she fed him through the Bureau of Prisons.

Holman said, 'Tough shit. I was downtown, too, thanks to your car. Did you bring my television today?'

'It's up in your room. You gotta play with the ears. The reception is off.'

Holman started up the stairs.

'Hey. Wait a minute. I got a couple messages for you.'

Holman immediately perked up, thinking that Richie's wife had finally called. He one-eightied back to the desk, where Perry was looking nervous.

'Gail called. She wants you to call her, man.'

'Who else called?'

Perry was holding a note slip, but Holman couldn't see what was on it.

Perry said, 'Now listen, you talk to Gail, don't tell her about the god-damned car. You shouldn't have been driving, and I shouldn't have rented it to you. Neither one of us needs that kind of trouble.'

Holman reached for the slip. 'I'm not going to say anything. Who was the other call?' Holman snagged the slip and Perry let him have it.

'Some woman from a cemetery. She said you'd know what it was about.'

Holman read the note. It was an address and phone number.

Richard Holman
42 Berke Drive #216, LA CA99999
213-555-2817

Holman had guessed that Richie had paid for his mother's burial, but this confirmed it. Holman's heart filled, and when he spoke his voice came in a whisper. 'Did anyone else call? I was expecting another call.'

'Just this. Unless they called while I was paying those fines.'

Holman put the slip of paper into his pocket. 'I'm gonna need the car again tomorrow.'

'Don't say anything to Gail, for Christ's sake.'

Holman didn't bother answering. He went upstairs, turned on the television—a small American brand twenty years out-of-date—and waited for the eleven o'clock news. The picture wavered with hazy ghosts. Holman fought with the antennas trying to make the ghosts go away, but they grew worse.

THE NEXT MORNING, after a fitful night's sleep, Holman climbed out of bed at a quarter past five. He went down for a paper and chocolate milk, then returned to his room to read the accounts of last night's developments.

The newspaper reported that three boys had discovered Juarez's body in an abandoned house in Eagle Rock, less than one mile from Juarez's home. Police stated that a neighbour living near the abandoned house reported hearing a gunshot early during the morning following the murders. Holman wondered why the neighbour hadn't called the police when he heard the shot, but he knew that people heard things all the time they didn't report.

Statements made by the boys and by officers at the scene described Juarez as having been seated on the floor with his back to a wall and a twelve-gauge shotgun clutched in his right hand. A representative of the coroner's office stated that death appeared to have been instantaneous.

Holman was thinking about the nature of Juarez's death when his phone rang. He answered tentatively. 'Hello?'

'Bro! I thought you was in jail, homes! I heard you got busted!'

'You mean last night?'

'What you think I mean? The whole neighbourhood saw you get hooked up, homes! I thought they violated your ass! Whatchu do over there?'

'I just talked to the lady. No law against knocking on a door.'

'I oughta come over there kick your ass myself, worryin' me like this!'

'I'm OK, bro. They just talked to me.'

'You kill her old man?'

'I didn't have anything to do with that. He killed himself.'

'I didn't believe that suicide shit. I figured you took his ass out.'

Holman changed the subject. 'Hey, I've been renting a guy's car for twenty dollars a day and it's killing me. Could you set me up with some wheels?'

'Sure, bro, whatever you want.'

'A driver's licence. A real one from the DMV.'

'I can take care of you, bro. I even got the camera.'

Back in the day, Chee had fabricated driver's licences, green cards and social security cards for his uncles. Apparently, he still had the skills.

Holman made arrangements to stop by Chee's later, then hung up. He showered and dressed. It was six fifty when he left his room.

Richie's address led to a four-storey courtyard apartment in Westwood near UCLA. Since the address dated from Donna's burial almost two years ago, Holman was worried that Richie had moved. He debated using the phone number, but Richie's wife had not called, so it was clear she wanted no contact. If Holman phoned now and reached her, she might refuse to see him and might even call the police. Holman figured his best chance was to catch her early and not warn her he was coming. *If* she still lived there.

The building's main entrance was a glass security door that required a key. Mail boxes were on the street side of the door, along with a security phone so guests could call to be buzzed in by the tenants. Holman went to the boxes and searched through the apartment numbers, hoping to find his son's name on 216. He did.

Donna had given the boy Holman's name even though they weren't married, and seeing it moved him. He touched the name—HOLMAN—thinking, *This was my son*, then felt an angry ache in his chest and turned away.

Holman waited by the security door for almost ten minutes until a young Asian man with a book bag pushed open the door on his way out to class. Holman caught the door before it closed and let himself in.

The interior courtyard was small and filled with birds-of-paradise trees. The inward-facing walls of the building were ringed with exposed walkways. Holman climbed the stairs to the second floor, then followed the numbers until he found 216. He knocked, wrapping himself in a numbness that was designed to protect him from his own feelings.

A young woman opened the door, and his numbness was gone.

Her face was focused and contained, as if she was concentrating on something more important than answering the door. She was slight, with dark eyes, a thin face and prominent ears. She was wearing denim shorts, a light green blouse and sandals. Holman thought she looked like a child.

She stared at him with indifference. 'Yes?'

'I'm Max Holman. Richie's father.'

Holman waited for her to unload. He expected her to tell him what a rotten bastard and lousy father he was, but the indifference vanished and she canted her head as if seeing him for the first time.

'Ohmigod. Well. This is awkward.'

'It's awkward for me, too. I don't know your name.'

'Elizabeth. Liz.'

'I'd like to talk with you if you don't mind. It would mean a lot to me.'

She suddenly opened the door. 'I have to apologise. I was going to call, but I just—I didn't know what to say. Please. Come in. I'm getting ready for class, but I have a few minutes. There's some coffee—'

Holman stepped past her and waited in the living room as she closed the door. He told her not to go to any trouble, but she went to the kitchen anyway and took two mugs from the cupboard.

'This is so weird. I'm sorry, I don't use sugar. And I have non-fat milk.'

'Black is fine.'

It was a large apartment, with the living room, dining area and kitchen all sharing space. Holman was overcome by being in Richie's home. He had told himself to be all business, just ask his questions and get out, but now his son's life was all around him and he wanted to fill himself with it: a mismatched couch and chair faced a TV in the corner; racks cluttered with CDs and DVDs tipped against the wall; a built-in gas fireplace with the mantel above filled with photographs. Holman let himself drift closer.

'This is a nice place,' he said.

'It's close to campus. I'm getting my masters in child psychology.'

'That sounds real good.' Holman felt like a dummy, and wished he could think of something better to say. 'I just got out of prison.' Stupid.

'I know.'

The photos showed Richie and Liz together, alone and with other couples. One shot showed them on a boat, another wearing bright parkas in the snow, another at a picnic where everyone wore LAPD T-shirts. Holman found himself smiling, but then he saw a picture of Richie with Donna, and his smile collapsed. Donna had been younger than Holman, but in the picture she looked old, her face was cut by deep lines and shadows. Holman turned away, hiding from the memories and the sudden flush of shame, and found Liz beside him with the coffee. She offered a cup, and Holman accepted it.

He said, 'I like the pictures. It's like getting to know him a little bit.'

'You look like him. He was a little taller but not much. You're heavier.'

'I got fat.'

She flushed. 'I didn't mean fat. Richard was a runner. That's all I meant.'

Her eyes filled then, and Holman didn't know what to do. He raised a hand, thinking to touch her shoulder, but he was afraid he might scare her.

Then she pulled herself together and rubbed her eyes clear with the flat of her hand. 'I'm sorry. This really sucks. This *so* really sucks. Listen—' She held out her hand. 'It's good to finally meet you.'

'You really think I look like him?'

She made a thin smile. 'Clones. Donna always said the same thing.'

Holman said, 'I know you have to get to class and all, but can I ask you a couple of questions about what happened? It won't take long.'

'They found that man who killed them.'

'I know, but I still have some questions about how this could happen.'

'Juarez blamed Mike for what happened to his brother. Do you know that whole story?'

'Yeah, it's in the paper. You knew Sergeant Fowler?'

'Mike was Richard's training officer. They were still really good friends.'

'Detective Random told me that Juarez had been making threats ever since his brother was killed. Was Mike worried about it?'

She frowned as she thought about it, then shook her head. 'Mike never seemed worried. It wasn't like I saw him that often, just every couple of months or so, but he didn't seem worried about anything.'

'Did Richie maybe mention that Mike was worried?'

'Richard never said anything, but he wouldn't have. He never brought that kind of thing home.'

Holman said, 'Another thing I'm wondering about—Random told me Richie wasn't on duty that night?'

'No. He was here working. He went out to meet the guys sometimes, but never that late. He told me he had to go meet them. That's all he said.'

'Did he say he was going to the river?'

'No. I just assumed they would meet at a bar.'

'What's bothering me is how Juarez found them. The police haven't been able to explain that. It'd be tough to follow someone into that river and not be seen. So I'm thinking, if they went down there all the time—you know, a regular thing—maybe Juarez heard about it and knew where to find them.'

'I just don't know. I can't believe they went down there all the time and he didn't tell me about it—it's so far out of the way.'

Holman agreed. They could have sat around getting drunk anywhere, but they had gone down into a deserted, off-limits place like the river bed. This implied they didn't want to be seen, but Holman also knew that cops were like anyone else—they might have gone down there just for the thrill of being someplace no one else could go, like kids breaking into an empty house or climbing up to the Hollywood sign.

'You said he almost never went out late like that, but on that night he did. What was different about that night?'

Liz appeared surprised, but then her face darkened and a vertical line cut her forehead. She seemed to be struggling with her answer. She said, 'You.'

'I don't understand.'

'You were being released the next day. That's what was different that night, and we both knew it. Richard never spoke about you. I tried talking to him about you—when Donna was still alive we *both* tried—but he just wouldn't. I knew your release date was coming up. Richard knew, but he still wouldn't talk about it, and I knew it was bothering him.'

Holman was feeling sick. 'Did he say . . . how it was bothering him?'

She cocked her head again, then put down her cup. 'Come see.'

He followed her back to a bedroom that was arranged as an office. Two desks were set up, one for him and one for her. Her desk was stacked with text books. Richie's desk was in a corner where corkboards were fixed to the walls. The boards were covered with clippings and slips of paper.

Liz pointed out the clippings. 'Take a look.'

THREE BANKS HIT IN ONE DAY, SHOOTOUT ENDS CRIME SPREE, TAKEOVER BANDITS STOPPED, BYSTANDER KILLED IN ROBBERY. The articles Holman skimmed were about a pair of takeover lunatics named Marchenko and Parsons. Holman had heard about them in Lompoc.

She said, 'He became fascinated with bank robberies. He clipped stories and pulled articles off the Internet and spent all of his time in here with this stuff. It doesn't take a doctorate to figure out why.'

'Because of me?'

'We knew you were approaching your release date. We didn't know if you would try to contact us or if we should contact you or what to do about you. It was pretty clear he was working out his anxiety about you.' Liz crossed her arms and her face tightened. 'When he told me he'd got a call and was going to see the guys, he had been in here all evening. I think he needed to talk to them. He couldn't talk to me about it, and now look—now look.'

Holman watched her eyes fill, but was scared to touch her. He said, 'I—'

She shook her head and Holman took it as a warning—like maybe she sensed he wanted to comfort her—and he felt even worse.

'Goddammit, he just had to go out,' she said. 'He had to go.'

'Maybe we should go back in the living room.'

She closed her eyes, then shook her head again, but this time she was telling him she was all right—she was fighting the pain and determined to kill it. She finally opened her eyes and said, 'Sometimes it's easier for a man to show what he feels is a weakness to another male rather than to a female. It's easier to pretend it's work than to deal honestly with the emotions. I think that's what he did that night. I think that's why he died.'

'Talking about me?'

'No, not you, not specifically—these bank robberies. That was his way of talking about you. The work was like an extra duty assignment. He wanted to be a detective and move up the ladder.'

Holman glanced at Richie's desk. Copies of what looked like police reports and case files were spread over it. Holman skimmed the top pages and realised that everything was about Marchenko and Parsons. A small map of the city was pinned to the board with lines connecting small 'X's numbered 1 to 13. Richie had gone so far as to map their robberies.

'I robbed banks, but I never did anything like this,' Holman said. 'I never hurt anyone. I wasn't anything like these guys.'

Liz's expression softened. 'I didn't mean it like that. Donna told us how you got caught. Richard knew you weren't like them.'

'He was working on this before he went out?'

'Yeah. He had been here all evening.'

'Were those other guys on the Marchenko thing, too?'

'Mike, maybe. He talked with Mike about it. I don't know about the others.'

Holman nodded, taking a last look at his dead son's workplace. He wanted to read everything on Richie's desk. He wanted to know why a uniformed officer with only a couple of years on the job was involved in a major investigation and why his son had left home in the middle of the night. He had come here for answers, but now had more questions.

'They haven't told me about the arrangements yet. For his funeral.'

'They're having a memorial for the four of them tomorrow at the Police Academy. The police haven't released them for a burial. I guess . . .'

Her voice faded, but Holman understood why. These officers had been murdered—the medical examiner was probably still gathering evidence and they couldn't be buried until all of the tests and fact-finding was complete.

Liz suddenly touched his arm. 'You'll come, won't you? I would like you to be there.'

Holman felt relieved. He had been worried she might try to keep him away from the service. It wasn't lost on him that neither Levy nor Random had told him about the memorial.

'I would like that, Liz. Thank you.'

She rose up on her toes to kiss his cheek. 'I wish it had been different.'

Holman had spent the past ten years wishing everything had been different. He thanked her again when she let him out, then returned to his car.

THE MEMORIAL SERVICE was held in the auditorium at the LAPD's Police Academy in Chavez Ravine, which was set between two hills outside the Stadium Way entrance to Dodger Stadium. When Holman passed the gate, he recalled how he and Chee had often cruised the parking lot for cars to steal during the middle innings.

Liz had invited Holman to accompany her and her family to the service, but Holman had declined. Liz's father was a physician and her mother was a social worker; they were educated, affluent and normal in a way Holman admired, but they reminded him of everything he was not. He had agreed to join Liz at the service, and drove himself to the academy in Perry's Mercury.

Holman parked off the academy grounds and walked up to the auditorium, following the directions Liz had given him. People were already streaming uphill to the academy. Holman glanced over their faces, hoping to spot Random or Vukovich. He had phoned Random three times to discuss what he had learned from Liz, but the detective had not returned his calls.

Liz had told him to meet them in the rock garden outside the auditorium. The flow of foot traffic led him up through the centre of the academy to the garden, where a large crowd of people stood in small groups. Holman felt self-conscious. Liz had lent him one of Richie's dark suits, but the trousers were too tight so Holman wore them unfastened beneath his belt. He had sweated through the suit even before he reached the garden, and now he felt like a wino in hand-me-down threads.

Holman found Liz and her family with Richie's commander, Captain Levy. Levy shook Holman's hand, then took them all to meet the other families. He introduced them to Mike Fowler's widow and four sons, Mellon's wife and Ash's parents. All of them seemed hollow and drained.

Levy led them inside. The auditorium was filled with chairs. A dais had been erected, with large photographs of the four officers draped by American flags to either side. Holman hesitated at the doors, glanced behind him and saw Random with three other men at the edge of the crowd. Holman immediately reversed course. He was halfway to Random when Vukovich suddenly blocked his way.

Vukovich was wearing a dark navy suit and sunglasses. He said, 'It's a sad day, Mr Holman. You're not still driving without a licence, are you?'

'I've called Random three times, but he hasn't seen fit to return my calls. I have more questions about what happened that night.'

'We know what happened that night. We told you.'

Holman glanced past Vukovich at Random. Random was staring back, but then resumed his conversation. Holman looked back at Vukovich. 'What you told me doesn't add up. Was Richie working on the Marchenko and Parsons investigation?'

Vukovich studied him for a moment, then turned away. 'Wait here, Mr Holman. I'll see if the boss has time to talk to you.'

Vukovich went over to Random and the three men. Holman guessed they were high-level brass. When Vukovich reached them, Random and two of the men glanced back at Holman, then turned their backs and continued talking. After a moment, Random and Vukovich came over.

Random didn't look happy, but he offered his hand. 'Let's step to the side, Mr Holman. It'll be easier to talk when we're out of the way.'

Holman followed the two detectives to the edge of the garden.

When they were away from the other people, Random crossed his arms. 'All right, I understand you have some questions?'

Holman described his conversation with Liz and the enormous collection of material pertaining to Marchenko and Parsons he had found on Richie's desk. He still didn't buy the explanation the police had put forth about Juarez. The bank robberies seemed a more likely connection if Richie was involved in the investigation. Holman floated his theory, but Random shook his head even before Holman finished.

'They weren't investigating Marchenko and Parsons. Marchenko and Parsons are dead. That case was closed three months ago.'

'Richie told his wife he had an extra duty assignment. She thought Mike Fowler might have been involved in it, too.'

Random looked impatient. The auditorium was filling.

'If your son was looking into Marchenko and Parsons he was doing so as a hobby or maybe as an assignment for a class he was taking, but that's all. He was a uniformed patrol officer. Patrol officers aren't detectives.'

'Richie was home all evening until he got a call and went to meet his friends at one in the morning. If I was him and my buddies called that time of night just to go drinking I'd have blown them off—but if we're doing police work, then maybe I'd go. If they were under the bridge because of Marchenko and Parsons, it might be connected with their murder.'

Random seemed to be studying him. He finally nodded as if he had come to a decision he didn't enjoy. 'OK, look, you know what the bad news is? They went down there to drink. I'm going to tell you something now, but if you repeat it and it gets back to me I'll deny I said it. Vuke?'

Vukovich nodded, agreeing that he would deny it, too.

Random pursed his lips and lowered his voice. 'Mike Fowler was a drunk and a disgraceful police officer. He radioed he was going to take a break, but he had no business telling those younger officers to meet him in an off-limits location. Fowler was a supervisor. He was supposed to be available to patrol officers in his area when they needed his assistance, but he went drinking instead. Mellon was on duty, too, and knew better, but he was a mediocre officer, also—he wasn't even in his assigned service division. Ash was off duty, but he wasn't in the running for Officer of the Year, either.'

'What are you telling me, Random? What does any of this have to do with Marchenko and Parsons?'

'You're looking to understand why those officers were under the bridge, so I'm telling you. I blame Mike Fowler for what happened, him being a supervisor, but no one was down there trying to solve the crime of the century. They were problem officers with shit records and a crappy attitude.'

Holman felt himself flush. His temples began to throb. 'Are you telling me that Richie was a rotten cop? Is that what you're saying?'

Vukovich held up a finger. 'Take it easy, bud. You're the one who asked.'

Random said, 'Sir, I didn't want to have to tell you any of this.'

The throbbing in Holman's head spread to his shoulders and arms, and he wanted to knuckle up. All the deep parts of him wanted to throw fists at Random and Vukovich for saying that Richie was rotten, but Holman told himself he wasn't like that any more. He forced down his anger and spoke slowly. 'Richie was working on something about Marchenko and Parsons. I want to know why he had to talk to Fowler about it at one in the morning.'

'What you need to do is concentrate on making good your release and let us do our jobs. This conversation is over, Mr Holman. I suggest you settle down and pay your respects.'

Random turned away and moved with the crowd into the auditorium. Vukovich stayed with Holman a moment longer before following.

Holman went to the double doors feeling brittle with rage. He watched people taking their seats. The four dead men stared at him from their giant pictures. He felt Richie's dead two-dimensional eyes.

He turned away and walked fast back to his car, tears filling his eyes with great hot drops that came as if they were being crushed from his heart.

Richie wasn't bad. He wasn't like his father.

Holman wiped the tears from his face and walked faster. He didn't believe it. He wouldn't let himself believe it.

My son is not like me.

Holman swore he would prove it. He had already asked the last and only person he trusted for help and had been waiting to hear back from her. He needed her help. He needed her, and he prayed she would answer.

4

FBI Special Agent Katherine Pollard (retired) stood in the kitchen of her small house, watching the clock above her sink. She watched the second hand sweep silently towards the twelve. The minute hand was poised at 11.32. The second hand touched the twelve. The minute hand released like a firing pin, jumping to 11.33—

Tock! The snap of passing time broke the silence.

Pollard wiped a ribbon of sweat from her face as she considered the debris that had accumulated in her kitchen: cups, grape juice cartons, open boxes of Captain Crunch and Sugar Stars, and bowls showing the first stages of whole milk curdled by the heat. Pollard lived in the Simi Valley where the temperature that day had already notched 104° Fahrenheit. Her air conditioner had been out for six days and wasn't likely to be fixed any time soon—Katherine Pollard was broke. She was preparing herself for the inevitable and humiliating call to beg her mother for money.

Pollard had left the FBI eight years ago after she married a fellow agent named Marty Baum and became pregnant with their first child. She had left the job for all the right reasons: she had loved Marty, they both wanted her to be a full-time mom for their son, and with Marty's salary they had enough money. But that was *then*. Two children, one legal separation and five years after the fact—Marty had dropped dead of a heart attack while scuba diving in Aruba with his then girlfriend, a twenty-year-old waitress.

Pollard had scraped by on Marty's death benefits, but more and more she required help from her mother, which was humiliating, and now the AC had been out for almost a week. One hour and twenty-six minutes until her children, David and Lyle, seven and six, would arrive home from camp, dirty and filled with complaints about the heat. Pollard wiped more sweat from her face, scooped up her cordless phone, then brought it out to her car.

The heat pounded down on her like a blow torch. Katherine opened her Subaru, started the engine and rolled down the windows. It had to be 150° inside the car. She maxed out the AC until it blew cold, then rolled up the windows. She let the icy air blow hard on her face, then lifted her T-shirt.

When she felt on the safe side of heat stroke, she turned on the phone and punched in a number. Her mother's answering machine picked up as expected; she usually screened her calls while she played online poker.

'Mom, it's me, pick up. Are you there?'

Her mother came on the line. 'Is everything all right?'

Pollard knew better than to make small talk. She steeled herself and got to the point. 'Our air conditioner went out. They want twelve hundred dollars to fix it. I don't have it, Mom.'

'Katherine, when are you going to find another man?'

'I need twelve hundred dollars, Mom, not another man.'

'You know I live to help you and those boys, but you have to help yourself sometimes, too, Katherine. You're not getting any younger . . .'

Pollard lowered the phone while her mother was still talking. She saw the mail van approaching, then watched the postman shove the day's ration of bills into her mailbox. When he drove away, Pollard raised the phone again.

She said, 'Mom, let me ask you something. If I went back to work, would you be willing to watch the boys?'

'Work doing what? Not with the FBI again.'

Pollard had been thinking about it. If she returned to the FBI, a position in the Los Angeles field office was unlikely. LA was a hot posting that drew far more applicants than available duty assignments. Pollard would more likely find herself posted in the middle of nowhere, but she didn't want to be just anywhere; Katherine Pollard had spent three years working on the

FBI's elite Bank Squad in the bank robbery capital of the world. She wished she had never left the Feeb. She missed the action. She missed the money.

'I might be able to get on as a security consultant with one of the banking chains or a private firm like Kroll.'

'How many hours are we talking about, me being with the boys?'

Pollard lowered the phone again. She watched the postman drive to the next house. When she lifted the phone again her mother was calling her.

'Katherine? Katherine, are you there? Did I lose you?'

'We need the money.'

'I'll fix your air conditioner. I can't have my grandsons living in—'

'I'm talking about me going back to work. The only way I can go back to work is if you help me with the boys—'

'We can talk about it, Katherine. I like the idea of you going back to work. You might meet someone—'

'I have to call the repairman. I'll talk to you later.'

Pollard hung up, then went to retrieve her mail. She shuffled through the letters as she walked to her car, finding the predictable Visa and Mastercard bills along with something that surprised her—a brown manila envelope showing the FBI's return address in Westwood, her old office. Katherine hadn't received anything from the Westwood Feebs in years.

When she was safely back in her car, she tore open the envelope and found a white envelope inside. It had been opened and resealed, as was all mail forwarded to current or former agents by the FBI. A printed yellow slip accompanied the letter: THIS PARCEL HAS BEEN TESTED FOR TOXINS AND BIOHAZARDS, AND WAS DETERMINED SUITABLE FOR REMAILING.

The white envelope was addressed to her, care of the Westwood office. It bore a Culver City return address that she did not recognise. She tore the end of the envelope, shook out a one-page handwritten letter folded around a newspaper clipping, and read: Max Holman, Pacific Gardens Motel, Culver City CA99999. She stopped when she saw the name and broke into a crooked smile, swept up in Bank Squad memories.

'Ohmigod! Max Holman!'

She read on—

Dear Special Agent Pollard,

I hope this letter finds you in good health. You arrested me for bank robbery. Please know I bear no grudge and still appreshiate that you

spoke on my behalf to the federal prosecutor. I have sucsessfully
completed my incarceration and am now on supervised release and
am employed. Again, I thank you for your kind and supportive words,
and hope you will remember them now.

Katherine remembered Holman and thought as well of him as a cop
could think of a man who had robbed nine banks. She felt no warmth
towards him for his robberies, but for how she bagged him on his ninth
caper. Max Holman had been famous for the way he went down, even
among the jaded agents of the FBI's Bank Squad. She continued reading:

My son was Los Angeles Police Officer Richard Holman, which you
can read about in the enclosed article. My son and three other
officers were murdered. I am writing you now to ask your help.

Pollard unfolded the article. She recognised it as a piece about the four
officers who had been murdered in the downtown river basin. Pollard had
seen coverage on the evening news. She didn't bother to read the clipping,
but she looked at the pictures of the four deceased officers. The last photograph was identified as Officer Richard Holman. A circle had been drawn
round his picture. Two words were written outside the circle: *MY SON.*
Pollard didn't remember that Holman had a son, but she also couldn't
remember what Holman looked like. As she studied the picture her memories returned. Yeah, she could see it—the thin mouth and strong neck.
Holman's son looked like his father. Pollard read on with interest—

The police believe they have identified the murderer but I still have
questions and cannot get answers. I believe the police hold my status
as a convicted criminal against me and that is why they will not
listen. As you are an FBI Special Agent I am hoping you will get these
answers for me. That is all I want.
*   My son was a good man. Not like me. Please call if you will help.*
You can also talk to my release supervisor, who will vouch for me.
*   Sincerly yours, Max Holman*

Beneath his name, Holman had written the phone number of the Pacific
Gardens Motel office, and his work number. Below the numbers he had
written the name and number of his federal release supervisor. Pollard
glanced at the clipping again and flashed on her own boys, older, and hoped
she would never get the news Max Holman had. It had been bad enough

when she was informed about Marty, even though their marriage was over and they were on their way to a divorce. In that singular moment, their bad times had vanished and she felt as if she had lost a piece of herself.

Pollard suddenly felt a rush of irritation and pushed the letter and the clipping aside, her nostalgic feelings for Holman and the day she bagged him gone. Pollard believed what all cops eventually learned—criminals were degenerates. You could bag them, house them and counsel them, but criminals never changed. It was almost certain that Holman was running some kind of scam, and Pollard had almost fallen for it.

She scooped up the phone and the bills, then shut down her car and stormed through the heat to her house. She had humiliated herself by asking her mother for money and now she had to beg the repairman to drag himself out here to make her nightmare house livable. Pollard was inside and dialling the repairman when she put down the phone, returned to her car and retrieved Max Holman's miserable, stupid-ass letter.

She called the repairman, but then she called Gail Manelli, Holman's release supervisor.

EARLY IN THE WEEK, Holman found Chee in the office of his East LA shop along with a pretty young girl who smiled shyly when Holman entered. Chee's face split into a craggy smile, his teeth brown with the morning's coffee.

Chee said, 'Yo, homes. This is my youngest baby, Marisol. Sweetie, say hi to Mr Holman.'

Marisol told Holman it was a pleasure to meet him.

Chee said, 'Baby, have Raul come up here, would you? In my office. Here, bro, c'mon inside.'

Marisol used an intercom to summon Raul as Holman followed Chee into his office. Chee closed the door behind them, shutting her out.

Holman said, 'Pretty girl, Chee. Congratulations.'

Chee went to a file drawer and pulled out a camera. 'Girl is my heart, bro, that one and the others. Here—stand right there and look at me.'

'You get me lined up with a ride?'

'Am I the Chee? Let's get you squared up with this licence.'

Chee positioned Holman before a dark blue wall, then lined up the camera. 'Digital, baby—state of the art. Goddammit, Holman, this ain't a mug shot—try not to look like you want to kill me.'

Holman smiled and the flash went off as someone knocked at the door.

A short, hard-eyed young man stepped inside. His arms and face were streaked with grease.

Chee studied the digital image in the camera, then tossed the camera to the new guy. 'California DL, date of issue is today, no restrictions.'

Raul glanced at Holman. 'Gonna need an address, his date of birth, the stats and a signature.'

Chee took a pad and pen from his desk and handed them to Holman. 'Here. Put down your height and weight, too.'

Holman did what he was told. 'How long before I get the licence?'

'Time you leave with the car, bro. It won't take long.'

Holman followed Chee out through the shop into a parking area, where a row of cars was waiting.

Chee eyeballed the Mercury. 'Man, no wonder you got pinched. That thing got "work release" written all over it.'

'Can you have someone bring it back to the motel for me?'

'Yeah, no problem. Here's what I got for you—a Ford Taurus or this Highlander, either one carry you in boring middle-class style, both registered to a rental company with proof of insurance, without wants, warrants or traffic citations. I'm loaning you a car, but you get stopped, it's rented.'

The Highlander was black and shiny, and sat high on its big tyres. Holman liked the idea of being able to see what was coming.

'The Highlander, I guess.'

'Sweet choice, bro—you gonna look like a yuppie on your way to the Whole Foods. C'mon, get in. I got something else for you, too, make your life a little easier now you back in the world. Look in the console.'

Holman climbed in and opened the console. Inside was a cellphone.

Chee beamed proudly. 'Got you a cellphone, bro. This ain't ten years ago, stoppin' at payphones and digging for quarters—you got to stay on the grid twenty-four seven. Instruction book's in there with your number in it. You plug that cord into the cigarette lighter to keep it charged up.'

Holman looked back at Chee. 'Remember when you offered to front me some cash? I hate to do it, man, you being so nice with the car and this phone, but I gotta go back on what I said. I need a pack.'

A pack was a thousand dollars. When banks wrapped used twenties, they bundled fifty bills to a pack. A thousand dollars.

Chee studied him, then touched his own nose. 'Whatever you want, homes, but I gotta ask—you back on the crank?'

'It's nothing like that. I got someone to help me with this thing about Richie—a professional, bro; she really knows what she's doing. I want to be ready in case there's expenses.'

Holman had been relieved when Special Agent Pollard contacted him through Gail Manelli. He hadn't held much hope he would hear from her. She had checked him out with both Manelli and Wally Figg at the CCC before calling him, and had refused to give him her phone number, but Holman wasn't complaining—she had finally agreed to meet him to listen to his case, at a Starbucks in Westwood, across the street from the FBI office where she had booked him on the day she arrested him.

Chee squinted at him. 'She? What kind of professional?'

'The Fed who arrested me.'

Chee waved his hands. 'Bro! Holman, you lost your mind, homes?'

'She treated me right, Chee. She went to bat for me with the Assistant US Attorney, man. She helped me get a reduced charge.'

'That's because you damn near gave yourself up! I remember that bitch runnin' into the bank, Holman! She's gonna set you up, homes!'

Holman decided not to mention that Pollard was no longer an agent. He had been disappointed when she told him, but he believed she would still have connections and be able to help him get answers. 'Chee, listen, I gotta go. I have to meet her. You going to be able to help me with that money?'

Chee waved his hand again, axing away his disgust. 'Yeah, I'll get you the money. Don't mention my name to her, Holman. Do not let my name pass your lips in her presence, man. I don't want her to know I'm alive.'

'I didn't mention you when they were sweating me, homes. Why would I mention you now?'

Chee looked embarrassed and waved his hand again as he left.

Holman familiarised himself with the Highlander while he waited. When Chee returned, he handed Holman a plain white envelope, the licence and some rental papers. Holman didn't look in the envelope. He tucked it into the console, then looked at the licence. It was a perfect California driver's licence, showing a seven-year expiration date and the state seal over Holman's picture. A miniature version of his signature was laid along the bottom of the plastic card beneath his address and description.

Holman said, 'Damn, this looks real.'

'*Is* real, bro. That's a legitimate Cal state driver's licence number straight up in the system. You get stopped, they run that licence through DMV, it's gonna show you at your address with a brand-new driving record. So, you give me the keys to that thing you been driving. I'll have a couple of boys take it back to your place.'

'Thanks, Chee. I really appreciate this.'

Chee put his hands on the Highlander's door and leaned into the window, his eyes fierce. 'Don't trust this woman, Holman. She put you in the joint once, bro. Don't trust her.'

'I gotta go.'

Chee stepped back, watching Holman with disgusted eyes, and Holman heard him mutter. 'Hero Bandit, my ass.'

Holman pulled out into traffic, thinking he hadn't been called the Hero Bandit in years.

HOLMAN ARRIVED fifteen minutes early and seated himself at a table with a clear view of the door. He wasn't sure he would recognise Agent Pollard, but he wanted her to have an unobstructed view of him when she entered. He wanted her to feel safe. He had shaved twice that morning, and polished his shoes. He had washed his clothes the night before and rented Perry's iron and ironing board for two dollars, so he would appear unthreatening.

The Starbucks was predictably crowded, but Holman knew this was one of her reasons for choosing it. She would feel safer with other people around. Holman settled in, expecting her to arrive late—to establish her authority. He didn't mind.

He was watching the entrance at twelve minutes after the hour when Agent Pollard entered. He wasn't sure it was Pollard at first. The agent who arrested him had been bony and angular, with light, short-cropped hair. This woman was heavier, with dark hair to her shoulders. She wore a straw-coloured jacket over slacks and a dark shirt, and sunglasses. Her expression gave her away. The serious game-face expression screamed FED. Holman wondered if she had practised it on the way over.

Holman didn't call out or stand. He placed his hands palms down on the table and waited for her to notice him. When she finally saw him, Holman offered a smile, but she did not return it. She stepped between the people waiting for their lattes and approached the empty chair opposite him.

She said, 'Mr Holman?'

'Hi, Agent Pollard. OK if I stand? It'd be polite, but I don't want you to think I'm attacking you or anything. Could I get you a cup of coffee?'

Holman kept his hands on the table and smiled again.

She still didn't return the smile or offer her hand. She took her seat, all business. 'You don't have to stand and I don't have time for the coffee. I want to make sure you understand the ground rules here. I'm happy you completed your term and you're set up with a job and all—congratulations. I mean that, Holman—congratulations. But I want you to understand— even though Ms Manelli and Mr Figg vouched for you, I'm here out of respect for your son. That's a terrible loss. But if you abuse that respect in any way, I'm gone.'

'Yes, ma'am. If you want to pat me down or anything, it's OK.'

Holman knew he wouldn't have long to make his case. Pollard was already antsy, and probably not happy she had agreed to see him. During their phone conversation, she had tried to reassure him that the murder scenario the police described and their conclusions regarding Warren Juarez were reasonable, but she hadn't been able to answer his torrent of questions or see the evidence he had amassed. Reluctantly, she had finally agreed to let him present his case in person—not, Holman knew, because she believed the police might be wrong, but to help a grieving father with the loss of his son. She probably felt he had earned the face time for the way he went down, but that was all. Holman knew he had only one shot, so he was saving his best hook for last.

He opened the envelope in which he kept his growing collection of clippings and documents and shook out the thick sheaf of papers. He said, 'Did you have a chance to review what happened?'

'Yes, I read everything that appeared in the *Times*.'

Holman fingered through his papers until he found what he wanted. He turned it so she could see. 'The newspaper ran this diagram of the crime scene. See how they drew in the cars and the bodies? I went down there to see for myself—'

'You went down into the river bed?'

'When I was stealing cars—that was before I got into banks—I spent time down in those flats. That's what it is: flat. The bed on either side of the channel is an empty expanse of concrete like a parking lot. Only way you can get down there is by the service drives the maintenance people use.'

Pollard leaned forward to follow what he was saying on the map. 'All right. What's your point?'

'The drive comes down the embankment right here in full view of where the officers were parked. See? The shooter had to come down this drive, but if he came down it they would have been able to see him.'

'It was one in the morning. It was dark. Besides, that thing probably isn't drawn to scale.'

Holman took out a second map, one that he had made himself. 'No, it's not, so I made this one myself. The service drive was way more visible from under the bridge than the newspaper drawing made it seem. And something else—there's a gate here at the top of the drive, see? You have to climb the fence or cut the lock. Either way would make a helluva noise.'

Pollard compared the two drawings. Finally she sat back again and shrugged. 'The officers left the gate open when they drove down.'

'I asked the cops how the gate was found, but they wouldn't tell me. I don't think Richie and those other officers would have left it open. If you leave the gate open, you take the chance a security patrol might see it and then you're screwed. We always closed the gate and ran the chain back through, and I'll bet that's what Richie and those other guys did, too.'

Pollard sat back. 'When you were stealing cars.'

'If the gate was closed, the shooter had to open it or go over it, and that makes noise. I know those guys were drinking but they only had a six-pack— how drunk could they be? If Juarez was stoned like you suggested on the phone, how quiet could *he* be? Those officers would have heard something.'

'What are you saying, Holman? You think Juarez didn't do it?'

'I'm saying it didn't matter what the officers heard. I think they knew the shooter.'

Pollard crossed her arms, the ultimate signal she was walling him off.

Holman knew he was losing her, but he was ready with his hook. He said, 'Have you heard of two bank hitters named Marchenko and Parsons?'

Holman watched her stiffen and knew she was finally interested. She took off her sunglasses. The skin round her eyes had grown lined and papery.

She said, 'I've heard of them. And?'

Holman placed Richie's map of Marchenko's and Parsons's robberies in front of her. 'My son did this. His wife, Liz, let me make a copy.'

'It's a map of their robberies.'

'The night he died, Richie got a call from Fowler, and that's when he left. He was going to meet him to talk about Marchenko and Parsons.'

'Marchenko and Parsons are dead. That case closed three months ago.'

Holman peeled off copies of the articles and the cover sheets of the reports he had found on Richie's desk and put them in front of her. 'Richie told his wife they were working on the case. His desk at home was covered with stuff like this. I asked the police what Richie was doing. I tried to see the detectives who worked on Marchenko and Parsons, but no one would talk to me. They told me what you just did, that the case was closed. But Richie told his wife he was going to see Fowler about it, and now he's dead.'

Pollard skimmed through the pages. She finally looked up. 'I'm not sure what you want from me.'

'I want to know why Richie was working on a dead case. I want to know how Juarez was connected to a couple of bank hitters. I want to know why my son and his friends let someone get close enough to kill them. I want to know who killed them.'

Pollard stared at him and Holman stared back. He didn't let his eyes show fear or rage. He kept that part hidden.

She took a breath and wet her lips. 'I guess I could make a couple of calls. I'd be willing to do that.'

Holman returned all his papers to the envelope, then wrote his new cell-phone number on the cover. 'This is everything I found in the library on Marchenko and Parsons, and some of the stuff from Richie's place. I made copies. That's my phone number at the motel, and my new cell number, too.'

She looked at the envelope without touching it.

He said, 'I don't expect you to do this for free, Agent Pollard. I'll pay you. I don't have much, but we could work out a payment plan or something.'

She shook her head. 'That won't be necessary. It might take a few days, but I just have to make a few calls.'

Holman nodded. 'Thanks, Agent Pollard. I really appreciate this.'

'You shouldn't call me Agent Pollard. I'm not a Special Agent any more.'

'What should I call you?'

'Katherine.'

'OK, Katherine. I'm Max.' Holman held out his hand.

Pollard did not accept it. She picked up the envelope instead. 'This doesn't mean I'm your friend, Max. All it means is I think you deserve answers.'

POLLARD WASN'T SURE why she had agreed to help Holman, but she was in no hurry to drive back to Simi Valley. Westwood was twenty degrees cooler and her mother would take care of the boys when they got home from camp, so it was like having a day off. Pollard felt as if she had been paroled.

She walked to Stan's Donuts and ordered one plain All-American round-with-a-hole glazed doughnut. Pollard hadn't been to Stan's since she left the Bureau. When she was working out of the Westwood office, she and another agent named April Sanders had snuck away to Stan's at least twice a week. Taking their doughnut break, they called it.

The woman behind the counter offered a doughnut off the rack, but a fresh batch was coming out of the fryer so Pollard opted to wait. She carried Holman's file to one of the outside tables to read while she waited, but found herself thinking about Holman. He had always been a big guy, but the Holman she arrested had been thirty pounds thinner with shaggy hair, a deep tan and the bad skin of a serious tweaker. He didn't look like a criminal any more. He looked like a middle-aged man down on his luck.

Pollard suspected that the police had answered Holman's questions as best they could, but he was reluctant to accept the facts. She had worked with grieving families during her time with the Feeb, and all of them had seen only questions in that terrible place of loss where no good answers exist. The working truth of every criminal investigation was that not all the questions could be answered.

Pollard finally turned to Holman's envelope and read through the articles. Andre Marchenko and Jonathan Parsons, both thirty-two years old, were unemployed loners who met at a fitness centre in West Hollywood. Neither was married nor had significant others. Parsons was a Texan who had drifted to Los Angeles as a teenage runaway. Marchenko was survived by his widower mother, a Ukrainian immigrant who, according to the paper, was both cooperating with the police and threatening to sue the city. At the time of their deaths, Marchenko and Parsons shared a small apartment in Hollywood's Beachwood Canyon, where police discovered twelve pistols, a cache of ammunition in excess of 6,000 rounds, and $910,000 in cash.

Pollard had no longer been on the job when Marchenko and Parsons blazed their way through thirteen banks, but she had followed the news about them, and reading about their bank hits now filled her with the same edgy juice she had known on the job. Pollard's life since Marty's death had been a nonstop struggle to pay mounting bills and single-handedly raise her boys. She had promised herself that, having lost their father, they would not also lose their mother to day-care and nannies. The commitment had left her feeling powerless, especially as the boys grew older and their expenses mounted, but just reading about Marchenko and Parsons revived her.

The articles Holman had copied included blurry security stills of black-clad figures waving rifles, but witness descriptions of the two men had always been sketchy. It wasn't until the eighth robbery that a witness described their getaway vehicle. The car wasn't described again until the tenth robbery, when it was confirmed as being a light blue Toyota Corolla. Pollard smiled when she saw this, knowing the Bank Squad would have been celebrating. Professionals would have used a different car for each robbery; use of the same car indicated that these guys were lucky amateurs. Once you knew they were riding on luck, you knew their luck would run out.

'Doughnuts ready. Miss? The hot doughnuts are ready.'

Pollard had been so involved in the articles she had lost track of time. She went inside, collected her doughnut with a cup of black coffee, then went back to her table to resume reading.

Marchenko and Parsons ran out of luck on their thirteenth robbery. When they took over a Culver City Bank of America, a joint task force of FBI agents and LAPD Robbery Special detectives was surveilling a three-mile corridor from downtown LA to the eastern edge of Santa Monica. As Marchenko and Parsons entered the bank, all five tellers tripped silent alarms. The bank's security contractor notified the LAPD, who alerted the Task Force. The Task Force teams converged on the bank, taking positions in the parking lot. Marchenko exited the bank first and opened fire. The surveillance teams returned fire, killing Marchenko and Parsons at the scene.

Pollard skipped through the articles covering the murders of the four officers and found what appeared to be several LAPD cover sheets from reports referencing Marchenko and Parsons and witness statements by the two men's landlord. These gave Pollard pause. Such reports were from the detective bureau, and Richard Holman had been a uniformed patrol officer. LAPD detectives used patrol officers to assist in searches and street interviews after a robbery, but those jobs didn't require access to reports or witness statements, and patrol officers rarely stayed involved after the first day or two following a robbery. Marchenko and Parsons had been dead for three months and their loot had been recovered. She wondered why LAPD was maintaining an investigation three months after the fact and why it included patrol officers. Pollard had got to know several LAPD robbery detectives during her time on the Squad. She decided to ask them.

Pollard phoned the LAPD's information office for their current duty assignments. The first two detectives she asked for had retired, but the third,

Bill Fitch, was assigned to the elite Robbery Special unit at Parker Center.

When she got Fitch on the phone, he said, 'Who is this?'

'Katherine Pollard. I was on the Bank Squad with the FBI. We worked together a few years ago.' She rattled off several of the serial bandits they had worked: the Major League Bandit, the Dolly Parton Bandit, the Munchkin Bandits. Unknown serial bandits were given names that made them easier to talk about. The Major League Bandit had always worn a Dodgers cap, the Dolly Parton Bandit had been an ex-stripper with huge breasts, and the Munchkin Bandits had been a team of little people.

Fitch said, 'Oh, sure, I remember you. I heard you quit the job.'

'That's right. Listen, I have a question for you about Marchenko and Parsons. You got a minute?'

'They're dead.'

'I know. Are you guys still running an open case?'

Fitch hesitated and Pollard knew this to be a bad sign. The rules stated you didn't share information with private citizens or outside agencies without a court order. He said, 'Are you back with the Feeb?'

'No. I'm making a private enquiry for a friend. I want to find out if the four officers killed last week were working on Marchenko and Parsons.'

Pollard could almost see his eyes roll by the tone that came to his voice. 'Oh, I get it. Holman's father. That guy is being a real pain in the ass.'

'He lost his son.'

'Listen, how in hell did he get you involved in this?'

'I put him in prison.'

Fitch laughed, but his laughter stopped as if he had flipped a switch. 'I don't know what Holman is talking about, and I can't answer your questions. You're a civilian.'

'Holman's son told his wife he was working on something.'

'Marchenko and Parsons are dead. Don't call me again, ex-Agent Pollard.'

The phone went dead in her ear.

Pollard sat reviewing their conversation. Fitch had repeatedly told her that Marchenko and Parsons were dead, but he hadn't denied that an investigation was ongoing. She wondered why and thought she might know how to find out. She opened her cellphone again and called April Sanders.

'Special Agent Sanders.'

'Guess where I am.'

Sanders lowered her voice. 'Oh my God—is that really you?'

'Are you in the office?'

'Yeah, but not much longer. Are you here?'

'I'm at Stan's with your name on a dozen doughnuts. Call down a pass.'

5

The Federal Building in Westwood was headquarters for the 1,100 FBI agents serving Los Angeles and the surrounding counties. It was a single steel and glass tower set amid acres of parking lots.

Pollard parked in the civilian lot, cleared the security station with April Sanders's pass, then took the elevator to the fourteenth floor. Pollard hadn't been to her old office since she cleared out her desk, but nothing had changed.

The Bank Squad occupied a small, bright room cut into cubicles for the agents assigned to the squad. Los Angeles suffered so many bank robberies that most of the agents were out in the field at any given time. Today was no different. Pollard saw only three people when she entered. A bald, light-skinned African-American agent named Bill Cecil was locked in conversation with a young agent Pollard didn't recognise. Cecil smiled when he saw her as April Sanders rushed forward.

Sanders, a profound paranoid, covered her mouth in case lip-readers were watching. She whispered. 'I should have warned you. Leeds is here.'

Christopher Leeds was the Bank Squad commander. He had run the Squad with a brilliant hand for almost twenty years.

Pollard said, 'You don't have to whisper. I'm OK with Leeds.'

'*Shh!*'

'No one's listening, April.'

They both glanced round to find Cecil and his partner cupping their ears. Pollard laughed. 'Stop it, Big Bill.'

'Big' Bill Cecil slowly rose to his feet. Cecil was not tall; he was called Big Bill because he was wide. He had been on the Bank Squad longer than anyone except Leeds. 'Good to see you, lady. How are those babies?'

Cecil had always called her lady. When Pollard first joined the squad, Leeds—then, as now—was as much a nightmare tyrant as he was brilliant. Cecil had taken her under his wing, counselled and consoled her, and taught her how to survive Leeds's exacting demands. Cecil was one of the kindest men she had ever known.

'They're good, Bill, thanks. You're getting fat.'

Cecil eyed the doughnut box. 'I'm about to get fatter. One of those has my name on it, I hope.'

Pollard held the box for Cecil and his partner, who introduced himself as Kevin Dillon. They were still chatting when Leeds came out of his office.

Dillon immediately returned to his desk and Sanders went back to her cubicle. Cecil, who had been part of the Squad for ever and was ripe for his pension, turned his letterbox smile on his boss.

'Hey, Chris. Look who came to visit.'

Leeds was a tall, humourless man known for immaculate suits and his brilliance in patterning serial bandits. Serial robbers were profiled, in much the same way as serial killers, to establish their patterns, and predictions made as to when and where they would strike again. Leeds was a legendary profiler. Banks were his passion, and the Squad's agents were his hand-picked children. The workload was horrendous, but the LA FBI Bank Squad was the top of the game, and Leeds knew it. Working with the Squad was an honour. When Pollard resigned, Leeds had taken it as a personal rejection. The day she cleared her desk, he refused to speak to her.

Now, he studied her as if he couldn't place her, but then he nodded. 'Hello, Katherine.'

'Hey, Chris. I stopped by to say hello. How've you been?'

'Busy.' He glanced across the room at Sanders. 'I want you in Monteclair. You should have left ten minutes ago.'

Sanders peeked over the top of her cubicle. 'On it, boss.'

He turned to Cecil and tapped his watch. 'Meeting. Let's go.'

Cecil and Dillon hurried towards the door, but Leeds turned back.

'It was good to see you, Katherine. I hope you still feel you made the right decision.' Leeds didn't wait for her to respond. He followed Cecil and Dillon out of the door like a gravedigger on his way to church.

Pollard took the doughnuts to Sanders's cubicle. 'Man, you know, some things never change.'

Sanders reached for the box. 'I wish I could say the same about my ass.'

They laughed and enjoyed the moment, but then Sanders frowned.

'Shit, you heard what he said. I'm sorry, Kat, I gotta roll.'

'Listen, I didn't stop by just to bring doughnuts. I need information.'

Sanders looked suspicious, then lowered her voice again. 'We should eat. Eating will distort our voices.'

'Yeah, let's eat.'

They fished out a couple of doughnuts.

Pollard said, 'Did you guys close the Marchenko and Parsons case?'

Sanders spoke with her mouth full. 'They're dead, man. Those guys were iced. Why you want to know about Marchenko and Parsons?'

Pollard knew Sanders would ask, and had worried over how she should answer. Sanders had been on the squad when they tracked and busted Holman. Even though Holman had earned their respect with how he went down, many of the agents had grown resentful because of the publicity he got when the *Times* dubbed him the Hero Bandit. Within the Squad, Holman's name had been the Beachbum Bandit because of his dark tan, Tommy Bahama shirts, and shades. Bank robbers were not heroes.

She said, 'I took a job. Raising two kids is expensive.'

Pollard didn't want to lie, but she didn't see any other way round it. And it wasn't like it was totally a lie. It was *almost* the truth.

Sanders finished her first doughnut and started a second. 'So where are you working?'

'It's a private job, banking security, that kind of thing.'

Sanders nodded. Retired agents often took jobs with security firms.

Pollard said, 'Anyway, I was told that LAPD was still running a case. You know anything about that?'

'No. Why would they?'

'That's what I was hoping you could tell me.'

'We're not. They're not. It's a done deal.'

'You sure?'

'Run a case for what? We bagged'm. Marchenko and Parsons had no accomplices inside or outside the banks. We ran this thing, man, so we know. We found no evidence of any other party being involved, so there was no reason to continue the investigation. LAPD knows that.'

Pollard thought back over her conversation with Holman. 'Were Marchenko and Parsons plugged in with the Frogtown gang?'

'Nope. Never came up.'

'Any gangs other than Frogtown?'

Sanders pinched her doughnut between her thumb and forefinger and ticked off the points she wanted to make on her remaining fingers. 'We questioned Marchenko's mother, their landlord and the three neighbours at their apartment house. These guys had no friends or associates. They didn't tell anyone—not *anyone*—what they were doing. And, except for a cheesy collection of gold necklaces and a two thousand dollar Rolex, they sat on the money. No flashy cars, no diamond rings—they lived in a dump.'

'They must have spent something. You only recovered nine hundred K.'

Pollard had done the maths when she read the articles at Stan's. Teller drawers could yield $2,000 at most, but a vault could net $300,000 and sometimes more. Marchenko and Parsons had hit twelve vaults, so that was $3.6 million, which left over $2.5 million missing.

Sanders finished her doughnut. 'They didn't blow it. They hid it.'

'How much was their take?'

'Sixteen-point-two million, less the nine.'

Pollard whistled. 'That's a lot. What did they do with it?'

'We found no evidence of purchases, deposits, fund transfers, gifts—no receipts, no conspicuous consumption. We ran their phone calls for the entire year, investigating everyone they called—nothing. We worked that old lady, Marchenko's mother—what a nasty bitch she is, but you know what? She couldn't even afford to buy medicine. We don't know what they did with the money. It's probably sitting in a storage shed somewhere.'

'So you let it drop?'

'Sure. We did what we could.'

Pollard said, 'Maybe LAPD is still running the case.'

'Nah, we were in with Robbery Special every step of the way, so we both hit the wall at the same time. That case is closed.'

Pollard considered her options. If Sanders said the case was closed then it was closed, but Holman's son told his wife he was working it. Pollard wondered if LAPD had developed a lead to the missing money.

'Listen, could you get a copy of the LAPD file on this?'

'I don't know. Maybe.'

'I'd like to see their witness lists. I'd like to see yours, too. I might have to talk to those people.'

Sanders hesitated, then suddenly stood to make sure the office was empty. She glanced at her watch. 'Leeds will kill me. I have to get going.'

'How about the list?'

'You'd better not let it get back to Leeds. He'll have my ass.'

'You know better than that.'

'I'll have to fax it to you.'

Pollard left the building with Sanders, then went to her car. It was one forty-five. Her mother would be hammering the boys to clean their room, and the day was still young. Pollard had an idea how she could find out what she wanted to know, but she would need Holman's help. She found his cell number on the envelope and placed the call.

HOLMAN WAS SETTLED in a Burger King with a Whopper and fries, and the instruction manual for his new cellphone. He had set up his voicemail and was programming the list of numbers he'd been keeping in his wallet into the phone's memory when the phone made a chiming sound. Holman thought he had pressed the wrong button, then realised he was getting a call. It took him a moment to remember to answer by pressing the SEND key.

He said, 'Hello?'

'Holman, it's Katherine Pollard. Have you spoken with Fowler's widow?'

'Yeah. I met her at the memorial.'

'Good. We're going to go see her. I want you to meet me in Westwood. There's a mystery bookstore on Broxton just south of Weyburn with parking next door. Park there and meet me outside the bookstore. I'll do the driving.'

'OK, but why are we going to see her? Did you find out something?'

'I asked two people if LAPD was running an investigation and they both denied it, but I think something was going on. She might be able to tell us.'

'Why do you think Fowler's wife knows?'

'Your son told his wife, didn't he? How soon can you get to Westwood?'

'I'm already there.'

'Then I'll see you in five.'

POLLARD WAS WAITING for Holman in front of the bookstore in an old blue Subaru with the engine running. He climbed into the passenger side.

She tore away from the kerb as he closed the door. 'Now, listen—we have two things to cover with this woman. Was her husband participating in some kind of investigation involving Marchenko and Parsons? And did he tell her why he would meet your son and the others that night, and what they were going to do? All right. She lives up in Canoga Park.'

'So why do you think something is going on even though your friends said the case was closed?'

Pollard swivelled her head. 'They never recovered the money.'

'The papers said they got nine hundred K in Marchenko's apartment.'

'Chump change. Those guys netted over sixteen mil. It's missing.'

Holman stared at her. 'Wow.'

'Yeah.'

They climbed the 405 into the Sepulveda Pass. The city spread out around them as far as Holman could see.

He said, 'All that money is just . . . out there?'

'Don't mention the money to this woman, OK, Holman? If she mentions it, fine, but the idea here is that we want to find out what she knows. We don't want to put ideas into her head.'

Holman was still thinking about the $16 million. His biggest single take had been $3,127. The combined take from all nine of his robberies had been $18,942.

'You think they were trying to find the money?'

'Finding money isn't the LAPD's job. Unless they had a lead to someone who had knowingly received stolen money, or was holding it for Marchenko and Parsons, or was in possession of the stolen cash.'

Holman said, 'You can't let that much money just go.'

Pollard laughed. 'Holman, you wouldn't believe how much dough we lose. Not with guys like you who we bag alive—you bag a guy, he'll give it up if he has any left, trying to cut a deal—but the takeover guys like Marchenko and Parsons who get killed? One-point-two here, five hundred thousand there, just gone, and no one ever finds it. No one who reports it, anyway. The banks don't want losses like that in the papers. It would only encourage more assholes to rob banks. Anyway, a friend of mine is pulling the LAPD file on this thing. As soon as we have it we'll know what's what.'

Holman nodded but did not answer. He watched the valley roll past; a pelt of houses and buildings covering the earth that reached to the mountains, cut by remote canyons and crevices and shadows. Some men would do anything for $16 million. Murdering four cops was nothing.

THE FOWLERS had a small house in a development of similar houses, all with stucco sides, composite roofs and tiny yards.

Jacki Fowler answered the door, but she seemed like a coarse version of the woman Holman met at the memorial. Without make-up, her wide face was loose and blotchy, and her eyes were hard. She stared at him without recognition. Holman wished they had called.

'I'm Max Holman, Mrs Fowler, Richard Holman's father. We met at the memorial service.'

Pollard held out a small bouquet of daisies. She had swung into a Ralph's Market to pick up the flowers when they reached Canoga Park. 'My name is Katherine Pollard, Mrs Fowler. I'm terribly sorry for your loss.'

Jacki Fowler took the flowers without comprehension, then looked at Holman. 'Oh, that's right. You lost your son.'

Pollard said, 'Would you mind if we come in for a few minutes, Mrs Fowler? We'd like to pay our respects, and Max would like to talk about his son, if you have the time.'

Holman admired Pollard. In the time it took them to walk from the car to the door, the fast-talking frenetic driver had been replaced by a reassuring woman with a gentle voice and kind eyes.

Mrs Fowler showed them into a living room. Holman saw an open bottle of red wine on a little table at the end of the couch, but no glass.

'This must be really hard for you right now,' Pollard said to Mrs Fowler. 'Are you doing all right? Do you need anything?'

'I have four sons, you know. The oldest, now he's talking the big talk about going on the police. I told him, are you out of your mind?'

'Tell him to be a lawyer. Lawyers make all the money.'

'Do you have children?'

'Two boys.'

'Then you know. This is going to sound terrible, but you know what I used to say? If he's going to get killed, please God let him get T-boned by some drunk-driving movie star. At least I could sue the sonofabitch. But no—he has to get killed by some cholo without a pot to piss in.' She glanced at Holman. 'We should still look into that—me, you and the other families. They say you can't get blood from a stone, but who knows? Would you like a glass of wine? I was just about to have one, first of the day.'

'No, thanks, but you help yourself.'

Pollard said, 'I'll have one.'

Mrs Fowler told them to take a seat, then continued out to her dining room. A second bottle of wine was open on the table. She poured two glasses, then returned, offering one of the glasses to Pollard. Holman realised it was a long way from being the first drink of her day.

As Jacki Fowler took a seat, she asked Holman, 'Did you know Mike?'

'No, ma'am. I didn't know my son very well, either. Richie's wife—my daughter-in-law—she told me that your husband was my son's training offi-cer. I guess they were good friends.'

'I wouldn't know. It's like we lived two lives in this house. Are you the one who was in prison? Someone at the funeral said there was a convict.'

Holman felt himself flush and glanced at Pollard, but Pollard wasn't looking at him. 'Yes, ma'am. That's me. Officer Holman's father.'

'Jesus, that must have been something. What did you do?'

'I robbed a bank.'

Pollard said, 'I used to be a police officer, Mrs Fowler. I don't know about you, but these murders have left Max with a lot of questions, like why his son went out in the middle of the night. Did Mike tell you anything about that?'

Mrs Fowler sipped her wine, then made a dismissive wave with the glass. 'Mike went out in the middle of the night all the damned time. He was hardly ever home.'

Pollard glanced at Holman. 'Max, why don't you tell Jacki what your daughter-in-law said? About the call he got that night.'

'My daughter-in-law told me your husband called. Richie was at home, but he got a call from your husband and went out to meet the other guys.'

She snorted. 'Well, Mike sure as hell didn't call me. He was working that night. He had the dog shift. The way it was around here, he came home when he came home. He never showed me the courtesy to call.'

'I got the idea they were working on something.'

She grunted. 'They were drinking. Mike was a drunkard. You know the other two—Mellon and Ash? Mike had been their TO, also.'

Holman shrugged. 'I didn't know that.'

Pollard said, 'Why don't you show her the phone bills?'

Holman unfolded his copies of Richie's telephone bills. 'These are my son's phone bills for the past couple of months. You see the red dots?'

'That's Mike's phone.'

'Yes, ma'am. Ash is the yellow dots and Mellon the green. Richie was calling your husband two or three times a day almost every day. He hardly ever called Ash or Mellon, but he talked to Mike a lot.'

Mrs Fowler pushed to her feet. 'I want to show you something. Just wait here. You sure you don't want any wine?'

'Thanks, but I've been sober for ten years. I was a drunkard too.'

She grunted again and walked away. She came back shuffling several pages and returned to her spot on the couch. 'Isn't it strange you checked your son's phone records? So did I. Not your son's, I mean, but Mike's.'

Pollard put down her wine. Holman saw that it was untouched. She said, 'Had Mike said anything to make you suspicious?'

'It was the not saying anything that made me suspicious. He'd get these calls on his cell. The damn thing would ring and he'd leave—'

'What would he say?'

'He was going out. That's all he would say. "I'm going out." What was I to think? What would anyone think?'

Pollard leaned forward quietly. 'He was having an affair?'

'That's what I thought, so I decided to see who he was calling and who was calling him. See, here—on his cellphone bill . . .'

Mrs Fowler bent forward to show him the pages. He recognised Richie's home and cellphone numbers and pointed them out to Pollard. She pulled a notepad and pen from her bag and jotted down the details of Fowler's calls.

Mrs Fowler said, 'I didn't recognise any of the numbers, so I called them. I thought he was calling women, but it was your son and Ash and Mellon. I asked him, "What are you doing with these guys?" He told me to mind my own business. It made me angry, but I didn't say much until he came home in the middle of the night tracking mud all over the house. I didn't find it until the next day and I was so mad.'

Holman had no idea what she was talking about, so he asked her.

Mrs Fowler pushed to her feet again. 'Come here. I'll show you.'

They followed her out through the kitchen onto a small covered patio in the back yard. A pair of Wolverine work boots stood on the ground beside a dusty grill, caked with dirt and dried mud and weeds. She pointed at them.

'Here—he came clopping through the house in the middle of the night with these things. I said, "Have you lost your mind?" I threw them out here and told him he could clean them himself. You should have seen the mess.'

Pollard stooped to look at the boots more closely. 'When was this?'

She hesitated, frowning. 'I guess it was Thursday, week before last.'

Five days before they were murdered. Holman wondered if Richie, Mellon and Ash had also gone out that night and come home muddy.

Pollard, reading his mind, straightened. 'Was that a night when he went out with the others?'

'I didn't ask and I don't know.'

Then Pollard surprised him. She said, 'Did Mike ever mention the names Marchenko and Parsons?'

'No. Are they on the police?'

Pollard studied her for a moment, then made the gentle smile. 'Just people Mike used to know. I thought he might have mentioned them.'

'Michael never told me a thing. It was like I didn't exist.'

Pollard glanced back at Holman, then nodded towards the house, the gentle smile deadened by sadness. 'We should be going, Max.'

When they reached the front door, Jacki Fowler took Holman's hand and held it an uncomfortably long time. She said, 'There's more than one kind of prison, you know.'

Holman said, 'Yes, ma'am. I've been there, too.'

HOLMAN WAS UNSETTLED when they left. He had wanted to find a grieving widow with answers to explain his son's death, but now he pictured Mike Fowler having secretive phone calls with his hand cupped over his mouth, slipping from his home too early for the neighbours to see and returning under cover of darkness. Holman had spent most of his life doing crime. Whatever had happened in the Fowler house felt like a crime in progress.

Pollard gunned her Subaru up the freeway access ramp into the thickening traffic. The drive back would be ugly, but when Holman glanced at her, she was glowing as if a light had been turned on inside her.

Holman said, 'What do you think?'

'Talk to your daughter-in-law. Ask if Richard went out that Thursday night and if she knows anything about where they went or what they did.'

Holman was thinking he wanted to drop the whole thing. 'I wasn't asking about that. I checked the call dates when she showed us her phone bills. All of the calling started on the eighth day after Marchenko and Parsons died, just like on Richie's bill. Fowler called Richie and Mellon and Ash, one right after another. Like he was saying, "Hey, let's go find some money."'

'Holman, listen—we've had exactly one interview with a woman who had a bad marriage. We don't know what they were doing, or why.'

'It feels like they were up to something. Would they get a reward if they found the missing money? A legal reward?'

'The banks award a recovery fee, but policemen aren't eligible.'

'This isn't what I wanted in my head.'

'Oh, for Christ's sake,' she said, 'we don't know enough for you to think any differently about your son, so stop it. You heard this depressed woman with her husband sneaking around and you know the money's missing, so you've jumped to this conclusion. Maybe they just liked to hang out. Maybe this fascination with Marchenko and Parsons was just a hobby.'

Holman felt irritated that she was trying to cheer him up. 'That's bullshit.'

'Just because they were sneaking around doesn't mean they were doing anything illegal. I can think of plenty of ways we might be able to tie in what they were doing with Marchenko and Parsons and Juarez.'

Holman glanced at her, doubtful. 'How?'

'If you've read Fowler's obituary, you'll know he spent two years on the LAPD's anti-gang unit. He'd have had experience with Frogtown. Marchenko and Parsons could have had an inside accomplice, someone who knew when the bank branches were scheduled to receive their shipments of new money—a secretary, a Frogtown home girl, say, and her boyfriend passed it along to Marchenko and Parsons to get cut in on the split.'

'But they hit different banks.'

'It only takes one inside job to have an insider, and then the Feeb and the cops are all over it. LAPD learns of a Frogtown connection, so they turn to the cops with Frogtown experience to develop or follow up leads. That could explain how your son leaving his house to discuss Marchenko and Parsons with Fowler led to Warren Juarez.'

Holman felt a flicker of hope. 'You think?'

'No, I don't think, but I want you to understand how little we know. When you're asking your daughter-in-law about that Thursday night, pick up the case reports your son had—the stuff he got from the detective bureau. You gave me the cover sheets, but I want to see what was in the reports.'

'OK.' Holman watched Pollard manoeuvring her car through the traffic. He said, 'Why do you drive so fast?'

'I have two little boys waiting for me at home. They're with my mother.'

'What about your husband?'

'Let's keep the personal stuff out of this, Max.'

Holman went back to watching the passing cars. 'One more thing—I know you said you didn't want me to pay you, but my offer is still there. I never expected you to go to all this trouble.'

'If I asked you to pay, I'd be scared you would have to rob another bank.'

'I'd find another way. I'll never rob another bank.'

Pollard glanced at him and Holman shrugged.

She said, 'Can I ask you a question?'

'So long as it isn't personal.'

Pollard laughed, but then her laugh faded. 'I put you away for ten years. How come you're not pissed off at me?'

Holman thought about it. 'You gave me a chance to change.'

They rode in silence after that. The lights were just beginning to twinkle.

PERRY WAS STILL at his desk when Holman let himself into the lobby. The old man's leathery face twitched and trembled.

Holman said, 'You get your car back OK?'

Perry leaned forward. His eyes were watery and nervous. 'Here's the money I charged you, the sixty bucks, those three days for the car.'

As Holman reached his desk, he saw the three twenties he'd given Perry laid out face up, waiting for him. Perry pushed the three bills towards him.

Holman said, 'You're giving back the money? Why?'

'Those goddamned spics said to give it back, so you tell'm I did.'

'The guys who brought back your car?'

'When they come in here to give me the keys. I was doing you a favour, man, renting out that car, I wasn't trying to rip you off. Those bastards said I should give back your cash else they'd fuck me up good, so you take it.'

Holman didn't touch the money. 'We had a deal. You keep it.'

'No, you gotta take it. I don't want that kind of trouble in my house.'

'That's your money, Perry. We had a deal, fair and square. I'll straighten it out with those guys. I'm sorry this happened.'

Holman left the sixty dollars on Perry's desk and went up to his room. The clunky old window unit had the place like a deep freeze. He looked at Richie's picture on the bureau, eight years old and smiling. He still had a bad feeling in his stomach that Pollard's pep talk hadn't been able to shake.

He turned off the air conditioner, then went downstairs again, hoping to catch Perry still at his desk.

Perry was locking the front door, but stopped when he saw Holman. He said, 'That sixty is still on the desk.'

'Then put it in your pocket. I wouldn't have you shaken down. My son was a police officer. What would he think if I did something like that?'

'I guess he'd think it was pretty damned low.'

'I guess he would. You keep that sixty. It's yours.'

Holman went back upstairs and climbed into bed, telling himself that Richie sure as hell would think it was low, shaking an old man for sixty damned dollars.

6

Every morning for as long as Pollard could remember—months; maybe years—she had woken feeling depleted and dreading the pain of beginning her day. She drank two cups of black coffee just to give herself a pulse. But when Pollard woke that morning, she jumped her alarm by more than an hour and immediately went to her little desk.

She had stayed up the night before until almost two, comparing numbers and call times between Fowler's and Holman's phone bills, and searching the Internet for information about Marchenko and Parsons. She had reread the material Holman had given her, but was frustrated by not having the complete LAPD reports. She hoped Holman would get them from his daughter-in-law soon. Pollard admired Holman's commitment to his son. She felt a sudden sense of satisfaction that she had spoken on his behalf to the Assistant US Attorney all those years ago. Leeds had been pissed for a month but Pollard thought the guy had earned a break, and she felt even more strongly about it now. Holman had been a career criminal, but the evidence suggested he was basically a decent guy.

Pollard set about drawing up a work plan for the day. She was still working at it when her oldest son, David, pushed at her arm.

'Mom! We're gonna be late for camp!'

Pollard glanced at her watch. It was 7.50. The camp bus arrived at eight. She hadn't even made coffee or felt the time pass, and she had been working for more than an hour.

'Get your brother dressed, David.'

She pulled on a pair of jeans and a T-shirt, then slammed together two baloney sandwiches.

'David, is Lyle ready?'

'He won't get dressed!'

Pollard heard the fax phone ring as she was packing the sandwiches into paper bags. She ran back to the office bedroom to see a page emerging. She smiled when she saw the FBI emblem—Sanders was delivering the goods.

Pollard ran back to the kitchen, topped off the sandwiches with two containers of fruit cocktail, two bags of Cheetos and cartons of Orangina.

David pounded breathlessly in from the living room. 'Mom! I can hear the bus! They're gonna leave us!'

Sending David out to stop the bus, she forced a T-shirt over Lyle's head. She had Lyle and the lunches through the door as the bus rumbled to a stop.

Lyle said, 'I miss Daddy.'

Pollard squatted down so they would be the same height. She touched his cheek. 'I miss him, too, little man. What are we going to do about that?'

It was a script they had played before. 'Keep him in our hearts?'

She smiled and touched her youngest son's chest. 'Yeah. He's right here in your heart. Now let's get you on the bus.'

Pollard walked Lyle to the bus. She kissed her boys, saw them away, then hurried back to the house. She went directly to work, skimming through the fax. Sanders had sent sixteen pages, including a witness list, interview summaries and a case summation. Pollard was going to compare the phone numbers on the witness list against the calls appearing on Richard Holman's and Mike Fowler's phone bills. If Holman or Fowler were running their own investigation into Marchenko and Parsons, they would have called the witnesses. If so, Pollard would ask the witness what they talked about.

She called her mother and arranged for her to stay with the boys when they got home from camp.

Her mother said, 'Why are you spending so much time in the city all of a sudden? Did you take a job?'

She had always resented her mother's questions. Thirty-six years old and her mother still questioned her! 'I have things to do. I'm busy.'

'Doing what? Are you seeing a man?'

'You'll be here at one, right? You'll stay with the boys?'

'I hope you're seeing a man. You have to think of those boys.'

'Goodbye, Mom.' Pollard hung up and went back to her desk.

She studied the map of the murder scene that Holman had sketched, then compared it with the drawing that had appeared in the *Times*. The Feeb had taught her that all investigations begin at the crime scene, so she knew she would have to go and see for herself. Alone in her house, Pollard smiled.

She felt as if she was in the game again. She was back in the hunt.

PERRY WASN'T AT HIS DESK when Holman came downstairs that morning. Holman was relieved. He wanted to pick up the reports from Liz before she left for class and didn't want to get bogged down in another argument. But when Holman stepped outside, Perry was hosing off the sidewalk.

Perry said, 'You got a call yesterday I forgot to tell you about. Tony Gilbert at that sign company. Said he's your boss and wants you to call. Sounded pissed off.'

Holman went round the side of the motel to his car. He hadn't been to work in a week and didn't want to lose the job. Holman climbed into his Highlander to make the call. As soon as Gilbert came on the line, Holman knew the man's patience was wearing thin.

Gilbert said, 'Are you coming back to work or not? I need to know.'

'I'm coming back. I've just had a lot to deal with.'

'Max, I'm trying to be a good guy here, what with your son and all, but what in the hell are you doing? The police were here.'

Holman was surprised. 'What did the police want?'

'They wanted to know if you'd been coming to work and what kind of people you've been associating with. Whether or not you've been using. If I knew how you were supporting yourself. What am I supposed to think? I'm trying to run a business here and you disappeared. I told'm I gave you some time off for your son, but now I gotta wonder. It's been a week.'

'Who was it asking about me?'

'Some detectives. Now listen, are you coming back to work or not?'

'I just need a few more days—'

'Ah, hell.' Gilbert hung up.

Holman put away his phone and headed out. He called Liz to let her know he was coming.

When she answered, he said, 'Hey, Liz, it's Max. I need to stop by to see you for a few minutes. Can I bring you a coffee?'

'I'm on my way out.'

'This is kind of important, Liz. It's about Richie.'

She hesitated, and when she spoke again her voice was cold. 'I don't want to see you any more. Please stop bothering me.' She hung up.

Holman was only five blocks from Liz's apartment by then, so he drove on.

The usual morning rush of students on their way to class meant that Holman didn't have long to wait before he could get inside her building. He took the stairs two at a time, but slowed when he reached her apartment, catching his breath before he knocked.

'Liz? Tell me what's wrong.' He knocked softly again. 'Liz? This is important. Please, it's for Richie.'

She finally opened the door. Her face was tight and pinched, and she was already dressed for the day. Her eyes seemed hard with a brittle tension.

Holman didn't move. He said, 'Did I do something?'

'Whatever you're doing, I want no part of it.'

Holman kept his voice calm. 'What do you think I'm doing? I'm not doing anything, Liz. I just want to know what happened to my son.'

'The police were here. They cleaned out Richard's desk and they questioned me about *you*. They wanted to know what you were doing.'

'Who did? Levy?'

'No, Detective Random. He wanted to know what you were asking about and said I should be careful around you. They warned me not to let you in.'

Holman took a step away from her and spoke carefully. 'I've been inside with you, Liz. Do you think I would hurt you? You're my son's wife.'

Her eyes softened and she shook her head. 'Why did they come here?'

'There was someone with Random?'

'I don't remember his name. Red-haired.'

Vukovich.

'What did they tell you?'

'They didn't tell me anything. They said they were investigating you.'

The apartment next door opened and two young men came out, book bags over their shoulders. Holman and Liz stood quietly as they passed.

When they were gone, Liz said, 'I guess you can come in. This is silly.'

Holman stepped inside and waited as she closed the door.

'They asked if you said anything to indicate you were involved in criminal activity. I didn't know what in hell they were talking about. What would you say to me—"Hey, you know any good banks to rob?"'

'You said they took things from his desk? Can I see?'

She brought him to their shared office, and Holman looked at Richie's desk. The LAPD reports and documents were gone.

'They wanted to know if you'd been in here. I told them the truth.'

Holman nodded. 'That's OK. Let me ask you, did Richie go out with Fowler on the Thursday before their murder? It would have been at night, late.'

Her brow furrowed. 'I'm not sure . . . I think Rich worked that night.'

'Did he come home muddy? Fowler went out that night and came home muddy. It would have been late.'

She thought more. 'No, I—wait, yes, it was Friday morning I took the car. There was grass and dirt on the driver's side floor, not mud but grass and dirt. Richie had the shift Thursday night. He said he'd chased somebody.'

'Listen, I don't know what Random was talking about, all that stuff about investigating me. I haven't done anything illegal and I'm not going to, you understand? I wouldn't do that to you and to Richie. I couldn't.'

She stared up at him for a moment, then she nodded. 'I know. I know what you're doing.' She rose up on her toes to kiss his cheek. 'You're trying to take care of your little boy.'

Richie's wife hugged him long and tight and Holman was glad for it, but he cursed himself for being too late.

HOLMAN WAS FURIOUS as he crossed the street, heading back to his car, furious that Random had warned Liz not to trust him. The detective had jeopardised Holman's only remaining connection to Richie, and Holman didn't know why. He wanted to drive to Parker Center to confront the man, but by the time he reached the car he knew this would be a bad idea. He needed a better sense of what Random was thinking before he called him on it.

Holman got into the Highlander and was thinking through the rest of his day when a blue car slid up fast beside him, blocking him against the kerb. Random and his driver stepped out of the blue car as Holman caught a flash of movement from the kerb. Vukovich and another man were stepping off the sidewalk, one from the front and one from the back. They were holding pistols along their legs.

Holman put both hands on the steering wheel, in plain sight.

Random pulled open the door, then stepped aside. His driver was shorter than Holman but as wide as a bed. He jerked Holman out from behind the wheel and shoved him face-first against the Highlander.

Holman didn't resist. The short guy patted him down.

Random said, 'Nice car. Where'd you get a car like this? You steal it?'

'I rented it.'

Random said, 'Vuke, run the car. You can't rent a car without a driver's licence and a credit card. I think he stole it.'

Holman said, 'I got a driver's licence, goddammit. It came yesterday. The rental papers are in the glove box.'

Vukovich opened the far passenger door to check the glove box as the short guy pulled Holman's wallet. Random pulled Holman around so they were facing each other while the short guy brought the wallet to his car and went to work on their computer. Three students stopped on the sidewalk, but Random's eyes were dark knots focused on Holman.

'You don't think Jacki Fowler is suffering enough?'

'What are you talking about? So I went to see her? So what?'

'Here's a widow with four boys and a dead husband, but you had to invade her privacy. What do you expect to gain by upsetting her, Holman?'

'I'm trying to find out what happened to my son.'

'I told you what happened when I told you to let me do my job.'

'I don't think you're doing your job. I don't know what you're doing. Why did you go to my boss asking if he thinks I'm on drugs?'

'You're a drug addict.'

'Was. *Was.*'

'Drug addicts always want more. I think that's why you're leaning on the families. You're looking to score. Even from your own daughter-in-law.'

'That's my son's wife, you sonofabitch. Now it's me telling you to stay away from her. You goddamn leave her alone.'

Random stepped closer, and Holman knew he was being provoked. Random wanted him to swing. He wanted to take him inside.

'You don't have a right to tell me anything. You were nothing to your son. You didn't even meet the girl until last week, so don't pretend she's family.'

Holman felt a deep throbbing in his temples. Random floated in front of him like a target, but Holman told himself no. Why did Random want him inside? Why did Random want him out of the way?

Holman said, 'What was in those reports you took?'

Random's jaw flexed, but he didn't answer, and Holman knew the reports were important.

'My daughter-in-law claims you took something that belonged to my son from her house. Did you have a warrant, Random? Did it list what you went there to find or were you grabbing whatever you wanted?'

Vukovich came back out of the car with the rental papers. He held them out to Random. 'He's got a rental agreement here in his name. Looks legit.'

Random studied the papers. 'Quality Motors of Los Angeles. Never heard of them.' He called over his shoulder, 'Teddy? You get the plate?'

The short guy was Teddy. Teddy returned and handed Holman's licence and wallet to Random. 'Vehicle registered to Quality Motors, no wants, warrants or citations. His DL shows good, too.'

Random glanced at the licence, then Holman. 'Where'd you get this?'

'The Department of Motor Vehicles. Where did you get your warrant?'

Random put the licence back in Holman's wallet. He had backed off because he didn't want Holman to make a stink about the reports.

'I want to make sure you understand,' Random said. 'I asked you one time nice. This is me telling you a second time. I'm not going to let you make it more difficult for these families. Stay away from them.'

'I'm one of those families.'

Random stared for a moment, then something like a smile played at his lips. He stepped closer and whispered. 'Which family? Frogtown?'

'Juarez was in Frogtown. I don't know what you're talking about.'

'You like White Fence any better?'

Holman kept his face empty.

'How's your friend Gary Mareno—L'Chee?'

'I haven't seen him in years. Maybe I'll look him up.'

Random tossed Holman's wallet and rental papers into the Highlander. 'You claim you want answers, but you have made it harder for me to find those answers, and I take that personally.'

'I thought you knew the answers.'

'Most of the answers, Holman. Most. But now because of you an important door just closed and I don't know if I'll be able to open it again.'

'What are you talking about?'

'Maria Juarez disappeared. She split, man. She could have told us how Warren put it together, but now she's gone and that one's on you. So if you feel like undercutting me with your daughter-in-law again, you get the urge to make these families doubt what we're doing and keep their grief fresh, you explain to them how you delayed the case by being an asshole. Are we clear?'

Holman did not respond.

Random went back to his car. Vukovich and the other guy vanished. The blue car pulled away. The three kids on the sidewalk were gone.

Holman didn't believe Random's false concern for the families, or even that Random believed he was looking to score. Holman had been fronted and leaned on by a hundred cops, and he sensed something deeper was at play. Random wanted him out of the way, but Holman didn't know why.

POLLARD WAS ON HER WAY downtown to check out the crime scene when April Sanders called. 'Hey. You get the faxes OK?'

'I was going to call you to say thanks, girl. You really came through.'

'Hope you still think so after I tell you the rest. LAPD froze me out. I can't get their file.'

'You're kidding! They must have something in play.'

Pollard was surprised. The Feeb's Bank Squad and the LAPD's Robbery team worked together so often they shared information freely.

Sanders said, 'I don't know why they wouldn't come across. I asked the putz—you remember George Hines?'

'No.'

'Probably came on after you left. Anyway, I said, what gives with that? What happened to agency cooperation? He said after they closed the file someone upstairs pulled the whole thing. I'm like, *who* upstairs, the chief, God? He said it wasn't their case any more and that's all he could tell me.'

'How could it not be Robbery's case? It was a *robbery*.'

'If those guys knew what they were doing they would be *us*, not them. Shit—gotta run. Leeds—'

The line went dead in Pollard's ear.

If LAPD had closed the book on Marchenko and Parsons, it increased the odds that Richard Holman had been involved with Fowler and the others in something off the books. It was bad news for Holman, but Pollard already had bad news—Sanders's witness list included the names and numbers of thirty-two people who had been interviewed by the FBI in the matter of Marchenko and Parsons. Marchenko's mother, Leyla, was among them. Pollard had checked the thirty-two telephone numbers against the outgoing-call numbers on Richard Holman's and Mike Fowler's phone records. Fowler had phoned Marchenko's mother twice. It was highly unlikely that a uniformed field supervisor would have a legitimate reason to contact a witness, so Pollard felt sure that Fowler had been conducting some kind of rogue investigation.

Pollard cruised over to the east side of the river, an area thick with warehouses and train yards. She felt queasy. The LA River was a restricted area. Jumping the fence to check out the crime scene would be a misdemeanour, but Pollard had to see for herself if Holman's description held up.

She drove along Mission Road until she found the service gate. She parked beside the fence, locked her car, then went to the gate. She was wearing jeans and Nikes, and had a pair of Marty's work gloves in case she had to climb. The gate was locked and had been secured with a secondary chain. The river bed was a wide concrete plain cut by a trough and bordered by concrete banks crowned with chain link and barbed wire. She could see the Fourth Street bridge from the gate, but not well enough.

Pollard climbed the gate, then walked down the service drive. Entering the river bed was like lowering herself into a trench. Concrete walls rose around her, cutting off the city from view. The channel walls in this part of the river were twenty-foot verticals topped by the fence. They were designed to contain the river during the rainy season.

As she made her way to the bridge, Pollard stepped out of the sun into the shade. She had brought the *Times*'s drawing of the crime scene and Holman's sketch, but she didn't need them to see where the bodies had been. Four shining, irregular shapes were visible beneath the bridge, each shape brighter and cleaner than the surrounding concrete. After the bodies had been removed and the crime scene cleared by the police, a Hazmat crew had disinfected the area. Pollard had once seen them work. Blood was soaked up with absorbent granules, which were vacuumed into special containers. Contaminated areas were sprayed with disinfectant, then scoured with high-pressure steam. Now, more than a week later, the ground where each man had died glowed like a shimmering ghost.

Pollard stood between the body marks and considered the service ramp. It was about eighty yards away, and sloped towards her. She had an uninterrupted view of the ramp, but she knew this was in broad daylight with no cars parked in the area. Perspectives often changed in the darkness.

No marks remained to locate the positions of the cars, so Pollard opened the *Times* map. The three cars were pictured under the bridge in a loose triangle between the east columns and the river. The bodies were located in the drawing relative to the cars and columns. Mellon and Ash had been together at the back of Ash's radio car, at the top of the triangle. A six-pack of Tecate had been found on their trunk with four bottles missing. Fowler's car was the left base of the triangle, under the bridge and nearest the river. His body was near the right front fender. Richard Holman's car formed the triangle's right base, with his body midway between his car and Fowler.

Pollard tried to picture how the four men were standing at the moment they were shot. If they were talking, both Fowler and Holman would have had their backs to the ramp and wouldn't have seen someone approaching. The shooter had come from behind.

She moved to stand with Mellon and Ash, positioning herself where their car had been parked. They had been facing south towards Fowler. Mellon and Ash had a clear view of the ramp.

Pollard wanted to see if there was another way down to the north, but the walls were hard verticals all the way to the Fourth Street bridge and beyond. She was still searching when she heard the gate clatter. She walked back under the bridge and saw Holman coming down the ramp. Pollard was surprised. She hadn't told him she was going to the bridge. She was wondering what he was doing here when she realised she had heard the gate. Then she heard his shoes scuffing on the gritty concrete surface. He was half a football field away, but she heard him walking, and then she knew why. The towering concrete walls trapped sound and channelled it like the river.

When he arrived, Pollard gave him her expert opinion. 'You were right, Holman. They would have heard him coming, just like I heard you. They knew the person who killed them.'

Holman glanced back at the ramp. 'Once you're down here there's no other way to see it. And at night it's even more quiet than this.'

Pollard crossed her arms and felt sick. That was the problem—there was no other way to see it, but the police claimed they saw it another way. She was still trying to decide what this meant when Holman interrupted her thoughts.

He seemed nervous. 'Listen, we shouldn't spend too much time down here. Someone might call the police.'

'How'd you know I would be here?'

'Didn't. I was up on the bridge when you came down the ramp.'

'You just happened to be up there?'

'I've come here a dozen times since it happened. C'mon, let's go back up. I was going to call you—'

'Wait a minute, Holman. You've been here at night?'

Holman stopped. 'Yeah. Two or three times.'

'How's the light at that time of night?'

'They had a three-quarter moon with scattered clouds on the night they were killed. I checked the weather report. You could've read a newspaper down here.' He turned back towards the gate again. 'We better leave.'

'You go on. I'm thinking.'

Holman didn't leave. 'Listen, I went to see Liz this morning, but the police got to her first. They cleaned out Richie's desk. They took the reports.'

'How did they know she had them?'

'I don't know if they did, but they knew she's been helping me. They

made it sound like they had to search his things because I'd been there—
like they wanted to see what I was up to. Maybe they saw the reports then.'

'Who?'

'Random, the homicide detective who's running the task force. When I
was leaving, he and three other guys jumped me. They told me that Maria
Juarez split and they're blaming me for it, but I don't think that's why they
jumped me. They knew we went to see Mike Fowler's wife and they didn't
like it. They didn't mention you, but they knew about me. And they warned
me to stay away from her and the other families.'

Pollard didn't give a damn if they knew about her, but she wondered why
a homicide detective had taken robbery reports about Marchenko and
Parsons. The same reports that Sanders had told her were no longer available from Robbery Special because they had been pulled upstairs.

Pollard asked, 'What did Liz say about that Thursday night?'

'The floorboard of his car was messy with dirt and grass, she said.'

'So Richard was out with Fowler. Someplace muddy.'

'I guess. You think they were down here?'

'There's no grass and damned little mud. Even if they waded around in
the water, they wouldn't pick up mud and weeds like we saw on Fowler's
boots.' Pollard stared at the ramp, then looked at Holman. 'Here we are in
the kill zone, and it's obvious the shooter could not have approached without being seen. This is freshman detective work. Fowler, your son, Mellon
and Ash—they let him get close. The cops who came down here would
have seen that, too. They'd know Juarez could not have ambushed these
guys, but their statements in the press claimed that's how it happened. So
either they're lying about it or there's some mitigating factor, I cannot
imagine what.'

Holman stepped into the shade. 'I understand.'

Pollard said, 'OK, here's where we are. I went through the witness list
from the Marchenko case and checked the witnesses against the calls your
son and Fowler made. Fowler called Marchenko's mother two times.'

'That means they were investigating the robberies.'

'It doesn't tell us whether they were doing it in an official capacity or for
themselves. We should talk to this woman, find out what Fowler wanted.'

Holman looked away. 'Maybe tomorrow. I can't do it today.'

Pollard felt a tick of irritation. 'You know, I don't have all the time in the
world for this, Holman. I'm set up to help you today.'

Holman's mouth tightened and he turned red. 'You're really going above and beyond. I appreciate this—'

'Then let's go see her.'

'I gotta go see my boss. I haven't been to work in a week. The guy's been really good to me, but Random went to see him. I just can't lose this job.'

Pollard felt like an idiot for pressing him. She also wondered why Random was coming down so hard on a poor bastard who had just lost his son. 'OK, we can go see Marchenko's mother tomorrow. I know a man who might be able to help get the reports. I guess I could do that today.'

Neither spoke as they walked back, but their footsteps were loud in the silence. With every step, Pollard grew more convinced that the investigation into the murder of the four officers was bad. She wanted to find out the truth.

POLLARD LEFT HOLMAN at the river, drove back over the bridge, then north into Chinatown to a tall glass building where Pacific West Bank kept their corporate HQ. She believed she had a way to see the reports Random had confiscated from Richard Holman's apartment—if she could pull it off.

She called information and was connected with a Pacific West receptionist. Pollard said, 'Is Peter Williams still with the company?'

It had been twelve years, and she hoped he would remember her.

A second voice came on the line. 'Mr Williams's office.'

'Is he available for Katherine Pollard? Special Agent Pollard of the FBI.'

'Hold, please, and I'll see.'

Pollard's most dramatic bust during her time with the Bank Squad was taking down the Front Line Bandits, a team of Armenians who were later identified as Lyle and Jamison Bepko, their cousin Andre and an associate named Vlad Stepankutza. Leeds tagged the Front Line with their name because of their size; Andre Bepko, the lightest, weighed in at 264 pounds. The Front Line Bandits hit sixteen branches of Pacific West Bank in two weeks, a reign of nightly news terror that became a public relations nightmare for Pacific West, a small regional chain with only forty-two branches.

Leeds assigned the case to Pollard. By the seventh robbery, she had a good fix on how she would identify the bandits. First, they were only hitting branches of Pacific West Bank, indicating a connection to Pacific West, and likely some kind of grudge. Second, they recognised and discarded the explosive dye packs disguised as cash that tellers slipped in with the money. Third, after demanding the money, the bandits never stayed in a bank longer than two minutes. Pollard was convinced that a Pacific West employee had taught these guys about the dye packs and the Two Minute Rule. She began screening the bank for disgruntled employees. On the morning of the day that the Front Line Bandits committed robbery sixteen, Pollard and April Sanders questioned Kanka Dubrov, a middle-aged woman who had recently been fired as an assistant manager from a branch of Pacific West; the moment they flashed their creds and told Ms Dubrov they wanted to ask her about the recent robberies, she burst into tears. Stepankutza was her son.

Later that day, when Stepankutza and his associates arrived home, they were met by Pollard, Sanders, LAPD detectives and a SWAT Tactical Team. The general manager of Pacific West, Peter Williams, presented Pollard with their Pacific West Meritorious Service Award of the Year.

'This is Peter. Katherine, is that you?'

'The very one. I wasn't sure if you'd remember.'

'I remember those monsters who almost put me out of business. After you brought them down, we nicknamed you Kat the Giant Killer.'

'Peter, I need five minutes with you. Can you make time for me now?'

'May I ask what this is regarding?'

'Marchenko and Parsons. I need to discuss them with you, but I'd rather do it face to face. It won't take long.'

'Sure, Katherine. I can do that. When can you be here?'

'Five minutes.'

Pollard left her car in a parking lot next to the building, then took an elevator to the top floor. When she got off the elevator, she saw that Williams had been promoted. A burnished sign identified him as the president and CEO.

Peter Williams was a fit man in his late fifties, short and balding with a tennis player's tan. He seemed genuinely pleased to see her, and took her into his office to show off the sweeping views of the LA basin. Then he brought her to a wall covered by framed photographs.

He pointed at one of the pictures. 'You see? Here you are.'

It was a picture of Williams presenting her with the Pac West award twelve years ago. Pollard looked a lot younger in the picture. And thinner.

Williams offered her a seat on the couch, then sat in a leather club chair. 'All right, Agent. What can I do for Kat the Giant Killer after all this time?'

'I'm not with the FBI any more. That's why I need your help.'

He seemed to stiffen, so Pollard gave him her most charming smile.

'I'm not talking about a loan. It's nothing like that.'

Willliams laughed. 'Loans are easy. What can I do?'

'I'm interviewing with private contractors as a security specialist. Marchenko and Parsons have the highest profile of the recent takeover teams, so I need to know those guys inside and out.'

Williams was nodding, going along. 'They hit us twice.'

'Right. They hit you on their fourth and seventh robberies. I need the back story in detail, but LAPD won't share their files with a civilian.'

'But you were an FBI agent.'

'From their side I can see it. They have to dot the "i"s and cross the "t"s, and the Feeb is even worse. Leeds hates it when an agent goes into the private sector. He considers us traitors. But I have two kids to support and I want this job, so if you can help me I'd appreciate it.'

Most major banks had their own security office, which worked with authorities to identify and deter bank robbers, openly sharing information; what was learned during robbery number 2 or 6 might help the police capture the bandits during robbery number 12 or 16, or help the banks prevent future robberies. Pollard knew the Pacific West security office had probably been copied on all or part of the LAPD's detail reports as they were developed. They might not have all of it, but they would have some.

Williams frowned, and she could tell he was working it through. 'You know, we have security agreements with these agencies.'

'I know. You signed some of those forms for me when I was profiling the Front Line gang and I shared our interview summaries. With you.'

'They're supposed to be for our internal use and ours alone.'

'If you want me to read them at your security office, that would be fine. They don't have to leave the premises. And if you'd like me to sign a confidentiality agreement, of course I'd be happy to sign it.'

Williams made a noncommital shrug. 'Tell you what. Leave your contact information with my assistant. Let me think about it and I'll be in touch.'

He stood, and Pollard stood with him. Williams walked her out. She left her information and rode down in the elevator alone, feeling like a brush salesman who had struck out for the day.

HOLMAN DROVE AWAY from the river towards Culver City, and reached the sign company a few minutes before quitting time. He parked in a red zone across the street and stayed in the car, waiting for the day shift to end.

He checked the dashboard, then called Chee on his cell.

'Homes! 'Sup, bro? How you like those wheels?'

'I wish you hadn't sent your boys after the old man.'

'Homes, please! Billin' you twenty a day for a cop magnet like that, a man in your position! I couldn't let him get away with that.'

'He's an old man, Chee. We had a deal. I knew what I was getting into.'

'You knew he had warrants on that piece of shit?'

'No, but that's not the point—'

'What you want me to do, send him flowers? A note sayin' I'm sorry?'

'Look, I'm not asking you to do anything, I just wanted to mention it.'

'I got your back, bro, don't ever forget that.'

'This other thing, I heard Maria Juarez left her cousins. The cops issued a warrant, and now they're blaming me for making her run. Think you can ask around?'

'Whatever, bro. I'll see what I can see.'

Holman said, 'Something else. I got fronted by the cops today about this Juarez thing. Have they been talking to you?'

'Why would the cops be talkin' to me?'

Holman told him that Random had mentioned Chee by name.

When Chee spoke, his voice was quiet. 'I don't like that, bro.'

'I didn't, either. I don't know if they've been following me or they're into my phone at the room, but don't call me on that phone. Just on the cell.'

Holman put down the phone. At exactly five o'clock, men and women came out of the printing plant and filed through the parking lot to their cars. Holman watched Tony Gilbert go to a Cadillac. Three minutes later he watched Pitchess exit the building and get into a Dodge Charger.

Holman followed the Charger until he was sure no one else from the printing plant was around. He accelerated round the cars ahead, swerved back into the lane so he was directly behind Pitchess, and tapped his horn. Pitchess's eyes went to the rearview mirror. Holman tapped his horn again, and when Pitchess looked, Holman gestured for him to pull over.

Pitchess turned into a Safeway parking lot and stopped near the entrance. Holman parked behind him, got out and walked forward. Pitchess's window rolled down as Holman approached.

Holman said, 'Can you get me a gun?'

Pitchess smiled. 'You got the money?'

'Yeah.'

'Then I can get whatever you need. Get in.'

7

When Holman got home that night, Perry's usual parking spot was empty. The Mercury was gone.

Holman let himself in through the front door like always. It was almost ten, but Perry was still at his desk, reading a magazine.

As Holman moved towards the stairs, Perry put down his magazine with a big smile. 'Hey, those boys came back today. You must've straightened'm out real good, Holman. Thanks.'

'Good. I'm glad it worked out.'

Holman kept going, but Perry swung his feet from the desk.

'Hey, wait—hang on there. What's that in the bag, your dinner?'

Holman stopped, but held the paper Ralph's Market bag down along his leg like it was nothing. 'Yeah. Listen, Perry, it's getting cold.'

Perry pushed the magazine aside. 'If you want a beer to go with it I got a couple in my place. We could have dinner together or something.'

'It's just a little bit of chow mein. I already ate most of it.'

'I'm just trying to thank you for whatever you did. Did you notice that ol' Mercury is gone? They're gonna fix it up for me, kind of like an apology.'

'That's real good, Perry. Listen, I want to get this upstairs.'

Holman went up to his room and turned off his AC unit to cut the noise, then returned to his door. He heard Perry lock the front door, then move through the lobby turning off lights before heading back to his room. When He heard Perry's door close, he slipped off his shoes, then crept down to the utility closet at the end of the hall where Perry kept cleaning supplies.

He had raided the closet a couple of times, looking for disinfectant and a plunger, and had noted a water shut-off valve in a rectangular hole cut in the wall between two studs. Holman pushed the bag into the hole beneath the valve. He didn't want to keep the gun in his room or car. The way things had been going, the cops would search his room.

THE NEXT MORNING, Pollard called to tell Holman that they were on with Leyla Marchenko. Mrs Marchenko lived in Lincoln Heights, so Pollard would pick him up at Union Station and they would drive over together.

Pollard said, 'Here's the deal, Holman—this woman hates the police, so I told her we were reporters doing a story about how the cops mistreated her when they were investigating her son. That's why she's willing to talk to us.'

'I don't know anything about reporters.'

'Well, why don't I do this without you? No reason you have to tag along.'

'No—no, I want to go.'

Holman took a quick shower, then went to meet Pollard.

He had always liked Union Station. He liked the old Spanish look of the place, with its stucco and tile and arches. After parking in the lot alongside the passenger terminal, Holman walked over to the main entrance. Pollard picked him up and they drove to Lincoln Heights, only a few minutes away.

Andre Marchenko's mother lived in a low-income neighbourhood near Chinatown. The houses were tiny and most were poorly kept. They would be overcrowded with two or three generations and sometimes more than one family, and it took everything they had just to hang on. Holman had grown up in a similar house.

Pollard reached round to the back seat and brought out a folder. She put it in Holman's lap. 'Carry this. Try to act like a reporter.'

Leyla Marchenko was short and squat, with a wide Slavic face showing small eyes and thin lips. When she answered the door, wearing a thick black dress and fluffy slippers, she looked suspicious.

'Are you the newspaper people?'

Pollard said, 'Yes, that's right. You spoke with me on the phone.'

Mrs Marchenko pushed open the door and told them to come in. Her living room was very small, with furnishings pieced together from sales and secondhand stores. Her house wasn't air-conditioned. Three electric table fans were set up around the room, churning the hot air. A fourth fan sat motionless in the corner, its safety cage broken and hanging on the blades.

Mrs Marchenko dropped into a chair like a dead weight. Pollard took a seat on the couch and Holman sat beside her.

Pollard said, 'All right, Mrs Marchenko, like I told you on the phone, we're going to do a story exploring how the police mistreated—'

Needing no more than that, Mrs Marchenko launched into her complaints. 'They were nasty and rude. They came in here and made such a mess. They broke my fan.' She waved at the motionless fan. 'They stomped around the house. I don't believe any of those things they said. Andre did not commit all those robberies—maybe that last one, but not the others.

They blamed him so they could say they solved all those cases. This man on TV, he said Andre was trying to surrender when they killed him. They over-reacted, he said, and used too much force, and they told those terrible lies to cover themselves. I am going to sue the city. I am going to make them pay.'

The old woman's eyes reddened, and Holman found himself staring at the broken fan. It was easier than seeing her pain.

'Max? Could I have the folder, please?'

Pollard had her hand out, waiting for the folder. Holman handed it to her. Pollard took out a sheet and passed it to Mrs Marchenko.

'I'd like to show you some pictures. Do you recognise any of these police officers? Did any of them come to see you?'

Pollard had clipped the pictures of Richie and Fowler and the others from the newspaper and taped them to the sheet.

Mrs Marchenko peered at the pictures, then tapped the one of Fowler. 'Maybe him. He wasn't wearing the uniform. He was wearing a suit.'

Holman glanced at Pollard, but she showed no reaction. Holman knew it was a telling moment. Fowler had worn civilian clothes because he had been pretending he was a detective.

Pollard said, 'How about the others? Were any of them here?'

'No. Another man was with him, but you don't have his picture here.'

Holman wondered who in hell this fifth man was.

Pollard asked, 'Do you remember his name?'

'I don't give those bastards the time of day. I don't know.'

'About when were they here, you think? How long ago?'

'Not long. Two-three weeks, I think. Why are you asking about them? They weren't the one who broke my fan. That was another one.'

Pollard put away the pictures. 'Let's just say they might be nastier than most, but we'll focus on everyone in the story.'

Holman was impressed with how well Pollard lied. It was a skill he had noticed before in cops. They often lied better than criminals.

Pollard said, 'What did they want?'

'They wanted to know about Allie. Andre's lady friend.'

Holman was surprised. The papers had described Marchenko and Parsons as a couple of friendless loners.

Pollard stared down at the folder for a moment before continuing. 'What did the officers want to know about her?'

'Just questions. They asked—did Andre see her a lot, where she lived, like that, but I am not going to help these people who murdered my son. I said I don't know any girl named Allie.'

'We'd like to speak with her for the article, Mrs Marchenko. Could you give me her phone number?'

'I don't know the number.'

'That's OK. We can look it up. How about her last name?'

'I am not making this up. He would call her when he was here watching TV. She was so nice, she was laughing when he gave me the phone.'

Holman saw how desperately Mrs Marchenko needed them to believe her. She had been trapped in her tiny house by the death of her son, and no one had listened for three months.

Holman felt badly but he smiled and made his voice gentle. 'We believe you, Mama. We just want to talk to the girl. When was this you spoke to her?'

'Before they murdered Andre. He would come and watch TV. Sometimes he would call her and put me on the phone—"Here, Mama, talk to my girl."'

Pollard pooched out her lips, thinking. 'Maybe if you showed us your old phone bills we could figure out which number belongs to Allie. Then we could see if Detective Fowler treated her as badly as he treated you.'

Mrs Marchenko brightened. 'Would that help me sue them?'

'Yes, ma'am, I think it might.'

Mrs Marchenko pushed up from her chair and waddled out of the room.

Holman leaned towards Pollard and lowered his voice. 'The papers didn't say anything about a girlfriend.'

'She wasn't on the FBI witness list, either.'

Mrs Marchenko interrupted them by returning with a cardboard box. 'The bills I put in here after I pay them. It's all mixed up.'

Holman watched them go through the bills. Mrs Marchenko didn't make many calls or phone many different numbers. Whenever Pollard found a number Mrs Marchenko couldn't identify, Pollard called it on her cellphone, but the first three she dialled were two repairmen and a Domino's.

Mrs Marchenko remembered the repairmen, but frowned when Pollard reached the Domino's. 'I never have pizza. That must have been Andre.'

The Domino's call had been placed five months ago. The following number was also one Mrs Marchenko couldn't identify, but then she nodded.

'That must be Allie. I remember the pizza now. When the man brought it, Andre gave me the phone when he went to the door.'

Pollard smiled at Holman. 'Well, there we go. Let's see who answers.'

She dialled the number and Holman watched as her smile faded. She closed her phone. 'It's no longer in service.'

Mrs Marchenko said, 'Is this bad?'

'Maybe not. I'm pretty sure we can use this number to find her.' Pollard copied the number into her notebook, then smiled at Mrs Marchenko. 'I think we've taken enough of your time. Thank you very much.'

Mrs Marchenko's face folded in disappointment. 'Don't you want to talk about the fan and how they lied?'

Pollard stood and Holman stood with her. 'I think we have enough. We'll see what Allie has to say and we'll get back to you. Come on, Max.'

Mrs Marchenko waddled after them to the door.

Pollard walked out to the car, but Holman hesitated. Pollard was waving for him to join her, but here was this old woman with her pleading eyes, thinking they were going to help her and they were going to leave her with nothing. Holman felt ashamed of himself.

He looked at the broken fan. 'You couldn't fix it?'

'Andre is dead. How could I get it fixed until I sue and get the money?'

'Let me take a look.'

Holman went back into the house and examined the fan. The safety cage was supposed to be attached at the back by a little screw, but the head of the screw had popped off and its body was still in the hole. It would have to be drilled and rethreaded. It would be cheaper to buy a new fan.

'I can't fix it, Mrs Marchenko. I'm sorry.'

Pollard beeped the horn. Holman went back to the door and saw her waving, but he still didn't leave. Here was this woman with her son who had robbed thirteen banks, murdered three people and wounded four others; her little boy who had modified semiautomatic rifles to fire like machine guns and shot it out with the police, but here she was defending him to the last.

Holman said, 'Was he a good son?'

'He came and we watched the TV.'

'Then that's all you need to know, Mama. You hang on to that.'

Holman left her then and went to join Pollard. He pulled the door closed and Pollard roared away from the kerb, then turned to head back towards the station. 'Max, why'd you go back inside?'

'To see if I could fix her fan.'

'We have something important here and you're wasting time with that?'

'The woman thinks we're helping her. I didn't feel right just leaving.'

Pollard went silent. When Holman glanced over, her mouth was a hard line. 'It might not have dawned on you, but I did not enjoy that. I don't like lying to some poor woman who lost her son and I don't like sneaking around pretending to be something I'm not. I don't need you making me feel worse.'

Holman felt like a moron. 'I'm sorry. I didn't mean it like that.'

Her mouth tightened, so he decided to change the subject.

'Hey, I know this Allie thing is important. Can you find her with a disconnected number?'

'I'll have a friend of mine at the Feeb do it. They can run the number through a database that will show prior subscribers.'

'Why wasn't she on the witness list?'

'Because they didn't know about her, Max. That's why this is important. They didn't know about her, but Fowler did. That means he learned about her from some other source.'

'Fowler and the new guy.'

Pollard glanced over at him. 'Yeah, and the new guy. I'll go back through his phone bills to see if and when they made contact, and I'll see if we can trace her. I'll call you later with whatever I find.'

Holman watched her drive, feeling guilty that she would be spending her afternoon with this. 'Listen, thank you again for going to all this trouble. Your husband doesn't mind you spending all this time?'

'Let's not talk about my husband.'

Holman sensed he had stepped over a line. He had noticed she didn't wear a ring the first time he saw her at the Starbucks, but she had mentioned her kids so he didn't know what to make of it. He regretted bringing it up.

As they crossed the river, Holman was surprised when Pollard spoke. 'I don't have a husband. He's dead.'

'Sorry. It was none of my business.'

'It sounds worse than it was. We were separated, on our way to a divorce we both wanted. How about you? How'd it go between you and your wife?'

'Richie's mom and I never got married. If I could go back I would have married her, but that was me. I didn't learn my lesson until I was in prison.'

'Some people never learn, Holman. At least you figured it out.'

He glanced over and saw Pollard was smiling. She said, 'I can't believe you went back to fix her fan. That was cool, Max. That was very cool.'

Holman watched Union Station swing into view, and realised he was smiling, too.

HOLMAN DIDN'T IMMEDIATELY leave Union Station after Pollard dropped him off. He bought a churro and moved through the crowd. He breathed the air and felt the sun and enjoyed the snack. He felt a lightness he hadn't known in a while. Freedom gave a man choices and every choice was a potential step back towards prison. But now Holman knew he was putting it behind him. He was becoming free again and it felt good.

It occurred to him he could have asked Pollard to join him for lunch. He imagined the two of them having a French dip up at Phillippe's or a taco plate at one of the Mexican restaurants, but then he realised he was being stupid. She would have taken it wrong and probably wouldn't have seen him again. Holman told himself to be careful with stuff like that. Maybe he wasn't as free as he thought.

He picked up his car and was heading home when his phone rang. The caller ID showed it was Chee. Holman opened the phone. 'Hey, bro.'

'Where are you, Holman?' Chee's voice was quiet.

'On my way home. I just left Union Station.'

'Come see me, bro. Drop around the shop.'

Holman was certain that something was wrong. 'Are you all right?'

'I'll be waiting.' Chee hung up without waiting for an answer.

When Holman reached Chee's shop he pulled into the lot and was parking his car when Chee came out, his face grim. He motioned Holman to stop, then climbed into the passenger seat.

'Let's take a little drive, bro. Swing on around the block.'

As they pulled into traffic, Chee swivelled his head left and right, and adjusted the outside passenger mirror so he could see behind them. He said, 'It was the cops told you Maria Juarez went on the run?'

'Yeah. They put out a warrant.'

'That's bullshit, man. They bagged her in the middle of the night. People saw it happen, ese. They heard the noise and saw her shoved in a car.'

'A police car?'

'A car car.'

'How do they know it was the police?'

'It was that red-haired guy, homes—that same guy who jumped you. That's how they know. These are the people who told me that you got bagged, homes! They said it was the same guy who grabbed you.'

Holman drove in silence for a while. The red-haired man was Vukovich and Vukovich worked for Random.

POLLARD BLASTED UP the Hollywood Freeway, feeling the electric buzz that had always come with making a breakthrough in a case. Now she wasn't just covering someone else's case notes—the girlfriend was new. Pollard had turned a new lead and now the investigation felt fresh and totally hers.

She called April Sanders. 'Hey, girl, where are you?'

Sanders came back whispering. 'Office. You got more doughnuts?'

'I have an out-of-service phone number and I'm in my car. Can you pull the subscriber for me?'

'Yeah, sure. What is it?'

Pollard read off the number. 'Three-ten area code.'

'Stand by. I show a Verizon account for one Alison Whitt, W-H-I-T-T, billed to a Hollywood private mailbox service.'

'What was the date of termination?'

'A couple of weeks ago.'

Pollard thought about it. If Fowler had discovered her number at about the time he visited Leyla Marchenko, he would have been able to contact her. Maybe Fowler's contact is why she dropped the number.

'April, see if she has a new listing.'

'Ah . . . hang on. No, negative. No Alison Whitt in the listings.'

'Listen, one more thing. I hate to ask, but could you check this girl in the DMV system? I'm trying to find her.'

'Is this something I should know about?'

'If it turns out to be, I'll let you know.'

Sanders hesitated, and Pollard thought she might be peeking at the office. Running a government database check couldn't be handled at her desk.

Sanders returned to the line. 'I can't right now. Leeds is here but I can't see him. I don't want him to ask what I'm doing. I'll call you later.'

Pollard knew she might not hear back from Sanders until the end of the day, so she went to the supermarket. She stocked up on food and toilet paper and bought treats for the boys. She wondered if Holman had once bought bags of JuJuBees for his little boy, and suspected that he hadn't. This left her feeling sad. Holman seemed like a pretty good guy now she had got to know him, and it was a shame he hadn't had a second chance with his son.

Once she had the groceries away, she straightened the house, then sat on the couch with Fowler's phone bills. She read through the outgoing numbers, beginning with the date Fowler visited Mrs Marchenko, and found Alison Whitt's phone number a few days later. He had called her on the

Thursday he and Holman's son went out late and came home muddy. Mrs Marchenko claimed she had not given Fowler any information about Allie, which meant that Fowler had got her number from another source. Pollard scanned the rest of Fowler's bills, but the Thursday call was the only one.

She was curious about how Fowler had learned of Alison Whitt and was still thinking about it when her doorbell rang. She pushed the papers together, went to the door and squinted through the peep hole.

Leeds and Bill Cecil were standing at the door. Leeds was scowling.

Though Cecil had been to her home on several occasions when Marty and she entertained, Leeds had never been to her house. She had not seen him outside his office since she left the Feeb.

Pollard opened the door. 'Chris, Bill, this is—what a surprise.'

Leeds didn't look happy to see her. He said, 'May we come in?'

'Of course. Absolutely.' She stepped out of the way to let them in.

Leeds entered first. As Cecil passed, he raised his eyebrows, warning her Leeds was in a mood.

Pollard moved to join Leeds in the living room. 'I'm stunned. Were you in the area?'

'No, I came up here to see you. Have you lost your mind?'

'Excuse me?'

'Why on earth would you get involved with a convicted criminal? I know you're helping Max Holman.'

'Chris, he lost his son. He asked me to talk to the police about it—'

'Katherine, the man is a criminal. You should know better than this.'

'Than what? I don't know why you're here, Chris.'

'Because you were on my team for eight years. I picked you and I was goddamned sorry and pissed off to lose you. I could never forgive myself if I let you do this to yourself without speaking up.'

'I'm just trying to help the man get answers about his son.'

Leeds shook his head, and said, 'Have you gone Indian?'

Pollard felt a surge of blood brighten her face. It was an old expression. A cop went Indian when he turned crooked . . . or fell in love with a crook.

'No! This is really none of your business—'

'Your personal life is *absolutely* none of my business, yes, you're right— but I still give a damn so here I am. Have you given him money?'

'Chris? You know what? You should go—'

Cecil said, 'Maybe we should leave now, Chris.'

'When I'm finished.' Leeds didn't move. He stared at Pollard.

'I'm not doing anything wrong. I haven't broken any laws.'

'Do you really know what this man wants?'

'He wants to know who killed his son.'

'Is that *really* what he wants? I've spoken with the police—I know what he's told them and I'm sure he's told you the same thing, but can you be sure? You put him in prison for ten years. Why would he turn to you for help?'

'Maybe because I got his sentence reduced.'

'And maybe he sought you out because he knew you were soft. Maybe he thought he could use you again.'

Pollard felt a growing tickle of anger. Leeds had been furious when the *Times* dubbed Holman the Hero Bandit, and he had been livid at her for speaking in Holman's favour with the Assistant US Attorney.

'He didn't use me. We didn't discuss it and he didn't ask me to intervene. He earned that reduction.'

'He isn't telling you the truth, Katherine. You can't trust him. The police believe he's consorting with a convicted felon and active gang member named Gary Mareno, also known as Little Chee or L'Chee. They believe Mareno has funded Holman with cash, a vehicle and other items for use in a criminal enterprise.'

Pollard tried to keep her breath even. Here was Holman fresh out of prison with a brand-new car. He had told her a friend had loaned it him.

'Why?'

'You know why. To recover the sixteen million dollars stolen by Marchenko and Parsons.'

'I don't believe it. He didn't even know about the money until—' Pollard realised she was saying too much.

Leeds gave her a sad but knowing smile. 'You told him?'

She took a slow breath, but Leeds seemed able to see her fears.

'It's difficult to think when your emotions are involved, but you need to rethink this, Katherine.'

'My emotions aren't involved.'

'You felt something for the man ten years ago and now you've let him back into your life. Don't lose yourself to him, Katherine. You know better.'

'I know I would like you to leave.' Pollard kept her face even.

The phone rang. Not her house phone, but the cell.

Leeds said, 'Answer it.'

Pollard didn't move towards the phone. It sat on the couch near the file with Holman's papers, chirping loudly.

'Please go. You've given me a lot to think about.'

Cecil looked embarrassed and went to the door. He opened it, trying to get Leeds out of her house. 'Come on, Chris. You've said what you had to say.'

Leeds studied the phone as if he was thinking of answering it himself, but then he joined Cecil at the door. He looked back at her. 'Agent Sanders will no longer be helping you.'

Leeds walked out, but Cecil hesitated, looking sad. 'I'm sorry about this, lady. The man—I don't know, he hasn't been himself. He meant well.'

'Goodbye, Bill.'

Pollard watched Cecil leave, then went to the door and locked it.

She walked back to the phone. It was Holman.

HOLMAN DROPPED Chee a block from his shop, then turned towards Culver City. He replayed the news about Maria Juarez, trying to cast it in a light that made sense. He wanted to drive to her house to speak with her cousins, but was afraid the cops would be watching. Why would they bag her then claim she had split? Why would they issue a warrant for her arrest if they had arrested her? News of her flight and the warrant had been in the paper.

Holman didn't like it. The police who thought she had fled had been lied to by the cops who knew different. The police who obtained the warrant didn't know that other cops already knew her whereabouts. If cops were keeping secrets from other cops, that could only mean one thing: bad cops.

Holman drove a mile from Chee's shop, then turned into a parking lot. He speed-dialled Pollard's number and finally she answered.

'Now isn't a good time.'

Pollard didn't sound like Pollard. Her voice was remote.

'Katherine? What's wrong?'

'Now isn't a good time.'

She sounded terrible, but Holman believed this was important.

'Maria Juarez didn't run. The cops took her. That same cop with the red hair who bounced me—Vukovich. It isn't like the police have been saying. Vukovich and another cop took her in the middle of the night.'

Holman waited, but heard only silence. 'Are you there?'

'How do you know this?'

'A friend knows some people who live on her street. They saw it.'

'What friend?'

Holman hesitated. He still didn't know what to say. 'Just . . . a friend.'

'Gary Mareno?'

Holman knew better than to ask how she knew. 'Yeah, Gary Mareno. He's a friend. Katherine, we were kids together—'

'So tight he gave you a car?'

'He runs a body shop. He has lots of cars—'

'And so much money you don't have to work?'

'He knew my little boy—'

'A multiple felon and gang member and you didn't think it worth mentioning? What are you doing, Holman?'

'Nothing—'

'Don't call me again.'

The line was dead. Holman hit the speed-dial, but her voicemail picked up. She had turned off the phone. He spoke as fast as he could.

'Katherine, listen, what should I have said? Chee's my friend—that's Gary's nickname, Chee—and yes he's a convicted felon, but so am I. I was a criminal all my life; the only people I know are criminals. Now he's straight like I'm trying to be, and he's my friend so I went to him for help. Katherine, please call back. I need your help to get through this. Please—'

Her voicemail beeped, cutting him off. Holman lowered his phone. He didn't know where she lived or how to reach her except through her phone. She had kept it that way to protect herself.

POLLARD'S MOTHER called at dinner time. That's the way they had been working it. Her mother would meet the boys when they were brought home from camp, then take them to her condo in Canyon Country where the boys could play in the pool while her mother played online poker.

Pollard, knowing it would be awful and steeling herself for the pain, said, 'Could they camp out with you tonight?'

'Katie, do you have a man there?'

'I'm really tired, Mom. I'm just beat, that's all. I need the break.'

'Why are you tired? You're not sick, are you?'

'Mom, could they stay? Missing camp tomorrow won't kill them.'

'I don't understand a mother who needs a break from her children. I never needed a break from you or wanted one.'

'Thanks, Mom.'

Pollard put down the phone and went back into the living room, wondering if Leeds was right. She had felt a kind of admiration for Holman both back then and now, for how he went down and how he had brought himself back. And she had felt a kind of attraction, too. Pollard didn't like admitting to the attraction. Maybe she had gone Indian without even knowing it.

Sixteen million dollars was a fortune. Holman had robbed nine banks for a total of less than $20,000. He had pulled ten years and come out with nothing, so why wouldn't he want the money? Pollard wanted the money. She had dreamed about finding it, a huge vacupacked block of it. She would be set up for life. The boys would be set. Her problems would be solved.

Pollard, of course, would not steal it. Keeping the money was just a fantasy. Like finding Prince Charming. But Holman was a lifelong degenerate criminal who probably wouldn't think twice about stealing the money.

The phone rang. Her house phone, not the cell. She answered.

April Sanders said, 'Are you really helping out the Hero?'

Pollard closed her eyes. 'I am so sorry, April. Are you in trouble?'

'Is it true about the Hero?'

She sighed. 'Yes. April—'

'I found Alison Whitt.'

'Are you still going to help me?'

'Of course I'm going to help you, Pollard. Give a sista some credit.'

Pollard reached for a pen. 'OK, April. I owe you, girl. Where is she?'

'The morgue.'

Pollard froze as Sanders's voice turned sombre and professional.

'What have you got into, Pollard? Why are you looking for a dead girl?'

'She was Marchenko's girlfriend.'

'Marchenko didn't have a girlfriend.'

'He saw her on multiple occasions. Marchenko's mother spoke with her at least twice.'

'That flabby bitch. She didn't mention a girl and I specifically asked her. And Bill and I ran his phone logs, Kat. If we had ID'd a potential girlfriend on the call-backs we would have followed up on her.'

'Maybe he never phoned her at home, or maybe he only called her from his mother's.'

'Whatever. The sheet shows a couple of busts for prostitution, shoplifting, drugs. She was just a kid—twenty-two—and now she's been killed.'

'She was murdered?'

'The body was found in a dumpster in Hollywood. She was stabbed twelve times in the chest and abdomen. Yeah, I'd call that murder.'

'Was there an arrest?'

'Nope.'

'When was she killed?'

'The same night Holman's son was killed.'

Neither of them spoke for a moment.

Finally, Sanders asked, 'Kat? Do you know what happened to this girl?'

'No. What was the time of death?'

'Between eleven and eleven thirty that night.'

Pollard hesitated, unsure what this might mean or how much she should say, but she owed Sanders the truth. 'Mike Fowler was trying to find her.'

'Who's that?'

'One of the officers killed with Richard Holman that night. He was the senior officer. Fowler approached Marchenko's mother between two and three weeks ago. He asked for information about a girl named Allie. He knew that Allie and Andre Marchenko were linked.'

'What did Mrs Marchenko tell him?'

'She denied knowing the girl.'

'What did she tell you?'

'She gave us the first name and allowed us to look through her phone bills to find the number.'

'You mean you and the Hero?'

Pollard closed her eyes again. 'Yeah, me and Holman.'

'Huh. When were the four officers killed that night?'

'One thirty-two. A pellet broke Mellon's watch at one thirty-two, so they know the exact time.'

'So it was possible Fowler and these guys killed the girl earlier. They had time to kill her, then get to the river.'

'It's also possible someone killed the girl, then went to the river to kill the officers. Listen, April, can you get the police report on Alison Whitt?'

'Already have it. I'll fax you a copy when I get home.'

'Thanks, babe.'

'You and the Hero. Man, that's a shiver.'

Pollard put down the phone and went through the kitchen into the garage. It was hotter than hell, even though the sun was down and night had fallen. She waded round bicycles and skateboards to a battered filing cabinet layered with dust. She hadn't opened the damned thing in years.

She pulled the top drawer and found the folder containing old press clippings from her cases and arrests. She had almost tossed the stuff, but now was glad she hadn't. She wanted to read about Holman again. She needed to remember why he deserved a second chance.

She found the clip, and smiled at the headline. Leeds had thrown the paper across the room and cursed the *Times* for a week, but Pollard had smiled even then. The headline read: BEACH BUM A HERO.

Pollard read the clippings at her kitchen table and remembered how she and Holman had met . . .

THE WOMAN AHEAD of him shifted irritably, making a disgusted grunt as she glanced at him for the fourth time. Holman knew she was working herself up to saying something, so he ignored her. It didn't do any good.

'I hate this bank,' she finally said. 'Only three tellers, and they move like sleep walkers. Why three tellers when they have ten windows? Shouldn't they hire more people? Every time I come here it sucks.'

Holman kept his eyes down so the bill of his cap blocked his face from the surveillance cameras.

The woman spoke louder, wanting the other people in line to hear. 'I have things to do. I can't spend all day in this bank.'

She was a large woman wearing a purple muumuu, orange nails and an enormous shock of frizzy hair. Holman crossed his arms and tried to become invisible. He was wearing a faded Tommy Bahama beachcomber's shirt, cream-coloured Armani slacks, sandals, and a Santa Monica Pier Beach Bum cap pulled low over his eyes. He was also wearing sunglasses, but so were half the people in line. This was LA.

The woman harrumphed again. 'Well, finally. It's about time.'

An older man with pickled skin in a pink shirt moved to a teller. The large woman went next and then it was Holman's turn. He tried to even his breathing, and hoped the tellers couldn't see the way he was sweating.

'Sir, I can help you over here.'

The teller at the end of the row was a brisk woman with too much make-up. Holman shuffled to the window and stood as close as he could. He was carrying a sheet of paper folded round a brown paper bag. He put the note and the bag on the counter in front of her. The note was composed of words he had clipped from a magazine. He waited for her to read it.

THIS IS A ROBBERY. PUT YOUR CASH IN THE BAG

Holman spoke softly so his voice wouldn't carry. 'No dye packs. Just give me the money and everything's cool.'

Her features hardened. She stared at him and Holman stared back, then she wet her lips and opened her cash drawer. Holman glanced at the clock behind her. He figured she had already pressed a silent alarm, and the bank's security company had been alerted. An ex-con Holman knew cautioned him you only had two minutes to get the cash and get out of the bank. Two minutes wasn't long, but it had been long enough eight times before.

FBI SPECIAL AGENT Katherine Pollard stood in the parking lot of the Ralph's Food Store in North Hollywood, sweating in the afternoon sun.

Bill Cecil, in the passenger seat of their anonymous beige g-ride, called out to her. 'You're gonna get heat stroke.'

'All this sitting is killing me.'

They had been in the parking lot since eight thirty that morning, half an hour before the banks opened for business. When Pollard got out of the car to stretch her muscles, she left the driver's window down to monitor the two radios on her front seat, even though Cecil remained in the car. Cecil was the senior agent, but he was only on hand to assist. This was Pollard's case.

They had been hovering in the Ralph's lot for three days, praying the Beach Bum would strike again. Leeds had dubbed this one the Beach Bum Bandit because he wore a Hawaiian shirt and had shaggy hair in a pony tail.

A voice crackled from one of the radios. 'Pollard?'

It was Leeds on the FBI channel.

Pollard dropped into her car and scooped up the radio. 'Hey, boss.'

'LAPD want their people on something else. I agree. I'm pulling the plug.'

Pollard had been dreading this moment. Forty-two known serial bank robbers were operating in the city. Many of them used violence and guns, and most of them had robbed way more banks than the Beach Bum.

'Boss, he's going to hit one of my banks. Every day he hasn't drives up the odds that he will. We just need a little more time.'

Pollard had patterned most of the serial bandits operating in LA. The Beach Bum's pattern was more obvious than most. The banks he hit were all located on major intersections and had easy access to two freeways; none employed security guards, Plexiglas barriers or 'bandit trap' doors; and all his robberies had followed a progressive counterclockwise route along the LA freeway system. Pollard believed his next target would be near the Ventura/Hollywood split, and had identified six banks as likely targets. The 'rolling stakeout' she now oversaw covered those six banks.

Leeds said, 'I can't afford to have you and Cecil tied up any longer.'

Cecil took the radio. 'Give the girl one more day, boss. She's earned it.'

'I'm sorry, but it's done, Katherine. The plug has been pulled.'

Pollard was trying to decide what else to say when the second radio popped to life. The second radio was linked with Jay Dugan, the LAPD surveillance team leader assigned to the stakeout.

'Two-eleven in progress at the B of A. It's going down.'

Pollard dropped the FBI radio into Cecil's lap and snatched up her stopwatch. She hit the timer button, started her car, then radioed back to Dugan. 'Time on the lead?'

'Minute thirty plus ten. We're rolling.'

Cecil was already filling in Leeds. 'It's happening, Chris. We're rolling out now. Go, lady—drive this thing.'

The B of A was only four blocks away, but the Beach Bum had at least a ninety second jump on them and might already be exiting the bank.

Pollard dropped her car into gear.

HOLMAN WATCHED the teller empty her drawers one by one into the bag. He glanced at the time and smiled. The second hand swept through seventy seconds. He would be out in less than two minutes.

The teller pushed the last of the cash into the bag.

Holman said, 'Cool. Just slide it across to me. Don't shout and don't tell anyone until I'm out the door.'

She slid the bag towards him as Holman wanted, but that's when the bank manager brought over a credit slip. The manager saw the paper bag and the teller's expression, and that was all she needed to know. She froze. She didn't scream or try to stop him, but Holman could tell she was scared.

He said, 'Don't worry. Everything's going to be OK.'

'Take it and go. Please don't hurt anyone.'

The old man in the pink shirt had finished his transaction. He was passing behind Holman when the manager asked Holman not to hurt anyone. The old man turned to see what was happening and, like the manager, realised that the bank was being robbed. Unlike the manager, he shouted—

'We're being robbed!' His face turned deep red, then he clutched his chest.

Holman said, 'Hey!'

The old man made an agonised gurgle, stumbled back and fell. When he hit the floor his eyes rolled and the gurgle turned into a fading sigh.

The loud woman in the muumuu screamed, 'Oh my God!'

Holman snatched up the money and started towards the door, but no one was moving to help the old man.

The large woman said, 'I think he's dead! Someone call nine-one-one!'

Holman ran to the door, but then he looked back again. The old man's red face was now dark purple and he was motionless.

Holman knew the old man had suffered a heart attack. He said, 'Goddammit, don't any of you people know CPR? Someone help him!'

No one moved.

Holman knew the time was slipping away. He was already over the two minute mark and falling further behind. He turned back towards the door, but he just couldn't do it. No one was trying to help.

Holman ran back to the old man and went to work saving his life. He was still blowing into the old man's mouth when a woman with a gun ran into the bank, followed by this inhumanly wide bald guy. The woman identified herself as an FBI agent and told Holman he was under arrest.

Between breaths, Holman said, 'You want me to stop?'

The woman lowered her gun. 'No,' she said. 'You're doing fine.'

Holman kept up the CPR until the ambulance arrived. He had violated the two minute rule by three minutes and forty-six seconds.

The old man survived.

8

Holman was doing pushups when someone knocked at his door. He had been mechanically grinding them out for most of the morning. When he heard the knock he figured it was Perry.

'Hang on.' Holman pulled on his pants, opened the door, but instead of Perry he found Pollard. He stared at her, surprised.

She said, 'We need to talk.' She seemed irritated, and she was holding the folder with all the papers he had given to her.

Holman suddenly realised he was shirtless with his flabby, sweaty white skin, and wished he had pulled on a shirt.

'I thought you were someone else.'

'Let me in, Holman. We have to talk.'

Holman backed out of the door to let her pass, then glanced into the hall. Perry's head disappeared behind the far corner. Holman turned back into his room, but left the door open. He thought she wouldn't feel comfortable being inside alone with him. He pulled on a T-shirt to cover himself.

She went back to the door and closed it. 'I want to ask you something. What are you going to do with the money?'

'I don't know what you're talking about.'

'If we find the sixteen million. What do you want to do?'

She looked serious. Her face was intent, her mouth pooched into a tight little knot. She looked like she had come to cut up the pie.

Holman said, 'Are you kidding me?'

'I'm not kidding.'

'I just want to find out what happened to my boy. We find that money, you can have it. I don't care what you do with it. You want to keep it, I won't rat you out. But just one thing—I won't let the money keep me from finding Richie's killer. If it gets down to a choice—keeping that money or finding out what happened—then that money is going back.'

'What about your friend, Mareno? Maybe he expects a cut.'

'I never mentioned the money to him, but I don't give a rat's ass if he keeps it, either. What do you think we're doing, planning a capital crime?'

'How would the police have come to put you and Mareno together?'

'I've been over to see him. Maybe they have him under surveillance.'

'Why would they be watching him if he's gone straight?'

'Maybe they figured out he helped me find Maria Juarez.'

'Are he and Juarez connected?'

'*I asked him to help*. Listen, I'm sorry I didn't tell you Chee loaned me the car. I'm not looking for the money—I'm looking for the sonofabitch who killed my son.'

She was still staring at him, so Holman stared back. He knew she was trying to read him. She finally seemed to make up her mind.

'Nobody's keeping that money. If we find it, we're turning it in. You good with that?'

'I'm fine with that.'

Pollard studied him a moment longer, then took several sheets from the folder. 'Marchenko's girlfriend was named Alison Whitt. She was a prostitute. Approximately two hours before your son and the other three officers were murdered, Whitt was murdered, too.'

She continued, but the pictures snapping through Holman's mind drowned her out: Fowler and Richie in a dark alley, faces lit by the flashes of their guns.

Holman barely heard himself speak. 'Did they kill her?'

'I don't know. Fowler called her a few days before he was killed. They spoke for twelve minutes that afternoon. That was the night Fowler and Richard were out late and came back with the muddy shoes.'

Holman focused on the picture of eight-year-old Richie on his dresser, not yet a thief and a killer. 'They killed her. She told them where the money was or maybe she lied or whatever and they killed her.'

'Don't go there yet, Max. The police are concentrating on customers she might have met on her day job. The hooking was just a sometimes thing— she was a waitress at a place on Sunset called the Mayan Grille.'

'It's too coincidental, her getting killed on the same night like that.'

'I think so too. The guys running this case probably don't know about her connection with Marchenko. But don't forget, we have five people in Fowler's group, and only four are dead. The fifth man could be the shooter.'

Holman had forgotten about the fifth man, and he grabbed onto the thought like a life preserver. The fifth man had been trying to find Allie, too, and now everyone else was dead. He suddenly remembered Maria Juarez.

'Did you find out about Juarez's wife?'

'I talked to a friend this morning. LAPD still maintains she fled.'

'She didn't flee; she was taken. That guy who grabbed me took her— Vukovich—he works with Random.'

'My friend is following up. She's trying to get the videotape Maria made of her husband. I know you told me Random said it was faked, but our people can examine it, too, and we have the best people in the world.'

Our. Like she was still with the Feds.

Holman said, 'You're still going to help me?'

She turned back to the door. 'You'd better not be lying to me.'

'I'm not lying.'

'You'd better not be. Clean yourself up. I'll be downstairs in the car.'

Holman watched Pollard let herself out, then hurried into the shower.

THE MAYAN GRILLE was a diner on Sunset. Business was good. People were waiting on the sidewalk and the outside tables were packed with young, good-looking people eating pancakes and omelettes.

Holman followed Pollard through the crowd into the restaurant. Inside was crowded, too. There was a wall of people, all waiting to be seated. Most of the guys were dressed in baggy jeans and T-shirts, and most of the girls were wearing shirts that showed tattoos across the top of their butts. Everyone seemed more interested in schmoozing than eating. Holman decided that either none of them had jobs or they worked in show business.

Pollard said, 'The police identified one of the waitresses, a girl named Marki Collen, as having been close to Whitt. We just have to get her to talk to us. That's not going to be easy with them being this busy.'

Pollard worked her way forward to a hostess who was overseeing a sign-up sheet for the waiting customers. Holman watched them speak and saw someone who looked like a manager join them. The manager pointed towards a waitress who was helping a busboy clear a table in the rear, then shook his head. Pollard didn't look happy when she returned.

'They got twenty people waiting to be seated, they're short-handed and he won't let her take a break. It's going to be a while before she can talk to us. You want to go get a coffee and come back when she gets off?'

Holman didn't want to go anywhere else and dick around while a bunch of Hollywood wannabes ordered food they didn't eat. 'That was her, the one in the back he pointed out?'

'Yeah, Marki Collen.'

'Come on.'

Holman shouldered through the crowd past the hostess and went to the table. The busboy had just wiped it clean and was putting out new place settings. Holman pulled a chair and sat, but Pollard hesitated. The hostess had already called two men to be seated and she was glaring at Holman.

Pollard said, 'We can't do this. You're going to get us thrown out.'

'It's going to be fine. Trust me. They're actors.'

Marki Collen was delivering an order to the table behind Holman. She looked harried and pressed. Holman dug out Chee's money, keeping his wad hidden under the table. He leaned back and tapped Marki's hip.

'I'll be with you in a minute, sir.'

'Look at this, Marki.'

She glanced round at her name.

Holman showed her a folded hundred-dollar bill, then slipped it into her apron. 'Tell the hostess I'm a friend and you told us to take this table.'

The hostess had flagged the manager, and now they were steaming back towards the table. Holman watched Marki square things with the manager, then return to the table with a big smile and two menus.

'That was cool, sir. Have I waited on you before?'

'No, it's not that. We need to ask you about Alison Whitt. We understand you were friends.'

Marki just shrugged and held her pad as if she was waiting for them to order. 'Well, yeah, kinda. We were buds here at the grill. Listen, this isn't the greatest time. I have all these tables.'

'A hundred covers a lot of tips, honey.'

Marki shrugged again and shifted her weight. 'The police already talked to me. They talked to everyone here. I don't know what else I can say.'

Pollard said, 'We don't want to know about her murder so much as a former boyfriend. Did you know she worked as a prostitute?'

Marki giggled nervously. 'Well, yeah, sure. The police told everyone about it. That's what they asked us about.'

'Her record shows two arrests about a year ago, but none since. Was she still working?'

'Oh, yeah. That girl grooved on the life. She had all these great stories.'

Holman was keeping an eye on the manager, who was watching them. He said, 'Tell you what, Marki. Put in a couple of orders so your boss doesn't freak out, then come back for the stories. We'll look at the menus.'

When she went away, Pollard leaned towards him.

'Did you give that girl a hundred dollars?'

'What of it?'

'Jesus Christ. Maybe I should have let you pay me.'

'Chee's money. You wouldn't want to get contaminated.'

Pollard stared at him. Holman stared at the menu until Marki returned. Marki told them she could hang for a minute, and Pollard went back to the point as if Holman hadn't just made an ass of himself.

'Did she ever tell you about her johns?'

'She had funny stories about her johns. Some of them were celebrities.'

'We're trying to find out about a guy she was with four or five months ago. He had an unusual name—Andre Marchenko. A Russian dude?'

Marki smiled, recognising the name right away. 'That was the pirate.'

Her smile morphed into a giggle. 'Allie said he couldn't get off without pretending he was this bad-ass pirate, you know, yo ho ho and a bottle of rum, how he lived a life of adventure and had all this buried treasure.'

Holman smiled. 'He told her he had buried treasure?'

'He used to take her to the Hollywood sign. That's where he had to do it. They had to go up to the Hollywood sign so he could make these speeches and look out over his kingdom.' Marki giggled again.

Holman saw a problem. 'Allie told you they went to the sign?'

'Yeah. Four or five times.'

'You can't get to the sign. It's fenced off and covered by security cameras.'

Marki shrugged. 'That's what she told me. She said it was a pain because you have to hike up, but the guy was loaded. He paid her one thousand dollars for sex. She said she'd hike up there all day for a thousand dollars.'

A nearby table waved Marki over, leaving Holman and Pollard alone. Holman was starting to doubt Allie's story about going up to the sign.

'I've been up there. You can get close, but you can't get to the sign. They have video cameras all over up there. They even have motion detectors.'

'Now, wait a minute, Max—this is making sense. Marchenko and Parsons lived in Beachwood Canyon. The sign is right at the top of their hill. Maybe they hid the money up there.'

'You couldn't bury sixteen million dollars anywhere around that sign. Sixteen million dollars is big.'

'We'll see when we get there. We'll go take a look.'

When Marki returned Pollard resumed her questions.

'We're almost finished, Marki. We'll be out of your hair in a minute.'

'Like he said, a hundred covers a lot of tips.'

'OK, you mentioned speeches. What kind of speeches did he make?'

Marki scrunched her face, thinking. 'Not really speeches, maybe—more like pretend. Like if he was a pirate and kidnapped her, he would screw her on all his stolen treasure. She had to act like that would be this big turn-on.'

Pollard nodded. 'Like it was his turn-on, to do it on the money?'

'I guess.'

Pollard glanced at Holman, but he still couldn't see planting sixteen million in cash in such a public place. Then he remembered that Richie and Fowler had come home covered in grass and mud.

He said, 'When the cops were here, did you tell them about Marchenko?'

Marki looked surprised. 'Should I have? It was so long ago.'

'No. I was just wondering if they asked.'

Holman was ready to leave. But Pollard wasn't looking at him.

She said, 'OK, just one more. Did Allie have a madam or work for an outcall service?'

'She had someone looking out for her, but he wasn't a pimp or anything.'

Holman said, 'What does that mean, someone looking out for her?'

'It sounds kinda silly. She told me I wasn't supposed to tell anyone.'

'Allie's gone. The statute of limitations ran out on that one.'

Marki glanced at the nearby tables, then lowered her voice again. 'OK, well. Allie worked for the police. She said she didn't have to worry about getting trouble 'cause she had this friend who could make it go away. She even got paid for telling about her clients.'

Pollard had turned white. 'Alison was a paid informant?'

Marki gave an uneasy grin. 'She wasn't getting rich or anything. She told me they had some kinda cap or something on the amount. Every time she wanted some money this guy hadda get it approved.'

Holman said, 'Did she tell you who she worked for?'

'Uh-uh.'

Holman looked back at Pollard, but she was still pale. Holman touched her arm. 'Anything else?'

Pollard shook her head.

Holman peeled off another hundred and slipped it into Marki's hand.

A DEPRESSED ACTRESS named Peg Entwistle had killed herself by jumping from the top of the letter H. The letters were fifty feet tall, and the sign stretched some 450 feet across the top of Mount Lee in the Hollywood Hills. After years of neglect, the Hollywood sign was rebuilt in the late seventies, but vandals took their toll, so the city closed the area to the public. They surrounded the sign with fences, CCTV cameras, infrared lights and motion detectors. It was like they were guarding Fort Knox, which wasn't lost on Holman as he directed Pollard up to the top of Beachwood Canyon. She had picked him up from the motel at first light that morning.

Pollard looked worried. 'I thought we had to go through Griffith Park.'

'This way is better. We're looking for a little street I know.'

Holman still didn't think they would find anything, but they had to look. If Alison Whitt had told her contact police officer about Andre Marchenko, the cops might have known about the Hollywood sign. Putting the sign together with Marchenko's fantasy would have inspired them to search the area. Richie might have been part of the search. Whitt had probably seen Marchenko in the news, realised that her pirate was the bank robber, and offered up what she knew to her cop. This had probably inspired her death.

They wound their way up through narrow residential streets higher into Beachwood Canyon. The Hollywood sign grew above them, sometimes visible betweens houses and trees and sometimes hidden by the mountain. When they reached the top of the ridge, Holman told Pollard to turn.

'Slow down. You can pull over in front of these houses.'

Pollard pulled over and they got out of the car. The road ended abruptly at a large gate, which was locked and hung with a sign reading CLOSED TO THE PUBLIC. On the other side, the surface was gravel and dirt.

Pollard looked dubious. 'This is your short cut? It's closed.'

'It's a fire road. We can follow it up round the peak to the back of the sign. This way cuts a couple of miles off going up through Griffith Park. I've been coming up here since I was a kid.'

Pollard tapped the CLOSED sign. 'Have you *ever* obeyed the law?'

'No, not really.'

'Jesus Christ.'

Pollard squeezed round the side of the gate and Holman followed. The road was steeper than he remembered, but he was older now and in lousy shape. He was breathing hard before long, but Pollard seemed to be doing fine. The road curved round to the back of the peak and the Hollywood sign disappeared from view, but the radio tower perched above it grew.

Holman said, 'No way those guys brought all that money up here.'

'Marchenko brought his girlfriend up here.'

'She could walk.'

The road continued round the mountain as they neared the peak and suddenly all of LA spread out before them as far as Holman could see.

Pollard said, 'Wow.'

Holman didn't give a damn about the view. The radio tower waited at the end of the road, surrounded by fences. Another ten-foot chain-link fence ran on the downhill side of the road, with the tops of the Hollywood letters visible through the fence. Holman waved his hand at the sign.

'There it is. You still think they buried the money up here?'

Pollard hooked her fingers into the fence and gazed down at the sign. The slope was steep. The bases of the letters were too far below them to see.

She said, 'Can you get down there?'

'Only if you climb the fence, but it isn't the fence you'd have to worry about. See the cameras?'

Closed-circuit television cameras were mounted on fifteen-foot metal poles dotting the fence. The cameras were trained on the sign.

Holman said, 'They have cameras along the length of the sign and more down at the base so they can see it from all angles. They're also set up with infrared so they can watch it at night, and they have motion sensors.'

'Who's on the other end of the cameras?'

'The Park service. Rangers are watching this thing twenty-four/seven.'

Pollard squinted up the road at the communication station. A bristle of cameras sprouted at the station, too. Uphill from the road was a steep slope climbing to the summit. She asked, 'What's up there?'

'Weeds. It's just the top of the hill.'

Pollard set off towards the communication station and Holman followed. He tried to picture Richie and Fowler and the other two cops coming up here in the middle of the night, and just couldn't see it. If they suspected Marchenko had hidden the money at or near the sign, where and how would they search? The Hollywood sign covered a lot of ground, and even policemen couldn't approach it without being seen by the Rangers. They might have tried telling the Rangers they were conducting an official police investigation, but Holman thought the chances of that were slim. The Rangers would have had questions, and stories of the late-night search would have spread beyond the park. If they had tried to bluff their way through the Rangers they would have made their search during the day. Coming out at night meant their search had been a secret.

Pollard said, 'You know what I'm thinking about?'

'What?'

She turned in a little circle, spreading her arms at their surroundings. 'So Marchenko brings her up here to have sex, what did he do? Cameras are everywhere. There isn't any privacy. This is a lousy place for it.'

Holman was uncomfortable with Pollard talking about sex. He glanced at her, but couldn't bring himself to make eye contact.

She suddenly turned and stared up the steep slope rising above them. 'Is there a way up to the top?'

'Yeah, but nothing's up there.'

'That's why I want to see it.'

Holman realised her instincts were right. The summit was the only private place on the hill.

They squeezed between the hillside and the corner of the fence by the communication station, then followed a narrow path round the side of the peak. The soil was loose and the trail was steep, but pretty soon they crested the summit and emerged from the brush into a small clearing.

Pollard looked around at the 360-degree view that surrounded them and smiled. '*That's* what I'm talking about! This is where they were doing it. Right here.'

She was right. From the clearing, they could see if anyone was approaching on the fire road. The cameras that dotted the fences were below them, and pointed downhill towards the sign. No one was watching the summit.

But Holman still didn't believe Marchenko and Parsons had buried their money up here. Carrying that much cash would have taken several trips, and each trip would have increased the odds they would be discovered. Even if they were stupid enough to bring the money up here, the hole needed to bury it would have been the size of five or six suitcases. It would have been difficult to dig in the rocky soil, and anyone else who visited the summit would have easily noticed the large area of disturbed soil.

Holman pointed out the heel prints and scuff marks that had been scratched into the clearing. 'Hikers come up here all the time. Maybe he had the girl up here, but there's no way they brought the money. '

Pollard gazed down at Hollywood. 'Why did he have to come up here to be with the girl? He could've pretended to be a pirate anywhere.'

Holman shrugged. 'Why'd he rob thirteen banks dressed like a commando? Freaks happen.'

She shook her head. 'No, Max, coming up here was important to him. It meant something. Even madness has meaning.'

'You think that money was up here?'

'No. No, you're right about that. They didn't bury sixteen million dollars up here, and Fowler and your boy sure as hell didn't find it and dig it up. That hole would look like a bomb crater.'

'OK.'

She pointed down towards the city. 'But he lived right down there in Beachwood Canyon. See it? Every day when he stepped out of his apartment, he could look up and see this sign. Maybe they didn't hide the money up here, but something about this place made him feel powerful. That's why he brought the girl up here. Remember what Alison told Marki? It had to be here. He couldn't perform without his fantasies, fantasies about treasure—having sex on the money. Money equals power. Power equals sex. Being here made him feel close to his money, and the money gave him the power to have sex.' She looked at him. 'Fowler and your son could have picked up mud and grass in any vacant lot in LA, but if they knew what Alison knew, they would have come up here. Look around. It isn't that big. Just look.'

Pollard walked off into the brush, scanning the ground. Holman thought they were wasting their time, but he turned in the opposite direction.

The only man-made artefact on the summit was a wire cage that had been set into the ground years ago. It contained scientific equipment bearing US Geological markings. Holman guessed it was for monitoring seismic activity. The equipment and locks on the cage appeared undisturbed.

He was in a brushy area ten feet in front of the cage when he found the turned earth. 'Katherine!'

It was a small oval depression about a foot across. The darker turned earth stood out from the surrounding undisturbed ground.

Pollard appeared at his side, then knelt by the depression. She probed the turned soil with her fingers and tested the surrounding area. She scooped loose soil from the centre, revealing a hard perimeter. She continued clearing loose soil until she finally sat back on her heels. It hadn't taken long.

Holman said, 'What is it?'

She looked at him. 'It's a hole . . . See the hard edge where the shovel bit? Someone dug up something. And because they removed it, there wasn't enough dirt to refill the hole. Hence the depression.'

'You couldn't fit sixteen million dollars in a little tiny hole like that.'

Pollard stood. 'No, but you could hide something that led to the sixteen million—GPS coordinates, an address, keys, even a pirate's treasure map.'

Holman glanced up, but Pollard was walking away. He looked down at the hole again as an emptiness grew in his heart.

Richie had not been a good man. Richie had made a play for the money.

Holman heard Donna's voice echoing across the cavernous emptiness that filled him, the same four words over and over: *Like father, like son.*

POLLARD LOOKED DOWN at the cameras perched on their fifteen-foot poles. She decided that they probably included views of the fire road as it approached the sign and the antenna, but no one was watching the road on the back side of the mountain. She moved to the edge of the summit and studied the rear facing slope. It was steep and brushy, but do-able. Scrambling up the slope on a dewy night probably even explained the mud on Fowler's boots. They could have avoided the cameras.

Pollard opened her phone and punched up Sanders's cell number. She knew Sanders wasn't in the office because she answered in a normal voice.

'Let me ask you a question, Pollard—what in hell are you and Hero doing?'

Pollard glanced across the clearing at Holman, who was still standing by the hole. 'The same thing we were doing yesterday and the day before. Why?'

'Leeds has been getting serious heat from the police is why. Parker Center has been calling and Leeds is going to meetings he won't tell anyone about and he's coming apart at the seams.'

'Has he said anything specifically about me?'

'He said if any of us were contacted by you we were to report that contact immediately. He also said if any of us were using government time and resources to aid a civilian endeavour—he looked at me when he said it—he would bring disciplinary charges and transfer our asses to Alaska.'

'Are you going to report this call?'

'Are you breaking the law?'

'For God's sake, no, I am not breaking the law.'

'Then I just want to know what's going on.'

'I'll tell you, but have you been able to get a copy of the Juarez tape?'

'They told me the tape had been erased. An unfortunate accident.'

Pollard took a breath. Maria Juarez had disappeared, and now her tape had been destroyed, the tape Maria claimed as her husband's alibi.

She said, 'Who's calling Leeds?'

'I don't know. The calls come from Parker Center. Leeds doesn't tell us.'

'All right. I think we're looking at a criminal conspiracy among police officers growing out of the Marchenko and Parsons robberies. That conspiracy includes the murder of the officers under the Fourth Street bridge.'

Pollard's phone beeped with an incoming call. She didn't recognise the number so let it go to voicemail, and resumed her conversation with Sanders.

'We believe the four dead officers plus one additional officer were conducting an off-the-books investigation to find the missing sixteen million.'

'Did they find it?'

'I believe they did or identified its location. My guess now is that once the money was found, one member of the conspiracy decided to keep everything for himself. I don't know that yet, but I'm positive about the conspiracy. I believe this fifth person was connected with Alison Whitt.'

'How does Whitt fit into this?'

'She claimed she was a registered police informant. If that's true, she might have told what she knew about Marchenko to her contact officer.'

Sanders hesitated. 'You want me to identify her contact officer?'

'If she's registered, she'll be on an informant list and so will her sponsor.'

'This is going to be tough. I told you how they're coming down on us.'

'Parker Center is coming down on you. Whitt's murder is being handled out of Hollywood Station. You might still be able to get some cooperation.'

'OK, I'll see what I can do. You really think this is cop on cop murder?'

'That's the way it's shaping up.'

'You can't sit on this. You're a civilian. You're talking about murder.'

'When I have something that stands up I'll give it to you. You can bring it forward through the FBI. One more thing—Mike Fowler left a pair of dirty boots on his patio. Soil and vegetation samples from his boots should be compared with samples from the summit above the Hollywood sign.'

'*The* Hollywood sign? Why the friggin' sign?'

'That's where I am. Marchenko and Parsons hid something related to their robberies up here. I believe Fowler and Richard Holman came here searching for it, and I believe they found something. If you end up bringing this thing forward, you'll want to see if the soil samples match.'

'OK. I'm on it. You keep me advised, OK? Stay in touch.'

'Let me know when you get something on Whitt.'

Pollard ended the call, then retrieved the incoming message. It was Peter Williams's assistant, calling from Pacific West Bank.

'Mr Williams has arranged for you to access the files you requested. You'll have to read them here on our premises. Please contact myself or our chief security officer, Alma Wantanabe, to make the arrangements.'

Pollard put away her the phone, sensing that they were close to making a breakthrough. She hurried over to Holman. He was now squatting beside the hole, pushing dirt back into it with measured mechanical motions.

'Stop playing in the dirt and let's go. Pacific West has a copy of the police summaries. This is good, Holman. If we can match your cover sheets with the reports, we'll know what Random took from your son's desk.'

Holman stood as if he was made of lead and started back down the trail. Pollard related what she had learned about Maria Juarez's videotape.

'We're getting close, Holman. We catch a break with these reports or with Whitt being an informant, and everything will come together.'

She got pissed off when he didn't answer. She was about to say something when Holman finally spoke.

He said, 'I guess they did it.'

Pollard realised what was bothering him. Holman had probably been holding out hope his son wasn't a bad cop but now that hope was gone.

'I'm sorry, Max. We still have to find out what happened.'

'I know.'

When they reached the car, Holman got in without a word. Pollard tried to be encouraging, telling him what she hoped to find at Pacific West Bank.

He said, 'Listen, I don't want to go. I'd like you to bring me home.'

Pollard said, 'We won't be at the bank that long.'

'I have something else to do. Just drop me home first.'

'We're halfway to Chinatown. If I have to bring you to Culver City it's really out of the way.'

'Forget it. I'll ride the bus.'

With no warning, Holman suddenly pushed open the door and stepped out into traffic. Pollard was caught off guard, but she jammed on the brake.

'Max!'

Horns blew as Holman darted through the traffic.

'Max! What are you doing? GET BACK IN THE CAR!'

He didn't look at her. He kept walking. The cars behind her lit up their horns and Pollard finally crept forward. She didn't turn onto the freeway. She let the traffic flow round her, then eased to the kerb, letting Holman walk, but keeping him in sight. She thought he looked furious.

Pollard watched Holman board a bus. She believed he was going home, but she couldn't be sure, so she followed the bus, wedging her Subaru to the kerb each time it stopped.

Holman left the bus two blocks from his motel. When he reached it, she expected him to go inside, but he continued round the outside and got into his car, and then she was following him again.

He picked up Sepulveda Boulevard and dropped south through the city. Pollard stayed five or six cars back, following him steadily south until Holman surprised her. He stopped near a freeway exit ramp and bought a bouquet of flowers from a vendor.

A few blocks later he arrived at the cemetery.

THE MORNING SUN was breathtakingly hot as Holman turned into the cemetery grounds and followed the road up to Donna. Only a few other visitors were scattered through the cemetery. A burial was taking place on the far side, with a small crowd of mourners gathered around a tent.

Holman parked and carried the flowers to Donna's grave. His earlier bunch were still on the bronze plaque, now black and brittle. Holman took the dead stuff to a trash can by the drive, then put the fresh flowers on the plaque. He felt bad that he hadn't brought some kind of vase. In this heat, without water, the flowers would be dead by the end of the day.

Holman squatted and pressed his hand onto Donna's marker. The hot metal burnt his palm, but he pressed harder. He whispered, 'I'm sorry.'

'Max?'

Holman glanced over his shoulder to see Pollard coming. He stood.

She stopped beside him and gazed at the grave. 'Richard's mother?'

'Yeah. Donna. I should've married this girl, but . . . you know.'

Pollard looked up and seemed to study him. 'You OK?'

'Not so good. She was proud of him. So was I, but I guess the kid never really had a chance, not with the way I was.'

'Max, don't do this.' Pollard touched his arm, but he barely felt it.

'I tried to believe in God when I was in prison. I really wanted there to be a heaven, man—heaven, angels, God on a throne.' Holman shrugged. 'Now I hope there's no damn Heaven. I don't want her up there seeing all this, knowing he turned out like me.'

Pollard was as rigid as a statue. Her mouth was a tight line and her face was grim. When Holman glanced at her, a tear leaked down from behind her sunglasses and rolled to her chin.

Holman lost it when he saw the tear, and a sob shuddered his body. He tried to fight it, but he gasped and heaved as tears flooded his eyes, and all he knew in that moment was how much pain he had caused.

He felt Pollard's arms. She murmured words, but he did not understand what she was saying. She held him hard, and he held her back, but all he knew were the sobs. He wasn't sure how long he cried. After a while he calmed, but he still held her.

Then Holman realised he was holding her. He stepped back. 'Sorry.'

Pollard's hand lingered on his arm, but she turned aside to wipe her eyes.

Holman cleared his throat. He still needed to talk with Donna. 'Listen, I want to stick around here for a while. I'll be OK.'

'Sure. I understand.'

'Why don't we call it quits for today?'

'No. No, I want to see the reports. I can do that without you.'

Pollard touched his arm again and he reached to touch her hand, but she turned away. Holman watched her walk to her car in the brutal heat and watched as she drove away, then he looked back at Donna's marker.

His eyes filled again, and now he was glad Pollard had gone. He squatted once more and adjusted the flowers. 'Bad or not, he was ours. I'll do what I have to do.'

He smiled, knowing she wouldn't like it, but at peace with his fate. You just couldn't beat the bad blood.

'Like son, like father.'

Holman heard a car door close behind him and glanced up into the sun. Two men were coming towards him when a third called his name.

9

Vukovich and Fuentes were coming from one side and two more from the other. Holman could not reach his car. They spread apart as they came like they expected him to run and were ready for it. Holman stood anyway, his heart pounding. The empty plain of the cemetery left him exposed like a fly on a dinner plate, with no place to hide and no way to lose them.

He started for the gate, and all four men suddenly ran forward.

Holman shouted at the burial party. 'Help! Help me!'

Mourners at the far tent turned as the first two officers converged on him. Holman lowered his shoulder at the last moment and drove into the smaller guy hard, then spun, making a sprint for his car.

Someone slammed into Holman from behind, but he kept his feet and turned as Fuentes charged from the side.

Vukovich was shouting, 'Stop it, goddammit—give it up!'

Everything blurred into bodies and arms. Holman swung hard, catching Fuentes in the ear, then someone tackled his legs and he went down. Knees dug into his back and his arms were twisted behind him.

'Help! Help!'

'Shut up, asshole. What do you expect those people to do?'

'Witnesses! People are watching, you bastards!'

'Calm down, Holman. You're being dramatic.'

Holman didn't stop struggling until he felt the plastic restraints cut into his wrists. Vukovich lifted his head by the hair and twisted him round so they could see each other.

'Relax. Nothing's going to happen to you.'

'What are you doing?'

'Taking you in. We tried to be nice, but could you take the hint?'

When they lifted him to his feet, Holman saw that everyone in the burial party was now watching them. The two motorcycle cops who had escorted the hearse were walking over, but Fuentes was trotting out to meet them.

Holman said, 'They're witnesses. They're gonna remember this.'

'All they're going to remember is some asshole getting arrested. Stop being stupid. You're going to be fine.'

Holman didn't like the way Vukovich told him he was going to be fine. It sounded like something you heard before you were murdered.

They stood him up outside their car and went through his pockets. They took his wallet, keys and cellphone, then checked his ankles, waist and groin. Fuentes came back and the motorcycle cops returned to the funeral.

Vukovich said, 'OK, load'm up.'

'People know, dammit. People know what I'm doing.'

'No, Holman, no one knows anything. Now shut the fuck up.'

Fuentes drove away in Holman's Highlander as the two new guys pushed him into the back seat of their car. The larger man got into the back with Holman and his partner climbed in behind the wheel. They pulled away as soon as they had the doors locked.

Holman knew they were going to kill him. He studied the two cops. They were both in their thirties, with solid builds. They were fit men and young, but neither had Holman's heavy shoulders and weight.

He said, 'Did either of you know my son?'

The driver shot a glance in the mirror, but neither answered.

'Was it one of you gunned him down?'

The driver started to say something, but the back-seat man cut him off.

'That's up to Random to tell him.'

Holman figured Random was probably the fifth man, but now Vukovich,

Fuentes and these two guys were also part of the action. Add in Fowler, Richie and the other two, and that made nine. Sixteen million was a lot of money. There was still plenty to go round. Holman wondered what they knew about Pollard. They would have seen her at the cemetery. They probably didn't like the idea of stirring up the FBI, but they would be willing to take the chance. When they got rid of him they would get rid of her.

They drove for about fifteen minutes. Holman thought they would take him out to the middle of nowhere, or maybe a warehouse, but they turned onto a middle-class street in Mar Vista. Small houses set on narrow lots lined both sides of the street. Holman saw his Highlander parked at the kerb. Fuentes wasn't in the car and no one was nearby. Holman's heart started to pound and his palms grew cold. He would have to make his move soon. His life was on the line.

They pulled across the drive of a small yellow house. The drive ran past the side of the house under an arching carport to a garage at the rear of the property, and a blue sedan was parked beneath the arch.

The driver shut off their car and unlocked the back doors. He got out first, and opened Holman's door. 'OK, dude. Get out, but don't move away from the car. When you're out, turn to face the car. You understand?'

'I think I can handle it.' Holman got out of the car and turned.

The driver immediately stepped up behind him and took a firm grip on his wrists. 'OK, John.'

John was the back-seater. He got out, then moved to the front of the car, waiting for Holman and the driver.

Holman took in the surrounding houses. Bikes in the front yards and knotted ropes hanging from trees told him this was a family neighbourhood. An outboard powerboat was parked in a drive two houses away and he glimpsed low chain-link fences through breaks in the shrubs. No one was outside, but people would be inside with their air conditioners, mostly women with small children this time of day. He could scream his ass off, but no one would hear. If he ran, he would have to go over fences.

He said, 'You better tell me what you want me to do so I don't fall.'

'We're going round the front of the car. Down the drive to the carport.'

Holman had guessed they would use the carport. The front door was exposed, but the kitchen door would probably be hidden under the arch. He wasn't going to let them bring him into the house. He figured he would die in the house. If he was going to die he wanted to die in the open where someone might see, but Holman didn't plan on dying that day.

He stepped away from the car. The driver closed the door, then nudged him towards the front. Holman shuffled forward. John waited for them at the drive, then walked ahead.

The driver said, 'Jesus, you can walk faster than that.'

'You're bumping my feet. Why don't you back off and give me some room, for Christ's sake. You're going to trip me.'

The driver moved closer behind him, which was what Holman wanted.

John stepped under the arch, in the narrow space between the house and the blue sedan, and went to the door. He waited for Holman and the driver, then opened the screen door, leaving him on one side of it and Holman and the driver on the other, sandwiched between the house and the car.

Holman didn't wait for the door to open. He swung his right foot high against the house and shoved the driver back into the sedan as hard as he could. He jerked his left foot up to join his right, and with both legs pressed so hard that the sedan rocked. He slammed his head back and the solid bone-on-bone impact made his eyes sparkle. He felt the driver go limp.

John realised what was happening. 'Hey!'

He scrambled to get the door closed, but Holman was already running across the front yard. Then he turned for the back yard, wanting to get out of sight. He ploughed through bushes and shrubs and fell across a fence. He heard someone shouting inside the house but didn't stop. When he reached the rear of the house he rolled over another fence into the neighbour's back yard. Branches tore at him but he kept going. He sprinted across the neighbour's yard and kicked his way over another fence, then struggled to his feet and ran across the next yard. He heard shouts two houses away and knew they would be coming, but he moved up along the side of the house towards the street, because that's where he had seen the boat.

Holman crept to the corner of the house. Vukovich and John were in the street by their cars, Vukovich holding a radio.

Holman crept over to the boat with its big outboard motor. He twisted round to push the plastic wrist tie onto the edge of the propeller blade and sawed it back and forth. He pushed so hard the plastic cut into his skin, but then the tie on his right wrist popped and his hands were free.

Fuentes and John were now moving in the opposite direction, but Vukovich was walking down the middle of the street towards him.

Holman crabbed backwards away from the boat, then slipped across the back yard in the direction he had come from. They were fanning away from the house and wouldn't expect him to double back. He jumped back over the fence into the next yard and saw a stack of patio bricks. He took one, and continued across the yard, moving quietly. He eased over the fence and was again behind the yellow house. The back yard was empty and quiet.

He slipped along the side of the house towards the street, listening, staying beneath the windows. He couldn't take too much time because Vukovich and the others would return when they couldn't find him. They would probably see him when he made his move, but if he got lucky they would be too far away to stop him. He edged closer, and that's when he heard a woman's voice coming from inside the house. The voice was familiar. He slowly raised himself up enough to see into the house.

Maria Juarez was inside with Random.

Holman should never have looked. Random caught the movement. His eyes widened, and he turned for the door. Holman lurched to his feet.

He ran for the Highlander and heard the front door open behind him. Vukovich was already on his way back and broke into a run. Holman shattered the Highlander's passenger side window with the patio brick, then reached in and unlocked the door, Random screaming behind him.

'He's here! Vuke! Johnny!'

Holman threw himself inside. Chee had given him two keys, and he had left the spare in the console. He jacked it open, fished out the key, then pushed himself into the driver's seat and ripped away from the kerb.

He turned at the next intersection, punched out of the turn and powered up the street. When he hit Palms Boulevard, he headed off towards the freeway, then jammed into the first and largest shopping centre he found, an open-air monster anchored by an Albertson's supermarket.

The Highlander was easy to spot, so Holman didn't want to leave it in the main parking lot. He swerved into the service lane behind the shopping centre, pulled over and shut the engine. Then he looked at himself. His face and arms were scratched and bleeding, his shirt was torn and streaked with dirt, and the restraint was still attached to his left wrist, the strands from the severed loop dangling like spaghetti. He studied the clasp. The plastic tie had to be cut, only now Holman didn't have a blade.

He restarted the engine, then pushed in the cigarette lighter. When it popped out, he pulled the tie away from his skin and pressed the glowing end onto the plastic. He clenched his jaw, but it burned like a sonofabitch.

He had to heat the lighter three more times before the tie melted through.

Vukovich had taken his keys, wallet, money and cellphone. Holman searched the floorboards and console, and came up with seventy-two cents. He had stashed some cash with the gun at the motel, but he couldn't get it yet.

He locked the Highlander and walked away. He found a payphone outside the Albertson's. He wanted to warn Pollard but when he reached the phone he couldn't remember her number. He had programmed it into his cellphone's memory, but now his phone was gone.

Holman started to shake. He slammed the phone into its cradle and cursed. Three people entering the store stared at him.

Telling himself to calm down, he decided to call Chee. He didn't remember Chee's number, either, but Chee's shop was listed. Holman fed in his coins, then waited while the information operator made the connection.

Chee's phone rang a long time, then a young woman answered in a tentative voice. 'Hello?'

'I'm calling for Chee.'

'I'm sorry, we're closed.'

Holman hesitated. It was the middle of the day. Chee's shop should not have been closed.

'Marisol? Is this Marisol?'

Her voice came back even more tentative. 'Yes?'

'This is Max Holman—your dad's friend. I need to talk to him.'

Holman waited, but she didn't respond. Then he realised she was crying. 'Marisol?'

'They took him. They came—' Her crying, clogged voice broke into full-blown sobs and Holman's fear level spiked.

'Marisol?'

Holman heard a man saying something in the background and Marisol trying to answer, and then the man came on the line, his voice also guarded.

'Who is this?'

'Max Holman. What's she talking about? What's going on over there?'

'This is Raul, man. You remember?'

Raul was the kid who put together Holman's driver's licence.

'Yes. What was she talking about? Where's Chee?'

'They hooked him up, man. This morning—the cops arrested him.'

Holman's heart started pounding again and he once more scanned the parking lot. 'What happened? Why did they arrest him?'

Raul lowered his voice like he didn't want Marisol to hear, but his voice became strained. 'I don't know what happened. They came in this morning with warrants, dogs, assholes with machine guns—'

'The police?'

'LAPD, FBI, SWAT, even the ATF—if it's in the alphabet they were here.'

Holman forced himself to breathe. 'OK. What were they looking for?'

'Assault rifles and explosives.'

'Jesus Christ, what was Chee doing?'

'*Nothin'*, bro! Chee's not into anything! His daughter works here. You think he'd keep explosives? Chee won't even let us deal stolen air bags.'

'But they arrested him?'

'Hell, yes. They put him into the car right in front of his daughter.'

'Then they must have found something.'

'I don't know what they found. They loaded some shit into a truck. They had the Bomb Squad here, Holman! They had those dogs sniffin' everywhere, but we didn't have anything like that.'

A computerised voice came on the line, telling Holman he had only one minute left. He was out of quarters. His time was running out.

Holman said, 'One more thing. Did they ask about me?'

The line was already dead. Raul had hung up.

Holman put down the phone and studied the parking lot. He believed Chee had been set up, but he didn't understand why. Holman hadn't even told Chee about the missing $16 million and his suspicions of a police conspiracy, but maybe someone thought Chee knew more than he did.

Holman returned to the Highlander, opened the rear cargo door and pulled out the emergency tool kit. Holman hadn't stolen a car in a dozen years, but he still remembered how.

POLLARD ARRIVED at the Pacific West building in Chinatown forty-five minutes after she left Holman at the cemetery. Alma Wantanabe, the Pac West chief security officer, showed her to a windowless conference room. Two institutional blue boxes were waiting on a table.

Wantanabe explained that the LAPD summaries were divided into two distinct groups. One consisted of divisional files specific to the robberies within those divisions. The second group was files compiled by Robbery Special, who had synthesised the divisional reports into their larger, citywide investigation. Wantanabe cautioned Pollard not to remove or copy any material from the files, then left her alone to work.

Pollard opened her own file for the cover-sheet copies Holman had made before Random confiscated the reports. The cover sheets told Pollard nothing except the case and witness numbers. She hoped to identify the witnesses through the witness lists, then see what they said.

She started by emptying the box of divisional reports. She found three witness lists, but it was soon apparent that the numbering system did not match that of her cover sheets. She put the divisional files aside and turned to the box of Parker Center reports. Her interest spiked the instant she opened it. The first page was a case file introduction signed by the commander of Robbery Special and the two lead detectives in charge of the case.

The second lead detective was Walter B. Random.

Pollard stared at his name. She knew Random from his investigation into the murder of the four police officers. She had assumed he was a homicide detective, yet here he was in charge of a robbery investigation. The same robbery that now overlapped with the murders.

She flipped through the reports until she found the witness list. It was a thirty-seven page document listing 346 names beginning with witness number 1, identified as a teller at the first bank Marchenko and Parsons robbed. The lowest witness number on Pollard's cover sheets was 318, followed in consecutive order by 319, 320, 321, 327 and 334. All of her witnesses had come late in the case. She began matching the numbers on her cover sheets to names, and immediately saw a pattern.

Number 318 was identified as Lawrence Trehorn, who managed the apartment building in Beachwood Canyon where Marchenko and Parsons lived. The next three witnesses were their neighbours. Number 327 was an attendant at the West Hollywood health club that Marchenko visited. And 334 was Andre Marchenko's mother.

Pollard located the individual summaries, but did not read them straight away. She checked for the names of the detectives who conducted the interviews. Random had signed off on Trehorn and Mrs Marchenko, and Vukovich had signed off on one of the neighbours. Vukovich had been one of the officers with Random who confronted Holman outside his daughter-in-law's apartment—another detective investigating the murders who had also investigated Marchenko and Parsons.

Fowler and the fifth man had gone to see Mrs Marchenko. Pollard wondered if Fowler had also gone to see these other five people.

She copied the five new names and contact information, then read the summaries. They provided nothing except as a list of people who were personally known to Marchenko and Parsons. Pollard decided this was the key. None of these summaries was specific to the robberies, but all were potentially relevant to establishing what Marchenko and Parsons had done with the money. This would have been why Richard Holman had them, but the questions still remained: how had he got them and why had Random removed them from Richard's home? It was as if Random didn't want anyone to have proof that Fowler and his group were trying to find the money.

Pollard returned the summaries to the file, then placed the files in their boxes. She thanked Alma Wantanabe, who walked her to the elevators. As Pollard rode down, she checked her messages, but Sanders hadn't yet called. She felt a flash of frustration, then realised she had something almost as good as an informant list to work with—Mrs Marchenko. If Random was the fifth man, Mrs Marchenko would be able to identify him, which would put Random together with Fowler. Finding Alison Whitt's contact officer would then be icing on the cake.

Pollard decided to call Holman. She was dialling his number when the elevator opened.

Holman was in the lobby, filthy and streaked with dried blood.

HOLMAN REMEMBERED that she was going to the Pacific West building, but he didn't know if she was still there or how to reach her. He didn't want to go to the building. If someone had followed Pollard from the cemetery, Holman would be giving himself back to them, but he didn't know how else to reach her. He circled the building until he was scared he would miss her, then cowered in the lobby like a shivering dog. A security guard questioned him twice. He was about to leave when the elevator opened and Pollard stepped out. In that double-take moment when she saw him, her face went white.

'What happened to you? Look at you—what happened?'

Holman was still shaking. 'We gotta get out of here. Vukovich and those guys—they grabbed me again.'

Pollard saw the guard, and lowered her voice. 'You're bleeding—'

'They might have followed you. I'll tell you outside.'

'Who?'

'The cops. They jumped me at the cemetery after you left.'

The shaking grew worse. Holman tried to bring her towards the door, but she pulled him the other way.

'This way. Come with me—'

'We have to go. They're looking for me.'

'You're a mess, Max. You stand out. In here.'

Holman let her pull him into the women's bathroom. She jerked paper towels from a dispenser and wet them in the sink.

'They brought me to a house. It was Vukovich and . . . Random was there. They didn't arrest me. It wasn't a goddamn arrest. They *took* me—'

'Shh. You're shaking. Try to calm down.'

'*We have to get out of here, Katherine.*'

She wiped blood from his face and arms, but he couldn't stop trembling. Then he remembered his phone was missing and the terrible helpless feeling he had when he couldn't reach her.

'I need something to write with—a pen. You got a pen? I tried to call you, but I couldn't remember your number. I couldn't remember—'

The trembling grew worse until Holman felt he was shaking apart.

Pollard tossed the bloody towels, then gripped his arms. 'Max.'

Her eyes seemed to draw him. She stared into his eyes and Holman stared back. Her fingers dug into his arms, but her eyes were calm and her voice was soothing. 'Max, you're here with me now—'

'I was scared. They had Maria Juarez—'

'You're safe. You're with me now, and you're safe.'

'Jesus, I was so scared.' Holman stayed with her eyes, but the corners of her lips held a gentle curl that slowed him like an anchor would slow a drifting boat. His shaking eased.

'You OK?'

'Yeah. Yes, I'm better.'

'Good. I want you OK.'

Pollard found a pen in her jacket, then took his arm. She wrote her cell number on the inside of his forearm, then looked up again with softer eyes.

'Now you have my number. You see, Max? Now you can't lose it.'

Holman felt that something was different. She moved closer to him, then slipped her arms round him and rested her head on his chest. Holman stood stiff as a mannequin. He was uncertain and didn't want to offend her.

She whispered into his chest. 'Just for a moment.'

Holman hesitantly touched her back. She didn't jump away. He put his arms round her and laid his cheek on her head. Little by little, he let himself hold her and breathed her in and felt the badness drain away. After a bit Holman felt her stir, and they stepped apart at the same time.

Pollard smiled. 'Now we can go. Tell me in my car what happened.'

She was parked in the building's basement. Holman described how they had taken him at the cemetery and how he had escaped and what he had seen. She made no comment even when he told her he had stolen a car. She didn't speak until he was finished.

'All right, it was Vukovich and three other men—one named Fuentes and one named John—who arrested you at the cemetery?'

'They didn't arrest me. They hooked me up, but they didn't bring me to a station—they brought me to a *house*. This wasn't any damn *arrest*.'

Pollard frowned. 'All right, and Random was at the house?'

'Yes. With Maria Juarez. Chee said the cops took her and he was right. And now they have Chee. They arrested him this morning.'

Pollard shook her head. 'I don't get what's happening here.'

Holman thought it was obvious. 'They're getting rid of everyone who's rocking the boat about Random's case against Warren Juarez. Think about it. Random put the murders on Juarez and closed the case, but Maria said Warren didn't do it—so they grabbed her. Then I didn't buy the story they floated, either. They tried to make me back off, and when that didn't work they bagged me, too. Now they have Chee.'

'Random arrested him?'

'A task force raided his shop this morning. One of Chee's guys, he told me they found guns and explosives. I've known Chee my whole life and I am telling you that's bullshit. These bastards must have set him up.'

Pollard still didn't seem convinced. 'But why involve Chee?'

'Maybe they think I told him about the money. Maybe because he's been helping me. I don't know.'

'Could you find the house again, the one where they took you?'

'Absolutely. I can take you there right now.'

'We're not going there now—'

'We have to. Now that I know where they have her, they'll clear out. They'll take that woman with them.'

'Max, listen to me—you're right. They left as soon as you left and if they were holding Maria Juarez against her will then they took her with them. If we go back now we'll find an empty house. If we go to the police about this, what can we tell them? You were kidnapped by four LAPD officers?'

Holman knew she was right. He was a criminal. He had no proof, and no reason to think anyone would believe him. 'Then what can we do?'

'We have to find the fifth man. If we can prove Random is the fifth man we can tie him to Fowler and make our case—'

Pollard paged through her folder and pulled out a newspaper clipping about Richie's murder. The clipping included a picture of two cops making a statement at Parker Center and one of the cops was Random.

'I want to show this picture to Mrs Marchenko. If she fingers Random as the fifth man, I can take what we know to my friends at the FBI.'

Once more, Holman knew she was right. He reached out to touch the curve of her cheek. She didn't move away.

'Funny how things work.'

'Yeah.'

Holman turned to open the door. 'I'll see you over there.'

She grabbed his arm. 'Hey! You're coming with me! You can't drive around in a stolen car. You want to get bagged for grand theft auto?'

Pollard was right again, but Holman knew he was right in a different way. Random and Vukovich had come for him. They would come for him again. For all he knew, every cop in the city was looking for him, and they would set him up just like they set up Chee.

Holman gently lifted her hand. 'I might have to run, Katherine. I don't want to run in your car. I don't want you caught with me.' He squeezed her hand. 'I'll see you at her place.'

He didn't give her a chance to respond. Holman slid out of her car and jogged away.

HOLMAN LEFT the parking lot as if he was sneaking away from a bank he had just robbed. He still worried that someone had followed Pollard from the cemetery, so he studied the cars and pedestrians outside the building but found no one suspicious. He waited in his stolen car until Pollard pulled into the traffic, then followed her to Mrs Marchenko's house.

Holman felt better now that he had spoken with Pollard. He sensed they were close to finding out who had murdered Richie, and why. Random had been a major player in the Marchenko case and now he controlled the investigation into the murder of the four officers. Random would have known about the missing $16 million and had probably put together a team to find it that included Fowler, Richie and the others. Random wanted to pin the murders on Warren Juarez; Maria Juarez had proof her husband wasn't the shooter, so the proof disappeared and so did Maria Juarez. Richie had been in possession of reports Random had written, and Random had made the reports disappear. Holman had asked too many questions, so they tried to scare him off, then finally tried to make him disappear, too.

When they reached Mrs Marchenko's house, Holman parked across the street and joined Pollard on the sidewalk. When she opened her front door, Mrs Marchenko didn't seem happy to see them. She looked suspicious.

'I been lookin' for that article. I don' see it.'

Pollard smiled brightly. 'Soon. We're here to tack down a few last details. I have a picture I want to show you.'

Holman followed Pollard and Mrs Marchenko into the living room.

Mrs Marchenko dropped into her usual chair. 'What picture?'

'Remember the pictures we showed you last time? You were able to iden-tify one of two officers who came to see you. I'm going to show you another picture. I want to know if he was the other man.' Pollard took the clipping from her folder and held it out.

Mrs Marchenko nodded. 'Oh, him I know, but that was before—'

Pollard nodded, encouraging. 'Right. He interviewed you after Andre was killed. Did he come back to see you with the other man?'

Mrs Marchenko settled back in her chair. 'No. It wasn't him.'

Holman felt a swirl of anger. They were close. They were at the edge of breaking this thing open and now the old lady was being a road block.

'Why don't you look again?'

'I don't need to look again.'

'For Christ's sake, lady—'

Pollard held up a hand, warning him to stop. 'So think about the other man, Mrs Marchenko. Try to remember what he looked like. He didn't look like this man?'

'No.'

'Can you describe him?'

'He looked like a man. I don't know. A dark suit, I think.'

Holman suddenly wondered if the fifth man might have been Vukovich.

'Did he have red hair?'

'He was wearing a hat. I don't know. I tol' you, I not pay attention.'

Holman's certainty at nailing Random fell apart like a dream shattered by an alarm clock. He stalked out of the house and didn't stop walking until he reached the street.

When Pollard came out he said, 'How could it not be Random? It *had* to be Random! He's what ties this all together.'

'Just stop. All right, so the fifth man wasn't Random or Vukovich. We know he wasn't your son or Mellon or Ash, but he had to be somebody.'

'Random had three or four other guys with him at that house. Maybe it was one of them.'

'We still have Alison Whitt—' Pollard already had her cellphone out and was speed-dialling a number.

'If Random was her contact officer, we can still—'

She held up a hand, cutting him off as the person she called answered. 'Yeah, it's me. What did you get on Alison Whitt?'

Holman waited, watching as Pollard stiffened. He knew it was bad even before she lowered the phone.

Pollard stared at him for a moment, then shook her head. 'Alison Whitt was not a registered informant with the Los Angeles Police Department.'

'So what do we do?'

'I have her arrest record at my house. I can see who the arresting officers were. Maybe we were wrong in thinking she was a registered informant. Maybe she was just feeding some guy on the sly and I'll recognise a name.'

Holman smiled, more for himself than her. He took in the lines of her face and the way her hair fell, and remembered again the first time he saw her, pointing a gun at him in the bank. 'I'm sorry I got you into this.'

'We are *not* finished with this, Max. Random is all over both sides of this thing and all we need is the one missing piece to have it make sense.'

Holman nodded, but he felt only loss. He had tried to play this the right way, the way you're supposed to play it when you live within the law, but the right way hadn't worked out. 'You're a special person, Agent Pollard.'

Her face tightened and she was that young agent again. 'My name is Katherine. Call me by my name.'

Holman wanted to hold her again. He wanted to hold her close and kiss her, but doing so could only be wrong. 'Don't help me any more, Katherine. You'll only get hurt.' He started towards his car.

Pollard followed him. 'Wait a minute. What are you going to do?'

'Get new stuff and drop off the grid. They had me and they're going to come for me again. I can't let that happen.'

He got into his car, but she wouldn't let him close the door. Holman wedged his screwdriver into the busted ignition and twisted it.

'I have to go, Katherine. Please.'

'Max!'

He looked up at her. Pollard stepped back and closed the door. She leaned in the window and touched his lips with hers. Holman closed his eyes. He wanted it to go on for ever, but knew that, like every other good thing in his life, it would not last. When he opened his eyes, she was watching him.

She said, 'I'm not going to quit.'

Holman pulled away. He glanced in the mirror and saw her in the street, watching him, this incredible woman who had almost been part of his life.

They hadn't been able to put the pieces together, but that no longer mattered. Holman was not going to let them get away with Richie's murder.

10

Pollard brooded as she drove home, her thoughts swinging between her disappointment that Alison Whitt had lied about being an informant and her surprise that Mrs Marchenko had not identified Random as the fifth man.

It was as if she and Holman had uncovered two separate cases with Random on both sides—Fowler's search for the missing money and the murder of the four officers. Random had been a principal in the Marchenko investigation and he controlled the murder investigation, which he had closed by naming Warren Juarez the assailant, even though unanswered questions remained. He had denied that Fowler and the others were connected to Marchenko and had actively suppressed further inquiry.

Only Fowler and his boys *had* been searching for the money, and they hadn't been searching alone. At least one other person was involved—the fifth man. Pollard believed this was same person who provided Fowler with information learned from Alison Whitt. She believed Whitt was the key and would still connect everything to Random.

Pollard pulled into her drive, hurried through the hellish heat and let herself into the house. She stepped through the front door, lost in thought, when a red-haired man waiting inside pushed the door out of her hands, slamming it shut.

Startled, Pollard jerked backwards as another man stepped from the hall.

'Walt Random. We're the police.' He held a credential case with a badge.

Pollard spun into Vukovich, driving her elbow hard into his ribs.

Vukovich grunted and jerked to the side. 'Hey—'

She spun in the opposite direction, thinking she had to get to the kitchen then out of the back door, but Random was already blocking her path.

'Hold it! We're not going to hurt you. *Hold it!*'

Pollard's heart was pounding, but Random had stopped between her and the kitchen and had come no closer. He was holding up both hands with his badge dangling over his head and Vukovich had made no further move.

Random said, 'Take it easy now. Just relax. If we wanted to hurt you would we be standing here like this?'

Pollard edged to the side, eyes going between them. 'What do you want?'

Random put away his badge. 'Your cooperation. You and Holman have been messing things up for us, lady. Will you give me a chance to explain?'

'Is that why you grabbed him, to explain?'

'I wouldn't be here now and telling you what I'm about to tell you if you hadn't forced my hand.'

Vukovich was leaning against the door, watching her, but his eyes were curious and his manner relaxed. Random seemed irritated, but his eyes were tired and his suit was rumpled. Nothing about their body language was threatening. Pollard felt herself begin to relax, but she was still wary.

She said, 'Question.'

Random opened his hands, saying go ahead, ask.

'Who murdered those men?'

'Warren Juarez.'

'Bullshit, Random. I don't believe you and I don't believe they just happened to be under that bridge. They were looking for Marchenko's money.'

Random shrugged. 'Yes, they were looking for the money, but Juarez was the shooter. He was hired by someone to kill them. We're trying to identify the person who hired him.'

'Stop lying to me. Holman saw Maria Juarez with you at the house.'

'That house is a safe house. She was there voluntarily at our request.'

'Why?'

'Juarez didn't commit suicide. The person who hired him murdered him.

We grew worried that this person might also murder Juarez's wife. We brought Holman to the house so Maria could tell him herself. I didn't expect him to believe me otherwise.'

Pollard watched Random as he spoke and believed he was telling the truth. She nodded. 'All right, I buy that, but why did you have Chee arrested?'

Random frowned, then glanced at Vukovich before looking back at her. He shook his head. 'I don't know what you're talking about.'

'Holman's friend, Chee—Gary Mareno. He was raided this morning and taken into custody. Am I supposed to believe it was a coincidence?'

Random looked blank, but he glanced at Vukovich again. 'Vuke, see what you can find out.'

Vukovich took out a cellphone and drifted into the dining room. Pollard could hear him mumbling as she continued with Random.

'If you knew another person was involved, why did you close the case?'

'Juarez's killer set up the murder to look like a suicide. I wanted him to think we bought it. I wanted him to feel safe.'

'Why?'

'We believe this person is a high-level police officer.'

This was exactly what she and Holman had been thinking, only they had figured it was Random. Pollard suddenly realised how the disparities between the two Randoms made sense.

'The fifth man.'

'What's the fifth man?'

'We knew someone else was involved. We called him the fifth man. We thought it was you.'

'Sorry to disappoint you.'

'You've been running an investigation within an investigation, one public, the other secret—a secret investigation.'

'There was no other way to approach this. The only people who know what we're doing are my team, the chief and one assistant chief. This investigation began weeks before these guys were killed. I was informed that a group of officers were making a play for the money. We identified most of them, but someone with an intimate knowledge of Marchenko and Parsons was feeding information to Fowler, who was protecting the sonofabitch like a pit bull. Fowler was the only one who knew this person, the only one who spoke or met with him, and that's who we were trying to identify.'

'And then the shooting started.'

'Yes. Then the shooting started, and you and Holman have been kicking so many rocks even divisional officers are beginning to notice. I need you to stop, Pollard. If this guy starts feeling the heat we'll lose him.'

'How is it you know so much about what Fowler did and didn't do? How do you know Fowler was the only one?'

For the first time, Random hesitated.

Pollard felt a growing knot in her stomach. 'You had someone inside.'

'Richard Holman was working for me.'

The house filled with silence. Everything Holman had told her about his conversations with Random flickered in her head.

'You sonofabitch. You should have told him.'

'Telling him would have compromised this investigation.'

'You let the man think his son was dirty. Do you have any idea how much this has been hurting him? Do you give a shit?'

'Rich Holman contacted me when Fowler tried to recruit him. Rich had refused, but I convinced him to call Fowler back. I put him in with them, Ms Pollard, so, yes, I do.'

Pollard thought about Holman: Richie wasn't a bad guy any more; Richie was good. Holman wouldn't have to apologise to his wife.

Random said, 'Do you see why it had to be this way?'

'If you're looking for absolution, forget it. Maybe it did have to be this way, Random, but you're still an asshole. The man lost his son. All you had to do was talk to him like a human being instead of a dirtbag and none of this would be happening.'

'Will you call him?'

Pollard laughed. 'Well, I would, but I can't. Your guys took his cellphone at the cemetery. I have no way to reach him.'

Random clenched his jaw. Vukovich returned from the dining room saying someone would call him back, but Pollard paid no attention. She was wondering if everything she and Holman had done was pointless.

'Well, did they find the money or not? I'm guessing they must have else this suspect you're looking for wouldn't have killed these people.'

'We're not sure.'

'They must have found the money, Random. What did they find at the Hollywood sign?'

Random was clearly surprised. 'How did you know about that?'

'Kicking rocks, you asshole. What was it they found?'

'Keys. They found twenty-two keys in a blue metal Thermos bottle.'

'Just keys? What kind of keys?'

'Rich didn't see them. It was Fowler who opened the Thermos. He told the others what they had, but kept them in his possession.'

'There was nothing about how to find the locks?'

'Just the keys. The next day, Fowler told the others his partner thought maybe he could figure out what the keys opened. That's why the meeting was called on the night they were murdered. The last report I got from Rich, he said everyone thought they were going to learn about the money.'

Pollard realised that almost everything Random knew came from Rich Holman. But Fowler kept secrets. Pollard suddenly wondered if she didn't know more about this case than Random.

'Do you know why Marchenko hid those keys at the Hollywood sign?'

Pollard could see by his expression he didn't have a clue. He guessed.

'Remote. Close to his apartment.'

'Alison Whitt.'

Random was lost.

'Alison Whitt was a prostitute. Marchenko used to have sex with her up at the sign. You didn't know this?'

Vukovich shook his head. 'That's not possible. We interviewed everyone even remotely connected to Marchenko and Parsons. Everyone we talked to said these clowns were eunuchs. They didn't even have *male* friends.'

'Holman and I learned about her from Marchenko's mother. Listen to this—approximately two weeks before the murders, Fowler and another man went to see Marchenko's mother, specifically to ask about Alison Whitt. The man with Fowler wasn't Rich or Mellon or Ash. She didn't have a name for him, but you could work her with an artist.'

Random glanced at Vukovich. 'Have someone go with an artist.'

Vukovich turned away again with his cellphone.

Random turned back to Pollard. 'What's the story on Whitt?'

'Bad. She was murdered on the same night as the others. Whitt's the connection here, Random. Fowler and his friend knew about Whitt *before* they saw Marchenko's mother. Whitt claimed she was a registered informant, so I figured the fifth man might be her contact, but that didn't pan out.'

'Wait a minute—how did you find out all this if Whitt was already dead?'

Pollard told him about Marki Taylor at the Mayan Grille and Alison Whitt's stories about Marchenko and her being an informant.

Random took out a pad and made notes. When she finished, he studied what he'd written. 'I'll check her out.'

'You won't find anything. I had a friend at the Feeb run her name through the roster at Parker. She isn't on your list.'

Random smiled. 'Thank your friend, but I'll check it myself.' He took out his phone and went to the window as he made his call.

Vukovich returned to Pollard. 'Got word on your boy, Chee. It was a righteous bust. Bomb Squad got a tip from the Feeb. They pulled six pounds of C-4 plastic explosive and some det cord out of his shop.'

Pollard stared at Vukovich. 'The FBI put them onto this?'

'What the man said. Part of a conspiracy investigation, he said.'

'When did the call go in?'

'This morning. Early sometime. Is that important?'

Pollard shook her head, feeling numb.

Random finished his call, then took a business card from his wallet and brought it to Pollard. 'Holman will want to talk to me. That's OK. Once you reach him, call me, but you have to make him understand you have to back off. That's imperative here. You can't tell anyone what I've said, and Holman can't tell his daughter-in-law. You see why we're playing it like this, don't you? I just hope it's not already too late.'

Pollard nodded, but she wasn't thinking about how Random was playing it. She waited stiffly at the door as they walked away, then turned to face the emptiness of her home.

A tip from the Feeb.

Pollard knew she might have made a serious mistake. Marki told them that Whitt was a registered informant with a cop taking care of her, but the word 'cop' wasn't necessarily a policeman and LAPD wasn't the only law-enforcement agency using registered informants.

Alison Whitt could have been an informant for the FBI. And if she had—

The fifth man was an FBI agent.

Pollard hurried out into the heat and drove into Westwood.

THE INFORMATION that registered informants provided was included as part of the legal record in investigator's reports, writs, warrants, grand jury indictments, motions, briefs and ultimately trials. Since many of these documents were in the public record, the true names of informants were never used but were replaced by code numbers, and the codes were held under lock and key to protect the anonymity of the informants. Where and how this list was safeguarded varied by agency, but no one was guarding nuclear launch codes; all an agent had to do was ask his boss for the key.

Pollard had used informants only three times during her years on the Squad. On each of those three occasions she had requested the Bank Squad's informant list from Leeds and watched him open a locked file box in which he stored the papers. Each time, he used a brass key taken from a small box he kept in his upper-right-hand desk drawer.

The sky over Westwood was a brilliant clear blue when Pollard rolled into the parking lot. The black tower shimmered against the late afternoon sky; an optical trick played by the sun.

Pollard opened her phone to call Sanders. She needed a pass into the building, but Sanders did not answer. Her voicemail picked up on the first ring, indicating she was probably at a crime scene.

Pollard dialled the Squad's general number. When the Squad was spread through LA, a duty agent remained in the office to field incoming calls.

'Bank Squad. Agent Dillon.'

Pollard remembered the young agent she met with Bill Cecil.

'This is Katherine Pollard. I met you up in the office with the doughnuts.'

'Oh, sure. Hi.'

'I'm downstairs. Is April up there?'

'I haven't seen her. I'm pretty much alone here. Everyone's out on a call.'

'How about Leeds?'

'Um, he was here earlier—no, I don't see him. It's pretty busy today.'

Pollard tried to sound disappointed. 'Damn. Kev, listen—I have some things for Leeds I wanted to drop off along with a box of doughnuts for the Squad. Would you call down a pass?'

'Sure. No problem.'

'Great. I'll see you in a minute.'

Pollard had picked up a box of doughnuts from Stan's. She carried the box and her file into the building, then picked up her pass, cleared security and rode up to the fourteenth floor.

She let herself into the Squad and scanned the room. Dillon was in a cubicle near the door and another agent she didn't recognise was in a cubicle near the wall. They both looked up. Pollard nodded at the agent near the wall, then flashed a big smile at Dillon as she approached him.

'Man, I used to *hate* having the duty. I think you need a doughnut.'

Dillon fished a doughnut from the box, but seemed uncertain where to put it. His desk was covered in paperwork.

Pollard said, 'You want me to leave the box with you?'

Dillon glanced at his desk. 'Why don't you leave it in the coffee room?'

'You bet. I'm going to drop these things in Leeds's office, then I'll be out of your hair.' She gestured with the file so he would see it, then turned away.

She dropped the doughnuts off in the coffee room, then stole a glance at the two agents as she stepped back into the squad room. Their heads were down and neither was paying attention.

Pollard went to Leeds's office. She opened the door without hesitation and entered the dragon's lair. Pollard had not been in Leeds's office since the day she resigned, but it was as intimidating now as she remembered. Pictures of Leeds with every president since Nixon adorned the walls.

Pollard was relieved to see the filing cabinet was still in the corner and Leeds's desk unchanged. She hurried to the desk and opened the upper-right-hand drawer. Several keys were in the box, but Pollard recognised the brass key. She went over to the cabinet, unlocked the security file, opened the drawer and scanned through the folders, which were divided alphabetically. She found the W folder, then searched the files until she saw the name.

Alison Carrie Whitt.

Pollard opened the file to the cover sheet, containing Whitt's identifying information. She bent over it, scanning the page, searching for the fifth man's name—

'*What in the hell are you doing?*'

Pollard jerked at the sound of his voice.

Leeds filled the door, his face furious. 'Pollard, *stand up!* Get away from those files. Dillon! Get in here!'

Pollard slowly straightened up, but she didn't put down the file. Dillon appeared in the door behind Leeds. She studied them. Either of their names might be on the sheet, but she didn't believe it would be Dillon. He was too new.

She looked Leeds in the eye. 'An agent in this office was involved in the murder of the four officers under the Fourth Street bridge.'

Even as she said it she thought: Leeds. It could be Leeds.

He advanced towards her across the office, moving carefully. 'Put down the file, Katherine. What you're doing now is a federal crime.'

'Murdering four police officers is a crime. So is murdering a registered federal informant, name Alison Whitt.' Pollard held out the file. 'Is she your informant, Chris?'

Leeds glanced at Dillon, then hesitated. Dillon was her witness.

Pollard went on. 'She's in your file—Alison Whitt. She was a friend of Marchenko's. An agent in this office knew that. That agent was involved with Fowler and the other officers in trying to find the sixteen million.'

Leeds glanced at Dillon again, but now Pollard read his hesitancy in a different light. He didn't seem threatening; now, he was curious.

'What kind of proof do you have?'

She nodded towards the file of Holman's notes, articles and documents. 'It's all in there. You can call an LAPD detective named Random. He'll back me up. Alison Whitt was murdered on the same night as the four officers. She was murdered by the person named in her file.'

Leeds stared at her. 'You think it's me, Katherine?'

'I think it could be.'

Leeds nodded, then slowly smiled. 'Look.'

Pollard skimmed the cover sheet until she found the name.

Alison Whitt's recruitment officer was Special Agent William J. Cecil.

Bill Cecil. One of the kindest men she ever knew.

HOLMAN HEADED for Culver City. He did not like the idea of returning to his apartment, but he needed the money and gun.

The traffic was thick when Holman reached the Pacific Gardens. He circled the block twice, looking for loiterers and people waiting in parked cars. Then he left the car on the side street alongside the motel and entered through the rear by Perry's room.

Perry wasn't at his desk. Holman crept up the stairs to the second floor. He checked that the hall was empty, then went to the utility closet and eased open the door. He pushed the mops out of the way and reached into the wall beneath the water valve. The wad of cash and the gun were still behind the pipe. Holman was fishing them out when the muzzle of a gun dug hard behind his left ear.

'Leave go whatever you've got in there, boy. Nothing better come out of there but your hand.'

Holman didn't even turn to look, but went rigid with his hand in the wall.

'Pull that hand out slow and empty.'

Holman showed his hand, opening his fingers wide so the man could see.

'That's good. Now stand there while I cop a feel.'

The man felt Holman's waist and his crotch and the seat of his pants, then checked down along the inside of his legs to his ankles.

'All right then. You and I have a little problem, but we're gonna work it out. Turn around slow.'

Holman turned as the man stepped back—a wide, light-skinned black man with a bald head and tired eyes, wearing a blue suit. He slipped his pistol into his jacket pocket, but held on to it.

It took a minute before Holman recognised him. 'I know you.'

'That's right. I helped put your ass away.'

Holman remembered—FBI Special Agent Cecil had been with Pollard that day in the bank. He wondered if Pollard had sent him, but the way Cecil was holding the gun told Holman he was not here as his friend.

'Am I under arrest?'

'Here's what we're going to do—we're going down those stairs like we're the best buddies in the world. That old man down there says anything or tries to stop us, you tell him you'll see him later and keep walking. We get outside, you'll see a dark green Ford Taurus parked out front. You get in. You do anything but what I'm telling you, I'll kill you in the street.'

Cecil stepped out of the way and Holman went down the stairs and got into the Ford, wondering what was happening. He watched Cecil cross in front of the car then get in behind the wheel. Cecil took the pistol from his pocket and held it in his lap with his left hand as he pulled away from the kerb. His breath was fast and shallow and his face sheened with sweat. His eyes darted between traffic and Holman like a man watching for snakes.

Holman said, 'What are you doing?'

'Going to get us sixteen million dollars.'

Cecil was the fifth man. Cecil had killed Richie. Holman glanced at the gun. When he looked up Cecil was watching him.

'Oh, yeah. Yeah, yeah, I was in with them, but I didn't have anything to do with those killings. That was that stupid bastard, Juarez. Me and your boy were partners until Juarez lost his mind. The man went nuts, killing everybody, figuring he could keep the money, I guess. That's why I took him out. I took him out for killing those people.'

Holman knew Cecil was lying. He saw it in how Cecil made eye contact, arching his eyebrows and nodding his head to fake sincerity. Fences and dope dealers had lied to Holman the same way a hundred times. Cecil was trying to play him, but Holman didn't understand why. Something had driven Cecil into revealing himself and now the man clearly had a plan that included Holman.

He glanced at the gun again, wondering if he could get it or push it aside. Everything he had done since that morning in the CCC when Wally Figg told him Richie was dead had led to finding this man. If Holman could keep from being shot he might be able to punch Cecil out, hammer him hard in the head. But then where would he be? The cops would come and Cecil would flash his creds—who would they believe?

Holman thought he might be able to jump out of the car before Cecil shot him. They had just turned onto Wilshire Boulevard where traffic slowed.

'You don't have to jump. We get where we're going, I'm gonna let you out.'

'I'm not going anywhere.'

Cecil laughed. 'Holman, I've been hooking up guys like you for almost thirty years. I know what you're going to think even before you think it.'

'You know what I'm thinking right now?'

'Yeah, but I won't hold it against you.'

'I'm thinking why are you still here if you have sixteen million dollars?'

'Know where it is, just couldn't get it. That's where you come in.' Cecil took a cellphone from the console and dropped it in Holman's lap. 'Here. Call your boy Chee, see what's shaking.'

Holman caught the phone but did nothing. 'Chee was arrested.'

'You already know? Well, good, save us a call. Chee was in possession of four pounds of C-4 and a laser-siting device. Among the evidence confiscated from that dump he calls a body shop are the telephone numbers of two people suspected of being Al-Qaeda sympathisers and the plans for building an explosive device triggered by the aforementioned laser.'

'You set him up.'

'Ironclad, baby, ironclad. And only I know who planted that shit in his shop, so if you don't help me get this money your boy is fucked.'

Without warning, Cecil slammed on the brakes. The car screeched to a stop, throwing Holman into the dash. Horns blew and tyres screamed behind them, but Cecil didn't react. His eyes were hard black chips that stayed on Holman.

'Do you get the picture?'

More horns blew and people cursed, but Cecil's eyes never wavered. Holman wondered if he was crazy.

'Just take the money and go. What in hell do I have to do with this?'

'Told you—couldn't get it by myself.'

'Why the hell not? Where is it?'

'Right there.'

Holman followed Cecil's nod. He was looking at the Beverly Hills branch of Grand California Bank.

11

Cecil pulled his car to the kerb outside the flow of traffic and stared at the bank as if it was the eighth wonder of the world.

'Marchenko and Parsons hid all that money in twenty-two safe deposit boxes, the big kind, not those little ones.' Cecil reached under his seat and took out a soft pouch that tinkled. He dropped it into Holman's lap and took back the phone. 'Got the keys here, all twenty-two.'

Holman poured the keys into his hand. The name MOSLER was cut into one side along with a seven-digit number. A four-digit number was on the opposite side. 'This is what they hid at the Hollywood sign.'

'Guess Marchenko figured if he got pinched for something, those keys would be safe up there. Wasn't anything saying which bank, either, but the manufacturer keeps a record. One phone call, I had it.'

Holman shifted the keys in his hands like coins. Sixteen million dollars.

Cecil said, 'So now you're thinking, if he had the keys and knew where it was, why didn't he just go get the damn money.'

Holman already knew. Every bank manager in LA would recognise Cecil and the other Bank Squad agents. A bank employee would have to accompany him into the vault with the master key to the safe boxes, and he would have to sign their ledger. Sixteen million spread through twenty-two safe boxes was a lot of trips in and out of a bank where you were recognised by the employees and everyone knew you had rented no boxes. Cecil would have been questioned. His comings and goings would have been recorded by security cameras. He would have been made.

'I know why you didn't get the money. I was wondering how much sixteen million dollars weighs.'

'I can tell you exactly. Bank gets hit, they tell us how many of each denomination was lost. Tally that up, you know how many bills; each bill weighs a set amount—you just do the math. This particular sixteen million weighs eleven hundred forty-two pounds.'

Holman glanced back at Cecil. The man was still staring at the bank. Holman would have sworn his eyes glittered green.

'Did you go look at it?'

'Went in one time. Opened box 3701. Took thirteen thousand dollars and never went back. Too scared.' Cecil frowned at himself, disgusted. 'Even wore a disguise.'

Cecil had gold fever. Men in the joint used to talk about it, trying to make their bad decisions sound romantic by comparing themselves to Old West prospectors. They thought about the pot of gold until they thought about nothing else; they became desperate for it until their desperation made them stupid. This idiot was looking at six first-degree murder hits and all he could see was the money. Holman saw his way in. He smiled.

Cecil said, 'What are you smiling at?'

'I thought you knew what I was thinking before I thought it.'

'I do. You're thinking, why on earth pick me?'

'That would be right.'

Cecil's wet eyes hardened with anger. 'You think this is my *preferred* plan of action? Believe me, I was going to work this out. I had all the time I needed, but you and that bitch got me jammed in a corner. A week ago I had forever; now, I got fifteen minutes, so who in hell *should* I ask? My brother in Denver, maybe the kid who caddies when I play golf? And say *what*, come help me steal some money? This shit is on *you*! I will *not* walk away from sixteen million dollars. I refuse! So here we are. It's you because I don't have anyone else. Except for your friend Chee. I own that boy. You fuck me over, I swear that boy will pay the price.'

'You'll be gone. What could you do for Chee?'

'You bring out this money, I'll give you the man who planted that stuff—tell you when he got it, where, how—everything you need to clear the boy.'

Holman nodded like he was thinking about it, then stared at the bank. He didn't want Cecil to read his face. Cecil could shoot him now or wait until he brought out the money, but Cecil was going to shoot him either way—this stuff about dealing for Chee was bullshit. Holman thought about pretending to go along so he could get away, but then Cecil might escape. Holman wanted the sonofabitch to answer for killing his son.

'How do you see this playing out? The bank's about to close.'

'Go to the customer service manager. Tell'm right up front you're going to be making a lot trips—you're picking up tax records and court documents you put here for safe keeping. You know how to lie.'

'Sure.'

'You're going to open four boxes at a time. I figure the bag in each box weighs about fifty pounds, two on each shoulder, two hundred pounds, a big guy like you oughta be able to handle that.'

Holman wasn't listening. He was thinking if he could put Cecil together with the money, Cecil wouldn't be able to explain it away. 'It's going to take a long time, man. I hate being in a bank that long. I have bad memories.'

'You just think about Chee.'

Holman stared at Cecil, then he got out of the car and walked towards the bank. His stomach was cramping as if he was going to throw up, but he told himself he could make this thing happen.

He stepped inside and took in his surroundings. Five customers were waiting in line for two tellers. Two manager-types were at desks behind the teller cages and a young man who was probably a customer service rep manned a desk on the lobby floor. Holman went to the head of the customer line, glanced at the customers, then turned to the tellers and raised his voice.

'This is a robbery. Empty the drawers. Give me the money.'

Holman checked the time. It was 3.56. The clock was running.

LARA MYER was in the final hour of her shift as a security dispatcher at New Guardian Technologies when her computer flashed, indicating a 2-11 alarm from the Grand California Bank on Wilshire Boulevard in Beverly Hills. The time log on her screen showed the time at 5:26:27.

On any given day, half of the incoming alarms received by New Guardian were false, triggered by power surges, computer glitches, electrical failure or human error. Lara followed procedure. She brought up the Grand Cal (Wilshire/BH branch) page on her screen. This page allowed her to run a system diagnostic particular to the bank. The diagnostic would check for system problems that could trigger a false alarm.

Lara clicked the button labelled CONFIRM. The diagnostic automatically reset the alarm as it searched for power anomalies, hardware malfunctions or software glitches that could have caused a problem. If one of the tellers had accidentally triggered the alarm, they sometimes reset at the bank, which automatically cancelled and cleared the alarm.

The diagnostic took about ten seconds.

Lara watched as the confirmation appeared. Two tellers at the Grand Cal Beverly Hills branch had both triggered their silent alarms.

Lara called over her shift supervisor. 'Hey, Barry. We got one.'

Her shift supervisor came over and read the confirmation. 'Call it in.'

Lara pressed a button on her console to dial the Beverly Hills Police Department's emergency services operator. The phone rang four times.

'Beverly Hills emergency services.'

'This is New Guardian operator four-four-one. We show a two-eleven in progress at Grand California bank on Wilshire Boulevard in your area.'

'Stand by one.'

Lara knew the emergency services operator would now have to confirm that Lara was for real and not making a crank call. No cars would be dispatched until this was done. Lara glanced at the clock: 5:28:05.

HOLMAN THOUGHT it was going pretty well. No one screamed or made a break for the door or fell out with a heart attack like last time. The tellers quietly emptied their drawers. The customers stayed together in their line.

Holman said, 'Everything's going to be OK. I'll be out of here in three or four minutes.' He pulled the pouch of keys from his pocket and went to the young man standing at the customer service desk. Holman tossed him the pouch. 'What's your name?'

'Please don't hurt me.'

'I'm not going to hurt you. What's your name?'

'David Furillo. I'm married. We have a two-year-old.'

'Congratulations. David, these are safe box keys. Take your master and open four of these boxes, any four, doesn't matter.'

David opened his desk for the master box key, then hurried towards the box room.

Holman turned back to the customers. 'I need a phone. It's important.'

They milled uncertainly until a young woman tentatively drew a cell-phone from her bag.

'You can use mine, I guess.'

'Thanks, honey. Everybody stay calm. Everybody relax.'

Holman checked the time as he opened the phone. He had been in the bank two and a half minutes. He was past the window of safety.

Holman held out his arm to read the number on the inside of his forearm.

He called Pollard.

LEEDS HAD CAUTIONED Pollard that Cecil's connection to Alison Whitt did not ensure a conviction, so they were making arrangements to see if Mrs Marchenko could pick Cecil's picture from a six-pack. In the moments when Leeds was placing his call to Random, Pollard had tried to reach Holman by phoning his apartment. She got no answer.

Now, Pollard was sitting in a cubicle outside Leeds's office when her phone rang. She checked the caller ID, but did not recognise the number. She decided to let it go to her voicemail, then changed her mind.

Holman said, 'It's me.'

'Thank God! Where are you?'

'I'm robbing a bank.'

'Hang on—' Pollard called out to Leeds. 'I've got Holman on the phone.'

Leeds left his desk as Pollard returned to the call. He stood in the door, murmuring into his phone as he watched her.

Pollard said, 'The fifth man is an FBI agent named Bill Cecil. He was—'

Holman interrupted her. 'I know. He's in a dark green Ford Taurus outside the bank right now. He's waiting for me—'

She interrupted him. 'Whoa, wait a minute. I thought you were kidding.'

'I'm in the Grand California on Wilshire Boulevard in Beverly Hills. Marchenko stashed the money here in safe deposit boxes. Cecil had the keys—that's what they found at the sign—'

'*Why are you robbing the bank?*'

Leeds frowned. 'What is he doing?'

She waved him quiet as Dillon came over to watch.

Holman was saying, 'You know a faster way to get the cops here?'

Pollard cupped the phone, glancing at Leeds and Dillon. 'Grand California on Wilshire in BH. See if they're reporting a two-eleven.'

She returned to Holman as Dillon ran for a phone. 'Has anyone been hurt?'

'It's nothing like that. The cops will be here soon. I want you to tell them what's happening. I figure they won't listen to me.'

'Max, this is a *bad* idea.'

'I want the cops to catch him with the money in his possession. He was scared to come in, so I'm gonna bring the money to him—'

'Where's Cecil now?'

'Parked outside, in a dark green Ford Taurus. He's waiting for the money.'

Pollard cupped the phone and spoke again to Leeds. 'Cecil's in a dark green Ford Taurus in front of the bank.'

Leeds relayed the information to Random as Dillon returned, excited.

'Beverly Hills confirms a two-eleven alarm at the location. Units en route.'

Pollard went back to Holman. 'Stay in the bank, OK? Do *not* go outside. This is dangerous and I'm not just talking about Cecil—the responding officers don't know you're a good guy. They will not know—'

'You know.' Holman hung up.

She struggled to her feet. 'I'm going to the bank.'

'Let Beverly Hills handle it. You don't have enough time.'

Pollard ran as fast as she could.

HOLMAN CLOSED the phone, then glanced out the front, worried the police would arrive too soon. He had been in the bank two minutes longer than for any of his robberies except the one in which he was arrested. He thought back. It had taken Pollard almost six minutes to arrive and they had been on a rolling stakeout, waiting and ready to go. He still had a few seconds.

He went back to the customers and returned the girl's phone. 'Everyone OK? Everybody still cool?'

A man in his forties with wire-rimmed glasses said, 'Are we hostages?'

'No one is a hostage. Just stay cool. I'll be outta your hair in a minute.'

Holman called towards the vault. 'Hey, David! How we doin' in there?'

David's voice came from the vault. 'They're open.'

'You people just stay where you are. The police are on the way.'

Holman trotted across the lobby to the vault. David had four large safe boxes open and had dragged four nylon gym bags into the centre of the floor. Holman lifted the bags one by one, hooking the straps over his shoulders, staggered out of vault room and immediately noticed that two of the customers were missing. He thought, oh shit.

CECIL DECIDED to see what was taking so long. He shut off the engine as a man and woman ran out of the bank. Cecil immediately started the engine, ready to drive away, but no one else emerged. The bank was quiet.

He shut the engine again, slipped his pistol into his holster, then got out of the car. He glanced up and down Wilshire, but saw no lights or police cars. He looked back at the bank, but now Holman was in the glass door with all these big nylon bags hanging from his shoulders—just standing there. Cecil waved him over, but Holman didn't leave the bank. He dropped two of the bags, then gestured for Cecil to come and get them.

Cecil kept thinking about the two people running away. He flipped out his cellphone and hit a speed-dial button he had already programmed.

'Beverly Hills Police Department.'

'FBI Special Agent William Cecil, ID number six-six-seven-four. Suspicious activity at the Grand California on Wilshire. Please advise.'

'Copy. We have a two-eleven alarm at that address. Units en route.'

Cecil felt a burning knot in his chest. Everything he wanted was just feet away, but now it was gone. Sixteen million dollars—gone.

'Ah, confirm the two-eleven. Suspect is a white male, six-two, two-thirty. He is armed. Customers in the bank appear down and disabled.'

HOLMAN HAD the skin-prickling sense something was wrong, then Cecil turned back towards his car. A heartbeat later, red and blue flashes reflected off the glass buildings across the street, and Holman knew time had run out.

He shoved through the door, the heavy bags of cash swinging like lead pendulums. The police cars would be here in seconds.

Holman ran at Cecil as hard as he could. Cecil reached the Taurus, threw open the door and was climbing inside when Holman caught him from behind. He pulled Cecil backwards and both of them fell.

As Cecil tried to climb back into the car, Holman dragged himself up Cecil's leg, hammering at the man with his fist.

Holman should have been more afraid. He should have realised Cecil was a blooded FBI agent with thirty years training and experience. But all Holman saw in those moments was Richie running alongside his car, red-faced and crying, calling him a loser; all he knew was the eight-year-old gap-toothed boy in a picture that would continue to fade; all he felt was the blind-furious need to make this man pay.

Holman didn't see the gun. He was still punching, still blindly trying to anchor Cecil to the street, when Cecil rolled over. An exploding white light flashed three times and the sound of thunder echoed on Wilshire Boulevard.

Holman's world stopped. He heard only the sound of his beating heart.

He stared at Cecil, waiting for the pain. Cecil stared back, his mouth working like a fish. Behind them, the patrol cars slid to a stop as an officer's amplified voice shouted words Holman did not hear. He looked down. The bags of money were wedged in front of his chest, scorched where the cash had trapped the three bullets.

Cecil shoved the gun across the money into Holman's chest, but this time he didn't fire. He dropped the gun into Holman's arms, then rolled away, coming to his knees with his FBI credential high over his head.

'FBI! FBI agent!' He pointed at Holman. 'He's got a gun! I've been shot!'

Holman glanced at the gun, then at the four uniformed officers crouched behind their patrol cars. Young men about Richie's age. Aiming.

The amplified voice boomed again in the Wilshire canyon, now behind the sound of approaching sirens.

'Put down the weapon! Drop the weapon but make no sudden moves!'

Holman wasn't holding the weapon. It was on the money bag directly under his nose. He didn't move. He was too scared to move.

People had spilled out of the bank. They pointed at Holman as they shouted to the officers. 'That's him! It was him!'

Cecil staggered to his feet, crabbing away as he waved his credentials. 'I see his hand! I see it, goddammit! *He's reaching for the gun!*'

Holman saw the young men shift behind their weapons. He closed his eyes, held himself perfectly still, and . . .

Nothing happened.

He looked up, but now the four young officers had their guns in the air, surrounded by milling officers. Other officers with rifles and shotguns ran towards Cecil, shouting for him to get down on the ground. They tackled him, proned him out, then two of them peeled towards Holman.

Holman still didn't move. One of the tactical officers stayed back with his shotgun up and ready, but the other approached.

Holman said, 'I'm the good guy.'

'Don't move.'

The near officer lifted away Cecil's pistol, but he didn't slam down on Holman or prone him out. Once he had the gun he seemed to relax.

The cop said, 'You Holman?'

'He killed my son.'

'That's what they tell me, buddy. You got him.'

Pollard and Leeds shoved through the growing crowd of officers. When Holman saw Pollard he started to rise, but she motioned him to stay down so he did. Holman figured he had come too far to take any chances.

Leeds went to Bill Cecil, but Pollard came directly to Holman, breaking into a run as she came. She was wearing a blue FBI windbreaker like the first time he saw her. When Pollard arrived, she gazed down at him, breathing hard but smiling, then held out her hand.

'I'm here now. You're safe.'

Holman slipped out of the money bags, took her hand and let her help him up. He stared at Cecil, still spread-eagled on the street. He watched the officers fold his hands behind his back to bind his wrists, then turned back to Pollard. He wanted to tell her why everything that happened here and everything that led up to it had been his fault, but his mouth was dry.

She held tight to his hand. 'It's OK.'

Holman shook his head and toed the bags. It wasn't OK.

He said, 'Marchenko's money. This is what Richie wanted.'

She touched his face, turning him. 'No, honey. Oh, no, Max, it wasn't that way.' She cupped his face in both her hands. 'Richie wasn't doing what we thought. Listen—'

Pollard told him how his son died and, more importantly to Holman, how Richie had lived. Holman broke down, crying there on Wilshire Boulevard, but Pollard held on tight, letting him cry and keeping him safe.

WHEN HOLMAN got downstairs, Perry was at his desk. Perry usually took a break at seven o'clock to hole up in his room to watch *Jeopardy*, but here he was. Holman figured Perry was waiting for him.

Perry wrinkled his nose. 'What in hell are you wearing, perfume?'

Holman decided to fess up. 'I bought this new shampoo. It's supposed to smell like a tropical garden.'

Perry leaned back and cackled. 'I guess it does. And what flower would that be—pansies?' Perry was killing himself laughing.

Holman glanced out of the front door, but the kerb was empty.

Perry, still enjoying himself, said, 'Look at how slicked up you are. My, my—I guess we have a date.'

'It's not a date. We're just friends.'

'That woman?'

'Stop calling her "that woman". I'll knock you on your ass.'

'She looked pretty fine to me. I was you, I'd tell people this was a date.'

'Well, you're not me, so shut up. I'll have Chee send those boys back, bust up your fancy car.'

Perry stopped laughing and scowled. Once everything about Chee had been straightened out, his boys rebuilt Perry's old beater like they promised. Perry took great pride in tooling around in the pristine classic.

He leaned forward. 'You think you got a future with this woman?'

Holman went back to the door but Pollard still had not arrived. He glanced at his father's watch. He had finally had it repaired and now it kept time pretty well. Pollard was running late.

'Perry, I have enough trouble with the present. Katherine is an FBI agent. She has two little boys. She doesn't want anything to do with a guy like me.'

After the fallout from Cecil, Leeds was left with an opening on the bank squad and had offered it to Pollard. Allowing an ex-agent to return to such a sought-after post was highly unusual, but Leeds had the clout to make it happen. Pollard would be able to apply her prior service towards her seniority and eventual retirement. Holman thought it was a good deal and encouraged her to take it.

Perry said, 'Well, Jesus Christ, that new pansy shampoo must have made you stupid. The woman wouldn't be coming here if she didn't want anything to do with you.'

Holman decided to wait on the sidewalk. He went outside, but thirty seconds later Perry appeared in the door. Holman raised both palms.

'Please, I'm begging you—let it rest.'

'I just want to tell you something. All you know about me is I'm a cranky old man in this shitbag motel. Well, I wasn't always this way. I was young once and I had chances and opportunities in my life. I made choices that put me here. I sure as hell would make different choices if I had it to do over. You think about that.' Perry stomped off into the empty motel.

Holman stared after him, then heard a horn. He looked up the street. Pollard was a couple of blocks away, but she had seen him. Holman raised his hand and saw Pollard smile.

Holman thought about what Perry said, but Perry didn't understand— Holman was afraid. Katherine Pollard deserved a good man. Holman was trying hard to be better than he had ever been in his life, but he still had a long way to go. He wanted to earn Katherine Pollard. He wanted to deserve her. And he believed—one day he would.

ROBERT CRAIS

Home: Santa Monica
Interests: flying, cooking, backpacking
Website: www.robertcrais.com

RD: What was the starting point for this book?

RC: For me, a book always begins with a character and this book began with Max Holman. When you are the victim of a crime, you go to the police, but what if you were someone with whom the police would not cooperate? You want answers, but the police won't give you answers. The cops ignore you. You think they're maybe even lying to you. I was working on this character when I realised that only one type of person could be so totally alienated from society, on the outside of the system, and friendless—a criminal. That's when I had Max Holman.

RD. At the centre of the novel is the mystery of the missing money. Was this inspired by a real event?

RC: Yes. In the late nineties, six men robbed the Dunbar Armored Car company here in LA of $18.9 million. The six were caught and are now in prison, but the police were only able to account for about four and a half million dollars. The rest of the money is still missing. Fifteen million in cash, and it might be anywhere. Learning about the Dunbar case led me to research other robberies where large sums went missing and haven't been recovered. A hundred thousand here, two or three hundred thousand there—missing cash that might be buried in someone's yard or forgotten in a storage facility or waiting in a dusty attic. Fun to think about it.

RD: Do you ever use aspects of your own life in your fiction?

RC: Absolutely. To create Max Holman, I had to tap into my own feelings of alienation, loss, and regret. It's the job of the writer to use those personal experiences and transform them into fiction.

RD: Is *The Two Minute Rule* real or something invented for the book?

RC: It's a term coined by the FBI. It's a reference to the minimum arrival time for first responders to a robbery-in-progress call. In reality the time will vary according to locale and traffic conditions and other factors, but two minutes is the usual rule of thumb.

RD: Holman is a former bank robber and yet he's a very sympathetic character. Was it a difficult combination to achieve?

RC: You know, when I first told my publisher the concept for *The Two Minute Rule*, they were concerned that Max would be unsympathetic, but I never saw him as anything other than heroic.

RD: What is it that gives him that quality?

RC: He's learned from his mistakes, and his commitment—at the point in his life when we meet him—is to be a good and better man. Holman carries the burden of his sins not with pride, but with shame. He regrets the choices he made and suffers the losses that came with those choices without making excuses for himself. He doesn't try to justify his past crimes. He has taken responsibility for the mess he's made of his life and paid the penalty that society demanded—the time he's served in prison—and now he's trying to move forward and build a worthwhile life. I admire his courage.

RD: Los Angeles almost seems like another character in your books. How important is it to you to get the location and sense of place right?

RC: Character and place are one and the same. You cannot have a fully formed character—a living, breathing character—unless he or she reflects the place in which they live. Take Holman, for example. He's been in prison for ten years. When he returns to Los Angeles, the city he returns to is different to him. He sees it with a newcomer's eyes. Even sites that he grew up with like Union Station and the views of the city from the Hollywood sign—he views them from a new perspective.

RD: Would you be happy living anywhere else in the world?

RC: No. I love Los Angeles. I would not be me without it.

RD: Does writing fiction get harder or easier as time goes on?

RC: More difficult. Definitely more difficult. The more I learn about writing, the more I realise that I don't know a damned thing, so I dig harder and deeper to write well.

RD: Life as a best-selling writer must have many things going for it. What do you like best about it?

RC: Knowing that I've been able to touch so many people in so many parts of the world, and that they dig what I'm doing. I get mail through my website from England, France, Italy, Japan, China, Australia, Israel, and all over—I'm in twenty-six or twenty-seven countries now, and it's quite amazing.

RD: If you hadn't been a writer what would you have like to have been?

RC: An Astronaut.

RD: And if you had to sum yourself up in a single word, what would that be?

RC: Writer.

1

That Thursday evening in December I was working late, removing the skull of a dead owl. At my workbench, the heat from the lamp was making my fingers sweat. I was at the hardest part of the whole operation, but I could sense it was going well, and when I heard the telephone grumbling at the back of the workshop I decided to let it ring. Even though I'd removed myself from the Yellow Pages, the pranksters ('I've got this chicken that needs stuffing . . .') would still occasionally get through. This was their time to call, but tonight I wasn't in the mood. Until I remembered Katya.

Katya was the latest student to rent the flat at the top of the house. It was always students because I kept the rent low to make up for any dead animals they might meet in the hallway. They were prepared to overlook a bit of that because the location was central and because my own students in the Natural Sciences department were prepared to vouch for my character. Students will overlook a great deal if you have a reputation as a rebel, and I qualified by riding a motorbike and refusing to toe the university line on current conservation theory. It was that easy.

The top-floor flat was self-contained. Katya and I had a front door and a staircase in common and very little else—in the couple of months since she'd moved in we'd exchanged some polite smiles and rather fewer words. Every ten days or so her mother would ring from Sweden and I'd dutifully take down a message on a yellow pad and leave it at the bottom of the stairs, along with the suggestion that Katya might give her mother the number of the upstairs phone. The next day the note would be gone but her mother would continue to ring downstairs. She was a polite woman, who struggled not to let any anxiety show. I felt sorry for her.

Which is why I peeled off my gloves and answered the phone.

It wasn't Katya's mother. It was a voice I hadn't heard for fifteen years. A scarcely remembered, totally familiar, soft, low voice.

'Fitz,' it asked, 'is that you?'

'Gabriella.' A rhetorical statement, if such a thing is possible.

'Yes, it's me. It's been a long time, Fitz.'

It wasn't clear if that was a reproach or an apology.

'Yes, a long time.' The words came out sounding defensive. 'Though I got your letters.'

'You didn't reply.'

'You know I'm not a great one for writing.'

She couldn't deny that. I was famous for it.

'Look, Fitz, I'm over in London for a few days and there's someone I want you to meet, a collector. He's got quite a good story to tell and I think you'll be interested. What are you doing tomorrow?'

I looked at the remains of the owl on the workbench. It would just have to take its chance in the freezer.

'I think tomorrow is reasonably free,' I said.

'Good. Can we say seven in the bar at the Mecklenburg? It's off Oxford Street, just by Selfridges.'

How like Gabby to realise that the Mecklenburg Hotel was not among my usual drinking venues.

'All right. Seven tomorrow . . .'

'It will be good to see you. I've told Karl that if anyone can help him, you can.'

'Karl . . .?'

'Karl Anderson.'

'Ah, yes. The collector. And what sort of help would that be?'

She paused. She had never liked talking over the phone.

'Not now. Wait for tomorrow. But I promise you'll be interested, Fitz. It's about the Mysterious Bird of Ulieta.'

SHE WAS RIGHT, of course. I *was* interested. In all sorts of ways. Abandoning the owl to the darkness, I climbed the stairs to the room where I did most of my living. It was untidy, comfortable and warmly lit and smelt of old paper. The bed was permanently unmade and the desk was littered with dusty notes for a book I wasn't really writing. One whole wall was taken up with shelves of carefully ordered books, but I didn't need to look anything up to know that Gabby wasn't being melodramatic. Despite its name, the bird was real enough, or had been once. I'd even made some notes about it for an article, back in the days when I was going to be famous.

And now, all these years later, she wanted to ask me about it. She and her friend Karl Anderson. I'd seen a picture of them together once, taken by a mutual friend at one of the big summer lectures in Salzburg. She was leaning very lightly on his arm, dark and slim and calm, with that familiar half-questioning smile.

I settled down on the bed and looked thoughtfully at the trunk in the corner of the room. What they wanted to know was probably in there along with everything else—the dodo, the heath hen, the passenger pigeon—the lost and the forgotten, all mixed together, years of jotted notes and observations still waiting to be given a shape.

But instead of thinking about them, I thought again about Gabby and the man she wanted me to meet. I'd read a lot about Karl Anderson over the years but everything I knew really came down to three things: he was a man with a reputation for finding things; he was used to getting what he wanted; and nowadays he was far too successful to do his searching in person.

I wasn't sure I liked the sound of him.

2

It was raining heavily by the time I reached the Mecklenburg Hotel. After abandoning the bus at Oxford Circus, I arrived wet and out of breath, but at least I was on time. The hotel turned out to be ugly, concrete on the outside and expensively mock Edwardian beyond the revolving doors. I stood dripping for a moment in the lobby, slightly disappointed. Then, suddenly self-conscious, I followed a sign to the gents, where I dried my hair and pushed it into some sort of order. When I'd finished, I looked better but still underdressed. Among academics I considered myself reasonably stylish. Here I just looked like someone who might steal the towels.

I paused in front of the mirror to collect my thoughts. It was hard to imagine what Anderson might want. The bird from Ulieta was an enigma, one of nature's conjuring tricks—a creature that had disappeared as if with a wave of the conjuror's hand. The disappearance had been final and there would be no coming back. The audience was left looking for feathers that had long ceased to exist. Not even Anderson could do much about that.

Upstairs, in the Rosebery Bar, despite the cigarette smoke there was a smell of expensive perfume and leather. Not the sort of desiccated leather that featured in my jacket and shoes. This leather was new and expensive and smelt soft, if that's possible. Its effect was to make me aware of the smell of rain I'd brought in with me. Among these dry, groomed people it was the odour of not quite belonging.

Gabriella was easy to spot. She was sitting in a corner under a soft lamp, framed in best cinematic style by a twisting curve of smoke. She was, as before, dark and slender, so neat as to seem flawless, and in her slim black dress there was no question of her being out of place. Beside her was a tall, blond man in his early fifties, constructed in straight lines. A good-looking man. He had turned to Gabby and was talking eagerly as I edged towards them, past a group of pre-theatre Americans.

Then Gabby looked up and noticed me. 'Hello, Fitz,' she said quietly as I arrived at their table, and suddenly I was annoyed with her for still being so beautiful, and annoyed with myself for noticing. And annoyed that an impeccably suited arm was being advanced to shake my hand.

'Fitz, this is Karl Anderson,' she said, as if that would make it all right.

I nodded at him, not caring much, and turned back to Gabriella. She was so startlingly familiar it was hard to breathe.

'Perhaps we should all sit down?' suggested Anderson calmly. 'I'm sure Mr Fitzgerald would like a drink.'

He was right. A drink was exactly what I wanted.

AND SO I SAT down and joined a painfully well-mannered conversation that tiptoed carefully around any awkwardness. A waiter brought me a beer, and more drinks were ordered. I was aware of Gabby being close enough for my hand to fall on hers if I let it drop from the table. Anderson was drinking as quickly as I was and ordered deft refills whenever our glasses were nearly empty. I watched him while Gabriella talked. A tall, well-proportioned man—a maverick, a charmer, a big personality in a dusty discipline.

Beside him, Gabriella seemed tiny, like a bird. It was as if she'd slipped through the years without friction, her freshness and vitality untouched.

She must have been ten years younger than the big man next to her, and yet they matched. They made a good-looking couple.

'So what are you doing with yourself these days, Mr Fitzgerald? Your withdrawal from field work is a great loss to us all.' He was a Norwegian by birth but his English was only very slightly accented.

'Oh, I keep myself busy. Teaching mostly. "Natural History: the historical context". It's a compulsory module, so the students have to turn up, even if I'm no good.'

'And are you good?'

'Well, I'm controversial, which is the next best thing.'

At that moment Anderson was diverted by the waiter and Gabby caught my eye. 'I'm glad you could come, Fitz,' she said, and she sounded as if she meant it. Personally, I was withholding judgment.

It wasn't until the third drink that Anderson turned to the subject we'd all been waiting for. 'You must be wondering why I'm here, Mr Fitzgerald, intruding on this meeting of old friends.'

I raised an eyebrow, but didn't reply, so he carried on.

'I was lucky enough to hear Gabriella speak in Prague a few years ago and we have been friends ever since. She mentioned you to me as a man with a great deal of knowledge in one of the areas I am interested in. She thinks you may be able to help me . . .' He paused to put his glass down neatly on its paper coaster. 'I am a collector, Mr Fitzgerald. I am here because I am looking for something incredibly rare. Something that may not even exist any more.' His eyes lingered on my face for a moment. 'What do you know of the Mysterious Bird of Ulieta?'

'Not much,' I told him truthfully. 'Rather a fanciful piece of naming, I've always thought.'

Again his intent, searching gaze. 'Perhaps not so fanciful.' He rubbed the back of his neck with his fingertips. 'Let us talk about it a little.' He placed his fingertips softly on the edge of the table in front of him. 'The rarest bird ever recorded, Mr Fitzgerald. Seen only once, in 1774, by Captain Cook's second expedition. A single specimen captured during a routine collecting party on a South Sea island known then as Ulieta. Preserved by Johann Forster and brought back to England. No bird like it was ever found again, on Ulieta or anywhere else. Extinct before it was ever really catalogued.'

His eyes dropped to the table top, where he ran one fingertip across a drop of liquid. 'On his return, Johann Forster gave away the preserved specimen. .

The *only* specimen. Of course he had no way of knowing its rarity then. Nor did the young man he gave it to, the naturalist Joseph Banks.'

He looked up at me with excitement in his eyes. 'Yes, Mr Fitzgerald. It is more than two hundred years since that one specimen went missing from Banks's collection. I think it's time it was found, don't you?'

ANDERSON HAD DONE his research. He knew all there was to know about the bird, which frankly wasn't that much. In May 1774, Captain Cook had brought his ship, the *Resolution*, to the small island of Ulieta, one of the spattering of islands in the Pacific that came to be known collectively as the Society Islands. Cook stayed there several days, to make repairs and trade with the local people. On June 1, Johann Forster, the ship's naturalist, took an expedition ashore to gather specimens. A number of birds were shot and killed that day but there was only one that Forster didn't recognise. After he had recorded his observations of it, the specimen was passed to his son, Georg, one of the ship's artists, who made a drawing of the bird. Immediately afterwards it was cleaned and preserved for mounting.

It was not an unusual day's work for either father or son, and would have been of no great interest to anyone if it hadn't been for one thing: that single specimen remains the only one of its kind ever recorded, anywhere. Consequently no one will ever know if the species was once widespread, how its song sounded, the shape of its nest, or the mating rituals it acted out. The bird handled by Forster was one of the very last of its kind.

When the Forsters returned to Britain the following year, the specimens they had collected were theirs to dispose of. Johann Forster was permanently in financial difficulties and he sought help from Joseph Banks, the naturalist on Cook's previous voyage. Banks was a young man with money and a future and he was generous towards Forster. In return Forster presented him with specimens, one of which was the bird from Ulieta. A naturalist named Latham saw the bird in Banks's collection at some point in the 1770s and recorded it as *Turdus ulietensis*, the Ulietan thrush, in his book *A General Synopsis of Birds*. After that, there is no further record of the specimen. Like the species itself, it simply disappeared.

The Rosebery Bar was no less full when Anderson finally finished speaking but the atmosphere had changed. The after-work drinkers with trains to catch had moved on, while those who replaced them were relaxing into the evening. Somewhere out of sight a pianist had started to play.

I drained my drink slowly. Gabriella and Anderson were watching me, but if they were looking for a reaction all they got was a raised eyebrow. I can't deny I felt a little buzz of excitement at the story Anderson was telling, but anyone interested in extinct birds would know that the idea of finding the Ulieta specimen was a joke. No one *seriously* imagined it still existed. Museum records are full of eighteenth-century specimens that simply fell apart after about seventy or eighty years. The bird from Ulieta was just one of thousands of species that didn't make it.

'Tell me, Anderson,' I asked, 'why would a man like you suddenly decide to look for something like that?'

'What if I told you I was an enthusiast?'

'I wouldn't believe you. You're a businessman. You find things on commission for the sort of people who can't enjoy anything unless they own it. Cash for dinosaur remains, endangered species on demand, that sort of thing. Why would you spend time looking for something that probably disintegrated two hundred years ago?'

He smiled, a quiet, confident smile. 'It might have survived. Specimens of that age do exist.'

'Very, very few. Perhaps a dozen. It's hard to imagine this was one of them. Joseph Banks was the pre-eminent scientist of his generation. He didn't just lose rare birds. If this one blipped off the radar at some point, it's because it fell apart. If it had survived, there'd be mention of it in records.'

Anderson had caught the waiter's eye again and more drinks were arriving. 'You may be right, Mr Fitzgerald,' he said. 'And yet I intend to find it nevertheless. The rewards for doing so would be . . . considerable.'

'Yes?' It seemed unlikely. 'Who's interested in stuffed birds nowadays? Oh, I don't deny it would be quite a coup—the natural history establishment would be overjoyed. But there's no money in museums.'

'Sadly true, Mr Fitzgerald. But museums were not the market I had in mind.' Anderson took another sip and sat back, as if that was all he had to say on the subject.

It was left to Gabby to explain. 'Fitz, have you ever heard of the Ark Project? Or the Gene Ark, to give it its full title. It was set up in Canada by Ted Staest. Have you heard of Staest?'

Only vaguely. A Canadian. A man famous for being rich. I passed.

Anderson pushed himself back into the conversation. 'Ted Staest owns one of the big North American pharmaceutical companies. His big thing now is DNA. The Ark Project is basically his own personal DNA bank. He collects genetic material from rare and vanishing species and stores it, holding it against potential increases in value.'

Gabby sensed my scorn. 'It's true, Fitz. I know it sounds crazy but there's a scramble going on to own genetic coding. Even the pharmaceutical companies aren't sure of its value, but no one wants to let the others get it first, so they're spending now and they'll ask questions later. They keep the public interested with talk about rebreeding extinct species, that sort of thing. But it's the bioengineering possibilities that they're interested in.'

'But the Ulieta bird would be more than two hundred years old. There couldn't possibly be material of any value in that, could there?'

Anderson shrugged. 'Who knows? Techniques develop all the time. And to be frank, Mr Fitzgerald, I don't think Ted Staest cares much either way. He's taken by the story of the Mysterious Bird of Ulieta and he knows the value of publicity. Turning up a specimen like that would get the Ark Project in the news. The rarest bird in the world, patented by Ted Staest.'

'And he is paying you to find it?'

'He is paying me to find it *first*. It's hard to keep that sort of thing quiet. Where there's a market, there are always others hoping to cash in.'

'OK,' I said carefully, trying to draw it all together, 'so a rich Canadian wants to find a nonexistent bird specimen because he thinks it will boost his share price. That's bizarre but I can just about get my head round it. What I can't see is why you're telling me about any of this.'

It was Gabby who answered. 'Karl won't be the only one to contact you, Fitz. People remember your work on extinct birds. They'll want to know what you can tell them.'

Anderson nodded. 'Fifteen years ago, Mr Fitzgerald, your research was known to everyone in the field. We know you visited museums and collections all over the world, collections that no one else has ever properly studied. You collected maps, drawings, inventories, letters. We all waited for you to publish but you never did. If anyone has any information that might lead to the Ulieta bird, it would be you.'

'So you think I might be able to help you find it?'

'You have contacts. You know the sort of people who might have heard rumours. I'm sure you could make some calls, see what you could find.'

'And if I can't find anything?'

He looked unconcerned. 'To be honest, Mr Fitzgerald, I have a lead already. But I thought you'd be interested in joining me in this. And if you can make the search quicker and easier for me, that's all to the good.'

'And why did you think I'd be interested in looking for it?'

He paused and looked me directly in the eye. 'Because you never found anything like the Ulieta bird. Oh, you found some rare specimens all right, but never the specimen of a bird lost without trace, a bird seen only once . . . Think of it! This is your chance, Mr Fitzgerald.' He sat back and let his words sink in. 'As long as I get the bird, I'm happy for you to have the headlines. And I would, of course, pay you for your time. Fifty thousand dollars was the sum I had in mind.'

I tried not to show my incredulity. Instead I took a long swig of beer and did some rapid calculations. Fifty thousand dollars was a pretty significant sum. If Anderson was prepared to send that sort of money in my direction, how much was he expecting to make?

'I don't get it,' I said. 'I figure for you to come all this way on the offchance that it might still exist, that must mean someone's offering some pretty weird money for it. How can it possibly be worth that much?'

Anderson smiled and shook his head. 'Let us not exaggerate its importance. It would be an amazing find, yes, and Ted Staest would pay well for it. But I'm over here on a different piece of business and looking for the Ulieta bird is really just a favour for Ted Staest. As a client, he could mean a great deal to me in the long term. So if I can sort this for him, then that's good business. I'm not even too bothered about covering my costs.'

I was still suspicious. 'What brings you here, then, if not the Ulieta bird?'

'Oh, various things. Botanical art, mainly. There are one or two eighteenth-century works that I'm hoping to pick up while I'm over here, which I suspect could be very valuable indeed. Very fashionable, particularly in the States, and extremely rare. The best possible combination.'

He spoke as if the paintings were without interest to him so long as a profit was assured. I looked across at Gabby and then looked back at him.

'What happened to you, Anderson?' I asked softly. 'Once upon a time you were a pioneer. I saw you interviewed when you found those plesiosaur remains. You *glowed* with pleasure. It wasn't about money back then.'

Anderson looked a little annoyed, but his tone was unruffled. 'We all make our choices, Mr Fitzgerald. After all, you were a serious scientist once.'

He let his hand fall back to the table so that it rested against Gabby's.

I'd like to say it was his first mistake, but even before his hand touched hers I knew I wasn't going to help him. That just made it easier.

I stood up. 'Look, there's nothing in my notes that will help you. They're just a lot of observations about some old specimens no one cares about any more. I'd be taking your money under false pretences.' I swallowed. I was trying hard to keep my voice low. 'There's another thing I should say. If by some miracle that bird *has* survived, I shudder to think of it being pulled apart in a lab, tested and analysed in pursuit of some genetic conjuring trick.' I met his eyes as calmly as I could. 'I think it might be you who doesn't understand its value, Mr Anderson.'

I nodded to Gabby as I turned away, but I didn't look back. Fifteen years on, and she still had the same effect on me. Now she was with Anderson. And I was glad there was nothing I could do to help them.

Beyond the Mecklenburg's revolving doors the rain had almost stopped, leaving the roads shiny under the street lamps. The buses were still running but I chose to walk, my mind turning over everything I'd heard.

Halfway home I stopped at a late-night coffee place. It was still empty, waiting for the post-pub crowd to pass through. In two hours it would be packed. I claimed a corner for myself and thought about Gabby—how she'd looked, how I felt, how Anderson had sat so comfortably beside her. Gradually, I began to think about the lost bird that had brought them to London. Anderson's search seemed too bizarre to be true. A unique bird, an infinitesimal possibility that somewhere the specimen might still exist. It was the sort of discovery I'd dreamed about once. But surely not possible?

My mind was still turning over that thought when I left the café. It took me a little while to walk home, and when I got there it took me even longer to grasp the meaning of the broken front door pane that greeted me. It had been smashed through to the hallway, and beyond it Katya was sitting at the foot of the stairs, looking at me over the shattered glass.

*J*ourneys begin in many different ways. It was Captain Cook, a man experienced in preparations for long sea expeditions, who persuaded Joseph Banks to return home to Revesby two months before they sailed. In the summer of 1768, he made the journey back to Lincolnshire, back to the woods and fields that were to fill his dreams of home for the next three years.

As his carriage arrived, people spilled out in welcome: familiar, friendly faces whose greetings were already tinged with goodbyes. In the days that followed, his expedition was the subject of every conversation, and every person who spoke of it took care to speak confidently of his return. Revesby, it seemed, was proud and anxious in equal measure.

That first night there was dancing. Gentlemen flushed by music and wine thumped his back and wished him luck and noticed the bright spirits he was in. And they were right. He felt strong and vital and talked of great discoveries, and when the music played he danced wildly. The gentlemen's daughters were a blur to him: bright satins, soft hands, and always a hush of whispers behind him, speculating and excited.

The next day, while the house drowsed in the summer heat, he left the talk behind him and set out on foot for the cool of the woods.

HE KNEW she was there before he saw her. At first she was only a movement, some way off, as if a deer had shied away from the corner of his vision. Later he found twigs broken and grass cushioned into a hollow.

Then he saw her again, at a distance against the trees on the edge of a meadow, too far away for him to see her face. She moved easily through the long grasses, slipping between sun and shadow like a white thread stitching the trees to the meadow. Her form struck him as uniquely graceful, and its promise more than once brought him back to the woods in the hopes of satisfying his curiosity.

On first seeing her face, he decided that she was not, after all, beautiful.

His disappointment kept him on the edge of the clearing in the cool of the oak trees. Beyond their shade, where the young woman now sat drawing, he could smell the sun on the hot earth. The afternoon light showed her clearly: a slim figure in white muslin, her skin slightly freckled, a frown of intense concentration on her forehead as she drew. Her hair was brown, her figure slight, her features neat but ordinary. With his wood nymph exposed as a mere sunbrowned girl he hesitated, and might have turned away had she not, at that moment, looked directly at where he stood.

Her gaze embarrassed him. She was alone in the woods and he had been observing her openly. A gentleman, he thought, would bow and withdraw. And yet he stepped out into the sunshine, clearing his throat and looking down as he did so to hide his confusion. When he looked up again she had risen to her feet and was facing him.

'My apologies if I have disturbed you,' he said, advancing. 'I often walk this way and did not think to find this remote spot so happily tenanted.' He extended his hand. 'My name is Joseph Banks.'

She looked down at his hand but didn't take it. When she spoke her voice was quiet. 'I know who you are, Mr Banks. Revesby is too small to permit otherwise. Even those who wish to avoid each other are not always able to do so.'

'Then I am pleased that is not the case today.' He smiled, and indicated the drawing book she held against her bosom. 'I see you are an artist.'

For a moment she looked down, and Banks studied her face. Then, when he realised that she intended to make no reply, he bowed and smiled into the silence she had left for him.

'I shall wish you goodbye,' he said. 'I am sure we shall meet again soon.'

NEXT MORNING Banks took his sister, Sophia, to pay visits in the village. Ahead of them the sun was shining and the meadows were full of the scent of summer. Both air and sunshine felt fresh on his cheek. With the danger of his great voyage looming, he had never felt more alive.

The various calls were made in good humour. Banks was pleased to be with his sister and she was pleased to show him to their neighbours. When Sophia made to turn back, Banks stopped her and indicated a small stone-built house that lay ahead of them at the end of the village.

'I'm told the black sheep of the parish is unwell, Sophia. They say he is dying. I would like to call to find out how he fares.'

'No, really, Joseph!' She pulled on his arm and her face was suddenly serious. 'Since the *incident* it is not proper to call. And besides he has suffered a seizure that leaves him insensible to the world around. Even, one fears, insensible to his own disgrace.'

But he was not to be dissuaded. With a firm arm he steered her towards the house. The old woman who answered the door informed them that the daughter of the house was not at home and that the master was unable to receive.

'Do you think you might keep my card, nurse, so that he is aware of my visit?' Banks asked.

'I fear he will know nothing of it, sir.'

Banks nodded, the card still between his fingers. He might have spoken more but Sophia's pressure on his arm persuaded him to turn for home.

As they walked back through the place called Slipper Wood, Banks spied a movement in the shadows. They watched for a moment until it became clear to Banks that they were glimpsing the figure of a woman dressed in white. As they looked, she stopped by the trunk of a tree with her face turned towards it. For some seconds she was motionless, then she began to circle the tree, her face still close to the bark. When her circuit was complete, she moved to a neighbouring trunk, and repeated the ritual.

'I fear that is the invalid's daughter,' Sophia said, and told him her name. 'She is often to be seen alone in the woods. It does little to redeem her family's reputation in the eyes of the village.'

'What does she do in the woods?' he asked.

'Really, I have no idea. Perhaps she is hoping to catch the attention of a passing gentleman of susceptible disposition. Though her looks are sadly ordinary and she has no prospects whatsoever.'

That evening, Dr Taylor from the village joined the party at the Abbey. Sophia related what they had seen in Slipper Wood and turned to the doctor to gain his support for her disapproval.

'Indeed. That young girl is most difficult,' he confirmed. 'Since her father's disgrace she shuns us all most markedly. It is as if misfortune has aged her and hardened her. She is alone a great deal too much, I fear.'

Banks nodded and the conversation turned to other subjects. But she preyed upon his mind for reasons he didn't understand. He had the impression of a person hidden, and found himself speculating about the emotions beneath her shell.

The next morning he took a magnifying glass from his study and returned to the place in Slipper Wood where he had seen her, to study the lichen there. So great was his absorption there that his business correspondence of the morning went unattended, and a letter to London beginning '*My dearest Harriet . . .*' was left unfinished on his desk all day long.

3

I was feeling distinctly uneasy as I sat in my small back kitchen and watched Katya make tea. Opposite me, across the table, a young police man was asking the usual questions, and making notes. No, nothing was missing. No sign of any disturbance at all. No damage, nothing.

'Passport, cheque book, post office book . . . All all right, sir?' He made me feel like somebody's grandfather.

'Yes, all still here.'

'Do you keep money on the premises?'

'I'd like to but I never seem to manage it.'

'Well, if you're sure, sir.' He looked up as Katya approached with three mugs of tea on a tray. 'I know this must be very disturbing for you both.'

The remark was intended entirely for her, and it made me glance up at her as she turned for the sugar, my attention caught by the young man's interest. I hadn't seen much of Katya since she moved in and I'd never looked at her very carefully before. Now I saw how tall and slim she was, attractive in a youthful, slightly angular way. She was wearing black and her hair was dark too, long and straight with a fringe that framed her face. A strange thing, I thought, how little I'd noticed her.

She answered the officer's questions with a faint Swedish accent, but she spoke English naturally, as if she'd grown up with it. Her story was simple. She had returned a little before twelve and had found the glass in the door broken. She'd called the police immediately and waited on the stairs. She hadn't touched anything. She had lived here only two months. She had seen no one acting suspiciously near the front door.

At this point, something bleeped in the officer's pocket and he put away his notebook. 'There's nothing much else I can do here, sir,' he told me neutrally. 'Probably just kids. But I'm afraid you'll need to take steps to make these premises more secure. With a front door like that it's only surprising it didn't happen sooner.'

I got up to show him out and when I returned to the kitchen Katya was still sitting in the chair opposite mine at the old wooden table. The downstairs kitchen was my kitchen—Katya had her own—and it felt strange for us to be alone together there. Nevertheless, it was a good place to sit—an ageing boiler kept it warm and a quirk of the ventilation meant it always smelt of coffee from the offices next door. Even tonight it felt immune from the sense of intrusion that hung in the hallway.

Neither of us spoke for a moment. When I looked up from my tea, she was watching me from under her fringe.

'Is it true?' she asked. 'Is there really nothing missing?'

I paused before I replied. 'No, nothing missing. But there's something I noticed. Something a bit odd.'

She was looking at me carefully. 'What sort of thing?'

I didn't attempt to explain until she'd followed me upstairs and we were standing facing the bookshelves that covered one wall of my bedroom.

'Have you ever seen any of those old films where the detective comes back to find his office has been ransacked? Well, this is exactly the opposite.'

She slowly shook her head, not understanding.

'Here, run your finger along my desk. What happens?' I asked.

She picked up her finger and blew on it. 'Nothing happens. Just dust.'

'Exactly. Now do the same on the bookshelves.'

She didn't need to. 'Nothing. They've been dusted.'

'Take a look around. Do I look like a man who dusts?'

It wasn't hard to see what I meant. Everything in the room that wasn't in daily use was covered with a thin layer of dust—the chairs, the wooden chest, the photograph by my bed. But the bookshelves were immaculately clean. Someone had dusted them.

It was really too absurd to believe. My first thought on finding it had been that something must be missing, that perhaps someone had wiped for fingerprints after a theft. But I knew the contents of those shelves so well I could almost recite them, and nothing was missing.

To my surprise, Katya began to giggle. 'So,' she began, trying to restrain herself, 'you think someone would break in to do your cleaning? I mean, it isn't *that* messy.'

It was about then that I found myself liking her. I think it was her laughter, the way she kept things in proportion. The break-in was confusing, and the conversation with Anderson was still on my mind. I needed someone to listen while I tried to manufacture a little cosmos out of the chaos. So that she wouldn't go away, I cleared her a seat and began to tell her about my evening at the Mecklenburg Hotel. But to make sense of that I found I had to tell her about the book I'd never written, the ultimate book about extinct birds. A book that was going to make each one, in a little way, live again. I told her about some of the birds: the Stephen Island wren, entirely wiped out by a single domestic cat; the spectacled cormorant, eaten to the brink of extinction by Arctic explorers and finished off by a fleet of Russian whalers in the course of an afternoon.

Katya listened with her elbows on her knees and her hands round the tea she'd brought up with her. She didn't seem bored, and once her tea was finished I fetched two glasses and a bottle of vodka from the freezer.

When I returned I closed the curtains. The street outside lay in darkness and it had started to rain again.

'Why did you never finish it?' she asked as I filled the glasses.

It was hard to explain. I picked up the bottle, still four-fifths full, and put it between us. 'Look,' I said, pointing to the empty fifth at the top of the bottle. 'When I set out, I thought all I had to do was describe the gap here.'

She looked at the empty part and nodded.

'But after three years I was further from finishing than when I started. The level in the bottle keeps falling and the rate at which it drops gets faster and faster. Each year there are more and more species on the brink. And then there are the empty bottles we don't even know about, the birds extinct before we even noticed them. One day, I suddenly realised that I'd never catch up. There's never going to be a definitive work about extinct birds. All we can do is record the handful we happen to know about.'

She pursed her lips. 'I hadn't thought of it like that. But what has this got to do with the dust on your shelves?'

So I told her about my meeting with Anderson and his plan to hunt for the remains of the rarest bird in the world. The room got warmer as we talked, and every now and then Katya sipped her drink. The idea of the lost specimen seemed to fascinate her.

'I can see why it's valuable, but fifty thousand dollars is a huge amount for a dead bird.'

I shrugged. 'That depends on how you look at it. If you came across a preserved dodo you'd be able to retire for life. Seriously. You see, there's no such thing as a preserved dodo skin, only bones and beaks and things. Something genuinely unique does have a huge value.'

Katya looked unconvinced.

'You see, for a species to officially exist, there has to be something called a *type*,' I went on. 'That's a sample specimen, one that's held to be typical of the species. Without a specimen, there's no type, and without a type, science doesn't really recognise that something exists. So if we're strictly scientific about it, the Ulieta bird isn't even extinct. It just never happened. There's no physical evidence, no bones, no feathers, nothing. Just a drawing in the Natural History Museum, a few lines of writing and one lost bird.'

Katya nodded slowly. 'But where do your books fit in?'

'I've absolutely no idea. None of them is very special.'

We stayed there drinking until the bottle was two-thirds empty. Her face lit up every time she spoke, and her vitality was infectious. Our conversation went from birds to history, the subject of Katya's masters degree, and we rambled happily about the way things in the past come to be recorded, about the way time takes things away from us if we don't fight to keep them. It was common ground of sorts.

'My father teaches history at the university in Stockholm,' she told me. 'He used to be a brilliant historian, the sort who went off and found things out. When he met my mother he was going to be the most brilliant historian in Sweden. Now he's never out of TV studios and he writes the books the publishers tell him to write. He's too busy doing interviews to care any more.' She shrugged. 'We don't get on. That's why I came to England. I want to do the research for myself.'

'And is that why you don't ring your mother?'

She paused, frowning. 'My father walked out on her when I was a teenager. She didn't even fight. Not even for my sake. She just let him go.'

It was too harsh a reason to reason against. We'd been talking for a long time now and it had made questions easier. Now it was her turn.

'Why didn't you take the money you were offered?'

'If I wanted money I wouldn't be doing what I do. Besides, there was something about Anderson. I didn't like his suit.'

At that Katya began to laugh again and we were both still laughing as we swept up the glass in the hall and tried to seal up the broken windows with drawing pins and plastic bags. Finally we stood by the semi-repaired door, facing each other, smiling. Despite the break-in I felt oddly light-hearted.

'Why don't *you* go and look for this bird?' she said, her voice serious.

I shook my head. 'I wouldn't know where to start. The trail went cold more than two hundred years ago. And, besides, Anderson is a professional. He knows what he's doing.'

Those words ran through my mind again in the early hours of the morning when I finally reached my bed. It was an impossible task, surely. But Anderson's confidence disturbed me. Could he be right? Could it really be that the bird had somehow survived in some unknown collection, untouched since the days of Cook and Joseph Banks? I tried to put the thought away, tried to remind myself that life had moved on. But Anderson must have known the effect his story would have on me. He knew I'd feel that I'd left something unfinished, that I'd never make a find like the one he was intending. The lost bird of Ulieta would be the most remarkable find of all.

My mind kept turning, and as the night began to change into the grey light of a winter dawn I realised I had one small, faint hope, something I knew that Anderson couldn't possibly know . . .

*T*hree days later she returned to the clearing where Banks had watched her sketch. It was a day to savour. The sky was an unblemished blue and the sun was hot on her skin. Without any great preparation she began to draw. As she worked, the silence of the woods turned to small noises—the water in the stream, the darting of unseen birds.

She had learned that only when she was in the woods could she be the person she knew herself to be. As her father's daughter she had needed to protect herself from the world she lived in.

She didn't hear him approach. The sound of his voice made her start.

'*Lichen pulmonarius*,' he said simply, and her eyes went to the place on the edge of the clearing where he stood. 'The name of the lichen on the trees in Slipper Wood,' he added.

With that he stepped forward into the sunlight and she saw he was smiling. Later she always remembered that moment, that smile.

'That *is* what you were looking at.' His voice betrayed no doubt. 'It grows only on the trees you were examining and on no others.' He stood before her, his smile both a greeting and a challenge. His shirt was open at the neck, his hair unkempt. In one hand he swung a leather collecting bag.

'I don't know its Latin name,' she replied. 'They call it tree lungwort. It's different from the lichens around it. But you're wrong to believe it grows nowhere else in these woods.'

'I am?' He placed his bag at his feet and looked at her again.

She remained seated, looking back at him. If she had flushed on his arrival there was no sign of it now.

'I was sure I had examined each tree most particularly,' he said.

'It grows on just those twelve trees in Slipper Wood,' she stated, studying him with cool and thoughtful eyes. 'But you've certainly seen it elsewhere. You will find traces of it on nearly every tree in your home park.'

The naturalist in him shook his head. 'I had not observed it. Or rather, if I had, I had not noted it. Do you believe what they say, that it is a cure for sickness of the lungs?'

'No, that's surely not true,' she said, her gaze turning for the moment to the trees all around them. 'They say so because of its appearance—like the texture of a lung. But that is coincidence, surely. I cannot believe that Providence felt it necessary to illustrate its workings in such a literal way.'

'I confess I am surprised. And overjoyed. I had no idea Revesby contained a fellow natural philosopher.'

THE CONJUROR'S BIRD | 183

Embarrassed at towering over her, yet unable to sit without being invited to do so, he sank to his haunches as though he wished to study something on the ground in front of him.

She rose to her feet and prepared to depart. 'I am hardly that, Mr Banks. I have no books to study and my tutor is no longer able to instruct me.'

'Your tutor?' he asked, rising hurriedly, caught off balance.

'My father, sir.'

'Of course. My apologies. I did not mean to pry.'

'And yet your presence here would suggest the opposite.'

It was not said coldly but with an air of detachment that made him step backwards. 'My apologies, madam. I had not realised my presence here was objectionable to you.'

And as he spoke, she saw the sunlight go out of his face. The sight stopped her even as she began to move, since she had not intended to wound, only to safeguard her own retreat. Around her the summer morning was still sweet. So, although she understood the risk, she turned back and met his eye.

'I am not used to company, Mr Banks. I have known these woods since I was a child and I was taught to notice what I saw around me. It would be a great luxury to talk further on these things. But today I have this drawing to complete. Soon this flower's season will be past and my opportunity will be lost.'

'Of course,' he responded. 'It was selfish of me to interrupt your work. Please be seated again,' and he gestured at the grassy mound.

As she seated herself she took care that her dress fell properly to the ground, then she turned to the page of her unfinished drawing.

'I shall bid you farewell and leave you to your work . . .' he began.

But his sentence trailed away and she did not sense that he was withdrawing. Instead she felt him move forward. When she looked up she saw his eyes fixed intently on the drawing in her hand. The expression on his face sent a flash of joy to her heart.

SHE STAYED in the woods until the light began to thicken into dusk, then she returned home with the stars already showing above the trees. On reaching the house at the edge of the village, she paused with the door open, then let it close softly behind her, knowing that in the whole village her door was the only one shut against the night air. Inside the house the shutters were fastened, and it was suffocatingly hot. She put her drawing book down on the bare table, then went upstairs to the room in which her father was dying.

Martha, the nurse, greeted her with a nod and a smile as she entered, and briefly the two sat in silence on either side of the sleeping man.

'Thank you, Martha,' she said eventually. 'You can leave me for a while. You must get yourself some supper.'

The older woman paused. 'Mr Ponsonby called again today, miss.'

'Then it's fortunate I was not at home, Martha.'

The two exchanged a look, then Martha spoke again. 'He has not asked for rent these twelve months, miss.'

'I know he has not.' She lowered her head. She might have said more but she was eager to be left alone that evening. When Martha had gone downstairs, she sat for a little, listening to her father's breathing.

She had been upstairs, sleeping, the night they brought him home. At first she thought it was drink that had affected him and she had been ashamed. Then she saw that his hair was matted with blood and they told her how he had been found. He had been drunk, they said, and had interrupted the Ponsonbys at dinner. He'd been thrown out by the servants and had wandered into the darkness. The men who found him had been returning horses to the stables at Highwold when they noticed him in a ditch, his head hard down on a stone.

That night she had tended him, an ache of anxiety deep in her stomach. She tried to force a little brandy between his lips, waiting for him to open his eyes.

The doctor came the next day, even though she had not sent for him. He was a good man: there were few who would come willingly to their door.

'You must try to feed him,' he said. 'Anything he can swallow without choking. You need him to keep up his strength.'

In the days that followed, she found he would swallow what she could force between his lips, but at other times he lay inert, unconscious of her touch. After a week, Dr Taylor returned with Martha, a nurse from the next village who had once nursed his own children. At the doctor's request she was willing to accept work in the house of a sinner and a heathen.

'You must understand,' he said, when Martha had gone downstairs to store away her things, 'that the longer he sleeps the less likely his waking.' She nodded at that but he could see she hadn't heard.

'Doctor,' she said when he came to leave, 'my father has debts. I have nothing to pay the nurse.'

He looked at the troubled green eyes. 'Martha will come to me for her wages,' he told her.

'But I cannot . . .' She looked up at him, wordlessly asking him to understand.

But he was a study of concentration, fastening his glove, and he paused only to add that he would call again when he could.

The day of his next visit he found her changed. She was neatly dressed and she did not smile as she greeted him. As she led him upstairs she explained there had been no change, but he could see for himself the alteration in her father's face, the grey pallor of his skin and his sunken cheeks. He was inching away from life. Dr Taylor knew she had seen it too, knew by the way she tended him, softly now, like a caress.

'Doctor,' she whispered, 'is it possible that my father may not recover?'

'I fear that is possible,' he replied, wishing she had a mother to place an arm round her. 'The wound is more profound than was first apparent.'

'Will it be long?' Her voice was smaller than he had ever heard it.

'I cannot say. I have known men in his state survive for many weeks. Recover too, sometimes. You must tend him well and keep him comfortable.'

'I shall,' she said. 'And then . . .' But neither of them cared to complete the sentence, and after only a few words more the doctor withdrew.

The next day she stood on the edge of the wood and let the sun warm her face, as if its touch might smooth away every thought. She felt the roughness of the grass on her fingertips and made herself memorise the pattern of leaves on the forest floor and the way the saplings twisted towards the light. And to keep these things for ever, to have them fill the emptiness inside her, she took up her pencil and drew.

4

It's a common thing for people to be fascinated by the ghosts that history leaves behind. Look in the public record offices on any Saturday and you'll find rows of them trying to summon up their ancestors, outlining with names and dates the shadows of individuals they can never truly find.

Hans Michaels was like that, but for him it was birds, not people. It was only by chance that I ever knew him. He wrote to me after reading an article I'd written about the spectacled cormorant, and after various letters had been exchanged he invited me to visit him to look at some of the research he'd done. It was a humbling experience. I was the professional and he was the amateur, but when it came to the two or three species he had really concentrated on, he had found sources and references that were completely new to me. I remember that as I left that day he asked me about the Ulieta bird. I told him what I knew and he nodded and then said something about an idea he'd been working on, something I didn't really listen to at the time. But it was that chance remark that had kept me awake until dawn, wondering what it was he had found so promising.

I was up early the next morning. I'd slept for no more than an hour, but my mind wouldn't rest and it was easier to get up and get on with things. After a shower and a coffee I felt surprisingly clear-headed. Outside it was cold but the air felt fresh on my skin. I fired up my motorbike and edged out into the traffic and headed south.

Hans Michaels lived in a red-brick villa in a village south of Guildford. I was there ringing the bell a little after ten.

'My name's Fitzgerald,' I told his wife, who opened the door. 'I was hoping to talk to your husband. It's about extinct birds.'

She looked at me evenly. 'My husband died five years ago, I'm afraid. But if you've called about his research, you'd better come in.'

The living room was cluttered with furniture and objects. 'Please take a seat,' she said, and waited until I was settled in one of the floral-print armchairs. 'I do remember you, Mr Fitzgerald,' she told me. 'You're the expert. Hans used to talk about you. You came here to look at his work once.'

'That's right,' I replied. There didn't seem much else to say.

She went to the kitchen to make tea, and when she returned I began to explain about the Ulieta bird. I told her I was after any information I could find and that I thought her husband might have been interested in the same area.

In response to that she waved a small, brown hand and gave a snort. 'If it was as obscure as you say, he probably did. He loved that sort of thing.'

'So tell me,' I asked, finally getting round to the question I'd been too polite to ask, 'do you still have his notes? Did you keep them?'

She leaned forward. 'When you get to my age you have very few things left of those you love and you hang on to them firmly. The bird notes were the thing he was proudest of. Of course I kept them.'

'And may I see them?'

'Yes. I'm sure Hans would have liked that.'

The notes were kept in a room on the first floor. She climbed the stairs slowly and led me into a large, book-lined room.

'Up there,' she said, pointing to the highest shelf. It ran all the way round the room, and instead of books it carried a series of box files, each carefully labelled by hand. There was one file per species and other files under subject headings, some of them named after collectors or collections.

'Did he show them to many people?' I asked, my eyes scanning the shelves.

'Just me,' she replied. 'And you.'

In my haste to read the labels I nearly missed it. The one I was looking for wasn't a box file at all, just a folder placed between two boxes. Even here, the Ulieta bird seemed determined to be elusive.

I paused beneath it and his wife nodded.

'Go on. You can stand on one of the chairs.'

As I lifted the folder down and felt its lightness, I thought it was going to be completely empty. But I was wrong. Hans Michaels had done some research after all and what he'd discovered was there on a single sheet of paper. There was no text. Only a simple pencil sketch of a woman's face.

Looking at it again in the brighter light of the living room, I was still at a loss as to what it meant. She was a young woman, not beautiful, but noticeable, with eyes that caught your attention and then held it. There was something vivid in them that made the face memorable. And something knowing in them that made it sad.

'It's definitely by Hans,' my hostess told me. 'He'd often make a sketch of things if he wanted to remember them.'

'You've no idea who she is?' I asked.

'Well, I don't *recognise* her, if that's what you mean. But then I wouldn't expect to. Don't you think there's something vaguely *period* about her? As if he's copied an old painting?'

'But who *is* she?' The question was to myself, but Mrs Michaels turned from the picture and looked at me.

'I rather think that is what you have to find out.'

I DIDN'T GO HOME until much later that day and by then it was dark. I'd arranged for someone to come and secure the broken front door and, in my absence, three boards had been nailed across the window, giving the place a more neglected appearance than usual. Once inside, however, the hallway felt warm and lived in. I'd spent the whole afternoon in various libraries and had a pile of books in my bag. The weight of them made me happy as I drew the curtains and shut out the night.

It was nearly eight o'clock when I was interrupted by the doorbell. I was slow rousing myself and before I reached the door the bell rang again, another long burst. The boarded-up window made it impossible to see who was outside so it wasn't until the door swung open and the light behind me touched the street that I realised it was Gabriella.

Her eyes met mine and she smiled.

*H*er drawings amazed Banks—he knew they were far better than any he had ever achieved for himself. Not just artistically better, but scientifically better, more closely observed and more scrupulous in their detail.

Because of her, the days that remained before his departure from Revesby were filled with botanical fervour. Inside him he felt something of his first, intense passion for living things. Even the most familiar specimen was fascinating, each one miraculous. Soon he would be thousands of miles away, under tropical skies, and it felt right that he should take with him these fresh memories of his home woods.

At first she had seemed reluctant to let him examine her work. She pulled the book close to her, and when their eyes met he understood instantly that there was nothing coquettish in her refusal. Her gaze held his, he thought she was about to speak—and then, quite suddenly, she yielded the book.

There in the woods, as the sun shone, she watched him as he turned the pages from one drawing to the next, his face full of wonder. It was then she felt the stirring wildness inside her that she didn't in the beginning understand. The shock of it made her silent. 'Remember this,' she told herself. 'Let me always remember this.' It was the first prayer she had uttered for a year that had not been for her father.

On each subsequent afternoon they had returned without prior arrangement to the same clearing. They worked through her drawing book, discussing the nature and characteristics of each plant. Banks's pleasure in her company was instinctive, and nothing made him pause and consider its implications. Even as she revelled in the sun full on her face, she marvelled at his blindness.

One afternoon he sat and watched her sketch. She had allowed it only after protest; he had no idea how much he asked of her. As she began to draw it felt like an unveiling and she was clumsy and tentative. But as she went on she felt a change inside her. As her concentration intensified, the turbulence within her calmed itself until soon she became unaware of his presence. He watched the familiar furrow appear and deepen in her brow and, for a moment, he wondered that he had ever considered her ordinary. When at last he disturbed her, the drawing was two-thirds complete.

'You have a gift,' he told her. 'I wish you could travel and paint the plants of the tropics. I can imagine you in the heat, drawing away, concentrating too hard to be concerned about the prowling tiger or the snake at your feet.'

He laughed, and she smiled, even though his words made the walls in her mind seem higher and closer.

So the afternoons passed. A week before his departure for London she pointed to one of the woodland birds in the trees and told him that such small brown birds were insufficient for him; his voyage was necessary so he could seek out birds of brighter colours and stranger shapes to satisfy him. At first he felt wounded. Then he sensed a meaning in her words that moved him to meet her eyes and smile. He was still smiling later, as he said his farewell and left her to her drawing. As he approached the shadow of the trees, she called out to him.

'Mr Banks.' He stopped and turned. 'Mr Banks. I'd like to thank you for the kindness you've shown me these few days.'

He shook his head, serious again. 'On the contrary, it is I who am in your debt. Your drawings have refreshed me in my calling. And the memory of these woodlands will sustain me when I am far at sea.'

She considered him carefully, her face made soft by the early-evening sun. 'I should like you to know I am grateful, all the same.'

He bowed and as he turned to leave he thought she would speak again. But when he paused she only nodded, and with another smile, he was gone.

On his return the following day he found the clearing empty. It was a surprise. There remained in her book a dozen drawings he had yet to study. He waited until the afternoon was far advanced but she did not come.

The next morning, in his hurry to return to the clearing, he almost missed the letter. The handwriting was unfamiliar but he knew at once it was hers.

'Sir,' she wrote, neatly and carefully. '*My father's health is declining and I must spend the days between now and your departure at his side. It would be a favour to us both if you did not call.*'

The letter was unsigned.

He strode into Revesby that same day, inclined to take her decision lightly, thinking it caused by a temporary sadness at her father's health that would end when the crisis passed. But at her door he was firmly turned back by the old woman who answered: her mistress was indisposed and would not receive callers.

He had planned, on his departure, to present her with a book, a copy of Gerard's *Herbal*. Now he decided that she should have it early and he left it at her door with his compliments. Within an hour the gift had been returned. The next day he walked the woods restlessly, hurt by her coolness. Whatever direction he took, he found himself back at her door. On two or three occasions he advanced and was rebuffed. On the fourth day he did not call.

In the darkened house she heard his footsteps come and go until they no longer came at all. Between his visits there was the steady breathing of her father and the creaking of the floorboards as they spread and contracted with the passage of the sun. The shutters let in little of the sunlight but trapped the heat at night so that her dampened handkerchief would sometimes dry before it had reached her father's brow.

The cessation of his visits was a sorrow and a vindication. In a few summer days she had learned to fear hope in the way she had once feared despair. And so she cut herself away from him and hoped that when he was gone the woods would be hers again, at least until the day that gentle breathing stopped and everything would change.

On the first day that Banks stopped calling at the house in Revesby, he kept mostly to his room. The following morning he rose early and marched to his study. There he took a piece of paper and began to write:

'*My dearest Harriet, I return to London forthwith. Although I have been, as always, the worst of correspondents, my time here has made many things clear to me. I wish to be allowed to call on you on my return to speak of certain matters that are better said than written . . .*'

5

I had met Gabriella over the remains of a dead macaw. I was younger then and still an optimist, and the Brazilian rain forest was uncharted in all sorts of ways. I'd gone there on an expedition, fresh from college and overconfident in my abilities. When the expedition's leader left, I stayed on, intending to join a group from Oxford that was due to arrive later that month. In fact the Oxford team took months to arrive as vital personnel fell sick or changed their minds and the funding kept falling through. But I was happy to wait. I had good contacts out there and through them I found a clean room with a desk and an electric fan. More importantly I had a chest full of jottings under my bed and an idea for a volume on lost avian species that would be my great work.

I spent most of the days sleeping or moving with a glass in my hand through consular garden parties, my nights scribbling away with undisguised passion on the fate of the passenger pigeon or the great auk.

It was one of the last days before the second expedition set out when Berkeley Harris, a fellow scientist, came to find me.

'You free, Fitz?'

Harris was one of those men who wore long shorts all the time and did everything with a pipe in his mouth except eat, a breed that became extinct in Europe shortly after the war but in those days still lingered in small populations on the postcolonial fringes.

'I only ask because there's rather a pretty girl over at the bungalow who wants some help with a parrot. I said you were the man.'

Although he was never right about anything, he was right about Gabriella. She was in the shade when Harris led me into the bungalow garden and all I could make out was a slim figure in the shadows. Then she stepped into the sunlight to meet us and I broke off from what I was saying and put out my hand. I'd met girls in the past who were considered beautiful and Gabriella was nothing like any of them. But there was something about her eyes and the way she held her head and crinkled her brow as she reached out her hand to shake mine.

'Miss Martinez, this is John Fitzgerald. I'm sure he'll be able to sort you out. Fitz, Miss Martinez works down at the zoo. Her parrot's died and she wants it stuffed.'

'The term is mounted. We only say "stuffed" if we're trying to be crude.'

'I dare say. Anyway, I'll leave you to it. Got an expedition to mount, don't you know.'

She waited until he'd gone inside before she spoke. 'He's quite wrong, Mr Fitzgerald. It's not a zoo and it's not a parrot.'

I laughed. 'That's about average for Harris. Just what is it that I can help you with, Miss Martinez?'

She looked very earnestly into my eyes. 'I've just lost one of the rarest birds in the world.'

She could hardly have picked a better introduction.

THE GABRIELLA who faced me now across the kitchen table had the same earnest eyes. She watched me with the same half-smile, studied my face with the same disarming care as I opened a bottle of wine.

'It's good to see you again, Fitz,' she said, raising her glass. 'We didn't get a chance to talk last night.'

'No, I noticed that.'

She cupped the glass in her hand and began to rock it gently so that the wine moved around in circles. 'I'd wanted to call before. You didn't reply to my letters, though. I wasn't sure. Then when Karl asked about you it seemed a good excuse.'

We sat for a second or two and looked at each other, not sure where to take up again. Eventually she began to talk, updating me on her project in the Amazon, how it had developed since we'd last seen each other, the work she was doing there. I could see she was relieved that I could still talk knowledgeably about the latest science—island biogeography, conservation corridors—the sort of issues that her project was grappling with. By mutual consent we avoided the other stuff, the things we'd never talked about— those last days, the photograph by my bed, a life we'd left behind us. Instead we talked ratios and pie charts and variable extinction rates. Eventually, the conversation edged round to the subject of the previous evening.

'There's something I wanted to ask you.' She put her glass down and moved both hands behind her neck, flicking her hair outwards as if to free it from her collar. 'You didn't like Karl very much, did you, John?'

'Was I supposed to?'

'Not really. But I thought you'd be interested.'

'It was interesting that he wanted to give me fifty thousand dollars for making some phone calls.'

'I told him the money was a mistake. I said you'd either help him or you wouldn't.'

'You were right. I wouldn't.'

She looked at me with that familiar questioning intensity. 'I want to tell you about Karl,' she said, leaning forward.

I tried to keep my voice level. 'I'm not sure I want to hear.'

'He isn't what you think, Fitz. He is an interesting man, a bit of a trouble-maker, and you should like that. He's always been given a rough time by the establishment. They won't take him seriously because he's not an academic, but he's still better at finding things than they are, and that makes them look stupid. You and he should be on the same side.' She paused. 'But that's not why I introduced you. You know the sort of work I've always wanted to do. Well, now it's happening. Good work. Valuable work. It's making a difference to the whole way people think about conservation areas. And when I met Karl, the project was hanging in the balance. We're broke, Fitz, and the grants we get from Europe don't even cover our computers. Karl pumped money in when we needed it and he's been doing it ever since. He hasn't asked for anything from us. Anything from me. He meets the bills when things get particularly bad, that's all.'

'And in return you're going to help him find Joseph Banks's lost bird?'

'He doesn't need my help. He has a lead, something that tells him where to look. But he can't be sure it's going to work out and that's why he wants you on his side rather than on someone else's. You see, he's sure you know something. He says you'll have read the right books.'

'It doesn't sound as though he really needs my help. And even if he did, I wouldn't help him.'

'Then help *me*.' Her grip on my arm was suddenly tight. 'I need to find this bird, Fitz. It means everything to the work we're doing.'

'I don't understand.'

She looked at me very hard, her head tilted towards mine. 'This is my introduction to Ted Staest. Karl is as generous as he can be, but Staest is in a different league. If we can help him with his DNA ark, by finding the bird, if I can get him to take an interest in the project . . . He gives out grants that would make your mouth water, Fitz, the sort of money that would keep the project going for years. Literally. Five years of good work. It could mean the survival of a dozen species. Think of that.'

The little kitchen suddenly seemed too hot. I moved from the table and walked round to the window where it was cooler. Helping her, helping Anderson, helping the project . . . I felt I was being drawn into a tangled net.

And then I remembered it was all built on a mistake.

'Gabby, there's a problem with all this. I don't know anything.'

'You have all the contacts. And your notes . . .'

I shook my head. 'I'm sorry. If you have any sense, you'll go back to Anderson and be very nice to him until he finds the bird.'

Gabby stood up. I watched her reflection in the kitchen window. She wasn't looking at me.

'Tomorrow I fly to Germany for some lectures,' she said, her voice neutral.

'I'll be back in a couple of weeks. If I find out anything useful in the meantime, I'll pass it on. You can choose what you want to do with it.'

She moved to the door but didn't go through it. I turned to look at her and found she was looking at me, her expression suddenly sad.

'Do you remember when we first met, John? The bird I brought you?'

'Yes, I remember. A Spix's macaw.'

'Do you know the latest?'

I nodded. The bird Gabby had found dying in a market cage had been one of the last of its kind. Ten years ago the total number of Spix's macaws in the wild was down to three. Eight years later there was only one, a single ageing male. When it was gone, there would be thirty or so specimens left in captivity. None of them were breeding pairs.

'I'll call you when I get back, John. I'd like to talk again.'

I waited by the window until I heard her pull the front door shut behind her. It was only as I cleared up the glasses that I noticed her raincoat on the hook behind the door. Like a promise, I thought. Or just a careless goodbye.

THAT WASN'T QUITE the end of my day. I needed some sleep, but the books on my wall wouldn't let me rest. What had Anderson said? Something about reading the right books. I tried to imagine I was finding out about the Ulieta bird for the first time. Where would I look? There were two books that would be the obvious places to start and I had them both on my shelves. I took them down. The first was easily the most authoritative: *Extinct and Vanishing Birds of the World* by James Greenway. I opened it carefully and turned to the page about the Ulieta bird. The little that was known was laid out with admirable clarity.

The second book, *Some Notes on Rare Avian Species* by R.A. Fosdyke, was quirky where Greenway was scientific, slapdash where Greenway was rigorous. The book didn't pretend to be comprehensive, but anyone who was serious about the subject had a copy because every now and then Fosdyke came up with a reference that no one else had. I opened the book carefully. Mine was a first edition, signed by Fosdyke himself shortly before he died. Was a signed first edition worth anything? Worth breaking in for? Apparently not, because this one was still here, very unstolen. Inside, Fosdyke listed two references to the bird—both also listed in Greenway—and limited himself to the same conclusion: last seen in the collection of Sir Joseph Banks.

I closed the book wearily. Those two entries were the sum total of my knowledge and neither offered any help at all, except a vague indication of where to start. And that was with Joseph Banks, the naturalist, sometime in the late 1700s.

London was stifling after the shady woods of Revesby, but Banks was too busy with the practicalities surrounding his departure to stop and take note of it. There were bills to be paid, tradesmen to interview, provisions to be secured and innumerable letters to be written.

His engagement to Harriet Blosset was settled a few days after his return to London. He had met her only a few months earlier and his flirtation with her had not seemed beyond the commonplace. But on the day his place on Cook's expedition was first discussed seriously, he was due to call on her guardian and, left alone with her in the garden, he found himself observing her in a different way. It was as if the prospect of his journey gave him a new, clearer perspective. He watched her lean forward and was struck by the incredible beauty of her form, by the perfect line that curved from her neck to her shoulder. And when she looked at him, he saw in her eyes such pleading that he reached out and took her hand. That she should look at him in that way seemed both astounding and wonderful.

He knew full well the expectations he had raised by his letter. When the demands on his time allowed him to call on her family, it was a short interview. She was flushed but contained, and in her kiss there was a girlish elation that touched him and sent him on his way feeling wise and a little paternal. No announcement was to be made until his return, when such things could be done properly. Even so, those who saw them together thought them very much in love. Only when she talked of his return as if it was certain and imminent did his smile fade a little. And when he tried to speak of the dangers of the voyage, and of his hopes for it, she silenced him by taking his hand and kissing each of his fingers.

When he was not with Harriet, Banks sought the company of men. Cook was stern and practical and Banks warmed to him. His plainness and his sense stood out among the noise and excitement of the many. When the day finally came, Banks and his friend Daniel Solander, the botanist, travelled together from London to Plymouth, where they were to meet Cook and join the *Endeavour*. The journey took four days and it was a sombre one. Both now had to face the reality of the danger ahead of them. It was not until they were both on board, at anchor off Plymouth and looking out at the country they might never see again, that an enquiry from Solander made Banks think of Revesby.

'Things were well there,' he replied, and looked across to the busy docks. 'I was able to say my farewells to both the place and the people.' A smile crept into the corner of his mouth. 'And I was given a lesson in lichen by a student of the local flora.'

'Indeed?' Solander smiled. 'I had not realised that Revesby was such a centre of learning.'

'Oh, you underestimate Revesby at your peril, my friend. What would you say if I told you I discovered a botanical artist there whose skill is the equal of any of those who go with us?'

'I should say you exaggerate. Did you bring any examples of his work that might support such a claim?'

Banks's face grew serious. 'No, I have none of that work to show you. And who knows? Perhaps I was mistaken.' He looked out to where the sun was low in the sky. 'It is time for us to go below, my friend. They will be waiting for us.'

IN THE HOUSE at the end of the village, the summer would continue to beat on her door, and every evening she would sit with her father until nightfall. Then she would tiptoe down the corridor to her bed and sit at the open shutter for a time, looking at the dark trees rippling in the breeze. She heard rumours of Banks's engagement to Harriet Blosset only after the *Endeavour* had sailed, and in the slow hours between sunset and dawn she would imagine him journeying with that unknown woman close to his heart. She thought of him standing on the edge of new worlds, hungry for life, drinking in the sights and the sounds as a gift to bring back for that one who was waiting for him.

She knew that his presence that summer had changed things for her. After he'd gone, she paid the price she had expected to pay: without him the woods seemed far emptier than before, indeed the whole of Revesby seemed to shrink, and her loneliness increased.

BANKS FOUND HIMSELF writing to her one evening during the first weeks of his voyage. The sea was a deep blue and there was no scent of land on the breeze. But most of all, the night was clear and when he stood near the prow of the ship he felt the huge arch of the sky embrace him. The air was warm against his skin and the stars were bright, and as he stood there he felt a huge burden of responsibility fall from his shoulders. All at once he felt free to be happy.

Slowly the light faded. He watched until the blue was truly black and the sky and the sea merged at the horizon. Then he went below and lit his lamp and wrote to her.

The sea turned green today, just for a moment in the morning light, a deep, deep green of the sort you never see from land. Above the sea, high above it, a single swift. I watched, amazed to find it so far from solid earth. It seemed to wave a last farewell from all things to do with land.

I have little time here to think of Revesby but when I do I am saddened at the manner of our parting. But most I am saddened that you cannot see this sky. The colours seem to change every instant as the clouds pass and the moon begins to rise. You would wish to paint this sky . . .

At that point there were sounds outside his cabin and he wrote no more that night. The letter was never finished.

6

The following Monday, Katya and I met in the café of the Natural History Museum. Katya was neat in jeans and trainers with her hair pulled back. I was scruffy and slightly unkempt in an old jacket. The Natural History Museum welcomed both of us equally, and if anyone thought we made an odd couple, no one showed it.

I'd bumped into Katya that morning in the hallway as she was leaving for a lecture. Slightly to my surprise, I started telling her about Hans Michaels's widow and the sketch. I was faced with a puzzle and I suppose I just wanted someone to help. It was Katya who had suggested meeting there and I was pleased with the idea: it was one of my favourite places, elegant and airy and stuffed full of wonders. She'd said she would drop into the university library first thing and get some information on Banks.

Over frothy cups of coffee we shared what we'd found out—the main facts of the case, if you like. We started with the early life of Joseph Banks. He was a good subject—charming, dashing, good-looking and the leading natural scientist of his generation. Oh, and rich too. By the age of twenty-eight he'd been round the world with Captain Cook, established

198 of M ART IN DAVIES

himself as the darling of society and become one of the leading members of the Royal Society.

After twenty minutes we'd come up with this:

1743		*Joseph Banks born. Grew up in Lincolnshire (Revesby Abbey).*
1760	*Age 17*	*At Oxford. An avid naturalist.*
1766–7	*Age 23*	*Expedition to Newfoundland.*
1768	*Age 25*	*Engaged to Harriet Blosset. Departed with Cook on the* Endeavour. *Gathered specimens. Helped map coast of Australia.*
1771	*Age 28*	Endeavour *returns. Banks a huge hit in top social circles.*
1772	*Age 29*	*Cook's second voyage. Banks drops out at very last minute. Replaced as ship's naturalist by Johann Forster.*
1775	*Age 32*	*Cook returns. Forster gives (only ever) specimen of bird found on island of Ulieta (now Raiatea) to Banks.*

'How does that look for background?' I asked.

Katya nodded. 'It's good. We can call it "Events Leading up to the Crime".'

I looked at the list again. 'Actually, there are a couple of things in there I don't really understand,' I said. 'We've put down "*1768—Engaged to Harriet Blosset*". But he never married her, did he? What went wrong?'

Katya looked down at her notes again. 'Not sure. Seems like the engagement was never announced—it was all arranged just before he sailed off with Cook. And it seems to have been broken off soon after he got back.'

'Any pictures of her?' I wondered.

'Not in the books I've read so far.' Katya looked worried. 'We should be able to find one though, shouldn't we?'

I wasn't so sure. After some discussion we agreed to alter our list:

1771	*Age 28*	Endeavour *returns. Banks no longer engaged (why?).*

My other question was about Cook's second voyage, a year later. Banks had been all set to go, with his provisions bought and arrangements made, only to pull out on the very brink of departure over an argument with Cook about cabin space. It seemed a strangely petulant piece of behaviour from an otherwise good-natured man.

Katya agreed. 'You can tell it took people by surprise. Look at this.'

She reached into her bag and pulled out a photocopy. It was the text of a letter from Captain James Cook to the Secretary of the Admiralty, sent from Madeira on August 1, 1772, quite early on in his second voyage. The letter was printed with Cook's original punctuation.

. . . Three days before we arrived a person left the Island who went by the name of Burnett. He had been waiting for Mr Banks arrival about three months, at first he said he came here for the recovery of his health, but afterwards said his intention was to go with Mr Banks, to some he said he was unknown to this Gentleman, to others he said it was by his appointment he came here as he could not be receiv'd on board in England. At last when he heard that Mr Banks did not go with us, he took the very first opportunity to get off the Island. He was in appearance rather ordinary than otherwise and employ'd his time in Botanizing &ca—Every part of Mr Burnetts behaviour and every action tended to prove that he was a Woman, I have not met with a person that entertains a doubt of a contrary nature.

Katya grinned as I finished reading. 'What do you think? A Joseph Banks groupie?'

I smiled. 'It could be. Or just gossip? Banks was a dashing young man with a bit of a reputation, so he was fair game for rumours. And the two men had fallen out. Perhaps Cook couldn't resist dishing a bit of dirt on Banks to the folks back home.'

'Either way, it doesn't get us anywhere,' said Katya. 'The bird hadn't even been discovered then. But when Cook passed that way again at the end of his voyage, he had the Ulieta bird on board. What do we know after that?'

All that we knew was that the bird had been given to Banks shortly after the *Resolution* returned to Britain. Latham saw it in Banks's collection in the couple of years that followed. After that it was never mentioned by anyone again. Banks kept records of any specimens presented to fellow collectors and scholars, but the Ulieta bird wasn't listed. At some point, therefore, it was either destroyed or carried out of Banks's house. And then, if Anderson was to be believed, it had spent more than two hundred years quietly waiting to be discovered by someone who knew where to look.

'So what do we do next?' Katya asked.

I smiled and pulled out a blank sheet of paper. 'We play a game. According to Michaels's drawing there's a woman involved. Now, what women were there in Banks's life at the time the bird disappeared? We write down all the ones we can think of. They're all suspects. And if the bird was given to one of them, we could check to see what happened to *their* collections. Assuming they had collections.'

Katya gave me a bright smile. 'I like it,' she said cheerfully, reaching for her notes. '*Cherchez la femme.*'

The first three or four names came quickly: Banks's mother, his sister Sophia, Harriet Blosset, one or two society hostesses whose names we had noted. Somewhere there would be portraits of them all. After that we paused.

'Anyone else?'

'There was a mistress,' Katya said at last. 'After his engagement. I read about her but I didn't write down her name.'

'Was she still around in 1775?'

'I don't think so, but put her down if only to . . . What's the phrase?'

'Eliminate her from our enquiries?'

She smiled. 'That's the one. Then we go and find their portraits!'

At the bottom of our list of suspects I wrote the words *Joseph Banks's mistress*. Then, as an afterthought, I added a question mark.

WE TOOK a quick tour of the Natural History Museum, beginning in the main hall, under the skeleton of the giant diplodocus. We moved haphazardly from room to room, past fossil plates of great sea creatures and under the ribs of long extinct mammals, then came back to the main hall, and the carefully reconstructed skeleton of a dodo.

'There you go. When people say "dead as a dodo", that's what they mean.'

Katya nodded, reading the label. 'Three hundred years dead.'

'And speaking of dead birds.' I looked at my watch. 'We've got an appointment to keep.'

I led her through the main hall to the back of the museum and into its small General Library, where Geraldine, the librarian, was expecting me.

'They're just fetching it, Mr Fitzgerald,' she told me. 'Should be ready for you in a few minutes. And I've put out the Banks biographies you asked for on the table over there.'

Katya and I sat down next to each other and went through the pile of books, looking for the name of Joseph Banks's mistress. I took photocopies of two pages that referred to her, but no one seemed to know her name, and the more we looked for her the less visible she became. We'd made no progress at all by the time Geraldine returned with the object I'd requested, and left it on a table near us, covered only with a loose sheet of clear plastic.

It was a drawing of a bird, expertly done, its colours apparently as fresh as they had been on the June afternoon in 1774 when Georg Forster had sat drawing in his cabin. Through the plastic you could even glimpse traces of the artist at work—the corrections to his original outlines, the places where his sweating hand had smudged his own pencil lines as he drew. It made that hot afternoon suddenly seem very close, the bird very real.

'The bird itself . . .' Katya breathed.

'Yes, that's the one. The one that ended up in Joseph Banks's collection. We don't know how many of them there once were, or how they lived or anything. All we know of them is this one individual.'

We sat together in front of that picture, musing, until the room began to grow gloomy around us and Katya looked at her watch.

'I've got to go,' she said. 'I've got a tutorial.' She pulled on her coat. 'We should . . .' She trailed off. 'Well, whatever. I'll see you later.'

By the door she turned and waved.

After that I found it hard to settle. I let Geraldine remove the picture and then returned to the reference books, still curious about the missing mistress. The next twenty minutes or so threw up a couple more mentions of her, which I photocopied, but I still couldn't find her name.

When I got home I found a plain, unmarked envelope had been pushed through the door. Two things struck me about the document inside. The first was that it had been sent anonymously. The second was that it looked remarkably as though it might be Anderson's secret clue.

*D*r Taylor called less frequently once winter arrived, but he came early one morning in February when the village was still white with frost and there was ice on the path to their door.

Inside he found the house cold, the fires small and newly lit. In the hallway, where he laid his hat and gloves, he could see his breath in short white bursts in front of his face. He found that only the sickroom was truly warm, and he could tell by the ash that the fire there had been tended through the night.

His patient had, month by month, confounded the doctor's expectations, but today he saw at once that it could not be very much longer. For many months his visits had been for the sake of the daughter, not the father.

'What will you do?' he asked her quietly, his examination complete. 'It will be soon now.'

'I will not think of it,' she said. 'I won't think him gone.' She reached out and took her father's hand.

The doctor nodded but after a short silence he spoke again. 'I know of someone . . . a family . . . children to teach . . .'

She looked up. 'You know what is said of me,' she said. 'They could not take me. They simply could not.' It was spoken quietly, without emotion.

The doctor nodded again. 'I'm sorry,' he said, although what aspect of the world he was regretting he did not say.

On his way out, the nurse, Martha, detained him at the front door with a hand on his arm and a gesture in the direction of the kitchen.

'I can borrow no more in the village on her father's name,' she said softly.

'I'm sorry,' he said again and hesitated. He was not a wealthy man and he had a family of his own. But he would not have her bury her father for want of food. 'Then you must borrow on my name,' he told her and stepped outside into the frozen morning.

THAT NIGHT she sat in the dark of her room and thought of the question the doctor had posed. She had opened the shutters and could feel the cold pressing in on her from the window. Beyond the glass a half-moon lit the meadow but left the great stand of trees in darkness. The grass was already sparkling with frost. She shivered and pulled her shawl closer to her neck. She knew there was only one answer to the doctor's question, one that many would think she was lucky to have. It didn't seem to matter to her so much now, as she sat there alone in the night with everything coming to an end.

For a moment she thought of Joseph Banks sailing through a southern summer, and she was happy to think that, unlike her, he was not cramped by the cold and the long hours of darkness. And with the loss of her father so close and so real, she found herself for the first time glad of Banks's engagement, glad that he had found his happiness. It was then that she understood the gift her father had given her by clinging so tenaciously to life. He had given her time. Time before their world fell apart for her to enjoy the woods and the summer; time to love a little; time to understand her loss so that the great, empty ache she would feel on his death was one she had already learned to carry.

Lent came in with streams still frozen and the ground too hard to dig, and she became determined that her father should feel one last spring. As he fought painfully for each breath, she would talk of the coming thaw, painting warm, bright pictures, as if her words could breathe into him the need to be alive.

However, the first death in Revesby that year was not the one most expected. At the end of March, Dr Taylor died, outlived by the man he had paid to keep alive. The village was stricken and the funeral was attended by mourners from five parishes. She sat at home and grieved by the bedside where he had so often sat. The shock of his death brought a new dimension to her loneliness.

Martha looked at the pinched face of her mistress and the ice on the windows and decided to stay. Since the incident, there had been no money to pay the interest on her master's debts to Mr Ponsonby, who now all but owned the house. It was only through his goodwill that the family had been allowed to remain. There was food in the larder to last until spring, but Martha had begun to worry where further money would come from.

In London, Harriet Blosset was also waiting. In the first months of Banks's absence she wore her situation like a mourning gown. At balls and dances she was fetching and prettier than ever in her desolation. But as the season progressed she proved too pretty a widow to remain in black for ever. No one she danced with was quite like Banks, she told herself, but they were pressing and charming and a great deal closer. She suffered in her own way, and on the day when her closest friend's betrothal was announced she wept.

In Revesby, perhaps the dying man had listened to his daughter's exhortations. There were yellow crocuses outside his front door on the morning when his daughter woke at his bedside and found him gone.

7

I was in the kitchen, boiling the kettle, when Katya came in. I intercepted her in the hallway, then made her a cup of tea before I pushed the envelope over to her. She opened it cautiously.

There were two photocopied sheets inside. The first showed the front of an envelope, the George V stamp clear, the postmark smudged and illegible. The envelope was addressed to: *Miss Martha Ainsby, The Old Manor,*

Stamford, Lincolnshire. The second sheet was a copy of a letter written in the same strong, sloping handwriting on Savoy Hotel notepaper.

January 17th, 1915

My dear Martha,

Colonel Winstanley was as good as his word. Though I have been here in London little more than eight hours, at dawn tomorrow I set off to rejoin the regiment.

Your letter only caught up with me two days ago. What sad news! The old man was a great character and a good friend to us both. I'm glad the end was peaceful. He deserved as much.

It was great quick thinking to secure that precious bird of his. You know I have always coveted it. Even without the connections to Cook and Banks, it would still be the most remarkable and romantic object.

When I return, you and I shall write to the Natural History Museum. It's only fair they are made aware of the survival of this unique specimen. Until then, guard it with your life—I don't want to return and find that young Vulpes of yours has snatched it from my grasp!

This brief glimpse of London has done me a power of good. My spirits are high and I'm certain this job will be done shortly so I can return to your side.

Remember me to everyone.

Your loving brother, John

When Katya had finished reading we looked at each other across the table. She was sitting quite still but I could feel her suspense.

'The Ulieta bird,' she said quietly. 'That's what he's writing about, isn't it?'

'It could be.'

She made an impatient face. 'What do you mean? It *must* be.'

'No, it just *could* be. And this letter *could* be the lead Anderson mentioned.'

'Then it *can* be found!' She clutched my arm. 'It means we've got as much chance as he has!'

I held up my hand. 'Wait a minute, a lot has happened since 1915. The Blitz, death duties, an awful lot of rising damp. We can't be sure of anything.'

'But if it was still in one piece back then . . .'

'Yes, if it survived till then there's a chance it might still be around. But if this is Anderson's big clue, who sent it to us? I can't imagine Anderson dropping it in just to make sure he doesn't have an unsporting advantage.'

Katya was still looking at the photocopied sheets in front of her. 'I don't know.' She hesitated. 'Who else knew about it?'

I immediately thought of Gabby. She'd promised to pass on anything she found, and it looked as though she was keeping her word. I reached over and took the papers out of Katya's hands.

'What are you going to do?' she asked.

'I'm going to Stamford,' I told her, ' to find out if these are real.'

'Very good,' she replied brightly. 'I'm coming too.'

WE PACKED A BAG each and set out the next morning, just as the rush hour began. Now that there were two of us travelling I couldn't use my bike, but Geoff from the Hammer and Sickle lent me his car—a small rusty object the colour of a fading lemon.

It was a slow journey, the radio didn't work and the heating did only enough to stop the windows from steaming up, but we were childishly elated. On the outskirts of London we pulled over and put on our coats. Katya's was long and black, with the collar turned up round her face. Mine was old and tatty and made me look like an extra from *Dr Zhivago*.

'You know this is crazy, don't you?' I said, though there was a little pulse of optimism inside me that refused to be dampened.

'Of course.' She smiled. 'But it feels good, being in search of something.'

'That's what I always used to say to people. I spent six years in the rain forest, looking for things.'

'What sort of things?'

'Birds, plants. Connections. It was a genetic impulse. My grandfather was the same. And my father. Do you know, they both have beetles named after them? How could I possibly follow that?'

Katya laughed. 'So what did *you* discover?'

I shrugged. 'Nothing much. When I was twenty-five I published a paper that showed how a certain species of tree frog was being badly affected by logging operations. It was quite big news at the time—well, big news if you were into that sort of thing. The thing is, they carried on logging anyway. When I next went back there were no frogs left.'

Katya looked at me. 'But still, you'd done good work, hadn't you?'

'In an academic sense. But that didn't do the frogs much good.' I paused. 'I suppose that's when things began to go wrong between me and Gabriella. We began working together, setting up rain-forest reserves. But after the frogs, I began to wonder if we'd got it all wrong. I began to believe that reserves weren't the solution at all. They were just sticking plaster for our consciences. We should have been putting all that funding into tackling the causes—population growth, consumer demand, that sort of thing.'

Katya was still looking at me from under her fringe. 'And that's why you two fell out? You weren't really on the same side?'

'It wasn't only that. There were other things . . .' I thought of saying more but I was too slow or too shy, or out of practice. 'There always are, aren't there?' I concluded lamely. 'Anyway, we went our separate ways. Gabby stayed in the rain forest and I set off to track down the remains of all the birds we'd already lost. I figured we owed it to the future to preserve the evidence, to show what they'd been like.' I smiled ruefully. 'I was a bit manic really. After a couple of years I calmed down and came back here to sort myself out. It was all a long time ago now.'

Before Katya could reply, it started raining and the pained creaking of the windscreen wipers put an end to conversation.

It was lunchtime by the time we made our way into the centre of Stamford. We found a pub near the station called the Railway Tavern, and since it had a sign that read BAR MEALS, SNACKS, BED AND BREAKFAST I booked two rooms. Leaving our bags still packed, we found a café for lunch and sat down to do some planning. Before eating, I rang the university and told them where they could contact me in case Gabby tried to get in touch.

Buoyed by a flood tide of confidence and two strong cups of coffee, we agreed to split up. Katya would visit the local record office while I'd try to find the Old Manor.

At the tourist information office, I waited politely until a would-be rail traveller finished monopolising the woman behind the counter. She looked up and caught my eye as he let the door bang behind him.

'I'm not supposed to do trains,' she said with a sad smile.

She stopped smiling when I told her I was looking for the Old Manor. 'What *is* all this?' she asked. 'I had someone in here a couple of days ago asking about just the same place.'

I felt a slight stir of anxiety. 'And is that unusual?' I asked.

'Well, yes,' she replied, 'especially as I'm not sure it exists.'

The disappointment she saw in my face was enough to persuade her to tell me about the previous visitor. She illustrated her story with a succession of leaflets advertising old houses in the surrounding area.

'This one seemed the best bet,' she told me, indicating one of them. 'The Old Grange. Tudor, mostly. It's just north of here.'

I nodded politely. 'And was this visitor a tall man? A Scandinavian?' I asked, pretty sure of the answer.

'No, not at all. He was an American. Very polite. Little round glasses. Getting on a bit. Now, are you going to tell me what all this is about?'

I explained I was trying to trace a family called Ainsby that had lived in the area in the early 1900s. The name didn't ring any bells with her but she told me how to find the record office. Which, she said, was the same thing she'd told the polite American.

THE RAIN CONTINUED for most of the day. At six o'clock that evening, Katya and I retreated to the bar at the Station Tavern. It looked better after dark, with a gas-flame fire and lots of small red lampshades making it harder to see the marks on the walls. It was gloriously warm, too, after the cold rain of a Lincolnshire evening, so we risked ordering food at the bar, then retired to the corner by the fire with a large glass of red wine and a pint of something dark and local.

The record office had told Katya what I'd already begun to fear. There was no trace of any family called Ainsby in or around Stamford in 1915 or, as far as they could see, at any other time. It had taken Katya three hours and the urgings of two different librarians to accept the fact. We had drawn the most emphatically featureless blank imaginable.

As we ate our meal we speculated furiously. Did this mean the letter we'd been sent was a fake? Neither of us wanted to believe that. Apart from Hans Michaels's drawing, it was the only clue we had. We decided to try again the next day, to dig a little deeper.

After that we suddenly grew awkward with each other, and when Katya opted for an early night I stayed behind for another pint. When she'd gone I took out the tourist leaflets and spread them across the table. I was contemplating the possibility of a third pint when an unpleasant breath of cold air made me look up. A small, round man had come into the pub and, judging from the state of his raincoat, the weather outside was getting worse.

'No good, any of them,' he said with an American accent as he made his way over to my table, where he flapped the water off the sides of his coat.

'I'm sorry?' I replied, as coldly as a man can when he's just been caught reading a leaflet titled 'The Pixie Glen and Elves' Grotto, Fairbank'.

'None of them is the place you're looking for,' he replied. 'You're Fitzgerald,' he added. 'Mind if I join you?'

He was already pulling up a chair. The removal of his coat revealed a woollen three-piece suit of the sort worn by country doctors in the 1930s. His hair was grey and slightly curly and he wore thick glasses in old-fashioned frames. He looked absurdly un-American.

'I think you'd better start again. Who are you?'

'The name's Potts,' he said, holding out his hand. 'I called the university and they told me I'd find you here. I'm staying at the George on the High Street. I guess we're here for the same reason.'

'You're looking for a lost bird?'

'That's the one.' He reached into his jacket and handed me a card.

It didn't give much away: *Emeric Potts. Art, Antiques, Ephemera.*

'You're an art dealer?' I asked, looking at him more carefully.

He pursed his lips as if to blow the idea away. 'Not exactly. But you could say that art dealers are my business. I find the things they want to sell. Looking for a lost Van Dyck? Want a first-edition *Ulysses*? I'm your man.'

I gave him back his card. 'Isn't this outside your normal line of work?'

'Oh, I prefer to call it a natural diversification. After all, you could say taxidermy is just sculpture in another form.'

'So you know someone who wants to buy the Ulieta bird?'

Potts looked pained. 'Such directness, Mr Fitzgerald. Let's just say that I'm very interested in finding it. And people seem to think you're the best person to help. I rang you a few times in the last few days but you were always out.'

I wasn't sure what to make of him. 'So what are you doing here in Stamford? Not just looking for me, surely?'

He reached into his pocket again and pulled out a folded piece of paper. 'You've seen this?' he asked.

'I'm not sure,' I lied, recognising instantly the photocopied sheet he placed in front of me. It was another copy of John Ainsby's letter.

'Of course you have.' He leaned back. 'I sent it to you myself.'

I admit that took me by surprise, and my face must have shown it.

'Who did you think sent it, Mr Fitzgerald? Karl Anderson?'

'No. Well, I mean . . .'

He chuckled softly to himself. 'Well, it's Anderson's letter, all right. This is what's brought him over here in a hurry to try to find the thing.'

'He told me he was coming over anyway. Something to do with botanical paintings. The Ulieta bird is just a sideline to him.'

Potts was still smiling affably, but I felt that he was studying me carefully. 'He told you that, did he? Well, who's to say?' And with that he took his glasses off and began to polish them, apparently having no further interest in Anderson and his motives.

But I couldn't let him stop there. 'I'm sorry, this doesn't make sense. Why would *you* send me that letter?'

He shrugged in a way that suggested the answer was obvious. 'I reckoned that when you saw John Ainsby's letter, either you'd ignore it, in which case I'd know it's a dead end, or you'd come running up here, in which case we might be on to something. And here you are.'

He was clearly a man who liked to talk. As he warmed up in front of the fire, he began to tell me a lot more about the Ainsby letter. Apparently, Anderson had been put onto it by an academic doing research into the First World War. He grasped the letter's significance at once and his first step was to take a copy to Ted Staest. The two men came to some sort of agreement about the bird's value—though Potts seemed rather vague about exactly what they agreed. It wasn't until rumours about the bird began to leak out that Potts got hold of his own copy of the letter.

'Not through official channels, you understand, Mr Fitzgerald.'

'You mean you bribed someone?'

He looked offended. 'Please, Mr Fitzgerald, there's no need for us to go into the details. Suffice it to say that I have a copy. And now, so do you.' He indicated the piece of paper in front of him. 'Intriguing, isn't it? The references to Cook and Banks, the unique specimen . . . All very promising. There's one bit though— "*I don't want to return and find that young Vulpes of yours has snatched it from my grasp!*" What do you make of that?'

I shrugged. '*Vulpes* means fox, so I expect he means someone cunning and a bit predatory. The way he uses it sounds affectionate though, doesn't it? I wondered if it was a suitor of hers—someone prowling around while her brother's away.'

'A suitor. A lover . . . Yes, I can see that. Interesting . . .'

Behind his glasses, his eyes seemed to cloud with thought, but a second later his unflappable exterior was back in place and he was telling me he'd drawn a blank in Stamford. No trace of the Ainsbys, no trace of the Old Manor, no stuffed bird. No trace of Anderson either.

'That was beginning to worry me most,' he confided. 'I figured if I wasn't where Anderson was, I was in the wrong place. Then on my fourth day here I noticed a guy in the George.' He took a card from his wallet. *Edward Smith, Discretion Guaranteed, 63 North Hill Road, London N17.* 'This guy Smith is working for Anderson. He admitted it quickly enough when pressed. Seemed to hint it was pretty much all over.'

'What's Smith actually doing?' I asked.

Potts shrugged. 'Goes out early, comes back late. Takes his car. I tried tailing him one day but he must have spotted me. We drove around the county for six and a half hours. Jeez, the roads here are really something, aren't they?' He sat back and looked at me pleasantly. 'You know, if it wasn't for noticing Smith I'd have quit by now—if there's anything here to find, I can't find it.' He then leaned forward, almost conspiratorially. 'Listen, we may as well be straight with each other. I'm very, very keen to find that bird before Anderson does. Now, here's the deal. You find me that bird and we can go to Staest together. You can deal with him direct. All I ask is a small cut, say five per cent. Call it an introduction fee, if you like.'

It was then I began to understand the real purpose behind Potts's avuncular demeanour. For the next twenty minutes or so, very gently and with the greatest politeness, he interrogated me about the whereabouts of the Ulieta bird. Like Anderson, he seemed reluctant to believe how little I knew. Even my empty glass wasn't enough to stop the questions, until finally I insisted on going to the bar to buy myself another pint. When I came back he was squeezing himself into his raincoat. He paused to shake my hand.

'Remember what I've said tonight, Mr Fitzgerald. My job here is to find that bird before Anderson. But if you get to it before either of us, remember that I'll be happy to help you get the best price for it.'

When he'd gone I drank my pint in silence, feeling sure there was something going on that I wasn't quite grasping. Potts seemed eager enough to get hold of the bird, but, like Anderson, he didn't seem too bothered about making money out of it. Was this really all about pleasing Ted Staest? How much is the goodwill of a Canadian billionaire worth?

As I went to put the leaflets back in my pocket, I found the photocopies I'd made at the Natural History Museum, the two references to Joseph Banks's mistress. I looked around. The bar was still warm and still serving. It seemed a shame to go to bed. So I settled down again and started to read them properly for the first time.

*T*he last days of a journey can be the hardest. At sea every one on the *Endeavour* had an order to live by and clear duties to perform. They knew their routine and their instructions and at all times they had a destination ahead of them. With the approach of land, these certainties began to dissolve. As the Channel drew nearer, men would pause in their work to scan the horizon. Banks was one of them. He knew, long before they arrived in London, that their return would be momentous. They had seen and recorded things beyond the imaginations of the people who had sent them. He had brought back with him a collection—specimens, plants and artefacts—that was unlike anything that had ever been seen before. He was too young not to enjoy the anticipation of triumph. And too human not to be a little changed by it.

Nevertheless, he was nervous and found himself envying Cook. Banks knew that the Yorkshireman's reputation was made, and he found that he envied him his wife at home and his sturdy sense of belonging. The aspects of home that Banks had cherished in the South Seas began to seem subtly different as he edged nearer to reality.

He found it easy to imagine himself in the salons of London, recounting his voyage and meeting the great philosophers of the day on equal terms. But when he tried to imagine Harriet with him in that world, the picture would begin to fade. She seemed to him to sit uneasily beside these men of serious science, and he was ashamed to find that, when he remembered her, instead of recalling her face he found his pulse quickening at the recollection of a neck as smooth as pale china, of his fingertips trailing gently down the line of her soft, bare shoulders. These images returned to him over and over, as he tried instead to remember her voice or her smile. Disconcerted, he swept such thoughts away until the time came when he would meet her in person.

When the *Endeavour* finally anchored in Deal they had been away almost three years. The return of the expedition was an even greater sensation than Banks could possibly have imagined. Within days of their arrival he had become its public face, the young man who had combined daring and adventure with the most dedicated pursuit of knowledge. While Cook sank quietly into the routine debriefings of the Admiralty, Banks entered polite society and opened its eyes to a new world. Carried to fame by both the novelty and the daring of the tales he had to tell, he was rushed through parlours and dining rooms, scarcely able to believe the honours paid him.

At first he rode this wave of celebrity as a small boat rides the storm, lifted from wave to wave without control of his direction or destiny. For five days after his return he did not visit Harriet Blosset. When she sent him a hurt, reproachful letter complaining of his very public negligence, he went to see her, and each found the other altered, so that the interview was awkward and unsatisfying. She found him constrained and uncertain where before he had been easy and amusing, and his talk of distant islands was less interesting to her than talk of a future with her in London and the shires. She greeted him coldly, unaware of how much of her attraction had been in the openness with which she showed her feelings for him. This proud, resentful Harriet was a stranger to him. As their interview progressed he found her less striking than he remembered, the creamy white of her skin less perfect, her gait less graceful and natural. They sat together for a painful, inconclusive half-hour and then he excused himself. His time was not his own, he told her, and he was bound in a few days' time to go to Revesby to enquire into the management of his estates. On his return, he promised, he would call again and then there would be time to talk of the future.

Perhaps it was the excitements of London society or the rigours of the voyage that had affected him, but as he journeyed back to Revesby he barely thought of his last visit there. His mind was on the improvements he might make and the decisions that needed to be taken about rents and rates.

He was surprised on his arrival to be greeted by smiling and eager faces he hadn't thought of for over three years. Amid all the greetings there was a moment of sadness for him when he heard of Dr Taylor's death two years before. The doctor's family, he was told, had left Revesby shortly after, their circumstances much reduced.

Banks felt genuine sadness at the news, but comforted himself with the discovery that his estates had been well managed in his absence: after three days of accounts and rent books, he was satisfied that there were no acts of neglect that needed remedy, and he headed into the sunshine with his steward, Nicholson, to see for himself how things stood. The tenant farms and cottages were inspected and found satisfactory.

It was a hot afternoon in late summer, and as they returned on foot from their expedition, and turned their attention to the woods that lay between the Abbey and the village, the shade was welcomed. A few minutes into the trees Banks paused, as if surprised at where he stood. With Nicholson at his side, his thoughts had been entirely on business, and it came to him as a shock to recognise the place in which he found himself.

'This way, if you will,' he muttered to Nicholson, and struck off to his right.

The steward followed him until both emerged into a clearing between the trees. Banks was smiling quietly to himself.

'After so many years away,' he murmured, 'it is strange to find the paths, even the shapes of particular trees, exactly as they were when I stood here last.'

Nicholson nodded. 'There's no denying the woods change slowly, sir.'

'Tell me,' Banks said after a while, 'when I was here last there was a young lady who used to roam these woods as if they were her own. Her father had the house at the end of the village. He was something of a freethinker, much given to drinking, and there was always scandal attached to his name.'

'Yes, sir, I know the gentleman you mean. Unpopular in these parts. He died a couple of years back, in the spring.'

'And the daughter? Where is she now? Is she married?'

'She's gone, sir. I don't know where. Not married though, I'll warrant. Not if what they say is true.'

Banks looked at him sharply. 'What do you mean by that?'

'Well, sir,' the steward began uncomfortably, 'I don't pretend to know anything for certain but there was a lot of talk. About where she went and who she went with. There was no talk of her marrying, sir.'

'Really, Nicholson! That sounds like no more than common gossip.'

'I don't know to be sure. But I saw her for myself, sir, just once since she left here. It was up in Louth on market day. I saw her quite plain up near the church and, well, she was very smartly dressed, sir. Not like we'd ever seen her here in Revesby when her father was alive.'

Banks looked down at his feet while he digested this. 'And she was alone?'

'With Martha, sir. The woman who used to look after her father.'

Banks looked up, his features firmly set. 'Thank you, Nicholson. That is very interesting. But of course it is taking us very far from a proper valuation of all this timber . . .'

With that the two men turned towards the Abbey and continued their inspection, leaving the clearing empty but for the sunshine and a pair of small birds that fluttered quickly to the forest floor when they were gone.

IT WAS ANOTHER three days before Banks was able to find the time to ride to Louth. His return to the woods had stirred memories, and he was in a reflective mood as he guided his horse into the town's marketplace and dismounted. He called on friends and enquired after her by name. They were delighted to see him and insisted on his taking tea, but none of them could help.

Uncertain how to proceed, and feeling a little foolish at the rashness of his expedition, he made his way across the market square towards the church where Nicholson claimed to have seen her. It was late afternoon and the town smelt hot and airless. Coming to the churchyard, Banks was happy to sit for a moment in the shade of the lich gate.

He looked out across the gravestones of the parish. Some were fallen at an angle and near obliterated by lichen, others clean and poignant. A private, hidden place. Leaving the shade, he began to make his way round the church, pausing at some of the stones to read their messages, pleased to be thinking of something other than his own foolishness. After a leisurely circling of the church, he returned to a long green stone sunk into the grass near the lich gate. Unable to decipher its inscription, he lowered himself onto his haunches and began to scrape with his fingernails at the lichen that hid the names of the souls at rest. The first name was almost legible when a voice spoke behind him.

'*Lichen pulmonarius,*' it said.

He turned and looked up so abruptly that he almost lost his balance. She was standing at the lich gate, slight and straight, watching him. She was partly concealed by shadow but was instantly familiar, her figure and her face exactly as he remembered. A beautiful face, he thought suddenly, though he had not always thought so. Then she moved into the sunshine and he noticed that she was paler now, as if she had been too much indoors.

As he began to step towards her, she seemed to move back but then stopped and stood her ground, her face serious and her eyes meeting his. He opened his mouth to speak, to call her by her name, but as he began she shook her head and held up her hand.

'No, you must not call me by that name. I have a different name here.'

He stopped, no more than a pace away from her. 'Then you are married?'

The shake of her head was almost imperceptible. 'No, I'm not married. Here I am known as Miss Brown.'

He looked around awkwardly, then met her eyes again. 'Our acquaintance was very short, Miss Brown. There are too few botanical artists in the world for me to neglect them when I meet them. I would very much like to hear how things have been with you.'

She looked back to the seat near the lich gate. 'Martha,' she said. 'Please wait for me here. I have something to say to Mr Banks.'

He held his arm out to her. When she took it he paused at the touch of her hand and then they set off together.

8

Katya and I spent the next day on the tourist trail, driving from Tudor manor to Georgian pile, paying entry fees and asking questions. We were full of energy and our spirits never flagged. Katya was particularly good. When we found the Old Grange closed for the season, she stepped boldly up to the front door and roused a startled woman in pearls. At Pulkington Hall she discovered a bald, red-faced man who seemed so charmed by her interest that he insisted on showing us his greenhouse. Neither of them had ever heard of the Ainsbys. We even found one house that was liberally supplied with cases of stuffed birds, which, to the surprise of the caretaker, we studied with enormous care.

It was dark as we drove back to Stamford, our world shrunk to the tunnel of light dug by our headlamps.

Suddenly Katya began to laugh. 'Did you see the look on that woman's face when you congratulated her on her stuffed grouse?'

I grimaced. 'Well, what else could I say? She'd just caught me standing on an antique chair, peering at it.' I began to laugh too. 'Anyway,' I retaliated, 'at least I didn't flirt with anyone. You and that old man in the tea room . . . I thought he was going to insist on coming home with us.'

The oncoming headlights lit up her smile. 'I had to be nice. And since you mention it, the woman at the Old Grange definitely liked you.'

We parked the car near the station and found an Italian restaurant, where we settled down with a bottle of wine, still laughing at ourselves. After a couple of glasses I got out the photocopies I'd read the night before.

'You remember Joseph Banks's mistress?' I asked. 'After he came back from his voyage with Cook?'

'Yes. We couldn't find out who she was.'

'That's what's interesting. In all the books about him she only seems to exist between the lines. People refer to her but no one tells us anything. They don't even know her name. Here, read this.'

The first sheet was a page from an ageing biography of Banks by a man called Havelock. It described the couple of years after Banks's return from his round-the-world expedition with Cook. I'd marked a passage.

Little is known about Banks's personal life after the end of his engagement to Miss Blosset. It seems he was content to postpone thoughts of matrimony and concentrate his energies on his scientific calling. However, it is unlikely that a young man of such wealth and good looks would have ignored the fairer sex entirely, and it is perhaps unsurprising that there was talk of a mistress. The Town & Country Magazine *referred to her only as Miss B—n, and suggested that Banks was sufficiently attached to her to install her in rooms in Orchard Street. It proved a transient affair, however, and after 1774 she is not mentioned again. Happily adventures such as this one did not distract Banks from his scientific duties . . .*

'*Scientific duties* indeed! Patronising sod,' Katya growled. 'I hope none of the fairer sex ever tried to distract Havelock from *his* work.'

'Unlikely, if his prose is anything to go by.'

She turned to the second sheet, a page from a more recent biography.

Although Banks died without children, his affair with Miss B—n seems to have resulted in a pregnancy, at least according to the gossip columnists of the time. On this occasion, the gossip may not have been entirely malicious. In 1773, a letter to Banks from Johann Fabricius, who spent a lot of time studying Banks's collection in the 1770s, seems to confirm the rumours: 'My best compliments and wishes in Orchard Street. What has she brought you? Well, it is all the same, if a boy he will be clever and strong like his father, if a girl, she will be pretty and genteel like her mother.' For all that, there is no further mention of either mother or child and, whether the affair was ended by mutual agreement or by death in childbirth, it is clear that by 1774 it was indeed over.

'Sad story,' Katya said, 'though from a practical point of view we can cross her off our list of suspects if she was gone by 1774. The Ulieta bird didn't even arrive in the country until a year after that.'

I nodded. 'It *is* sad,' I agreed. 'Sad that no one even knows her name.'

Katya refilled our glasses and held up hers for a toast. 'To solving mysteries,' she said.

'And finding things,' I added.

That night we both got outrageously drunk. Towards the end of the first bottle, Katya began to tell me about herself. She told me her family had spent eight years in London while her father taught here. She'd been fourteen when they went back to Sweden and her parents' marriage broke up. She'd spent four or five years rebelling—dropping out of school, living in a squat, doing all the things that parents like least.

'So what changed?' I asked her.

'I did, when I was about nineteen.' She smiled a half-smile and gave a slight shrug. 'One day I realised that my life was just boring and miserable. I began to spend whole days in the library, reading. I pretended it was just a way of keeping warm when I had nowhere else to go, but then I found myself sneaking books out at night so that I could carry on. It made me stop and ask who I was trying to punish. A week later I signed up for school again. First, I wrote a long, angry letter to my father telling him it didn't mean I was forgiving him.'

After that the evening grew hazier. Tables began to empty, but in our little pool of candlelight we scarcely noticed. We talked about history and politics and wondered aloud whether Joseph Banks had loved his mistress. At some point Katya eyed me solemnly from under her fringe and asked me why I'd changed my mind about finding the bird.

'Who says I changed my mind?'

'You *have* changed your mind. Definitely. The night of the break-in you weren't very sure.'

'I suppose I thought Anderson would get there first. And it's like he said. This sort of discovery is the kind I was always looking for. I suppose I knew I had to give it another try.' I paused and thought for a moment. I'd reached that point in the evening where it didn't seem to matter if I was making sense or not. 'You know, sometimes someone's born and then they die and they're gone for ever. I mean, however hard you try to remember them, you begin to lose them. In the end you're left with something that's made up of fragments of them, little bits of memory and feelings.' I shrugged. 'And those are all we have and we should keep them.'

'People? Or do you mean birds?'

I shrugged. 'Both, I suppose.'

She touched my hand then, but didn't say anything. She looked very lovely in the candlelight.

'And there's another reason for finding it, of course,' I went on solemnly. She took her hand away and frowned. 'What's that?'

'Well, if that bird outlived Cook and Banks and survived all the wars and fires and floods since then, I'm damned if I'm going to let Anderson flog it off to somebody in a lab in the vague hope that by tearing it apart they may some day come up with a slightly modified chicken.'

She laughed at that and I laughed at myself, and I don't remember much afterwards, not even how we got back to our rooms, only that I stood for a moment at the top of the stairs looking at Katya, thinking how easy it was becoming to forget the photograph by my bed. Easy to forget everything, in fact. A hazy, fleeting moment, gone before I even thought to grasp it.

A very few hours later I was woken by a rap on my bedroom door and Potts's American accent summoning me to breakfast. When I finally made it downstairs, dry-mouthed and croaky, Potts was settled in the bit of the lounge bar where they served food. By daylight the bar seemed stained and tatty again and the air smelt of stale cigarette smoke.

'Over here, Mr Fitzgerald,' he said, beckoning me. 'I've already checked out of the George, and I thought I'd get these folks to cook me breakfast. I thought we could talk while we eat.'

He was as immaculate as before, this time dressed in a suit of purple and green tweed, as if for a grouse shoot. As he helped himself to coffee, he explained that Anderson's detective had left Stamford the night before.

'That means the letter looks like a dead end,' he told me. 'I'm off to London to look for Anderson and check out a couple of other things.'

While I nibbled at a triangle of cold toast, Potts demolished an enormous cooked breakfast.

'No matter how you look at it,' he said, dabbing the corner of his mouth with a paper napkin, 'neither of us is doing much good round here, peering into priest-holes and at rare breeds of sheep. The answer's somewhere else.'

When he'd mopped the last traces of baked beans from his plate, he pulled a ten-pound note out of his wallet and pushed it under the salt pot.

'That should cover it,' he announced. Then he looked at me for a moment and pulled something else out of his wallet. 'Know who this is?' he asked.

I recognised her at once. It was a photocopy of an old print, the sort of cheap, printed portrait that was common in the eighteenth century. It was a neat, small-featured, unremarkable face, yet the artist had caught something in the eyes that made the portrait oddly striking; something intelligent and compelling.

I looked up at Potts. 'Where did this come from?'

THE CONJUROR'S BIRD | 219

'It was lying around in Anderson's hotel room.'

'I didn't know you'd seen Anderson.'

'I haven't. I've no idea where he is. But I went into his room at the Mecklenburg, and had a look through his papers.' Again that benign smile. 'Oh, don't look so shocked, Mr Fitzgerald. I just wandered around the corridor looking lost until a maid with a vacuum cleaner let me in.' He gave a slightly rueful smile. 'There wasn't much to see. A copy of the letter we already have, a big bundle of photocopies from books and articles about Joseph Banks. Nothing very exciting. This picture was near the bottom and it kinda caught my eye. So I brought it with me.'

I gave him the picture back as coolly and as carelessly as I could manage. 'I'm sorry,' I said, 'I've no idea who she is.' And then I took a long, slow swig of tea. Because whoever she was, Hans Michaels had found her. And he had made a sketch of her portrait because she was the clue he thought would lead him to the Ulieta bird.

Potts shrugged and put the picture away, then stood up and shook my hand. As he headed for the door with his bags, I called after him.

'Mr Potts?' He turned back to me. 'That picture. Would you mind if I took a copy, just in case I come across it again?'

He put down his bags and took out the picture again, looking at it with new curiosity. 'Well, well,' he muttered. 'So it *is* important.'

'I don't know any more than you do,' I told him, almost truthfully. 'It just . . . Well, I don't have many leads.'

He placed the piece of paper on the table. 'It's yours. Keep it.' He picked up his bags again. 'I always keep copies.'

When he'd gone I stayed in the bar, drinking tea until Katya joined me. She looked amazingly fresh after her late night. She helped herself to fruit juice and cereal, and as she ate she listened to my account of breakfast with Potts.

*T*hat afternoon in Louth, the sun shone and the little churchyard seemed heavy with summer. They sat side by side near the long grass, and from time to time she paused in her explanation to study his profile, still wondering at his being there.

'When we last met,' she began, 'my father was dying. He fell on the road when he was both drunk and angry. It's known by everyone in Revesby that he struck John Ponsonby at his own table, in front of his wife and daughters. You must have heard that. It was what they expected of a man like my father: a nonbeliever, a man who let his daughter run wild in the woods. What they don't know is why my father went to the Ponsonby house that night. It was because everything he owned he'd sold to Ponsonby, and that day he realised the sale included his own daughter.'

He was sitting leaning forwards, his forearms resting on his knees. She couldn't see his eyes but she could see the tension in the line of his jaw and the way he rubbed the knuckles of one hand with the fingers of the other.

'John Ponsonby is not all bad,' she continued, 'though I have not always thought so. I felt his interest in me from the first, when he began calling on my father, something few in the village would do. Many of his visits involved the signing of papers, and after those visits my father's spirits would rise and he would drink more freely. As my father's debts grew, Ponsonby's visits became more frequent. One day he waited until I was alone and then he called. He told me that when my father could no longer protect me, when I had nowhere else to go, I was to come to him. He would take me away from Revesby. He told me I was wasted there, nobody recognised my value. I was fifteen.'

She paused in her story. Instead of responding, Banks stood up and took a few slow steps away from her. She waited, watching him.

'All those weeks in Revesby I was so blind,' he said at last. 'I should have seen, should have taken steps . . .'

She shook her head. 'No, please do not say so. Those days in the woods . . . None of the rest of it seemed to matter. There were only my drawings and the plants around us. Those days gave me more than you can know. They let me see that there will always be some things that are my own.'

And sitting there on the cold stone, waiting for him to speak, she realised she had misunderstood. It was *he* who needed comforting, he was the one lost, the one struggling to understand.

She rose and went to him and held out her hand. 'If you do not have to go, let us walk a little as we talk.'

He found it difficult to speak. Instead, when she came level with him, he allowed her to take his arm and guide him along the path round the church.

As they walked, she finished her story. Her father's drinking increased and she began to fear for his health. He grew short-tempered and was unable to rest. Then one evening Mr Ponsonby called and spent an hour with her father. When he was gone her father emerged from his study transformed, almost euphoric in his good humour. 'That man Ponsonby is a good fellow but a fool,' he declared. 'He has agreed to advance me a substantial sum against the sale of certain books in my library. Oh, I don't doubt the value of the volumes under discussion. I'm sure his money is secure. But in the matter of interest he is unnecessarily restrained. He says he does not wish to profit from a neighbour. And that must surely make him a fool.'

She listened to his words and felt sick inside. It was his blindness that hurt her most. Before she was able to pause and think, the words escaped her.

'I'm sure Mr Ponsonby sees his interest paid in a different currency.'

It was an ugly scene. At first he raged and she tried to explain away her words, but there was no escaping what she'd said. Her father was relentless: he pushed her and pushed her, drawing out the truth in tiny drops even as she begged him not to believe her. When he had heard everything, he turned his invective on his neighbour, spluttering with rage. It took her an hour to calm him.

'Leave me for a while,' he said at last. 'You have given me a great deal to think about.' And as he retired to his study she even dared to hope that her outburst had done some good, that he might at least reconsider any further borrowing.

She did not hear him go out. She only became aware of his absence when she began to prepare for bed. Her knock on his door went unanswered and, afraid that he had drunk himself to sleep, she entered and found him gone. Three hours later the men brought him home and carried him to his room.

'And so,' she said now, leaning a little more heavily on Banks's arm, 'I was to blame. And when you become accustomed to that, there is little else with the power to hurt.'

They walked on. The sun was still warm but the shadows were longer now and she felt a shiver growing inside her. She had reached the part of her story that could not be avoided. She waited for him to speak, to tell her to go on.

'And so,' he began awkwardly, 'when your father eventually died . . .'

'Yes,' she said simply. 'There was nowhere else to turn. There was no money for the funeral, so he provided it. Everything I thought of as mine was really his.'

'So he made you—'

She stopped him then, pulling his arm so they came to a halt in front of the church door. 'No,' she said, looking up at him. 'I had nothing. A young woman with no money and no character, not fit to teach the children of decent people because she was raised with no religion and no morals. A woman known to meet a man in the woods and to return smiling each day. Do you see? He didn't make me. He didn't need to. I sent for him. All I asked was to live under a different name so that my father's critics would not hear of it and jeer.'

She was looking up at him with eyes full of fire. He had never before considered the price she might pay for their meetings, but he thought of it now. In his eyes she could see the pain and uncertainty.

'He was gentle with me. Do you understand? He did all he could to make it right for me. His demands were never excessive. He has never alluded to my poverty, never reminded me of what I owe him. He tries to make me happy. And I let him try because it is all I can do in return.'

As he looked down at her, the light in her eyes seemed to burn into him. He had never seen eyes blaze as hers did.

She saw the struggle in his face, saw the words forming on his lips, and she braced her shoulders. When he spoke, his voice was raw with emotion.

'Come away with me,' he said. 'You have an alternative now.' Suddenly he smiled. 'I swear I will ask nothing of you but that you talk to me of lichen. And that you draw every day until your drawings astonish the world.'

As he spoke she felt such warmth rushing into her that she shivered. The fierce urging she had tried to forget was raging inside her again. Whatever price she had to pay she would be alive again. Wondrously, wildly alive.

9

Journeys do not always lead where one expects. We'd been looking for a bird, but we'd found a face: the face of a woman with striking eyes and no name. For the next couple of days, pictures obsessed us. We returned to London and began with a morning in the National Portrait Gallery. There were many more portraits of men than women in the eighteenth-century galleries and after less than an hour we'd run out of suspects.

As we headed towards the exit we found ourselves, by accident, in front of Joshua Reynolds's portrait of Joseph Banks.

It's a striking portrait. It shows Banks as a young man recently returned from his great voyage. He is seated in his study and there are papers on his desk, but his body is turned away from them, as he engages the painter directly with his eyes. His expression seems solemn at first, but as you look properly you can detect the trace of a smile on his lips. It's the same with his eyes: behind the direct gaze there is a lightness that belies his gravity, a laughing young man peeping out from behind a serious façade.

'Mmm,' murmured Katya. 'Attractive. Not handsome but definitely attractive. It's the good humour in his face. And the intelligence. You just know he was interested in things. The sort of man a girl could like.'

As we looked at him and he looked back, I knew she was right. Reynolds had captured on the canvas an aura of confidence and vitality that shone through the paint. It was hard to imagine that this man's company would ever be dull. Easy to imagine him living and loving. We stood and watched him with our shoulders touching until, with a silent nod, we agreed to go.

That night I cooked Katya dinner. We lit a candle and drank cold beer and sat up late talking about sex and politics in the 1780s. At one point she sat back in her chair and smiled.

'What?' I asked. 'What's so funny?'

'We are,' she said. 'Come on, let's have another beer.'

The next day we went to the British Library and searched through every book of portraits we could find. When we'd exhausted them, we returned to biographies. After the biographies of Banks we began on the biographies of Banks's friends and associates—anything with pictures.

It took me a little while to realise that Katya had stopped turning the pages of the large volume she was poring over. I looked up and saw that she was sitting very still, her dark hair falling away from her face as she leaned over the worn leather binding. Her eyes were full of wonder.

'I've found her,' she said softly.

I got up and moved round the table to see what she was looking at. A page from a *Town & Country Magazine* of 1774. I could tell at once she was right. It was definitely the original of the grimy photocopy we had in front of us, the same picture that Hans Michaels had once sketched.

'His mistress.' Katya was scarcely audible. 'Miss B.'

Her face was small, ordinary, but her eyes held you. Perhaps, in a crowded room, when you grew tired of the noise and the social niceties, perhaps this was the woman you'd seek out.

'So we've found her,' I said, resting my hand on Katya's shoulder. 'What the hell do we do now?'

IT WASN'T UNTIL we'd left the British Library and were standing facing each other outside that Katya answered the question. 'I'll tell you what we do,' she began. 'We track her down. We find out who she really is and where she lived and what happened to her.'

'And you have a plan for how we do that?' I wasn't feeling optimistic.

'No, but I will.' Her enthusiasm was burning bright again. 'Look, I have an idea. I'll see you at home this afternoon. By then I'll have worked it out.'

So Katya and I said goodbye, and I watched her dark head bobbing along until I lost it in the eddying crowds of the Euston Road. Then I thrust my hands a little deeper into my pockets and tried to refocus my thoughts. By rights I should have been going home to catch up on some work. Instead, I found myself a pub, and settled down with a pint and the notes I'd made about the item in *Town & Country Magazine*.

It seemed a simple enough tale. Miss B—n was an orphan; Banks had known her when she was a girl, before his voyage on the *Endeavour*; on his return he had sought her out. There was no clue as to where she had come from or where she might have disappeared to in the months after the magazine was published. For society gossip, it was a surprisingly modern piece of work: moral righteousness on the surface, sly innuendo underneath.

And this was all we had. Without this one piece of writing there would be nothing to tell us that she had ever existed. And that was not a comforting thought. A little deflated, I headed home to look for Katya, but when I got there she'd already gone. The only sign of her was a note pinned by the stairs: *City of Westminster Archives, 10 St Ann's Street, SW1.*

WE LIVE in a society that is strangely superstitious about written records. Even while we're content to countenance the tearing down of rain forests and the destruction of countless unknown organisms every day, we hold on grimly to our documents and papers. Few of us are immune to this. I keep notes about dead birds for a book I won't write. Other people keep bills or bank statements or the menus of long-closed takeaways. Our national archives bulge with ephemera that may one day transform themselves into history.

I found Katya in the research room of the Westminster archives, tucked away in a corner behind a large microfilm reader. She scarcely looked up when I walked over to her. She just smiled and pointed to a chair, then carried on, spinning the reels of the microfilm viewer deftly backwards and forwards with both hands.

'Am I interrupting something?' I asked, but she carried on turning. Pages of old copperplate handwriting skidded across the screen.

'Shit!' she said, loudly enough to make an elderly woman sitting nearby turn and look. 'You've made me miss what I was looking for.'

'I'm sorry,' I said, and our eyes met and held for a moment.

Abruptly she turned back to the screen and smiled to herself. 'So you should be. Leaving me to do all the work.' She began to rewind the film, much more slowly now, until she found the place she was looking for. 'Here, look at this. Marylebone Parish rate books for 1774.'

Lit up in front of me were the pages of an old ledger, a photographic image of the time-stained, torn-edged original. The left-hand column was a list of addresses and next to each was a name, a date and a sum of money. Halfway down the page I saw the words *Orchard Street* and the date *April 30th 1774*. Each house number in the street had a name beside it except one. Next to Number 24 the space was blank.

'If the gossip is true, Orchard Street is where Miss B lived,' Katya reminded me, turning to see my reaction.

'So what does this mean?' I asked her, not sure of her point.

'Number 24 Orchard Street is blank. That means it was vacant when the collector called. But one year earlier, in June 1773, the place was taken by Banks, just like the gossip column said. So the affair was over by 1774.'

'He could just have moved her somewhere else.'

Katya shook her head. 'She's never mentioned again, is she? Perhaps she went to another man. Or Banks got bored of her and paid her to leave town.'

'There is another option, you know.'

She pulled a face. 'I know. Death during childbirth.'

'But there's no mention of him having children, even illegitimate ones.'

Katya turned back to the screen and began to rewind the film. 'At least I can check that. I can go to the Marylebone Parish registers of births and deaths and look for any woman whose name begins with B and ends in N who died in 1773 or 1774.'

'You might find dozens.'

'At least that would give us some real names to check out, wouldn't it?'

I considered that. 'OK . . . And what if you don't find any names that fit?'

She looked me very firmly in the eye. 'Then we look somewhere else.'

KATYA AND I spent a morning up near Farringdon checking the parish deaths registers but astonishingly there were no entries that matched the name 'B—n'. Which, as Katya pointed out, could just mean she died some-where else. But even though we were running out of ideas about what to do next, neither of us seemed able to give up the chase.

That Monday evening was stormy and the rain was lashing the windows of my kitchen when I began to cook dinner, having spent my day in various London archives, flapping like a bird of ill omen over long lists of the dead. The ancient boiler was muttering throatily in response to the weather, and the pans were beginning to bubble as Katya came home. We ate together with the lights low and the rain pleasingly impotent against the windows. Neither of us had anything to report, so we opened a bottle of wine and didn't talk about the bird at all. The wine perked us up and soon we were chatting happily.

'About the bird,' Katya said eventually. 'You're going to have to do the searching without me for a day or two. I've got to go back to Sweden. There's a couple of things I need to do.'

'That's a bit sudden, isn't it?' I asked.

She poured herself another drink. 'It's probably all a waste of time but it's stuff I've got to do. I'll tell you all about it when I get back.'

Although the rest of the evening went well, the kitchen seemed a slightly sadder place. Searching for the bird by myself didn't seem so appealing.

And when I woke up the next morning, Katya was already gone.

*R*ichmond. Fashionable and discreet, where an orphaned young lady staying with a respectable old woman could live a quiet and genteel existence. Where, properly chaperoned, she could walk on the hill or draw in the woods to her heart's content. Where an old friend from London could visit from time to time and take tea before returning home. Richmond, where, in the summer of 1771, the arrival of the quiet and unremarkable Miss Brown to live with elderly Mrs Jenkins, widow of a Revesby pensioner, went largely unnoticed.

She took Martha with her as her attendant, and they learned to respect conventions and exercise freedoms that neither had encountered before. Banks visited rarely but wrote often, anxious that the two women should have all the things they needed. That was why, one morning three weeks after their arrival from Lincolnshire, five large packages arrived addressed to Miss Brown containing all manner of materials for drawing and painting. She spent a morning unpacking them, running her fingers over each one as it was removed from its paper, lost in awe that she should be the object of such fortune. Many years later, when she recalled those weeks, they seemed to her to have happened to someone else. From the moment she had seen Joseph Banks kneeling in Louth churchyard, as if she had somehow summoned him, nothing seemed quite real.

He had acted swiftly after that encounter. In casting around for a family with whom she could stay respectably, he had quickly thought of Mrs Jenkins, the widow of a long-serving steward to his father, whose small cottage on the edge of Richmond was paid for by the Revesby estate. She was neither a gossip nor a busybody and was pleased to have genteel company. That settled, he set about arranging a carriage and funds for the journey.

It was left to her to decide how she would manage her departure from the house where John Ponsonby had installed her. She decided to write to him, informing him that she was to leave for London.

Within hours he arrived, and shouted, questioned, paced, begged her to tell him what she planned. This she would not do, and watching his angry gesticulations she felt an overwhelming sadness at the thought of the intimacy she had shared with him—this flawed, confused stranger. She waited for him to threaten her, perhaps to forbid her to leave, to remind her of the debt she owed him. But after a time he became quiet and turned from her. She could hear him taking deep, slow breaths and she waited.

'To lose you so suddenly is hard to comprehend. But I have always been waiting for this. I told you once you were wasted on Revesby; I never dared to tell you how much you were wasted on me. It was only a matter of time before someone saw that, as I once saw it. I hope he knows your worth.'

He turned and tried to smile, but there were tears in his eyes as he spoke. 'You owe me nothing—and I owe you a great deal. Two years of your company I have never deserved and will not forget.'

She looked at him as he stood, suddenly small and unhappy in front of her, and part of the great barrier of reserve she had held so firmly between them began to tremble at its edges. There were so many things for which she would never forgive him but, at the last, she felt more forgiveness than she had ever thought possible.

The next day she had left Lincolnshire.

EACH TIME HE VISITED Richmond, Banks planned to play the part of the modest benefactor, cutting short with proper grace any unbecoming shows of gratitude. But that was never how things were. The second time he called on her, when she had been in Richmond seven weeks, a very young maid he didn't recognise answered the door and showed him into a small front parlour. There he waited, for what seemed an unpardonable amount of time, his rehearsed speech fading from his thoughts.

At last the door opened enough for a head to fit round it.

'I'm afraid, sir, you are the victim of a misunderstanding.' She laughed. 'Have you been waiting here a *very* long time?'

He attempted to muster some dignity. 'A full ten minutes, I believe.'

She laughed again and came into the room properly. 'I'm sorry. I told Jenny I was working and would be down shortly, and then I lost myself in what I was doing. In any case, I assumed that after a time you would find your way up. You have watched me draw before, as I recall. And I give you full licence to interrupt me without invitation.'

'I should never dream—'

'Of course not,' she interrupted him, laughter in her voice but her face serious. 'That would be to take advantage of your position. I should have understood that you would never do that. But truly, sir'—her voice was now bright again—'I release you from that scruple. If I am to draw well I cannot always be running down here to make conversation.'

He hesitated, wrestling with his inner youthful self. Then he smiled. 'I would very much like to see your work,' he said.

She showed him the upstairs room where she had laid out her materials. She explained that Mrs Jenkins used little more than one room at the back of the house where she largely kept to her bed. 'Having me here gives her licence to be an invalid,' she said. 'I spend the morning sitting with her and running errands, but she sleeps at this time of the afternoon so it is a good time to work.'

They discussed some drawings of oak leaves and acorns that she had been working on. The drawings seemed very fine to him: fresh but intricate and correct in their detail.

She kept pressing him to comment, as if she wanted him to go further. Finally she turned to him and said, 'It is good of you to comment on my work, but if it does not draw your attention to its subject then it is not a success.'

He looked again at the image she had created, his eyes flicking from the picture in front of him to the woman behind it. 'Very well. You have drawn a collection of oak leaves and acorns. Both are brown but that is because they are last year's. Each leaf shows the standard indentations and each . . .' Suddenly he paused. 'I see,' he said. 'You are right to be impatient with me. The acorns have no stalks, they are connected directly to the twig. And the leaves have long stalks. This is a sessile oak, not an English oak. And found in the park, you say? I have never heard of sessile oak occurring here.'

She nodded, her eyes bright. 'It *is* interesting, is it not?'

From that conversation they moved on to other native trees, and Banks soon forgot the mood of his arrival. They were discussing a study she had done of beech leaves when she suddenly turned to him and said, 'You must not think me ungrateful.'

For a moment he was unbalanced by her directness.

'All this, I mean.' She waved her hand as if to embrace the room, the house and everything around them. 'I thank you for it every day. More often than that. And you scarcely know me. I must be for you a random act of kindness.'

He was honest enough to nod at this. 'That is how I explain things to myself. I call it a making good of Revesby's faults.' He paused, still looking at her. 'And yet there is something in the time we spend together that marks it as different. I came here today to patronise you. I know I did. But within moments of seeing you I remembered why it is not possible. You have never given me the opportunity.'

She smiled a little sadly. 'This place. My position here. It is the model of respectability. I look after an infirm old woman. I walk in the fresh air, properly accompanied. I draw a little. I dress respectably. Strangers might take me for a saint. But we both know that isn't true. There is something we have never spoken of . . .' She looked away, uncertain. 'Of the fact that the object of your charity is no longer what they call a maiden.'

Suddenly the joy went out of him. 'Please,' he said, standing abruptly. 'We have no need to talk of it. It pains me to think of it.'

She moved a little further away from him. 'I cannot help but think that the pain is more mine than yours,' she said softly. She paused a little while her words hung in the air between them. 'And you do me no favour by pretending I am what I am not.'

He rode back to London that evening a more thoughtful man.

EVEN THOUGH he was only three months returned from the *Endeavour*, he began to plan for his next long voyage. Cook had received word from the Admiralty to prepare for a second expedition, and Banks was invited to go with him. The success of their first venture had been so spectacular that a second had never been in doubt, but he was surprised how quickly it was proposed, with less than a year between their return and their next departure. It never occurred to him to decline the opportunity. Yet it came too soon. There was much work to be done on describing his *Endeavour* collection.

And then there was Harriet. Relations between them had never recovered from their three years apart. On his return from Lincolnshire he had called on her promptly. He explained to her his plan to go abroad again, used it to show the impossibility of his ever making a proper husband. The news of a second expedition so quickly after the first was not well received. There were tears when he spoke of it and reproaches that it was an excuse to break his promise. He pointed out that his ambition to travel had never been a secret. He declared that on his return he had fully intended their nuptials to go ahead, but had found such a change in her that he hardly felt it right to go on.

An interview with her guardian followed, very tense and formal. Banks regretted that he was not, as he had hoped, in a position to marry at this time; his travels prevented it. As he knew it was unreasonable to make the lady wait, he sought to be freed from his engagement. Frank words were exchanged. An agreement was reached. Banks left feeling guilty and miserable—and, to his own shame, greatly relieved.

One of the few places where his spirits were never low was the little house in Richmond, where the fears and concerns he took with him appeared petty on his arrival. She would listen to him quietly when he wanted to talk, but more often he found himself dismissing it all from his mind and talking about science and ideas again, newly alive with optimism. When he left her his half-formed plans were always a little more ordered, a fraction closer to being ready for the scrutiny of his peers.

When his plans for a second voyage began, of necessity, to take shape, she wanted to know everything: what orders Cook sailed under, what course was to be set, what his own hopes and aspirations were for the voyage. He found himself discussing at length the possibilities of new continents in the southern latitudes, what conditions might exist there, what life such land might support. When he finally made to leave she turned to him and said, 'One thing disappoints me. You seem too little excited at the prospect ahead of you. Were I a man there would be nothing else I could talk about.'

'Is that so? Yet when we first met in the Revesby woods, I was only a few weeks away from such an expedition and I remember that we scarcely talked of it. Our conversation was of lichen and woodland flowers.'

'Oh, but do not tell me you were not excited! You had a shine about you then that spoke of excitement in everything you did or saw or said.'

'And do I not have that shine now?'

She looked at him, her eyes suddenly tender. 'You are different now. It was new to you then. Now you have the world a little on your shoulders.'

It was a cue to pass to another subject but he felt a sadness at her words that seemed to prevent it. 'So I shine to you less?'

She wanted to reach out and take his hand and tell him that nothing shone in her life so brightly as he. But instead she searched for words that she was permitted to say. 'You shine with a different lustre now,' she said softly. 'You have less time for the things most real to you.'

'Yes,' he said after a moment's thought. 'I think that's true.' And suddenly, looking into her green eyes, without planning or reason, he went on, 'And I discover that one of the things most real is you.'

They were seated close to each other, and when he saw she was silent in surprise he reached across and let his fingers touch her cheek. A voice in his head he had never heard before told him, '*This is what love is.*' He leaned forward, and as she felt the first, warm touch of his lips she found her own mouth moving softly under his and heard somewhere far removed the words '*I love you.*'

10

Katya flew to Sweden and left me fretting. If Miss B hadn't died, where had she gone? She could have moved anywhere in London, to another man, under another name, to another parish. Even if we knew what the B stood for, it would still be impossible to find her. So after banging my head against the futility of the question, I decided to speculate a little. If it was impossible to find where she'd gone, perhaps we could at least find where she had come from. That prospect didn't seem so unlikely. According to the *Town & Country Magazine*, Banks had known her before he sailed with Cook, when she was of school age. When he got back three years later she was old enough to become his mistress. That would make her between thirteen and sixteen in 1768. Where might the wealthy Joseph Banks meet someone of that age whom he felt the need to rescue from economic distress? She could have been a tradesman's daughter or the daughter of one of the professional men he met in his day-to-day affairs. But I wasn't convinced that young aristocrats formed relationships so easily with the daughters of their tradesmen. For now I was prepared to hope they didn't. The option I kept coming back to was very different.

Banks inherited Revesby Abbey when he was a young man, and took his responsibilities seriously. He'd have been aware of the financial predicaments of the families around his estates, and it wouldn't be unconventional for a beneficent landowner to concern himself with the plight of an orphaned girl whose family had once been his neighbours. The village of Revesby would have been a relatively small place, after all. Small enough, in fact, to make a search through the parish records a reasonable idea.

I had a couple of days ahead of me with no teaching to do, and I still had keys to the rusty yellow car. I set off the following day.

LINCOLN IS a striking city. The hill it stands on lurches out of the surrounding flatness, topped by a cathedral that is all vertical lines reaching for the sky. The modern town is sprawled around its base and contains, along with a lot of shops, a labyrinthine one-way system, which eventually led me to a long-stay car park.

By then it was already after four and too late to begin at the archives, so instead I hauled my bag out of the car and set off up the hill to find myself somewhere to stay. It felt like a holiday and I was going to enjoy myself. Eventually I found a small, plush hotel near the top of the hill, tucked into the knot of old streets immediately below the cathedral. The reception area was thickly carpeted in red and the desk was the old-fashioned type with a bell and a visitors' book instead of a computer. It felt warm and smelt of wood fires, and somewhere out of sight there were bottles clinking gently as though someone was restocking the bar. It was also phenomenally expensive, but just then it didn't seem to matter. I was feeling reckless, and if this was all just folly, let it be folly on a noble scale.

That night I had dinner in a little restaurant close to the hotel, and afterwards I sat up late by the fire in the hotel bar, drinking big glasses of brandy and feeling that all was well with the world.

The following morning I checked out, left my bag at reception and strode off to find the county archives. Once I got there, a pleasant-faced woman with glasses sorted out my reader's card and showed me where to find the relevant microfilms, then left me to get on with it.

I'd been right about Revesby being a small place. It was the record of births that I was interested in, and it wasn't a long or difficult morning's work to find all the girls born in the 1750s whose names might fit the bill. My list for Revesby came out like this.

Jan 1st 1750	Mary, bastard daughter of [blank]
Sept 29th 1752	Mary, daughter of Richard Burnett & Elizabeth his wife
April 18th 1756	Mary, daughter of James Browne & Susanna his wife
Feb 20th 1757	Mary, daughter of William Burton & Anne his wife
Jan 18th 1759	Elizabeth, daughter of James Browne & Susanna his wife

When I sat back and looked over it I wasn't sure what I'd found, apart from a clear fondness among the Revesby parishioners for the name Mary. The name that leapt out at me was Burton, but there was a Browne there too and I wasn't too worried about the E on the end—spelling was fluid back then and the E might easily have got lost later. And although Mary Browne and Mary Burton were both on the young side, only twelve and thirteen when Banks set off on his voyage, either of them could have grown up to become Miss B. I felt I was getting somewhere.

My next step was to look at Revesby's record of deaths, as I knew from *Town & Country Magazine* that Miss B had become an orphan while Banks was away. This wasn't foolproof, of course—Miss B's father could have died somewhere quite different. But it was worth a try. A quick check came up with the deaths of only four adult males, but William Burton was one of them.

Jan 12th 1768	James Turner
Nov 7th 1768	William Burton
March 25th 1769	Dr Taylor
April 12th 1769	Richard Burnett

I noted the names down and looked at them, excitement growing inside me. James Browne had disqualified himself, it seemed, by living on for another eighteen years. But William Burton had died three months after Banks sailed, so his daughter Mary fitted on both counts . . . It wasn't much to go on, but my hands were sweating a little as I noted down the dates. If I was right, and Mary Burton was the woman in the picture, I could go back to London and try to trace her through the records. And if Hans Michaels was right, then finding her was the key to finding the Ulieta bird.

I found myself scanning through the remaining records, my eyes still hungry for detail. And it was that careless impulse that brought my whole theory crashing to the ground. The excitement was blown away in an instant because Mary Burton had been buried in Revesby alongside her father only six months after Joseph Banks returned to Britain.

I could have stayed longer and tried to think up some new theory, but I had a long drive home ahead of me, so I stored the lists I'd made in my jacket pocket, thanked the librarian, then set off back towards the cathedral in the mild, damp, deeply grey afternoon.

It was three fifteen by the time I arrived back at the hotel to collect my bag. Three fifteen is a ghostly time in county town hotels. Lunch is over and all the guests who plan to go out are out, and those who plan to stay in are probably snoozing in their rooms. A thick silence falls on everything except the clocks, which seize their moment and begin to tick louder.

It was just that sort of silence that greeted me when I reached the reception desk and my defiant striking of the bell did very little to dent it. I could see my bag behind the desk but it seemed hasty, somehow, to go round and fetch it, so I waited, leaning on the dark oak counter, looking idly at the various leaflets displayed there. After a few moments my eye fell on the guest register, still open at the page where I'd been the last person to sign. A familiar word caught my attention—*Mecklenburg*. My eye leapt to it and my blood began to pump a little faster: *Mecklenburg Hotel*. The words were written under the column headed 'Address', and to their left, in beautiful handwriting, was the name *Karl Anderson*. I checked the dates. He'd arrived a week ago and hadn't yet checked out.

This was the place where he'd come to find the bird.

IT WAS LATE when I got home. The phone was ringing as I opened the front door, but by the time I'd closed it behind me the ringing had stopped. I knew as I stood there in silence that something was wrong.

There was no mess this time, no broken window or shattered glass. Only a broken catch on a kitchen window where the ill-fitting frame had been levered open. I took it in with a dull sense of incredulity, then suddenly I felt angry, full of choking rage at the effrontery of it all. How *dare* someone come forcing their way in here?

I pulled the window closed, and began a quick, clinical inspection, my brain racing. There was no sign of any disturbance in the kitchen, and none in the hallway. My workshop seemed untouched too, the tools and chemicals still neat in their cupboards. My bedroom, then . . . I climbed the stairs two at a time, impatient to know the worst. This time, there was to be no lucky escape, no cryptic overtidiness. The room had been ransacked.

The worst thing was the paper. My old trunk had been pulled into the centre of the room and the contents scattered over every surface. All those old notes on extinct birds, never properly sorted but piled together with some rudiment of sense, were flung in all directions, a random diaspora of lost species. Someone had been through them all. And they had found nothing. I knew that. There was nothing to find.

I sat down on the edge of my bed and took a deep breath. It occurred to me that despite the chaos there may actually be nothing missing. If I rang the police, what would I report? Another theftless break-in. Yes. I'd report it. But first I wanted to think.

Initially, Anderson's story about the lost bird had stirred up old emotions, probably better left where I'd buried them. But now with my anger came a clarity. Looking around the bedroom, I realised why finding the Ulieta bird was important to me. Not for posterity, not for science, not even for the fame of being its finder. But to fill a hollow of discontent that had lain inside me too long; the same discontent I felt whenever I looked at the photograph by my bed, or thought of my days in Brazil. Finding the bird—holding it in my hands—would be my proof that even the most fragile things can sometimes cheat oblivion.

I was checking through the rest of the house when the phone rang. It was Gabby. Her lectures were over early, and she was flying back to London. We arranged to meet the following afternoon in a café near Queensway.

*T*hey lay in bed, naked together, long into the evening. It was a small bedroom, low-ceilinged, hung in shades of green and russet; the autumn light was fading quickly around them yet still touched her skin with the palest hint of gold. After the urgency of their first passion came a long, slow time of discovery in which they lay, hardly talking, each from time to time running their fingertips over the other as if to memorise an outline or reassure themselves that what they felt was real.

When the day was quite gone she rose to light the lamp. He watched as she swung herself upright and moved soundlessly, still naked, across the room. As the lamp flared she saw him watching her, his eyes moving over her body.

'I never learned to be coy,' she said simply.

'I would not change the way you are,' he replied. Then he held out his hand and pulled her back under the sheets and into his arms.

'And what of Mrs Jenkins?' she asked, teasing. 'Do you not consider this an abuse of her hospitality?'

'She will no doubt scold me for being alone with you,' he said with a shrug, 'but she will probably think the better of me.'

'She will do neither. She is asleep in her room and she won't emerge till morning. Martha told her we were taking tea in the drawing room.'

'What about Martha? Is she discreet?' he asked.

'Oh, yes. And she has been waiting for this for weeks. If half of what the gossips say is true, about what you got up to in the South Seas, you can hardly blame her for expecting a little more impatience and a little less scruple.'

He found himself blushing. It made her smile.

'They slander me abominably,' he said, 'but there *were* occasions . . . I'm prepared to admit I was not chaste for the entire duration of the voyage.'

'Ah . . .' She ran a hand across his chest. 'I'm glad you are prepared to admit that.' He waited for her to tease him, but in the silence that followed he realised her mood had changed. 'After all,' she said quietly, almost to herself, 'I have already admitted the same.'

She felt his body tensing, then he turned onto his side so that they lay facing each other, heads on the same pillow. 'I cannot imagine what it must be like knowing no alternative but to give yourself in that way,' he said quietly.

'No. But people suffer much worse. I've been lucky.'

'Men place such great store on virtue,' he continued. 'When you told me what had happened . . . it hurt me.'

'Yes, I saw. It surprised me. Why did it hurt?'

'It's hard to say.'

'Say it anyway.'

'When you told me about Ponsonby, I realised I was jealous.'

'Jealous of *him*?'

'Yes. I realised that I'd always thought of you as my discovery. Mine, not his.' Her smile made him smile back. 'But must I always be someone's?'

'Of course not.'

She smiled again. 'Know this.' She took his hand and placed it against her naked breast. 'Here, now, for as long as this night lasts, I *am* yours.'

'And beyond that?'

She shook her head. 'I can't tell you what lies beyond tonight. Not out there beyond this room.'

'I wish the rest of the world would vanish and leave us here for ever.'

She reached round him and ran the flat of her hand down his spine. 'None of it is there until you look at it,' she said, pulling him closer.

'I'll never look,' he said.

'You will,' she said, 'but kiss me first.'

'Always,' he whispered, and they could almost believe the world outside had fallen still for them.

That night, as Banks travelled back to London, he felt he had stumbled on something he had never imagined, someone who asked the questions he needed to answer and knew better than him whether his answers were true. And now he found . . . He blushed as he thought of how she had been with him that night, so alive and loving and challenging.

At New Burlington Street he got down from the carriage and walked the few streets to his friend Daniel Solander's dwelling. He shouted and knocked until the door was opened, then leapt up the stairs three by three. When he tumbled into his friend's study, Solander looked up from his desk and smiled.

'Which is it this time, Joseph?' he asked. 'A new idea or a new woman? Whichever it is, it is a more than usually exciting one by the look of it.'

And then, seeing his most trusted friend, Banks felt a change in himself so sudden that it was like missing a step that has always been there. He could only shake his head and say, 'Solander, I'm the most confounded fellow and I find I have completely forgotten why I called. No, please don't move. I have drunk too much brandy. It is far, far better I should leave.'

And Solander, to his astonishment, found himself looking at a closing door and listening to the sound of running feet descending his stairs.

11

Gabby's choice of café wasn't random. It was a place from our early days, back when we were setting up the project that later became *her* project. There was no denying that in those days we had been impossibly in love. Each step we took together seemed natural and automatic, from our very first meeting over the remains of the Spix's macaw, to our times in London, lobbying and fundraising and embracing a future together that even fifteen years later we had still not fully disentangled.

That life seemed hard to imagine now, I reflected, as I made my way up the Bayswater Road to meet her. When things went wrong between us we'd discovered the sort of differences that made all the good things unimportant. It had been me who walked away, but it was Gabby who had been most deceived: she thought she was linking her life to one like her own. She discovered, devastatingly and beyond all doubt, that I simply didn't share her single-mindedness. In fact I came to resent it with a fierce passion. I was emotional where she was professional, erratic where she was objective. By the time I began to question the work we were doing in the rain forest, the gap between us was too wide to bridge.

That afternoon I arrived slightly late at the café, having spent the morning shovelling my notes back into the trunk.

It was a small place: a counter and a coffee machine and five or six tables tucked away from the door. She was sitting at the far end, where we used to sit, and when she saw me she stood up.

'Hello, John,' she said, and that was all, but when I made my way to where she was standing she reached up and pressed her cheek against mine. I caught the scent of her hair, familiar and disorientating.

We ordered coffees and sat down, then looked at each other across the little round table.

She gave me that familiar half-smile. 'It feels strange to see you again so soon. After so long not seeing each other.'

It didn't feel strange to me. If anything it seemed frighteningly normal to be sitting with her again. She looked well and I told her so, though what I really meant to say was that she hadn't changed.

'You look well too,' she said. 'More relaxed.'

'Well, I've had fifteen years to work out what I want from life.'

She nodded. I was glad she didn't ask me what.

'I wanted to ask . . .' she began, and I could see her struggling for the right words. 'Do you still think of . . .?'

It was the subject that was always between us. Would always be between us. 'Yes,' I said slowly. 'I think of her all the time.'

She looked away briefly. Outside I could see cars and buses splashing through the December gloom.

'It's been a long time since then, John. We should have sorted things out before this. You've never met anyone since?'

'I suppose I haven't wanted to. What about you?'

She looked down at her coffee and shrugged. 'I've been busy.'

'Karl Anderson seems to like you.'

'He does.' Her voice was hard, defensive, but then she caught hold of herself and began to relax again. 'He's a good man, Fitz. Oh, I know he's gone commercial and that's unforgivable to some people. But they made that happen—all those academics who wouldn't give him a chance. Underneath he still cares. He just can't afford to let it show.'

'Does he want to marry you?'

She shrugged again. 'It isn't an issue. For either of us.'

I put down my coffee cup and looked at her. 'Look, Gabby, I need you to tell me what's going on.'

'What do you mean? Between me and Karl?'

'I mean about the Ulieta bird. There's something you're not telling me.'

She blew onto the top of her coffee. 'I don't know what you mean.'

'Someone broke into my house that night we met. And someone broke in again yesterday and riffled through my notes. Someone's going to a lot of trouble to find that bird. Why? What's it really worth? I can't work it out, but I'd be an idiot not to realise it's worth more than anyone's telling me.'

Gabby shook her head. 'No, Fitz. It's true what Karl told you. That specimen's worth a lot, but not much more than Karl offered you.'

'So why does everyone seem to want it so badly?' I could feel myself growing angry. 'Look, I'm not just going to sit here like a fool. There *must* be something about that bird that makes it valuable. I want to know what.'

Gabby leaned forward and touched my hand. 'Oh, Fitz, you really don't get it, do you? Can't you see? This is about more than just your precious bird. No one really cares about that. Oh, I know you do, and it's true that Ted Staest will pay a few thousand dollars for it. But Karl isn't stuck over here in the middle of winter for that. It isn't the bird he's after.'

'Then what . . .?' I was blinking at her now, feeling foolish.

Gabby reached out and uncurled my fingers from my cup, then took them between hers. I thought about moving them away, but I let them stay.

'I shouldn't tell you,' she said. 'I promised not to.'

'What?' I tightened my fingers round hers.

'It's quite a tale. Have you ever heard of a French artist called Roitelet?'

Something stirred in my memory. 'Vaguely. It rings a bell.'

'Don't worry, no one knows much about him. He was a botanical artist in the last half of the eighteenth century. He isn't recorded as being on any of the major expeditions, but we know he travelled because he came back with a collection of amazing botanical paintings. Twenty-four of them. Apparently they were brilliant, the finest anywhere at a time when botanical art was flourishing.'

'What do you mean, "apparently"? What happened?'

'The owner kept them in his town house in Paris, and the place was ransacked during one of the Paris uprisings. Only three survived. Last year one was auctioned in New York for over a hundred thousand dollars.'

'OK . . . So what's that got to do with the Ulieta bird?'

Gabby smiled. 'This is where it all gets complicated. You see, all through the nineteenth century there were rumours about another collection of Roitelet paintings that had ended up in England. In about 1850 a gentleman called Finchley wrote a jokey letter to a friend about something that had happened when he was touring Lincolnshire. He'd heard tell of a local man who reputedly owned a preserved specimen of a rare bird, and out of curiosity he found the man and saw the specimen for himself. From his description, it seems certain that this was the Ulieta bird. But what intrigued Finchley was that the owner of the specimen insisted on opening up the glass case and showing Finchley some papers that had been hidden under the green cloth the bird was standing on. To Finchley's amazement, the papers were a collection of studies of English wildflowers by Roitelet—twelve of them in pristine condition. The man had no idea what they were worth, and wasn't very interested when Finchley told him. He insisted that the bird was a family heirloom, and the pictures could happily stay where they'd been put. Finchley found the whole thing amusing, assuring his friend that the stubbornness of the man had been more than a match for the generous offers he had made. He thought it was unlikely that any amount of wealth in the world would be enough to move the pictures from the spot.'

'I see . . .' I murmured. 'But isn't that all too tenuous for words? Even if we believe in a collection of French paintings turning up in some backwoods part of Lincolnshire, surely there's no way they'd still be there? And not still with the bird? There have been generations of people since then who've had the opportunity to sell them off.'

Gabby nodded, still cradling her coffee. 'You'd think so, wouldn't you? But the thing is that no other Roitelets have ever come to light. Also, Finchley's letter gives no details of where he'd found the bird or who owned it. It's almost as if he was deliberately teasing his friend by not telling. So there's still the possibility that the paintings are out there somewhere.'

'So Karl wanted to use me to find the pictures.'

'Not use you, Fitz. Karl knew you'd be interested in finding the bird and he was happy to let you have the money for it. He's found a clue that he thinks points him to where the bird might be.'

'I know. A letter.' I looked at her. 'But Anderson's a businessman. I can't see him spending money on something as vague as this. His chances of finding anything at all must be tiny.'

'Twelve paintings by Roitelet, Fitz. If each of them went for a hundred thousand dollars . . . Well, you can do the sums. And as a collection, they'd probably be worth even more. There's just one snag.'

'What's that?'

'Karl's having problems finding the bird.' Gabby leaned a little closer to me, earnest and intense and beautiful. 'It was all to do with a house sale. Karl traced the bird to a big house somewhere that was broken up after the war. He thought it was all sorted. But apparently the bird wasn't where he expected it to be. Now his people are going through all the sale records again, trying to find out what they've missed.'

'Interesting. Do you know where this house was?'

'Karl didn't say. But he's in Lincolnshire at the moment.' She paused, looking at her hands. 'Have you thought of anything at all that might help?'

I decided to trust her. 'Look, Gabby, I'm not pretending I know anything useful but I've got an idea I'm going to follow. It's about a woman Joseph Banks knew when he was young. I think there may be a connection with the bird. It might come to nothing but I'll see what happens.'

'And if you find it?'

I looked down. 'Let's find it first. We can talk about it then.'

She flashed me a warm, affectionate smile. 'Well, seeing as there's no one in your life to be jealous, I think you could buy me dinner tonight.'

GABBY HAD ALWAYS BEEN good company, and that night she was at her most entertaining. We drank white wine and talked about things that had nothing to do with Karl Anderson. As the evening mellowed around us, she became quite daring, telling me a series of scandalous and probably slanderous tales about acquaintances we had in common. Even when we talked about conservation, the mood of the evening stayed the same. Gabby leaned forward and spun her dreams, and as she talked I found the sounds and the colours of the rain forest coming back to me. The wine must have made me sentimental and I found myself missing them.

There were still difficult things between us, but that night they didn't seem to matter. The old warmth flowed without friction.

As we said goodbye outside the Mecklenburg there was a pause when an unasked question seemed to pass between us. I hesitated, and Gabby smiled sadly, then kissed me on the cheek.

'Good night, Fitz,' she said, and stepped away.

I stood in the dark and watched her disappear behind the inviting lights of the waiting hotel.

As I walked back home I switched on my mobile and found a voicemail message from Katya. She sounded excited.

'Fitz, I think I may have found something.'

KATYA CAME HOME the following day. She looked tired and a little worn.

'Sit down,' I said, 'and I'll get you a beer.'

'That sounds good.'

In the kitchen she dropped into a chair and was watching me open the bottles when she noticed the twisted window-catch. She was on her feet immediately, peering at it. 'Someone's broken in again? Did they take anything?'

I shook my head and smiled. 'Nothing to steal.'

'But why?'

'It turns out that finding our bird might be worth rather more than we thought. It's a long story. But first I want you to tell me what you've been up to. Here, drink this.'

'OK.' She stretched and looked happy. 'Well, I've been digging around. In the Fabricius papers. You remember—the naturalist who knew Banks. There's an archive of his stuff in Denmark. My father arranged for me to get access to it. I was there for two whole days. But I found something.' She picked up her bag and took out a notebook. 'It was one of the first letters I looked at. I almost didn't notice it.'

'Go on. What did you find?'

'A letter to Fabricius dated 1778 from a Frenchman called Martin. Apparently, Fabricius had tried to buy some drawings from him and this was a letter of refusal. There was a PS at the bottom, and I wrote it down: "I assume from your last letter that the picture of *Turdus ulietensis* you have received from Lincolnshire is by the same artist. I wish you joy of it. I'm sure it is fine work." *Turdus ulietensis*—that's our bird, isn't it?'

I could barely reply. Katya had stumbled across proof that our lost bird had survived its time in Joseph Banks's collection. A year or so after it was last seen there, someone had been making a painting of it—someone somewhere in Lincolnshire.

'That's stupendous,' I managed at last. 'It proves the bird survived Banks's collection. *And* it gives us a good idea about where to look.'

'Yes, I got really excited, and I thought I'd find a lot more. But I don't think there's anything else.' Katya told me about the rest of Fabricius's papers. As she talked, the tiredness left her and she became animated. Most of the correspondence she'd been through had been about scientific issues, and none of it mentioned Banks. 'Do you mind me doing all that?' she asked when her account was over.

'No, of course not.'

'I felt a bit embarrassed, as though I was barging in . . .' She looked at me for a moment. 'Anyway, tell me what's been going on here.'

'Hard to know where to start. I suppose the real discovery came yesterday, when I met up with Gabby.'

'Oh?' She took a swig from her beer but didn't look round.

'Before that I'd been up to Lincolnshire. And guess who I found there?'

Katya sat and listened while I told her how I'd ended up in Lincoln, and about my discovery of Karl Anderson's whereabouts.

'Anyway,' I concluded, 'I didn't come up with anything amazing.' I reached into the jacket on the back of my chair. 'Though for a moment I thought I had. Here, take a look. These women were all born in Revesby.'

I spread the paper on the table.

Jan 1st 1750	*Mary, bastard daughter of [blank]*
Sept 29th 1752	*Mary, daughter of Richard Burnett & Elizabeth his wife*
April 18th 1756	*Mary, daughter of James Browne & Susanna his wife*
Feb 20th 1757	*Mary, daughter of William Burton & Anne his wife*
Jan 18th 1759	*Elizabeth, daughter of James Browne & Susanna his wife*

'I got quite excited by Mary Burton. When I found her father had died while Banks was away, I really thought I was on to something . . .'

I looked up and realised that Katya wasn't listening. She was staring at the paper, her lips moving as if she were calculating something.

'Here, Fitz. Look here.' She pointed at the second name on the list. 'That's roughly the right year, isn't it? That would make her about sixteen when Banks left, about nineteen when he got back?'

'Yes . . .' I wasn't sure where this was leading.

'*Mary Burnett.* You see?'

'But *Burnett* doesn't end in an N.'

'That letter . . . The letter written by Captain Cook at the start of his second voyage. About a woman pretending to be a man. *Remember*?'

I remembered the letter but I still didn't see the connection.

'*Burnett.* I'm sure that's what the woman was calling herself. *Mr Burnett.*'

In the end we had to go upstairs and find the photocopy of the letter before I was convinced. But Katya was right: '*Every part of Mr Burnetts behaviour and every action tended to prove that he was a Woman, I have not met with a person that entertains a doubt of a contrary nature.*'

'What do you think?' she asked triumphantly.

'It's hard to tell. It could just be a coincidence.'

'And look here.' Katya picked up the other piece of paper that I'd laid out on the table. 'Her father died while Banks was abroad. What if she and Banks were being discreet when she became his mistress and used a name that wasn't hers? That would make sense. And Burnett isn't too far from Brown, is it? *Burnett, brunette, brune, brown . . .*'

I sat back and looked at her before replying. 'We need to go back to Lincoln. How soon can you leave?'

WE DROVE NORTH through the grey light of a day that never seemed to get started. The flat Lincolnshire plain slipped past in various shades of ochre and brown, and mostly we were silent beneath the throaty straining of the engine, comfortable enough with each other to retreat into separate places.

We arrived in the middle of the afternoon but it felt later. The lights of the small, plush hotel where I'd stayed before were already on, and inside there was warmth and the immediate promise of comfort. A dreamy trickle of piano music came from the wood-panelled bar and somewhere close we could smell a wood fire.

Katya looked around her. 'Wow,' she said. 'Very nice. And very English. Can I afford it?'

'On me,' I said. 'When we find the bird I'll dock it from your share.'

She looked at me, but didn't argue. It was just another thing I was happy to let go, another reckoning to be dealt with later.

We checked in and dropped our bags in our rooms, then returned to the streets so Katya could get her bearings. It was a Sunday and the town was quiet, but it was bitterly cold now that the light had faded. Old-fashioned lamps lit the narrow streets around the cathedral and the places still open—a café, a bookshop, a restaurant—threw welcoming glances onto the cobbles. Looking up, we could see the cathedral outlined against the sky and behind it the clouds, now broken into fragments and giving way to stars. There would be a frost.

When we reached the cathedral close we could hear organ music.

'Do you want to go in and listen?' I asked Katya.

'Not my thing, I think.' Katya put her hand on my shoulder. 'But you go if you want to. I'll head back and have a shower. I'll meet you in the bar.'

So I went alone and sat in the shadows of the dimly lit cathedral and let the music envelop me. There was no service, just the organist practising for evensong. By the time I left I felt relaxed and soothed and found myself looking forward to a glass of wine in the hotel bar.

I wasn't anticipating what I found when I got there: in one corner, near the fireplace, Karl Anderson was lounging in one of the big leather arm-chairs. Opposite him, in a slim red dress, was Gabby. And between them, poking its head out of a large silver bucket, a bottle of champagne.

Snow fell in Richmond in late November and lingered until February, a white cloak drawn over their past and muffling the present. He would arrive on horseback, a dark figure against the white, the snow turning to ice in the folds of his cloak. Inside he'd find the fires crackling and the smell of hot wine and spices thick in the air. Even when he travelled at dusk he would find the lamps burning for him, the windows glowing with welcome, and always in the green bedroom a single lamp and a fire that turned the russet drapes to amber. The place seemed timeless, wrapped in winter and wood smoke as if nothing that happened in the rest of the world would ever change it.

She never looked out for his coming but came to recognise the sound of his approach. First the chimes of a harness, a boy running to take his horse, then footsteps, a firm knock, and Jenny the maid scampering eagerly to answer it. Then she would hear his voice—always indistinct but low and merry—and would put down her things so that when he entered she was free to rise and welcome him. But best of all was his arrival in darkness when the house had settled for the night, the times, always unexpected, when he had risen in the middle of a London evening and, making his excuses, returned to his house, there to cause consternation among his ostlers by calling for a horse.

When he arrived in daylight she put away all thoughts of her work and they spent the afternoons by the fire or walking through the frozen woods, talking of things that mattered less than the fact of their talking. Sometimes their conversation was brilliant—about ideas beyond every bound of reality. Sometimes they talked of things that made them laugh for reasons they could never explain.

And as they talked, she would forget the past that had brought her there and any fears for the future. The trees and the fields around them, even the cart-pocked tracks, seemed to lie unconscious, waiting for spring to restart their clocks.

For him the snow seemed to obliterate the stains of the past, all the things that marred his perfect happiness. At night they would lull themselves by the fire and dream of a world where everything, including themselves, could be anything they wished.

'You would stay here and grow plants,' she said, 'and devise a way to farm pineapples on your precious Fens.'

'Too cold,' he said.

'You would heat the water with underground pipes and people would come from Brazil to bathe there.'

He mused on the thought. 'In that case, you would tour the shires of England and produce the definitive work on mosses and lichen. And for your pains you would be elected unanimously to the Royal Society.'

'Too young and a woman.'

'You would write under the name of Tom Brown the Elder.'

'Ah! And am I only ever to paint lichen?'

'Very well, you would travel with me and you would draw while I collected. Between us we would create a collection that would be the wonder of the world.'

'A woman at sea?'

'I should disguise you as a boy.'

'For the sake of art only?' She reached her face up to his and very lightly brushed her lips against his neck.

'Well,' he mused, beginning to smile, 'perhaps not purely for your drawings.' And he pulled her to him and kissed her while she laughed.

WHEN FEBRUARY drew to a close, the snow began to give way to water and their time together became quieter, parting more painful. It was only four months until he was due to leave on the *Resolution*. Neither wanted to think of it ending, but each day they did. It made both of them less playful. When they did laugh together there was a wildness about them, a desperation to seize the moment and hold it for as long as it could be held.

They lay close to each other one night with only the fire lighting the room and he said, 'Come with me.'

She was lying half on him, her head on his chest. She might have been asleep but at his words she raised her head to look at him. He expected her to laugh, to tease him, but instead she held his gaze for a long time.

'I couldn't,' she replied at last.

'You could!' With sudden energy he rolled her onto her side, then moved to kneel beside her. 'You could join the ship in Madeira, away from prying eyes. I would tell Cook that one of my draughtsmen was joining us there.'

'Joseph! It isn't possible, a woman at sea pretending to be a man. The arrangements on board . . .'

'I will have more space for my party this time. It is already being arranged. I will demand an extra cabin, next to mine. They won't refuse me that.'

She looked away from him, trying to imagine herself with cropped hair, tightly jacketed.

'Just think!' he cried. 'You could see the oceans and the tropics for yourself, see all the things we talk of with your very own eyes. You could stand with me on unmapped lands, pick out the Southern Cross in the night sky. You could smell the brine in the wind as we round the Cape. All those things you've imagined, you could see them for yourself! Think of it!'

It was impossible, she knew, madness born of the long nights and the winter stars. Yet the firelight wove his words into bright images and her dreams seemed, for a moment, close enough to reach. She would be prepared to risk a great deal to touch just one of them. And what did she have that she was putting at risk? Only him. And she would lose him anyway.

She knew they were deluding themselves. On the passage to Madeira she might pass unnoticed, but once they were there it would be impossible to avoid the speculation of others, even if she spent her days botanising in the hills. And even if she were not exposed immediately, discovery would come when the *Resolution* arrived. There would be no fooling Cook; Banks had always talked admiringly of his perspicacity. At some point he would know the truth and what then? If it was before they departed from Madeira she could slink away blushing and leave Joseph to repair his fences and continue the journey. At the end of a three-year voyage it would all have been forgotten. But if it was when they were at sea, what then? Could she live with the thought of discovery, of humiliation? There could be no quick escape. Yet even if Cook insisted on her leaving the ship when they put into Rio de Janeiro, she would already have lived dreams she had never dared to believe in.

Banks thought less of these things. It can be dangerous to be in love and an optimist. He was still a little intoxicated by his own successes and he knew his plan would work because he would make it work. The realities were less important than his determination to overcome them. But there were moments when even he became suddenly uneasy. The pressures of preparing for a second voyage were different. Last time he had not been burdened by the attentions of countless botanists, taxonomists, philosophers, priests, chandlers, inventors, artists, merchants, beggars and optimistic younger sons, all eager to claim acquaintance, to offer advice, to detail their talents or to ask most blatantly for preferment. And worse, his plans for his party and their accommodation on board were not going as he had wished.

He felt strongly that the problem was Cook. For their first voyage, the captain had opted for a squat, round-bottomed Whitby collier, a boat as slow as it was stable. The *Endeavour* had served them well but such ships were small and cramped, and not large enough to accommodate Banks's ambitions both scientific and personal. Yet, to his dismay, Cook refused the frigate offered by the Admiralty and insisted on another collier. Banks's frustration at this decision began to manifest itself in increasingly peevish letters to the Admiralty arguing his need for an expanded entourage and the space to accommodate them. This time around, Banks had influence and the Admiralty agreed to certain alterations and additions to the *Resolution* in order to increase the space available. Banks would, after all, have the accommodation he demanded.

The result was a victory of sorts but he still felt wounded that his recommendation of a larger vessel had not been given more weight. Worse than that, the whole issue had brought him into conflict with Cook, a man he respected and with whom he had always previously been in accord. This shook Banks's confidence a little and made him wonder if Cook would be quite so quiescent in the matter of the extra passenger as Banks had anticipated. Yet even as he paced the floors of his house in New Burlington Street, he knew that a little of his anger had its source elsewhere. The thought that he proposed at best to deceive Cook, at worst to place him in a position that would both embarrass and anger him, was not a pleasant one. Banks had always esteemed the navigator and been inspired by his leadership and honesty. Smuggling his mistress on board ship was hardly a demonstration of such qualities. And the more guilt he felt about his own behaviour, the more Cook's virtues began to irritate him.

Strangely, as his doubts grew, she became more reckless. Summer came early and the days became hot. Her passage to Madeira was confirmed, the arrangements made for money and accommodation. It was a fantasy that seemed to have its own life and logic. She rehearsed in her mind every step of the journey: the carriage to Southampton, embarking on the *Robin*, her voice as she did so, her name, her manner, her conduct. She practised her lines and stared down her fears before they grew tall enough to engulf her. During that period, Banks needed to be so much in London that his visits became shorter and irregular. That made it easier for her to imagine how her Richmond refuge would be if he were gone and she remained. The more she reflected, the more she knew she could not stay without him. It mattered to her less and less what happened next as long as it was not that.

BY THE TIME he rode to meet her, four days before she was due to depart, he had made his decision. The excitement of the game had gone on long enough but now they could maintain it no longer. They had planned that night as their last together before he saw her on her way. Now he would tell her she must not go, forbid it if necessary. It had been a mirage of his creation and the fault lay at his door: he would beg her forgiveness and they would plan instead their lives on his return. His decision brought with it an immeasurable relief.

On his arrival in Richmond, Martha met him solemn-faced and handed him a note written in a now familiar, sloping hand.

My darling, forgive me. If I spend another night in your arms you will make me change my mind. It is too easy to be afraid with you beside me. Alone, I must be brave. And I know that you will tell me not to go. So I have gone already. It is what I must do. I will wait for you in Madeira. Find me there.

There was no signature, but at the foot of the page there was one more line of writing which, at the last, she had added in small, less certain letters:

It is dark now and there is something in the wind that makes me afraid. Whatever befalls us I will always think of you. If you can, think of me.

12

B y checking into Karl Anderson's hotel again, I had planned to disconcert him. I'd hoped that it might persuade him I was hot on the trail, perhaps fluster him into making a mistake. As things turned out, the confusion was all mine.

Anderson rose to his feet as soon as he saw me, then came forward with a smile, his hand extended to shake mine. 'Ah, Mr Fitzgerald! We saw from the book that you had checked in. Welcome.' He might have owned the place. His grip was firm and suitably proprietorial.

'Hello, Fitz. I thought I might see you here.' Gabby was also on her feet.

'I thought you were in London,' I replied, trying to sound casual and almost certainly failing.

Anderson was quick to ooze unction over any trace of awkwardness. 'I rang Gabriella today and urged her to join me here to celebrate. I have a feeling that this may be a good week.'

Gabby rested her hand on his elbow. 'Karl thinks he may have found the bird.' Her eyes met mine. Beautiful eyes. But hard to read.

Anderson signalled for an extra glass, then put his hand on my shoulder and guided me over to where they'd been sitting. 'Come and drink. You have to admit that the recovery of such a rare specimen is worth celebrating.'

'You've actually seen it?' I asked, still standing.

'Not yet.' The smile didn't flicker. 'But I expect to.'

'I see.' I dropped into an armchair. 'Then there's still hope.'

'Hope?' Anderson feigned surprise. 'Ah, of course! A few minutes ago I bumped into your charming companion. Katya, I believe her name is. I understand that you have been making investigations of your own.'

'I have one or two ideas,' I told him.

'Ideas about the Fabricius papers?'

That caught me off-balance. It hadn't occurred to me that Katya would tell him about her trip to Denmark.

'I can assure you that trail doesn't lead anywhere,' he went on. 'Joseph Banks's mistress and all that. I've been down all those alleys and they're all dead ends. If you'd told me I could have saved you some trouble. You see, I know exactly where the bird was at the turn of the century and I think I know where it went after that. Remember, I've had a team of researchers working on this for months. Today they spoke to someone, a farmer whose family once lived near here. Soon I may be able to show you the bird itself.'

'And the pictures?' I asked, watching him closely.

'Pictures?' He looked calmly across at Gabby. 'Ah, yes. The paintings by Roitelet. You will forgive me for not mentioning them earlier. In such situations a degree of discretion is always sensible.'

'And you think you'll find them when you find the bird?'

'It seems a reasonable hope. Of course, they may not be by Roitelet at all. But the rumours are most persistent and Finchley is a reliable witness. I hope to know tomorrow for certain. But I have a very good feeling.'

At that point a movement behind me caught Anderson's eye and he rose to his feet again. I turned round to see Katya hesitating at the door of the bar, all in black, her hair very dark. Anderson beckoned her over.

'Join us,' he said. 'We'll open another bottle.'

I can't say it was the easiest of evenings, though Anderson seemed relaxed. He kept the conversation away from the Ulieta bird, telling us instead about his time as a young palaeontologist in America. The stories were good ones and they made Katya laugh. But when he began to make arrangements for the four of us to eat together I'd had enough, and was quick to tell him that Katya and I had booked a table elsewhere. Outside, when we'd both found our coats, I had to admit to Katya that it wasn't true.

'I just didn't want to spend the evening with Anderson,' I told her.

She looked at me a little strangely. 'He seems very friendly. And he's entertaining too. Not how I imagined at all.' She put her hand on my arm and squeezed it slightly, guiding me down the narrow street. 'But he's very used to winning,' she said. 'I'm not sure that's something I like.'

There was something else I had to say. 'I didn't think you'd tell him all about your Fabricius research. I thought that was between us.'

She looked hurt. 'Of course it is. I only told him I'd been looking at those papers. I didn't tell him what I'd found.'

'He seemed to know all about it. He said it was a dead end.'

She stopped and looked up at me. 'Did you tell Gabriella about it?'

'Gabby?' I felt myself blushing. That afternoon in the Queensway café . . .

Katya watched me for a moment, then shrugged and walked on. Dinner that night wasn't a great success.

THE NEXT DAY we were in the county archives practically as soon as they opened. The librarian recognised me.

'People beginning with B, isn't it?' she asked with a smile as we began to move towards the microfilm readers.

'Not this time,' I told her. 'This time it's only people called Burnett.'

She nodded at that. 'Did you have a particular one you're looking for?'

'Not really. We're going to start off with a Mary Burnett. After that we'll take any we can find.'

That was all we had by way of a plan. It didn't seem much, especially given Anderson's display of confidence the night before, but I was living in hope that his plan might go wrong, that something in all his relentless research might prove flawed.

We found the relevant rolls of film and checked them intently, edging slowly down the parish lists. We checked all the deaths for the next hundred years. There was no further mention of Mary Burnett. Then, still hoping for a miracle, we began to check the records of neighbouring parishes. We stopped for sandwiches at lunchtime, then carried on. Next to me Katya was all bristling efficiency. Somehow the night before had broken the flow of our understanding.

By four o'clock our eyes were aching from the screens, and the list of Burnetts we'd found was becoming increasingly meaningless. And we still hadn't found any other references to Mary Burnett.

At four thirty we called it a day and packed up our notes. While Katya disappeared to find the ladies, I lingered by the main desk where the library staff were beginning to pack up.

The librarian we'd spoken to earlier clearly thought I looked downcast. 'No luck?' she asked.

'I'm afraid not. We found some Burnetts but not the ones we wanted.'

She looked around the reading room. 'There's a gentleman who often comes in here to do his family tree. He was telling me the other day that he was looking for Burnetts. It struck me this morning as soon as you said the name. I was going to point him out to you if he came in. He's here quite often, so perhaps if you come back tomorrow . . . His name's Bert.'

Before we left the building, Katya and I agreed to split up and meet again at seven to go through our notes. That arrangement made, she didn't wait for me: I watched her step out into the gathering gloom, her face buried in the collar of her coat. Twenty yards down the road she turned and saw I was still watching her. She raised her hand and gave me a shy wave. A moment later she was out of sight.

It lifted my spirits, and I was about to follow her into the dark when the friendly librarian called out to me. 'Excuse me, sir. I thought this might help.' She pushed a scrap of paper into my hand and gave me a rather surprising wink before bustling away.

The paper, when I unfolded it, had the name *Bert Fox* written on it, and next to it, a phone number. I hadn't anything better to do, so I took out my mobile and called it. After three or four rings a male voice answered.

'Excuse me,' I began, realising I hadn't worked out what to say. 'Is that Bert Fox?'

'Yeah.' His voice was gruff but not unfriendly.

'Look, you don't know me. My name's Fitzgerald. I've spent all day in the county archives and the librarian there said you might be able to help me. I'm trying to trace someone called Burnett.'

'That would've been Tina. In the library, I mean, I always tell her what I'm working on. Which one are you looking for?'

I told him I was looking for a woman who'd lived in London in the 1770s, someone who might be the Mary Burnett born in Revesby in 1752.

He thought about it. 'Well, I'm afraid Revesby isn't really my area, but if you want to talk family trees come round. I'm in all evening.'

He lived a bus ride away, in a street of tall red-brick Edwardian villas. The front gardens were bounded by dark hedges spotted with laburnum trees or yews, still dripping after the last shower of rain. I rang the bell.

My host turned out to be someone quite unexpected. He was tall and wiry but slightly stooped, and the little hair he still had was tied back in a long silver ponytail. He was wearing a white, baggy, collarless shirt and a brown suede waistcoat, and his face was creased with lines that suggested both smiles and frowns.

'You're the Burnett man?' he asked and beckoned me indoors. 'Come on in. I'm working, but I can talk.'

At first glance, the room he showed me into seemed to be in chaos. There were shelves and tables everywhere, each one densely packed with ancient wind-up gramophones. Scattered around, on the tables and on the floor, were screws and levers and moulded chunks of metal in weird shapes. An enormous Anglepoise lamp shone brilliantly onto the table in the centre of the room where a gramophone appeared to lie in a thousand pieces.

'This is what I do,' he said. 'Gramophones. You'd be surprised how much work there is.' He indicated the pieces on the table, near a large sofa. 'Some gent brought this one up from Kent. Here, take a seat.'

I found an empty patch of sofa large enough to sit on and perched myself there. A record tipped from the arm of the chair and slid into my lap.

'A seventy-eight,' I commented, peering at it.

He waved his hand around the room. 'All of them are. Great sound. The only way you can hear them properly is on one of these.'

I waited patiently while he gave me an impassioned speech about the glories of early sound recording, smoking continuously as he talked.

'So tell me,' I said, eventually changing the subject, 'you're working on a family tree?'

He nodded, cigarette clutched firmly in the corner of his mouth. 'Yeah. I do it for my mum. She loves that kind of stuff. She's over a hundred. Still lively, though.' I made a hasty recalculation of his age. I'd taken him for about sixty but now I could see he was older. Late sixties, seventies perhaps. 'Can't say I don't enjoy it, though,' he went on. 'It's a bit like one of these things.' He indicated the work in front of him. 'Putting bits together in the right order. Finding what you need to fill the gaps.'

'And what's your interest in people called Burnett?'

'There's Burnetts on my dad's side.' He began rooting around among the bits on the table in front of him. 'I did my mum's side first. That was quite easy. They were local gentry really. Not that you ever really finish something like that, do you? There's always someone you haven't found.'

That seemed a good cue to tell him the little I knew about Mary Burnett of Revesby, and about our failed attempts to find any other references to her.

He shook his head. 'Don't think I can help you. She's earlier than the ones I'm interested in, and Revesby isn't really my bit of the county. My family all come from further north, the other side of Lincoln. And I've never come across any Mary Burnett.'

'So it was your grandfather who married a Burnett?'

'Nah.' He took a swift drag at his cigarette. 'Goes back much further than that. It was my granddad's granddad, Matthew Fox, born 1764.'

'It must have taken some work to go back that far.'

'Nah, it wasn't too hard. Fox is an easy name, and the Foxes didn't move around much. Makes them easier to track. They were tenant farmers or the like. All in the Ainsby area.'

'Hang on, hang on. Did you say *Ainsby*?'

'Yeah, that's right. Ainsby.'

'You mean Ainsby is a *place*?'

'Yeah. Northwest of here. Small village. Not much of a place now.'

I stood up quickly. 'I don't want to be rude, Mr Fox, but do you mind if I rush off? There's something I really need to check. I think you might have told me something really, really important.'

If he was surprised at my sudden exit he didn't show it. He came to the door with me and then watched as I hurried out into the night. It was all I could do to stop myself from running.

*T*he days before the *Resolution* sailed were among the worst of Banks's life. The Navy Board had challenged the seaworthiness of the *Resolution*. The pilot charged with taking her out of the Thames had been so alarmed at her handling he had refused to take her beyond the Nore. She was branded crank and unseaworthy and the Admiralty had insisted that the changes made to accommodate Banks's party be reversed. The extra cabins were to be ripped out.

Bitterness began to consume him. Cook had been against him from the start, he decided. The Navy Board was made up of his enemies. People jealous of his success and resentful that a civilian should have any say in maritime matters. Lord Sandwich at the Admiralty was stubborn or misguided or ill-advised. All Banks's raging seemed unable to sway them. Nevertheless, he vowed to make his plan work and spent those final days restating his case in the strongest terms. Indeed, his temper became so out of check that each interview, each letter, began to teeter on the brink of angry confrontation.

Unsurprisingly, Cook's views prevailed. Banks was rich, famous and well connected, with prominent friends and a good deal of influence, but when it came to dispatching an expensive expedition to the other side of the world, the opinions of the professional seafarer held sway. Banks fumed.

Later—many years later—he was better able to understand the emotions that gripped him in those few days. At the time, however, nothing was clear. Banks had spent *his* money and *his* time putting together a team of unparalleled talents to advance the course of human learning and now he was to be thwarted by stubbornness and ignorance. He felt deeply let down, hurt on the most personal level that his opinion had been so easily set aside. He could never again sail with Cook after such an act of perfidy.

And underneath it all was the thought of that slim figure sailing to Madeira on board the *Robin*. How could he arrive and tell her she was to return alone while he went on? How admit to her that he had been so publicly humiliated in his attempt to secure her quarters? Their meeting in Madeira had been one he had been anticipating with a sensual thrill. Now it simply tasted bitter.

He continued to reason and rage right to the brink of departure but there were to be no more changes of heart. A letter to the Admiralty from the Navy Board dismissed his objections out of hand. It implied that Banks was not fit to comment on naval matters. Furthermore, the Board argued, even after the alterations were reversed, Banks's accommodation on the *Resolution* was very nearly everything he had asked for, save for the loss of one small cabin.

One cabin! Banks found it impossible to describe his emotions. That cabin meant everything. White-faced with anger, he wrote to the Admiralty saying that the treatment he had received made it impossible for him to achieve the goals he had set himself. He had no alternative but to withdraw. At the same time he wrote to Cook and asked that all his equipment and effects be removed from the ship.

The letters dispatched, Banks remained in his study, thinking of her at sea, travelling ahead of him, dressed as a young man about to begin his studies in botany. She would arrive there in little more than a week. And how happy that arrival would make her.

13

The bus got me back to the centre of Lincoln a little after seven, and Katya was already waiting for me in the hotel bar. I'd dreaded finding Anderson there too, but the room was nearly empty. I think Katya knew that something had happened when I didn't even stop at the bar, just went straight to her and sat down, placing two pieces of paper in front of her.

'We've been very stupid,' I said.

She peered forward to look at the things I'd brought, then she looked up, her eyes bright with curiosity. 'These are the photocopies we were sent,' she said. 'The letter to the woman in Stamford.'

'That's right. And where does it say that she was living in Stamford?'

She scanned the paper again. I could sense her mind already leaping ahead. 'Nothing in the letter,' she concluded. 'Only on the envelope.'

'Exactly.'

I pushed forward the photocopy of the envelope addressed to: *Miss Martha Ainsby, The Old Manor, Stamford, Lincolnshire.*

'We never saw the original,' I went on. 'Potts just had a photocopy. Now, what if I tell you there's a *place* called Ainsby in Lincolnshire?'

She hesitated for a moment. 'You mean it's a local name? I don't see . . .' She carried on peering at the envelope as if for inspiration, and then suddenly it seemed to fall into place. 'Of course! Someone swapped the names!' She was looking at me, her eyes wide with discovery. 'The writing on the envelope looks genuine because it *is* genuine—it just had two words changed around. A bit of cutting and pasting.'

'And both of them are really grey, grainy copies that would hide a lot of mischief,' I agreed.

Katya looked back at the papers. 'So we were looking for the wrong person in the wrong place. We should have been asking about a family called Stamford that lived in Ainsby.'

'That's right. That's why there was nowhere called the Old Manor in Stamford. But I bet you anything you like that we'll find one in Ainsby.'

'I'm afraid not, Mr Fitzgerald.' The voice came from behind me. 'The Old Manor in Ainsby burned down during the last war.'

I looked up to see the rotund figure of Potts approaching. His voice as he introduced himself to Katya was full of its usual lazy drawl.

'I'm Potts,' he told her, offering his hand. 'We didn't meet before but I saw you in Stamford. When we were all being made fools of.'

Katya told him her name and he twinkled back merrily, a slightly flirtatious favourite uncle.

'I didn't mean to overhear,' he told us, 'but I take it you two have just got as far as working out about Ainsby village. Give me a moment to go to the bar and we'll drink to that.'

We watched him patter to the bar and return with a bottle of red wine and three glasses.

'Don't get the idea I'm ahead of you,' he explained as he poured the drinks. 'I only sussed it out yesterday. Do you believe in coincidence? I was outside a shop in Covent Garden that sells maps and stuff, thinking about packing it in, when I looked up and saw it was called Stamford's. You know it?'

I nodded. 'It's quite a famous shop. It's called *Stanfords*. With an N.'

'It is? Well, it was close enough to give me the prod I needed. You see, as soon as I saw the name above the shop I realised what a fool I was. I blushed, I can tell you. It must be time for me to retire.' He raised his drink to us and smiled. 'Anyway, since it was a map shop I went in and checked some maps. Sure enough, there it was: Ainsby, Lincolnshire.' He shook his head ruefully. 'Anderson must still be laughing.'

I was not sure how much of what he said I should believe. 'So what brought you here?' I asked. 'You're not telling us that's coincidence too?'

'Oh, no. Not at all. I know Anderson's taste in hotels. I just phoned around all the most expensive ones in Lincolnshire until I found him. Does he know that you two are here as well?'

'We met him last night. He expected to have the bird in his hands sometime today.'

'Did he indeed?' Potts looked a little pensive at this. 'Well, we can ask him all about it in a moment. I called him late last night and arranged to meet him here at eight.' He pulled a fob watch out of his waistcoat pocket and flicked it open. 'While we wait for him, we can all have a drink.'

IT WAS ANOTHER strange evening. Anderson arrived twenty minutes later with Gabby in tow and I think they were both a little surprised at the committee assembled to greet them. Anderson responded with typical unruffled ease and insisted on ordering more wine—French and expensive.

We were a curious group. There was Anderson, immaculately dressed, and next to him Gabby, who couldn't help but challenge the popular image of a conservationist. She was too perfectly at home in a cocktail dress, too instinctively chic to be imagined sweating and dirty in a makeshift field lab, and she'd always been that way, even in the hottest and dirtiest of times, always somehow cooler and neater than the rest of us. Next to those two, Katya looked younger and less confident. Potts, sitting beside her, looked vaguely cherubic. What people would have made of me, I couldn't guess.

It was Potts who began the real business of the evening, leaning back and pushing his thumbs firmly into his waistcoat pockets.

'We've just been admiring your handiwork, Mr Anderson.' He indicated the photocopied sheet that was still lying on the table. 'You used the Stamford letter to get Ted Staest interested in your little expedition, but you wanted to make sure he couldn't leak the information to anyone else. So you moved the names around on the envelope. Very neat. Simple, clever, effective. You must have had a good laugh at our expense.'

Anderson looked at the paper and smiled, but when he spoke it was with his usual calm politeness. 'On the contrary, it never pays to belittle the competition. But you're right about me moving the names. I knew Staest would be interested in the bird, but he knew the story about the pictures too, and I couldn't be sure he'd keep quiet about it. It's amazing what you can do with tracing paper and a hotel photocopier. And then, when I heard someone had got hold of the photocopy I'd left with Staest . . .' He tailed off and gave us an apologetic shrug, leaving Potts to finish the sentence.

'When you heard that, you sent a man to Stamford so that I had someone to follow around. Nice touch.'

Anderson graced us all with his most charming smile. 'Not strictly necessary, I think. By then I was already six months ahead of you.'

Potts was looking a little rueful. 'I guess you're right about that. To the victor the spoils.' He took a generous swig of red wine. 'May I ask if you actually *have* the spoils yet?'

'Not today. But I'm confident I'll have the bird soon.'

'Pah! The bird. No one cares about the bird.' Potts looked up and corrected himself. 'Excepting Mr Fitzgerald here, of course. Now what about the pictures? Have you found them?'

'The man I'm meeting tomorrow doesn't know anything about the pictures. All he knows is that he has a very old stuffed bird.'

'So you haven't mentioned to this guy that his bird might be sitting on a million dollars' worth of art?'

Anderson clearly thought the question in poor taste and he looked up at the clock above the bar. 'Was there anything in particular you wanted to see me about tonight, Mr Potts? Because if not . . .'

The American nodded. 'Sure. No need to get touchy. Look, Anderson, you may be an expert in your own area, but I know about art. Trust me, if you go public with those paintings over here, you'll find yourself in a lot of trouble. They'll ban the export of the Roitelets quicker than you can dial a lawyer. But I could get them to the States in no time, complete with documents to show that they've been in an attic in Pennsylvania all these years. No costs to you, no delays, no lawyers' fees. Only a modest commission.'

Anderson exchanged a glance with Gabby. 'I'd like to wait until I actually have them in my hands before discussing anything like that.'

Suddenly I felt very weary. I looked over at Katya, but she wasn't looking back. I turned to Gabby, but she was watching Anderson, her face strangely serene. I was seized then by an urge to get away from them all, out of the hotel, out of Lincoln. Anderson would get his pictures; Gabby would get the money to keep her project going for a few more years; Katya would go back to college and all this would become an intriguing anecdote for her. And the Ulieta bird—what would happen to that? It was an afterthought now, destined to end its story in a freezer in Ted Staest's lab.

'There's one thing I'd like to ask,' I said before I got up to go. 'How did you find the bird?'

The warmth with which Anderson greeted the question surprised me. Beneath his smooth exterior, I could see he was excited by it, pleased at his own detective work. 'My researchers found that John Stamford was killed on the Western Front in 1917,' he told us. 'He never had the homecoming he'd looked forward to. And by the end of the war, the family's fortunes had collapsed. The contents of the Old Manor had to be auctioned off.'

That sale had been Anderson's real starting point. He obtained the catalogue listing the various lots, and concentrated on all the ones including mounted birds and animals. The catalogue recorded the purchaser of each lot and Anderson's people set about tracing them. Miraculously they managed to track the history of all the lots he was interested in.

'The listings in the ledger just gave descriptions like "a collection of songbirds" or "four doves and pigeons". Even so, once I'd discounted the items it couldn't have been, I was left with seven items. Gradually we tracked them down to where they are now. All seven of them. Can you imagine the odds against that? That's when I decided to come over. My only concern then was that someone might beat me to it.' He looked across the table at me. 'But it seems I needn't have worried.' He paused briefly, like a magician waiting for his moment. 'Now we've seen six of them, and none is the bird we're looking for. Tomorrow I'm getting photographs of the final one. I'll have an answer then.'

'Photographs?' Potts sounded astounded. 'Why not the real thing?'

'The last specimen ended up a long way from Lincolnshire. My researcher saw it today and is bringing over the Polaroids tomorrow.'

'And if the photos you see tomorrow are not the Ulieta bird?' I asked.

Anderson looked at me steadily. 'Then it is lost. Unless you have any ideas how to progress the search?'

Everyone looked at me again. I looked down at my lap where my fingers were laced around each other.

'No,' I concluded. 'If it wasn't part of the sale it could be anywhere.'

And, for some reason, that thought made me feel much happier.

*F*rom her first glimpse of land, from the first scent of it unannounced on the breeze, the sheer wonder of it entranced her. As the *Robin* drew nearer and she began to make out the details of trees and farms, an unfamiliar joy seized her. She knew as she looked that she was being touched by something so profound that she would never be the same again.

For the last mile or so, the *Robin* hugged the coast and she let the parade of shore and straggling houses roll past her, always with green, sloping mountains behind them. On reaching port she expected to be overwhelmed with panic. Instead, she disembarked almost in a trance, barely noticing the bustling crowds shouting their exhortations in tumbling, foreign tongues. The town seemed to her brilliant and exhilarating, though the accounts she'd read had called it neither. The houses that clustered round the harbour were either bright white squares or haphazard compilations of weather-worn timber. She watched a fellow passenger put a handkerchief to his nose, but she was happy to breathe in the smell of tar and heat and humans, mixed with the stench of mud and floating waste, and record it in her memory.

The boy from the *Robin* saw her bags unloaded, and another boy, from the house where she was to stay, was there to greet her.

'Senhor Burnett?' he asked, looking not at her face but at her bags. 'You are to come.' He led her through the crowd to a waiting carriage then leapt up behind her. 'Your bags, they come,' he told her earnestly before the driver picked up the reins and manoeuvred them through the chaotic traffic of the port.

The driver was a man of around fifty, his face creased by the sun into a smile. Did he look at her too carefully? Was there a flash of curiosity in his eyes as he nodded his greeting? Did he note the slimness of her figure? She simply didn't care. She was busy taking in a whole new world.

As they drew away from the sea, buildings became fewer and she was lost in the lush greenery of an unfamiliar landscape. There seemed to be trees everywhere of every kind, and above them, clearer now, she could see the mountains. With a surge of exhilaration she realised that tomorrow she could walk among them. It seemed miraculous.

This daze of wonder and excitement helped her through the arrival at the neat stone villa where she was to live. Mrs Drake, the plump widow of a Bristol wine agent, was to be her hostess during her stay on the island. Wiping her hands on her apron, Mrs Drake launched into a complicated speech of welcome as the carriage drew to a halt in front of her house. When she saw the face of the figure that was handed down to greet her, she seemed to pause for a moment.

BANKS'S DECISION to withdraw from Cook's expedition caused a sensation. On hearing it, his entire party—Solander, Zoffany and the rest—had little alternative but to stand down, too. What had promised to become the greatest scientific expedition ever mounted was suddenly reduced to a series of empty berths. Not even the hasty recruitment of a replacement naturalist called Forster and his son, an artist, was sufficient to disguise the fact that things had changed considerably. For Banks's friends it was baffling. They knew he could be volatile but they also knew of his ambition, of the towering hopes he had for the voyage of the *Resolution*. It seemed inexplicable that he would sacrifice it entirely over a few feet of cabin space.

They were equally confused by Banks's reaction to his own decision. They had expected him to be defiant, resilient, full of alternative schemes. The stores and equipment were all assembled and ready to go. Surely something could yet be salvaged? Instead, Banks seemed lifeless and enervated. He was bitter towards the Admiralty and vengeful towards the Navy Board, but at other times he seemed subdued and detached.

Eventually Solander went to New Burlington Street and challenged him to act. 'Come, Joseph, these last weeks have seen great setbacks to your plans, but the South Seas are not the only places of interest in the world. You have an expedition ready to depart, your equipment assembled at considerable expense. Many of your friends have made a great sacrifice to stand beside you in this matter. They are asking what you intend to do.'

'Do?' The word seemed to puzzle him.

'For instance, Wainwright tells me of a ship available to us bound for the West Indies. There is a great deal of work still to be done in collecting and identifying the flora and fauna there. You might consider that a possibility.'

'The West Indies?' Banks looked out of the window as if unable to concentrate on his friend's words. 'No, it's not to be thought of. For it to be of any value we would have to be away a year.'

'We had planned to be away three.'

'I'm sorry, Solander, it's out of the question.'

Solander paused and seemed at a loss. 'The Royal Society will think it most surprising if, after all your promises and with a party assembled, you choose to do nothing at all.'

'The Royal Society be damned. I shall do as I please.'

Solander tried another tack. 'Inactivity at this time is going to invite a great deal of speculation. A lot of people will wonder what it is that keeps you here, what is more important to you than the increase in knowledge which you have made such a public show of advocating.'

After a long silence, Solander continued. 'The important thing is to do *something*, Joseph. You have to prove that this dispute with the Admiralty is their loss, not yours. To divert the resources you have assembled into an expedition of your own will underline your own seriousness.'

Banks nodded slowly. 'Yes, I can see that. Even so . . .'

'The expedition need not be a long one. Perhaps just a few months away.'

'You have somewhere in mind?'

'If a short expedition is the thing, one could do worse than Iceland. It's a comparatively short voyage yet the island still demands considerable study. It would be a fitting object for your attentions.'

Banks turned back to the window. 'When would we depart?'

'As soon as we could. The Icelandic winter arrives early.'

Banks began to calculate. It would take perhaps twenty days for his letter to reach Madeira. She would then have to book a passage back to England. Then another twenty days before she could reach London. He must be waiting here for her on her arrival. He must.

He turned back to Solander. 'Two months,' he said.

'Impossible. Our supplies are ready now. If we wait two months we may as well not go at all. There are men here who have given up the opportunity of a lifetime out of loyalty to you. You have a duty to them, Joseph.'

Banks flinched at the word.

'Besides,' Solander continued, 'if we go now, quickly, we can be back in three months' time. Whatever business it is that has arisen to unsettle you will have to wait that extra month or you will fail the friends who have trusted you. On my honour, you have no choice.'

Banks listened in silence, and when Solander finished speaking he remained quiet, his eyes shut. 'Honour, is it?' he said eventually. 'That is to be the banner under which I sail? Very well. I thank you for your concern and I own the truth in what you say. Let me know what needs to be done.'

And Solander departed hastily, before whatever anguish gripped his friend could return to change his mind.

The plans for Iceland developed despite him. The charter of a ship, the *Sir Lawrence*, was negotiated largely by Solander, the itinerary was decided almost without Banks noticing, and the movement of supplies on board began while he watched the calendar and waited, hoping for a wind to speed her return. Yet while part of him longed for her to arrive before he sailed, another part seized gladly at the idea of escape.

He sailed on a grey morning tide when the wind dropped long enough for the *Sir Lawrence* to creep out to sea. Most of his last hours in England had been spent either drunk or ashamed and he had begun to blame both on her. By running off ahead of him she had placed him in an impossible position and as a result he had been forced to give up his greatest adventure. If he had sailed with Cook, he reasoned, all would be well. But her rashness had made it impossible. It was intolerable and it was not of his making. And now he must sail if he was not to betray his companions; must stay if he was not to abandon her a second time. The misery of it all confounded him and it seemed to him that the intimacy of their Richmond winter had been blown away for ever. It was easier to drink and forget. When the wind dropped they sailed for Iceland. All the way to the Lizard and then up the Irish Sea the wind fought against the *Sir Lawrence*. Those on board were forced to focus on the struggles of the ship and Banks, the great circumnavigator, was wretchedly seasick. A landing on the Isle of Man had to be abandoned because of the rough seas. It was not until they neared the Hebrides that the weather relented and Banks, after the darkest month of his life, found the sun shining again.

HER FIRST DAYS in Madeira passed largely in a state of wonder. Rising early, she would leave the villa at dawn and head for the mountains. There she would follow the *levadas*, the ancient irrigation channels that snaked round the contours of the hills, until she found the place where she had been working the previous day. On the first two mornings the houseboy had shown her certain paths, but thereafter she found her own way, under cinnamon trees, amid mangoes or bananas. She sketched flowers and leaves she had never seen before, and after a long morning of walking and drawing she would settle in the shade and look out over the sea and eat the food she had brought with her. Then she would often doze for a little, lulled by the heavy scent of the afternoon and the music of the goat-bells on the mountainsides above her.

If her days seemed perfect they were doomed to end with the ordeal of the dinner table. Of the two other English visitors in the house, Mr Dunivant, a Bristol merchant with interests in Madeira wine, seemed the less curious about his new dining companion. The second guest, Mr Maddox, was a much younger man, slim and handsome with enquiring eyes that seemed frequently to linger on his new acquaintance.

Other members of the English fraternity also came there to pay their respects. She told them that she hoped to join Banks's party when it arrived in Madeira. They all asked about her plans, and under pressure she began to contradict herself. Some came away believing that awkward Mr Burnett was already assured a place with Banks, others that he scarcely knew him. And as she struggled, Maddox, who claimed acquaintance with Banks himself, watched her, half amused, intervening from time to time and deftly turning the conversation to different channels.

Then came the day when she was interrupted in her drawing. She had returned to a favourite place and was making a study of guava leaves. It was late morning and the air was already still and weighty with heat. Beyond the shade the light was dazzling and she could hear water flowing through a nearby stream and into a stone basin cut into the hillside. Engrossed in her work, she did not hear anyone approaching, and the first she knew of Maddox's arrival was the sound of his footsteps behind her.

'I confess I owe you an apology,' he said, stepping out of the shadow and into the sun. 'I was inclined to disbelieve your claims to be a draughtsman. There are so many who believe they can draw, I find, and I thought you would be one of those. But I can see that you really are an artist. Perhaps you really do plan to join Banks's party after all.'

She felt the heat in her cheeks. 'As I told you, sir—'

'Oh, I don't mind very much what you told me.' He threw himself down on the bank beside her, so close that she drew away from him. 'So this is where you pass your time,' he said. 'I admit that I bribed the boy to point me in the right direction. I find you a most interesting character, Mr Burnett.'

She ignored him, apparently intent on her work.

'It is getting hot, is it not?' Maddox continued. 'Are you not warm in that jacket?'

'I am very comfortable, thank you.'

'Really?' He pondered this. 'I know . . .' He pointed to the water, cool and green in the shade. 'Do you swim?'

She carried on drawing. 'No. I have never learned.'

'Come!' He reached out and took her by the elbow. 'It is not deep and wonderfully cooling. And there are no peasant girls here for us to shock, are there?'

She shook him away. 'No, really, Mr Maddox. I don't care to swim.'

He smiled back at her, amused. 'Then you won't object to my carrying on without you?'

She looked at him steadily, not prepared to blink. 'Why should I? You may do as you please.'

He jumped to his feet and, standing in front of her, began to unbutton his shirt. He continued to undress, and when he was naked he turned his back to her, walked slowly to the water's edge and lowered himself in. As he bathed she returned to her drawing, unsettled but determined not to show it. When Maddox emerged from the water he took his clothes and retired a discreet distance to dry himself and dress. When he'd finished, he returned to where she sat and resumed his position on the bank beside her. She carried on drawing as though he wasn't there, and for a while there was silence between them.

When he spoke his mocking tone was gone. 'Who are you?' he asked quietly.

'My name is Burnett,' she replied.

'I thought you would scream and run away,' he said, smiling a little to himself. 'You called my bluff.'

'Why should I run?'

He looked at her carefully. 'I took you for a lady.'

She already knew he had guessed. But the words still made her tremble. 'Well, you were wrong. It's obvious that I am not.'

He raised his eyebrow again. 'No, it is clear you are quite another sort of woman. I find that even more intriguing, I confess.'

For a moment she wanted to strike him, to deliver a blow across his face that she knew he deserved. But there was a calmness inside her now. She would not break. She would not run. 'I think, sir, it would be better if you were to leave me now. I have work to complete.'

To her surprise, he rose to his feet. 'Very well, *Mr* Burnett.' He seemed about to go, but he hesitated. 'Mrs Drake knows. They've all guessed. Are you aware of that?'

She continued to draw, the blood hot in her cheeks, her eyes very firmly fixed ahead of her.

'Oh, one other thing, Miss Burnett.' Maddox reached into his jacket. 'A letter for you. It arrived this morning. From Mr Banks. About plants, no doubt.'

He dropped the letter onto the grass in front of her and she left it there until she had watched him go out of sight round the curve of the mountain. Then, still shaking, she reached down and opened it.

After reading its contents she sat for a long time, very still inside. She would finish her drawing before dusk, she decided. The next day she would look for a passage to England.

14

I woke up the next morning still determined to get away from Lincoln, having no desire to hang around and witness Anderson's triumph. When I was dressed, I set out to look for Katya. I wasn't sure what she'd say when I told her I was going back to London, but I expected her to be disappointed. Tracking her down, however, proved difficult. The woman at the reception desk told me she had gone out early without leaving a message.

I tried the county archives and the public library, and then a couple of cafés we'd been to. Not finding her left me at a loss. I was anxious not to hang around Lincoln, but I couldn't go without Katya, and I hadn't a clue where she was. For want of a better plan I decided to drive out to Revesby. It crossed my mind to go to Ainsby, but Ainsby was all about the bird's recent history, and it was the bird's distant past that interested me, the half-glimpsed story in the background—the one that Hans Michaels had had in mind when he made his drawing of the woman with no name. What was the story there? How had the Ulieta bird become a part of it? These things were interesting in a way Anderson's search would never be, and when I came to the road that led to Ainsby I ignored it and drove south, towards Revesby.

I reached the village some time after three, with the sun already low in the sky so that the church stretched a long shadow over the corner where I parked my car. Revesby was a small, not very significant sort of place: no pub to offer welcome, no shop that I could see, just silence and a large, square green area, bordered by a long row of single-storey cottages— almshouses, judging by their shape and design. On a stone set above one of the doors I could make out the name BANKS and a date. I did a quick calculation. My man's grandfather, perhaps.

There was no real reason for my visit, only a curiosity to see where the lives I'd read about had once been lived. Revesby Abbey, the house where Banks had lived, had lain outside the village, but had burned down in the 1840s. Its replacement was a private house, aggressively signed as such. So instead I turned to the village church as a focus for my musings. Even that turned out to be a different building from the one Banks had known. His church had been torn down in the nineteenth century to make way for something more spacious. But the graveyard was older than the building it surrounded and I made my way through it, walking between gravestones that had been there when Banks was alive. Even in the gloom I could still make out names and dates where the moss had not yet overwritten them. But eventually the brambles and the darkness combined against me and forced me to step away.

The quietness of the day had put me in the mood for company, so I got in the car and drove four or five miles along the Lincoln road until I saw the sign of a roadside pub. I pulled in, aware of the cold in my fingers and toes. Inside it was too early for more than a couple of drinkers to have gathered at the bar, but there was already a good fire going and I settled myself into a corner seat with a pint of beer. It was an old-fashioned, ungentrified country pub with no make-over and no menu. This was fox-hunting country and the walls were decorated with glass cases containing creatures that had fallen foul of the fact, testimonies to the age-old conflict between the Lincolnshire farmer and *Vulpes vulpes*, the red fox.

Vulpes vulpes, the red fox.

For a moment I was completely still, and then came a rush of amazement at my own stupidity. When I did move, I was clumsy with haste. That letter—did I still have it with me? I groped in my pocket for the sheet. Where was that line I'd talked about with Potts? That line that I'd taken as nothing more important than a casual quip. There it was . . .

Until then, guard it with your life—I don't want to return and find that young Vulpes of yours has snatched it from my grasp!

I'd thought he meant it loosely, a jocular reference to a suitor at his sister's door. But what if he hadn't? A young *Vulpes*. A young Fox.

I got out my mobile. At first I couldn't find the number I wanted and then I misdialled twice before I got it right. I almost punched the air when I heard his voice at the end of the line.

'Hello? Bert? It's John Fitzgerald here. I came round yesterday about your family tree. I know it's an odd question, but in your time in the archives have you come across the name Martha Stamford?'

There was a pause. I thought I heard him chuckle. 'Yeah, you could say I've come across it. Martha Stamford's my mother.'

*J*uly was a month of winds. On the Thames, white water and ships uneasy on the swell. In Lincolnshire, floods. In the Bay of Biscay, bound for Portsmouth, a small ship, the *Saffron*, driven off course and forced to hug the coast. On board the *Saffron*, tired and sick, a small figure watching the sea-flecked wind and longing for home. But a three-week voyage turned to four and by the time she reached England he was already gone.

She came ashore in Portsmouth under grey skies with rain in the air and the night already falling. The town looked drab, the streets dirty, and there was no welcome. She had not written ahead to advise of her coming, but even knowing he couldn't be there, she stood in the rain and looked for him.

She spent the night in a cheap inn and arrived in Richmond the following day, in late evening sunlight. In the time she had been away, England had drifted into the folds of full summer. The fields were higher, the hedges less kempt and the fresh playbills on the tavern door had begun to peel from their moorings. But nothing else seemed different. In the time she had been away, Richmond had done no more than stretch itself in the sun. Startled by the familiarity around her, avoiding the riverside, she made her way up the hill in the fading light to the discreet place where Martha, forewarned of her arrival, was waiting to greet her. After a warm clasp of hands and some soft words of greeting, Martha passed her a letter.

She broke it open and began to read aloud. '*My dearest, writing this causes me great distress. I have had no choice but to undertake another voyage . . .*' She read no further then, but held the letter for a moment before folding it into her pocket. 'Come, Martha,' she said, 'the letter will wait and I need to wash. And when I am clean and fed we have a great deal to talk about.'

There followed some months in which the two women in Richmond heard nothing of Banks. By the time word reached her that Banks's expedition was at an end, and that he was in Scotland, her hair was growing long again and the notes and sketches she had made in Madeira were being transformed into colour. Still he did not write, and if she thought of him at all it did not seem to unsteady her hand or distract her from her strict regime of work.

He reached London in early December and was glad to find that in his absence the acrimony of his departure had largely been forgotten. A friendly letter from Cook awaited him. Lord Sandwich called on him. But he made no attempt to write to her. By now she must know of his arrival, he reasoned. If she chose to ignore him, it told him what he needed to know. If she wrote, her letter would tell him how he stood. And if it proved she harboured no grudge, he would call when his business in London allowed it.

After two weeks of hearing nothing, he rose one morning, called for his horse and set out for Richmond.

The door was opened by a servant he did not recognise. 'If you'll wait here, sir,' she told him. The girl returned a moment later. 'Miss Brown says you're to go up, sir. She's painting, sir.'

So, heavy-footed, he made his way upstairs, rehearsing his words as he went. When he came to her door it was open and he saw the room flooded with sunlight. She was standing near the window with her back to him, intent on the picture before her. She was dressed in green and her brown hair, loosely pinned, tumbled over her collar in places. He barely had time to note the slimness of her figure before she turned and the light fell golden on her face.

'Hello, Joseph,' she said and he saw a light in her eyes that made him cross the room in two strides and take her in his arms.

'How is it that you are able to forgive me?' he asked.

They lay again in the green bedroom, little more than a year since the first time. Outside, the afternoon sun glowed against the windows and threw ripples of light onto the bedclothes. They had barely spoken as they tugged and hurried each other out of their clothes, but as their eyes met they laughed and paused to kiss. When they stumbled to the bed their bodies found a dialogue of their own and their whispered endearments were broken and half formed. Only after they had fallen still in each other's arms did the time for talking arrive.

'Forgive you for what?' she asked.

'For letting you go to Madeira. For failing to join you there because I was too proud and too angry to sail.'

'I understand. I know what happened. The hard part was coming back and finding you gone.'

His arms tightened a little round her. 'I was ashamed to see you. And I had to go. They were waiting for me to do something.'

'I know. I guessed. But by then I was tired of being a boy. I wanted to be a woman again.'

'And did you make a good boy?'

Her head lay on his shoulder and he could feel her smile. 'Not really. Anyone who bothered to look seemed to guess. But not many looked. In a crowd I was quite anonymous.'

He tightened his arms a little more and bent his head to kiss her. He felt he had come home.

AND YET IT WAS not quite the same. While Cook was abroad with the *Resolution*, Banks found it hard to settle. His career in London continued to take up a good deal of his time, building his influence in philosophical circles, establishing his reputation with the Royal Society. There were fewer spontaneous visits to Richmond and now there was no sense when they were together that time was standing still.

Their time apart seemed to have changed her. The wildness in her feeling for him seemed gone, and he began to sense a doubt in her that had not been there before. At night she held him no less tenderly, but when mention was made of the future he thought he saw a hesitation in her eyes. Then he would laugh and take her in his arms and tell her that she must never leave him, that he was only happy when she was with him: things that were both true and untrue.

When he asked her how she had spent her time when he was in Iceland, she would answer with a shrug and say, 'I painted.'

By the early days of the New Year, Richmond had become impractical. To keep her close to him while he continued his work he persuaded her to move to London. She came to rooms above Orchard Street where she could hear the street criers on Oxford Street and the bells of fifty churches and where, when the wind blew from the west, she could think she caught the scent of open fields. The rooms were new and slightly grand and the day she looked at them for the first time was the day she first felt she'd become his mistress. She had made a great point of protecting her family name but here her caution seemed unnecessary: she had no name. She was Joseph Banks's mistress. The tradesmen who called knew it and the women in the street knew it and neither her name nor her past mattered to them.

Yet London had its compensations. Joseph was growing into his new life. His house in New Burlington Street was becoming a focus for all London's thinkers and philosophers and his collection there drew people from across

Europe. Ideas whirled around him like a rising tide, and he shared it all with her, the two lying together at night, discussing and disputing, until they would notice the fire burning low and would roll contentedly into each other's arms.

She knew to count those days as precious. In February and March he travelled to Holland and left her alone in Orchard Street. Knowing that she was there made it easier for him to go; he knew that when he returned she would be there still, wise and lovely in equal measure. After two months of male companionship nothing could be better than returning to her. And in a different way, his being gone was good for her. As soon as he departed, she took out her materials and painted.

He returned at the end of March, playful and loving, younger than ever in his energy and affection. He was to go to North Wales in the summer, he told her, to tour the country there. He would bring her back tales of the dark Welsh mountains. And then next time, if the place did not prove impossible, they would go together and she would see the wild moors and the famous Mount Snowdon. In the meantime he had someone she must meet: a Dane, a student of insects called Johann Fabricius who would be spending the summer studying Banks's collection.

If she was a little more serious than usual on his return, he did not notice. She waited until the first bustle of his arrival had subsided before she told him. By then she was already three months pregnant.

15

It was two in the morning before I returned to the hotel. A small lamp still lit the reception desk but the rest of the lobby was in shadow. The hotel's warmth wrapped itself around me and I paused for a moment to enjoy it, rubbing my hands together and loosening my scarf. Until then, I hadn't really noticed the cold, such was the excitement running through me. I felt more alive than I had for many years.

In my euphoria, it would have been easy to miss the figure in the darkness, but a movement in the shadow caught my eye as I was heading towards the stairs. Through a doorway to my left lay the hotel bar and in that patch of blackness I saw a small pinprick of light rise and glow brightly, then fall back out of sight. Someone was sitting there, smoking in the dark.

I moved forward to the doorway. 'Katya?' I asked, but the reply came in Potts's American drawl.

'She's gone to bed, Mr Fitzgerald. A couple of hours ago.'

'What about the other two?' I asked, pausing in the doorway, wondering where the light switch was, trying to make out his outline and failing.

'Anderson and your Gabriella? He's not here. He's driven up to Durham. She went to bed early. They've had a long day.'

'No news on the bird then?' I tried to keep my voice calm.

'Apparently not. You want to hear what happened?'

'Go on.' I could still make out nothing but the tip of his cigarette.

'Well, at one o'clock they left here in Anderson's car. They drove to a village called Storeby, where they had lunch in a pub called the Bell. Anderson held her hand between courses and kissed her quite a bit. I've seen a lot of that sort of stuff over the years, Mr Fitzgerald, believe me. You'd be amazed at some of the things I've had to sit through.' Potts sighed and raised his cigarette back to his invisible lips. 'At twenty to three they were joined by two men, both of them people who've worked for Anderson before.'

'You've been following him?'

'Of course I have.' There was a faint trace of impatience in his voice. 'That's what I do. Do you want to hear the rest of it?'

I said nothing so he carried on.

'One of the two men produced a pile of photographs and the four of them went through them. Anderson got quite excited, but not in a happy way. After half an hour he got up and walked into the village and smoked a whole lot of cigarettes.' A little chuckle came from the darkness. 'Between you and me, Mr Fitzgerald, I'd say he was mightily pissed.'

'You think it was the wrong bird, then?'

'You can be damned sure it was.'

I let out a long breath. 'Just think of that. All that research, and nothing to show for it.'

'That's right. No bird, no paintings, nothing.'

I watched the tip of the unseen cigarette flare brightly again. By now I could make out the shape of Potts's body, very faint in a deep armchair.

'I spoke to one of the guys working for him, got the full story. It turns out the Polaroids came from a big house near Durham, where they've got quite a few things that came from the Ainsby manor. And they've a few botanical paintings, too. That's why Anderson was so keen. But according to the photos, none of the birds is *the* bird, and the paintings aren't right either.'

'So the stuffed bird's still out there.' I pondered for a moment. 'And what about you now, Mr Potts? Why are you sitting in the dark?'

'I was waiting for you, Mr Fitzgerald. I was interested to know where you've been. Jeez, all that business of the Stamford letter has led us precisely nowhere. And I guess that means you're about our best hope for finding those pictures. You're the one who knows about stuffed birds. Perhaps you know more than you say.'

I was about to reply when a cigarette lighter clicked open and lit up Potts's face. I realised it wasn't a random act. He was using it to study mine.

'Who knows?' I turned away. 'I'm going to bed.'

I left Potts sitting in the dark and it was all I could do not to run up the stairs. The adrenaline was still flowing and the strain of maintaining a calm exterior was almost more than I could bear.

On reaching my room I washed in cold water, waited five minutes, then turned off the lights. I sat down with my back against the door and waited some more. It was forty-five long, cold minutes before I heard Potts come upstairs. I made myself wait another hour before I dared move. Then I picked up the bedside phone and rang Katya's number. I let it ring for a fraction of a second before I hung up. Then I waited a few seconds and did it again. On the sixth attempt, Katya answered, sleepy and confused.

'Don't say anything,' I whispered to her. 'Just get dressed as quietly as you can. We're going to London.'

AT FOUR THIRTY in the morning the roads were empty and the frost was white between the carriageways. We drove with our coats and scarves on.

'So what's going on?' Katya asked when we'd successfully negotiated the outskirts of the town.

'Not yet,' I told her. 'I'm still piecing it all together.'

She thought for a moment. 'Tell me about Gabriella then.'

'Gabby? You know most of it already.'

'Tell me the rest.' She looked at me. 'I can't work out what you feel for her.'

I didn't answer for a few seconds, waiting while a fat Mercedes rushed past. Then I said, 'I suppose it took me a while to work it out myself. I needed to see her again before I really knew.' I hesitated. 'So much that means a lot to me is tied up with her. That makes it hard to let go.'

'Do you want to let go?'

'Yes. It's time.' My eyes were still on the road ahead.

'Because you found out she's with Anderson?'

'No, I knew before then. I was just scared to believe it.'

She considered that. 'And what about Gabby? Has she moved on?'

'In one way. She still has her work, though. That doesn't change. It's what really matters to her. More than people do.'

'You sound quite harsh.'

'I don't mean to. Gabby really loved me once, I know that. But it was when I was part of her work. When I stepped away from it I stopped being part of her world. She couldn't understand that I had feelings more important to me than the whole bloody rain forest.'

After that Katya seemed content to huddle into her coat and sleep. Gradually, as the miles clicked by, the car grew warmer.

We'd been driving for more than an hour when Katya stirred and asked the time and said she was hungry. A little after that we pulled into a Little Chef for breakfast. Katya waited until the coffees were steaming in front of us before she placed her chin on her hands and said, 'So?'

We talked for nearly an hour, until the night sky was liquefying at the edges, its colour draining into the fields below. By the time we climbed back into the car, Katya understood the bargain I had struck that evening in Lincolnshire and knew I had no more than a couple of days to come up with what I'd promised. There was no time to waste.

We drove in silence until we reached home. When I turned the engine off, Katya didn't move.

'What?' I asked.

'I was thinking about Karl Anderson. I think it's real, what he feels about Gabby. The way he looks at her.'

I thought about it. 'I don't see their lives fitting together very well.'

Katya shrugged. 'Perhaps she's changed. Perhaps she's ready to do something different. Perhaps she'll marry Anderson and settle down.'

I shook my head. 'What she does now is too much a part of her.' I paused. 'With Anderson's money behind her, perhaps she'll save the planet after all. But she won't marry him. At least not for a while.'

'How can you be so sure?'

I kept my eyes very firmly ahead of me. 'Because at the moment she's still married to me,' I said.

WHEN WE WENT INSIDE I showed Katya the photograph on my bedside table.

'My daughter,' I told her. 'She was just under a year old then. She died a few weeks after this was taken.'

We were sitting on the bed in my crumpled, comfortable room, our knees and elbows touching.

'I'm so sorry,' she said. She held the picture gently between her fingertips.

'There are hundreds of things in Brazil that can kill a child. It's a fact of life out there. But it was more than that to me. It just changed everything.'

She touched my hand so I carried on. 'I wanted us to leave, to come back here. I couldn't bear just going on as if nothing had changed. But Gabby's work was a place for her to hide. She needed it more than ever then, I suppose, just when I stopped caring about it completely.'

For a moment I found myself back in that plain room, its window half covered by a dirty net, an electric fan turning endlessly. The small bed, empty; the blankets still curved into a child's shape. And Gabby downstairs, her voice flat, making the arrangements that had to be made.

'So you left her?'

'I was in her way. Everything she did I held against her as a sign of her not caring enough. It wasn't fair, but that's how it was. We were in danger of hating each other. I had to go.' I looked at the picture in front of me, feeling the emptiness all over again. 'We called her Celeste, after Gabby's mother. This photograph is all there is of her now.'

We both sat silently for a little before Katya spoke. 'So that was when you started tracking down extinct birds?'

'That's right.' I gave a sort of off-beam smile. 'It all seems a bit obvious now, doesn't it? Refusing to let things go. But it didn't at the time.'

'And Gabby?'

'She got on with her work. She dealt with it like a grown-up, I suppose. While I was just angry about everything. In the end I was too exhausted to feel angry any longer so I came here and started stuffing birds.' I pointed to the corner of the room. 'I put all the papers for the book away in that trunk and began a different life. I don't feel angry any more. I just feel so incredibly *sorry* that she never had a chance to grow up. There's so much that's wonderful in the world that she'll never see.'

'And you and Gabby never saw each other until this month?'

'It sounds ridiculous, doesn't it? I suppose I was angry with her. But she'd write to me and I'd read the letters and keep them. And while she was writing and I was reading there was still a link. I knew there were men sometimes but while she was still writing that didn't seem to matter.'

'Because you still loved her.'

'No.' My voice was firm. 'That vanished somewhere. But she was the only other person who remembered Celeste. That was what mattered.'

We sat in silence for another moment before I spoke again.

'I wasn't trying to hide being married to Gabby. It just didn't seem to matter. It sounds stupid, but I find myself forgetting.'

Katya was looking out of the window, her face turned away from me. I thought at first she wasn't going to reply but then she turned and squeezed my hand. 'OK,' she said.

We didn't say much more after that, but Katya's hand stayed in mine. Then we got up and set about getting hold of the Ulieta bird.

*P*regnancy suited her. Even in the early months, before it showed, before Banks left for North Wales, she was aware of a warmth within her as if the life stirring there was already part of her future. She worked from early each morning until the heat of the afternoon, often dressed in nothing more than her nightdress, sometimes with a jacket of Banks's wrapped round her. In the afternoon, when the heat became unbearable, she rested quietly in the shaded drawing room. Martha would often find her at the window with the shutters a little open, watching the crowds of strangers below her, a calm, contented smile on her lips.

Even when Banks left for Wales her life felt no less complete. His absence was a relief, a chance to work uninterrupted. She had been very quickly aware of how her announcement had affected him. She had seen him touched with wonder, moved by pride and excitement, and she had seen those things fade as he began to ponder what it meant and how things would change. She watched the explorer and the statesman struggle inside him, and that conflict pained her more for his sake than for her own. For her it made things easier. His departure for Wales was both a confirmation and a release.

And then there was Fabricius. He first came to the rooms in Orchard Street soon after she had moved there, a pale, shy, serious young man. She sensed he came reluctantly and at Banks's insistence. At first he seemed loath to notice her, his attention directed at Banks, his only apparent interest the taxonomy of insects. Then one afternoon he called at Orchard Street in search of Banks and found only her. She was painting, her hair loose around her shoulders. He attempted to withdraw. Amused by his embarrassment, she insisted that he wait, settled him in a chair and, while she worked, asked him questions that required him to talk. He answered carefully and precisely and eventually with growing animation, surprised to find that the slight figure in front of him understood the basic anatomy of insects and seemed to know a good deal about Linnaean principles. Lulled by the fact that her back was turned, he found himself explaining his life in Denmark, his aspirations and hopes. When Banks's return interrupted him he grew confused, and the formality of his farewell made her smile.

After that he began to call more often, always in the afternoons when the heat made it difficult for either of them to work. He would usually find her alone, as Banks was seldom there at that time of day. When Banks departed for Wales, Fabricius became her only visitor.

At first this dedication amused her and the shyness of the Dane made her mischievous. He hovered a little awkwardly in the background while she painted, and she would tease him with personal questions, then smile to herself at his attempts to answer. But gradually she began to find his presence restful, part of her daily routine, and she began to listen for his arrival.

Her work fascinated him and what he saw on her easel astounded him. He had seen the work of Parkinson and Masson, of all the botanical artists of the day, but hers stood out. Her subjects seemed to live on the page as if they were still growing, still stirred by the breeze or freshened by dew. He would watch her paint, her body now curved with child, her small face furrowed with concentration, and feel intensely moved by what he saw.

As June turned into July his visits grew longer. They began to laugh together: uncertainly at first, then more often and more comfortably. It marked a new easiness between them. She began to call him by his first name, and he found that when he took his leave in the evenings his mind was no longer disposed to study.

One day, as he admired her work, she turned to him. 'Do you know that this one is the last? After this the work from Madeira will be complete.'

'I had not realised,' he replied solemnly, his eyes still on the painting in front of him. 'It is the very finest body of work. It will grace the collection of botanical paintings that Mr Banks is assembling.'

She shook her head slightly. 'We have not talked of that,' she said.

'But surely? Where else would it go? It must certainly be displayed.'

She began to put away her brushes, her back turned to him so that he could not see her face. 'Tell me, Johann,' she said, 'have you ever heard of a Frenchman called Martin? He is in London quite often.'

'I have met Monsieur Martin,' he replied. 'He is in London at the moment.'

'I have met him too,' she said. 'Joseph brought him here once.'

'And what of him?' His tone was short and suspicious.

'I don't know yet,' she replied and continued to put away her things.

That day Fabricius began to feel a disquiet that marred his time with her. Outside the summer was still growing, but he felt himself gripped by a sense of ending. Banks would return from Wales soon and here in London the companion of his summer was finishing her paintings. Soon she would be a mother, Banks a father. And he would be returning to Denmark and his studies.

Before departing he decided to speak. They were sitting in the drawing room, high above street level. The room was shaded against the heat, and at the hour when he usually took his leave they were sitting together quietly in the shadow. Instead of rising and making his farewells, he reached out and took her hand, gripping it much harder than he intended.

'I need to know,' he said simply. 'When your child is born, what will happen?'

Very gently she detached her hand from his but she smiled as she returned his look. 'What usually happens will happen. I shall become a mother and do the things that mothers do.'

'And Banks? What will he do?'

'He is generous with his feelings. It is a good quality in a father.'

'And will you stay here? In Denmark it is one thing for a man to maintain a mistress, another to raise a family under the noses of his peers.'

She looked down. 'Things will be different in the future, yes.'

'You will leave London?'

'Yes, I will leave London.'

'And raise his child somewhere more discreet. I see. It is not uncommon for a man in that position to . . .' He tailed off, suddenly embarrassed.

'To find companionship with another?' She was still looking down. 'A woman unencumbered with the cares of motherhood, perhaps?'

'Forgive me,' he said, and took her hand again. This time she let him retain it. 'I should not have spoken in that way.'

She looked up and smiled again, her eyes slightly misted. 'You must understand. In the future his life will be full of people and plans and social niceties that he will have no choice but to observe. But I also know there will never be a time when he does not think of us, of his child and me.'

It was Fabricius's turn to bow his head. 'Of course. How could it be otherwise? He is a lucky man. Though I hope he understands his good fortune. If I were he, I would not leave you alone at a time such as this.'

'I am not alone, am I?' She pressed his hand a little tighter then moved away from him. He saw she was smiling to herself, a sad, uncertain smile.

FABRICIUS BEGAN to make plans to leave London before the autumn. His visits to Orchard Street had a different feel to them now. The Madeira paintings were finished and her afternoons seemed busy with quite different things. On one occasion he arrived and found her with the Frenchman, Monsieur Martin, who seemed to be elaborately polite and solicitous of her comfort. Fabricius had the feeling he had interrupted two people who shared an understanding. When he called the following day and found the Frenchman there again, taking his leave, he felt hurt and suspicious. He waited until they were alone then demanded a reason for the visits.

'Monsieur Martin is an admirer of my paintings,' she replied. She came up to him and slipped her arm through his. 'Do not be anxious for me, my friend. A woman in my position needs friends. He will help me.'

'If you need assistance . . .' he replied.

'Oh, I know you would help me. But you have your studies. And I am not really a part of your life, though I have helped you to pass the dreariness of a hot summer in London.'

'Dreariness? You have done much more than that. You have . . .'

'No, do not say it. You will be gone from London soon. Joseph will be back. Let us leave these strange summer afternoons as they have always been, something gentle and good and not quite real. That is how we should remember them when we journey in our different directions. It is a consolation that I shall be able to follow your career from a distance. I know it shall be distinguished.'

He cast his eyes down at that. 'I see. And I shall of course follow your future path. I am sure Mr Banks will keep me informed of how you fare.'

Still with her arm in his, she led him across the room to the window. Looking out, her eyes on the people below, she spoke to him softly. 'It may be that these are the last moments we spend together. Whatever happens, promise not to be sad for me.'

'The thought of you suffering any hurt leaves me desolate.'

'Do not let it. You must believe that I intend to be happy.'

He said nothing for a long time. 'I shall try,' he said at last.

16

Time was tight. I reckoned I had two days at the most to call in favours and scrape together what I needed before Potts and Anderson decided something was up and came looking for me. The plan was for Katya to be back in Lincoln by evening to make sure that Potts, Anderson and Gabby stayed there—we'd worked out what tale she'd spin—but we had other things to do before then. First, still a bit groggy from lack of sleep, we went back to the Natural History Museum.

We had to wait about half an hour before Geraldine the librarian brought the picture to our table again—the Mysterious bird of Ulieta, drawn on the day it was last seen alive. Katya studied the picture then looked up at me.

'It's so *plain*, isn't it? When you first told me about it, I expected something really exotic. You know, bright colours and fancy feathers.'

'I know. Just a small, brown bird. There's nothing very striking about it. But when you look at it closely, it changes. See? The beauty's all in the detail. Things you only notice when you look properly.' We let our eyes wander over all the tiny vagaries of shape and markings that made the bird beautiful and unique, burning the image into our minds. We took notes. We measured.

'Would you recognise the real thing if you saw it now?' I asked.

Katya nodded solemnly. 'Yes, I'm sure I would. What about you?'

'Yes, it's clear in my mind. Of course, we have to allow for the colours having faded. And the eyes won't look like that. They'll be eighteenth-century glass gone cloudy with time. Come on, let's go.'

Outside the museum we went our separate ways.

'Good luck.' Katya smiled.

'Thank you.' I smiled back, awkwardly, not sure what we did at moments of parting. In the end I just nodded a little foolishly and waved as I walked away. My plan was to spend the rest of the day on the phone asking favours.

AT TWO O'CLOCK Katya called me from the London archives, where she was back on the trail of Miss B. Her voice was clipped, a flood of excitement held back by crisp efficiency. 'I've found them,' she said. 'She went south of the river for the baptism. To be discreet, perhaps.'

'What does it say?'

'Sophia, daughter of the late Joseph Burnett and his wife Mary. September 1773.'

'So she pretended the father was dead? That would be so the real Joseph wasn't implicated.'

'What about you? How are you doing?'

'I think I'll be able to get most of what I need. It's outrageous, really. I'm trying people I haven't seen for years. But most of them are being very generous. The trouble is that I'll have to spend most of tomorrow driving round to collect. Bristol, then Dorset, then a couple of places on the way back.'

'Will you have enough time?'

'I don't know. And if I don't pull it off, Anderson is going to get wind of what's going on and blast us out of the water. You've got to get up to Lincoln quickly to keep his nose out of things.'

'I'm going there now,' she promised.

KATYA WAS BACK in Lincoln in time for a pre-dinner drink. Before visiting the bar, however, she stopped at reception and told them I'd been called away suddenly but was keeping on my room for the next two days. Then she went upstairs and knocked on Anderson's door.

The previous twenty-four hours hadn't been Anderson's best. He'd been forced to accept that his research had led to nothing, that the Ulieta bird hadn't been part of the sale at the Ainsby manor. By the time Katya arrived in Lincoln, he and Gabby were beginning to pack their bags.

But his plan changed when he opened his door and found Katya standing in front of him.

'How much will you pay for the bird?' she asked.

HALF AN HOUR LATER she found Potts in the bar.

'Ah, greetings.' He beamed and bobbed to his feet. 'You and Mr Fitzgerald made a very early start this morning. I've been looking for you.'

'And here I am.' Katya smiled brightly.

'And Mr Fitzgerald? Is he here?'

'He's been held up. He'll be back later, I think.'

'I see. Back from *where*, I wonder.'

'I promised not to say,' she teased.

'I see. Well, in that case I have all evening to persuade you otherwise.'

Katya raised an eyebrow and looked deliberately enigmatic. 'There was something else I promised not to say too,' she told him.

'Is it very pointless to ask what?'

'That depends.' She studied him for a moment. 'Are you likely to pay more for the Ulieta bird than Karl Anderson will?'

THAT NIGHT I MANAGED to snatch a few hours' sleep. It was my first for forty hours and I knew I was going to need it. The next day would be long and difficult. I wasn't sure how it would turn out.

At 7 a.m. I was heading west towards Bristol. The morning was a bright one, but when I got beyond the London sprawl there was frost on the fields and the branches of the bare trees were white. With the sun shining and the sky a pure blue, I sensed my tiredness slipping away and felt a deep stirring of exhilaration. I knew what I was doing and where I was going. And that morning, when I thought of the face looking out of the photograph by my bed, I thought perhaps it wasn't wrong to smile back.

I COVERED A LOT of miles in the rusty lemon car that day and called in more favours than I had ever earned. I visited squat Victorian suburbs and villages with frosty village greens and ice-fringed ponds. Some of the people I met were able to offer me material assistance, others had nothing to give but advice on how an eighteenth-century specimen would be preserved and what state it would be in now. I listened to it all, and when there was nothing more I could possibly collect or learn, I drove home.

I didn't reach London until about ten that evening, but instead of feeling tired my mind was alert and full of restless energy. I knew I should try to sleep so that I could start the next day fresh, but time was so critical that the idea of sleep seemed laughable; instead I dug out the keys to my workshop and worked long, long into the night. The next day, I reviewed what I'd accomplished; it was some of the best work I'd ever done.

I set out for Lincoln later that day.

*H*er child was born early, kicking and coughing in the dust and heat of late August. The birth was a difficult one and for a month after it she was too weak to leave the house, too exhausted to go on with the plans she had laid. Instead she nursed her baby and herself through sleepless nights and long, breathless days when the stench of London seemed to boil up to their windows.

Banks had returned from Wales barely three weeks before his daughter was born. On his arrival, he found the rooms in Orchard Street changed. Her artist's clutter was tidied away and the walls were now bare. The sole example of her work that remained on view was the collection of brown oak leaves and acorns that she had painted in her first months in Richmond. For all its plainness, it was her favourite: the first she had hung on arriving in Orchard Street.

'The Madeira work is put away,' she explained. 'It felt right that it should all be kept together and I don't want to be distracted by it. You would not have me neglect our child for thoughts of line and shading?'

He concurred, but her words saddened him and the removal of her paintings left the rooms subdued and empty. Even the arrival of a new life, for all the noise it brought, never seemed to Banks to fill the rooms as they once had been filled, when he had her undivided love. Perhaps because of that, his daughter failed to move him in the way he had expected. He found the little distance that had come to exist between father and mother came also between father and child. He willed her well from his very heart but it was as if the knot of uncertainty that twisted inside him prevented him from loving. He was a man who found it easier to love when he was loved, and this was a time of doubt. They named her Sophia after his sister.

As she began to recover her health he would watch her laughing with the small bundle on her lap and at first he was jealous. He tried to entertain himself elsewhere, telling himself that her fascination with the child would dwindle with time. But the memory of the look on her face as she smiled down would haunt him. She was still a miracle to him. He wanted to take her in his arms and tell her so but found he didn't know how.

Eventually there came a day when he found her alone, arranging flowers in a bowl, her hair neatly tied up and her dress crisp and fresh. She looked as she had looked in their first days in Richmond, and a rush of tenderness carried him across the room to stand behind her, his hands resting gently on her waist.

'It has been a long time since we were alone,' he whispered.

She laid the flowers down and leaned back so that her cheek was touching his. 'Things are changed,' she said.

'You are not changed. You are more lovely than I can ever tell you.'

'We are both changed, Joseph. Things are different.'

'How are they different?'

She moved her cheek from his and twisted around within his embrace until she was facing him. 'You had no doubts then.'

For a moment he held her gaze, then he looked down. 'I don't doubt you,' he said quietly. 'I know I love you. But I don't know what happens next.'

She leaned closer to him so that her lips almost touched his ear. 'You have things to do, Joseph. A world to change. You have to do all the things we have talked about.' She moved her cheek gently against his. 'I like to think I was a help to you once. Now, with Sophia, I'm in the way.'

'It isn't true.'

'And I must do my best for her.'

'Meaning?'

She broke away from him. 'Have you thought how it will be for her to be known as the daughter of your mistress? The daughter of a kept woman? It will be used against her for the rest of her life.'

He refused to believe that his daughter's life could not be lived in London, discreetly, acknowledged by him, unseen by others. But she knew he was wrong. She thought back to her own childhood: she had been shunned and scorned for being her father's daughter, then later for being John Ponsonby's mistress.

She came back into his arms and held him tightly before she said quietly, 'I have promised Sophia that in her whole life she will never be scorned or shamed by anyone,' she said. 'You must let us go.'

FABRICIUS LEFT LONDON shortly after Banks returned there. He went back to Denmark, where the air was clean and the light shone off water that dazzled with its clarity. In London he had missed the great arching Danish sky and now he found himself frequently looking up or stopping to scan the horizon with a sense of simple joy.

The close, confined afternoons in Orchard Street began to seem increasingly unbelievable, an episode in life that had come from nowhere, led him nowhere and left him back where he had begun. It seemed remarkable that he had felt so much and been prepared to show his feelings. He thought of her often. Sometimes, when he was concentrating on a difficult piece of work, a word or a phrase would come into his head, and for the briefest of moments he would be back in London where a slender young woman stood before him, painting.

Banks had been generous with access to his collection, and the examination of it that summer had left Fabricius with a great deal of work to do and much to ponder. Nevertheless he found himself shy of Banks now, as if his visits to Orchard Street had been an undiscovered betrayal. Perhaps that was why he waited until November to write to Banks, and even then he had to rework the letter several times. '*My best compliments and wishes in Orchard Street,*' he wrote. '*What has she brought you? Well, it is all the same, if a boy he will be clever and strong like his father, if a girl she will be pretty and genteel like her mother.*'

Banks's reply was short. He was the father of a daughter. Both mother and child were well.

When Banks next wrote to Fabricius it was February and the sky over Denmark was low and heavy with snow clouds. Banks's letter said nothing of Orchard Street, nothing of either mother or child. When Fabricius made his own discreet enquiries, he learned that Banks had been deserted by his mistress. Miss Brown and her daughter had disappeared.

IN JANUARY OF 1774, four months after her daughter's birth, she left her rooms to walk in the nearby gardens. It was cold and the ground held a stiff frost, but she was accompanied by Martha and, despite the chill, the two were talking comfortably when she heard her name spoken.

'Miss Burnett, I believe.'

It was a man's voice and there was something in the way it lingered over the word *Miss* that made her turn sharply. Not since the day she left Revesby to become John Ponsonby's mistress had anyone addressed her by that name, and her shock was great.

At first she didn't recognise him in his heavy winter coat, but when she thought of Madeira she remembered his face laughing at her.

'Mr Maddox,' she replied instinctively, surprise making her incautious.

'So you remember me?' He smiled that lazy, confident smile. 'As I recall, I am dressed rather differently today from our last meeting. But then I would have to remark that the same is equally true of you.'

She felt herself blushing, suddenly aware of people within earshot.

'I'm afraid, sir, that Burnett is only the name under which I travelled,' she said quietly. 'Now if you will excuse me . . .'

He kept pace with her effortlessly. 'Such haste to be gone is most unflattering. The time was when you were not so shy. I feel it would be quite wrong to end our acquaintance so soon after rediscovering it, Miss Burnett. Especially under such *different* circumstances. And as you see, I have no alternative but to call you by that name until you furnish me with another.'

'My name can be of no interest to you, sir.'

'On the contrary, I find you most intriguing. I have often regretted that I never had the opportunity of coming to know you in quite the same way as you came to know me. Perhaps now that we are both in London we may be able to make good that omission.'

'I hardly think so, sir.'

He was still walking alongside her and in her hurry to get away from him she had left Martha slightly behind.

'Really?' She could hear the mocking smile in his voice. 'I wonder if your current gentleman knows of your former exploits? Perhaps you do not care for him to know. After all he may not wish to think he is in the company of a former ship's boy?'

'Sir!' She stopped walking and Martha came up puffing to her side.

He eyed them both. 'Come now, you must admit that good reasons for your extraordinary behaviour are hard to come by. I'm sure your current protector would not enjoy trying to discover them.'

She spoke as slowly and calmly as she was able. 'Sir, I would ask that you leave us at once. I'm sure you have business to attend to elsewhere.'

His smile widened. 'I'm pleased to see that your spirit has not been diminished by your abandonment of male clothing. It was your spirit I admired that day you watched me bathe. I was convinced you would blush and run away.' He made a little bow. 'As you have asked me to leave you, I shall. But I assure you that none of my business affairs are nearly so interesting as the surprising Miss Burnett. I shall be looking out for you. London is poor at keeping its secrets.'

At that, with another bow, he turned and walked away.

SHE WROTE to Joseph telling him of her encounter, telling him that she feared a scandal if Maddox told the story of her journey to Madeira. She begged him to visit so that she could explain the danger. And then she waited. For five days he did not come. He had been out of town, he explained, when he finally appeared, sulking like an adolescent, petulant at being summoned but embarrassed at his petulance. When she saw how he carried himself, she turned and tried to leave the room, but this dismissal piqued him further and he caught her before she reached the door.

'I am here because you wished to talk to me.'

'There is no point,' she replied. 'I can see you are not to be talked to.'

'That is insulting. I have come away from the household of very good friends. They do not value my conversation so lightly.'

'Oh, Joseph!' She looked him in the eye and shook her head, suddenly weary. 'Then go and talk to them. We would both prefer it.'

The sharpness of her words shocked them both into stillness. At that moment, in the sadness of his face, she saw clearly the young man she loved; saw him hurt and confused and uncertain of her. For an instant she felt her resolution waver. She reached up and touched his face.

'My love, this isn't how it should be.'

He took her hand in his and pushed it to his lips, his eyes shut. They stood like that until she freed her hand.

'How has it come to this?' he asked. 'I know I love you now as much as I have ever loved you. Sometimes I forget that. I blame you because things are not as they used to be. I feel such resentment. But even as I do, another part of me thinks of you with such longing that I end up hating myself.'

'Perhaps love is always honest in the end.'

'Is that true?'

'I don't know,' she said. 'I would like it to be.'

'I seem always so weighed down by the world. There is so much to do that I can do none of it well. There are so many things I want to be, and sometimes it is easier to pretend those things when I am not with you. You know me too well.'

'You can be anything. I've always told you that.'

'Yes, you make me believe that. But it comes at a price.'

She leaned against him then, her forehead resting lightly on his chest. 'Yes,' she said. 'It all comes at a price.'

That night he slept with his body pressed close to her. His sleep was peaceful and even, and in sleep he seemed young again, his face as uncreased as in the Revesby woods. She slept too, but intermittently, feeling the warmth that always filled her when they were together at night. But when it came, the dawn on her skin was like an icy breath.

She fell eventually into a deeper sleep. He woke and watched her sleeping. He began to reach out to wake her but her sleep seemed too perfect to disturb. The morning was a bright one. A new day beckoned. He hurried to meet it, and when she woke he was gone.

HER LETTER reached him at New Burlington Street three days after that.

My love, I have sold my Madeira paintings. I did it while you were away and did not tell you. They are gone abroad. They are signed with a name that is not mine so they will never reappear to embarrass you. The terms were generous and I have commissions for more—I cannot help but be a

little proud of it. With the money, I have prepared a home for our daughter.
A quiet place where she will grow and be loved. All her life she will be loved.
That is my promise.

    Goodbye, Joseph. I will love you for ever.

WHEN HE REACHED the house in Orchard Street he found she had left everything. She and Martha were gone and Sophia's cot was empty, but not even her clothes were gone. The servants were as surprised and mystified as he. Only later, when the light was fading, did he notice that where her painting of oak leaves had once hung, there was now an empty space.

17

The journey to Lincoln felt like a fresh start. I called in on Bert Fox on the way to make arrangements, and arrived at the hotel just before six. By that time another cold evening had settled on the streets and the hotel fires were stoked up high. I stepped quietly into the lobby in my big overcoat, its collar high around my face, and found Potts sitting there, reading a Raymond Chandler novel and watching the door. His eyes ran quickly over me when I came in, but I carried nothing. He looked disappointed, but when he rose to greet me he was all old-world charm in a new-world accent.

'Mr Fitzgerald! How very mysterious you're getting to be!' He waved in the direction of the reception desk. 'I guess you'll want to freshen up after your journey. After that I'd very much like to have a word with you alone.'

'I could meet you in the bar in half an hour.'

'Perhaps somewhere with a little more privacy?'

'No, I like the bar. That's about as private as I want to be.'

He nodded, accepting my terms. 'Sure. The bar then, in half an hour.' He pottered back to his sofa and his book.

I told the woman at reception that I was expecting someone to arrive with a parcel for me. 'When he comes,' I asked her, 'could you let him drop it off in my room, please? His name's Fox.'

When I got to my room I rang Katya, then Anderson. Five minutes before I was due in the bar, Katya knocked at my door and let herself in.

'Phew!' she gasped, flopping dramatically onto the bed in mock exhaustion. 'They've been on at me all day, trying to persuade me to put in a word for them. The bidding is ferocious.' She pushed herself upright. 'Did everything go all right?'

I sat down next to her. 'It went well. Look at this.' I pulled a piece of paper out of my pocket. 'It's my receipt. I'll only show it to them if they demand to see one. I don't want them giving Bert Fox any hassle about this.'

Katya looked down at it and laughed. 'Five thousand pounds! That's going to make them *so* mad.' We both laughed then, and with the laughter came a warm thrill of complicity. 'Where is it now?' she asked.

'With Bert. He's going to bring it round later.'

'What about the pictures?'

'The case is all sealed up. You can't tell if there are any paintings in there until it's opened.'

Katya looked at her watch. 'We should go down. The others are in the bar. Except Potts. He's hanging around at the end of the corridor.'

'OK, then.' I stood up and gave her my hand to help her up. 'Let's collect him on our way.'

Potts showed no surprise when he found that Anderson and Gabby waiting for us in the bar. He merely took off his little round glasses, rubbed them vigorously on his waistcoat and said, 'You'd have been much better to talk to me by myself, Mr Fitzgerald. But, hey, let's see what happens.'

We gathered round the same table as before, but this time everyone was looking at me, not Anderson. And for once he didn't wait for the drinks to be ordered before getting down to business. He wanted to know about the Ulieta bird? Was it true? Did I have it?

'Yes,' I told him. 'It's true. I bought it this afternoon for five thousand pounds. The owner was quite happy with the deal.'

'Who was the owner?' That was Potts cutting in but Anderson waved the question away impatiently.

'Did he have the pictures, too?'

'No, he'd never heard of the pictures. But the seal of the case hasn't been broken for years. Probably not since the last century.'

'And you're sure it's the real thing?' he asked.

'You'll have to make up your own mind on that,' I told him. Then I turned back to Potts. 'As for the owner, it doesn't matter. I own it now.'

'And what will you do with it?' Gabby asked softly.

THE CONJUROR'S BIRD | 291

'Well,' I began, 'that's one of the things I thought we'd talk about this evening. But first there's a couple of questions I wanted to ask. Which one of you broke into my house?' I turned to Potts. 'Was it you?'

He was leaning back in his chair, hands joined over the generous curve of his stomach. 'Ah, Mr Fitzgerald! Just a little research. I would have liked to have left things tidy but you'll understand that I wasn't keen to linger. It was important for me to see what you really knew about the Ulieta bird.'

'Why didn't you do that the first time? What was all that stuff about dusting the bookshelves?'

He looked back at me blankly.

'I don't think he can answer that.' Anderson sounded his usual calm self. 'It was *you*?'

'That's right.' He seemed amused by my surprise. 'That night, after you left the bar, I tried to catch up with you. But when I reached your house no one was in. And your front door was practically inviting me to look around.'

'But what were you looking for?'

Anderson stared at me as if he was seeing me clearly for the first time. And then he began to laugh: big, genuine gusts of laughter that made his whole rib cage heave. When the laughter subsided, he shook his head. 'You really *don't* know, do you? The world famous authority on extinct birds, and somehow you still don't know.'

'Know what?' At that particular moment I disliked him more than ever. And his laughter was having an effect. Although they had no idea what he was laughing at, Gabby and Potts, even Katya, were beginning to smile.

He gave a few more shakes of his head and then composed himself. 'OK, I'll start at the beginning. When we met at the hotel you said you knew nothing about the Ulieta bird—but I didn't believe you. There was one basic thing that you *had* to know, and when you pretended not to, I just assumed you knew a lot more besides.'

I was completely confused now and my expression made Anderson laugh some more.

'When I found you weren't there that evening, I thought I'd go in and try to take a look at your famous notes. But when I got to your room something on the bookcase caught my eye: your copy of Fosdyke's *Notes on Rare Avian Species* is an out-of-date edition.' He paused to let the comment sink in. 'Perhaps you stayed with that edition because it was signed by the author, I don't know. But then it suddenly dawned on me that perhaps you hadn't been pretending after all. Perhaps you really didn't know anything.'

I shrugged, still not comprehending.

'You see,' he went on, 'Fosdyke brought out a second edition a few years after the first. He'd added one or two new bits of information, including one about the Ulieta bird.' He turned now and looked at Katya. 'Fosdyke had found that letter, the one you saw in the Fabricius archives. The letter mentions a drawing of the Ulieta bird made in Lincolnshire. So that's why the letter sent to Martha Stamford was so exciting. Because it fitted with what we already knew—that the bird had somehow ended up in Lincolnshire.'

'So you put the book back, dusted the shelves so I didn't know which book you'd looked at, and left me to wallow in my ignorance?'

'More or less. I certainly wasn't going to point out the Lincolnshire reference to you.' He turned to Katya. 'Considering you hadn't read Fosdyke, I was very impressed by the way you found it for yourself. Now, tell me, Mr Fitzgerald, what was the other question you wanted to ask?'

I reached into my pocket and pulled out the crumpled picture of Miss B that Potts had removed from Anderson's room. 'Do you know who this is?'

Anderson barely glanced at it. 'Joseph Banks's mistress. His first mistress. He went on to have others, of course.'

'Didn't you think she was important in some way?'

'In finding the bird? No, of course not. She was interesting because she knew Fabricius, and Fabricius knew about the bird. But she's a dead end. No one even knows who she was.'

I looked across at Katya. 'No, I suppose no one will ever know who she was.'

Before Anderson could reply, the receptionist appeared at our table. 'The gentleman has left the parcel in your room, sir,' she said.

'Thank you.' I smiled, and turned to the others. 'What do you think? Is it time for us to go upstairs and inspect the merchandise?'

I'D LEFT one small lamp on in my bedroom, so when we all filed in, the room was washed with a low, reddish light. It was a small room and there was just about enough space for the five of us to stand in.

Bert Fox had left his parcel in the centre of the bed and we instinctively spread out around it. It was a couple of feet tall and about the same across, wrapped in brown paper under a layer of bubble wrap and crisscrossed with belts of heavy-duty tape. No one spoke at first, but Anderson gave a little sigh on seeing it. It was a sigh that told me something. Before then I'd taken him for the ultimate professional, a man who looked for rare things purely for profit. But now I wondered if Gabby might have been right. Perhaps he really was a man who just loved the search.

'You might need this.' Potts had taken a penknife out of his pocket.

I started forward, suddenly full of doubt about the whole enterprise. But now I had no choice but to show them what was in the package. Slowly, I cut away the tape, then removed the wrapping and uncovered the object beneath.

The case was built of old, dark wood with a glass pane set into each side. One of the panes was cracked and another was misted with a haze of tiny flaws so that it was almost opaque. Inside, perched on a wooden branch, was a small brown bird, its head cocked slightly towards us as if in surprise. A very ordinary bird, like a thrush or a blackbird or something in between. It could have landed in a suburban garden without exciting much notice.

'Jeez!' exclaimed Potts. 'Is that it? All this fuss for that?'

But Anderson and Gabby were both crouching down, studying it intently through the two clear panes. I took a deep breath and turned on the overhead light so they could see it properly. And that made a difference.

It was easy to see that the bird wasn't in a good state. It was a little shapeless, as if its body had begun to sag with gravity, and the once rufous feathers had faded to grey in places. But the better light showed the shadings of colour that distinguished it, that made it neither a blackbird nor an ordinary thrush but something different and unknown.

Anderson turned to me, his eyes shining. 'Is it the one?'

I shrugged. I wasn't enjoying this as much as I'd hoped. 'It could be.'

He turned back and began to point out the details to Gabby. She was nodding, scrutinising it minutely. Neither of them was a specialist but they both knew about birds, and they knew what they were looking for. Potts watched them, observing their reactions.

Anderson was murmuring under his breath, repeating Forster's description of over two hundred years ago: 'Head dusky marked with brown . . . Wing dusky, primaries edged with brown . . . Twelve tail feathers . . .' Eventually he stood up. Something of his usual manner had returned. 'Of course it's nothing without provenance,' he said. 'There would need to be tests done.'

'Of course. The lab people will want to do their bit of poking around.'

He bent down and looked at it again. 'It's a miracle that it's survived.'

'It's certainly an amazing piece of luck.'

'Jeez!' Potts snorted. 'Are we doing business here or not? What about the pictures? We need to open the case.'

'No.' I held out my hand to keep him away from the bed, and the authority in my voice seemed to surprise him. 'Nobody's opening up the case until we have the right conditions, the right humidity, the full works. That's the deal—whatever happens, the bird is dealt with properly. Now, let's go back downstairs and talk figures.'

Back in the bar I watched Anderson settle back into one of the hotel sofas, and Gabby sat close to him. This time I didn't resent it. I just sat quietly and waited for someone to speak.

'Well, Mr Fitzgerald,' Potts began, 'what's the deal here? Are you selling the bird now and the paintings later, if they turn out to be there? I'm not prepared to bid blind.'

'I don't care about the pictures. It's the bird that I'm interested in. I'm prepared to sell the bird to either of you, but these are my terms: as soon as we agree a price, we take the bird to the Natural History Museum, and the case is opened there, in proper conditions. The bird itself is donated to the Natural History Museum, but you get to keep the case and anything in it. And if the pictures are there, one per cent of anything you get for them goes to the museum for the upkeep of the bird.'

Potts snorted. 'You're joking, Mr Fitzgerald. No one can do business on those terms. There may not *be* any pictures!'

I looked at him steadily. 'I guess that's the risk you have to take.'

'You're living in dreamland if you think anyone will touch a deal like that. It stinks.'

But Anderson was watching Potts and smiling. 'Oh, I don't know,' he mused. 'I like what you're saying, Mr Fitzgerald. You're right to want to safeguard the bird. So, let's see. Let's say I promise to make a donation to the Natural History Museum to cover all the costs incurred in restoring the bird and in keeping it on display in proper conditions, plus fifty grand more for the upkeep of other rare specimens. In return, if the pictures are there, I get to keep them. The risk is all mine.'

I nodded and turned to Potts.

'Frankly, this is all bullshit,' he told me. 'Look, Mr Fitzgerald, here's my offer. You open up the case. If the pictures are there, I look after the business of getting them over to the States nice and quiet. I take a ten per cent cut. A private sale, discreet, tax-free. No questions, no red tape, no mark-ups to anyone else. Plus you get to keep the bird. If they're not there, we go our separate ways and you can give the bird to who the hell you like. Think of it, Mr Fitzgerald. Ninety per cent of a million dollars is going to pay for some pretty good bird preservation. And what's he offering you? Not a dime.'

'My offer's on the table, Mr Fitzgerald,' Anderson said evenly.

I turned back to Potts. 'He's guaranteeing the future of the bird, pictures or no pictures. I need you to do the same.'

'Oh, for chrissake!' He stood up, clearly agitated. 'This is crazy. Give me ten minutes. I need to think.' He stalked out of the bar.

When he was out of sight, Anderson chuckled. 'I guess I've just matched his highest bid.'

I looked over at Katya, who raised her eyebrows at me questioningly. I answered her with a nod and turned back to Anderson. 'Let's have a drink.'

'Yes, of course.' He reached into his jacket pocket for his wallet. 'Assuming Mr Potts doesn't change his mind, we'll need something in writing about all this,' he said.

'OK, start writing. Put down exactly what you've just said. Tomorrow I'll get it checked over by a solicitor.'

He produced a sheet of paper from his briefcase and began writing. 'It's amazing,' he mused. 'Seeing that bird. Who would have believed it? Even if we don't find Roitelet's paintings, it was worth coming over just for that.'

He wrote in silence for a while, then pushed the paper over to me, smiling contentedly.

'Where's Potts?' he wondered idly. 'He's taking his time.'

For three or four seconds that statement hung in the air before anyone reacted. Then we all moved at once. Anderson was first to his feet and first to the door of the bar. I was a couple of yards behind him as he launched himself up the hotel stairs. And I was still behind him when he reached my room and found the lock forced, the bed empty, the bird gone.

*I*n the years after her departure, Banks pursued both his work and his pleasures with a grim vehemence. He laboured tirelessly at his scientific projects, impressing all who met him with his fierce commitment to the advancement of knowledge. His career flourished. A man who is so busy can allow himself little time for introspection, and Banks had little need for it. In his own mind he had already answered the question that so beset him in the days after her departure: the two of them, he knew, would never meet again.

But in that he was wrong. He was to see her one more time, some three years later, on a bright spring morning. It was one of the last days he spent in the house on New Burlington Street, and his mind was fixed on the many matters squabbling for his attention. There were arrangements to be made, papers to be signed and formalities to be overcome. As a result, he had no intention of receiving callers and it was only by chance that he appeared on the stairs at the moment the front door was opened to her. She did not see him at first, but he saw her, and with the shock came a tightness in his lungs. Then she looked up and their eyes met.

He brought her into the house himself, all the anger he had manufactured in the years since she'd left suddenly dissipated by the touch of her gloved fingers on his hand. All the recriminations he had rehearsed were replaced by speechlessness; all the coldness he carried in him changed to raw feeling.

'I was in London,' she said. 'I came to thank you.'

He looked beyond her, into the street where a carriage was waiting.

'To thank me?' he asked, still confused by her presence.

'For not following us.'

'I'd promised I would not.' Then he shook his head and found he could smile. 'In truth I was too resentful. I wanted you to return to me unbidden.'

She looked up and he could no longer avoid her eyes.

'You knew I would not,' she said.

'Yes. I think I knew that.'

She reproached herself for the visit, for the lack of warning she had given him. 'I would not have come, but I had need to be in London and I wanted to tell you that Sophia is well and happy. Only that.'

He nodded. 'I think of her more often than you would believe.'

'No, I would believe it.'

They stood still and looked at each other. From outside, the bright spring day cast a silver light in the space between them.

'Do you blame me for what I did?' she asked.

'For three years I have. But I was not then looking at your face.'

'Then I am glad that I came.'

They passed an hour together that morning, surrounded by his collection, the great store of curiosities that had become the wonder of Europe. They drifted from exhibit to exhibit, each more aware of the other than of the marvels before them. From the great display of implements and memorabilia of his days in the South Seas to the herbarium, where they flitted from plant to plant and back again. There were pictures too, wild landscapes and the faces of strange men and women, and of course the botanical works, the incomparable collection of drawings made by Parkinson during the first expedition of the *Endeavour*. Finally, they came to a room of animal specimens, some mounted, many of them only skins stored flat. He showed her the greatest curiosities, the novelties that had become the talking point of his museum. Towards the end of that final room she came upon a mounted bird of no great distinction. The label showed that it came from the South Seas, from an island near Otaheite.

'Such a plain bird to be so displayed,' she said.

'Indeed. I don't know why Forster mounted it. I remember he talked of some new practice in preservation that he wished to try. Perhaps he chose something unexceptional lest the experiment failed.'

She was still looking at the bird. 'But I like it,' she said. 'A plain, brown bird amongst all this glory. It has its own beauty, I think.'

'Take it,' he said urgently, seized with the desire that she should have an object to remind her of that day. 'Or I can have it sent to you.'

'But that would diminish your collection,' she replied.

'By a fraction. Who will notice?'

In the end he insisted and she gave him an address in Soho where it could be sent. 'The house of Monsieur Martin,' she told him. 'It is he who buys my work.'

And so, when she had gone, the brown bird was taken down and prepared for dispatch. And soon it was forgotten.

18

Katya and I were up half the night, calming Anderson and shaking our heads while the police were called. I tore up my agreement with Anderson and gave the pieces back to him. I had sufficient respect for Potts to know that it was highly unlikely we would ever see the bird or its case again. At about three o'clock, groggy from lack of sleep, Katya and I left Gabby and Anderson in the hotel bar and went to bed. I can't speak for the rest of them but that night I didn't even dream.

The next day we checked out of the hotel as snow was beginning to fall. The drift of snowflakes onto the cobbles was strangely soothing. I think we both felt the same. Katya put her arm through mine as we walked to the car.

'What will Potts do with it?' she asked.

'I don't know. When he finds there are no pictures, he might just dump it. Or he might sneak it to America to see what Ted Staest will pay for it.'

'And Anderson?'

'He'll write it off as a business loss, I guess. And something tells me that, bird or no bird, he'll find the money to make sure Gabby's project carries on. I don't think that's a business thing for him.' I smiled at my own contradictions. 'They make a good couple,' I said.

'Seeing that bird last night mattered to him, didn't it?'

'I know. It makes me feel bad.'

Katya gave my arm a little squeeze. 'Tell me, did you really need to go to such trouble? All that work . . .'

'I think so. Otherwise Potts and Anderson would never have stopped looking. This way they can forget about it and leave us all in peace.'

Snowflakes were lingering in her hair as we talked and she pulled her coat collar round her face. 'And Gabby? Did you say goodbye to her?'

'Sort of.'

We reached the car and found its windscreen wipers edged with a delicate line of snow.

'What would you have done if Potts hadn't stolen it?' she wondered.

'I've no idea. But I was sure he'd try something. He's that sort of guy.'

We got in and began the practised routine of buttoning our coats and pulling our scarves tighter. It felt familiar and comfortable.

'Is it far?'

'About forty minutes in this thing.' I grinned, patting the steering wheel affectionately. 'Come on, let's get moving.'

As we nudged our way out of Lincoln into the countryside, we were caught in an unannounced flurry of proper snow, thick flakes falling heavily and making the windscreen wipers do their job. Then, almost as suddenly, we drove out the other side and into sunshine. Around us, patchy white furrows scored the fields.

We talked as we drove, light-hearted now, taking our time to understand everything that Bert Fox had told me about his family history.

'So Bert Fox's great-grandfather married a Sophia Burnett?'

'Yes, except it was his great-*great*-grandfather. Fox told me about it when I first went to see him, but I got so excited when he mentioned Ainsby that I never asked myself if his Burnett and our Burnett might be related.'

'So Mary Burnett brought Sophia to Lincolnshire. I wonder what became of her after that.'

'I don't suppose we'll ever know. But we know Sophia married Matthew Fox, a farmer. Guess what their son was called?'

'Not . . .?'

'Yup. Joseph. Joseph Fox's son was another Matthew Fox and he ended up as steward to the Stamford family. He had a son called Henry, who grew up with the Stamford children. They all knew the stories about the stuffed bird Matthew had in his cottage. And Matthew Fox is the old man John Stamford was talking about in his letter. He died while Stamford was at the front.'

'And Martha Stamford grabbed the bird for safekeeping?'

'That's right. She already had an attachment to Henry Fox, the old man's son. The two of them had grown up together. He's the "young Vulpes" mentioned at the end of the letter.'

'And at the end of the war?'

'Martha gave the bird back. Henry Fox had been in France when his father died. But it was his bird. And that's why it missed the sale of everything in the Old Manor. When the dust settled after the war, Henry and Martha married. She'd moved to Cornwall to live with a cousin when the house was sold, and he went to find her there. In a way, the loss of all the family money must have helped them. If it hadn't been for the war they'd probably have been kept apart.'

I drove in silence then, pondering the vagaries of chance. Soon we were on the outskirts of the next town, and a few minutes later I pulled up outside a terrace of smart Georgian houses, on a quiet street near the centre.

'This is it. Where the last of the Stamfords ended up.'

On the pavement in front of the house a figure I recognised was lurking, smoking a roll-up. Bert Fox's silver ponytail was squashed down by a faded baseball cap and hidden under the collar of a saggy overcoat.

'Just having a fag,' he explained when I introduced him to Katya. 'Mum doesn't like me smoking at her place.' He dropped the cigarette onto the pavement and pressed it with his toe. 'You'll like my mum. She's a laugh.'

We went inside. The hallway had been built to feel spacious but the effect was undermined by the mass of objects squeezed into it. An umbrella stand by the door sprouted walking sticks and old-fashioned canes. Next to it, a small table was covered with a cigar box, an ashtray-with-lighter, a gold photograph frame, an ebony camel. The walls were studded with pictures from waist height upwards so that the wallpaper beneath them was all but obscured.

'Mum!' Fox shouted as he closed the door behind us. 'John's here again. Remember? To see the bird. Got a friend with him.'

We were shown into the front room, which, like the hallway, was packed with objects. Amid the clutter, tiny under a pink blanket in a large green chair, sat the woman whose letter had first made us believe in the Ulieta bird. She was old now—so old that it had occurred to none of us that she might still be alive—but Martha Stamford had aged into a happy, laughing old lady. All around her were the mementoes of another age, but she herself was so alert it seemed impossible to believe that she had danced and flirted with men on leave from Passchendaele.

She greeted Katya with a nod, then looked up at me. 'So you've come for another look? It's a dull old thing, that bird, but I'm not surprised it's valuable. We've always treasured it in our family.' And she began to tell me again how old Matthew Fox had called it his grandmother's most precious possession. 'She loved it because it was *her* mother's, you see. Her mother had been given it by a lover—at least that's what Matthew used to say. We all thought it was terribly romantic. And I remember Henry—that's Bert's father—telling me how it was so valuable because of Captain Cook finding it. But none of them would ever sell it because it was a love gift.'

'And what about the pictures, Mum? Tell them about the pictures again.'

'Ah, yes. Those. Henry found them, not long after we were married. Beautiful things they were. All local wildflowers. There were harebells and bluebells and all sorts. So bright, they were. Lovely things. Henry had them all framed and we had them on the walls. But when we moved here there was no room, so he sold them to the family that had bought the Old Manor. Got a few pounds for them, he did.'

Katya turned to me breathlessly. 'So they could still be there now?'

I shook my head and looked across at Bert Fox.

'The Old Manor burned down during the war,' he said.

'Lovely things, they were,' his mother went on. 'Lovely bright colours. Better than having fresh flowers in the house, I used to say . . . But of course you don't want to listen to me going on. It's the bird you're interested in. Go on up and take a look at it.'

Fox led us upstairs to the first-floor landing and the strange little room they called the Book Room. He showed us in and turned on the overhead light.

The room was narrow, about five feet wide but perhaps fifteen feet long. Both long walls were covered with bookshelves, which meant that only the far wall and the area above the door had any space for decoration. The far wall was empty but for a rather drab study of oak leaves. I turned. There, above the entrance, in a clear glass case, stood the lost bird of Ulieta.

It wasn't unlike the bird I'd made in its image but it was far, far better preserved. To create mine I had been forced to beg and buy very old specimens of thrush and blackbird and it had taken all my skill to combine them believably into a counterfeit bird: where things proved difficult, I had simulated decrepitude to mask my failings. But this specimen had none of the torn feathers, none of the shapelessness. It was in a remarkable, almost incredible, state of preservation.

Katya and I both stood and wondered.

'How can it be so perfect?' she said at last.

'I don't know. It must be the most amazing fluke.'

But Bert Fox pointed around him. 'No outside walls to this room, you see. My father kept it in here with the books because this room never gets damp. And the temperature is always the same. Always cold. I think each generation has done what it could to look after it.'

'So that's why,' said Katya as if a missing piece had just fallen into place. 'That's why this one's still here when all those other specimens fell apart.'

She paused and looked up at the bird again before she realised we were both watching her, waiting for her to explain.

'Because of all that love,' she said simply.

WHEN WE WENT downstairs again, we found Martha Stamford asleep under her pink blanket. Above us Joseph Banks's bird had been restored to the stillness and the darkness of its sealed room. There seemed no reason to disturb either.

Before stepping out into the street, Katya and I stood in the doorway, trying to gauge the temperature. I waited while she buttoned up her coat and pulled her collar up to her nose, and we stood close to each other for a second or two, looking up at the sky.

Then we stepped out together into the winter sunshine.

MARTIN DAVIES

Born: Cheshire, December 7, 1965
Home: Putney, west London
Profession: television producer

'Extinction is a fascinating concept,' says Martin Davies of the inspiration behind his first 'serious' novel. 'The Dodo, dinosaurs . . . people are intrigued by them. The notion of loss, that something can disappear and that once it's gone, there's no getting it back, interested me. There's a parallel, too, in human relationships, of course.'

The Conjuror's Bird combines a present-day hunt for a lost bird specimen with a tale of thwarted love, set in the eighteenth century. It is based on a mix of historical fact and conjecture and grew out of several ideas that piqued Davies's curiosity as a history graduate. His curiosity about extinct creatures prompted him to buy a copy of James Greenway's *Extinct and Vanishing Birds of the World*, which, he recalls, 'read like a thriller.' He then read a biography of Joseph Banks, the naturalist who sailed with Captain Cook, but he was left wondering about the unanswered questions in the history books, such as the speculation about what might have happened to the 'Mysterious Bird of Ulieta', and why Banks inexplicably pulled out of a second voyage with Cook. Davies decided to go on a research mission to the naturalist's home village of Revesby in Lincolnshire. 'When I found that there was a Miss Burnett who could quite conceivably have been Joseph's mistress, I knew I had the makings of a novel.'

Back in London, in the archives of the Natural History Museum, he got permission to view the original drawing of the Bird of Ulieta (shown on page 163), which is kept in the archives there, and his enthusiasm grew. 'It was so exciting to see it in front of me—seeing the actual pencil marks made at the time.'

One of the hard things about being an historian *and* a writer, in Davies's view, is that you're very aware when you move beyond the facts into the realms of speculation, 'that you're blurring the rules a bit,' as he puts it. 'On the other hand, history is, after all, made up of good stories. And it's the half-stories, those that aren't fully told, that are particularly fascinating.'

Long walks, such as those along the Norfolk and Devon coastal paths, and on a guided exploration of Greenland recently—are Martin Davies's way of clearing his mind.

'It takes about two days to get rid of all the stuff like "have I left the iron on?", and then the ideas start to flow. One of the best things about being a writer is that it is a fantastic excuse to go off and be by yourself for a bit without appearing to be anti-social.' Last summer, his destination was Sicily. 'Just me, with my pen and pad, for a week, sitting in a bar with a fantastic view, and writing.'

He used to run half-marathons and says that the knowledge that he could 'go the distance', helped him to get started on *The Conjuror's Bird*. Although he'd had two light-hearted pastiches of Sherlock Holmes stories published in Holland and America ('enjoyable but essentially frivolous'), the challenge of a 'proper' novel still lay ahead. 'I got bored hearing myself talking about wanting to write, without ever doing anything about it. I just wanted to prove to myself I could do it. Like a marathon, or a mountain you're going to walk up, it seems daunting, but once you break it down, determine that you'll do this much each night, you reach a point when you know you will finish.'

The next book is taking shape during the three evenings a week that he devotes to writing, once his day job is done. It, too, is inspired by a fascinating, relatively unknown historical curiosity—this time a language developed in China centuries ago that was only spoken by women. The story's hero is a 'Marco Polo-style explorer' who follows a trail of mysterious graffiti . . .

JOSEPH BANKS 1743-1820

Joseph Banks, who was passionate about natural history from an early age, acquired a large inheritance in his twenties that enabled him to lead explorations to Newfoundland and Labrador. In 1768, he successfully lobbied the Royal Society for permission to take part in Captain Cook's first great voyage to the South Seas. He came back with a vast collection of some 1,300 new specimens, including the Ulieta bird, and was considered a national hero. As well as appointing Banks adviser to the Royal Botanical Collections at Kew, George III made him a baronet. This portrait of him by Joshua Reynolds is in the National Portrait Gallery, London.

BENEATH
THE SNOW

CAROLINE CARVER

It's one thing to be on the run. It's quite another to be fleeing for your life in one of the most inhospitable places on earth—the frozen Alaskan wilderness.

But scientist Lisa McCall knows how to survive the difficult terrain, which may just give her the edge over her pursuers . . .

One

It was just past midnight and Lisa was exhausted. She'd been on the run for five hours and the storm was still blowing hard, the temperature dropping. Recently even −20° Fahrenheit had become a rarity in Alaska, but this storm was from the old days; it had to be at least −30°F with the wind chill. Her attempts to keep warm were no longer working, and if she didn't find shelter soon she knew that she and her dogs would die.

Through the roaring wind she could hear the rattle of snowflakes on the hood of her parka, the dogs' harnesses creaking, her skis rustling on snow. She couldn't hear any engines, but she didn't doubt her pursuers were close behind. She could still hear the crack of the .45 calibre semi-automatic in her mind, see the white winter-camouflaged figure swinging the pistol her way. If it hadn't been for her huskies, Roscoe and Moke, she'd already be dead.

Don't think about it. Push it aside and keep running. A snow machine can only go so far on a tank of gas, but my dogs can go much further. And once we're safe, then I can think about what I'm going to do.

They came to a frozen river. She urged the huskies across, checking ahead for dark, tell-tale cracks. Break-up had started last week when the 40°F mark had been reached, and she could barely believe that the river felt solid beneath her skis. One day the countryside had been gently thawing in the sunshine, the next it had been thrown straight back into the deep freeze.

She had just turned towards Wildwood Ridge when the world closed in on her. The horizon vanished between the snow clouds and the endless white line of the Imuruk Hills. There were no shadows or edges and she could no longer tell whether there was a dip or bend ahead.

It was a whiteout. She had lost the trail, and could not retrace her tracks because they were already covered. Her pursuers would lose her spoor, but she might never find her way to safety. A chill crept deep into her bones. Her face was numb, and her feet and hands were frozen. It became more difficult to push each ski forward, and the desire to lie down and sleep was almost overwhelming. She had nothing left to draw on but sheer will, but she would not let them win. She would perish with her dogs rather than give up.

The wind was now nearly head-on, pounding her with ice pellets. Then the terrain shifted, forcing them to climb. Roscoe and Moke stopped and looked over their shoulders at her, their expressions puzzled and faintly hurt, telling her they wanted to rest. Out of nowhere, Lisa wished Abby was with them. She'd know how to get them climbing to the top of the hill.

And there she was. Her sister. Standing right in front of her. She'd forgotten how broad Abby's shoulders were, how statuesque her figure. She looked like a Nordic athlete, and Lisa felt a rush of admiration.

Memories of Abby grinning at her in her pram; playing hide and seek; extracting little green caterpillars from garden cauliflowers and throwing them at each other; water fights; painting each other's toenails. Abby walking out of Lisa's cabin four years ago, the air between them bitter as acid.

Abby seemed oblivious of the storm and was smiling. Lisa was so relieved she'd been forgiven that she wanted to weep, but her tear ducts were frozen. She wanted to tell Abby how tired she was, but she couldn't form the words. Slowly, she fell to her knees. A mantle of snow started to cover her, and it was strangely comforting, as though Abby was tucking her under the duvet at night. A great tranquillity suffused her. Snow clogged her eyelashes, blanketing her vision, but Abby was still there, smiling.

Lisa didn't see her two huskies standing over her, didn't feel their anxious faces pushing against her. All she could see was her sister. Abby.

ABBY LOPED down Cowley Road, ignoring rush-hour stares. Her suit was drenched by the rain, her hair plastered against her scalp, but the bliss of wet pavement against her stockinged feet was exquisite. No amount of money would make her wear high heels again.

She couldn't wait to get out of her suit and into something comfortable. She never normally dressed up to impress clients, but this time her boss had insisted that she forgo her usual uniform of jeans and work boots for something more businesslike. How women could wear high heels all day defeated her. Abby felt as though she'd been weightlifting all day instead of presenting restoration plans for a nineteenth-century garden.

She padded into the house. 'I'm home!' she called, dumping her briefcase. Her mother's voice floated down the hall. 'See you when you're ready!'

Abby ducked under the beam above the kitchen door and took her shoes to the bin, then hesitated. What if she needed to wear them again in the future? She decided to be prudent, and put them by the Aga to dry out.

The phone started to ring, but she ignored it. Her priority was to get changed. Besides, her mother had a phone within reach; if it was for Abby, she would yell. Or she could press the little emergency button on a chain round her neck.

Heading upstairs, Abby looked forward to stretching out in front of the TV. She had just hung her sodden jacket in the airing cupboard when the house gave a polite buzz. The emergency button.

She piled down the stairs, shouting, 'I'm coming!'

Her mother had suffered from multiple sclerosis since Abby was a child, stoically enduring her progressive physical decline. Although she had been forced to give up her biological sciences tutorial post at Christ Church College, Professor Julia McCall had no intention of retiring. She was currently researching four academic papers, one of which was scheduled to appear later in the year, launching an attack on creationism and rebutting 'intelligent design'.

Abby rocketed into Julia's room to see her sitting up in bed, computer glowing on her lap, pencils and reference books everywhere. For a second she thought it was a false alarm, until she saw how pale her mother was.

She tightened inside. The last time she'd seen Julia looking so shell-shocked was when she and Lisa had returned from school to discover that their father was abandoning them for another woman. He'd gone to Australia on a business trip, and returned in love with an Australian fitness instructor. There had been rows and tears and bitterness, and when he eventually left even the house seemed to heave a sigh of relief. Julia had encouraged her daughters to stay in touch with their father, but it had been difficult. Not just because the sisters were desperately hurt and angry, but because he didn't seem that enthusiastic about maintaining contact.

'What is it?' Abby said. 'What's wrong?'

'It's Lisa. She needs your help.'

Abby stared at Julia. She hadn't spoken to her sister for four years, and her mother was clearly trying to patch things up between them again.

She was about to walk out when her mother added in a whisper, 'A policewoman just called. From Alaska. She says Lisa's missing.'

Belatedly, Abby saw that Julia was trembling, her mouth working to stop herself from crying.

'Oh, Mum.' Abby sat on the edge of her bed. 'You know what Lisa's like. She'll turn up within the next few hours, guaranteed.'

Julia shook her head and tried to speak, but a sob choked the words. Abby gently took her mother's hand. It was cold and thin. She brought it up to her cheek and pressed it there to warm it. Julia gave her a watery smile, took a deep breath and steadied herself.

'She went skijoring,' she managed, 'with her dogs. She got caught in a bad storm up in the mountains. She's been out there for four days.'

Abby's eyes widened. 'You're kidding.'

Julia shook her head. 'She was meant to show up at a friend's place on Saturday, but she didn't. He waited a couple of hours, then went to her cabin. He found equipment gone from her shed, along with her dogs . . .'

'I bet she's tucked up in a bar somewhere, along with her equipment and her dogs. Anything's possible with Lisa.'

'Abby, I know you don't have any patience for your sister, but this time I need you to listen. The friend, who's a ranger, reported her missing. They've got people out looking for her, but I'm worried they're not telling me everything. I want you to go over there. Liaise with the police in Lake's Edge and keep tabs on how the search is progressing.'

'Lake's Edge?' Abby's voice rose a notch higher. 'I thought she was moving back to Fairbanks to live with Greg.'

Julia looked away again. 'She and Greg split up. She stayed.'

'You want me to go to *Lake's Edge*?'

Julia wouldn't meet her eyes. Abby's brain was clogged with disbelief. Why hadn't Lisa gone missing someplace else?

'What about Thomas?' She was referring to Lisa's boss at the University of Alaska, Fairbanks. 'Doesn't he mind her living in the back of beyond?'

'No.' Julia pulled a tissue from the box on her bedside table and blew her nose. 'Lake's Edge is in the middle of some powerful magnetic field, which is what they've been researching. She goes to Fairbanks every month, and he puts her up while she's there. You know how she loves the wilderness, and it's not like she has to be at the lab full time. She does the majority of her work on a computer, after all.'

Julia scrunched up the tissue. She was still pale but she had regained her composure. 'Darling, I know you don't want to go back there, but maybe this isn't such a bad thing. Perhaps it will do something to bring you back together. Please go, Abby.'

A small, angry child's wail started up inside her: *But I don't want to!*

'Ralph will take care of me.'

An army colonel, widowed and recently retired, Ralph lived at the end of their street and had been part of Abby's life ever since she could remember. After her father left, he'd asked Julia out. She turned him down, but he hadn't seemed offended, and cheerfully offered to look after the girls while Julia went to a conference in Venice. Abby had been thrilled when Julia agreed. She adored Ralph, and over the next few years allowed him to take on the role of part-time surrogate father.

'I thought Ralph was going to France on some reunion thing.'

'That's not the point.' Julia took a shaky breath. 'Darling, this is not the time to be stubborn.'

'I'm not being stubborn! I'm just not sure if my going over there will change anything.'

'She's your sister, Abby. She needs your help.'

Abby thought about the local council who were screaming for the landscaping plans for their riverside park. Then she looked at her mother, the anxiety already etched into lines round her eyes and mouth, and she knew she didn't have a choice. 'All right.' Her voice was quiet. 'I'll go.'

Julia's eyes filled with tears. She gripped Abby's hand. 'Darling, thank you.'

Two

Abby shivered and stamped her feet, trying to bring them to life. She breathed into her gloves, pulled her turtleneck up to her chin. She could see why the guy loading the plane wore ear muffs; her ears were aching with cold. The wind sliced through her paltry layers of sweater and waterproof jacket, and she wished she was snug inside a fur-lined parka like everyone else.

It was April, and she'd expected the country to be melting into spring, but a series of late-winter storms had altered the season dramatically. She'd never felt such cold before.

A queasy feeling grew in the pit of her stomach as she surveyed the rusting ski plane. The skis were tiny, and looked as though the lumpy runway of frozen lake would rip them apart on takeoff, and she bet the aircraft didn't have heating. Not like Wright's Air's nice big Camel plane parked alongside, but they weren't flying to Lake's Edge until the end of the week.

'Try Mac,' a girl with black braids had told her cheerfully. 'He's flying a friend up near Lake's Edge today. He'll drop you off, I'm sure.'

Abby hated flying. She had wanted to hire a car, but since the road north was shut due to the storm, she was trapped. Bush flying may be a way of life in a state twice the size of Texas, but no way was it for her.

Not like Lisa, who loved not only to fly, but to glide, parachute and skydive. The closest Abby got to adventure was hill walking in Wales.

She stamped her feet again, looking at the distant mountains, their white fangs gouging the sky. Was Lisa *really* lost up there somewhere? Abby had stepped off the plane in Fairbanks looking for an apologetic official of some sort cringing over an absurd mix-up. When no one had appeared, she had sighed and gone to collect her bag. Someone would turn up at some point with an explanation for Lisa's disappearance. She just hoped it would be sooner rather than later, preferably before she got to Lake's Edge.

Pulling up her scarf to cover her nose and mouth, she lugged her single bag to Mac, a broad bear of a man with a haystack of blond hair and a bristly moustache. He took her bag, hefted it briefly as though gauging its weight, then dropped it to the ground.

'Just three of us today,' he said. 'Glad you travel light. Not like my other passenger.' He nodded to a pile of gear: shovels, axes, skis, snowshoes, rifles, boxes of ammunition, a tarpaulin and a variety of unmarked crates.

She was wondering if she was sharing the flight with an arctic explorer when the passenger turned up, shotgun in hand. He had a fur cap with ear flaps, blue padded trousers tucked into wide-legged rubber boots, and a red padded jacket. His scruffy dusting of grey stubble seemed incongruous against the neatly cropped iron-grey hair and military set of his shoulders.

'What are you staring at?' His tone was aggressive.

'Nothing. Sorry.'

Shrewd eyes raked her up and down. 'Christ,' he growled. 'I had no idea.'

Abby was working up to bite back, but the man had switched his attention to her bag. He was scowling at it as though it was a sack of snakes.

He said, 'Hope we don't come down out there 'cause you're going to be a real liability, aren't you?'

'You're assuming we'll get airborne with all your clobber on board,' she replied, stung. 'Do you *really* need three crates of Alaskan Amber?'

'Six,' he corrected. 'I'll squeeze 'em in once Mac's cleared his reserve fuel out.'

Abby thought it was his idea of a joke, but to her horror ten minutes later Mac removed his reserve drums and in their places went the beer.

'Not scared of flying, are you?' the man asked.

She stuck her chin in the air. 'Not at all. I was just concerned about what would happen if we're forced to land off-course and need to refuel.'

'We'll have to walk,' was the laconic response.

She glanced at the forbidding, snow-laden mountains and couldn't prevent a shiver.

'You wouldn't last three seconds, would you?'

'No,' she admitted.

He cocked his head and studied her. 'Not like your sister, are you?'

She felt as though he'd punched her in the midriff. 'My *sister*?'

'You're Abigail McCall, right?'

'How on earth—?'

'Saw the flight plan. Abigail McCall flying to Lake's Edge, where Lisa McCall's gotten herself in trouble.' The man gave a little sneer. 'Don't have to be a detective to put two and two together.'

'Yo, Victor!' Mac called out. 'You really need that canoe? We can strap it below, but it's gonna play hell once we're up.'

Canoe jettisoned and everything securely roped down, Mac wedged her firmly behind Victor, who was in the co-pilot's seat, and passed her a headset before running through a speedy preflight check. The next she knew they were skittering down the ice-packed lake with the throttles wide open, and she readied herself for the swoop as they lifted into the air, but the plane remained firmly lake-bound.

She was beginning to panic, a scream building in her throat as the end of the lake approached with alarming speed, when Mac said, 'She's a bit heavy, but we *should* be OK,' and at the same moment the aircraft reluctantly lumbered skywards.

Abby sat rigid, teeth gritted, concentrating on slow, steady breaths.

'Abby?'

She started as Mac's voice came through her headset. She twisted the mouthpiece round and said in a hoarse voice, 'Yes?'

'Victor tells me you've been here before?'

A jet of panic rocketed through her veins. How the hell did Victor know that? Would everyone in Lake's Edge remember her?

'Conservationist or some such?' Mac prompted.

'I came out to do a feasibility study four years ago.'

For two months that summer, July and August, she had joined a group of scientists in one of the world's last, great unspoilt wildernesses. Their chartered helicopter had flown them from Lake's Edge right into the heart of the Brooks Range, where they set up camp. Each morning, it would fly them to a different area, and they'd spend the day sketching and mapping, packing samples of plants and taking notes of wildlife. In the evening, the chopper would fly them back to the campsite. When she returned to Lake's Edge she didn't think she'd been happier. Not only had she been sun-browned and fit, but she'd been in love.

Abby flushed as she remembered those two months with Cal. He'd been the group's professional hunter and wilderness guide, teaching them about the web of life in the Arctic, and making sure they didn't get too close to any bears. What a cliché, falling for the guide. She still felt so *stupid*.

Mac twisted in his seat to look at her briefly. 'A feeza-what?'

'Background research in the field. Looking at tundra and its context to see if we could duplicate it in England for the general public to look at.'

Mac snorted. 'They want to look at tundra, may as well come out here.'

Which was what the Eden Project in Cornwall had decided in the end.

Not only was human habitation minimal in the Arctic, they said, but the plants weren't as sexy to the average punter as, say, cacti.

Steeling herself once more, she peered outside to see they were heading north over the Chena river. The plane gave a little bump, then resumed its smooth ride. It wasn't warm in the plane but she was sweating.

He's an experienced pilot, she lectured herself. *You're in good hands*.

'Keep a lookout,' Mac told her as he banked northwest, the city starting to fall behind them. 'You might get to see a bear or two. It was warm enough last week to get them moving. Hibernation's over.'

Abby gazed down but couldn't see anything, thanks to an opaque grey cloud. They droned on for another two hours. She tried to doze, but each time the plane lurched she'd been convinced they were about to crash.

How she wished she was more like her dauntless sister. Not for the first time, Abby wondered at their differences. Unlike Lisa, a physicist and mathematician whose research was impenetrable to Abby, she'd never been interested in delving into abstractions. Her thinking was solid and practical, her feet planted on terra firma.

Her eyes snapped open as Mac suddenly put the aircraft into a steep dive. 'Victor's dropping-off point', he yelled. 'Destination nowhere!'

As they emerged under the cloud, Abby gave a muffled yelp. Holy cow! They were barely a hundred feet above the ice-covered lake. Mac inched down further and kept cruising. Abruptly, he pulled the nose up.

'Nope. Soft ice ain't safe.'

'Come on, Mac!' Victor protested. 'It's frozen solid as my front drive.'

'So what are those cracks at the edges? Native art?'

'For Chrissakes, at least let's have another look.'

Mac turned his head to look at Victor. 'You that desperate to get away you want the cost of hauling this thing from the bottom of the lake?'

'Yup.'

'Jesus.'

The wing dipped and they were turning, scooping low again, skimming over the ice. She could see the sinister black fissures Mac had mentioned and was waiting for him to abandon all pretence of landing when he throttled back. Abby couldn't believe it. They were about to land.

A yell stuck in her throat, and seconds later they were bouncing and sliding across the surface until the aircraft came to rest beside a tall cliff.

The whole area was frozen under a cape of snow. A tiny log cabin was tucked beneath the cliff, but there was no other form of human habitation. No birds were in the sky. It was a bleak desert of cold, and Abby couldn't think what Victor was doing all the way out here.

Mac didn't cut the engines. 'Better get a move on! Not long till dark!'

Abby sprang into life, realising that the sooner they got rid of Victor and his equipment, the larger the window of safety she'd have on the next leg of the journey. Hauling a crowbar and pickaxe from the back of the plane, she edged her way onto the creaking ice and to shore.

'See ya,' Mac told Victor. 'Watch out for grizzlies.'

Victor patted his rifle and, without even glancing at Abby, crunched away. Abby scowled. If she never saw Victor again it would be too soon.

THEY FLEW WEST for another ten minutes before Mac pointed out Lake's Edge. The queasy feeling returned as Abby looked down at the remote outpost clinging to the side of a lake, in a deep valley between two mountains.

Mac began to drop altitude, and as they approached she recognised the main street and the spiderweb of trails that connected the various dwellings. At the southern end of town, Abby spotted a dirt runway.

'Since when did Lake's Edge get that?' she asked, pointing down.

'Couple of years back.'

She looked across at him. 'Don't you have a plane with wheels?'

'Sure, but it wouldn't have got Victor to his cabin, and he was that desperate for a break . . .' He trailed off as the lake began to approach.

Abby held her breath as he set the aircraft down, gently as a feather, but she didn't unclench her fingers until he'd cruised to a stop beside a pontoon. She reckoned she was coping pretty well with enduring this terrifying bush flight, but when she took in the vast expanses of snow and ice reaching as far as the eye could see, the snow pluming off the tops of the mountains, jagged rubbles of rocks forming landslides on their flanks, she felt as though her mind was going to implode. Lisa had gone missing up there somewhere. Like it or not, this was for real.

Abby clambered out of the aircraft. Hands tucked beneath her armpits, breath steaming in the freezing air, she looked around. Buildings, sheds and trees were all slumped under a coating of fresh snow. There were no cars or snow machines or people. The place was deserted.

Engine still running, Mac jumped out with her bag and dropped it on the pontoon. Abby felt dismayed when he held out his hand for a shake.

She looked at the light bleeding out of the sky. 'Aren't you staying? I didn't think pilots out here flew in the dark.'

He grinned. 'It's only a short hop. It'll still be light when I get there.' He turned to go, when she stopped him.

'I don't suppose you know where the police station is?'

'There isn't one. Nearest is Coldfoot.' Mac jerked his chin towards the village. 'You needn't worry, Trooper Demarco's on her way.' She was about to turn to look for the trooper when he added, 'Hope you find your sister.'

'Me too,' she murmured.

Mac headed for his plane, calling, 'Good luck!' over his shoulder.

Engine bellowing, he slipped to the end of the lake and turned, accelerating until the air was under his wings and he lifted off. The engine's roar faded, leaving a dense silence that made her ears ring.

'Miss McCall?'

The voice was threaded with confusion, and Abby felt the familiar surge of irritation that the trooper had assumed she and Lisa would look alike.

Abby was different from the rest of her family, with their compact bodies, curly dark hair and wild gestures, but it wasn't until she was thirteen, when Julia had a clear-out one wet weekend, that she'd fallen on a yellowing photograph of her great-grandmother. And there she was, right down to the slightly tilted, intense blue eyes and tiny birthmark at the corner of her mouth. If she hadn't known it was Marijka Schikora, Norwegian bride to Dewitt McCall, she'd have thought it was a picture of herself.

'Yes,' she said now, 'I'm Abby McCall.'

Abby looked down at the uniformed trooper. Dark blue trousers with gold stripes down the sides, matching blue padded parka with lots of pockets. Pistol on one hip, walkie-talkie on the other. Curly brown hair peeking from beneath a hat made of beaver fur. She was staring at Abby's hair, and Abby felt like saying no, it wasn't dyed, and that yes, she liked it short-cropped and spiky like a bleached-white hedgehog.

'Ma'am,' she said, giving up her hair inspection, 'I'm Trooper Demarco.'

'Hi.'

'Hope the trip was OK.' The trooper kept her intelligent brown eyes on Abby's. 'It's a long way to come.'

Abby knew this was the coded version of *You should have saved yourself the trouble*, and refused to drop her gaze.

Demarco smiled, as though she'd heard Abby's thoughts. 'I've a car,' she said amiably. 'I flew up from Fairbanks in the heli, but folk are generous round here and I've been loaned a vehicle.'

They crunched along the pontoon to the Ford Explorer Demarco had pointed out. 'I'll take you to the school and fill you in,' the trooper said. 'As a temporary measure, we're using one of the teachers' rooms. We don't have a trooper post here. Just a VPSO. A village public safety officer.'

With the heater on full blast, the trooper bounced her loaned Ford Explorer from pothole to pothole, crunching on muddy ice and fresh snow. A snow plough had gone through recently, piling banks of snow five feet high on either side. 'I understand you've been here before,' Demarco said.

Abby nodded but didn't say anything. She didn't want the past dragged up. Turning her attention outside, she wondered where everyone was. It was like a ghost town. There was nobody about. Not even a dog.

They passed snow-covered log cabins, and the Moose bar with its neon-pink sign flashing, *Hot coffee, all-day breakfast, Budweiser, B & B*. It was familiar but also strangely alien. The only change she could see was that the visitor centre had expanded to take over the shop next door.

Finally the trooper slowed to a stop outside a single-storey building. Abby followed Demarco through some double doors. Walls were covered in drawings of bears, whales and flowers, and Abby could hear children chattering, their bright, happy voices infusing her with a sense of normality. But where were the parents? Why did the town appear abandoned?

At the end of the corridor, Demarco pushed open a door and ushered Abby into a stuffy, overheated square box with white walls. She could see four plastic chairs, an aluminium desk piled with paper, a filing cabinet, and a small table overflowing with paper cups, packs of sugar and teabags.

Demarco went to the coffee machine and poured them a cup each. She offered Abby a chair, which she declined. She'd been travelling for twenty-four hours, and she knew that if she sat down she'd fall asleep.

The trooper settled behind the desk and reached for a green folder. Ran a finger down the front page as though gathering the facts, then looked up with a sombre expression.

'You've found her?' Abby's voice was hoarse.

Demarco shook her head. 'Not yet. Everyone's out there now. Looking.'

Abby glanced through the window at the empty street. 'Everyone?'

'Pretty much. Folk from Wiseman and Coldfoot are chipping in too. We've dogs on the ground, and Ron and Lou . . . I mean Mr and Mrs Walmsley, are scouting in their aeroplane.' Demarco glanced at the phone sitting on the desk, then away. 'They'll be back after dark.'

'Where are they looking?'

The trooper picked up a crumpled map from the floor, spread it across her desk. 'We're here.' She showed Abby where Lake's Edge was, and then swept her finger southwest. 'And we're searching here.' She pointed to an area marked with big black letters: WILDERNESS.

Abby studied the areas shaded in green, white and brown, denoting glaciers, glacial moraines, crevasses and springs, woodland, waterfalls, and mile upon mile of cramped contour lines rising to various mountain tops.

'Your sister was supposed to meet Joe Chenega at the weekend. Joe's a forest ranger. He and your sister go fishing from time to time. He taught her survival skills. She was supposed to collect a dog sled he was fixing up for her. When she didn't turn up, he went and checked her place. From the equipment missing in her shed, he was of the opinion she'd gone skijoring.'

'Skijoring?' Abby repeated. Julia had mentioned something about skis, but she hadn't taken it in.

'Skiing behind a couple of dogs, with supplies either on her back or tied to a small sled. She's known for taking off like that from time to time, but it's the first time she's been in trouble.'

No it's not, Abby thought. 'You know my sister?' she asked.

'Never met,' the trooper admitted. 'But she's well known round here . . .' She reached into a pocket and withdrew a tissue, blew her nose. 'One of her dogs turned up. Chewed through its harness to get back home. He's got frostbite. He's still pretty weak after his ordeal . . . That dog had been on the mountain a long time.'

The trooper was still talking but Abby's mind had frozen on the vision of Lisa crawling through the snow, her elfin face blackening with frostbite. She swallowed drily, pushing the picture away. Lisa was a survivor. Just because her dog had broken free didn't mean Lisa was dead.

'Joe knows the score when someone goes missing. He did a recon when the storm cleared.' The trooper pushed her finger at a small black square on the map. 'He ascertained someone stayed here recently . . . it's a wilderness cabin. Your sister likes M&Ms, right? Smokes Marlboro?'

Yes and yes, Abby replied silently, but a stubborn cynicism made her say, 'My sister can't be the only person in the world who smokes that particular brand of cigarette and eats chocolate-coated peanuts.'

The trooper reached into the desk drawer and pulled out a small, clear plastic bag and passed it over. 'We found this, too.'

Inside the bag was a slender silver chain with a turquoise drop. It was Abby's necklace, the one she'd bought with Granny Rose's money for her sixteenth birthday. Lisa used to drive her mad, borrowing it without asking. Abby hadn't worn it for years and had had no idea it was missing.

'It's Lisa's, right?' The trooper was watching her closely.

'Actually, it's mine.' Abby gave a tight smile. 'But I guess it means the same thing as far as you're concerned.'

The trooper gave a nod and popped the necklace back inside the drawer.

'This is where she'd be headed next, but it looks like she never made it.' Demarco had returned to the map. 'It's been untouched all winter, still is.'

Abby traced the route. It was fifty miles from one cabin to the other across valleys and lakes, through forests. 'She couldn't do this in one day, surely.'

'She'd camp out. There's an old trail linking the cabins. See, it makes a nice loop back to Lake's Edge, an easy three or four days. I gather she'd often head out there after a trip to Fairbanks. Said it cleared her head.'

Nothing had changed, obviously. Abby could remember Lisa coming home from school, dumping her bags in the kitchen and disappearing into the garden for at least half an hour before she'd talk to anyone.

'Joe says Lisa got back from town late on Friday, so it makes sense she left Saturday morning. She obviously forgot she was supposed to be meeting up with Joe later the same day.'

Abby looked through the window at the colourless street, wondering if it would brighten up in the morning. She flinched when the phone rang.

Demarco picked it up. Listened briefly. 'You've found *what*? Jesus . . .' She tucked the phone between her ear and shoulder and pulled the map across. 'But that's miles away . . . Yup. OK. Will do.' She dropped the receiver into the cradle and bent over the map, studying it with a frown.

'What is it?' Abby asked. 'Is it Lisa?'

The trooper raised her head and looked at Abby straight. 'They've found something . . . But nowhere near where your sister went missing. I'm sorry.'

'What have they found?'

'I'm sorry,' the trooper said again, refolding the map. 'Miss McCall—'

'Abby, please.' She didn't like the trooper's evasiveness.

'Abby. I was thinking you could stay at your sister's for the night. It's not far; I'll drive you. Then we can meet tomorrow when you've rested up.'

Abby followed Demarco outside into the still, cold silence. The trooper's steps were light in the snow, her spine erect. Something close to a smile tugged the corners of her mouth and her eyes were overbright. With a shiver Abby recognised what it was: adrenaline.

LISA'S CABIN wasn't a prefab like some of the other homes in Lake's Edge, but a traditionally built log cabin with solar collectors on the snow-covered roof. A dozen black dishes the size of dinner plates nestled alongside, faces turned to the sky. They hadn't been there when Abby last visited.

Demarco drew up outside the cabin and handed her a door key. 'Diane keeps a spare.' She sent Abby a sharp look. 'She's the owner of the Moose. You remember her?'

'Not really,' said Abby, cringing. 'I only stayed there a couple of nights.' She turned away to hide her flush at the sudden memory of Diane, fresh sheets in hand, catching her and Cal in bed the morning after the expedition returned. Cal was meant to be staying with friends, but he'd sneaked into her room after midnight. Diane had taken one look at them, thrown the sheets on the floor and stalked out, slamming the door behind her.

'You'll be OK?' the trooper asked, and stuck the gear into drive.

Abby climbed out and Demarco rocketed back down the trail.

The sky still held a little light and stars edged the horizon. Abby picked up her bag and crunched over to the deck at the front of the cabin. To one side of the front door, on a small circular table, was a rusting gold pan full of grey sand studded with cigarette butts—a makeshift ashtray. Abby's head buzzed, her vision wavering. Lisa had wanted badly to give up the last time they saw each other. It was as if time crumpled, as if the last four years' silence had never been. Abby could feel the shape of Lisa's small, strong body when they'd hugged on her arrival at Fairbanks airport. Her laughter was infectious, and people looked at them, smiling as they always did.

A deep, dragging ache started in Abby's heart. She couldn't believe it. Lisa was too ebullient, too full of life. She was indestructible.

Abby unlocked the front door and gently pushed it open. The silence pressed on her ears. She knocked her boots against the doorstep to shake off the snow, then stepped inside. The air was freezing. It felt as though the stove hadn't been fired up for months. She fumbled until she found the light switch. A single light came on at the far end of the room.

She scanned the room. As usual, the place was a mess. There were piles of washing up, packets of cereal spilling flakes all over the counters, toast crumbs, open jars of jam. Drawers were open, magazines and papers tossed on the floor. Abby's skin tightened as she looked around. Oh, God, she thought. It's not just that it's a mess. *It's been ransacked.*

A gust of cold air reached her from the stairway ahead. She trotted down the stairs to find the mud-room door wide open. Then she saw that the lock had been forced, the wood around it splintered. Cautiously she stepped outside, but there were no fresh footprints in the snow. Just a snowy pile of what appeared to be an old fire set away from the cabin to her left. Why, she wondered, had Lisa built a fire at this time of year? If she wanted to burn anything, wouldn't she have used her wood stove?

Abby crunched over, and kicked some snow aside to find a charred, twisted mess of computer discs and ring binders. Abby stared, astonished, then hurried inside to check the cabin. Lisa's bedroom, ransacked. Her office, also ransacked. No notebooks littered the desk, no files sat in the cabinets, no papers in the desk drawers, no computer or computer discs.

She could feel her heart pumping as she looked again at the broken lock on the mud-room door. Someone had definitely broken in here. But why had Lisa's work been burned? Had she done it herself, or was it the burglar?

Abby headed back upstairs for the phone. Mobile phones didn't work out here, which is why she'd left hers at home. Even land-line telephones were unreliable, which was why a lot of people in rural areas had ham radios.

She found the phone and dialled the number Demarco had given her.

A woman came on the line. When Abby explained who she was and what had happened, her tone turned brisk. 'I'll radio Demarco. Hang on a sec.'

Abby heard the woman talking, but the only words she could make out were her and Lisa's names. There was a clatter, then the woman returned.

'She says she'll be with you as soon as she's free.'

DEMARCO STAYED barely half an hour. She checked the broken lock, made a handful of notes in her notebook, and told Abby that break-ins were highly unusual in places like this, but not unknown.

As the trooper headed for the front door, Abby said, 'Aren't you going to get someone to dust for prints?'

'It's just me up here, Abby.' Her tone was dry. 'If and when I feel it's warranted, I'll bring the Crime Lab folks in.'

Abby got the point. She nodded.

'I'll be getting on, then.'

She watched the trooper leave, boots crunching in the snow. Demarco hadn't made much of the bonfire of discs and files, but Abby had already learned that the trooper didn't like giving anything away.

After she had fixed the mud-room door, Abby decided to take a shower. Lisa's bathrobe lay on the floor like a pool of spilt yellow paint. She loved bright colours. A man's blue robe was slung over the towel rail, and Abby wondered who it belonged to.

She heated up a can of tomato soup. She barely had the energy to lift the spoon but she knew she had to ring her mother. Checking her watch, she counted back eight hours, making it 2 p.m. English time.

'Mum? It's me.'

'Where is she? Is she with you?'

Deep breath. 'They're still looking.'

Abby hadn't expected Julia to break down, but when her voice remained calm, even if a bit wobbly, she felt a rush of relief.

'And you, Abby? How are you?'

'Tired. Weird.' She rested her head on her hand and closed her eyes as she described her bush flight, then her meeting with Trooper Demarco. She didn't mention Lisa burning her files, or the break-in. 'I saw this map, Mum, where they reckon she went. Skijoring, they call it—'

'She loves those dogs,' Julia said. 'But Roscoe's her favourite. I've a picture of him here. Darling . . .' She hesitated. 'I want you to know how glad I am you're there. You know that if I could have gone—'

'I know. And I'm glad I'm here too,' she lied. 'How's Ralph?'

'Driving me mad with his appalling jokes.'

Abby felt a rush of love for Ralph. He'd dropped everything to help out. He knew as well as Abby did that if left to her own devices Julia would forget to care for herself. That was why, after graduating with her landscape architect's degree from Leeds, Abby had found a job in Oxford and moved in with Julia. She worried far less knowing she could keep an eye on her.

After speaking with Ralph for a while, Abby hung up. Feeling unsettled and restless, she busied herself washing up the piles of dishes, then tackled the mess the burglar had made. As she tidied, she tried to get a sense of her sister but it was like being in a stranger's home. On Lisa's bedside cabinet stood a glass lamp in the shape of a leaping orca and a soft-backed beige book, well thumbed and filthy.

Abby picked it up. *Survival in the Arctic*, published in 1970. It covered everything from orientation and patrolling to making fires and building shelters. There were countless diagrams and sketches of traps, snares and tree pits. Not her type of bedtime reading, but typically Lisa's. She'd been fascinated by survival ever since Abby could remember.

She put the book aside and opened the top drawer. She found herself staring at her own handwriting.

Steeling herself, she took out the stack of letters and untied the ribbon that bound them. Some letters were on lined paper torn from school books and covered in childish drawings, some were neatly penned on thick vellum, others were postcards she'd sent from her travels.

She sank onto the bed, feeling dizzy. She hadn't kept any of Lisa's letters.

Her fingers felt numb as she opened the next drawer down. It was full of photographs of the two of them: riding bicycles, camping in the garden, opening Christmas presents. Her mind echoed with their happy shrieks.

She had loved her little sister so much, she was suddenly baffled how they had become estranged. Tears welled in her eyes and she brushed them angrily away. Jet lag was making her tired and emotional. She must get some sleep. Pushing the childhood memorabilia back into the cabinet, she wriggled under the covers and turned out the light.

ABBY AWOKE to the sound of hammering on wood. Her eyes snapped open to see pale arrows of sunlight falling coldly through the window.

Pulling the robe tight round her, Abby blearily checked the time on the VCR clock as she stumbled through the living area. Ten a.m.! She couldn't remember when she'd last slept in so late. Feeling every one of her thirty-one years, she peered through the window to see Trooper Demarco stamping her feet on the porch, vapour pouring from her nostrils.

Abby groaned. She'd arranged to meet Demarco at the Moose at nine.

She opened the door and gave an involuntary yelp. Christ, it was cold. She was about to urge Demarco inside and offer her a coffee when she took in the trooper's expression. Her heart faltered.

Demarco took off her beaver hat and held it formally in front of her.

Oh, God, please no. Please don't let Lisa be dead. She's my past, my history, she knows everything about me. Please God, she can't be dead.

'I'm sorry, Abby. We've found the body of a woman in the mountains.'

Three

Abby sat in the rear of the thundering helicopter, looking down at the icy tundra. She took a deep breath and tried to quell a rising tide of panic. The helicopter swooped to the right and began to descend. Demarco turned round with a sympathetic grimace.

'Nearly there,' she called.

Abby peered out at a ghostly white creek with a frozen waterfall. She couldn't see any vehicles or police and for the next few seconds she couldn't see anything at all as the rotors whipped up the snow into a thick white storm. Abby bit her lip to stop the whimper fluttering in her throat.

The engines wound down to a high-pitched whine as the snow resettled. Doors were opened, people jumped out. The pilot turned in his seat.

'Sure am sorry about this,' he said. His eyes were kind.

Abby nodded. Unbuckled her seat belt with stiff fingers. As she stepped out onto the soft snow, she felt her throat contract at the change in temperature. Wrapping a scarf round her face, she let Demarco lead her along the creek and past the frozen waterfall.

Round the corner was an Alaska State Troopers helicopter, its doors open. There were a couple of snow machines parked near by, and dozens of ski tracks leading to and from the chopper.

Breath clouding the air, two men stood beside a yellow plastic bundle lying on the ground. It was a body bag. Abby stumbled, but Demarco made soothing noises as she helped her upright and walked her towards the men.

Abby swallowed hard. Her legs trembled but she eased herself away from Demarco. She would do this alone and with dignity.

Slowly, her boots crunched through the snow. One man took a step back but the second raised his head and watched her. She was looking at a snow-sprinkled cap of short dark hair. The zip of the body bag was open to her chest, and Abby took in the red sweater, the single chunky gold earring in her left ear, and the gold cross nestled at the base of her throat.

Abby studied her face. The eyes were closed, eyelashes frosted with ice crystals. The skin was a mottled blue, the lips cracked and black.

Abby's mind was blank as she stared at the corpse that wasn't her sister.

WHEN LISA CAME round, she thought she was in a tomb.

She blinked and blinked, but she couldn't see anything. It was pitch dark and the air as cold and bitter as dry ice. She could hear that the storm was still raging, but she couldn't feel a single thing, no pain or discomfort.

She must be dying. She had heard death by hypothermia was relatively painless, that it began with a wandering mind, then apathy would set in, and a desperate desire to sleep. Eventually blood would stop pumping to the extremities, the breathing rate would slow, the pulse would weaken, and the limbs would grow rigid. It was death by freezing. Not such a bad way to go. But she hadn't finished yet. She had something important to complete.

Lisa tried to move to check her sled, to look for her research, but her body refused to respond. She had no heat in her core to spare. She was a lump of slowly freezing meat. Despite her best efforts, she had failed.

Distantly, she wondered when Abby would hear of her disappearance and whether she'd fly out. She doubted it, after the last time, but as her breathing started to slow she made a final effort. She prayed for Abby to keep hating her, so she wouldn't want to come and help her.

'YOU MUST HAVE some idea who she is,' Abby said. 'Hasn't anyone reported her missing?'

They were in the Explorer, skidding back down the road to Lisa's cabin while the woman's body was being flown to Anchorage, and an autopsy.

Demarco gave a noncommittal grunt. She obviously wasn't happy the body wasn't Lisa's. Her workload had just doubled.

'Was she alone?' Abby asked. 'Was there any sign of anyone else?'

The trooper braked for a corner and didn't reply.

'She wasn't wearing outdoor clothing,' Abby persisted. 'Or was she? Did you find a parka or anything?'

Demarco's chin jutted forward and for a moment Abby thought she was going to respond, but then she just gave a shrug.

'Maybe she drove there,' Abby suggested, 'Maybe she broke down . . .'

She turned her attention back to the map on her lap. She judged the distance between where Lisa had gone missing and where the body was found to be forty miles. She pointed this out. Demarco didn't say a word.

'Two women have gone missing in the mountains,' Abby said. 'It can't be a coincidence, surely?'

The trooper veered round a pothole, making the rear wheels slide briefly. She said, 'We'll be holding a public meeting at the Moose in half an hour or so. Shall I drop you at your sister's place so you can freshen up?'

'Sure,' said Abby, caving in against the trooper's immovability.

Some days, she wished she was more like her sister. Lisa wouldn't have let Demarco stonewall her; she would have been firing questions at the trooper, wearing her down until she'd got the answers she wanted.

AS SOON AS ABBY was back inside Lisa's cabin, she called home. She was still talking fifteen minutes later.

'Yes, I'm fine, Mum, I promise—'

'They don't know who this woman is?' Julia asked for the tenth time.

'Not yet, no. Look, Mum, I've got to go. You'll be OK?'

'Ralph's here. He's being very kind. Love you.'

Abby hung up and, grabbing her day pack, raced outside. She didn't want to be late for the public meeting. She glanced at the snow-topped vehicles in Lisa's driveway, one red, one beige, and went back inside to hunt for keys. She found a set on top of the microwave.

Grabbing a scraper from the deck, Abby went to the red SUV. No way would Lisa drive a beige car. The driver's door was unlocked. Breath steaming, Abby hopped inside. She tried to push the key into the ignition but it didn't fit. She crunched over to the beige car and tried the key in the lock. This time it worked.

She saw it the instant she started to climb inside. Lying on the passenger seat was a single chunky gold earring, identical to the one the dead woman had worn in her left ear.

She looked around and saw a rental-car tag dangling from the rearview mirror. Opening the glove box, she pulled out a flimsy white sheet of paper. The rental agreement. Made to a Marie Guillemote, from Virginia.

LIKE THE VILLAGE itself, the Moose hadn't changed. With its trophies of moose, Dall sheep and salmon displayed on the log walls, it still looked more like a hunting lodge than a bar. The place was empty aside from a big Native guy at the counter, drinking coffee.

'Trooper Demarco?' Abby asked him. 'She's gone?'

The big guy turned and peered at her from beneath a broad forehead and a pair of bushy black eyebrows. It was like being scrutinised by a buffalo.

'Where is she?' Abby shifted from foot to foot. 'Can I catch her up?'

'She asked me to take you to the Search and Rescue command post.' The big guy downed the last of his coffee and got to his feet. 'I'm Joe Chenega,' he said, and stuck out a paw the size of a frying pan. 'Most folk around here call me Big Joe.'

Abby blinked. 'You're the guy Lisa was meant to meet up with?'

He nodded.

Abby shook Big Joe's hand. It was strong and warm.

'I'll fetch the car,' he said. 'You wait here.'

A gust of fog blurred her senses as he strode away—jet lag kicking in. Abby watched a woman arrive, carrying a tray of glasses. She was small and strong-looking, but when she saw Abby she nearly dropped the tray.

'What the . . .?' she said.

'Diane,' said Abby cautiously.

'Abby.' The woman's dark, tilted eyes were appraising her warily. 'You want some coffee?'

Grateful for the peace offering, Abby said, 'Sure.'

Diane glanced away, then back. 'Go sit by the fire. I'll bring it over.'

Grateful for the woman's relative equanimity, Abby shrugged off her coat and settled into one of the leather armchairs round the fire.

Diane brought her coffee over and looked as though she was about to say something, then changed her mind and gave her a tight smile instead.

'Rest up all you want. You look like you need it.'

'Diane, I . . . Thank you.'

The woman walked off, her black plait twisting at her waist. Had she forgiven her? The Native woman had been apoplectic with rage when she caught her and Cal in bed that morning, but Abby hadn't understood why.

She leaned back in the leather chair and closed her eyes. The Moose smelt the same as it had when she'd been here with Cal: wood smoke, coffee and fried bacon. After Diane had slammed the door behind her, she could remember Cal flinging back the bedclothes and heading for his clothes, muttering something about coffee and muffins. He was away for nearly an hour, and it was only later that she realised he must have been talking to Diane. When he returned he was distant and distracted over breakfast. Eventually he'd said he had to go.

'Meet me for supper tonight?' she asked.

'I, er . . .' He ran a hand over his head. 'There's something I have to do.'

'What is it?'

'Nothing. I just need . . . a bit of time. I'll see you tomorrow, OK?'

She didn't make anything of it because he came over and pulled her close, pressing a kiss against her mouth. She felt more alive than she could remember, and an hour later, when she bounded into Lisa's cabin, she embraced her sister like she hadn't in ages.

'Blimey,' Lisa said, looking her up and down. 'What happened to you?'

'I met a man,' Abby blurted.

Lisa grinned. 'From the way your tail's wagging, this is cause for celebration.' She brought out a bottle of wine. 'Now start at the beginning.'

So Abby did. She'd only uttered a couple of sentences when Lisa said, 'What? Did I get his name right? Did you say *Cal*?'

'Cal Pegati was our guide. He's setting up an insurance company in Fairbanks, but he used to guide hunters—'

'Oh, shit.' Lisa was staring at her in open horror.

Abby blinked. 'What? What's wrong with that?'

'Why *him*, for God's sake?' She flung up her hands in despair. 'I don't believe this. You sitting smug as can be, carrying on like Saffron doesn't exist.' Lisa got to her feet, eyes glittering. 'One of the nicest, most beautiful women around, tossed aside in a moment.'

The name rang a bell but Abby shook her head. 'Who's Saffron?'

'Just my best friend in the whole wide world.'

Abby looked blank and Lisa flung up her hands again. 'She was the first person to make me welcome up here. Helped me find a cabin to rent, introduced me to everyone. We used to go picking berries, fishing together—'

'What has Saffron got to do with me and Cal?'

'Oh, just a small issue, like she's been Cal's wife for the past eight years.'

'He's *married*?'

'Oh, drop the bullshit, Abby. Married men stick out a mile.'

'But I honestly didn't know!'

'Saffron will *die* if she hears about this'

'I know he's a bit of all right, but to break up his marriage . . .'

Abby scrambled to her feet, face burning. 'How dare you! You've broken up more marriages than I've had hot dinners.'

'And you're a bossy, controlling cow who thinks she's so perfect looking after Mummy she can get away with anything.' Lisa's tone was like acid. 'Saffron doesn't deserve this and if you've fucked my best friend's husband to get back at me—'

'You self-centred little snake. It's *you* that's the issue here, isn't it? *You* who's never cared about anyone else, let alone your sister—'

'Too right. You're my sister but Saffron's a friend.' She ran a hand over her face. 'Why do you think I left England? For my career?'

A hot wave of horror rolled up Abby's spine. 'You left because of *me*?'

'Don't say you didn't break open the champagne the second you heard I was going.'

'I was *pleased* for you. I thought it was what you wanted.'

'That's what you always say. That you're *pleased* for me. I'm sick of it. I want you to leave. I can't bear the sight of you.'

A strange sense of calm descended over Abby as she looked at Lisa. She studied the raggedy home-cut hair, the little scar on her forehead, the sinewy strength in her arms, then she got to her feet and walked to the door.

'Goodbye,' she said.

By three o'clock that afternoon, Abby was on a plane, flying out of Alaska.

ABBY WAS DREAMING of the dead woman. The blue of her skin, the ice crystals on her eyelashes and in her hair.

'Joe. Dammit, Joe!'

The voice made her jump and Abby blinked, wondering how long she'd been asleep. Big Joe was approaching her armchair, Demarco hot on his heels.

'She's got something to tell you,' Big Joe said, looking at Demarco. 'And if she doesn't, I will.'

Demarco gave Big Joe a long, hard look, then said, 'Let's have a seat.'

'You've found Lisa?' Abby asked.

Demarco shook her head as she took the armchair next to Abby. Big Joe stood to one side of the fire, snow melting from his white bunny boots.

'I didn't tell you before,' Demarco started, 'because it . . . wasn't entirely necessary. Not when you saw the body wasn't your sister's. But we're now pretty sure who the woman is, and that she was visiting your sister.'

'Marie Guillemote,' Abby said.

'You know her?' Demarco asked, excited, expectant.

'No. I just found out she rented the car parked outside Lisa's cabin.'

Twin spots of red appeared on Demarco's cheeks. There was a small pause while Abby watched the trooper trying to hold on to her composure. 'As I was saying . . . I didn't say anything before. But I guess you should know that the woman you saw on the mountain had been shot, twice in the chest at close range. Murdered.'

A chill raced across the back of Abby's neck. 'Murdered?' she repeated.

'The body was hidden beneath the snow,' Demarco continued, 'wedged in a crevasse, but a wolf, maybe a wolverine, managed to free a section of the body. Someone with Search and Rescue found part of an arm, and after an extensive search we found the rest of the remains. Her indoor clothing and the lack of blood at the scene suggested murder. She hadn't been killed on the mountain, but had been moved there from the scene of the crime.'

Demarco held Abby's gaze. 'The tags on the Chevy Blazer match up with the car Marie Guillemote rented from Fairbanks. We're in the process of getting a search warrant for your sister's cabin.'

Abby forced herself to speak, and when it came out it was a croak. 'You don't think Lisa's been shot too, do you?'

'We can't say. Which is why we need to check her place out. And we'd appreciate it if you didn't return to the cabin for the moment.'

'What about my stuff?'

'We'll let you have it when we're finished. Meantime, we'd prefer it if you wouldn't mind finding alternative accommodation.'

The trooper got to her feet and, with a nod to Big Joe, walked outside.

Abby folded into the armchair, trembling. She could hear Big Joe talking to Diane, but not what he said. She looked up when Big Joe came back and squatted in front of her, holding out a glass of what looked like whisky. Abby swallowed it in one, feeling it burn all the way down.

'Lisa's not dead,' he said.

Abby stared into his unfathomable eyes. 'How do you know?'

'I just do.'

The calm passivity of his gaze gave her an inordinate rush of relief.

Big Joe gave a nod and rose to his feet. 'Let's go get your gear.'

'But Demarco said—'

'She doesn't have the search warrant yet. Let's get there before she does.'

Abby followed him out to the car park, feeling peculiarly light-headed. *Lisa is alive, Big Joe said so*. A trickle of hope seeped inside her.

They got to Lisa's cabin in Big Joe's white Dodge Ram. A uniformed trooper was stationed outside. He looked about sixteen. He introduced himself as Trooper Weiding and was polite but firm. He couldn't let them inside. Orders, he said, sorry.

With Abby cursing under her breath, Big Joe turned his Dodge around. At the bottom of the trail, Abby asked him to stop at a row of mailboxes. She knew which one was Lisa's because it was painted yellow. Abby crunched over, removed the stack of mail and stuffed it into her day pack. Big Joe headed south for his place, where he said he had something to do.

'Could we stop at the supermarket first?' she asked. 'I need supplies.'

While Big Joe waited in his car, Abby hurriedly bought the basics: toothbrush and paste, undies, shampoo and soap, deodorant. She hoped Diane wouldn't mind if she stayed at the Moose. Nowhere else was open. At the checkout, she asked for two packs of Marlboro Lights and a lighter, though she'd given up over five years ago.

Back in the Dodge she held up her cigarettes and asked if Joe minded, and when he shook his head she cranked open the window and lit up. The cigarette tasted of burnt rubber and ash and chemicals, which made her feel fractionally better, like she was punishing herself.

Big Joe lived just outside town, and Abby spent the five-mile journey trying to ignore the fear building inside her. When they arrived at his small, sturdy cabin Joe didn't invite her in, just dropped the tailgate and vanished.

Abby climbed out into the cold air and stood listening to nothing. Her stomach growled, reminding her she hadn't eaten. She lit another cigarette.

She stamped it out when Big Joe reappeared, hefting a bundle of blankets spilling fur, which he shifted carefully into the back. For a moment she thought it was a dead animal, but then she saw a bright blue eye wink at her. It was the colour of blue glacier ice, rimmed with black.

'Same colour,' said Joe, watching her.

'I'm sorry?'

'You and Moke. Same eyes.'

'This is Lisa's dog? The one that chewed through its harness?'

'Yup.'

'Hey there,' she said to the dog. A faint thump of metal told her it was wagging its tail. 'You did good, you know.'

FOUR DOORS DOWN from the Moose, Big Joe parked outside a little log cabin with red curtains in the windows and snow swept from the porch.

'All yours,' he said, tilting his chin at the cabin. 'It's been shut all winter so it'll take a while to warm up; just keep the wood stove burning.'

Abby stared at him in astonishment.

'It belongs to a friend of Lisa's. Michael Flint. He said you can stay as long as you like.'

'Who's Michael Flint?'

'I just said. He's a friend.'

Abby joined him on the boardwalk. 'What about rent?'

'You can figure it out when you see him.'

The cabin consisted of a single room with colourful Native rugs on wooden boards, a comfy-looking sofa, and a kitchenette with stools. In one corner was a shelf with a double mattress. Abby was so relieved to have somewhere nice to stay she could barely speak.

'Bathroom's out the back,' he said. 'Can't miss it.'

He strode back outside. Abby hurried after him.

'I'll pick you up in twenty minutes,' he told her. 'Take you to where Search and Rescue have set up. They'll tell us where they want us looking.'

'Joe, I can't tell you how grateful I am.'

He gave her one of his nods and she leaned over the tailgate and stroked the thick fur over Moke's head and ears. The dog closed his eyes and made a rattling sound deep in his throat. It was, she realised, a doggy purr.

'Where are you taking him?'

'Vet.'

Moke was nuzzling her hand. 'He'll fix him up?'

'With a lethal injection.'

She could feel the horror on her face. 'You can't do that!'

'It's just another dog to feed. A useless one at that.'

She hadn't taken Big Joe to be heartless, but out here she guessed that if an animal couldn't pay its way then it was deemed worthless.

'Can't we, er . . .?' Abby bit her lip. 'I mean, won't Lisa be upset when she discovers you've destroyed her dog?'

Big Joe raised his eyebrows. 'You want him?'

'I'm not sure about that. I wouldn't have a clue how to—'

She swallowed her words when he snapped open the tailgate, hefted Moke in his arms and carried him into the cabin, easing him down on what looked suspiciously like a dog bed already prepared in the kitchenette.

'All yours,' he said.

'But Michael Flint might not want—'

'Mike said it was fine.' He passed her a tube of ointment, then gestured at a sack on the counter. 'Dog food. Make sure he's got lots of water.' He flicked his gaze to her feet. 'And get yourself some decent gear for the mountain. Sports store's open down the road. Your boots are rubbish.'

With that Joe walked back to his car, leaving Abby open-mouthed.

THE SEARCH AND RESCUE command post was a motor home parked on a campground, with forest along one side, a frozen creek on the other. Come June the site would be packed with hikers and their tents, but right now it was littered with an assortment of four-wheel drives and snow machines.

Big Joe gave her new Sorrel boots the once-over. 'Good choice,' he said as he marched towards the motor home. 'Let's see where they want us.'

Abby followed, feeling snug in her new gear. She was wearing padded trousers, a parka with fur trim round the hood and wrists, a thick soft hat that covered her ears, as well as some gloves with mittens over the top.

People were eating sandwiches and drinking from Thermoses, voices ringing in the icy air. Occasionally someone would catch her eye, and give her a nod or lift a hand in a faint salute, to show they recognised who she was, but didn't want to encroach on her emotions.

She felt a rush of warmth for these people she didn't know. People who had come from miles away, people who had never met Lisa, but who knew what it would be like to be out there in the cold and all alone.

Inside it was hot and stuffy and chaotic. Maps were stuck on walls and thrown across tables; hats, gloves and jackets stacked in piles everywhere.

Abby's eyes snagged on a guy at the far end talking into a radio. When the man glanced round, her heart stopped. It was Cal Pegati.

Abby jerked her gaze away, her heart kicking back into action at triple-rate. What the hell was he doing here? He'd said he was giving up guiding and going into insurance, and was leasing offices in Fairbanks.

Out of the corner of her eye, Abby saw Cal put down his radio and get to his feet. She pretended to study a map on the wall.

'Abby.'

'Hello, Cal.' She fought to keep outwardly calm. 'How are you?'

'Like everyone else.' He nudged his chin at the team, who appeared to be filling Big Joe in on what was happening. 'Concerned about your sister.'

'Good of you to chip in,' she said. 'Especially all the way from Fairbanks. You are still based in Fairbanks, I take it?'

'Yes, I am.' Cal ran a hand over his head and back, making his hair stick up in tufts. He hadn't shaved for a couple of days and she could see speckles of white dotting his stubble that hadn't been there before.

'Look, Abby, you need to know . . . I'm here in an official capacity.'

'You didn't set up your business?'

'Sure I did, but I've taken on some other stuff—which involves Lisa.'

He took a step towards her, and he was so close she could smell the scent of wood smoke rising from his parka. She scooted sideways in order to put some distance between them.

'OK.' Cal held up his hands. 'Let's do this outside.'

The icy air had little effect on Abby's nerves. She leaned against the flank of the motor home and crossed one boot over the other. 'You went into the insurance business?' she asked, pleased with her tone: politely interested.

'Yup.'

'It's a long way from walking the wilds with the earth beneath your feet and the sky on your shoulders.'

'That's what weekends are for.' His expression turned rueful. 'Besides, the thought had crossed my mind that when I'm old and grey, I might not be as nippy around a grizzly.'

There was a silence, broken by the roar of a snow machine.

Abby forced herself to keep going. 'You said you're here officially?'

'I'm acting as Insurance Investigator. For one of the big firms, Falcon Union. They've used me before. We have a good relationship.'

'Hope they pay you well.'

'Oh, yes. Money's not a problem.' Cal dragged his hand back and forth over his head again. He looked uncomfortable, embarrassed even.

'So?' she said.

More head dragging. 'I've been retained to investigate your sister.'

For a second she just stared at him. 'You've *what*?'

'She took out a life insurance policy six months ago.' Another drag of the head. 'A big one. And Falcon Union is . . . concerned.'

Abby narrowed her eyes. 'And what does that mean?'

'There's a lot at stake. Two point four million dollars, to be precise.'

The penny dropped. 'You think Lisa has disappeared *on purpose*?'

Cal shuffled his feet and looked away.

Suddenly Abby stopped worrying about her own vulnerability and thrust her fingers hard against Cal's chest. 'How dare you even think it? Lisa may be a bit wild, but trying to rip off an insurance company by pretending she's died on some mountain? Give me a *break*.'

'Some people would do a lot for that sort of money.'

'Oh, come on, Cal. Listen to yourself, will you? Lisa is not *some people*.'

'The guy who sold Lisa the insurance told me she said that when her beneficiary got the money she'd rise from the dead to share it with them.'

'For God's sakes, it was a *joke*! If she really wanted to rip off the insurance company, she'd never say anything like that. She's not stupid.'

'That had occurred to me,' he said stiffly.

'Oh, good!' She beamed at him, sarcasm dripping. 'So you're looking at both sides of the coin. That makes a change.'

He glanced down at her fingers resting on his fleece. 'Finished?'

Abby snatched her hand back. 'So you'll return to Fairbanks? Tell them it's not a scam?'

'No. I've a job to do—and I'm going to do it, whether you like it or not.'

Silence fell. Abby was trying to think of a way she could persuade Cal to go home when he did the head-hand thing again.

'Abby? Can we talk about when you were last here?'

She spun on her heel and stalked away, speaking over her shoulder. 'What's to talk about? You conned me and I fell for it. End of story.'

ABBY FELT WRECKED the next morning. Her muscles ached from floundering through deep snow alongside Big Joe and two other guys all afternoon, stopping only to peer through binoculars, trying to see a trace of anything that might lead them to Lisa. No one had found anything.

Moke stood by the door, looking hopeful. Struggling up, she pushed him outside, then put a pan of milk on the stove and hunted through the cupboards until she found a sachet of chocolate.

She fed some kindling into the wood stove, then read the instructions on the tube of ointment that Big Joe had left her. She let Moke back in and smoothed silver sulfa diazine over his frostbite. She made some buttered toast, but the instant she bit into it her appetite vanished. To Moke's delight, she chucked both slices into his bowl.

Settling herself on the sofa, she turned her attention to the mail she'd swiped from Lisa's mailbox. There was a lot of junk mail, and a handful of bills, which she put to one side. There was one personal item.

It was from someone called Tessa, who'd signed off with *lots of love*. It was headed in capitals: *DON'T LET THE BASTARD GET YOU DOWN*.

Abby scanned the letter, but it didn't make much sense. It ended with: *It was only a minor offence, remember, so don't panic and blow it out of all proportion. We all love you. Who cares what happened some other place, some other time? We certainly don't.*

Abby turned the paper over and then back, but there was no address or telephone number. Frustrated, she checked the envelope, and her spirits lifted. Dated April 2, it had been franked by a company called Peak Adventure in Fairbanks. She grabbed the phone and dialled.

'Peak Adventure,' a woman said brightly.

'Hi, can I speak to Tessa?'

'She's not in today. Can I take a message?'

Abby introduced herself and the woman immediately said, 'Oh, heavens. Have you found Lisa?'

'Not yet.'

'Dear Lord, I hope you do. We're all so fond of her . . . Look, give Tessa a ring at home. She's not flying this week. She'll be glad to speak to you.'

Abby lit a cigarette before she dialled again. Tessa picked up on the second ring, and when she heard who Abby was and that Lisa was still missing, launched into a tirade of anxiety. Abby managed to interject some questions, learning that Tessa and Lisa had struck up a friendship through Peak Adventure, where Tessa flew clients in the company helicopter to peaks and glaciers around the country for mountain climbing and hiking.

'She did Denali last year,' Tessa was saying. 'If she can do Denali, she can survive some tin-pot mountain. She'll be walking out of there.'

Abby made a neutral sound, then braved herself to confess she'd read Tessa's letter. Tessa didn't sound annoyed as much as puzzled.

'How's that going to help?'

Abby stubbed out her cigarette and told her about the murder of Marie Guillemote. There was an appalled silence, which Abby hurriedly filled. 'Which is why I need to know some stuff. Like did you know Marie?'

'Never heard of her before. Shit, I can't believe this.'

'And what do you mean by "Don't let the bastards get you down"?'

'Bastard. Just the one.' Tessa sighed. 'Peter Santoni. He used to work with Lisa. They've never liked each other, and she likes him even less now he's found out about her court case.'

'What court case?'

'She told me not to tell anyone . . . but I guess you'd better know. Well, six years ago, your sister was summoned to the US District Court to face charges made by a professor at her university. Professor Crowe.'

Six years ago Lisa would have been twenty-three and in the middle of the PhD she never finished in Washington, DC.

'What charges?'

'Crowe took Lisa to court to get a restraining order against her. The professor won. Lisa couldn't go within a hundred yards of Crowe without risking a jail sentence.'

'What on earth was Lisa doing?'

'She accused Crowe of murder.'

Abby couldn't think of a word to say.

'Fifteen years ago,' Tessa continued, 'a student called Jared—can't remember his surname—died in a climbing accident. He was a genius, apparently, but he died before his PhD thesis could be submitted. Nobody knew what happened to it . . . Anyway, his buddy at the time, who shared a tutor with him, was Crowe. The thing is, Lisa unearthed a copy of Jared's thesis, don't ask me how, and it bore an uncanny resemblance to the one Crowe submitted after Jared died. When Lisa heard that Crowe had gone climbing with Jared the day he fell to his death, she went nuts. She accused Crowe of pushing Jared off the mountain and stealing his thesis.'

Abby was in a state of shock. If what Tessa said was true, both Lisa and the professor had been forced to leave the university.

'Who else knows about this?'

'Nobody as far as I know. Santoni used it as something to bait her with.'

Eventually Abby hung up, and began to pace the room, Moke's vivid blue eyes following. Lisa had lied to her and Julia. She hadn't been offered a dream job in Alaska, she'd been *thrown out of uni*.

HANDS COSY in her mittens, Abby walked to Lisa's cabin. The trail was filled with vehicles, the last in line being a black Dodge Ram, identical to Joe's aside from the colour. Lines of bright yellow police tape, strung between metal poles, formed a tenuous fence round the property.

Trooper Weiding appeared, beaver hat low on his forehead, and Abby asked if Demarco was around. Weiding trotted off and she surveyed the view beyond Lisa's cabin, past lines of spruce trees and across the lake to the cliffs opposite. She could see why Lisa had bought a place out here. She would have revelled in the space. Lisa needed a lot of space.

To Abby's dismay, the trooper returned with Cal.

'Where's Demarco?' she asked.

'Busy,' said Cal.

'Why are you allowed in? You're not a policeman.'

'I'm considered part of the investigative team. This doesn't mean I get to tramp all over the crime scene. I hang well back and out of the way.'

'Crime scene?' The words came out high-pitched with anxiety.

Cal studied her at length. 'I'll let you know what's happening, but only if you have a drink with me.'

Abby rallied enough strength to say, 'Blackmail.'

'Call it what you will, but the cops aren't going to share much with you.'

'All right,' she snapped. 'So long as you're paying.'

'I've been paying for the past four years,' he said, his voice low and hard.

IN THE MOOSE, Abby took her mug of chocolate to one of the leather chairs by the fire, and busied herself stirring the cream into her chocolate.

'Look, Abby.' Cal leaned forward, cradling his coffee mug in both hands, 'I really wanted to talk to you about Lisa's insurance policy—'

'Please'—Abby held up a hand—'I don't want to hear your accusations. I want to know what's going on. What's happening with the crime scene?'

Cal picked up his mug, put it down again, and cleared his throat. 'Well,' he said, 'first up, the cops have found a bullet lodged in the wall of Lisa's cabin. From a .45 calibre semiautomatic weapon. They've sent it to ballistics to see if it matches the one that killed Marie Guillemote.'

Abby was glad she was sitting down. 'Marie was shot in Lisa's cabin?'

'They found some blood. It's gone to the lab for analysis.'

She had to struggle to get the words out. 'I didn't see any blood.'

'Luminol,' Cal replied. 'You spray it on an area and shine a black light on it, and minute traces of blood will fluoresce back at you.'

Abby's mind became a desperate whirl. What if the blood was Lisa's? Had she been killed too? But what if it was Marie's? What would that mean? Had the two women fought over something?

'How did Marie know Lisa?'

'It looks like she was a friend. We found her bag behind the couch.'

'But how did they know each other? I mean, Marie lives in Virginia.'

'Through work, maybe at a conference. They're both into science.'

Abby thought of the burnt mess of computer discs and files in Lisa's yard and her mind turned to Lisa's boss. 'Does Thomas know Marie?'

'I don't know.'

Abby resolved to talk to Thomas later that day. He might have some idea why Lisa's work had been destroyed.

'What about the guy's robe in her bathroom?' Abby asked.

'They're not sure. After Lisa split with Greg, she went out with Jack Molvar. She dumped him over a year ago. There hasn't been anyone since.'

Abby found that hard to believe. Lisa always had a man on the go.

They sat in silence a long while. Abby could hear the other men talking in low voices, the clatter of their forks, a piece of wood hissing on the fire.

'Abby.' She turned to see Cal was leaning forward, his expression wary. 'About Lisa's insurance policy.'

'Oh, for God's sakes, Cal—'

'Her beneficiary,' he went on quietly, 'is you.'

Four

C al insisted on walking her to her cabin, and she didn't have the strength to object. Her limbs felt loose and rubbery.

Demarco's Explorer was parked outside her front door. Trooper Weiding climbed out as they approached. Apparently the ABI—Alaska's Bureau of Investigation—wanted a word. Would Abby mind accompanying him to the briefing room where Demarco and a sergeant from Fairbanks were waiting?

'Give me a second,' she told the trooper. 'I just need to give the dog a quick walk.'

He gave a nod, and hopped back into the warmth of the car.

Abby opened the door of the cabin, utterly unprepared for the blur of snarling fur and teeth that pushed her aside and flew straight for Cal.

'No! Moke, no!' she yelled.

The dog stopped inches short of Cal's legs, stiff-legged, ruff standing high, and growling deep in his throat.

'Jesus Christ!' Cal stared at the dog.

Abby put a hand on Moke's neck. 'Leave, boy,' she told him. 'Leave.'

Moke's hackles dropped and he stepped round Cal's legs, sniffing his ankles and knees, the back of his thighs. Then he sauntered two paces and, still looking at Cal, lifted his leg against a shrub. Abby couldn't help the snort of laughter that escaped.

'You think that was funny?' Cal said. 'Setting your dog on me and nearly giving me a heart attack?'

'Sorry,' she said. 'I didn't know he was going to do that. So far he's been a big softie, but I guess he's feeling better. I'll be more careful in future.'

'That would be wise,' Cal said drily. 'I wouldn't want you up under the dangerous dogs act.'

He was smiling now, his eyes crinkling at the corners, and she felt a swoop in her lower belly. She had to look away.

'See you later?' he said.

'Sure.'

Still smiling, he stepped warily round Moke, and strode off.

WHEN TROOPER WEIDING ushered her into the briefing room that had been set up at the school, she was surprised it was so quiet. She'd expected the place to be bustling. In fact the only evidence it was a briefing room at all was a single portable white board that was hurriedly being turned round. She just managed to catch the headings of three columns before it faced the wall. *Scenario*: *one*, *two* and *three*.

Three scenarios and just two cops. Alaska obviously didn't have the resources of Scotland Yard.

Demarco dropped her hands from the white board and swung to face her, looking at her colleague then back at Abby, suddenly uncertain.

Abby stared at Demarco's colleague. The last time she'd seen him he'd had a couple of days' stubble, a shotgun in one hand and antagonism at the back of his eyes. Now he was a clean-shaven, brisk-looking man in neatly pressed trousers and a thick fleece the colour of slate.

'Victor?' she said hesitantly.

He gave a grunt and came over to shake her hand. 'Sergeant Pegati.'

A distant bell rang. Cal hadn't talked about his parents much, but she could remember his mother was half Athabaskan and that when he was born his father had swapped his army fatigues for a policeman's uniform.

'You're Cal's *father*?'

A curt nod. 'Trooper Demarco's helping me with the investigation.'

Demarco gave her a half-smile, and took up position by the window.

Victor took a seat behind the metal desk and indicated she take the one opposite. When Abby didn't move, he leaned back and steepled his fingers in front of his face. 'We'd like to ask you a few informal questions.'

She repressed the urge to ask him if she needed a lawyer, and nodded, studying him and his change of persona. He even spoke differently.

'Let's start with this: why did your sister have one hundred and twenty-three thousand dollars in her account?'

'What?' Abby was astonished.

Victor stonily repeated the question.

'God knows,' Abby shrugged. 'I haven't spoken to her for four years.'

'Ah, yes. I heard about that. What was the disagreement over?'

Abby could feel the heat rise to her cheeks. 'Nothing much. We always had them. This time I'd had enough.'

'That's not what my son tells me.'

Abby sat down, concentrating on picking clumps of dog hair from her knees. 'If your son had worn a wedding ring, we'd all still be one happy family, wouldn't we?' She fixed him with as arctic a gaze as she could manage with her cheeks flaming red. 'I'd like to see men like that branded with the word "married" on their foreheads. It'd make life much easier for single women.'

'I see,' he said, and for the first time his voice lost its certainty.

'I doubt you do.' Her voice was cold.

He watched her closely for a few seconds, then cleared his throat. 'Right,' he said. 'How do you plan to spend the money? Two point four million is quite a lot to get through.'

Abby's blood pressure started to rise. 'I've already told Cal it's a load of rubbish that Lisa planned to fake her own death. Besides which,' she added, 'how can you possibly think I'm in cahoots with Lisa when we haven't even spoken for—?'

'What I find interesting,' Victor cut in smoothly, 'is how people envision spending their windfall.' He pulled out a piece of paper. 'A Dutch barn in Somerset with fifteen acres of woodland costs nearly two million dollars.' He tossed the piece of paper across so she could see it.

It was a page that had been ripped out of her sketch book. Inspired by an advert in *House & Garden* on the flight over, she'd stuck it in her book, then spent the next two hours designing the perfect garden for the barn.

'That's personal,' she snapped, overcome with anger that her belongings were being pored through.

'Nothing's personal in a murder investigation.'

Abby snatched the sketch, folded it in four and stuck it in her pocket. She waited for him to object, but he didn't. No doubt he'd copied it earlier.

'Quite ambitious, aren't you?'

'Dreaming isn't a crime. Don't you have dreams, Sergeant?'

'Not of ripping off an insurance company for two point four million.'

'Oh, come on, you can't be serious.'

'Tell me, did Lisa have any enemies that you know of?'

'Everyone loves Lisa,' she said automatically, then remembered the professor at her sister's university. 'Well, there is someone. . .' Abby trailed off. She couldn't see that Lisa's old professor had anything to do with this.

'An enemy?' Victor's interest quickened.

'Well, it got pretty acrimonious. The police even got involved at one point. It was six years ago. They slapped a restraining order on my sister.'

Victor's eyebrows shot up.

'Lisa accused a professor at her university of murdering a fellow student and stealing his PhD thesis.' Abby retold the story she'd heard from Tessa.

'And the name of the professor?'

'Crowe. I don't know the Christian name, sorry.'

Victor made a note. 'Should be pretty easy to follow up. Anything else?'

'Not really,' she said vaguely. She could still hardly believe Lisa had accused someone of murder.

She flinched when the phone rang. Victor snatched it up, listened briefly, then rose to his feet and nodded to Demarco. 'Carry on.' He left the room.

The trooper shed her jacket and put it over the back of Victor's chair. 'Wish it were as warm outside,' she said affably.

'You know Victor well?' Abby asked. 'I mean . . . the sergeant.'

'We've worked together before.' Demarco came and sat next to her, hip propped on the corner of the desk.

'Is this the good-cop scene?' Abby wanted to smile but couldn't.

Demarco chuckled. 'He's not a bad guy once you get to know him.'

'I can't make any sense of it,' Abby said. 'Lisa was reported missing up a mountain, but you find Marie Guillemote murdered instead . . . I feel like I've stepped into a nightmare. He surely doesn't think I'm working with Lisa to rip off the insurance company.'

'Don't let it trouble you. He just likes rattling people's cages.'

When Abby's head snapped round the trooper added carefully, 'That doesn't mean we're not curious about the insurance policy. It would be nice to know your sister's mindset when she took it out.'

Abby gave the trooper a startled look. Had Lisa known she was going to die? She couldn't believe that Lisa had organised any of this, she honestly couldn't. Lisa didn't plan as much as *react* to life.

'Abby, didn't you resent Lisa going to college in Washington, DC, leaving you behind to care for your mother?'

'No,' she said, which was true.

'You've borne a load of emotional burdens,' Demarco observed. 'Your loyalty to your family would break the back of anyone else.'

Abby blinked. 'Loads of people out there do much more than I do.'

The trooper looked thoughtful. 'Tell me about Lisa's old university friends,' she said. 'Would they help her if she turned up on the doorstep?'

Startled, Abby said, 'You think she's left Alaska?'

'Not that we know of,' she admitted. 'We've covered the airports, but she might have bribed a private pilot to fly her out. Or driven across the border.' Demarco sighed. 'You've got my number here. You hear anything, call me, would you?'

The door banged open and Victor beckoned Demarco outside. The door closed behind them with a little click. Abby couldn't hear what they were saying. She walked to the door and pressed her ear against it, but she couldn't make out any words.

Their footsteps gave a brief clatter and she managed to scoot into her chair as the door opened and both cops came back inside.

Victor cleared his throat. 'Do you know what Lisa was working on?'

'No,' she said.

'Has Lisa ever mentioned the name Meg to you?'

'Not that I remember. Why?'

Victor leaned forward, put his hands on the table. 'You know that we found some blood in your sister's cabin,' he stated. Abby gave him a nod, and he continued, 'It belongs to Marie Guillemote. The bullet we found lodged in your sister's cabin belongs to the .45 semiautomatic that killed her.'

Abby felt the blood draining from her face.

'We've issued a warrant for your sister's arrest in connection with Marie Guillemote's murder.'

LISA WALKED up the slope with grim-faced determination, Roscoe padding at her side. She concentrated on putting one foot in front of the other, fighting waves of dizziness brought on from exhaustion and hunger.

The area they were crossing was a mind-numbing series of mountains, valleys and creeks, of climbing up one ridge and heading down the other side, hour upon hour. The only consolation was that she hadn't seen anyone behind her yet. That didn't mean they weren't trying to follow. They were determined and ruthless. They had proved that by killing Marie.

However, it appeared her enemies didn't know much about the bush. They might be dressed in white winter camouflage snow suits, but she hadn't seen any sign of the three men since she'd fled her cabin. But then she had the advantage of knowing the area. She knew how to navigate using landmarks, to guide herself by the sun and the stars. All the men had were her footprints, and sometimes not even that when she cut across a glacier.

Roscoe paused to glance over his shoulder with a mournful expression.

'Moke's gone home, boy.' She tried to comfort him. 'Sorry.'

It was thanks to Moke that she hadn't frozen where she'd fallen. Through the storm her numbed senses had registered something tugging at her waistline. She'd looked down to see the dog trying to chew through his harness. Moke appeared to believe she'd reached the end and was determined not to die alongside his mistress. His condemnation had forced her to act.

She had dragged herself on until, amazingly, Roscoe led her to a fissure in a rock face, with just enough room for her to squeeze inside. As soon as she was out of the wind, the temperature seemed to soar twenty degrees. She wanted to light a fire but, as she pulled the sled towards her, her body shut down at the effort, and she lost consciousness.

Lisa didn't wake until dawn, and for a second she thought the cave had collapsed. Her ribs were being crushed. She could barely breathe. When she tried to roll onto her back, the cave parted and looked down at her. She'd been wedged in a doggy sandwich for most of the night. The dogs had saved her life with their body heat.

It took her a long time to get her numbed hands to release her emergency pack and light a fire. She melted snow in her tin pan and drank it as hot as she could to warm her core. Then she melted some more for the huskies. Ate some chocolate. Outside, the storm continued to howl.

Her cheeks were burning. Searing hot, her skin felt as if it was going to melt from her bones. She had frost nip, but there was little she could do aside from wrapping her face in her scarf to protect it from the cold.

As her brain began to function, she thought about how to divert her pursuers. Bringing Moke close, she studied his harness where he'd tried to chew through it. Using her knife she finished the job, then chewed the end vigorously. It wouldn't fool Big Joe, but it might convince everyone else.

She took Moke to the cave's entrance and pushed him outside. 'Home, boy,' she commanded, pointing back the way they'd come.

Eyes squinting against the driving snow, Moke refused to move. Lisa picked up some loose rocks and made to throw them at him. He bolted.

Huddled against Roscoe on the frozen cave floor, she prayed that Moke would make it. She hadn't had him long, but he seemed fit enough, with a coat thick enough to insulate him should he be forced to curl up and rest. She knew he would return to Lake's Edge; he had nowhere else to go.

Now she found herself in a forest. She moved slowly, stopping periodically to listen and take her bearings, careful not to disturb any birds or animals that might reveal her position. Here and there squirrels and rabbits had left their retreats to forage for food, and coyotes, lynx and wolverines added their trails to those of deer and moose.

She stopped when a shadow crept like smoke between the trees ahead. From behind a snow-covered boulder came another dark object. She looked over her shoulder to see four shadowy figures creeping up behind her.

Lisa grabbed her rifle from the sled. Loaded it. Chambered a round. Her fingers were stiff with cold but her heart was hammering.

Roscoe was growling and snarling as the wolves slunk forward. They were thin after a hard winter, their shoulder blades and hip bones jutting through their coats. Most wolves would be too wary to attack a human, even if they were starving. The intended victim was Roscoe.

Lisa raised her rifle to her shoulder. She didn't want to fire in case someone heard the shot, but she had no choice; without Roscoe, her chances of survival would halve. Carefully she chose a big iron-grey female as her target. If she could scare the leader away, the others would follow.

Her finger was tightening on the trigger when another wolf walked through the pack and stood a little distance from Lisa, watching. A great creature the colour of platinum with a chest as broad as a mastiff's. One ear was slit, and there were old wound-marks on his neck and shoulders.

Lisa lowered her rifle a fraction. 'Hello, King.'

His fierce yellow eyes locked on hers.

'Joe's told me about you. He's a fan of yours. He's sorry he shot your father, but he was creating hell in the town. You know better, don't you?'

The wolf didn't look away.

'Big Joe wouldn't want me to shoot you. So find a nice caribou or a moose to satisfy your family's appetite. Roscoe's not up for grabs. Sorry.'

King stared at her, unblinking. Lisa didn't lower her rifle. She hoped he'd be nice enough to leave her and Roscoe alone. The minutes ticked past. Stand-off, Lisa thought. A goddamn stand-off. If the pack moved in one wave, Roscoe wouldn't stand a chance.

Suddenly King gave a single bark, and trotted away in the opposite direction. The rest of the pack followed.

Her hands were trembling as she strapped her rifle back onto the sled. Roscoe was panting hard and fast. She tried to settle him down.

'You may be big, but deep down you're a scaredy-cat,' she told him.

She hadn't walked far when her eyes snagged on something symmetrical:

a right-angle joint of wood. Lisa peered at it from behind the trunk of a jack pine. To her astonishment, the forest revealed a mossy log cabin. A wisp of smoke rose from a chimney made from a length of rusting pipe.

She'd heard of this place, heard the rumours about Mad Malone, but she'd never met the guy.

Mad Malone was a trapper. He didn't have running water or electricity, didn't believe in the finer things in life like cutting his hair or bathing, but if Joe was to be believed, he had a hobby that might just save her life.

Lisa eyed the cabin cautiously, weighing up the pros and cons.

'Stay,' she told Roscoe in a low voice as she kicked off her skis.

From the sled, Lisa extracted her laptop and discs—well wrapped in plastic and oilskin—and buried them in the snow, placing a twig where they lay. Picking up her rifle, she crept to the front of the cabin and looked around. Fresh prints led from the door and into the forest.

Lisa rapped on the door. Silence. There was no lock in the door, so, with pulse rocketing she turned the wooden handle and stepped inside.

It was dark and fetid, so she left the door ajar, waiting for her eyes to adjust to the gloom, her breathing shallow. Carefully she moved around the room. There was a stack of hides and pelts, and a freshly skinned rabbit lay on the floor in front of the wood stove. She'd swipe that on her way out.

She looked further right, there it was. A ham radio.

It took her a while to find the frequency she wanted, then she paused to gather her thoughts. People might be listening in. She'd have to be careful.

Covering her English accent by drawling a parody of broad American, she said, 'Bravo, Jericho, you read? This is King.'

Big Joe had told her he'd given the wolf its name on their last trip into the Brooks Range, adding that she reminded him of a wolf with her untamed ways and love of the wilderness. Lisa prayed he would remember.

Silence. She kept trying, until finally the radio crackled. 'King? As in the King who hates anchovies on their pizza?'

Lisa sagged with relief. 'You know I love 'em, because I ate all yours.'

'You OK?' Joe asked.

'Sure. Whass'appenin' your end?'

'Got a surprise waiting for you here.' Brief pause, then he added, 'A bitch called Alpha. Big sister of the pack.'

'Alpha?' Her voice was hoarse. Oh, dear God. Was he referring to Abby?

'Yup. She got here a couple of days ago. She'd do anything to see you.'

A rush of emotion rocked Lisa. Abby was in Alaska, looking for her.

'How is she?'

Before Big Joe could answer, she heard a soft crunch of snow.

She spun round. 'Quiet, Joe,' she told him.

The radio fell silent. Then she heard another soft crunch. Picking up her rifle, she tiptoed to the door, then poked the barrel cautiously outside.

Everything was still and silent. She inched the door wider, and suddenly a hand whipped out and grabbed the barrel, yanked the rifle from her hands and she was sprawling face down in the snow. Then she felt the rifle ram into the back of her neck. A rancid odour wafted over her, making her choke.

'Well, well, well.' His voice was hoarse, rusty from not having spoken for a long time. 'If all my Christmases ain't come at once.'

ABBY FINALLY gathered the courage to ring her mother. Beside herself with worry, Julia kept repeating herself. Abby knew the stress was affecting Julia's health, but she kept reassuring her that Lisa was bound to be OK, and that they had to concentrate on that and let the police unravel the rest.

'Do you know what Lisa was working on?' Abby eventually asked. 'The police asked me, but I haven't a clue.'

'Oh, darling, you know she was impossibly possessive about her work.' Julia sighed. 'She gets it from me, I'm afraid.' There was a short pause, then she added, 'Have you asked Meg?'

'Meg?' Abby repeated.

'She was part of their team. Lisa would phone when she was in one of her moods, and she'd always refer to Meg. She sounded a very awkward type of person to work with. Impossible one day and a delight the next.'

Meg sounded as though she could be Lisa's twin sister, and Abby almost smiled at the thought of Lisa having to take some of her own medicine.

'Do you know Meg's surname?'

'Lisa never mentioned it.'

'Mum, did Lisa ever mention a Professor Crowe at her uni?'

'Oh, yes. Best of friends at the start, I remember. They worked closely for a year or so, then had a falling-out. Lisa never told me what it was over.'

'Did she mention anything about going to court?'

'Court?' Julia repeated, sounding alarmed.

'Oh, it's nothing,' Abby said hastily. 'If you haven't heard about it, then it's not what I thought it was. How's Ralph?'

'He's just about moved in, but I don't mind. His fish pie is rather good.'

Abby blinked. Julia was letting Ralph cook for her? Talk about a turn-up for the books. 'Is he there?'

'No. He's gone to the corner shop to buy a newspaper.'

Eternally grateful to Ralph for stepping into the breach, Abby hung up and flicked through Lisa's telephone directory until she found the number for University of Alaska. She dialled the number and asked for Meg.

'Meg who? Which department?'

'I can't remember her surname. Maybe try the Sir John Ross Institute?'

After a short silence, the woman was back on the line. 'I can't find a Meg. We've a Megan Wilson in the Geophysical Institute. Shall I put you through?'

Lisa didn't work in geophysics, but Abby said, 'Yes, please.'

There was a click, and the sound of a phone ringing. Nobody picked up. Abby waited until it cut off. She'd try the woman later.

Meantime, she'd call Thomas, Lisa's boss, but when she got through she was told he was on vacation and not due back for three days. Before she could ask anything further, the woman hung up.

After doing a quick shop at the local supermarket—cigarettes, wine, bread, jam, canned food—she was about to try Megan again when Moke started barking. A big, deep *WOOF!* that had her heart hammering.

Grabbing Moke's ruff she told him to be quiet. Diane stood outside in the sunshine in jeans and shirtsleeves, looking uncertain.

'Stop it,' Abby told the dog, whose lips had peeled back into a snarl.

Immediately he stopped growling, and looked up at her.

'Well, that's a first,' said Diane. 'I've known him since he was a pup and he's never growled. Not once. Must feel protective of you or something.'

'Or something,' said Abby ruefully. 'I think giving him buttered toast for breakfast might have had an effect. You want a coffee?'

'No . . . But thanks. Appreciate the offer.' She gave Abby a thin smile. Shoving a piece of paper towards her, she said, 'I just came to bring this.'

Torn from a notebook, it was folded into four, and the instant Abby opened it, her trachea closed down. The air couldn't get to her lungs.

Meet me at Mad Malone's. Everyone knows where he lives. Don't tell anyone. I'll look after you, promise. Love you. Lisa.

Abby's breathing returned with a rush, making her head spin.
Lisa was alive.

'Where did you get this?' Abby pulled Diane inside and shut the door.

'My uncle.' Diane was looking at the floor. 'Malone Fischer. Known as Mad Malone round here. He's a trapper. Lives in the mountains. He came into town late last night, in a bit of a state.' She fiddled with her plait. 'He wanted help with "women's things". When I asked him if he had a girl-friend hidden in his cabin he just about had a heart attack. He made me swear not to tell anyone, especially not the cops . . .'

'You've read this?' Abby demanded.

'She's my friend too.'

'How do I find your uncle?'

Diane squinted at Abby. 'You're not going to tell the police, are you?'

Abby's mind was whirling. She ought to, she knew, but the instant the cops got their hands on her they'd throw her in a cell.

'Er . . .' she dithered, wondering what the hell to do.

'Malone will kill me if the cops turn up at his place,' Diane said. 'Can't you go alone, like she wants? I've got a snow machine you can use.'

ABBY TOOK ONE LOOK at the map and quailed. No way was she going out there on her own, no matter what danger Lisa might be in.

'Diane, you've got to come with me.'

'I can't. The bar won't run itself,' Diane said. 'Not until tomorrow when my cousin can take over.'

'I don't know the mountains. I'll get lost.' And what about bears? her mind yelled. Wolves and crevasses and weak ice?

They were standing in the car park at the back of the Moose, the sun warm on the back of their necks. Abby looked at the map again. Malone's cabin was forty miles northwest of Lake's Edge, a couple of hours away by snow machine according to Diane, but Abby had visions of it taking much longer, especially if she lost her way or got stuck in a drift.

'She's your *friend*,' she pleaded.

'She asked you to go alone,' Diane said, shuffling her feet.

Abby looked at the snow machine. She didn't even know how to start the damn thing, let alone drive it. She pointed at a symbol on the map, a U inside a circle, about ten miles from Malone's cabin. 'What's this?'

'Unverified landing area.' Diane peered closer. 'Looks like it belongs to Flint's hunting lodge.'

'Michael Flint?' Abby asked. 'The guy who owns my cabin?'

Diane nodded.

'Big Joe said he was a friend of Lisa's. Is he local?'

'He's well known around here. Bases himself between Anchorage and his lodge. He's got his own aircraft—makes it easy to flit in and out.'

'What does he do?'

'Lots of different things. He's into mining in a big way. Zinc and gold. He even owns a couple of hotels and guesthouses, and a canning company.'

'Fingers in all sorts of pies,' Abby mused.

'You got it.' A small smile was playing on Diane's lips. 'Lisa stayed there once, for kicks . . . They didn't see eye to eye, you see. Poor guy had no idea. She ate his cupboards bare, slept in his bed. She left a note saying, "Thanks, from the three bears." He didn't find it very funny. But that was back then. Before they, er . . . became friends.'

How typically Lisa, acting as though she were nine years old instead of twenty-nine.

'He's got some wilderness cabins through the forest. She uses them like they're hers . . .' Diane's smile suddenly broadened into a grin. 'God-dammit, why didn't I think of it before?'

'What?' Abby demanded. 'What is it?'

'Flint knows the area real well, and since Malone thinks the sun shines out of his proverbials ever since he turned a blind eye to Malone taking a moose out of season last year, he might not shoot him.'

'I can trust Flint? Won't he call the police?'

'Nah. He'll do what's right for Lisa. I'll go and call him now.'

MICHAEL FLINT had a pair of Sorrels like herself, padded trousers and a blue and yellow parka. Tall, dark-haired and freshly shaved, he would have been handsome if it weren't for his red-eyed and haggard appearance. The man looked as though he hadn't slept in a week.

He shook her hand, said it was nice to meet her, brushed aside her thanks for his cabin, ignored her offer to pay rent and got right down to it.

'Diane tells me Lisa sent you a note.'

'You're not going to tell the cops, are you?' Abby asked. He shook his head. 'Why not?' She was curious.

'They'll arrest her.'

'What about Marie Guillemote?' Abby pressed. 'Do you think Lisa killed her?'

'Of course not. Look, can we do the questions later? I'd like to get going.'

Flint double-checked Diane's snow machine and prepared a pack of emergency supplies—a knife and a flare, shotgun and shells, torch, dried twigs and, in his pocket, a waterproof container with matches and fire starters. He showed Abby how to use his handheld GPS unit.

She scowled. If she'd had one of those, maybe she could have gone alone after all. The Global Positioning System pinpointed your position anywhere on the globe within a hundred yards.

Snow machine ready, Flint studied the map at length. 'I don't like it.' He frowned. 'Malone's miles from where we've been searching.'

Abby saw he was right. The wilderness trail and the cabin littered with M&Ms was south of Lake's Edge. Malone lived in the opposite direction.

'Lisa couldn't have made it to Malone's,' Flint added. 'It's impossible.'

They all stared at the map in silence. Then Diane ran a tentative finger between Lisa's cabin and Malone's. 'Maybe she wasn't skijoring after all,' she suggested. 'Maybe she *wanted* to get to Malone.'

'But what about the dog harness?' Abby asked.

'What if someone's trying to put us off her scent?' Flint said.

Abby stared at him, apprehension crawling up her spine. 'Like who?'

He didn't answer, just refolded the map and stuck it in his parka pocket. 'If we're not back by tomorrow midday, come and get us,' he told Diane as he mounted the machine and started it up with a clattering roar. Abby climbed behind him, and they took off along main street.

Soon the town fell away and they were in a world of glittering white. They headed directly up the hill until it steepened, forcing Flint to zigzag. When they reached the top, he paused and looked back over his shoulder at the view. It was worth looking at—the spiderweb of trails connecting everyone's homes, the frozen river feeding into the lake and flowing out at the southern end. The entire landscape was jaw-droppingly majestic.

'OK?' Flint asked her.

'OK.'

'If it gets rough, put your arms round me. I don't want you thrown off.'

He didn't wait for her to reply but launched the machine over the crest of the mountain and hurtled down the slope. She decided to drop her English reserve and put her arms round his middle. It felt oddly intimate.

The miles flew past in a noisy blur of ice and snow. Everything sparkled, and she found herself smiling for the first time since she'd arrived in

Alaska, exhilarated by her surroundings, by the speed they were doing.

Eventually Flint slowed and began winding through a forest. Spruce branches whipped past, and Abby turned her head and ducked low. She didn't want to lose an eye. Soon Flint stopped the snow machine and switched off the engine. The sudden silence closed in on Abby. Climbing off the machine she had to steady herself against the seat, her muscles were so weak.

'I'm going to do a recon.' Flint picked up his shotgun, loaded it, snapped it shut and clicked on the safety catch. 'You stay here,' he said.

He crept to the left, between two spruce trees, then vanished. Abby listened for his boots crunching, but heard nothing. She didn't want to be alone. Chilled and uncertain, she began following Flint's tracks.

She stopped when she thought she heard something behind her. She swung round, eyes staring. Jesus. What if it was a bear? Hibernation was over and they'd be out and about foraging, hungry after their long winter.

Her heart hopping, Abby backed up against a tree trunk. She listened to the tiny drips of ice melting onto the snow, the faint rustle of pine needles.

She caught a waft of something rancid and foul and turned her head. She nearly screamed when she saw a man standing right next to her.

HE WAS DRESSED head to toe in animal skins and had what appeared to be a dead rabbit sitting on his head. He had a hungry look in his eyes, like a man who hadn't seen food for days.

'Shhh.' He had a finger to his lips and a shotgun at his side.

'What the . . .? Who are you?'

'Where is he? He gone to my cabin?'

'Are you Malone?' Her voice quavered. 'Where's Lisa?'

'He's come for her, hasn't he? I'll deal with him. Scum.'

Eyeing his gun, Abby thought it best to try and befriend him. 'I'm a friend of Diane's. Your niece? She gave me Lisa's note. I'm Lisa's sister.'

Malone studied Abby carefully. 'Don't look much alike,' he remarked.

'No,' she managed. 'We don't.'

'Stay here. I'll be back.' He turned and began to follow Flint's tracks.

'Malone, wait. Where's Lisa?'

He crunched away without responding. Abby followed, quietly as she could. She had to warn Flint, but couldn't think how. And where was Lisa?

Abby crept round a rock to see a shabby-looking log cabin nestling in a clearing. She couldn't see Malone, but she could see Flint, walking to the cabin, hands raised like a man under arrest. He no longer had his gun.

'Malone?' Flint called. 'You there?'

'Flint!' she called and he swung round, startled, at the same time that Malone appeared between the trees, shotgun pointed directly at him.

'Malone, put that thing down, will you? It's me, Mike.'

Malone approached him, keeping the gun steady.

'We're looking for Lisa McCall.' Flint's tone was conversational. 'She went missing recently. The note you gave to Diane told us she was here.'

Malone stuck the barrels of his shotgun into the front of Flint's parka. Abby's mouth dried up. What the hell was she supposed to do?

'We just want to know if Lisa's OK,' Flint continued in the same, steady tone. 'It was a rough storm and we've been worried for her.'

'Rough all right,' Malone rasped, but he didn't lower the gun.

'We won't trouble you any further if you could tell us if Lisa survived the storm. Everyone thinks she perished up here, you see.'

'Not dead,' he said, and lowered the gun a fraction. 'At least, not the last time I saw her.' The shotgun was now pointed at Flint's groin.

'When was that, Malone?'

'Yesterday. When I left for town.'

'You went to get things for her. Diane told us. That was good of you.'

'She's all right, for a woman,' Malone said.

'So is Abby.' Flint turned and beckoned her over, but she had no intention of getting any closer until Malone had disarmed.

'Yeah.' Malone flicked a look at her. 'Good lookin' pair, all right.'

At last he broke the shotgun and hooked it over his left elbow. He stuck out a hand and Abby crunched over to shake. The familiar foul stench wafted from his clothes as they shook and she tried not to recoil.

'Sorry she left,' he said. 'Your sister told me a couple of good jokes.'

'Where did she go?' asked Flint.

Malone squinted around the clearing. 'God knows. It snowed some last night. Covered everything.'

'But *why* isn't she here?' Abby wailed. 'Why didn't she wait for me?'

'Dunno. I only got back yesterday and she was long gone by then. So I couldn't give her the supplies I bought.'

'Did anyone else see this note?' Abby brought out the scrap of paper. 'Did you tell anyone, aside from Diane, that Lisa was here?'

Malone shuffled his feet. 'Well, I was in the Moose—haven't had a beer in that long, see—and I bumped into Hank and Billy-Bob, then Big Joe, and I knew how worried Big Joe would be . . . Then this woman got talkin' to me . . . Not bad looking either.'

Abby looked at him in horror. 'All these people knew Lisa was here?'

'No, no. Just Big Joe. He's her friend.'

For all Abby knew, Malone had got drunk and spilt the beans to the lot of them, which was why Lisa wasn't here. Someone else had got here first.

'How was she when you left?' Abby asked anxiously. 'Was she OK?'

'Tired as hell. Bit of frost nip here and there. Pretty weak.'

'She's in trouble, Malone,' Abby pleaded. 'She needs our help. A woman's been murdered. And Lisa is involved somehow.'

Malone looked up, surprised. 'You know who killed the woman?'

'Not yet.'

'Bet it was him, then.'

'Who?'

Malone shuffled his feet. 'The man she was running from. Her husband.'

Flint reared back in surprise as Abby blurted, 'Her *what*?'

'You hard of hearing?' Malone said.

'She's *married*?' Abby was stunned.

Malone gave her a sly look. 'Wonder why she didn't tell ya.'

'Who?' Abby demanded. 'Who's she married to?'

'Never said his name.'

'Is he local? American? English?' She could see Flint shaking his head but she ignored him. 'Come on, Malone, she must have let *something* slip.'

Malone thought some more, then said, 'He's a pilot.'

'Who isn't?' said Flint drily.

'Of what?' Abby asked. 'Commercial or private? Planes or helicopters? Or both?' Maybe she could track him down through a register of pilots.

'Mind if I have a look around?' Flint asked Malone. 'See if I can see which way she went?'

'I already did that.' Malone looked insulted, but Flint appeared oblivious and moved away without rancour.

'Can I see where she stayed?' Abby looked longingly at Malone's cabin.

'She's not chained up inside, if that's what you're thinking.' His tone had turned hostile. 'Shit. You live your own life and people think you're crazy.' Then he relented. 'Come on then. But don't touch nothing.'

Malone opened the door. Trying to breathe shallowly against the odour of unwashed clothes and drying animal skins, Abby moved inside. It was gloomy without any windows, and dusty, but it was surprisingly warm.

'Where did she sleep?'

A filthy forefinger pointed at a sleeping shelf in the corner, piled with pelts and blankets. 'I took the chair.'

Abby looked around the room and noticed the ham radio.

'Did Lisa call anyone?'

'She might have. But not when I was around.'

Malone started to edge her back to the door, unable to bear her inspection of his house any longer. 'Keeps me sane, that thing. Talk to all sorts of people. It's good in winter. Good company.'

Abby was still scanning the room. 'Did she leave anything behind?'

'Pretty much left with what she came with. Oh, she swiped an old shotgun of mine, and some ammo. But she left a note saying she'd pay me back.'

'Shotgun?' They were back in the hard, bright air now.

'Better for small game. Ptarmigan and the like.' He nodded approvingly. 'She'll be able to live off the land a while.'

Abby was still questioning Malone, trying to gather clues that would point her to Lisa or her husband, when Flint returned. He put a hand on her arm. 'She's not here, Abby. We've got to get back.' He put out a hand to Malone, which Malone shook.

Tears pricked at the back of her eyes. She didn't want to go, to lose the closest contact she'd had with her sister in years. She went and gave Malone a peck on the cheek. 'Thanks for looking after her.'

He put his hand where she'd kissed him, as though it burned.

Five

Abby spent the journey back to Lake's Edge with her mind spinning over everything Malone had said, but it inevitably circled back to a shocked explosion of amazement and relief: Lisa was *alive*. And *married*. But where had she gone? She couldn't have travelled far, with just one dog. Abby considered the ham radio in Malone's cabin, and wondered if Lisa had called someone for help, and who they might be.

By the time they arrived at Lake's Edge the sky still held a little light and the snowy trails glowed blue from the frosty clear sky. Exhausted and numb with cold, Abby struggled off the machine, and said between chattering teeth, 'Thanks for the ride.'

'Go and have a hot bath,' Flint told her. 'While you do that, I'm going to see Sergeant Pegati. Tell him we know Lisa's alive.'

An automatic protest formed on her lips.

'Look, Search and Rescue's still scouring the mountains. People are being inconvenienced for nothing, and besides'—he gave a quick grin—'she's long gone from Malone's. They'll never find her. She's far too good.'

'Really?'

'Yes, really. Could you give me the note? I'll need it.'

Abby didn't want to, but she took it out and passed it over. Hesitating, she said, 'Do you happen to know Meg? The woman Lisa worked with?'

There was a flash of something at the back of his eyes: horror, anger, she couldn't be sure. 'Meg?' he repeated. 'Why? Who's been asking?'

'The police.'

The seconds ticked past. 'Abby,' he said at last, his tone gentle. 'A piece of advice: be extremely careful who you say that name to.'

'Why? Who is she? What does she—?'

'Promise me you won't say that name again.' His expression turned fierce. 'I like you, Abby. I don't want you to get hurt.'

The snow machine's engine revved, drowning out her words, and before she could stop him, he roared away.

ABBY LAY in a hot bath in the outhouse, which stood ten yards from the back door of the cabin, luxuriating in the velvety heat.

A water storage tank, buried out the back, gave the cabin running water, which would no doubt be delivered regularly by truck. And she had a flush loo, which meant a septic system. She appreciated these amenities big time.

She had also appreciated the return of her bag from Lisa's, which she'd found dumped on her sleeping shelf. No note, no apology for the messy state everything was in, but she was inordinately glad to have it back. Aside from the sketch that Victor had swiped, nothing appeared to be missing.

After her soak she curled up on the sofa, wearing her favourite oversized cashmere sweater, thick socks and track-suit pants, and rang her mother. She'd barely said hello, when Julia butted in.

'Darling, I've had a man here, asking about Lisa's colleague, Meg.'

Alarmed, Abby asked, 'What man? Did he threaten you? Are you—?'

'Abby, *calm down*.' Julia's voice was brisk. 'The man said he was a friend of Lisa's, but I've never heard of him. I thought I knew all Lisa's friends. Those she likes, those she doesn't. But I've never heard of Matthew Evans.'

'What did he look like?'

'Quite a big man. American. Brown hair, brown eyes. Mid-forties. Receding hairline. And he wore tinted glasses. He wanted to know where Meg was. He also wanted to know what Lisa and I talked about the last time we spoke, whether she'd sent me anything . . .'

'Maybe he's a guy she had an affair with and kept quiet about?'

Julia gave a snort. 'Lisa's never been attracted to couch potatoes. Matthew Evans looked as though he'd expire on a walk to the local shops. Oh, and he chain-smoked. The house still reeks.'

Abby glanced at her cigarette stub on the saucer and then away. What her mum didn't know . . . 'This Matthew, what was he like?'

'Quite charming, I suppose, but there was something . . . not quite *right*.'

Abby took a deep breath, 'Mum, look. Before we go any further, I've got to tell you that Lisa's alive. Really, *truly* alive. She made it through the storm. As far as I know, she's OK. A bit of frost nip, apparently, but OK.'

'She's all right?' Julia sounded dazed. 'My baby's all right?'

By the time Abby had finished filling Julia in on Malone, and answered her questions, she'd drunk two glasses of wine and smoked five cigarettes.

When she finally hung up, she felt exhausted. She let Moke out briefly, topped up his water bowl, and crept into bed. She lay with her hand resting on the thick fur of the husky's belly as she stared into the darkness.

'ABBY? ABBY MCCALL?'

Abby opened her cabin door to an overweight figure with a bonfire of auburn curls. A multitude of scarves hung from the woman's shoulders, and she was clutching an enormous carpetbag.

'Yes. I'm Abby.'

'Oh, thank God I've found you. I'm Connie, a friend of Lisa's. Connie Bauchmann.' The woman dropped her bag to the ground, stretching out her arms to grasp Abby's hands. 'Look, I know you're probably going through hell, but I just wanted to hook up with you, see if there's anything I can do. I can still barely make sense of it. I dread to think how you're feeling.'

'A bit peculiar,' Abby admitted, instinctively liking the woman.

'I've been going quite mad with worry, ringing everyone I can think of who Lisa might have gone to.' The woman gave a slightly hysterical laugh. 'Nobody seems to know *anything*.'

Abby wanted to ask the woman if she knew Meg, but after what Flint had said, she held her tongue. Instead she said, 'Would you like a coffee?'

Beaming happily, Connie crossed the threshold and dumped her carpet-bag by the sofa, pulling off her knee-length down jacket. Moke looked up from his bed and growled lowly. Abby told him to be quiet.

'Oooh, don't they look good?' Connie said, when Abby brought some blueberry muffins out of the fridge.

Abby poured the coffee and put the muffins on a plate before settling with Connie on the sofa. She decided to plunge right in, 'So, how do you know Lisa? From the UK? You sound English.'

'Do I?' Connie blinked several times. 'Good heavens. I haven't been back there since I was a child. I guess it's hard to shake off your past.'

As if Abby didn't know. Before Connie could begin to fill her in on her English connection, she said again, 'How do you know my sister?'

'I've been working with her for the last six months. And Thomas.' Connie took a bite of muffin. 'You haven't heard from Thomas, have you? I really want to see him, but he's not answering his phone.'

'He's on vacation.'

'I don't even know if he's heard about Lisa's disappearance,' Connie said. 'He'll be devastated when he finds out. They're so close, those two.'

'He's like the father I should have had', Abby remembered Lisa saying.

'I'm worried about him,' Connie went on. 'I'm worried about Meg too.'

Abby reared back, startled. 'Meg?'

'Don't tell me you haven't heard the name.' Her eyes were sharp.

'No. I mean, well, yes, I have.' Abby was flustered. 'Who is she?'

'Look,' said Connie, 'I'd love to fill you in, but I promised Thomas—'

'A man went to my mother's home yesterday wanting to know about Meg. She felt threatened. *I have to know what's going on.*'

Connie hesitated. 'Abby, just *knowing* about Meg puts you in danger. Both Thomas and Lisa know this.'

Abby felt a creeping sensation. Michael Flint knew this too.

Connie took a deep breath. 'OK then. Since you insist . . . It's just that Meg is top secret. And if I hear you've breathed a word, Thomas and I, *and your sister*, will have your guts for garters. Understood?'

Abby sketched a cross over her heart.

'Good. Because we can't have *anyone* getting wind of Meg.' Connie leaned close. 'You see, Meg's not a who but a *what*. It heralds the Mega Engine Generation. MEG. Thomas and Peter—that's Peter Santoni—had been working on it for years. Santoni showed it to me once, but the technology was so shaky I couldn't see how they'd be able to make anything of it.'

Peter Santoni was the guy Tessa had referred to in her letter to Lisa. Santoni knew about Professor Crowe taking Lisa to court, and for the first time Abby wondered how he'd found out about it. By chance? Or had someone told him? She hurriedly switched her attention back to Connie.

'When Lisa joined them, she brought something fresh to the project. She can think so *laterally*, being totally unorthodox, and . . . Oh, dear, she had a terrible row with Santoni. He's methodical, deliberate, meticulous with his data, whereas Lisa . . . well, you know what Lisa's like. She used to call him Santoni Craponi. It drove him mad.' Connie took another bite of muffin.

Abby looked across as Moke went to his water bowl and had a drink.

'Santoni wanted Lisa off the project,' Connie continued, 'but Thomas didn't want to lose her. There was a huge fight, and in the end, Santoni walked out. Thomas and Lisa put locks on the door of their lab, locked their offices whenever they left . . . Poor old Santoni went from being an integral part of the team to a pariah. He's still bitter about it all.'

Abby could see why he'd treasure a piece of nasty gossip about Lisa.

'What does MEG do?'

'You know what she was obsessed with, your sister?'

'Flight,' Abby answered promptly. 'Telsa was her hero, but she admired the pants off Whittle. He invented the jet engine. . .'

Out of nowhere came Lisa's voice, clear as day. '*All we're doing now is building variations on a theme. We need another Whittle to take us forward, so we can fly London to Sydney in two hours without using fossil fuels.*'

There was a huge silence. A slow smile spread across Connie's face.

Abby's eyes widened. 'They've invented a new jet engine?'

'A jet engine with no moving parts whatsoever.'

'You're kidding.' Abby felt lost for words. Her mad, crazy sister had actually helped invent something *useful*?

Connie laughed. 'Aren't you excited?'

'Oh, yes,' Abby said hastily, but she felt a shot of fear. If what Connie said was true MEG was going to change the entire aeronautical industry. 'Connie, do you know what happened to Marie Guillemote?'

'But of course! The second I heard I was on a plane flying out of San Francisco! I was terrified all my money had gone!'

'Money?' repeated Abby.

'Dearest, I'm their business investor.'

ABBY LOOKED OUT over the frozen lake as she and Connie drank more coffee. It felt good having an ally. A cheerful ally at that, who appeared just as determined as Abby to find Lisa and get to the bottom of what was going on. Connie headed the research department for Brightlite Utilities, a forward-thinking electricity company who invested in ideas for future energy.

'But she's invented an aeroplane engine,' Abby said, confused. 'What has that to do with electricity?'

'MEG could herald a new age of energy, for domestic needs as well.'

At least Abby now knew where Lisa's $123,000 had come from. Good old Brightlite Utilities had stumped up the money three months ago, with another $100,000 promised the following year. Abby knew, however, that Connie wasn't as concerned for Lisa as for her company's money and, of course, MEG. Apparently, not only was the prototype missing, but MEG's lab books, which, Connie informed her, were almost as important as the prototype when it came to patenting the machine. Connie was petrified that both prototype and lab books had got into the wrong hands and someone was patenting MEG right that instant.

'It isn't patented?' Abby was horrified.

Connie groaned and pushed her head in her hands. 'Thomas wouldn't do it. He was paranoid someone would pinch their idea before they'd completed it. I told him time and again that the USTPO, that's the United States Trade and Patent Office, had changed their regulations recently, that it's not who files the *application* first for an invention any more, but who has the *idea* first that matters. Which is why the lab books are so valuable—they show Thomas's work since its inception thirty-two years ago.'

'And Marie Guillemote? Who's she?'

'A woman from the patent office in Arlington, Virginia. Lisa approached the USTPO a year ago, and when Thomas baulked at filing an application, Lisa and Marie struck up a friendship. They've kept in touch ever since.'

'Do the USTPO know about MEG?'

'No, thank God. Just Marie, who was very discreet. I spoke to her colleagues before I flew here, and, from piecing together various conversations, it's my theory that she came over to see the prototype, maybe persuade Lisa to take the first step in patenting the technology.'

'Why didn't Lisa meet Marie in Fairbanks, rather than have Marie rent a car and come all the way up here?'

'I'd like to get to the bottom of that too. There's one more thing you need to know, dearest,' Connie added, fiddling with her bangles. 'I've told the police I'm Lisa's business investor, but I haven't dared breathe a word about MEG. If we told them, it would be out all over town, spread across all the papers, and your sister would be in even more danger than she already is!'

'But if the cops know you're their investor, how can they not know about MEG?' Abby asked.

'I told them Brightlite invested in EVals. That's capital EV, in case you need to know.' Connie grinned. 'You should have seen that dim little trooper's face when I asked her how to get a hundred billion electrons to huddle together. She hadn't a clue what I was talking about.'

'Connie, who else knows about MEG?'

'No one, as far as I know,' she said, openly crossing her fingers.

A charge of apprehension tightened Abby's skin as she thought of Michael Flint. How did he know about MEG if it was so secret? She paused in the kitchenette, thinking hard. She had to speak to Thomas, she realised. MEG was his invention, and he may well shed some light on things.

'Connie, I'm going to call Thomas.'

'Good idea.' Connie started to get to her feet. 'Shall I leave you?'

'No, no. Stay.' Abby looked up his number and dialled.

An answering machine kicked in. 'Hi, you've reached Thomas . . .'

Abby left a message asking him to call her urgently. Then she rang the UAF switchboard, who told her that Thomas was on leave until the next day.

When she hung up, she saw Connie was looking alarmed.

'Oh, dear Lord,' she said. 'He can't know about Lisa yet, or he'd be back by now. I bet he's staying with those friends of his in the mountains. No TV or radio, let alone newspapers.'

Abby's heart sank. She didn't relish breaking the news to Thomas that his beloved protégée had gone missing.

'Dearest, shall I drive us to Fairbanks? It's not something I feel we can do on the phone. Then we can tell him together.'

Abby shook her head. Much as she felt for Thomas, she didn't want to leave the area. Lisa might send her another message. 'I'll call him.'

'That's all very well, but you do realise he'll refuse to discuss anything about his research over the phone. He's paranoid about security, remember?' Connie got to her feet and began gathering her belongings. 'I'll go down tomorrow. If seeing him is the only way to get to the bottom of all this . . .'

Abby dithered. She knew she could ask Connie to ring and tell her what Thomas had said, but she wondered if Connie would hide anything from her. If she met Thomas, she'd hear it from him straight.

'I'll join you,' she said.

'Oh, that's terrific,' said Connie. 'Let's meet after breakfast in the morning.'

After Connie had left, Abby pulled out Demarco's card and rang her. 'Just so you know where I am,' she told the trooper.

'I appreciate it.'

The temperature had risen a little, so Abby settled herself on the deck with another cup of a coffee. Moke's head lay in her lap. She gazed across the cold, white length of the lake, knowing she should be doing something to help Lisa, but she couldn't think what. She stayed around the cabin for the rest of the day in case Thomas rang, but deep down she knew she was making excuses. She was more scared than she wanted to admit.

IT WAS BRIGHT the next morning, and even Abby could feel how much warmer it was. At 35° it must have felt like a heatwave to the locals: everyone was in shirtsleeves. The main road out of town was slushy, spraying mud up the flanks of the car and, when they hit a pothole—which was frequently with Connie's haphazard driving—over the windscreen.

'Hey, take it easy,' Abby said after Connie had hurtled into another blind corner. 'There might be a moose standing in the way next time.'

Connie didn't take any notice, and Abby felt grateful she had an air bag in front of her. She peered into her wing mirror, hoping nobody was behind them in case Connie was forced to do an emergency stop. A white SUV was following, but luckily it was well behind.

'How's your mum taking all this?' asked Connie.

'Hard.'

'Must be tough with her MS, you looking after her the way you do.'

Wanting to distract herself from Connie's driving, Abby studied the emptiness around them.

'Is that why you and Lisa fell out?' asked Connie. 'Because she never came home to give you a break?'

Abby sighed. She and Lisa were so different, it was a miracle they'd ever talked at all. It was only being out here, trying to untangle what the hell was going on, that she realised how fundamentally dissimilar they were. Trying to work out what Lisa was doing and why seemed impossible.

Her thoughts suddenly evaporated when she realised that Connie was going to take the next corner far too fast.

'Connie, slow down, will you? There might be ice on the road!'

'You are so uptight!' Connie exclaimed, but she dropped her speed a fraction and took the corner without mishap. 'You're worse than Scott, and that's saying something. None of my other husbands minded my driving.'

'Husbands?' Abby tried not to sound surprised.

'Just the two before I met the love of my life,' Connie said drily. 'Third time lucky, that's what I always say. Some days I still can't believe it. We both play hockey, that's how it started. I whacked him one before shooting a goal.' She gave a chuckle. 'Talk about getting his undivided attention; the poor man couldn't walk for a week.'

Abby couldn't think of anything she'd done to get Cal's attention. She had, she recalled, simply stood there and looked into his eyes.

Connie had speeded up again, oblivious of the corner approaching.

'Can you slow down? Please?' Abby said.

'Are we nearly at the haul road yet?'

Abby checked the map. 'We've a couple of miles—'

Suddenly, Connie rammed both feet on the brake pedal, yelling, 'Shit!'

A tractor and trailer sat in the middle of the road. Brief snapshot of a guy watching them from a snow bank, then they were skidding straight for it, Connie and Abby yelling, and Abby was bracing herself for impact when the car slid to a halt just a couple of yards short of the trailer's rear tyre.

'Jesus,' said Abby.

'That *stupid* man,' gasped Connie. 'I nearly hit it. Are you all right?'

'Yes, but no thanks to you! Could you slow down a bit from now on? Like brake before a corner rather than right in the middle of it?'

'OK, OK, I'm sorry,' muttered Connie.

A shadow appeared at Abby's window. It was the guy who'd been standing on the snow bank, and he flung the door open and hauled her outside, yelling, 'Get in the car! The SUV behind you! Do it now!'

Abby fought off the hands grabbing the collar of her parka, her elbows. 'What the hell . . .? Get off me!'

The next instant she was face down in snow and her hands were being yanked behind her back and bound together.

'Fatso!' Another yell. 'Open the hood!'

Spitting snow, Abby twisted her head round to see a man pointing a pistol at Connie. Connie released the bonnet of her car, then he was leaning inside and ripping out a handful of wires from the engine.

'You're the lucky one,' he told Connie. 'You get to walk back to town.'

Abby kicked at one of the men, felt it connect, heard his grunt, and kicked again, but the other man yanked her upright, and then they dragged her to the rear of the white SUV. She fought every inch, yelling.

'Shut up!' one of the men shouted.

Suddenly the hands dropped away. She lurched sideways, trying to get her balance and make a run for it, when a fist landed on the side of her jaw.

Her head snapped back and she toppled to the ground. Her mouth was taped, then her eyes, and the men half carried her into the back of the SUV. She heard them lock the door.

Breathing fast, sweat pouring, Abby scraped her face against the rough carpet, trying to dislodge the tape across her eyes and mouth but it refused to peel off.

The car started up and pulled away. Curled on her side, she was sobbing with frustration and fear, trying to wrench her hands free, when one of the men said, 'Shut the fuck up, lady, or you'll get another thumping.'

Abby immediately fell quiet.

Shortly after, the car slowed, swung left and accelerated hard, gravel churning beneath the tyres. Onto the haul road, she assumed. The Dalton Highway. Oh God, where were they taking her? There weren't any towns along the road for at least 300 miles.

Abby dozed fitfully, her arms aching, her jaw sore. She reckoned they'd been driving for two, maybe three hours, when the car slowed and turned onto a rough surface, sliding and rolling. Abby realised from the motion of the vehicle that they were on an icy track.

'There it is,' said one of the men, as the car came to a stop. She heard the men climb out and crunch round to the back.

She wanted to try and run for it, but there was no point if she couldn't see. The door opened and a flood of ice-cold air rushed inside.

'Out,' said a voice.

Abby twisted round and swung her feet out of the car. A hand grabbed her elbow and hauled her to her feet. Her boots scrunched into stiff snow.

'Over here.' The same hand pushed her, stumbling, through the snow until her shin banged against something with a hollow knock. 'Get in.'

Get in what? Tentatively she raised her foot, and he added, 'It's a fucking sled, OK?' He yanked her forward, but she couldn't picture where to climb. He gave her a shove that had her sprawling forward and she dragged herself awkwardly into the sled. Hands tugged her boots until they rested against a plastic lip, about six inches high. 'You try and get out,' he warned, 'you'll fall a thousand feet, OK?'

She nodded.

Footsteps crunched away, then, with a clattering roar, an engine started. She felt a moment of terror. A snow machine? They were going to drag her behind them? Oh God, where were they taking her?

The engine engaged gear and the sled lurched forward, slowly at first and then picking up speed. Abby braced her feet, feeling the plastic rim of the sled dig into her bound wrists in the small of her back.

Almost immediately the sled dived to the left. Instinctively she leaned right, straightening it. The sled bounced, flinging her into the air, and she prayed she wasn't going to fly out and lunge to her death down a cliff face, but then she slammed back into the sled.

The sled veered sideways again and she tried to keep the sled straight and steady, but it was no use. With her hands tied and unable to see, all she could do was just try to remain on board. The effort took its toll, and she found her body rolling more and more. Suddenly another impact hit her and the sled jolted further to the left, almost spilling her out. The engine note dropped from a shriek to a roar and the sled eased into an unsteady rocking motion. Thank God, they'd slowed. Minutes later her weight was pushed to the back of the sled, and she knew they were climbing.

Her senses knew nothing but the cold smell of the snow, the occasional blasting stench of exhaust, the fear riding muscles that were stiff with cold, and when they slowed to a stop and shut off the engine, her ears rang.

'Out.' Hands heaved her frozen body upright, then the two men took up position on either side of her, gripped her upper arms and walked her forward, uphill, through deep snow.

They came to a halt. One of the men kept a firm grip on her while the other fiddled with something metallic. The sound of bolts being shot, a click and the creak of wood scraping on wood. A tug on her elbow.

'In you go.'

She fumbled ahead. The air suddenly smelt dense and musty. She felt hands on her wrists, then the tape was loose and she was bringing her arms round when a hand planted itself between her shoulder blades and gave her a hearty shove. She fell to her knees. Ripping the tape from her eyes and mouth, she swung round to hear the door being bolted shut.

Abby leapt for the door, hammered and pounded with her fists, but it was solid wood and didn't budge.

'Please!' she shouted. 'I've got lots of money! I won't tell anyone what you did if you let me go!'

She pressed her head against the rough wood, and continued to thump and yell, until she heard the roar of the snow machine moving off.

She listened until all she could hear was the deafening thud of her heart, the blood hammering through her veins.

Gradually she gained control and, at last, looked around in the gloom to see that she was in a single-room wilderness cabin. There was a waist-high stack of wood along one wall, a wood stove and chimney, a wooden shelf for a bed, a ten-gallon container of water, and boxes of canned food.

Abby stared and stared at the supplies, dread filling her heart.

She wasn't expected to leave for some time.

Six

Lisa pulled up Roscoe and searched the country with her binoculars. Since she'd moved out of King's territory, she noticed that deer and other animals were more numerous. In some places, the sun had melted the snow only to refreeze it at night, and she caught sight of a snow-shoe rabbit running across the equivalent of an ice rink. She smiled, thinking of Malone, who would have had the animal straight in his pot.

A good man, Malone. He'd gone into town to give her message to Abby. The only problem was that he'd stopped for a beer and told practically the whole town, as far as she knew, including Big Joe and Billy Bob, and some woman he'd taken a fancy to. And one of them had talked to someone else, who'd come straight to Malone's cabin.

Luckily, she'd been prepared, and was tucked up with Roscoe at the top of the hill behind Malone's cabin. Sheltered by the forest, she'd been impossible to spot from the air, but when she heard the buzz of an engine and the clatter of a helicopter's rotors, she loaded her rifle and hunkered down.

The chopper had banked sharply when it reached Malone's cabin, then hung over it like a great noisy hornet, almost brushing the tops of the spruce trees, then it banked a little, then a little more, and inched round the cabin. Lisa realised that whoever was inside was scrutinising the area minutely. For tracks. For small, woman-sized footprints.

She congratulated herself for sweeping her tracks clean as she left Malone's. Unless they walked the area, they'd never know she'd been here. And there was nowhere for them to land, not for at least a mile, and by the time they got here she'd be long gone.

The helicopter continued its slow scrutiny until suddenly it rose straight up into the sky, pushed its nose down, and accelerated away.

Now, she had reached her destination, and was by the back door, shovelling snow aside. The last time she'd been here it had been late summer, when she and Saffron had joined a group of friends picking cranberries.

She took a crowbar and levered off the bear shutter—a piece of plywood with nails pointing outwards. Once inside she headed straight for the kitchen, where she knew the radios were stored. Short-wave, long-wave, a ham radio as well. Radios for all eventualities.

'Bravo Jericho? You read? This is the King.'

Big Joe answered almost immediately. 'King, we've been worried.'

'Sorry about that. How's that new bitch of yours? Alpha, weren't it?'

'Alpha's gone. Everyone's telling me she's been stolen.'

Lisa felt as though she was in a ski-lift whose cable just snapped. Her greatest fear had just been realised. Abby had been kidnapped.

Even through the radio Lisa could hear the concern in Big Joe's voice. 'How are we going to get her back?'

ABBY WAS SHIVERING. It was probably from shock, but her bones were aching with cold, so she quickly turned her mind to practical things. Heat was a priority. After lighting the wood stove, she explored further to find candles, a can opener, a small saucepan and a down sleeping bag. So long as she kept the wood stove burning and kept herself warm, she could survive here for two weeks at least.

She checked the supplies again, searching for a knife, a piece of glass, anything she could use to chip away at the wood, but the only thing sturdy enough was the can opener, and she daren't break it or she couldn't eat.

Still shivering, Abby brought the sleeping-bag to the wood stove and huddled inside it, trying to get warm. She could have done with a cigarette to settle her nerves, but they'd been in her day pack. Abby gave a grim little smile. She'd given up before; she could do it again.

Resolutely, she turned her mind to Connie.

You're the lucky one. You get to walk back to town.

Had she reached Lake's Edge yet? Alerted the police? Were they now searching for her? What were the kidnappers' motives, their plans? Was she being held to be tortured, to give them information about MEG?

Suddenly a wild clamour made Abby's heart jump. She swung towards the door. Then the baying noise stopped. Absolute silence lasted for a minute, then it began again, clear in the night air. She stared at the door as though waiting for the pack to burst inside, they sounded so close. The hair stood up on the nape of her neck.

Abby hurriedly fed another log onto the fire, but it was damp and didn't take well. Christ, if she couldn't keep warm she'd die of hypothermia.

Damn Lisa. It was all her fault, running away and hiding. Tears filled Abby's eyes and she scrubbed them away. She mustn't get depressed. She had to keep her spirits up and prepare for an escape.

There was not another sound from the wolves, but for some reason she didn't think they'd gone away. She could almost feel them closing in. She wished Moke was cuddled beside her, to comfort her and keep her warm.

Abby eventually dropped into a light doze. She jerked awake when a solitary deep call broke out again outside the cabin. Abby strained her ears. Gently a barely audible sound reached her, of animals padding on soft snow.

Wolves, she recalled from what Cal had told her, rarely attacked humans unless they were snared, when they would—understandably—lash out. She closed her eyes and visualised Cal building up the camp fire each evening. For kindling he'd use hairy lichen and punk: dry, decayed wood that smoulders when ignited. Then he'd add birch bark for its fast-burning resin.

Abby picked out a big log, soggy and soft, and knocked away the outer portions until she got to the flaky, dry and rotted inside that was punk. Then she built a nest of bark, lichens and punk beneath the logs, added a tissue from her parka pocket, and lit the thing. Twenty minutes later it was crackling and spitting, and Abby banked it up with green branches to make sure it didn't burn too fast.

At some point she fell asleep. When she awoke it was dark, save for the fire. No light leached in through the cracks round the door. Night had fallen. She didn't add any more logs to the fire; the cabin had warmed enough for her to shed the sleeping-bag and her parka. She spent the night keeping an eye on her fire and listening to the wolves pad around the cabin.

THE NEXT DAY was spent trying to chip her way to freedom, working at the crack at the corner of the door with the edge of an aluminium can, but she made little headway. For lunch she heated a tin of chicken soup. Afterwards, she placed every item in the cabin where she could find it in the dark.

She spent a lot of time considering MEG, the replacement for the jet engine, and wondered what sort of fuel it might use. She kept hearing Lisa ranting about the oil industry, and puzzled over why, if Lisa was passionate about the environment, she had invented yet another engine. And what about her husband? Who the hell was he? Did he have anything to do with all this? Abby was still worrying over this the following afternoon. She had just finished a snack of warmed beans when she thought she heard something. She pushed her ear to the door, wondering if the men were returning. Eventually there was a faint crunching of snow, then a snuffling sound, and the door gave an almighty shudder.

Abby sprang back, a shriek on her lips.

A snort and a growl followed, then another pounding on the door.

It wasn't a wolf or a human, she realised. It had to be a bear.

'Go home, bear!' she yelled. 'This food's mine! Go home!'

The bear gave a grunt, and started to circle the cabin.

She recalled Cal telling her to store food so that bears couldn't smell or reach it. And not to keep food in her tent, not even mints, or toothpaste.

Abby hurriedly rinsed out the saucepan and can, but she knew it was too late. The animal would be hungry after its long hibernation.

'Go away!' Abby shouted frantically, as she heard the bear stop and thump on the wall of the cabin. 'Leave me alone!'

She pictured it searching for a fissure in the wood where it could hook in its claws. Bears were at least as intelligent as dogs, Cal said, and if a bear was determined to break in, it would find a way.

The door creaked and shook under another attack, then silence fell.

Heart pounding, Abby stared at the door. Maybe the bear was coming up with another plan. Maybe it was going to charge at the door. Maybe . . .

She flinched at the grunting and thumping scrunch of snow. Trembling, Abby listened to it diminish. It sounded as though the bear was departing, and in its place . . . Her heart skipped a beat . . . was the clatter of the snow machine. The men were back. They had scared the bear away.

Immediately she started thumping the door and yelling. 'Let me out! Please, I'll do whatever you want, just let me out!'

'Just calm down, will you? You don't, we leave you here.'

'I'm calm!' she assured them, glad she wasn't strapped to a lie detector.

'Look at these prints!' the other man said. 'They're big as an elephant's!'

'Shut up and cover the door. I don't want her breaking loose.' Abby heard the bolts being shot back, and then he barked, 'In the back of the room, hands up! If you try and make a break for it, we'll shoot you!'

'I'm right at the back, OK?'

The door inched open, flooding the cabin with bright light. Narrowing her eyes against the glare, Abby watched a man step inside, pistol in hand.

'Turn around. Hands on the wall.'

Abby complied.

'You move a muscle, you get one in the leg.'

'I won't move,' she promised.

She let him tie a cloth round her eyes, relieved it wasn't duct tape.

'Sit on the bed,' he commanded.

Abby sat. She heard him walk away. Then he said, 'Make the call.'

She was about to ask what call, when she realised he must be talking to his pal. Her thoughts went wild. Was she being ransomed?

Nothing happened for the next ten minutes. She smelt cigarette smoke and heard the odd crunch of snow as the men waited. Then a phone rang.

'Yeah. Right, OK.'

Boots rang against the cabin floor. Something pressed against the side of her head. For a second she thought it was a mobile, but then realised it was much larger: a satellite phone.

'Say, hello,' he told her.

'Hello?'

'Abby?'

She felt as though she were in free fall. It was Lisa.

'Abby, are you OK? Are you all right? Oh, Abby, are you there?'

'Yes,' she said. 'Yes, Lisa. It's me. I'm here. I'm fine.'

'I'll get you back, OK?' Lisa was talking fast. 'Where are you?'

The phone was snatched away and Abby lunged after it, yelling, 'The mountains! I'm north up the haul road in the mountains!'

An arm went round her neck, a hand over her mouth. '*Shut the fuck up.*'

Abby lay back, trembling, hands clenching and unclenching.

'Yeah,' he said, and she assumed he was talking to Lisa. 'Fiveways, like we said. Six o'clock. Be there or we'll start messing with her.'

There was a brief silence, then he said briskly, 'Get up.'

Abby rose, and she felt her parka and scarf shoved into her hand.

'We'll do it like before. You fuck us around, we shoot you. Got it?'

She quickly put the clothes on and he pushed her outside. Abby inhaled the tart, cold air.

This time, her hands weren't tied and it was just the one guy who gripped her arm as she stumbled down the steep, icy slope.

They hadn't gone far when over the rustle of branches came a piercing wail, like an injured animal. All three of them came to a halt.

'What's that?' one of the men said.

'Christ knows,' said the other. 'But let's get the hell out.'

Again the creature wailed, then came a snuffling grunt that Abby recognised. It was the bear. A blade of pure terror sliced through her. If the wail was what she thought it was, they were in deep trouble. Mother bears were fiercely protective and wouldn't hesitate to kill to defend their cubs.

'It's a bear,' Abby told the men, her voice high-pitched with fear. 'For Chrissakes don't move.' She scrabbled at her blindfold and it fell free.

Brief glimpse of two guys, one with a beard, one without. Neither was looking at her. They were staring at a grizzly no more than twenty yards away, a huge mother bear on all fours, who was staring back. Her coat was glossy and thick after hibernation, and she must have weighed 800 pounds.

From their left came the bawl of a cub.

'Don't move,' Abby pleaded, 'just don't move.'

'Fuck that,' the guy with the beard said, and raised his gun.

The bear raised herself on her hind legs and peeled back her lips, revealing two-inch-long teeth.

'Don't, please don't,' Abby begged, 'just keep still and she'll move on.'

She began inching backwards, praying the men wouldn't do anything stupid. They weren't between the mother and the cub, she was certain, but if the bear saw them as a threat she might attack.

The bear snapped her teeth together. It sounded like an oven door slamming shut.

'Shit,' the man said. And, to Abby's horror, he fired his gun.

The bear didn't hesitate. She dropped down to all fours and charged, spraying snow on either side. She was fast. Her huge, chunky body moved with more fluidity and speed than a greyhound.

Abby sprinted for the trees. She didn't look behind her as she ran.

Several shots rang out, followed by the outraged bellowing of the bear, and a scream lodged in Abby's throat as she plunged across the slope.

Another bellow. The bawling of a terrified cub.

She risked a glance over her shoulder to see one of the men firing wildly as he ran, the other pelting in her footsteps, the bear right behind him.

Gasping, adrenaline pumping, Abby pounded as hard as she could. No time to stop and look behind her. *She had to get to the trees. Try and hide.*

Another shot, and she was in the shelter of the forest, fighting through the undergrowth, branches snatching and tearing at her clothes and hair, fingers and knuckles split and bleeding. Then she heard the man scream.

'Shoot it!' he shrieked. 'For Chrissakes, shoot it!'

Through the brush she saw a blur of limbs and fur. The bear was all over the man, dwarfing him. Another blast of gunfire, but the bear wasn't stopping. It grabbed the man's right arm and with a sickening, wrenching sound, plucked the limb clear of his body.

Abby stood paralysed with horror as the snarling bear threw the man's arm aside and plunged on top of him, burying him deep in the snow.

Finally the bear dropped its prey and looked around, blood dripping from its jaws. Abby didn't think she'd moved, didn't even blink, but to her horror the bear snapped its head to the forest and looked directly into her eyes. They were no more than ten feet apart.

Abby remained motionless. The bear's eyes were locked on hers. Slowly, Abby let her gaze drop. A lowered gaze was less threatening, Cal had said.

'Keith! Keith, you OK?'

The tenuous truce between her and the bear was broken. The bear dropped her head, and came for her. Abby felt a moment's disbelief, and then her wits kicked in. *Play dead!* Cal yelled in her mind.

The bear was nearly upon her. Abby closed her eyes and flopped to the ground. The grizzly thundered right up to her and stopped, huffing.

Abby's throat tightened. Her limbs went numb. She felt the warmth of the bear's breath on her cheek. It smelt of rotting meat, but she didn't flinch.

I am dead, she told herself. *I am as dead as one of Malone's pelts.*

The bear shoved her, making her tumble onto her side. Then it sniffed her face. Abby knew it was trying to sense her breathing, to see if she was still a threat, so she tumbled herself further and buried her face in the snow.

More sniffing. Another almighty shove. From somewhere came a wail from the cub. The bear stilled. Then it growled and whacked Abby's shoulder with a skillet-sized paw, making the air rush from her lungs. She was bracing herself for a full attack when the cub wailed again.

Huffing and grunting, the bear moved away.

Abby lay there, trembling, until she couldn't hear the bear any more. Cautiously, she raised her head and peered around. Nothing. She clambered onto all fours. Her face felt wet and she wiped it. Her fingers came away coated in bloody spittle.

She looked around again, and that's when she glimpsed a second grizzly in the brush. Smaller than mother bear, its coat as blond as a haystack, it was creeping swiftly but silently in the direction of the cabin.

Abby urged herself to move. She stood up and slipped through the trees as fast as she could, until she came to the edge of the forest. She peeked out. She could see neither the grizzly nor the bearded man. But way down at the bottom of an almost vertical slope, she spotted the snow machine.

Arms flailing, she galloped straight for it, praying they'd left the keys in the ignition, praying she wouldn't meet another grizzly.

Jumping astride the snow machine, she gave a yelp of relief when she saw the keys were there, then flinched as another shot rang out above.

The bearded man was piling down the mountainside after her, yelling and brandishing his gun. He was moving fast. Very fast.

She turned the key and the engine roared into life. Abby accelerated cautiously, and U-turned the machine to head back down the mountain.

The man was just ten yards away, running hard and fast, pistol held low.

Clamping her thighs round the seat, she increased the throttle and the machine surged forward, spraying snow, and she was leaning into the first part of her turn when he brought up his pistol and aimed it straight at her.

'Stop,' he yelled, 'or I'll shoot you!'

She swung the machine back, straightened the handlebars and opened the throttle to the max. Then she accelerated straight for him.

'Stop!' he screamed.

Abby ducked as low as she could, engine howling, snow billowing.

Crack!

He hadn't hit her, thank God, and the snow machine was bouncing and leaping and she was aiming straight for him.

Crack, crack!

She heard a metallic clank and she was nearly on top of him when he sprang to his left, arms reaching, mouth stretched in a soundless yell.

He was too late. The snow machine hit him squarely in the pelvis and flipped him into the air. He seemed to hang for a second and then he was plummeting on top of her.

Abby let go of the handlebars and flung herself to one side. There was a long, shuddering thump. Then silence.

Gulping cold air, she tried to get up, but something was on her legs. Slowly she raised her head. The man was lying across her, face down, motionless. The snow machine was on its side, engine stalled.

Abby carefully tested her legs to see if they were broken, but, aside from an aching knee and a dull throbbing in her forearm, she'd come through unscathed. She wriggled free, heaving at the man's shoulders until she was on her hands and knees beside him, gasping.

She studied the man for a few seconds, knowing that she couldn't leave him as he was. She hadn't a clue whether he was alive or not, but she dug through the snow and found his chin, then levered his head until his face wasn't buried in it. She wasn't going to do anything else for him. He could take his own chances out here, along with his friend.

Abby glanced up the mountain, listening. Everything was quiet and still. Time to get the hell out. She tried to right the snow machine, leaning her weight on the upper ski, but it barely moved. It was buried in the snow.

She contemplated heading back to the cabin for supplies, but abandoned the idea. She didn't want to meet mother bear or her sidekick a second time, so she followed the snow machine's tracks down the mountainside.

The drive up here had taken around an hour—so she had roughly thirty miles to go before she hit the snowy track, then another mile or so to the haul road. She checked her watch—3.45 p.m. The sun would start setting around eight o'clock and the temperature would plummet to below freezing. She would have to walk through the night. And what about the wolves? She didn't dare think about bears, or she'd remain rooted to the spot.

Abby sped up. She had to get some miles under her belt. She might come across another wilderness cabin where she could hide up for the night.

She walked for an hour without seeing any evidence of humankind. If it wasn't for the ski tracks in the snow, she'd have thought nobody had ever been here. It was clean and pristine and beautiful, and terrifying.

Slowly, darkness fell. Abby banged her gloved hands together and wrapped her scarf round her head, but her fingertips were cold, the tips of her ears freezing. She was praying that it would cloud over for the night, give her an extra couple of degrees, when it happened.

She glimpsed it out of the corner of her eye, and thought it was a jet contrail, until she looked up. Her breath caught in her throat.

A great arc of translucent pale, whitish green light flowed across the sky. Unfurling into a broad, weightless curtain of silk, it rippled delicately through the air. Abby forgot all about the cold, the wolves and bears, and she stopped and stared, completely absorbed. The aurora borealis. Northern lights. She hadn't realised that it moved. It was like watching a ballet dancer in slow motion. The curtain undulated gently, and folded back on itself before unfurling again, creating huge scythe-like shapes.

A sense of awe seeped into her, and with it a deep peace.

It was a moment of epiphany. She found herself making promises as she watched the miracle curl and fluctuate. *I will reunite myself with Lisa and not force her to be someone I want her to be. I will let Cal say his piece and forgive him once and for all. I will go to midnight mass this Christmas and thank whoever you are for letting me live and see this miracle.*

She was thinking about Cal and wondering if she'd be able to keep that particular promise, when she heard a shushing, scraping sound coming up the mountain, and then the creaking of wood and the jingling of small bells. She immediately thought of Father Christmas on his sleigh.

'Haw, George, haw!' A man's voice cracked through the still air.

Suddenly eight dogs came pelting round the corner. The man was standing on a sled behind them, headlamp blazing as he urged them forward. The second he saw Abby he slowed his team to a stop. He fiddled with something near his knees, then came racing towards her, broad face anxious.

'I heard shots,' he panted. 'Are you OK? I saw the grizzly. I've got some binoculars, I was over there'—he waved a hand across the valley—'training my team. I've been going like hell to get here.'

Abby didn't think she'd ever been so glad to see anyone before.

'I'm Walter,' he added.

Walter was as wrinkled as a dried fig. Caverns and furrows were scored deep on his face, burned into the skin by the cold, the winds and the sun. Like Big Joe, he was a Native, with almond eyes and black hair, but he wore a westerner's down jacket and fleece-lined boots.

'You are a *star*, Walter!' she exclaimed, having to stop herself from hugging him. 'I thought I was going to have to walk through the night!'

'Where's your vehicle?'

'Stuck.' Abby told him about her chase off the mountain, and backtracked to include the grizzly's attack, and her kidnap.

Walter's mouth dropped open. 'You're the woman they grabbed?'

'That's me.'

'Well, holy heck!' He shook his head, grinning. 'And I get to be the hero who rescues you.'

They sped down the mountain, Abbey in the front of the sturdy wooden sled, Walter standing behind her, urging the dogs on. The motion of the sled was soothing, along with the hiss of the runners on snow. Clouds of steam rose from the dogs' mouths, evaporating above their ruffs.

Walter told her that his village was called Raven's Creek, and that he was the only Native there who still kept a team of dogs. 'Can't be doing with those snow machines,' he continued. 'They weigh a ton, they're impossible to manoeuvre over ravines and creeks, and as soon as it hits twenty below, the engine gets real cranky.'

When they reached the valley the team veered to the left, away from the kidnappers' ski tracks. Soon they were approaching a wide, frozen river.

'Short cut,' Walter said. 'If we go round it, we'll be here all night.'

Nervously she asked if it would hold their weight.

Walter chuckled. 'I learned to read the ice when I was knee high. But the best guides are the dogs. When they stray off course, it's because their paws feel changes in the moisture on the surface. A snow machine can't do that.'

After safely bouncing and sliding across ribs of frozen water, they raced towards Raven's Creek, bells jingling.

The first sign they were nearing town was when they passed a gritty airstrip, banks of snow piled on either side. Drifts of fog were closing in, blanketing the stars and covering the mountain tops with pale gauze.

At the end of the main street, the dogs veered left and slowed to a stop outside one of the cabins. Ten dog kennels were set among the spruce trees on the western side. Four huskies were pulling against their chains and yipping and baying, and the team happily joined in.

Abbey saw a satellite dish bracketed to Walter's front wall and, as she looked further, she saw just about every cabin had one, which meant everyone had electricity and, given the telegraph poles, phones as well.

'Get yourself indoors,' Walter told her, plucking her out of the sled as though she were as light as a strip of balsa wood. 'Get warm.'

Walter set the sled hook, commanded the dogs to stay put and ushered her inside. The first thing that hit her was the smell: unwashed bodies, meat stew, urine, and just as she thought she recognised the distinctive odour of a butcher's, she took in the fresh moose skin hanging on the wall, still seeping blood, and the huge sections of carcass lying on the floor.

Walter introduced her to his wife, Kathy, and his five children, who stared at her as though she'd landed from Mars. As she scanned the small room she realised that the kids shared one bed while their parents had the other. There was no kitchen to speak of, just a wood stove with a pot of some kind of meat simmering on its top. A honey bucket stood in the corner, and a colour TV blared out some game show.

'Kathy, this is Abby. She'll be hungry.' Walter thumped to the phone in the corner. 'I'm calling the troopers.'

Kathy gave her a bowl of watery stew while Walter phoned Sergeant Pegati to explain he'd rescued Abby, and that yes, she was just fine.

'No, we're a fly-in village . . . No. Fog is coming in. I wouldn't risk it till the morning . . .' He listened a bit longer, then said, 'OK,' and passed the phone to Abby. 'He wants a word.'

Victor wanted descriptions of her kidnappers, where exactly she'd been held, details of the white SUV, and how, precisely, she'd got away. Finally Abby managed to ask, 'Have you heard from Lisa?'

'She called to tell us she was in contact with the kidnappers and not to mess things up.'

'How did she—?'

'Through an intermediary. And don't ask; we don't know who they are.'

Abby's grip tightened on the phone. Who was this intermediary? Could it be Lisa's husband?

'Now, Abby, we'll send out an aircraft at first light to see if the kidnappers are still on the mountain. But we need to know where the rendezvous was to take place. We're hoping the third man might be there.'

Her mind galloped. Wouldn't Lisa still be at Fiveways? She wouldn't know Abby was safe. 'I don't know,' she lied.

She thought she heard a muffled curse, then the sounds of him talking to someone else. When he came back he said, 'We'll send our chopper in as soon as we can, OK?'

'Do you know where Connie is?' she asked. 'Is she all right?'

'Mrs Bauchmann is just fine,' he said. 'She's still shaken up about the attack, of course, along with having to walk over fifteen miles to get help. But she'll be glad to hear you're OK.'

She had, Victor went on to say, been abandoned by the third man the instant the kidnappers had driven off with Abby. He'd taken Connie's phone and gone off in the tractor, which they found later on the haul road. 'Quite a slick operation,' Victor remarked. 'Three or four guys. All to swap you for your sister.'

'What do you mean, swap us?'

'That's what we believe the kidnappers wanted. Your sister. Her research is valuable, apparently. Which is why you were snatched. To draw her out.'

Abby felt a wave of dizziness. The kidnappers really were after MEG.

'I know I asked you this before,' Victor said, 'but are you sure you don't know what Lisa was working on?'

'Sorry, no,' she lied, and hurriedly wound up the conversation. She was tired and might let something slip.

When she'd hung up, Kathy started bustling about, and despite Abby's protests, began preparing the kids' bed for her.

'They can sleep on the floor,' Walter said. 'They're used to it.'

The children didn't look at all perturbed, just continued to stare in fascination at her from where they sat in front of the TV. Finally Kathy spooned her into the kids' bed, which was a nest of rancid blankets and skins with a huge dip in its middle. She didn't care; she was safe at last, and warm.

She lay with her head on a wolf pelt and drifted into an unsettled sleep, waking occasionally to hear Walter calling his buddies on his ham radio, telling everyone across what sounded like the whole of Alaska what a hero he was. It wasn't until his rescue began to take on epic proportions that she finally slid into unconsciousness.

'FLARES!' Walter suddenly yelled, making Abby jackknife up in bed, hair in tufts, blinking wildly. 'Get the flares!'

The TV was still blaring, the lights still on. The kids scattered as Walter shouted. 'It's the middle of the night! What kind of crazy . . .? Kathy, bolt the door and get the gun ready.' He shot a look at Abby. 'Just in case.'

Then he was gone.

'What's going on?' she asked Kathy, but Kathy was busy bolting the door and loading a shotgun, which she then held in both hands, facing the door.

'Kathy?'

'Aeroplane,' the woman replied. 'Here, nobody lands in the dark.' She shot the kids a look that had them scurrying for their parents' bed.

'Walter, he go light the strip. Help pilot to land.' This time Kathy looked at Abby as she spoke. 'He not sure if good man or bad man.'

Abby tuned in to the buzz of a plane. Oh, God. Was it the kidnappers? She leapt out of bed and went to the window. She saw several guys at the end of the street, running behind Walter towards the airstrip. Each of them carried a gun. If it was the kidnappers, they'd have one hell of a welcome.

For the next twenty minutes Abby stood by the window, senses fixed on the street. She thought she'd heard the sound of an engine throttling back as the plane landed, but couldn't be sure, and now she couldn't hear it any more. Kathy stood patiently beside her, shotgun loaded.

Eventually a group of men appeared at the end of the street, walking easily, their guns held loosely in one hand or strung across a shoulder. Individuals peeled away to enter their homes, leaving Walter and a tall guy with a shotgun crooked in his elbow to walk on alone.

As they neared, Abby blinked, wondering if she was imagining things. The man with Walter was Cal Pegati.

She heard both men stamp their boots of snow outside, then the door swung open and Walter stepped inside with Cal on his heels.

'What in God's name are you doing here?' she asked him.

Cal propped his shotgun against the wall. 'Nice to see you too, Abby.'

'But nobody flies in the dark!'

'Believe me, I wouldn't have done either, but for some obscure reason people are worried about you, and I was told to get out here.'

'I can't believe you risked your plane,' grumbled Walter. 'You crazy?'

Cal's jaw tightened. 'Raven's Creek is a remote village, and it won't take the kidnappers long to find the place, along with Abby. And since some people'—he looked at Walter—'have been chatting like chimps on ham radios about her rescue, there's every chance they're already on their way.'

Walter hung his head while Abby stared at Cal. 'You came out here to protect me?'

'Have you heard from your sister?' he parried.

'You thought she'd be here? Well, she's not,' Abby snapped. 'So you may as well leave, now you've checked.'

'Lake's Edge isn't reachable under Visual Flight Rules any more. I'll leave when I've received clearance, and when I do, you're coming with me.'

'Your dad sent you, didn't he?'

Cal didn't respond, just stood looking fed up.

Kathy looked across at them as she tidied the smelly covers of Abby's bed. 'You two,' she said, 'you share. Big bed. No problem.'

ABBY LAY CLINGING to the edge of the bed, keeping as far from Cal as possible, fighting not to fall back into the dip in the middle. She'd rather have slept outside in one of Walter's dog kennels, but hadn't wanted to insult Walter and Kathy's generosity.

She peeped at the kids. Three of them had joined Walter and Kathy in their bed, and the eldest and youngest were snuggled in a pile of skins and blankets by the wood stove.

Abby could still feel the heat of Cal's body rolling over her, smell the adrenaline and dried sweat from what must have been a hair-raising flight.

Could he smell her? She hadn't dared use the water while she'd been incarcerated for anything but drinking, and she knew she stank. Then she remembered their sharing a tent on the expedition. She hadn't bathed for two days, and was coated in sweat and dirt, but he hadn't minded then.

Abby could feel the heat rise through her body at the memory. A log shifted in the wood stove, flaring orange. She wondered about Saffron, and what she would do if she heard they'd shared a bed.

Whatever Cal's reasons for coming, she felt strangely glad he had. Probably because of the big handgun he'd pushed beneath his pillow. At least if the kidnappers arrived he'd be ready for them.

She closed her eyes and tried not to think about Cal. Without realising it, she sighed.

'Can't sleep?' Cal whispered. 'Neither can I.' His voice was rueful. 'I wonder why.'

Abby concentrated on breathing evenly and deeply, even though her heart was banging away like a big bass drum.

'Sweet dreams, Abby.'

He rolled over, and although she felt icy air dart over her neck she didn't move. She had no idea how long she had lain there when she heard Cal's breathing turn deep and regular. She'd forgotten how quietly he slept.

Seven

T he sun had disappeared behind the horizon and it was getting colder. Roscoe had curled himself into a ball and tucked his tail over his nose to keep warm. Lisa wished she could do the same, but she couldn't relax, not yet. She'd arrived at Fiveways an hour early and scouted the area before choosing her vantage point: a small rise where she could see the track from the road as well as the rendezvous site. Three hours had passed since the deadline. A blue Ford Expedition had turned up on time with only one guy inside. She made a mental note of the number plate.

Anxiety rolled through her. Where was Abby? Why wasn't the man bringing her out for the exchange? Why was there only one guy?

He sat in his car for forty minutes before he climbed out, holding an assault rifle. She ducked low as he skirted the area. He didn't move far from his vehicle. Finally, he left. She listened to the engine fading to silence.

She wanted to scream with frustration, bang her fists on the ice, but she kept her anger and fear tight inside. Ranting and raving wouldn't help Abby.

Rummaging through her pack she pulled out a high-energy bar. Thank God for Big Joe. When they'd met up on the haul road, the first thing he'd done was hand her a box of goodies.

While she ate, Lisa ran through every 'what if' scenario she could think of, including Abby getting injured, Abby being tortured, Abby dying, but, ever the optimist, ended up with, 'what if Abby escaped'.

Lisa knew her sister was tenacious, determined and dependable. If Abby knew about the rendezvous, if she thought there was the remotest possibility Lisa was at Fiveways, nothing would stop her getting here.

Lisa decided to wait for her. For as long as it took.

CAL HAD HIS elbow crooked over her ribs and she could feel his breath against her neck. Momentarily confused, Abby wondered if she was dreaming, but then she glanced down to see she was holding Cal's hand in both of hers, tucked beneath her chin. Abby shot out of bed like a scalded cat.

Cal reared upright, eyes bleary. 'What is it?' he demanded.

'Nothing.' Abby tried to appear insouciant. 'Just need to go . . .' She looked at the honey bucket and amended it to, 'get some fresh air.'

'Not alone, you're not.' Cal scrambled out of bed and pushed his feet into his boots. The gun went into his waistband.

Abby followed him outside. As soon as the dogs saw them, they barked and whined and leapt around their kennels, their tails going like crazy.

She paused to pat one of them. 'Wish you were Moke,' she told the dog. She would miss him dreadfully when she went back to England.

Cal ushered her into a clump of poplars, and took a tree well away from her, giving her loads of privacy. She shivered as she pulled down her trousers, baring her behind to the chill air. Past the tree trunks she could see strings of fog clinging to the village, but just off the horizon a brightening haze indicated the sun was trying to break through.

Back in the cabin, Kathy gave her a cup of coffee and she took it outside.

'It'll be clear in an hour or so.' Cal was standing beside her, gesturing at the sky. 'I'll let the cops know I'll be flying you back.'

'Would you fly me somewhere first?' Abby said.

'Not until the ABI have debriefed you.'

'What if I told you I know where Lisa is? Would you take me there?' She told him then about the rendezvous the kidnappers had arranged, and how she didn't want the cops to arrest Lisa if she was still there. 'Do you know where Fiveways is?' she finished.

'Yes,' he said. 'It's where five trails meet just south of Glacier. I can't see anyone spending the night there. It's bleak as hell.'

'Come on, Cal. At least let's check the place out.'

Abby waited while Cal frowned, obviously weighing up the pros and cons. 'OK,' he said eventually. 'But you owe me.'

She turned to go back inside the cabin but stopped when he put a hand on her arm. 'I'd like to talk about what happened on the expedition.'

'Later, Cal. We've got to radio the ABI right now.'

She went back inside the cabin, but not before she caught the look of frustration on his face. She almost felt sorry for him, but mistrust had hardened her to a point where she found it easier to push him away. Sadly, the forgiving, beatific feeling she'd experienced when she'd seen the aurora borealis had vaporised, just like the magnetic cloud itself.

BY THE TIME they arrived at Fiveways, it was just after midday. Forty miles from Lake's Edge, the rendezvous point was just half a mile from the haul road and, as Cal had said, bleak as hell. Miles of snow-clad tundra stretched beneath a hazy white sky. There was nowhere to hide, no trees or bushes or piles of boulders, and Abby's spirits sagged. It was the perfect place for a rendezvous; you could see a vehicle approaching from any direction for at least two miles. Had Lisa turned up and been snatched by the kidnappers?

Head down, Cal started walking the area, studying various tracks and footprints while Abby waited at the point where the five tracks converged, but the snow was unmarked.

'Abby. See this?' Cal called her over. He was standing next to a set of vehicle tracks that stopped twenty yards short of the junction. 'They sat here a while with their heater running.' He pointed out icy patches in the snow where hot water had dripped from the exhaust. 'They got out, had a look around, but didn't go far.' He looked at the sky then back at her. 'Let's split up, cover more ground. See if we can find any evidence that Lisa was here.'

For more than an hour Abby crunched across the tundra, searching for tracks, but the place was pristine.

She heard a yell and turned to see that Cal was standing near a small rise. He was beckoning her over.

When she got there, he didn't say anything, just pointed at the ground where the snow had been compressed in a large circle. Cigarette butts littered the area. Marlboro. Lisa must have smoked a whole pack sitting here.

'She chose a good place, considering,' remarked Cal. 'She was behind them, and too far away for them to see her, if she ducked down.'

'The tracks look fresh,' Abby remarked.

He looked over to where their loaned four-wheeler sat near the tracks they'd found. 'Whoever was in that car probably left after you didn't turn up. There's only one set of prints leading to and from this hideout, so it's a safe bet Lisa wasn't seen and got away OK.'

Abby swung her gaze around the area, almost in hope that Lisa might pop up from behind a tussock, but nothing moved.

ABBY SPENT the short journey back to Glacier in silence, wondering where Lisa was now. Soon they were airborne again, clattering across a gleaming swath of white, only twenty minutes from Lake's Edge and a hot bath. She couldn't wait to smell like a human being again rather than a dead moose.

'Abby,' Cal spoke to her through her headphones, 'I want to talk about us. Look, something happened when we were on that expedition . . . I thought it was . . . well, just sexual attraction, but it was something more.'

She turned her head to look at him. He was staring straight ahead.

'How's your wife, Cal?' she asked him.

He closed his eyes briefly. 'Dead,' he said.

LISA ACCELERATED up the haul road, cursing at her own stupidity. Hadn't she learned anything over the past four years? Jesus. There she'd been, hunched in her shallow little hidey-hole, when Abby had rocked up. With Cal. She couldn't believe she'd made such a basic mistake.

She had assumed Abby would get someone to show her where Fiveways was on a map and come to the rendezvous alone, because that's what she would have done. But Abby didn't know the area, and she didn't feel comfortable in the wilderness. Of course she would bring someone.

Thank God she hadn't reacted instinctively when she'd seen Abby. For a second she'd nearly leapt to her feet with a shout of joy, but then she saw the tell-tale lump at the rear of Cal's jeans. He was carrying a gun.

Gravel spat beneath her tyres as Lisa accelerated round the next corner. She hadn't dared leave a message for Abby. She couldn't be sure that Cal hadn't been corrupted. MEG was worth such a lot of money, even friends could turn on their own. She would have to find another way of contacting Abby. And soon. Time was running out.

'SAFFRON DIED six months after you left Alaska. I wrote and told you, but like all my letters, that one came winging its way back unopened.'

A jet of horror as Lisa's voice echoed through her mind. *'Saffron will die if she hears about this.'*

'She knew?' Abby managed.

'No.' Cal shook his head. 'Why didn't you answer my calls, Abby?'

'I'm not a home wrecker,' she said. She wondered how Saffron had died, but hurriedly turned away from that train of thought. Although she felt unsettled by the news of the woman's death, she knew it wasn't her fault.

'Abby, you have to believe I had no intention of having an affair. But when we met I found myself doing something I thought I'd never do . . .'

He paused and Abby rolled her head back. A tidal wave of exhaustion washed over her. 'Oh, go on, then,' she told him irritably, 'get it over with.'

He glanced at the aircraft's roof as though choosing his words before he spoke. 'Saffron came from the Yukon-Kuskokwim delta—'

'She was a Native?'

'Yup. I won't say I didn't love her, because I did.' His tone wasn't defensive. He was simply stating the facts. 'But the thing is, and I'm not making excuses . . . Well, I guess I am, but . . . She was sick as a young kid, chronic asthma, respiratory problems, but when her parents moved her away from the area, she got better. When we met, she was fine. But then she got sick again. She was ill for six years before she died. We were married for eight.'

She felt him glance at her but she kept her gaze firmly on the horizon.

'It was awful. The doctors couldn't help . . . I looked after her as best I could, but there was nothing I could do. It was terrible to see her like that, someone who'd been so wilful, so *strong*, struggling for breath, day after day . . .' He closed his eyes briefly. 'And then I met you.'

'Yes.' Her voice surprised her. It was gentle and understanding. She knew what he must have been going through, having cared for her mother.

'I made a mistake.' His voice went flat. 'It was the first time in three years I'd spent time with people who didn't know about Saffron, people who didn't ask after her all the time or look at me with pity. I felt released, as though I had my life back. Of course I didn't, but I pretended I did. I hadn't felt so alive in so long. I didn't care that I hadn't been . . . entirely truthful. Until the day we came back. Then I realised what I'd done.'

Neither of them said anything for a few minutes.

'You left before I could explain,' Cal said.

'So I'm the one to blame?'

'No, I am. But if you hadn't stormed off and frozen us out . . .' He gave a long sigh, and fell silent.

Abby considered what might have happened if she'd confronted him instead of fleeing the country, but she didn't see that it would have made any difference. It came back to the same old thing. He'd been *married*.

'I wrote to you,' Cal said.

Three letters, which she'd sent back, unopened, then nothing more until two years later, when he'd sent one letter a month for almost a year. She now realised this must have been well after Saffron's death, when he'd finished grieving. She hadn't had the courage to read them. No matter what he had to say, she knew it would hurt too much to relive the past, so she'd sent those back too. Despite the whole sorry mess, she couldn't say he hadn't tried to make amends.

'So,' he said, 'can you forgive me?'

She twisted her fingers together, wanting to forgive him, unable to. She didn't respond, and Cal didn't push her.

They spent the remainder of the flight in uneasy silence.

DEMARCO AND VICTOR were waiting for them when they landed. Cal had contacted them to let them know their ETA, but hadn't explained why they had taken so long to get from Raven's Creek to Lake's Edge.

While Cal scribbled in the flight record book, Abby went to meet them.

'Glad to see you're OK,' Demarco said, and shook her hand. 'You did good to get away. Real brave.'

Victor cleared his throat before shaking her hand. 'You've got grit in you, girl,' he said. 'Nice going.'

Demarco escorted her to the Ford Explorer while Victor went and had words with Cal. Buckled up in the back, she couldn't hear what they were saying, but she could see they weren't happy with each other.

Abby studied the aircraft parking area, where the AST helicopter was sitting next to two other choppers: a Bell 205 and a red and white Astar 350B with OASIS OIL decals.

'Here, I brought this for you. They left it behind.'

To her amazement, Demarco brought out her day pack. Nothing was missing as far as she could tell.

Demarco turned and yelled at Victor to hurry up, which made Victor stab a finger at Cal's nose before sprinting for the car.

Victor sat with Abby in the back while Demarco drove. Behind them, Cal tagged along in his black Dodge Ram. When Demarco cracked open a window, tilting her head to catch some fresh air, Abby cringed.

'Sorry,' she said. 'I'll be fine after a bath, I promise.'

Demarco looked at her in her rearview mirror, her features softening. 'It must have been tough. Being alone, not knowing what was going on . . .'

'We'd like to discuss what happened at HQ,' Victor said. 'Do you feel up to it? We don't want to add to your trauma.' He was studying Abby carefully.

'Sure. If you can stand the smell.'

His eyes crinkled at the corners as he smiled. 'That's great.'

'I did some thinking in the cabin,' Abby ventured after the vehicle had stopped shuddering over a set of potholes. 'Want to know what I think?'

Victor widened his eyes slightly.

'I think Peter Santoni's behind all this. He's the disgruntled scientist Thomas and Lisa chucked off their project. He was very bitter about it.'

'So we heard.' Victor was nodding. 'Do you know what the project was? We're having trouble finding out anything about it. Both Thomas and your sister were obsessively secretive.'

Abby wanted to tell him about MEG, but didn't dare after Connie's warnings. Prudently, she muttered, 'No, sorry,' keeping her gaze outside.

The car made another turn, slush spraying up its sides.

'Santoni went to the same university as your sister,' Victor said. 'We thought he might have something to do with that professor your sister accused of murder, but it's no go. He'd left way before all that happened.'

'You've found Crowe?'

He shook his head. 'We did find one of the men who kidnapped you. He turned up at Fairbanks hospital this morning, mauled by a grizzly.'

'He's alive?' She was astonished.

'His friend obviously had some training. We're thinking maybe military. He would have died otherwise. He lost an arm in the attack.'

'What about the other guy? The one I hit with the snow machine?'

'We believe he rang the third man to collect them from the mountain. They dumped their pal outside the hospital, and vanished.'

'At least you've got one of them,' she said.

Before long they came to the scattering of homes that were the outskirts of Lake's Edge, and Abby felt a rush of affection for the place.

As Demarco approached the school, she stuck her foot on the brake. 'Ah, shit,' she said. 'How the hell did they know we were bringing her in? It's like a goddamn circus out there! Shall I go round the back?'

Abby saw that the school's steps were crowded with people. She recognised Big Joe, Connie, Diane, Mac the pilot, and most of the others by sight. All people who'd searched for Lisa on the mountain and who had, according to Cal, searched for her too.

'Back it is. Let's give her some time before—'

'No,' Abby interrupted. 'I want to go in the front. They're my friends.'

Victor cut her a sideways look and shrugged. 'Your call.'

When Abby stepped out of the car, the crowd gave a cheer. Connie swept her into an embrace. It was like being hugged by a giant pillow.

'Dearest, I've been so *worried*.'

'You're OK?'

'Aside from my feet being *covered* in blisters, I'm in the peak of health.'

Then Diane was there, hugging her tightly and kissing her cheek. 'I'm sorry,' Diane said. She was on the verge of tears. 'I just found it hard, you know, with Saffron . . . but when those men got you, I realised what a bitch I've been. Lisa would have me strung up if she knew.'

Abby didn't have time to reply, because the next second Mac had her in a bear hug that lifted her to the tips of her toes. 'Thought we'd arrange a welcome. Diane's doing a bit of a party for you later.'

'Thank you all so much,' she told them, impossibly moved, voice thick with tears. 'You're all wonderful, you really are.' She looked across the crowd to where Big Joe was standing. 'How's Moke?' she asked.

He gave her one of his enigmatic nods.

When they eventually stopped inside the school corridor, Demarco asked 'What can we get you? Are you hungry? Thirsty?'

'A biscuit or something would be good,' Abby said. 'I missed breakfast.'

While Demarco trotted off, she followed Victor to the briefing room. He sank into his usual place behind the desk; she took the chair opposite.

'The white SUV,' Victor prompted, and ran through her description of the car, what the men looked like, only pausing when Demarco arrived with a bag of freshly baked cookies. Abby ate two. They were still warm.

Victor scowled when the phone rang. 'Sorry,' he said as he picked it up. He barked, 'Pegati,' then listened, staring dead ahead, phone clamped to his ear. He closed his eyes. A low moan escaped his lips. 'I'll be there in two hours,' he said, and hung up.

Alarmed, Abby said, 'What's wrong?'

Victor looked at Demarco and Abby in turn, then fixed his gaze between them. 'Bad news, I'm afraid.' He picked up a manilla folder, put it down.

'Sir?' Demarco was staring at him. 'What is it, sir?'

'Thomas Claire's body was identified yesterday. He was found inside a burnt-out car in a remote area on the outskirts of Anchorage.'

Abby heard the words, but they were having trouble getting to her brain. The room suddenly felt overly hot and cramped. She could barely breathe.

'Lisa and Thomas left Fairbanks the same day.' Victor was talking to Demarco. 'Friday, April the second. They travelled separately in opposite directions. Lisa headed north to Lake's Edge, Thomas south to Anchorage. Apparently Thomas had someone called Meg with him.'

Abby tried not to start. Thomas had taken MEG to Anchorage? Did that mean his murderer now had the prototype?

'I'll chase it,' Demarco said.

Victor turned to Abby. 'How well did you know Thomas Claire?'

'I met him only a few times, but I liked him a lot.' Abby's voice was husky. He was one of life's gems, full of kindness and generosity.

Victor glanced at her, saw the tears hovering. 'I'm sorry,' he said, 'but I'd rather you hear this from me, now, than find out through the media.' He took a breath. 'Someone set fire to Thomas, to make sure he wouldn't be identified easily.' Victor's jaw clenched. 'He was chained to the car's steering wheel.'

Horror coiled itself around her heart. 'Are you sure it's Thomas?' Abby's scalp had tightened.

'The dental forensics are one hundred per cent conclusive.'

'They'd have to be mad to do that to him . . .'

'You haven't heard from your sister, have you?' Victor asked. 'By radio perhaps? We need to know where she is, make sure she's safe.'

She leaned forward. 'Do you still think she killed Marie?'

Victor spread his hands in a conciliatory gesture. 'In all honesty we don't. They were friends, working towards the same goal: to patent whatever technology she and Thomas had cooked up. But it's imperative we speak to her. Her scientific project is at the heart of this investigation.'

He got to his feet and shrugged on his jacket. 'Look, I'm sorry to have to cut you short, but I need to talk with Trooper Demarco before I go.'

'Wait.' Abby jumped up. 'What about Peter Santoni?'

Victor stuffed some manilla folders in a briefcase. 'Unfortunately, he went to Juneau last week and we're having trouble tracing him.'

Abby stared at him. 'Are you saying Santoni's vanished?'

Victor didn't reply.

ABBY SAT on the sleeping shelf in her cabin, her mind churning. How had it come to this? Marie and Thomas murdered, her sister on the run. Had the same person killed Marie and Thomas? Had they found Lisa and killed her too?

She didn't react when someone rapped on the door.

The door opened. 'In,' she heard a man say irritably. 'For Chrissakes, will you just do as I say and go *in*?'

There was a patter of claws and then a grey-and-white form catapulted against her legs, tail waving and tongue lolling. Moke wriggled and squirmed, burying his head in her lap, then he reared back and did a little prance before flinging himself at her thighs again.

'Friends reunited,' Cal said. 'I heard the news about Thomas. Thought you could do with cheering up.'

Abby pushed her fingers into Moke's thick ruff. 'Thanks,' she said and smiled. 'Hey, boy, how are you?' Moke wiped his tongue across her cheek.

'Mind if I come in?'

Belatedly she realised that Cal was hovering in the doorway. She got to her feet. 'I'll put some coffee on.'

They didn't speak while the kettle boiled, just stood shoulder to shoulder looking outside. The boardwalks were still icy, the trails snowbound, but the street was melting, glistening with slush. Break-up was well on its way.

Abby spooned coffee into mugs and poured the hot water and milk.

'I'm so sorry about Thomas,' Cal said.

'Me too.' She concentrated on stirring her coffee to prevent the tears rising. 'He was a lovely guy. He made me laugh.'

Moke was nuzzling her thigh. Cal looked at him. 'Don't forget you've a job to do,' he said, stroking Moke's thick ruff.

'What job?' she asked.

'To look out for you.' He ran a hand over his face. 'Demarco would love to have a team of cops protecting you, but since Trooper Weiding's returned to Coldfoot and Dad's flown to Anchorage . . . It's just her up here.'

The hair on Abby's forearms rose. She hadn't thought the men might come back for her.

'You'll keep him with you?' Cal said. 'Twenty-four-seven, no matter what?'

It wasn't a difficult request to accept. 'Sure.'

He nodded, took a sip of coffee. 'Abby.' His tone was cautious. 'Do you know what Lisa was working on?'

She turned away and rested her hands on the worktop, looking outside. 'She never said. Not to Mum, not to anybody.'

'Hmm,' said Cal. 'So how come you know?'

'I don't.'

'Hmm,' he said again, and added, 'Be careful, Abby.'

Something in his tone made her shiver inside. 'God,' she said, 'you're as bad as Michael Flint with the prophecy of doom.'

'Flint?' Cal repeated. 'How do you know Flint?'

'He's my landlord.'

'Jesus, that man gets everywhere. Be careful of him, would you?'

Abby stiffened. 'Why?'

'Dad pulled Lisa's phone records. Flint called her a lot.'

'So?'

'His family owns Oasis Oil. He's rich as hell and wants to get richer.'

She immediately recalled the red and white helicopter with OASIS OIL decals on its doors, parked by the airstrip.

'Alaska's economy depends on oil. Unfortunately, Prudhoe Bay is drying up. Production is less than fifty per cent of what it was fifteen years ago.' He dragged a hand over his head. 'Flint is heading the debate about opening up the coast of the Arctic National Wildlife Refuge to oil drilling.'

Her mind started to flail. 'I thought he was a friend of Lisa's.'

Cal looked astonished. 'Whoever told you that?'

'Diane.'

He frowned. 'Everyone knows Flint and Lisa hate each other.'

'So why was he ringing her?' Abby asked.

'He insists they were settling their differences. Having "spirited discussions" was how he put it. But we think he might have been badgering her about what she was working on with Thomas . . .' He paused. 'Abby, if you know what Lisa was working on, don't tell Flint, will you?'

Flint already knew, but Abby didn't react. She put down her coffee mug without taking a sip. 'Thanks for filling me in,' she said calmly.

Cal nodded, and downed the last of his coffee. 'I'll see you at the Moose later?' he asked. 'They're having a bit of a celebration for you, don't forget.'

ABBY TOOK A BATH, with Moke lying on the bath mat beside her, thumping his tail each time she looked across. Then, hair still dripping, she tore back through the snow to the cabin and got dressed—warm padded trousers, stretchy shirt, thick socks and boots; at night the temperature plummeted.

She just about leapt a foot in the air when Moke launched himself at the door, barking fit to burst.

'Jesus, Moke!'

She peered through the window. Two men in dark suits and ties stood on her doorstep. Both were around five ten in height, but one was in his early thirties and carrying a couple of stone of extra weight, mostly round his middle, while the other had to be twenty years older and looked twenty times fitter. A rush of relief flooded her that neither were her kidnappers.

Abby tapped on the window pane, calling, 'Can I help you?'

The men came over and studied her with unsmiling expressions. The fatter one pushed their badged ID cards to the window. Her skin tightened. NASA. National Aeronautics and Space Administration.

'We'd like a word regarding your sister,' he called.

Abby opened the door and had to grab Moke to prevent him from making a lunge for one of the guys' knees. 'Leave, Moke. *Leave.*'

'Nice dog,' said the fat one, but his voice was scratchy with fear.

'Sorry, he's a bit overprotective.' She shifted Moke aside with her thigh, and the dog gave the men a long look, then turned away.

'I'm Ben Elisson,' the fat guy said, 'and this is Felix Karella.'

As well as the spare tyre, Elisson had a raggedy-clipped black beard that was attempting to follow his jaw line. 'I understand you've undergone a fair amount of stress this week, but this is important and we won't keep you long.' His smile was sympathetic. 'Any chance of a cup of coffee?'

Abby was still dithering when Felix Karella gripped her upper arm and, without seeming to force her, managed to twist her neatly around. The next thing she knew they were all in her cabin with the door shut behind them.

Moke sprang to her side and started to growl.

'Nice doggy,' Elisson said, putting a hand out to Moke.

'I wouldn't,' Karella told him. He flicked his eyes to Abby. 'Call him off.'

'Moke, leave,' she said. She could, she supposed, put him into attack mode again if she wanted.

The dog's shoulders seemed to slump, but he didn't move from her side.

'Shall we sit?' Elisson hitched up his trousers and smiled at her.

She didn't smile back. 'Sure.'

Elisson sat down on a stool; Karella stood at his shoulder. Neither of them, it transpired, actually wanted coffee.

'We're sorry about Lisa, what's been happening,' Elisson said. He folded his hands in his lap. 'We like her enormously. She's a nice lady. Sparky.'

'You've met her?' Abby took a seat on the sofa.

'Oh, yes. Several times. You know about MEG?'

She made a little frown between her eyes. 'I've heard the name,' she said.

'Hmm,' Elisson said. 'Well, as you probably know, MEG is incredibly important. As far as space travel goes . . . it's mind-boggling what we could achieve. We might have mankind travelling outside our solar system within the next few decades.' He blinked several times as though bringing himself back to earth. 'We are, however, worried about the safety of the technology. Not only have the two scientists who've had the most input into MEG disappeared, but all their research has disappeared, too.'

Did they know that Thomas had been murdered? Abby decided not to mention it.

'What can you tell us about Marie Guillemote?' Karella asked.

She weighed her answer. 'She's a friend of Lisa's, the cops tell me.'

'And she works for the patent office, which you're aware of, right?'

Abby gulped. Gave a nod.

'We heard Thomas and Lisa created a prototype machine. Guillemote's parents say she came over here to collect something.' Karella looked at his partner. 'In this case two and two, for us, made a perfect four. Guillemote came to collect the prototype.' Karella looked hard at Abby. 'Agreed?'

She managed a nod. Marie must have come to take MEG to safety. But why hadn't Lisa flown MEG out of the state? Met Marie in Virginia? Was she worried she might be picked up at the airport? Maybe by these guys?

'And whoever killed her wanted it for themselves. What we don't know is where the prototype is now. Do you have any ideas where it might be?'

Abby shook her head. 'No idea. Sorry.'

Karella looked frustrated. 'It can't be that big or heavy if Guillemote was going to haul it back to Arlington with her.'

Abby hadn't given any thought to what the prototype might look like. Surely a jet engine had to be *huge*. 'How come you know about MEG?' she asked. 'Nobody else does, not even the cops.'

'It's no secret,' Elisson said. 'Lisa met one of our scientists, Perry Torgeson, three years back, at a conference. Perry worked on our Breakthrough Propulsion Physics project. They bandied ideas about. Eventually, we got to hear what she was working on. We, er, approached Thomas Claire, but he wouldn't see us. Your sister was more approachable. We offered her an extremely generous sum for the technology, but she turned us down, saying she didn't want her work to benefit anything that wasn't humanitarian.'

'I see,' said Abby.

'The offer we made to your sister,' said Karella, 'is still open.'

'We are still very keen to invest in Lisa's work,' Elisson added.

'Gentlemen,' Abby said, getting to her feet. 'I'm sorry, but you're wasting your time. I can't help you.'

Neither man got to their feet. 'The point is,' Karella continued, 'that the offer we made to Lisa would, of course, be redirected to yourself if you found MEG or the lab books.'

Her mouth turned dry. 'OK,' she said lightly, 'if I should fall on MEG or the lab books, how generous a sum are we talking here?'

The eight figure number that Karella gave her made her feel dizzy. No wonder people were getting killed. The stakes were astronomically high.

Abby walked to the kitchen, feeling numb and detached.

'That much money can go a long way,' Elisson said softly. 'You can help charities, save the whale, have round-the-clock nursing for your mother, which would free you up—'

'Get out.' Her voice was low and dangerous. People didn't care about Lisa. They just wanted her damned technology.

'Hey, don't be hasty here. I'm just telling you how it is—'

'Moke!' she yelled. The dog sprang to his feet, watching her. She pointed at Elisson, and Moke fastened his eyes on him and snarled.

Elisson blanched. 'OK, OK.' His breathing was uneven. 'We're going. OK?' He inched his way to the door and opened it. Karella followed.

Abby watched them scoot outside. When the door closed behind them, Moke came over and nuzzled her thigh.

'Good boy,' she said, her voice trembling. 'You see them again, bite them.'

Eight

Lisa opened a carton of long-life milk and put it on the stove to warm. She wished the cabin had a radio. She wanted to know how Abby was. She knew that she was back in Lake's Edge, but was she really OK? Kidnap victims needed hours of counselling, didn't they?

She poured hot milk over her powdered chocolate and gave it a stir. Tears pricked the backs of her eyes, so she turned her mind from Abby, and wondered whether Thomas had managed to deliver the lab books as they'd arranged. She had to pray he had, because if someone patented MEG tomorrow, she'd never be able to contest the application without them.

Oh, God. Everything was her fault. Thomas had told her to keep MEG quiet a while longer, but she hadn't been able to resist bragging to Santoni about how far they'd come without him. And Santoni had obviously gone to NASA and told them about MEG, because Perry had called to warn her that they had been asking about her.

Perry worked for NASA on their BPP project, Breakthrough Propulsion Physics, and they'd met at a conference in Salt Lake City a few years ago. Perry was tall, with floppy blond hair and a wicked sense of humour. They'd had a glorious fling, and if he hadn't been based in Huntsville, Alabama, it might have developed into something more serious.

Lisa finished her chocolate, looking at the frozen white forest outside.

If she hadn't boasted to Santoni, Abby would be safe.

Roscoe pushed his nose against her thigh, and she dropped to her knees and hugged him, burying her face into the warmth of his fur for comfort.

Goddammit. It was all her fault.

THE BAR was three deep when Abby arrived. Everyone wanted to give her a hug and buy her a drink, and, spirits buoyed, she hugged them back.

The first beer went straight to her head, and Abby felt something loosen inside. She wolfed down a steak and a bowl of fries, had two more beers, and she was dancing with Mac, feeling carefree and slightly crazy that she was *here*, and not locked in a wilderness cabin, when Connie arrived.

'Dearest!' she shouted. She was beaming from ear to ear, eyes shining.

Connie obviously hadn't heard about Thomas's murder. It seemed nobody had, except the cops, herself and Cal. Abby decided to keep it that way.

Hugging her back, Abby noticed a large, balding man hovering to one side, looking ill-at-ease. Bizarrely he had a pair of tinted glasses perched on his head. 'This is Scott,' said Connie, beaming, 'my husband.'

Scott put out his hand and Abby shook it.

'It's not really his thing,' Connie told Abby, 'but I wanted you guys to meet before we grabbed something to eat. He flew out the second he heard about our little escapade. He's real glad you got out.'

Abby smiled at Scott, who smiled back, then glanced around at the bedlam and raised his eyebrows at his wife.

'Tomorrow!' Connie called over the sound of the Dixie Chicks belting out full blast. 'I'll come round in the morning!'

Abby nodded and let Mac take her hand and twirl her in an unsteady circle. Cal had been skulking in the background since she'd arrived, and she wasn't sure if she found his presence an annoyance or a comfort. Most of the time he was scowling, especially when Mac put his hand on her behind and gave it a squeeze.

Happily drunk, Abby finally collapsed on a stool at the bar and mopped her forehead. Diane poured her another beer and yelled, 'On the house!' Abby raised the glass in thanks, and when she nearly dropped it, set it carefully back down on the bar, deciding she'd probably had enough.

Mac sank on the stool beside her and started telling her about his latest passenger, who'd been so crazy he'd had to be tranquillised and tied up. Halfway through the flight, the passenger recovered from his stupor and started thrashing about, and Mac had been forced to land on a lake, cut his passenger's lashings and throw him overboard. The 700-pound brown bear had hauled himself ashore and disappeared without any seeming ill effects.

They talked bears for a while, then a pretty girl with green eyes came and whisked Mac away to dance. A guy moved into Mac's place, said, 'Hi.' He was in his twenties, strong, muscular and tanned.

'Hi,' she said. She didn't recognise him, but he obviously recognised her.

'You wanna drink? I owe your sister several, maybe you could drink them for her.'

'I think I've probably had enough, but thanks.'

'Miss her, you know.' He peered into his beer. 'We had a big bust-up twelve months or so back. She kicked me out barefoot in the middle of winter. Thought I'd get frostbite and lose all my toes.'

Abby blinked. 'You're Jack? Jack Molvar?'

'That's me.' He grinned. 'Luckily my bunny boots came sailing out a minute later or we wouldn't have stayed friends.'

Abby wished she hadn't had so much to drink. She had loads of questions for Lisa's ex-boyfriend, but now she couldn't think of a single one.

'She always said you didn't look alike, but I had no idea,' he grinned. 'She is such a short-ass, whereas you . . . well, you're a goddess.'

Abby pointed ruefully at his beer. 'I think you've had enough too.'

'Hey, Abby.' A hand rested lightly on her shoulder. She glanced up to see Michael Flint. His eyes were warm. 'Boy, is it good to see you.' He kissed her cheek. 'I can't believe you got the better of those bastards. Well done.'

'If you don't mind,' Jack said, an edge to his voice, 'we were talking.'

Flint turned to give him a cool look. 'And you are?'

'Jack Molvar.'

The atmosphere was tense as Flint looked the younger guy up and down.

'You got a problem?' Jack growled.

'No problem.' Flint gave a sigh. 'I'll catch you later, Abby. OK?'

'Piece of shit,' Jack muttered as Flint vanished into the crowd.

'He seems nice enough to me,' Abby said, hoping to prompt Jack into spilling some beans. 'I like him.'

'Your sister didn't.'

'How come?'

'Because she's a greenie and he's an oil . . .' Jack paused, began digging in his pockets as a barmaid came over. 'Yeah, Doreen . . . a beer thanks . . .'

'At each other's throats they were,' a man interjected from Abby's left. He had whiskers the colour of wet ash and a foamy rim of beer round his lips. 'Lisa wantin' to protect the environment, Mister Flint Almighty trying to destroy it. It got real personal—a lot of mud slinging. Press loved it.'

'When was this?'

'A year or so ago. All died down in the end.' The man scrutinised her at length through a pair of rheumy eyes. 'You and Cal an item yet?'

'Certainly not.' She was indignant.

'Don't go all hoity-toity on me. Only askin'. I know there's others all disapprovin' of what you two got up to, but the guy needed cheerin' up.'

Abby looked at him blankly.

'You know,' he went on, 'it's not right for a guy to get married then have his wife fall sick. Broke your heart to see her go like that. A real beauty too, all eaten up by illness. She used to be such a sparky lass.' He looked wistful. 'Tough too. She could butcher a moose, fix an engine, make the best sourdough you could want. Good shot, and not a bad fisher, either.'

What in the world Cal had seen in her compared to this parody of self-sufficiency, Abby couldn't think. 'Shame she was so ill, it sounds awful,' she muttered into her beer, trying not to feel jealous.

The barmaid, a handsome woman with a black braid and a dusting of dark hair on her upper lip, cut in with a sneer. 'Don't tell me you cared.'

'Hey,' Abby reared back, 'hang on a second—'

'You outsiders are all the same. See one of our men and it don't matter if he's married. You want him, you just have him and high-tail it home without a care about any diseases you've given him he's gonna pass on to his wife.'

'Doreen,' the old guy said, 'butt out, I was talking—'

'She set her sights on Cal and the poor bastard didn't stand a chance—'

Abby stood up, said quietly, 'You say another word, and you'll regret it.'

'Shut up, Doreen,' came a voice from behind. 'It wasn't like that.'

Abby turned to see Flint clutching her parka in one hand and beckoning to her with the other. 'Let's get out of here! It's time you went home,' he said, grabbing her wrist.

They were nearing the door when Abby heard the barmaid yell, 'Not him as well! Can't you keep your hands to yourself for once?'

Abby tried to turn round to yell back at her, but Flint's grip was like steel and the next instant she was outside.

'Jesus,' she gasped. 'What the hell happened in there?'

'You were about to lose your rag.' Flint was eyeing her warily. 'Not without good cause, but on top of all that beer . . .'

'Oh, God.' She cringed. It was definitely time for bed.

'I'll walk you home,' Flint said. 'Make sure you get there unscathed.'

The cold air cleared her head a little, but her legs were behaving as though they weren't connected to her body.

'You're as bad as your sister,' he remarked, tucking her arm in his, but he didn't make it sound like a bad thing. Affection threaded his voice.

'She bad,' Abby said, 'me good.'

'Yes, I know.' He looked across at her. 'Incidentally, Lisa's not married.'

'How d'you know?'

'She made it up to gain Malone's sympathy. My guess is she told him her husband was abusing her, and that she was hiding from him.'

She remembered the hunger in Malone's eyes. *I'll deal with him. Scum.*

'He was going to shoot you. He thought you were Lisa's husband.'

'Clever old Lisa.' He looked pleased. 'She knew how to get him on side.'

When they got to her front door, he asked if she'd be OK. Abby nodded and fumbled for her keys. She tried to fit the key in the hole, but it kept slipping. Flint took the key from her and slotted it in, but as he turned the lock and made to open the door, she grabbed his arm.

'No, no,' she said. 'Dog is in there.'

She could hear Moke scrabbling and whining on the other side. Flint seemed unperturbed about the dog and turned to face her.

'Go home, Abby,' he told her gently. 'You're in over your head, and you're going to get hurt if you're not careful.'

Confusion swept over her. One half of her wanted to trust him, but the other insisted on caution. Peering blearily at him, she desperately tried to kick her alcohol-sodden brain into gear. 'I've heard you and Lisa had a bit of a . . . set-to. Her trying to protect the environment, you trying to destroy it.'

A flash of amusement crossed his face. 'We got through that, became friends.' He looked up and down the street, stepped closer. 'Look, there's something you should know.' He lowered his voice. 'But you can't tell anyone. It'll put you in danger. And me. Promise you'll keep it secret?'

Trying to hide her unease at this sudden switch to co-conspirator, she sketched an unsteady cross over her heart.

'I've filed an application with the USTPO on Lisa's behalf. All she needs to do now is get the MEG prototype to them, along with the lab books, and the technology will be officially registered.'

'They wouldn't let you do that for her,' she protested. 'She'd have to do it herself.'

'What if I told you I have Power of Attorney?'

Abby froze as if he'd just slapped her.

'We can take the prototype to the USTPO. Get the killers off our backs.'

'We?' she croaked.

'You and me.' He raised a hand, let it fall. 'Abby, where is it?'

'I don't know.'

'And even if you did know, you wouldn't tell me, am I right? You don't trust me.' His jaw flexed. 'Christ, Abby, why don't you just go home and stop making everything so difficult?'

Fear crawling through her, she took several steps back, but he had spun on his heel and was walking away, his long coat flapping like crow wings.

ABBY LET MOKE out for his pre-sleep amble and stood watching him sniff clumps of grass, trying to make sense of what Flint had said.

Had he really filed a patent application for Lisa or was it a ruse so he could get his hands on MEG? Swaying slightly, Abby considered Flint and her sister. He was, she admitted, extremely attractive. But Lisa was black and white about environmental issues, and anyone involved in anything she disapproved of always got short shrift. Abby couldn't see Lisa ever befriending a man involved in the oil industry.

She was attempting to recall exactly what Flint had said about the patent office when a shadow materialised just yards away. *Bear*! her mind yelled and she tried to turn and run, but all she did was trip over her feet and end up sprawled on the boardwalk.

'Jesus.' Cal bent over her and plucked her skywards. 'Talk about wasted.'

Abby peered round to see Moke watching him, no hackles or bared teeth.

Cal carted her inside the cabin and dumped her on the bed. He unpicked her laces and slid her feet free from her boots.

'Have a nice walk with Michael Flint?' His tone was acerbic.

She blinked a couple of times. 'Yup.'

'I thought I told you to be careful, Abby . . .' She heard him give an irritated sigh. 'Have you a spare blanket?'

She blinked a couple of times. 'What?'

'I'm taking the couch. I have no intention of freezing my butt off in my car, keeping an eye out for a bunch of potential kidnappers.'

Abby started to shake her head, but when the room began to spin she just crawled beneath the covers and closed her eyes. The last thing she heard was Cal filling Moke's water bowl.

AFTER CAL LEFT the next morning, Abby sat on the deck. Moke lay next to her. Cal had been making toast when she'd finally crawled awake, and to her relief he hadn't crowed over her condition, just passed her a glass of water and two double-strength painkillers and agreed some fresh air might help.

It didn't seem to be working. Her head throbbed, and her mouth felt as though it had been packed with sand. She felt hot and sweaty and wasn't sure if it was another hangover symptom or if the weather had warmed up that much. The street was now clear of snow, the sun blazing down, and she could hear the steady drip-dripping of melting snow from roofs and trees.

At her side Moke stiffened and started to growl.

She glanced at the figure approaching. 'Leave, Moke,' she told him and the dog fell silent.

'Dear Abby, how are you?'

Abby watched Connie glide towards her, her feet as sure as a speed skater's on the icy boardwalk, despite her bulk.

'You were drinking for England the last time I saw you. You must be feeling awful. I brought Tylenol and Coca Cola—the only cure, you know.'

Abby struggled up as Connie clumped onto the deck. 'That's kind of you.'

'I can't blame you for letting your hair down. It must have been such a *relief*. I simply can't imagine how you coped. I'd have gone quite mad.'

Abby led the way into the cabin, shut the door behind them.

'Thank heavens for Scott. He helped me be strong. He's gone back home today.' Connie dropped her carpetbag to the floor. 'I saw Michael Flint took you home. Don't you think you ought to be a bit more careful?'

'He just walked me to my door, that's all.'

'He didn't mention MEG, did he?' Connie looked anxious.

Abby busied herself in the kitchenette. Should she break her promise to Flint and tell Connie that he was applying for MEG's patent? Connie was Thomas and Lisa's investor after all, and if Flint had been lying . . .

'Abby,' said Connie. Her tone was sombre. 'Look at me.'

Abby turned and looked at the soft ruddy hair and big tawny eyes.

'I've something to tell you. It's an apology really. Because I haven't been absolutely up-front with you about MEG.'

'What do you mean?'

'You see, I thought if you didn't know exactly what MEG was, you'd be safe. But I was wrong. They kidnapped you anyway.' She put a hand to her forehead. 'I can't believe how stupid I was.'

Abby stared at Connie. 'You lied to me?'

'Yes, I did. And for nothing. It didn't protect you. Can you forgive me?'

Abby briefly closed her eyes, then said, 'Tell me what MEG really is.'

Connie pulled a stool towards her and hitched herself on top. 'MEG stands for Magnetic Energy Generator. Basically, it converts magnetic energy into electricity.' She leaned forward, expression earnest. 'Which means we will no longer need to rely on oil, gas or coal to power our world. Not only is it unbelievably cheap and efficient, it's carbon-free.' Connie spread her hands, her face slowly lighting with excitement. 'MEG is going to solve the pollution and global warming problems for the world. It'll power our cars and trucks, planes, even space rockets, without harming the earth's environment. And what it's going to do for the Third World . . . You know Lisa's dishes on her roof?'

Abby nodded numbly.

'Well, they collect magnetic energy when the sun's not out. There will be no more electric cables running to places like this; every house will have their own little MEG.' Connie's face split into a beam. 'Lisa even believes it will recycle free energy to repair our environment. Can you believe it?'

She could. Lisa's involvement in creating something that would help the environment made far more sense than her producing another jet engine.

'The oil industry will go bust,' she said faintly.

'Eventually,' Connie agreed. 'There are an awful lot of people who don't want this to happen, which is why Lisa's in such a lot of trouble.'

Abby thought of Elisson and Karella and NASA's eight-figure offer. 'There are also a lot of people who *want* it to happen,' she said.

'Whichever camp they're from, they all want to find MEG,' Connie said glumly. 'Either to destroy it or steal it to make themselves rich.'

Abby wrapped her arms round herself. She felt cold and shaky. Connie had, she realised, been very clever. She'd realised that Marie had been murdered because she'd known what MEG was, and by creating the jet-engine story she'd kept herself and Abby as safe as she could.

'Abby dearest, I heard a rumour yesterday. I was wondering if you knew anything about it.'

'What is it?'

'That Flint and your sister were sleeping together.'

Abby stared at her, speechless.

'You don't think it's true?'

'I just can't see it. Oil magnate and environmentalist . . .' Abby bit her lip.

'Then why has he been going to his lodge?'

'What do you mean?'

Connie hopped off the stool, pulled a map out of her carpetbag and unfolded it on the kitchenette counter. 'See this?' She planted a forefinger on a circle with a U inside it on the side of a mountain 4,053 feet high.

'Unverified landing area,' said Abby.

'Which belongs to Clear Creek Lodge,' said Connie. 'And the lodge belongs to Michael Flint. I think that's where Lisa is hiding.'

Abby ran her tongue over her lips. Why would Lisa be hiding there?

'Flint has never gone to his lodge before the first of June,' Connie went on. 'But this year it seems he's been going up there rather a lot.'

Abby concentrated on the map. Flint's lodge was around forty miles from Malone's cabin. Could Lisa have made it in her weakened state, with one dog? 'Wouldn't it be inaccessible this time of year?' she asked.

'My point exactly. It would be a tough journey in, then out. Flint would have to have gone there for something important.' Connie held Abby's gaze. 'To check if Lisa got there.'

Abby began to shake her head, then remembered Flint's certainty that Lisa wasn't married. Suddenly all the hairs on her body were standing up.

She could see Diane's smile playing on her lips. '*Lisa stayed there once, for kicks . . . She ate his cupboards bare, slept in his bed . . .*'

Lisa, playing hide and seek. Lisa, who always won.

'*Best place is always close to the enemy,*' she could hear her sister telling her. '*They never think of looking under their noses.*'

Holy cow. She'd bet her last pair of knickers that Connie was right. Lisa was hiding at Flint's place, but perhaps not for the reasons Connie thought.

'It's impossible,' Abby said. She made her tone brisk to cover the lie. 'Malone said she was really weak. There's no way she'd manage such a trip, breaking her own trail as well as detouring for miles round canyons and rivers.' She gave a dramatic sigh. 'She wouldn't have had the strength.'

Connie's shoulders slumped. 'I will throttle her when I see her.'

'Me too,' Abby said, sounding cross, but she was gazing at the map in wonder. Clever Lisa. She had found the perfect hiding place.

ABBY HEADED for the Moose to collect Diane's SUV. She'd rung her after Connie left to ask where she could hire or borrow a car and Diane had immediately offered her own vehicle and wouldn't hear of being paid.

'Just fill up the tank when you've finished with it.'

Since fuel cost a fraction of what it did in the UK, it was a bargain.

While Abby walked, she made a mental list. She'd fill up Diane's SUV tonight, and prepare an emergency pack—a torch, some matches, lots of warm clothing. Some chocolate bars. The next time Lisa got into trouble, she hoped she'd do it somewhere less inhospitable, like Dorset.

Flint's hunting lodge sat roughly thirty miles north of Lake's Edge and twenty miles west of the haul road, along a track that had to wind its way round rivers, forests, hills and a lake. No wonder Flint had an airstrip. Abby was tense at the thought of driving out there, but was determined to go alone this time.

To her surprise, as she neared the Moose, she saw that two souvenir shops had opened. Spring was here and welcoming the first visitors. She was passing a group of people buying postcards when she heard her name being called. Turning, she saw Demarco striding her way.

'Abby? Can I have a word?'

'Of course.'

Demarco walked a little further down the boardwalk, out of the tourists' earshot. 'The sergeant wanted me to tell you that we've talked to the injured man in Fairbanks hospital and he's taken the deal we offered. We've names and addresses for the other two guys, and we're chasing them up now. They were hired to kidnap you. They've done this kind of thing before. They knew what they were doing.' Demarco took a breath. 'They were also hired to kill Lisa. They didn't know about Marie when they got to Lake's Edge . . . They mistook her for Lisa. There was no research for them to steal—the cabin had already been cleared.'

Abby said, 'And Lisa burned what she couldn't take with her.'

'It looks that way.' The trooper's intelligent eyes fixed on Abby's. 'All communication was by email. Payment by wire transfer. Difficult to track down, but with our bird singing we're piecing it together.'

'Who hired them?'

'The email address belongs to Peter Santoni.'

As if she hadn't guessed. 'And have you arrested him yet?'

'Not exactly.'

'What do you mean by that? *Not exactly*?'

'It means we've found him . . .' Demarco looked past Abby's shoulder. 'But he's dead. The cops finally managed to identify him this morning.'

'He's *what*?' Abby was shaking her head in disbelief. 'How did he die?'

'He was chained to the steering wheel of a car just outside Juneau. Doused with gasoline and burned to death. Same way Thomas Claire was murdered.'

'Oh, God.' Abby's mind was scrambling. 'When was he murdered?'

'They think it was around the first, second of this month.'

Abby shivered. Santoni had been killed while Thomas headed for Anchorage, Lisa for Lake's Edge. 'So Santoni wasn't behind this after all?'

'We're finding it hard to take in too,' Demarco said. 'We need to talk to your sister. There's a lot we don't understand. She'll help fill in the gaps.'

Demarco looked at Abby while Abby stared down the street.

'You'll let us know should she contact you?' Demarco asked.

'Sure,' she said and gave the trooper a smile, making sure she injected it with warmth. 'Haven't you any other suspects?'

'We're considering one or two.'

'Michael Flint?' Abby suggested.

Demarco started. 'What do you know about him?'

'I heard he and Lisa were enemies.'

Demarco looked hesitant, then said, 'Michael Flint was seen on the UAF campus the day Lisa and Thomas split. He told us he was meeting with a professor of geology, and the professor confirms this.'

'But you're not sure?'

'I think you'd better talk to the sergeant. He's due up here later today.' Demarco scrubbed her face with her hands, then said, 'Look, there's something else. Through a public appeal, we spoke to a truck driver who was on the haul road at the time of the kidnappers' rendezvous at Fiveways. He spotted a vehicle parked in the area. A white Dodge Ram pick-up.'

IF BIG JOE was surprised to see her, she would never have known it. His broad, weather-beaten face perused her with its usual impassive expression.

'Coffee?' he offered.

'Love some.'

She went to the window to check on Moke. He was sitting in the driver's seat of Diane's ketchup-red SUV, peering through the windscreen.

Abby settled herself on one of the upended logs in the kitchen. There was a sink, an oil stove for cooking and the usual wood stove for warmth. The floor was strewn with shoes, socks, sweaters and toys, and she could hear the kids outside, playing with their mother in the sunshine.

The coffee gave her heart a solid jolt. 'That's good,' she told him.

Big Joe leaned against the wall, cradling his mug against his chest. 'They know who grabbed you?'

'They were professionals. Paid by a scientist Thomas and Lisa used to work with—Peter Santoni. You know the guy?'

Big Joe shook his head.

'Good thing, since he's dead.'

No reaction. Not a muscle on his face moved.

She decided on a different tactic. 'Joe, why was your car parked near Fiveways at the time of the kidnappers' rendezvous?'

Again, no response. Abby remembered him giving her whisky to drink after she'd heard about Marie's murder, and his quiet confidence that Lisa was alive. 'You've been helping Lisa, haven't you?'

Big Joe fixed his dark gaze on her and gave a nod.

She went and stood in front of him. 'Jesus, Joe, why didn't you tell me?'

'We were trying . . .' He seemed to struggle for words. 'To protect you.'

'Jesus,' she said again. 'How do you and Lisa keep in touch?'

'We don't.' He said it very flat. 'She's only called me a couple of times.'

'The cabins,' she said, breathing fast. 'You put the M&Ms and necklace there to put everyone off the scent.'

'No. Someone else did that.'

'Who?'

For the first time since she'd known him, his face held an emotion. He was, she realised with a start, worried. 'I don't know.'

'Did you know about Marie's murder?'

He shook his head. 'I knew something was up, though. Lisa entrusted something to me for safekeeping. When she didn't collect it that Saturday, I went to her place but she'd gone. That's when I hit the panic button.'

She stared at him in astonishment. 'You've got MEG?'

'Not any more. I met Lisa on the haul road and gave it to her for the Fiveways deal. She still has it.'

Abby's mind was galloping. 'Joe, I wish you'd told me this before.'

He looked away and scratched the back of his head. 'Lisa told me not to. She believes whoever's after it will kill anyone who knows what the thing really is . . . So when they patent it, there's no one to go against them.'

'Why tell me now?'

'Because you should know. In case Lisa . . . I'd help you. Goes without saying.' Big Joe shuffled his feet, and she realised he was trying to tell her that, if Lisa died, he'd want her to join him in taking up Lisa's cause.

Abby pushed her head in her hands. 'How long did you have MEG for?'

He thought it over a bit, then said, 'A couple of weeks. They thought someone was after it, so Lisa brought it up here. Gave it to me.'

'And while Lisa got Marie to come and collect MEG,' Abby thought out loud, 'Thomas went to Anchorage as a decoy. But their plan went wrong. Marie was killed before Lisa had a chance to give her MEG, which left Lisa running for her life while you had MEG stashed here.'

'Got it in one.'

'Where's Lisa now?'

'She didn't say.'

'OK, which direction did she go after the rendezvous on the haul road?'

'North.' Flint's place was north, up the haul road.

'And she was OK?'

'Bit of frost nip here and there, but pretty good.' Big Joe sighed. 'She's going to wait to see if the cops find the killer. Then she might be safe to show herself and get MEG to the patent office.'

'What about the lab books? Does she have them too?'

The worry returned. 'She never said.'

Abby ran her hand over the wooden table, wondering whether to keep Flint's supposed secret or not, and just as quickly decided: not. 'Michael Flint says he's already filed an application at USTPO on Lisa's behalf.'

Big Joe studied the space above her shoulder in silence.

Abby sat motionless, feeling unsure of anything. As she dragged her mind over what Flint had told her, she was struck with an idea. 'What if I took MEG to the patent office? The kidnappers knew I didn't have it, so why would they take any interest in me?' Her excitement grew. 'I could pretend to be flying back to England. I'd buy a ticket from Anchorage to Seattle and on to Heathrow, but I'd jump ship in Seattle and fly to Arlington, and patent it and we'd beat them!'

'Good plan,' Big Joe said. 'But first, you've got to find your sister.'

Abby's face split into a grin. 'Don't worry, Joe. I know where she is.'

Nine

J ust after midnight, Abby got out of bed in the darkness and reached for her clothes. Moke came over and, when she hushed him, he went and sat by the door, expectant. She checked she had her car keys and purse, then she pulled on her parka. She propped a brief note she'd written earlier by the kettle—a precaution should she get into trouble.

She opened the front door and stepped outside, dog at her side. The sky was clear and there was no moon. Stars shone hard and bright in the still air. She pulled the door gently behind her and walked over to Diane's SUV.

With Moke in the back, Abby drove slowly out of town. When she came to the haul road she swung left and powered the SUV north on the gravel road, stones clicking the bodywork, the headlights cutting through the darkness. By three o'clock her eyes were beginning to burn.

She kept an eye on her odometer, and when it had clocked forty miles she slowed and did a U-turn. Backtracking at half the speed, she spotted an area of snowy slush and stones at the side of the road. Driving cautiously off the highway, she placed her SUV's tyres exactly where the previous vehicle had driven: Michael Flint's tracks.

From time to time the car would slip and her heart would jump into overdrive, until the wheels gripped and hauled her forwards. Eventually the track swung north. On her left was a five-foot drop to the frozen lake, on her right planes of flat snow. She wanted to drive further away from the drop but didn't dare leave Flint's tracks. He knew the terrain. She didn't.

As she approached the northernmost end of the lake, a bridge finally came into view. Thank God. She was over halfway there.

Carefully she drove over the planks, hearing them rattle and creak under the tyres, headlights cutting to the corner ahead. A sharp bend up an icy slope meant she'd have to get a run-up to it or she'd slide back downhill.

Abby pressured the accelerator, changed up a gear, and she was doing around twenty miles per hour, turning the car cautiously into the corner, when suddenly the wheels lost their grip and the SUV went into a graceful, slow-motion slide, straight towards the drop to the lake.

'Nooo,' she wailed. She felt more than saw Moke sit up and take notice.

She tried the hand brake, then slowed the engine speed. No response. The car was gliding inexorably towards the edge of the frozen lake.

She was about to turn to open Moke's door, to let the dog out before she leapt from the car, when she spotted several dark patches on the ice, like scattered ash. She turned the steering wheel for the first patch and the tyres finally gripped. The car immediately stopped sliding. She had full traction.

Abby drove past the treacherous corner until she was safe, and pulled up.

'You stay, boy,' she told the dog.

She climbed out, her breath clouding the air, and walked back. Studied the patches of grit and gravel that Flint must have shovelled across the ice. Sweet Jesus. If she'd been going any faster the car would have sailed right over them and plunged into the lake. Had that been his intention? Not to grit the whole corner in order to trap the unwary?

A surge of anger helped steady her. She wouldn't be trapped when she returned. No way. Abby crunched up the bank and grabbed some boughs covered in dry needles, lugged them back and laid them across the ice.

When she climbed back in her car her trembling had ceased. Clever bastard, she thought, easing the car forward. Letting me follow your tracks like that. Well now I'm ready for you. I won't get caught out like that again.

There were no more death-traps as she drove down the other side of the lake, no icy corners as the track wound round the river, then the forest. Abby reached the hunting lodge amazed she'd made it in one piece.

The stars were fading and the deep blue-black of the sky had softened into grey. Dawn was approaching. She climbed out into the freezing air and looked around. The lodge was one big main house with five smaller log cabins set in a semicircle opposite. An open-ended building sat at the end of a snowed-over airstrip with two four-wheelers and a snow machine to take care of year-round transportation. In summer it would be thick with game; grizzlies, moose, eagles and salmon.

She let Moke out. He sniffed the air briefly, then rushed at her, bouncing joyfully across the snow before darting away and running for the lodge.

She'd forgotten Moke knew the area. Big Joe had told her that Moke used to be owned by a guy who looked after Michael Flint's hunting lodge during the summer. When he'd lost a leg to a chain saw, his dogs had been rehomed. Being here again must have felt like a kind of homecoming.

Moke bounded ahead as she crunched her way to the lodge. She peered through the windows to see a huge kitchen with granite worktops, a living room with lots of animal hides and heads on the walls, rugs everywhere. It was rustic and masculine and she could see that nobody was living here.

Abby walked to each cabin and had a look.

No Lisa, but she was here, somewhere. She knew it.

Abby crunched round to the rear of the lodge. Everything was still. No breeze stirred the branches. No birds called or cawed into the silence.

A bear shutter was propped against the wall. Someone had levered it off recently; the marks on the wood were still fresh. Abby tried the door and found it was unlocked. She shone her torch around. Her heart jumped.

Fresh snow-machine tracks led straight from the lodge and into the forest. As easy to follow as a lighted highway.

She could hear Diane's voice. '*He's got some wilderness cabins through the forest. She uses them like they're hers.*'

If Lisa was hiding in the forest, had she been forced to raid Flint's lodge for supplies? She'd better check the lodge first, to make sure she wasn't hiding there. No point in heading into the forest if she was.

Her breath poured clouds into the freezing air inside. No way would Lisa be able to hide in this cold, but she'd better check anyway. Speeding up her pace, Abby swept through the ground floor, then pounded upstairs, looking in wardrobes and cupboards in bedrooms and bathrooms. In the back of her mind she could hear Lisa shrieking, *Found you!*

Lisa always won hide and seek.

Abby heard Moke pattering on the wooden boards downstairs as she sped into the master bedroom. The bed was rumpled, and a red towel had fallen to the floor in the shower room.

Downstairs she found Moke checking out the mud room. Fishing rods and nets, waders, boots, fridges and chest freezers—all silent—and an empty gun cabinet. As she ran her eyes around, something niggled at her. She looked again at the waterproofs and walking sticks, the freezers.

The freezers.

All three had locks. Whether this was to prevent people nicking a haunch of moose or a side of a fifty-pound salmon in summertime, Abby didn't know, but what had caught her eye was that two of the freezers had keys in their locks but the third didn't. Also, it wasn't plugged in the wall socket.

Abby tried to open the freezer. It was locked. She opened the others to find them empty. She looked at the locked one. It was bound to be empty too, the fact it was locked an accident. Someone had probably lost the key.

Moke's bright blue eyes watched her, curious.

'I've got to open it,' she told him. 'Sorry.'

Abby put down her mittens and hunted around until she found a screwdriver and a hammer. Pushing the screwdriver into the lock, she whacked it with the hammer until it snapped.

With a rubber sucking pop, she opened the lid. Peered down.

Four cardboard cartons stared back at her.

Kershaw's Wholegrain Kibble—all the goodness a healthy dog needs.

'Shit,' she said. Michael Flint had obviously sealed the dog food inside the freezer to prevent a grizzly smelling it and breaking into the lodge. Like a kid who'd been given a present she didn't like and was hoping it might be something better in disguise, Abby ripped open one of the carton lids.

'Shit,' she said again.

Instead of dog food were stacks of zip discs. She felt her legs weaken. She opened the next box to find piles of ring binders. She pulled one out.

Monthly reports. Notes. Experiments. Results.

Each page had been dated and signed by a witness.

Each page was headed: MEG.

She'd found the lab books.

WITH MOKE TROTTING ahead, Abby started walking into the forest, following the snow machine's tracks. Had Lisa hidden the lab books at Flint's? If so, it was a daring, dangerous move. Typically Lisa. But then she remembered what Demarco had said: '*Michael Flint was seen on the UAF campus the day Lisa and Thomas split.*'

Had Flint stolen the lab books then gone after Thomas, believing he had MEG? She thought of how he'd warned her off MEG, told her to go home.

As she crunched through the forest, Abby dug in her pocket for her mittens, but found only one. She stopped and shone her torch backward but couldn't see the other. She'd live, she decided, and walked on.

The tenuous dawn light dimmed as the tracks wound through the forest. Trees loomed close on every side and her ears strained to register the slightest sound. Her skin was tight with fear. She'd rather face a band of kidnappers any day than a startled grizzly. Her breath came out in short gasps.

'Moke,' she commanded, tapping her thigh, 'stay close. Close.'

The dog paused and looked at her over his shoulder, puzzled, then trotted briskly forward. He obviously couldn't smell any bears. As Abby walked on, she became aware that the sky was lightening, but there was no dawn chorus to herald the rising of the sun. It was so silent it could have been the last dawn on earth.

Suddenly Moke stopped. Stiff-legged, he took two paces forward, tail flat, and stopped again. His hackles rose, and he gave a low growl.

To her horror, she heard an answering growl.

'Go home, bear!' she yelled. 'Leave us alone!'

The growl erupted into a roar and Moke responded with a series of barks that had his forefeet clearing the ground, his hackles erect, teeth bared.

'Leave, Moke. LEAVE!'

There was another roar and then a shadow burst from behind the trees, going straight for Moke.

She heard the soft *thump* as the two bodies collided. A blur of fur and teeth and snarling and Abby was backing up, tensing her muscles to sprint behind a tree, when suddenly, it was all over. The animals had separated and were standing opposite one another, touching noses.

It wasn't a bear. It was a goddamn *dog*.

Weak with relief, Abby watched the two animals sniff each other all over, then Moke gave a lunge and a deep bark that Abby knew was a greeting, and the next instant they were running alongside one another, biting each other's ruffs, tails waving, tumbling in the snow, tongues lolling happily.

'Roscoe?' she called hesitantly.

Both dogs immediately stopped their play and stood looking at her.

'Moke,' she commanded. 'Roscoe.'

They trotted over. Moke leaned against her legs, looking up at her while Roscoe did the head-to-toe doggy inspection.

'Well, boys,' she told them. 'We've another reunion to be getting—'

She never finished her words because there was a rush of air behind her and something crashed into the backs of her knees and she went down like a felled tree. She tried to struggle up but something lay across her chest, pinning her down. She was about to call for Moke when she took in the gun.

A double-barrelled shotgun. And although it wasn't pointed at her, she had no doubt it was loaded and ready to fire.

'Abby?'

A wave of relief crashed so hard over her she wanted to cry.

'Lisa?'

'Who's with you?'

'No one. It's just me,' she gasped. 'I came *alone*.'

She could see her sister's face now. She'd lost a lot of weight and her features had hollowed, and there were charcoal marks on her cheekbones.

Still straddling Abby's chest, clutching the shotgun, Lisa glanced around. 'You're kidding me. Abby shit-for-brains actually worked out where I was?'

Abby promptly lost all control.

'Fuck you!' she yelled, and it was as though a dam had broken. 'You think you're so fucking smart but I found you!' Then in a single movement she knocked the shotgun away and heaved her sister aside. With a small *oof* Lisa landed in the snow and Abby was on top of her but Lisa wriggled free and they were grabbing each other and hitting and pushing, and then Abby was kicking Lisa's legs from beneath her and pushing her head into a snow drift, and it was as though they were children again, scrapping in the snow.

Abby sat astride Lisa, panting heavily. 'Give up?'

'Never.'

'You are nothing but a pain in the arse,' Abby said. 'I do my best and all I get is a gun stuck in my face.'

Small silence.

'Sorry.'

'You're always sorry,' Abby said. 'But nothing ever changes, does it?'

'If that's a rhetorical question, can I get up? You're squashing me.'

'No.'

'OK.' There was a small pause, then Lisa said, 'It's good to see you.'

Abby didn't respond. She could feel Lisa's chest rise and fall beneath her, see her breath clouding the air. Lisa's face was open, trusting, the same as always. As though she didn't give a damn that Abby was twice her size and sitting on top of her. The same as always. Fearless and in command and not in the least bit apologetic. She was lying in the snow, waiting for Abby to come to her senses. Then they'd laugh and joke over what had happened. Put it behind them.

'Not this time,' said Abby.

'No,' Lisa agreed. 'It's gone too far for that.'

Abby blinked. 'Did you just read my mind?'

'Come on, Abby. I've known you since I was born. My first memory is of you peeking down at me in my pram. The next is you feeding me spinach—'

'You hate spinach.'

'Which is why I filled my mouth with the stuff then went to the loo and spat it all out.'

'Dad went ballistic,' Abby recalled.

'Not at you,' Lisa sighed. 'At me. Everyone's always angry at me.'

An explosion erupted inside her head and Abby suddenly found herself in Lisa's place. Four years old, six, ten, seeing their father yelling at her, face red with fury, veins popping across his forehead, sending her to her room again and again. Dad had never been angry with her. Only at Lisa.

'Oh, God,' she said.

'Yeah. He never got it. That I'm me. Different from him.'

'Different from me, too.'

'Not so different.'

Abby heard the words but didn't believe them.

'You and me,' Lisa said. 'We're a couple of stubborn old cows, don't you think? Believing we're right all the time? How I ever thought you'd have a fling with Cal if you knew he was married defies belief. I know how puritanical you are. I just had my head up my arse, as usual.'

'Is that an apology?'

'The second you left I knew I'd fucked up. I'd said too much in the heat of the moment . . . but you'd left the country before I could explain.'

'I couldn't bear it. I liked him *so much*.'

'Yeah, so I gathered.'

Roscoe nudged Lisa's shoulder and whined.

'It's all right, boy,' Lisa told him, then raised an eyebrow at Abby. 'Can I get up now? I'm freezing my bum off down here.'

Abby levered herself off and took Lisa's hand and lifted her to her feet.

'I'd forgotten,' Lisa said, sounding surprised.

'Forgotten what?'

'How strong you are.' She patted the snow off her thighs, dusted her jacket down. 'I always envied that. I used to dream of being you, tall and confident and calm and not needing to be the centre of attention . . .' She broke off suddenly and looked away. Abby saw the tears welling up.

'Fuck. How I wanted to be you.' Abby swallowed, a hard knot in her throat. Carefully she picked up the shotgun and broke it, resting it across her elbow, like she'd seen Malone do.

'I hated you,' Lisa said, voice rasping.

'I hated you too.'

Lisa turned and looked up at her, eyes wet, her mouth curved in a sad smile. 'Well, at least we have something in common.'

LISA'S CABIN was almost a replica of the wilderness cabin Abby had been incarcerated in. It had a sleeping shelf in one corner, a simple kitchenette in the other, and a wood stove churning out heat in the middle. But instead of a bucket there was an outhouse. Kerosene lamps licked warm yellow light over an armchair, two hand-hewn stools, faded curtains at the windows, and a big tree stump for a table, which had been ground and polished until its top gleamed. A duvet and four pillows lay on the sleeping shelf.

'Five star,' said Abby, impressed.

'Says the expert.'

Abby froze, stiffening up at the familiar dismissiveness in Lisa's voice.

'I'm sorry.' Lisa was scrubbing her face with both hands. 'I thought we'd be hugging each other to death when we finally got together. You know, all is forgiven, I love you, blah, blah, blah. But it's not that simple, is it?'

'No.'

'Bugger it.' Lisa went to the wood stove, fed some logs inside. 'And you know what really pisses me off?'

Abby looked down at her sister's strong small body, seemingly indefatigable, and suddenly felt exhausted. 'No.'

'That bloody dog of yours.'

Abby put her hand on Moke's ruff. 'He's not my dog. He's yours.'

'So why hasn't he moved an inch from you the past half-hour?'

'I feed him, I guess.'

Abby yawned and Moke looked up, mouth stretching wide in unison so she could see right down his throat.

'Oh for God's sakes,' Lisa said, half laughing. 'He even mimics you.'

Abby shrugged, jiggling the ejected shotgun shells in her pocket.

'Coffee?' Lisa offered, reaching for mugs. 'I've chocolate if you prefer.'

'Chocolate, please.'

Abby took a stool at the tree stump. Moke flopped at her feet while Roscoe took prime position next to the wood stove. Her eyes moved over Lisa's face while she opened a carton of long-life milk and put a pan on the stove. The smears on her cheekbones had to be frostbite.

'Nothing a cosmetic surgeon can't fix,' Lisa said brightly.

'Does it hurt?'

'Like buggery at first. But I was lucky. It's not frostbite as much as frost nip. I keep it smothered in Camomile lotion. Seems to do the trick.'

Once the milk was hot, Lisa poured it over the chocolate, stirred it vigorously and passed the mug over. Then she went to the window and looked outside before returning to the kitchenette and lighting a cigarette.

Abby held out a hand. 'Mind if I pinch one?'

'I don't want to be responsible for you taking up smoking again.'

'You already are.'

'Ah, shit.' Lisa chucked the pack over.

Abby lit up. She hadn't had a cigarette since the day of the kidnap, and the nicotine hit her system fast and made her feel giddy.

Upending an old mayonnaise lid, Lisa put it on the table, flicked a length of ash inside. 'Some predicament I got us into, huh?'

'Just a bit. Any ideas on what we should do next?'

'I've one or two,' Lisa hedged.

'Joe told me you've got MEG,' Abby said.

Lisa didn't say anything, but her eyes clouded.

'You know about Thomas?' Abby ventured gently.

'Yeah. Big Joe told me. I radioed him last night from the lodge.'

'I'm sorry.'

'Me too.' Lisa looked away. 'He was . . . like a father to me.'

'I know.'

'How's Mum?'

'She's doing OK. Ralph's been looking after her.'

Lisa gave a smile. 'Maybe he'll get that date he's always wanted.'

'And maybe pigs will fly.'

Lisa flicked ash into the lid. 'You sorted things with Cal yet?'

'What's to sort? He let me believe he was free and available and he wasn't. I'm not sure I can forgive that.'

'Judge and jury, are you?' Lisa took a pull on her cigarette and exhaled a stream of blue smoke. 'Poor bugger.'

Abby stared at her sister, skin prickling. 'What he did to me was unforgivable. And what about Saffron? What if she'd found out?'

Lisa took a long drag of her cigarette. 'Don't tell me you were never tempted to jump on a train and never return when Mum was sick.'

'That's *different*. I didn't lie to anyone!'

'Come on, Abby, can't you see the guy made a mistake? He knew he'd fucked up and was devastated when you left. But would you listen to him? Oh, no, you just—'

'He was devastated?' Abby gave a hysterical laugh. 'Give me a break.'

'SHUT UP!' Lisa roared, making Abby and both dogs jump. 'Will you listen for a minute? I've spent the last four years working out what the hell went wrong and I won't have you start this crap all over again!'

Abby's heart was jumping like a firecracker.

'I condemned you that day.' Lisa stared at her, her eyes challenging. 'And you condemned me. And Cal. Did you ever think you might have been a teeny bit precipitate?' Her cigarette had burned down to the filter, but she didn't notice. 'You lost two people who loved you in a single day because you were too stubborn, too *self-centred* to think of anyone but yourself.'

'Talk about the pot calling the kettle black.'

'Exactly,' Lisa said, looking satisfied. 'You ever wonder about the things you hate about me? Why you hate them so much?' She kept still, eyes fixed on her sister. 'Because they're the same traits *you* have. The ones you hate about yourself. They're the ones I hate about *me*, too.' Lisa ground her cigarette out on the side of the sink, lit another. 'Took me ages to work it out.'

'I'm not like you,' Abby said stiffly.

'No. You're not.' She gave a long, heavy sigh. 'But there's bits that you can't deny.' Lisa finished her cigarette in silence.

Abby's mind was crashing, reverberating over Lisa's words.

You condemned me.

'I'm sorry.' She heard the words as if they hadn't come out of her mouth.

Lisa came over and tucked a strand of hair behind her ear, a gesture Abby remembered from her teens, when she had long hair. 'It's OK,' she murmured. 'I forgave you ages ago. All you have to do now is forgive yourself.'

Abby felt her throat tighten.

Lisa opened her arms. 'Come here, big sis.'

Lisa felt as light as a sparrow but her grip was fierce. Abby's eyes began to fill. She hugged Lisa tightly, her eyes shut, every sense concentrated on the feeling of her little sister in her arms.

'So what's next?' asked Abby a little later, blowing her nose and wiping her eyes. She hadn't cried all the time Lisa was missing, and now she'd started, she was finding it hard to stop.

'We've got to get MEG to the patent office. It's the only way to get the killers off our backs.'

Abby outlined the plan she'd already made with Big Joe. Lisa immediately brightened. 'You'd do that for me? Really?'

'You'd trust me with MEG? Really?'

Lisa laughed. A joyous laugh that filled her belly and stretched her mouth wide. 'Yeah,' she said, still chuckling, 'I'd trust you with MEG.'

Suddenly Abby was dying to see the invention that had caused so much mayhem but she knew better than to ask.

'You want to see MEG?' Lisa asked, putting on her bunny boots and preparing to go outside. 'Then you've got to dig.'

MEG's prototype was buried beside an enormous jack pine near the outhouse. It was about the size of a shoebox, and weighed just over two kilos.

'It doesn't need any maintenance,' Lisa was telling her proudly, 'and it produces all the energy you need to run your home. Larger ones will eventually be used to run factories and cars. One day even planes. It doesn't have an engine, just uses the earth's magnetic energy.'

They were crunching back to the cabin, Moke and Roscoe mock-wrestling in the snow, Lisa cradling MEG in her arms, as she would a baby.

'And it doesn't produce any waste products, or contribute to any negative environmental impacts.' Lisa gave the machine a pat. 'Thomas's baby.'

Lisa kicked the snow off her boots and walked into the cabin and put MEG on the tree trunk.

Abby went and ran her fingers lightly over MEG's cool metal. 'Santoni's dead,' she said. 'He was murdered.'

Lisa swung round. 'You're kidding.'

'Burned alive.'

'Jesus. They caught who did it?'

Abby was opening her mouth to tell Lisa about her last conversation with Demarco when Moke started barking.

The sisters spun round to face the door. Moke kept barking, then Roscoe joined in. Lisa and Abby looked at each other in dismay.

Eyes wild, Lisa grabbed MEG and shoved it inside a backpack by the door. Tied it up tight and bundled it beneath her sleeping shelf. She put her finger to her lips and tiptoed to one of the windows.

Abby crept to the other. She looked at their twin sets of tracks leading from the forest, the compacted snow that led to the outhouse round the back. She scanned the forest, trying to spot some movement, praying that the huskies were yelling at a wild animal, maybe a wolf.

Suddenly the barks turned into a hysterical baying.

Abby gestured they should lock the door. Lisa shook her head, mouthing, *wilderness cabin*. Shit. That meant it was permanently open in case anyone was in need of shelter and was probably only lockable from the outside.

Suddenly, there was a *crack!* and the barking abruptly stopped. Then a scream ripped through the air that had the hair on Abby's neck standing up.

Lisa and Abby stood paralysed with horror as the screaming went on and on until there was another *crack!* and everything fell silent.

Abby brought her hand to her mouth, trying to stop the tears.

'Abby,' Lisa hissed, pointing at the door. 'Quick, *hide.*'

Abby's heart flipped. The door was opening.

She scurried behind the wood stove while Lisa took up position behind the door. Gradually it inched wider.

The man was standing well back but Abby could see his face. And his gun. The same matt black pistol she'd seen tucked under his pillow at Walter's was cocked and ready to fire.

It was then she realised that she'd left the shotgun on the porch.

'Abby?' Cal called urgently. 'You in there?'

Lisa shook her head violently, telling her not to answer. She had her legs spread wide and was holding a sturdy log in both hands like a baseball bat.

Cal pushed the door open a little more, took a tentative step inside.

'Abby? Lisa? Are you OK?'

Another tentative step, then another, gun held firmly in both hands. Then he saw Abby. His face started to relax, but he didn't put down the gun.

'Abby, what are you—?' he started to say when Lisa stepped forward, swinging the log with both hands, aiming it for the back of his head. Her face was tight and Abby knew she was putting all her force behind the blow.

Abby didn't move or say anything to protect Cal.

He'd shot one of the dogs.

Abby heard the *thunk* as the log connected with his skull. His head jolted forward, his mouth opened, as if in surprise, then his eyes rolled back and he folded to the floor with a dull thud. His pistol was buried beneath him.

Abby stared at the blood seeping from the wound beneath his thick hair. She knelt beside him and tentatively touched his hair.

'What's he doing here?' Lisa was staring down at him.

Abby remembered Cal's relentless hunt for Lisa, his warning her to be careful. He'd known that she knew what MEG was.

'I don't believe this,' Lisa said, and then she was belting around the cabin, flinging belongings into her backpack on top of MEG.

Abby remained crouched next to Cal, stroking his hair, her mind numb.

'He followed you,' Lisa was panting. 'You think you're so smart . . . Jesus, what did I do to deserve you? Who's with him, do you know? Christ, we've got to get out of here . . . Abby! For Chrissakes, *move.*'

Lisa had her backpack over one shoulder. She grabbed Abby's arm and tried to heave her upright, but Abby didn't want to move. She felt as though her heart was breaking all over again.

'If you don't come with me, they'll *kill you.* You know what MEG is, we've got to *get going.*'

At last a trickle of thought permeated her brain. She didn't want to die. Not really. Not even of a broken heart. Slowly, she struggled up.

'Put your parka on. I've a snow machine hidden round the back, ready to go. Wrap up tight, it's going to be cold.'

Abby did as Lisa said, watching her race across the room and grab an oil-skin parcel from a shelf that Abby knew would contain emergency supplies, when she heard a wet metallic click. Someone had just primed their gun.

Her skin went cold. She stood paralysed for a moment. Then she looked at the doorway, and almost fainted with relief when she saw who it was.

'It's OK, he's OK,' she gabbled. 'I mean he's not, since Lisa clubbed him with a log. But he hasn't moved. He might be dead.'

'Oh, thank goodness,' said Connie and stepped inside the cabin. She kept the gun in both hands, and although it wasn't pointing at her and Lisa, it wasn't exactly pointing at the ground either. Remembering the woman's appalling driving, Abby backed off. She didn't want to get shot by accident.

'You can probably put it down now,' suggested Abby.

'All in good time.'

'He shot Moke,' Abby went on. 'Or Roscoe. I must go and see—'

'I shot the dog,' Connie said calmly, 'and if you move I'll shoot your sister.'

Her gun wasn't pointed aimlessly any more, it was trained slap bang on Lisa, who was white as bone and looked as though she was going to be sick.

Abby stared at Connie. 'What the . . .?'

'I mean it,' snapped Connie. 'You twitch your eyelid and I'll blow a hole the size of a truck tyre through her chest.'

It was like looking through the wrong end of a pair of binoculars—the horror flooding through her, narrowing her vision, making her dizzy.

Lisa was staring at Connie. 'You,' she said. Just the one word, but Abby heard the emotions behind it: recognition, contempt and hatred.

'Oh, yes,' said Connie, smiling. 'It's me all right. But this time, I get to win. Where's MEG?'

'I'll never give it to you,' Lisa said fiercely. 'I'd rather die first.'

Abby couldn't make sense of it all. 'But Connie's your investor,' she said.

Lisa gave a hollow laugh. 'I see you haven't lost your touch,' she said to Connie. 'You always were the consummate liar.'

Abby looked between Connie and Lisa. 'Brightlite,' she managed, 'they gave you all that money.'

Lisa looked startled. 'Brightlite's Santoni's investor. For EVals. So that's how this piece of shit learned about MEG. Through Santoni.'

'Brightlite lied to the cops?' Abby said, then she remembered Scott, Connie's husband and she remembered what her mother had said about the man who'd asked all those questions about Lisa. *Quite a big man. Brown hair, brown eyes. Mid forties. Receding hairline. Wore tinted glasses . . .*

Scott's glasses had been tinted. It had to have been Scott who had gone to the UK. And Santoni had given him all the details he needed to make him sound like a genuine friend. Which left one last thing she didn't understand.

'So who's your investor if it's not Connie?'

Lisa sent her a venomous look and Abby shrank inside.

'I already know the answer to that one,' Connie said. 'It's so obvious a child could have guessed. I'm not stupid.'

'Yes you are,' Lisa glared. 'You haven't had an original idea in your life; you've cheated, bribed, *murdered* a fellow student for his PhD thesis—'

'Who cares? He's dead. And you will be too if you don't give me MEG.'

'So kill me,' spat Lisa, 'Professor Crowe. See if I care.'

Abby's whole body jerked. Sweet Jesus. Connie was Lisa's old enemy, whom she'd accused of murder when she'd been at university.

'You'll never find MEG,' Lisa was saying. 'I've hidden it, hidden the lab books, where you, with your pathetic little brain, will never think of looking. So you'll never be famous, never get the glory you've always wanted. You'll die fat and alone and unknown, just as you should.'

Abby was readying herself to leap and knock Connie, who was less than three feet away, to the ground, when Connie spun, fast as a cat. Abby put up her hands, trying to defend herself, but something thudded against her skull. Pain blasted through her head and her knees were buckling and the next thing she knew she was lying on the floor, and Lisa was screaming and through her blurred vision she saw Lisa fly at Connie.

She wanted to shout, *No*, and then Connie pulled the trigger. There was a terrible pause, then Lisa fell to the ground, clutching her stomach and groaning. Abby tried to get up, ignoring the waves of nausea, but a dark cloud was encroaching on the corners of her vision.

Ten

Abby thought she was suffocating. There was something against her mouth and nose and although she was sucking as hard as she could she wasn't getting enough air.

'Calm down, Abby.' She heard Connie's voice. 'If you stop struggling, you'll find you can breathe.'

As Abby turned her head, she became aware of the rope round her neck. It took her a moment to realise she was on the floor, her feet tied in front of her, her hands tied behind her and to the wall.

Immediately she kicked out, panic mounting. She had some kind of hood over her head. She couldn't fill her lungs. She was going to asphyxiate.

'Abby, do as she says,' called Lisa, her voice threaded with pain. 'You've had the pillowcase on for the last five minutes and you could breathe, OK?'

Gasping, sucking cloth against her mouth and nose, Abby tried to calm herself, but the smothering sensation made her struggle all the more.

'I'll take it off if you tell me where MEG is.'

'Outhouse!' Abby yelled, muffled.

'What? It's *here*?' Connie sounded astonished.

'Yes, yes!' Abby shouted.

'Is it buried in the snow? Or is it at the bottom of the drop? I do hope not. I really don't fancy having to face more of Lisa's shit.'

'Off!' shouted Abby, fighting for air. 'I told you. Take it off!'

'Not until you tell me *exactly*.'

'No!' Lisa called. 'Abby, don't!'

'Bottom of the drop!' Abby was panting, dragging the pillowcase into her mouth, blowing it out. 'Under the lime!'

She heard Connie's quick footsteps on the boards, heading outside.

'Take it off!' she yelled.

Connie didn't answer. She'd gone.

Abby wrenched and thrashed but her bonds were tight and didn't give.

'Abby, calm down,' Lisa told her urgently. 'You're just making it worse.'

Panting against the pillowcase, Abby lunged against whatever was holding her, hoping her strength might break it, pull it loose.

'You're tied to a ring in the wall. You won't be able to pull it out. She's got me strapped to the wood stove with duct tape.'

'Where are you hurt?'

'My tummy.'

Oh God, Connie's bullet could have perforated Lisa's stomach, her kidneys, liver or spleen or the whole damned lot for all she knew.

'Listen, Abby. Mike Flint is my secret investor,' Lisa went on. 'He didn't want his industry, or his family . . . knowing just yet. I didn't know how you felt about Cal until I met Mike. Made me realise why you went so berserk.'

Abby remembered Michael Flint crunching around Malone's cabin, searching for Lisa, the shadows round his eyes, his exhaustion. He must have been helping her all along.

'Thomas was going to give Mike . . . lab books. Don't know if he did.'

'They're at the lodge,' Abby assured her. 'Does Mike know you're here?'

'No. I didn't want him anywhere near me or MEG in case he got hurt. It was the only way I could think to keep him safe.'

It had worked. Connie had known it was odd that the oil man was hanging around Lake's Edge, but hadn't known why until she'd heard the rumour that he and Lisa were sleeping together.

'Cal,' Abby gasped against the hot cloth. 'He OK?'

'Hasn't moved a muscle since I whacked him.'

Shit, shit, shit. There had to be a way. She started yanking against the ring in the wall, but it held fast. She felt the exertion draining her of oxygen, and had to stop. She lay quietly, pulling hot wet cloth into her mouth, letting it out, until she felt her heartbeat settle, her lungs ease into a less frantic gasp.

I won't give up, I won't.

'Cal,' she said. 'He tied up?'

'Just his hands.'

'His gun? He fell on it . . .'

'Still there.'

'Cal,' she called. 'Wake up. Come *on*, you can hear me. *Wake up.*'

Nothing.

'Door's open?' she asked Lisa.

'Yes.'

'Moke!' she yelled. 'Roscoe! Cal! One of you, help us!'

Abby kept shouting, for the dogs, for Cal. Her throat started to ache but she didn't stop. Not until she felt a large, furry body brush against her.

'Moke,' she breathed, and put her head down. 'Pull it off, will you? Pull!'

Moke pressed against her, whining.

'Here, boy,' Lisa called. 'I'll show you what she wants.'

But Moke wouldn't leave Abby. He pawed at her legs and butted her shoulder as though telling her to get up.

Then Abby heard the familiar quick steps on the porch.

Moke growled.

'Good boy,' she encouraged him. 'Good boy!'

His growl grew to a subdued roar.

'Good boy! Now go sic her. GO!' She heard his nails clattering as he bolted for the door. Connie gave a startled yell.

Bang! A single gunshot, but no yelping, no scuffle. Abby held her breath.

'That bloody dog.' Connie was panting. 'When I get my hands on it, I'll slit its guts wide open.'

Connie had missed, Abby realised. Thank God, thank God . . .

She heard Connie walk over to her. 'You lied to me, Abby.'

She could smell the stench of human faeces on Connie, and while part of her mind thrilled that she'd sent Lisa's enemy to dig around in her loo, the other was quietly petrified.

'No, no,' she muffled. 'Lisa told me it was there.'

'Hmm.' She could almost see Connie looking around the cabin, calculating. Suddenly she felt a hand on her face and she jerked aside but Connie had pinched her nose between her fingers and was trying to force something into her mouth.

Lisa was shouting as Abby felt a metal bar mashing against her lips and teeth, and she wasn't going to let it in but she couldn't *breathe*.

'Open wide, Abby.' Connie kept up her pincer-grip on Abby's nose.

Lungs screaming, Abby was determined that she would pass out before she opened her mouth, but her body had other ideas. Against her will, she took a huge gulp of air, and the barrel of a pistol was pushed inside her mouth, the metal grating on her lower teeth. Her tongue tried to push the barrel away, but it felt as though it was touching her tonsils.

She wanted to be as strong, as tough as Lisa, but she couldn't help the whimper that fluttered from her throat.

'Lisa.' Connie's voice was conversational. 'Tell me where MEG is, or your sister's brains will be splattered over this wall. I don't care if Abby lives or dies, but if I leave with MEG intact, I'll let her live. I'm not saying I'll let *you* live—that would be pushing things too far, and you'd never believe that. But I've grown quite fond of Abby. And although she's gutsy in her own way, I can't really believe she'll have the strength to fight me once I get to Arlington. She'll be like a fish out of water.' She chuckled.

Abby knew Connie was bluffing. She'd never let her live, and she bet Lisa knew that too.

'So, Lisa, what's it to be?'

'You shoot her, and you know you're stuffed,' Lisa said. 'You've already said I'm not leaving here alive. So what's the point in telling you where MEG is if Abby's dead? I won't tell you until she's free.'

There was a long silence while Abby tried to keep still. Sweat trickled down her face, down her neck and back. She knew what Lisa was doing. She wanted Connie to free her so she could go for Cal's gun.

'No.' Connie's voice went flat.

Silence stretched. Abby found herself listening for Cal's breathing, but she couldn't hear anything above the pulse roaring in her ears.

'Sweetheart, Abby,' Lisa's voice was soft, 'I'm sorry. I really am. It's not that I don't love you . . .' Her voice cracked. 'Because I do. Desperately. But we've reached a stalemate.'

She heard Lisa gulp, then her voice rang out, hard and strong.

'So shoot her, Professor Crowe. Shoot my sister.'

WITHOUT WARNING, the pistol was removed from Abby's mouth so fast it knocked against her upper front teeth. She ran her tongue around her gums, trying to work saliva into her mouth. She felt Connie working at the rope round her neck, and suddenly it loosened. Then the pillowcase was pulled off. Blinking furiously, Abby gulped in lungfuls of blissfully cool air.

She saw her sister bent double by the wood stove, a dark bloody stain across her shirt and seeping into her jeans. Her gaze flew to Cal, who lay motionless, his hands tied behind his back. She couldn't see him breathing.

'Untie her,' Lisa said.

'I don't think so,' Connie replied and, to Abby's surprise, she left the cabin.

'You OK?' Abby asked Lisa urgently.

After a couple of seconds, Lisa said, 'I've been better.'

Her heart twisting, Abby turned her attention to Cal. 'Wake up, Cal Pegati. You're lying on your gun . . . for God's sake, Cal, WAKE UP!'

She thought she saw his fingers twitch but it must have been wishful thinking. She wrenched against the iron ring, forcing her aching muscles to keep fighting until they burned, but Cal didn't move. Then Connie returned.

She was lugging a jerry can with her.

Abby's insides abruptly turned liquid.

Uncapping the can, Connie went over to Lisa. She poured gasoline over her head, her shoulders, drenching her entire body.

Lisa was choking and gasping and kicking. 'Don't tell her,' she panted to Abby. 'Promise me. *Don't tell her.*'

Connie stood back and took out a box of matches. She opened it and withdrew a single match, then raised her hands, the match poised to strike.

'It's your turn, Abby. Tell me where MEG is or Lisa burns alive. It won't be very pretty, but it won't take long. She'll be in her own little hell, screaming just like Thomas did when I tossed the match into his car.'

'No,' Abby pleaded. 'Please, *no*.'

'You've five seconds, Abby.'

'Don't tell her,' Lisa begged.

'Four,' said Connie, 'three, two—'

'OK, OK! It's under the sleeping shelf,' Abby blurted.

'I don't believe you,' Connie said.

'It is, go and see,' Abby pleaded. 'It's in the backpack.'

Lisa slumped against the wood stove. She was sobbing quietly.

Connie returned with MEG in her hands. 'At last,' she breathed, almost in reverence.

Abby's breath caught. She was sure she'd seen Cal's fingers move! Get up, she yelled at him in her mind, get up and shoot the bitch!

'Dearest, Abby,' Connie said, stroking MEG, 'Thank you for leading me to the lab books.' She gave Abby a broad smile. 'I'd never have looked past the kibble if it hadn't been for you dropping a mitten.'

The look on Lisa's face was more than Abby could bear and she turned her head aside. A knife twisted in her heart. She'd failed her sister.

With MEG under her arm Connie walked outside, but within seconds she returned. She splashed gasoline around the cabin, soaking the rugs, the bedding. The acrid stench made Abby's nose burn, her eyes water.

'Please, Connie,' she began to plead, but then she stopped. Cal's shoulders had moved, and also his arms. Oh, please God make him shoot Connie.

'Just think. I'll be in Virginia tomorrow. Once I've seen to Michael Flint.'

CAL! yelled Abby in her mind. For Chrissakes, HELP US!

Connie went to Lisa and poured the last of the gasoline over her head. Then she brought out the box of matches. Abby was screaming as Connie dropped the lighted match into Lisa's lap.

WHEN ABBY came round, she was still screaming.

She never knew if she fainted from the shock of knowing her sister was going to burn to death, or whether her body had simply shut down, but by the time she regained consciousness the sleeping shelf was ablaze, sending clouds of thick black smoke through the cabin. An orange wave of flames began rolling down the shelf to the floor, licking the rug at her feet, and her skin felt as though it was blistering. Choking and gasping, she looked for Lisa through the billowing smoke, but she'd gone.

She stared in disbelief at Cal crawling towards her on all fours. His head was hanging. His clothes were burnt, his face bloody and smeared with ash. He was clutching a knife in his hand.

She felt a surge of wild hope. Had he saved Lisa?

Part of the sleeping shelf dropped in a shower of embers. A torrent of smoke and flame belched across the room, knocking him sideways.

'Hurry, Cal!' she croaked. 'For God's sake, hurry!'

Cal sawed through the tape at her feet, then he turned aside. She was yelling at him not to stop when his shoulders spasmed and he vomited.

The rug was burning fast, a jagged line of flames edging towards them.

'Cal! Quick!'

He struggled to cut the tape round her hands. The instant she was free she sprang to her feet. Crouching low, she headed for the door.

She glanced over her shoulder at Cal. He'd slumped to the floor, and his boots were on fire. Eyes streaming, Abby tore off her parka, dodged round a wall of fire that used to be the kitchen counter and raced for the sink. She dumped her parka in it and turned on the taps full blast. With soaked coat in hand she swerved back to Cal and threw it over his feet and legs. Then she grabbed his wrists and pulled. It was like trying to shift a buffalo.

Legs braced, she gathered all her strength and began dragging Cal towards the door, six inches at a time. She was yelling at him, coughing and choking, smoke searing her throat, flames licking all around.

'I will not let you die on me, you bastard!'

Another six inches. Then another. Sweat poured down her face. She braced herself again. Pulled another six inches. And again.

'Get up! It's not far!' She put her arms beneath his and let him push against her until he was on his knees. 'Come on, move!'

With Cal on all fours, she cajoled and yelled, pushing and pulling him until at last they were outside in cold clear air. Cal managed to get to his feet, but he only took six paces before he folded to his knees.

'Just keep going' she panted.

She made sure he was well clear of the cabin before she told him it was OK. Immediately he slumped into the snow. Abby bent over him.

'Cal?' She looked into his eyes. His pupils were pin dots.

A soft crunching sound from the edge of the forest made her spring into a crouch, fear rocketing that Connie had returned, but it was only Moke.

BOOM!

The cabin was a fireball. The roof had caved in, sending a column of black smoke into the sky. The radiant heat seared her face and she turned her head away, gagging at a terrible smell in the air, like scorched flesh.

Then she saw Lisa. She was lying in the snow where Cal had carried her. She had no hair. Her face was raw and bloody, like a piece of uncooked steak. Her clothes had melted and charred into blackened threads all over her skin.

Abby fell to her knees. She felt as though she was losing her mind.

Lisa couldn't be dead. She was indestructible.

'Abby.' It was a croak. 'Chrissakes . . . Abby.'

'Lisa? *Lisa?*' Abby scrambled over to her. 'You're alive. Oh, Jesus. You're *alive* . . . Christ, hang on, Lisa . . . We'll get you to a hospital, fix you up . . .'

'Abby . . .'

'I'll get the snow machine.' Abby stumbled to her feet. Her heart thudded against her rib cage. 'Ride to the lodge. Radio for help.'

'Wait . . .' Lisa reached out a hand. It was dripping blood. 'Need you . . . do something . . . first.'

'No time, Lisa.' Her sister couldn't survive much longer without a team of medics to hand. 'I've got to go *now.*'

'Please.' Lisa's eyes implored. 'You must . . . stop Connie.'

'Lisa, there's no *time* . . .'

'All time . . . in the world.' Lisa bared her teeth with the effort of speaking. 'Think of Thomas . . . our dream. We want to give MEG . . . to the world. For free.' Lisa tried to shuffle upright but fell back with a groan.

Abby dived to her side. 'Don't move,' she begged. 'Please, little sis. . .'

'MEG more important . . . than me,' gritted Lisa. 'You must see that . . . everyone needs MEG. The world—'

'No, no . . .' Abby's eyes flooded. '*I won't leave you to die.*'

'You must.' Lisa tried a smile but it vanished beneath a groan of agony.

'I can't.' Abby started to pour sweat.

'You don't stop Connie . . . I will never . . . speak to you . . . again.' Lisa closed her eyes. 'I will hate you . . . Always. You gave her . . . the lab books.'

'No,' bleated Abby. 'Oh, God . . . I don't want to leave you.'

'Yes,' said Lisa. 'You owe me.' Her eyes were filled with blood but they seemed to look right through Abby and into her soul.

Abby couldn't stop the keening sound that was coming from deep in her throat. 'Please . . . Oh, Christ. Lisa, only you could do this to me . . .'

Lisa's scorched and blackened lips twisted into a smile. 'You'll do it?'

Abby nodded, tears pouring down her cheeks.

'Cross your heart?'

She crossed her heart. 'And hope to die.'

THERE WAS NO WAY to estimate how long it took Abby to find Lisa's snow machine, bundle Cal behind her, and head to the lodge.

Her lungs kept spasming in the cold air, making her cough over and over, and she could feel the shock entering her body, weakening her limbs, but she forced herself to concentrate, yelling at herself not to give in.

She had wrapped Lisa as best as she could in Cal's parka before they left. They hadn't dared move her. Cal was going to return to Lisa once a medi-vac crew was on its way. Abby just had to pray she'd survive that long.

She followed the tracks back through the forest: hers, Cal's and Connie's. All of them had driven to Flint's, she realised, then followed the person before them on foot until, one by one, they came to Lisa's wilderness cabin.

Abby brought the snow machine to a halt at the front of Flint's hunting lodge and turned off the ignition. To the right of the front door a window was hanging open, its glass broken. It hadn't been broken when she'd been here earlier. She took in the woman's prints in the snow. Connie.

Abby jogged for the open window. She was about to pull herself through when Moke arrived. He'd fallen behind as she'd snaked the snow machine through the forest, and was greeting her as if he hadn't seen her for a year.

'Stay,' she rasped, and levered herself onto the sill, cautious of the broken glass. She then dropped inside and raced for the front door.

She pulled back the bolts on the door, yanked it open. Cal had the hood of his car up and was looking inside.

'I'm going to find a radio!' she yelled. 'Get help!'

Without turning, he gave her the thumbs up.

Moke's nails clicked behind her as she ran through the living room and into a den. No radio. She raced into the kitchen. There was a granite work-top covered in smashed pieces of plastic. More broken plastic lay on the floor and the kitchen table, the remnants of a ham radio intermingling with a variety of handsets and transmitters. Connie had covered all the bases.

Abby felt a wail building in her lungs. Lisa would die if she didn't get help soon. She tore through the rest of the lodge, Moke hot on her heels.

Tears scalding her throat, she belted outside to Cal, who'd abandoned their vehicles and was in the lean-to, fiddling with a snow machine.

'Cal, she's broken the radios. No way will any of them work.'

'Shit,' said Cal. He dropped the pliers and began twisting some wires. 'She's taken the alternators from our cars, and sabotaged this lot. I should be able to get this one going. Then I can go get help.'

'Are you sure you're up to it?'

'Yes,' he said.

She put her fingers on his jaw and brought his head round so she could look into his eyes. His pupils were still shrunken into pin points.

'You've got concussion.'

'I've had worse, Abby. I'll make it.'

Belatedly she looked past the blood on his face to see the burns beneath. His hands were also burned. A new panic seized her. 'You're hurt.'

'I'll be fine,' he insisted, and turned back to the snow machine.

'OK, tough guy,' she said, trying to keep upbeat, 'have it your way.'

He gave a grunt.

She checked her watch. Eight forty-three. She had to get moving. She needed a map. Abby bolted for the mud room. The chest freezer that had held the lab books gaped open, mocking her.

She pulled on a scarf, grabbed some gloves and a hat, and climbed into a snow suit. Then she put together an emergency pack. Matches from the kitchen wrapped in plastic, kindling, a knife, some chocolate, dried fruit.

Abby unfolded the map and ran her eyes over the winding track that led to the haul road. She couldn't be that far behind Connie because Connie had walked to Lisa's from the lodge and Abby had made up a lot of time by using the snow machine. She studied the map, trying to work it out. Connie would be approaching the forest by now. She'd have to skirt round it a couple of miles north, come all the way down, and do the same for the river and then the lake.

Abby pelted back to Cal. The wind was like frozen needles on her face.

'I'm going after Connie,' she told him. 'Will you be OK?'

He took in her snow suit. His eyes filled with alarm. 'No,' he said.

'I promised Lisa.'

Horror flooded his face. 'Abby, if I'm going . . .' he flapped a hand south, towards Lake's Edge, 'you can't possibly leave her. I could be *hours*.'

Abby's throat closed. 'I know.' She lifted her eyes to his.

'Oh, God.' His face spasmed. 'If I only came round sooner. I tried . . .' His voice broke. 'I'm so sorry.'

She brought up her hand but she didn't dare touch his burned and bloody cheek. 'I know.'

'I had no idea Connie had followed me.' He swallowed. 'I wish I hadn't reacted without thinking, but I was worried about you. I found your note. Rang Big Joe. He got worried too.'

'You give him a time you'd return?'

'Tonight.'

Cal would arrive before Big Joe rang the emergency bells. Would Lisa survive until then? She turned her mind away from that avenue of thought before it started to splinter her emotions into a thousand pieces.

Cal put his hand over hers. Cupped her fingers. 'I wish it were yesterday so we could start again.'

'Me too.'

She looked at the pain in his eyes, felt the warmth of his hand in hers, and knew her life had changed irrevocably. And as she recognised this, she felt a hand reach into her consciousness without warning, cutting off that restless, flickering part of her brain that processed everything—colours, images, feelings—leaving her thoughts distilled and cold.

It was time for her to fulfil her promise.

ABBY HAD GONE two miles before she realised Moke was following. She'd cut across a bend, trying to save time, and had automatically checked over her shoulder as she would in a car—to make sure there wasn't any traffic—when she caught sight of a small grey dot bobbing behind her.

She turned her back on him and throttled down the edge of the next hillside. Her heart was as cold and hard as if it had been buried in a freezer.

From time to time she clattered over the track, but mostly she was on snow and moving faster than she had in the SUV. Ahead of her, the wind grew stronger, the gusts more frequent. The horizon was piled with angry grey clouds. A storm was brewing. Yesterday she would have felt scared, but today she wondered how she could use it to her advantage.

Eventually she came to the river bank and paused, studying the smooth stretches of ice and the mass of boulder-like sculptures. Lumpy ice like this, Walter had told her, could support a seven-ton truck.

Abby eased the machine onto the ice. It rocked and slid over the rough terrain but the ice didn't creak or crack. As she pressed on, her confidence grew. She looked for Connie's car heading south, but didn't see it.

The river crossing took only ten minutes. She'd saved more time than she'd envisaged, and by going over the next hill and through the forest instead of skirting it she'd save another twenty minutes.

Abby accelerated up the slope, snow spraying, dodging trees. The snow got deeper as she climbed, the treads fighting hard to grip. She had to scramble the snow machine to the top. The wind howled unimpeded, knocking and punching her as she scanned the track below.

Moke came into her mind. There was no grey dot in the distance that she could see, but then she spotted a movement way below, halfway along the riverside. Her skin tautened. It wasn't Moke. It was Connie.

For a second she couldn't believe it. Connie was *behind her*.

A surge of triumph made her want to shout, but she bottled the energy inside, storing it, keeping it in reserve. Taking the hillside at an angle, she powered over the snow towards the plank bridge and the treacherous bend.

She was going so fast she didn't see the hillside fall away behind a lip of ice and snow, and the next instant she was airborne.

A moment of weightlessness, of sheer disbelief. Abby could see the lake below, the spruce trees at the base of the mountains, the dirty grey sky.

Engine shrieking, the snow machine plunged down. Abby leaned back, trying to keep the nose up so they wouldn't plough head first, and there was a *thud* that had her spine jarring and the snow machine spinning wildly to one side. Abby clung on as it veered again. Another thud and the snow machine straightened before it continued bouncing down the steep slope.

Abby had to force herself not to lessen her speed, to keep her eyes peeled for any more sheer drops. She risked a glance behind her, and saw that Connie was less than a mile away. Time was running out.

Abby belted down the hillside towards the bridge, bouncing and sliding, and finally she decelerated and eased the snow machine over the lip of the bank and onto the track. Gasping with relief, she bumped the snow machine to the bend that led down to the bridge. She parked it side on, almost filling the track, at a point where Connie would only see it at the last second.

Pocketing the snow machine's keys, she raced to collect the branches she'd laid there earlier. She pushed them down the riverbank. As the frozen stream re-emerged, slippery grey, she heard an engine approaching.

She had to get out of sight. She looked frantically around. It was too late to cross the track and hide in the trees. Abby plunged down the side of the lake, towards a tree stump twenty yards away.

She scurried behind the stump on all fours. Heart pumping, she peered round it, past a broken branch and some frosted twigs, to see Connie's car flash past, powering for the bend. Breathing hard, she scrambled up the slope and peeked over a crest of snow, just in time to see Connie enter the bend far too fast. Just as Abby had hoped.

She saw the brake lights come on, saw the car fishtailing for the snow machine, watched it slam into its flank. The snow machine spun to one side. The SUV veered to the other, tail end spinning. The front tyres were pointing left, away from the drop to the lake. Bad move. Always steer into a skid.

The brake lights were still on but the tyres weren't gripping. The SUV did a full circle, graceful as a dancer, then dropped its rear end over the lip of the lake. Engine rumbling, it sat there, rear tyres suspended in midair.

Seconds ticked past. The driver's window buzzed down, and she could see Connie peering out, looking at her predicament. It looked scarier than it was. With the weight of the engine in the front, the car wouldn't tumble into the lake. But Connie wouldn't know that.

Abby could see the fear on her face, but didn't feel any satisfaction or concern. Connie turned off the engine, opened her door and carefully inched out, easing her bulk round the door until she was in front of the bonnet, feet firmly on the track. She had her gun, Abby saw, but MEG and the lab books were still in the car.

Connie looked around. Abby slid to the bottom of the bank and, crouching as low as she could, stumbled over rocks and boulders, praying Connie wouldn't see her before she'd got enough distance between her and her gun. Then she could break cover and run for it.

'Who are you?' Connie shouted. 'What do you want?'

Abby detoured round a fallen log, then another pile of boulders. *Faster*, she told herself. *You've got to go faster*.

It started to snow, thin hard flakes that stung her face. Connie was running after her, just twenty yards away. She held her gun low at her side.

Abby studied the lake, water shining on its surface, the dark fissures that were cracks in the ice, then she looked back at Connie.

Could she draw Connie onto the lake?

Abby pushed a boot onto the ice. There was an ominous cracking and her boot was suddenly ankle deep in icy water. *Oh, Jesus*.

Quick glance behind her. Connie was slowing, bringing up her gun.

Lisa's voice. *'Cross your heart?'*

And hope to die.

Abby launched herself onto the lake, leaping for a patch of lumpy white that indicated the ice was thick enough to take her weight. It felt as solid as the path to the post box at the end of her mother's garden. She kept moving.

'ABBY!' It was a roar of rage, carried by the rising wind. Connie could have been yelling into her ear she sounded so close.

Wind tugging her snow suit, icy snowflakes pinging her cheeks, Abby kept sliding one foot in front of the other, watching for dark patches of ice, light patches, reading every nuance she could remember from Walter.

Crack! Crack!

The shots sounded oddly tinny, as though the oncoming storm had swallowed them. Skin tight across her shoulder blades, Abby looked back to see Connie on the edge of the lake, squinting against the swirling snow.

'Where's Lisa?' shouted Connie.

'You killed her!' yelled Abby. 'You killed Cal! I'm going to the cops! Get you locked up for life!'

Connie didn't move as Abby inched backwards.

'See you in jail, Connie!'

Abby turned and continued sliding. Snow pellets blew onto the ice with a *tat, tat* sound that grew in volume. Away from the trees there was little protection from the wind, and the temperature was several degrees colder.

Hunching her shoulders, Abby looked ahead and saw a long patch of dark ice, thin and unstable. She skirted it carefully and glanced over her shoulder. For a second, she couldn't believe her eyes. Connie was gliding gracefully, almost effortlessly, across the ice, as though she had skates strapped to her feet. She was moving at twice Abby's speed.

'We both play hockey, that's how it started,' Connie's voice echoed in her mind. *'I whacked him one before shooting a goal.'*

Connie hadn't just played hockey, she'd played *ice hockey*.

Abby urged herself on. Try and skate like Connie, and keep out of range!

Connie fired off three rounds in quick succession. Abby heard a *whap* and at the same time she felt something stroke the hair just above her ear.

She broke into a shuffling, stumbling run, a scream lodged in her throat. She couldn't die yet, *not yet*.

The wind's direction suddenly shifted. It was now blowing from the northeast and getting stronger, driving snow into her eyes.

Another *crack!* and then she heard a metallic clicking over and over again. She prayed Connie didn't have a spare clip.

She tried to read the ice through the flurries, but the snow was settling fast. She kept sliding forward, trying to head for patches of white, but it was becoming more difficult to discern colour. Blindly, she increased her speed.

She risked a backward glance. Her heart kicked. Connie was barely ten yards behind her, a flensing knife in her right hand.

Eyes stinging, Abby broke into a wild, shambolic gallop, desperately dodging patches of weeping ice as she came to them. She was going too fast to see a dark shadow until it was too late.

She felt the ice beneath her bend and break. For an instant she nearly stopped but her mind shouted instructions at her, like a drill sergeant, to bloody well keep moving! Abby spread her legs to distribute her weight and edged forward with both feet on the surface.

There was a deadly creaking sound beneath her, and she dropped down, stretched out her arms and legs, and started to shimmy for safer ground. Water spurted up through a crack and the ice heaved.

Her hand found a block of ice ahead and she grabbed it, pulling her body over it and onto a ridged and lumpy area. Lumps were good. Lumps meant thick ice. She was scrambling up when Connie gave a shout.

Abby turned. Connie was just three yards away and had stopped dead, right in the middle of the thin ice.

'Abby!' she called, panicky. 'It's moving, it's going to collapse, oh, no, please . . .' She dropped the knife. Both hands were outstretched.

Abby stared at her through the driving snow. An ice pick buried itself in her heart.

Connie eased herself to her knees, and started a slow-motion breast stroke for Abby. The ice gave a deep groan and Abby felt it reverberate through her boots. Then came a ripping sound, like a yard of silk splitting.

Connie's eyes widened in terror. She rose and flung herself towards Abby. There was a terrifying grinding noise as the ice finally collapsed.

A soft explosion as Connie's body hit the water.

Connie was thrashing and churning, trying to climb out, but the ice kept breaking up around her, driving her back into the freezing water.

'Abby,' she gasped, 'get me out.'

The ice pick shifted deeper, sliding into her entrails.

Connie was choking and sobbing, but it didn't take long before her thrashing slowed. Her legs dropped lower in the water, and her voice weakened. 'Help me. *Please*. I'll p-pay y-you whatever you w-want . . .'

Abby stood quietly, snow drifting over her, and watched as Connie fell silent. Soon, her head fell back, and water lapped the corners of her mouth. She'd fallen into a state of hypothermia.

Abby didn't wait any longer. She had to get back to shore before the storm hit, finish what she had started.

Only when she looked around to get her bearings did she realise her predicament. Cloud had enveloped the lake. She could barely see five yards ahead. And one thing she hadn't put in her emergency pack was a compass.

ABBY SKIRTED the ice hole and tried to pick up her and Connie's tracks. There! A footprint. Abby followed it to the next print, and the next, and then there weren't any more. The ice was covered in a thin layer of snow.

Wind driving against the side of her face, Abby studied the fresh snow for any indication of a footprint, but the entire area looked uniform, pristine. She decided that if she kept the wind on her right cheek, she'd be heading west and would eventually hit the shore. So long as the wind didn't change direction, like it had earlier.

She checked her watch. Ten thirty. Midmorning and it felt as dark as night. OK. If she didn't reach the shoreline by midday . . . Well, she'd think about that when the time came.

Slowly she shuffled forward, trying not to be overcautious. Despite her snow suit she was bitterly cold, and she flapped and swung her arms, trying to keep warm. She wished she could stamp her feet, break into a jog, but since that might break up the ice she settled on a rhythmic slide, keeping both feet on the ice at the same time, her weight distributed, senses alert.

Her world became a blur of swirling ash-coloured cloud, her lungs ached with cold. Her face was numb. And she was shivering. That was good. It meant she was still producing heat faster than she lost it.

For a blissful second, the wind paused as though taking a breath, and she looked ahead, searching for the shoreline. Nothing but thick cloud. Then the wind returned, full strength. The temperature dropped further.

Abby continued trudging, and when she came across a dark patch of ice she glanced at her watch. Nearly twelve o'clock. It felt as though she'd been walking far longer, like half the day. Pray God she was nearly there.

Then she could shelter in the forest and wait out the storm.

She skirted the thin ice, then she saw a gaping black hole of water with clumps of ice floating in it, and something shiny in one corner.

Abby stared and stared. It was Connie's body. She'd come full circle.

She fell to her knees. 'Shit!' she yelled. 'I'm going to die out here.'

The wind had obviously shifted. Without a compass she might walk in circles until her body froze solid. She tried to work out how it had come to this: her sister lying bleeding to death in the snow while she sat in the middle of a lake and froze to death. She didn't want to die, not until she'd finished what she'd set out to do.

Abby had just clambered to her feet when she thought she heard something through the blasting wind. It sounded like someone had coughed. She cocked her head, concentrating, but didn't hear it again. It was probably her imagination playing tricks.

She studied the shape of the hole where Connie lay, and tried to work out which way west was. She heard the coughing sound again. It was much closer. And it was real. And no way would it be a bear. They were far too sensible to be out on a crumbling lake in this weather.

'Hello?' she shouted. 'Hello?'

To her astonishment, a shadow materialised right in front of her and launched itself at her thighs.

'Moke? *Moke?*'

She collapsed on to the ice and the dog leapt into her embrace, tail wagging furiously, body squirming against hers. She pushed her numb fingers into his ruff and shook him from side to side. 'My God, you followed me all the way here. You crazy dog, what possessed you?'

His tongue slurped across her face.

'Yeah, I love you too. Now, are you going to show me the way back? Walter told me dogs are best at this sort of thing. So come on.'

Abby stood up and waited for Moke to move off, but he didn't. He stood right next to her, looking up into her eyes, tail waving at half mast. She began walking west. He didn't move. She tried heading north, but he just stood there, ears pricked, looking at her as though trying to read her mind.

She started walking south. Immediately he trotted past her and took the lead. Maybe it wasn't south, she thought. He obviously knew something she didn't. At least she hoped so.

Moke led her through the whistling, shrieking cloud, sometimes trotting, but as soon as she dropped behind he'd wait, watching her over his shoulder, until she caught up. Then off he'd go again, striding confidently ahead.

It was like following a meandering stream as it tried to find its way to the coast. She was sure they were walking in circles, but since they hadn't come across any treacherous ice she put her trust in the dog.

Abby could feel her toes and fingers growing numb. She windmilled her arms, trying to pump her fingers to bring the blood to them, but it wasn't paying off. She felt as though she was slowly freezing to death.

Moke paused and looked back at her. 'What is it, boy?'

He turned and broke into a canter, then he bunched his hindquarters and leapt into the air, landing awkwardly, half rolling, and then he was upright and looking back at her expectantly.

Abby hurried over to see a yard-wide fissure in the ice. Moke was standing on a rock-lined bank on the other side. The edge of the lake.

She couldn't leap as far as Moke and started skirting to her right. The dog went ahead. Then he stopped and walked back towards her. The ice went all the way to a boulder that came up to her waist. It was surrounded with frosted tufts of grass, flattened by the wind.

As soon as Abby felt her feet sink into soft snow she put every effort into scrambling up the bank, wanting to put distance between her and all that treacherous ice, and when the ground levelled out, she saw they had joined a track. She looked up and down the track but didn't recognise any of it. Where was she? Where was Connie's car, and MEG and the lab books?

Moke started down the track, steps purposeful, tail high, as though he knew precisely where he was going. She had no choice but to follow.

After two hours she was struggling to put one foot in front of the other. She had eaten the last of her chocolate, her legs were like lead, her heartbeat sluggish, and she didn't know how long she could keep going.

The wind had dropped, and there were snatches of blue in the sky, but it didn't lift her spirits. She was exhausted, and felt adrift and vulnerable.

She came to a halt. Looked around. All she could see was white and a few snatches of black where the snow had melted. Moke came up to her and snibbed her glove between his teeth. Darted away. Came back and barked.

Abby rallied her failing strength and trailed after the dog.

It was three p.m. when she heard a distant rumble, like a train approaching. In the cold, every sound reverberated between the warmer air above and the heavy, cold air below, but she knew an engine when she heard one.

My God, she thought. It's a truck, a goddamn truck.

She broke into a stumbling run and Moke sprinted ahead. She was gasping and panting when the track became a mess of churned snow and gravel. Abby slowed to a walk as she came to a T-junction.

Moke was standing slap bang in the middle of a road, snow banked on either side. He was looking at her, tongue lolling.

He'd only led her straight to the haul road.

THE TRUCK DRIVER—call me Jerry—who picked them up had bundled her quickly into his truck at her story of her snow machine turning over on top of her friend.

'Nearest place is Lake's Edge,' he said. 'They'll help.'

'Don't you have a radio?' she asked him.

'It's bust.'

Grinding through the gears fast as he could, Jerry gave her his Thermos of coffee and a stack of sandwiches, but it was the coffee that revived her. The hot liquid warmed her core. She was glad Jerry was concentrating on driving his truck close to its limit and left her alone. She didn't want to talk.

Finally he roared into the village, and came to a jerky stop outside the Moose. She clambered out, and shambled inside to see the fire roaring, the worn wooden floor freshly mopped. The place was empty aside from a big Native guy drinking coffee at the bar and a woman opposite him, talking.

Big Joe and Diane turned and stared.

'Your head,' Diane said, alarmed. 'Abby, there's blood . . .'

Abby touched the side of her scalp where Connie had hit her with the butt of her gun. The hair was matted with old blood. Almost immediately it started to ache. The cold must have anaesthetised it.

She dropped her hat and scarf to the floor. 'Cal here?'

Big Joe was on his feet. 'He's meant to be with you.'

'He hasn't made it?' Horror coursed through her, bundling her nerves into knots. 'Oh, God . . . We need to get help to him. And Lisa . . . Lisa's in a really bad way. They're at Flint's lodge . . .'

The story came tumbling out, and, as she spoke, tears filled her eyes and ran down her face, but she wasn't sobbing. She kept talking while Diane made phone calls, Big Joe holding her hands gently in his.

'Joe,' Abby said, 'I've something I want you to do for me. Straight away, and before the cops get to know I'm here.'

She told him what she wanted and he gave a nod, strode outside. She desperately wanted to collapse into the armchair by the fire and sleep, but she had to keep moving. She had to hold on.

She tied Moke to the bar's foot rail with her scarf, walked outside and headed down main street towards the southern end of town.

She paused when she reached the dirt airstrip. A snow machine buzzed in the distance, but otherwise it was quiet. Nobody seemed to be around.

Abby settled herself on a flaking oil drum. The sun was warm and she unzipped her snow suit to the waist, wondering how long Joe would take.

Half an hour later she heard an engine being pushed hard, the scrunch of stones and splash of slush. She edged off the drum. A four-wheeler was bouncing towards her. With a squirt of gravel it lurched to a stop. The man jumped off and ran for her, face bleached white with anxiety.

'Is she all right?' he asked.

'I don't know.'

Abby walked up to Michael Flint and wrapped him in her arms. His grip was fierce, like that of a drowning man. He was shuddering.

She held him tight. Told him what they had to do.

FLINT PREPPED his aircraft in three minutes flat. He didn't check the weather, nor did he announce his departure, before takeoff.

She kept her gaze outside, searching for Cal, a snow machine caught in a drift or toppled down a ravine, but as they roared north all she saw were blankets of white interspersed with patches of dead grasses and shiny rocks.

Soon, the lake came into view, with the bridge at the far end. Moke had, she saw, led her straight across the lake—the shortest route to the haul road. When she got back, she was going to give him a can of spaghetti bolognese.

Flint dropped altitude. The closest he could land was at the southern end of the lake, on a gravel beach. Abby stayed in the helicopter while he jogged away. Her reserves of energy had been used up. It took him forty minutes to collect MEG and the first few lab books, but it felt like forty days.

They arrived at his lodge in a flurry of snow and ice. Two guys had brought Lisa out of the forest on a stretcher and were loading her on board the AST chopper. Cal stood to one side, head hanging.

Abby ran across.

'It wouldn't start,' Cal kept saying over and over to his father. He sounded close to tears. 'The snow machine wouldn't bloody start . . .'

Victor had an arm round Cal's shoulders. 'You did the best you could, son. You did the best you could . . .'

'We're flying her straight to Fairbanks hospital,' Demarco said briskly.

Abby knew that Flint wasn't hearing a word. He was focused on Lisa.

Lisa was covered in gauze. Face, neck, shoulders and hands . . . only the tips of her fingers showed.

'Hey, sis,' Abby said softly, 'it's me. And Mike's here too. Don't talk . . . We've brought something for you . . .' Abby brought up the smooth metal box and brushed it against Lisa's fingertips.

Lisa made a gasping sound.

'I stopped Connie,' Abby said. 'I kept my promise.'

Eleven

Abby loped down the street, ignoring stares. The pavement was damp, her bare feet filthy, but she didn't care. When she came to a rubbish bin she flung the high-heeled shoes inside.

Five minutes later she was padding into the house, yelling, 'I'm home!'

'See you when you're ready!' her mother called.

'Red or white?' asked Ralph from the kitchen.

'White, thanks.' Abby gulped down half the glass before her equanimity began to resurface.

'Bad day?' Ralph squinted in sympathy. He didn't remark on her bare feet.

'Too many meetings.' She took another glug of wine. 'I'm not supposed to be locked up inside, I'm supposed to be *outside* doing my job.'

'You poor thing,' he commiserated. 'I'll make some fresh pesto to cheer you up. Spaghetti and pesto do you?'

'Lovely,' she said.

'Go and see your mother then,' Ralph told her. 'Supper in half an hour.'

Abby trailed down the corridor. She used to relish evenings at home, but since she'd returned from Alaska she'd felt cramped and claustrophobic, unable to settle for more than thirty minutes.

'Hi, Mum.' She went and kissed her cheek.

Julia, as usual, was working. 'Ralph looking after you?'

'Always.'

'You don't have to move out, you know. He loves having you here.'

'Of course I have to move out. Three's a crowd, remember?'

Julia snorted. 'It's not as though we're getting married or anything . . .'

'But you're living together,' Abby said for the hundredth time, 'which means you can't cavort naked if I'm hanging around like a bad smell.'

Julia burst out laughing. 'Now, there's a thought.'

'Anyway, I've found somewhere nice.'

'Just nice?'

Abby thought about the apartment she'd seen, a great lofty space with tall windows, but it still didn't feel big enough.

'It's perfect,' she lied.

She turned to head upstairs for a shower, but Julia held up a hand.

'Lisa rang.'

'How is she?'

'As well as can be expected.' Julia took off her glasses and pinched the bridge of her nose. 'She'd like you to go over for a couple of weeks. Nothing urgent. Help her with a bit of R and R. She's horribly bored.'

Abby felt a little hop of excitement. 'I can't. I've got three gardens to design by the weekend, and there's Lord and Lady Cunich's estate—'

'I told her you'd be too busy to go.' Julia had pushed her glasses back and was peering at a computer print-out.

'Yes, well,' Abby huffed, 'it's impossible.'

MAC FLEW LOW over the dirt runway and studied a wind sock in an alder.

'Looks good to me.'

At the end of the strip was a Cessna and a Piper Super Cub, and despite Abby telling herself that if they'd landed safely so would Mac, her knuckles were white. She'd forgotten how much she hated flying.

Mac dropped altitude. The plane skimmed a bluff and kissed the gravel, roared towards the parked aircraft, and swung round with ten feet to spare.

Mac looked around appreciatively. 'Nice place.'

When she'd last been here, she hadn't seen the beauty of Michael Flint's hunting lodge. Running on fear and adrenaline, she'd taken in the basics: one big main house with five smaller cabins opposite, and a lean-to housing the four-wheelers and snow machines.

The reality in the soft September sunshine was quite different. The trees were luminous in capes of golds and reds and greens and shiny globes of red berries clustered everywhere she looked. It was so still she could hear the buzz of a wasp, and the sound of water tumbling over rocks.

'Abby,' Mac's voice was a whisper, 'over there.'

As she hopped out of the plane she saw a female moose foraging at the edge of the forest. Suddenly the moose flung up her head as a large grey form burst from behind the lodge. The moose took one look, and fled. Abby was tempted to do the same. Facing a husky headed full speed for you wasn't for the faint-hearted.

Moke knocked her straight off her feet. Sprawled in the grass she was half laughing, half protesting as he nipped and slurped and made that doggy groaning sound deep in his throat.

'Told you he was your dog.'

Abby scrambled up to greet her sister. The last time she'd seen Lisa was in Los Angeles in July, just before her first round of plastic surgery. Mike Flint had told Abby it had gone well, but she hadn't realised how well until now. Lisa was no longer wrapped in gauze, nor was she wearing the gloves that used to protect her hands. Her skin still looked raw and was covered in lumps and caverns—deeply, irrevocably scarred—but her eyes sparkled.

'Like it?' she asked.

Abby studied the bright pink wig. 'Suits you.'

'Yeah, so Mike said.' Lisa turned to Mac. 'Fancy a coffee?'

'Nah. Got a pick-up in Lake's Edge I can't be late for. Good to see ya, though. Lookin' good as usual.'

Lisa chuckled. 'Sure, Mac. Sure.'

Abby stood with Lisa, stroking Moke, and watched Mac take off.

'See that?' Lisa said, waving at the Cessna at the end of the strip.

Abby nodded.

'Damned man landed without permission this morning . . .'

'Was he in trouble?'

Lisa studied her. 'No, but he might be.'

'Why? Who is he?'

'Cal Pegati.'

'For God's sake, Lisa, I thought I asked you—'

'I didn't tell him you were here. He would have heard from Diane. Or Victor or Mac or any one of that lot. You know what it's like out here.'

'Shit.'

'Yeah, well. I'm going to pick cranberries while you go and see him.' Lisa gave Abby a stern look. 'Just remember, *it wasn't his fault.*'

Part of her knew Lisa was right, but the other couldn't forgive Cal for not regaining consciousness sooner. She'd seen his fingers twitch barely a minute before Connie splashed the last of the fuel over Lisa. She kept replaying the scene, wishing with every fibre of her being that Cal had risen with his gun and shot Connie dead. But now she didn't think she could ever look at him without reliving what her sister had gone through.

When Cal stepped out of the lodge and walked her way, her heartbeat went into overdrive. She wasn't sure whether it was nerves, or simply because he looked so damned good. Moke bowled over and greeted him with a lolling tongue and waving tail.

'Hey, boy.' Cal patted the dog. 'She going to talk to us, you think?'

His shirtsleeves were bunched at his elbows, his shirt open at the neck, showing skin tanned from the summer. His burns had healed, and she had to stop herself from reaching up and touching the blemishes on his cheeks.

'You left before I could say goodbye,' Cal said. 'Again.'

Abby averted her eyes. 'Sorry.'

'I'd like to say goodbye now. Properly.'

Startled, her gaze flew to meet his.

'I won't badger you again. I know how you feel about me. I also know how I feel about you, and probably always will.'

He put his fingers on her jaw and gently raised her head. Pressed a kiss against her lips. His mouth cupped hers with easy familiarity. Warm and soft and tender. His eyes were closed.

She felt his lower lip catch hers, and she was about to part her lips, kiss him back, when he pulled away. Looked her straight in the eye.

'Goodbye, Abby.'

Stunned, she watched him head for his Cessna. Moke trotted after Cal, paused to look back at her, then stood undecided. Cal hopped into his aircraft, and Abby was wondering if she had the courage to go over when he started the engine, leaned outside and yelled, 'Moke!'

The husky looked between them. His tail was down. Abby suddenly realised that Cal must have looked after Moke since she left.

'Your call!' he shouted.

With a final glance at Abby, Moke burst into a gallop straight for the Cessna and sprang inside.

Abby took a step forward, hesitated. Cal still had to do his pre-flight check; she had a couple of minutes to think . . .

To her horror, the Cessna started taxiing. Cal wasn't hanging around.

Abby broke into a run. *Please God, let him see me, make him stop.* Breath hot in her throat, she raced after the aeroplane, bouncing along the strip. He'd see her when he turned. He couldn't miss her, surely.

She was halfway along the strip when Cal turned, and without pausing, pushed the throttle. He was glancing at his instruments, then glancing forward through the windscreen, then down at his instruments . . .

Abby was running and yelling. 'Stop, wait, Cal. Wait!'

The aircraft got enough air under its wings and he pulled back and began to soar. At the last second, Cal saw her. He smiled and gave her a wave.

Then he was gone.

SUPPER WAS BUTTERED salmon steaks and salad, followed by warm pecan pie and whipped cream. Abby's favourite food, but she found it hard to eat.

'It doesn't have to be over, *over*, just because he wanted closure or whatever he came here for,' Michael Flint remarked.

'You should go and see him,' Lisa added for the hundredth time. 'He's crazy about you, you're crazy about him, what the hell's the problem? I mean we all know he loved Saffron, but it's been nearly four years . . .' Lisa swallowed, then gave a wobbly smile. 'Sorry. I miss her sometimes.'

'She sounded like an amazing woman,' Abby ventured.

'She was. But then, so are you.' Lisa smiled.

Lisa finished her second helping of pie, then got to her feet. 'Let's forget about Cal a minute. Mike and I have a proposal for you. Come next door.'

Next door in his study there was a big table by the window, where a model village was displayed. Log cabins with thatched roofs, a stream and a pond with ducks, a church, fields of crops and horses grazing.

'This is Bearpaw,' said Lisa. 'The first fully sustainable ecovillage in Alaska.'

Abby raised her eyebrows.

'It hasn't been built yet, but we've got the land, and the permission.' Lisa's face was alight, and there was a gleam in Flint's eyes too.

'It's just north of Fairbanks. It's got fresh running water, a good variety of agricultural and natural resources . . . And you can guess where the power will come from.'

'MEG,' said Abby.

'Too damn right.'

While Lisa had been fighting for her life in hospital, Flint had registered the technology for patent, using Lisa's power of attorney. The patent had been approved two months ago, and hadn't been contested.

'We're going to make sure it works a hundred per cent before releasing it to the world,' Lisa added. 'And what better way to show MEG off than by using an ecovillage.'

She took a breath. 'We do, however, need some advice about stuff we're not that great at. I mean, I'm a scientist, Mike's an executive . . . We need someone who knows plants and what grows and what doesn't . . .'

'You need an environmental architect.'

Lisa swung to Flint. 'See?'

'Fine by me.' He nodded.

'Are you going totally green?' asked Abby, now curious. 'Using organic paints and stuff?' She glanced at the model village. 'How many people are you planning to have live here? You'll need some sort of social contract for them, or social management plan.' Abby sent them both a sharp look. 'Are you sure you've thought this through?'

'Oh, yes.' Lisa looked cheerful. 'But it's rather dependent on whether a certain person will work with us—someone we can trust to do a good job.'

Abby stared at her sister, then at Flint. Both were grinning.

'You can't mean me.'

'And why not?' said Lisa. 'You'd love it. You'd be outdoors and not stuck in an office. You'd be striding about overseeing the building, the planting . . .'

Abby couldn't quite believe it. 'I'm not sure.'

'At least, think about it,' Flint told her.

'Sure.' She stared at the ecovillage model, completely lost for words.

Through the hallway came the squawk of a radio.

Flint vanished, to return seconds later. 'It's for you,' he told Abby.

'What?' She couldn't think of anybody in Alaska who'd want to radio her. She trotted into the kitchen. Picked up the receiver. 'Hello?'

'Does your running after my aircraft mean you'll have dinner with Moke and me next week?'

CAROLINE CARVER

Home: Wiltshire
Former job: travel writer
Website: www.carolinecarver.com

RD: What inspired you to set a book in the Alaskan wilderness?
CC: It's always held a great appeal for me, not just because of its raw beauty but because of the danger. I love putting my characters somewhere inhospitable and seeing what happens next; whether they rise to the challenge or have a screaming panic attack. Alaska looked just perfect—how do you survive in subzero temperatures with a wind chill of −30° F?

RD: Did you manage to visit Alaska?
CC: How could I resist it? Breathtakingly beautiful, harsh and unforgiving, Alaska really is America's last great frontier. There's open tundra, glaciers and forests; there's gold, zinc and oil. And everything is enormous, including the mosquitoes. I just about fell over when I saw a 74lb salmon—almost as long as I am—caught on the fly.

RD: Is Lake's Edge, where the book is set, a real place?
CC: Lake's Edge was inspired by a mix of isolated bush villages that I saw when I flew north of the Arctic Circle. I hitched a ride with the mail plane, which was a pretty nail-biting experience, and even the two native guys and their huskies didn't look too happy as we bounced our way over the mountains. There are no roads to most of these villages, and without light aircraft they would be totally cut off—no mail, no groceries, no way to get to the big city. One in fifty residents holds a pilot's licence, and after my trip there, I could see why. If I lived there I'd get one, too!

RD: Is Lisa's invention of a new form of energy based on real science?
CC: I bet you that someone out there is working on an invention just like Lisa's as we speak. There are scientists worldwide searching flat out to find an alternative, sustainable, free energy source—and they are looking at everything from dark matter in space to perpetual motion machines. My brother's a scientist, and I ran Lisa's idea past him. With a surprised look in his eyes he said, 'yes, that could work.' Maybe I should patent it!

RD: Were Lisa and Abby based on anyone in particular?

CC: No, but I pulled together a lot of their disputes and difficulties from a variety of friends. Sisters, in my experience, can have extremely tricky relationships with each other, especially when they are growing up, I'm lucky, I have a brother, but my two closest friends have sisters, and boy, the fur sure can fly!

RD: Have you ever been faced with a ferocious wild animal?

CC: I once came face to face with one of the most dangerous animals in the African bush—a mature Cape Buffalo bull. I was with a professional hunter, trekking through a riverine, when this wall of black flesh rose ten yards in front of us, put its head down and gave an almighty snort. I have never experienced such terror. Immediately I looked at the hunter for guidance, but he was already in full flight, legging it who knows where. I pelted after him. There were no trees to climb, no bushes to hide behind. I have never run so fast in my life. And when I finally glanced over my shoulder, I saw the buffalo crashing through the reeds in the opposite direction. My relief was cosmic, he would have killed us.

RD: One of your interests is long-distance rally-car racing and you've taken part in two major races. What led you to do that?

CC: My mother was one of the first women racing drivers in the UK, and then set the land-speed record in Australia; my dad was a fighter pilot; and my brother tears around a variety of race tracks whenever he can. So my rallying is just an extension of my family's core personality.

RD: And what do they think of your writing?

CC: They are immensely proud, and thoroughly enjoy batting around new ideas for car-chase scenes and family rows, which we do not, I hasten to assure you, re-enact.

RD: You've worked as a travel writer in the past. Is that something you still do?

CC: I recently decided to relax a bit more when I go travelling, and put most of my creative energy into my books instead. I love sinking myself into the moment when I'm travelling and not having to worry about obsessively taking notes. This doesn't mean I don't absorb the atmosphere. I absorbed Alaska into my psyche so much I still dream about the place.

RD: Are you now writing full time?

CC: Yup. Lucky me, I get to drink my mug of tea in bed while I listen to everyone else driving off to work. And while I sip my tea looking over the garden, I mull the next chapter. Not a day goes by when I don't count my blessings.

RD: What would you have liked to have been if you hadn't become a writer?

CC: A helicopter pilot, an anthropologist. An explorer, deep-sea diver, game warden, photographer . . . the possibilities are endless!

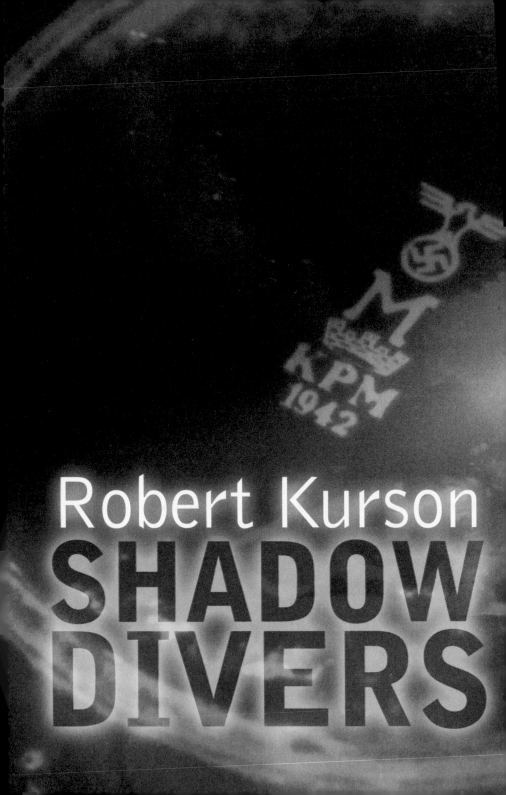

Robert Kurson

SHADOW
DIVERS

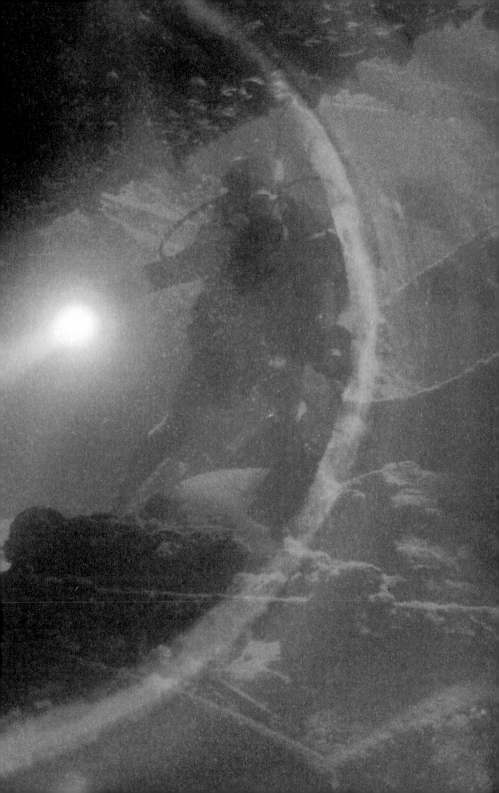

There was no mistaking the wreck's vintage. This submarine had come from World War II. Chatterton knew from his books that there were no American submarines in this area. For a moment, he dared not think it. But it was undeniable. 'I'm holding on to a U-boat,' Chatterton said out loud. 'I'm holding on to a World War II German U-boat.'

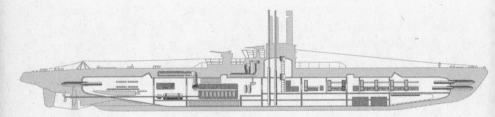

TYPE IXC U-BOAT

The Book of Numbers

Bill Nagle's life changed the day a fisherman sat beside him in a ramshackle bar and told him about a mystery he had found lying at the bottom of the Atlantic Ocean. Against his better judgment, that fisherman promised to tell Nagle how to find it. The men agreed to meet the next day on the rickety wooden pier that led to Nagle's boat, the *Seeker*. But when the appointed time came, the fisherman was not there.

Nagle paced back and forth, staring into the distance for the fisherman. He saw no one. The salt air blew against the small seaside town of Brielle, New Jersey, tilting the dockside boats and spraying the Atlantic into Nagle's eyes. When the mist died down, he looked again. This time, he saw the fisherman approaching, a small square of paper crumpled in his hands.

The *Seeker* towers above the other boats tied to this Brielle dock. Conceived in Nagle's imagination, she was built for a single purpose: to take scuba divers to the most dangerous shipwrecks in the Atlantic Ocean. Nagle was forty years old, a thin, deeply tanned former auto tools salesman. To see him here in his tattered T-shirt and thrift-shop sandals, the Jim Beam he kept as best friend slurring his motions, no one would guess that in his day Nagle had been great.

IN HIS TWENTIES, Nagle was already a legend in shipwreck diving, a boy wonder in a sport that regularly kills its young. In those days, deep-wreck diving was still the province of the adventurer. Countless shipwrecks, even famous ones, lay undiscovered at the bottom of the Atlantic, and the hunt for those wrecks was the activity that primed Nagle's imagination.

Treasure never figured in the equation for Atlantic shipwreck divers in the Northeast. Spanish galleons overflowing with gold doubloons and silver pieces of eight did not sink in this part of the ocean. Nagle's neighbourhood was the New York and New Jersey shipping lanes, waters that conducted freighters, ocean liners and warships. These wrecks occasionally surrendered a rare piece of china or jewellery, but Nagle and his kind were looking for stories in the broken ships, frozen moments in a nation's hopes or a captain's dying instinct, and they experienced these scenes unbuffered by curators or historians. And they did it to explore. Many of the deep wrecks hadn't been seen since their victims last looked at them, and would remain lost while nature pawed at them until they didn't exist any more. In a world where even the moon had been travelled, the floor of the Atlantic remained uncharted territory. It was still a wilderness in Nagle's prime, and it demanded of its explorers the same grit that the American West did of its pioneers.

In the 1970s and 1980s—Nagle's heyday—scuba equipment was still rudimentary, not much advanced past 1943 when Jacques Cousteau helped invent the system of tanks and regulators that allowed men to breathe under water. Even at 130 feet—the limit suggested by most scuba-training organisations—a minor equipment failure could kill. In searching for the most interesting wrecks, Nagle and the sport's other kings might descend to 200 feet or deeper.

One of Nagle's greatest finds was a four-foot-tall brass whistle from the paddle wheeler *Champion*. The whistle was majestic, but the most beautiful part of the discovery was that, under water, it looked like a worthless pipe. He knew the ship's anatomy, and as he imagined it coming apart, he could see the whistle settle, right where that seemingly worthless piece of pipe lay. Over the years, Nagle had devoured academic texts, reference works, novels, blueprints, any material he could uncover on historical ships, until he could have stood in the dockyards of a dozen eras and built the boats alongside the workers.

It was only time before Nagle's instinct delivered him to the *Andrea Doria*, the Mount Everest of shipwrecks. The grand Italian passenger liner had collided with the *Stockholm*, a Swedish liner, in dense fog off Nantucket Island in 1956. Fifty-one people died; 1,659 were rescued before the liner sank. The *Doria* made siren calls to great wreck divers—she was brimming with artefacts. But the ship's real challenge lay in exploration. The wreck rested on its side, making navigation dangerous and deceptive. A diver had to conceive the world sideways to make sense of doors on the floor and ceilings to the right. And she was deep—180 feet at her shallowest and 250 feet where she crushed the ocean floor. The wreck was so deep, dark and dangerous that decades after her sinking, entire decks remained unexplored. Those decks were Nagle's destinations.

Over time, Nagle penetrated the wreck in places long relegated to the impossible. His mantel at home became a miniature *Doria* museum. Soon, he set his sights on the bell. A ship's bell is her crown, her voice. For a diver, there is no greater prize. People thought he was nuts—scores of divers had searched for thirty years for the *Doria*'s bell.

Nagle studied deck plans, photographs, crew diaries. Then he did what few other divers did—he formulated a plan. He would need days, maybe even a week, to pull it off. No charter boat, however, was going to take a diver to the *Doria* for a week. So Nagle, who had saved a good bit of money, decided to buy a dive boat himself. That boat was the original *Seeker*, a thirty-five-foot Maine Coaster. In 1985, Nagle recruited five top divers, and he made this arrangement: he would take the group to the *Doria* at his expense. The trip would be a dedicated one, meaning the divers went with just one objective—to recover the bell.

For the first few days on the wreck, the divers stuck to Nagle's plan. They found nothing. Then Nagle abandoned the bow of the *Doria*, where he and his team had been searching, and rerouted to the stern. No one had ever been to the stern. On the fifth day, they hit pay dirt—there was the *Andrea Doria*'s bell. The men rigged it, and sent up the prize on a heavy-duty lift bag. Shock waves rippled through the diving community. Nagle insured the 150-pound bell for $100,000. He was among the immortals.

Soon an idea began percolating in Nagle's imagination. What if he could run the *Seeker* as a charter boat for divers? That would allow him to earn a living doing what he loved most. He could make a half-dozen trips to the *Doria* every year, then use his free time to search for great ships still missing decades after sinking. His wife and two children lived in Pennsylvania, but he resided in Brielle now. He dated other women and kept a bachelor pad, yet his wife held out hope that he would return someday. He commissioned a second *Seeker*, this one nearly double the length of the first.

Almost immediately, Nagle struggled with the business. It wasn't that he lacked for customers. It was that he couldn't abide them. Nagle had envisioned his business as an endless series of trips to dangerous wrecks like the *Doria*. But his patrons desired only easy, nearby sites. To Nagle, these people weren't divers; they were tourists, and he could not hide his contempt for them.

And Nagle was drinking. As the 1980s gave way to a new decade, Nagle's drinking began to bleach the greatness of his skills. His frame became emaciated, his skin jaundiced. He still swam beautifully but his *Doria* dives had become less strenuous. 'I just gotta get in shape,' he'd grumble to his few close friends, which they took as code for 'I gotta stop drinking.' By 1990, Nagle had made his last *Doria* dive. You couldn't challenge a wreck like that without every ounce of your faculties tuned high.

THIS WAS NAGLE'S LIFE and business in the late summer of 1991 as Brielle shut down for the season and returned to the rhythms of its regulars. Nagle had spent much of this August day washing the *Seeker* and contemplating his life. Now, with the sun setting, he took a short walk across the dock and into the Harbor Inn.

No one quite recalls when they started calling it the Horrible Inn, but everyone can tell you why. Hard-core smokers choked on the mushroom cloud of cigarette smoke that hovered over the bar. Drunken fishermen painted the names of sweethearts on greasy walls. And there was the clientele. The Horrible Inn didn't serve many, but its faithful were hard-core and local.

This evening, Nagle took his usual place at the bar and ordered a Jim Beam. A half-hour later, a thirty-eight-year-old fishing-boat captain ambled in. Everyone knew the man as Skeets. His business was small, but he ran it well, which in the charter fishing trade meant two things: he knew where the fish were; and he knew how to keep his mouth shut.

Finding fish, of course, was critical. Guys like Skeets had to be able to sniff the air, look at the sky, and say, 'Gentlemen, today I smell tuna.' And then the captain had to take his customers to little sites recorded in tattered notebooks. Sometimes this meant a location along the beach; other times it meant a long journey offshore to one of the underwater canyons. Most often, it meant a trip to the shipwrecks.

To fishermen, shipwrecks mean life. Shipwrecks are where the food chain poses for a snapshot. Tiny creatures attach themselves to solid objects. Those creatures attract predators, which in turn attract their own predators, and so on. Soon the wreck has become its own ecosystem. The pelagics—open-water travelling fish like tuna, codfish and pollack—visit and get fat. Fishing-boat captains get fatter. Every fishing-charter captain kept a book of public wrecks—the ones everyone knew about. But it was the secret wrecks that mattered, and the secret wrecks made the captain.

For the last few years, Skeets had been fishing a once-in-a-lifetime spot, a site about sixty miles off the Brielle coast. He had come upon the place one foggy day while trolling for tuna. Because the fishing boat is moving while trolling, the captain must keep alert for other boats in the vicinity. In the fog, he does this by scanning his radar. Skeets scanned his radar. Soon he spotted another boat on the screen. But its green blip never moved, meaning that this boat was anchored. To Skeets, that meant one thing: the boat on his radar was fishing a shipwreck.

Skeets set course for the anchored boat. Before that boat could respond, Skeets had 'jumped it' and had the numbers. The boat turned out to belong to a friend. The friend radioed to Skeets, 'Don't tell a soul about this site, Skeets. This one is special.'

A few days later, Skeets returned to the site, and the place was glorious—fishermen needed only to cast their hooks before fat tuna and sea bass leapt onto their lines. The best part was that only Skeets and his friend knew about it. But Skeets could not stop himself from wondering about the object at the soul of this underwater bounty. It was big—that much he could see by the crude green blob the mass painted on his bottom finder's screen. It was deep, at least 190 feet. And it was made of steel. He could tell that by inspecting the rust flakes that sometimes stuck to his fishing lures. Beyond that, he could divine nothing.

For years, when Nagle had seen Skeets in the parking lot or washing his boat, he had asked this question: 'Say, Skeets, you come across any wrecks out there that haven't been hit by divers?' For years, Skeets had given this answer: 'Sorry, Billy. Nothing.' Today, however, Skeets looked over to Nagle in the Horrible Inn and said something different.

'Billy, I've been fishing this site. You can't believe it. Big fish.'

Nagle raised an eyebrow. 'Oh, yeah?'

'Yeah, Bill. About sixty miles offshore. And deep, your kind of deep, maybe two hundred foot of water. Something's down there. Something big. You should check this thing out.' Then Skeets made an offer. 'Billy, I'm looking for a little inshore blackfish wreck that I know you dive every so often. Give me those numbers, and I'll give you my numbers.'

The two men agreed to exchange the numbers the next day on Nagle's boat. That night, Nagle could not sleep in anticipation of the appointment. The next day, he arrived an hour early and paced the rotted wooden pier that led to the *Seeker*. This meeting was about more than just an object at the bottom of the ocean. This meeting was about the tides turning. When Skeets finally arrived, Nagle invited him into the *Seeker*'s wheelhouse.

'Bill, I gotta tell you something,' Skeets said. 'This part of the ocean is a bad place. It's in a little depression. There's an edge there, with a huge current coming up over the continental shelf, lots of moving water. Your guys gotta be top-shelf divers. And it's deep. I'm thinking two hundred feet. I don't know anything about diving, but you better watch your guys.'

'Yeah, Skeets, I know. Don't worry. Let's swap the numbers.'

Nagle reached into his pocket and pulled out two cocktail napkins from the Horrible Inn. He wrote down his numbers for Skeets, then Skeets began to copy his Loran-C time differentials. Skeets handed over the napkin. 'Keep it to yourself,' he said. 'And for God's sake, be careful.'

'Don't worry, Skeets.'

Skeets let himself out of the wheelhouse and returned to his boat. Nagle followed a short time later. He walked to the Horrible Inn and ordered a Jim Beam. Then he called John Chatterton.

If Nagle saw himself in any other diver, that diver was John Chatterton, a tall and ruggedly handsome forty-year-old commercial diver. By day, Chatterton worked underwater construction jobs around Manhattan, the kind that required a brass helmet and a 10,000-degree Broco torch. On weekends, he masterminded some of the most daring shipwreck dives ever executed on the eastern seaboard. When Nagle looked into Chatterton's eyes, he saw his own best days staring back at him.

They had met in the mid-eighties aboard the *Seeker*. Chatterton had signed up simply to observe Nagle, the legend. Soon after, Chatterton took a *Seeker* charter to the *Texas Tower*, an old air force radar installation about sixty miles offshore. The tower had collapsed in a 1961 storm, killing its crew. Its bottom lay jackknifed in sand at 200 feet, making it too dangerous for all but the most accomplished divers. But its top could be easily explored at eighty-five feet, appropriate for every diver on this trip.

One man got cocky. He concocted a plan to dive the bottom. He became obsessed with removing a brass window. His air was short, but he tried to finish anyway. He drowned. That's how fast it happens at those depths.

Now there was a corpse on the bottom of a very dangerous wreck. Someone had to go get him. That was Nagle's job. Ordinarily, he or one of his assistants would make the recovery dive. But they had just completed their own dives and could not return to the water until their bodies had off-gassed

SHADOW DIVERS | 459

built-up nitrogen. Chatterton volunteered. Nagle asked if Chatterton knew the mangled topography of the wreck.

'Not really, but I'll go anyway,' he said. That answer spoke to Nagle.

Chatterton found the diver. He tied the man's tanks to a 200-pound lift bag and inflated the bag with air until the body began its ascent. Nagle reeled in the body when it surfaced. 'You did a good job,' he told Chatterton. 'You are a good diver.'

Before long, Chatterton was crewing on the *Seeker*. In 1987, he made his first trip to the *Doria*. He swam around but did nothing more. The wreck was so dangerous, so terrifying, that he vowed never to return. He shook Nagle's hand, thanked him for the opportunity, and said, 'Bill, I've made my trip to the mountaintop. Once is enough.' Nagle, however, knew better.

Chatterton couldn't forget the wreck. He returned. Soon he was going places and finding things on the *Doria* no one had before, not even Nagle. Chatterton's reputation wafted across the bows of dive boats along the eastern seaboard. And he continued to absorb Nagle. He and Nagle shared a philosophy. To them, diving was about exploration, about the unknown. There were a lot of impossible places to go, but you had to try. What were you doing alive, these men thought, if you didn't go and try?

The day after Skeets revealed his secret, Nagle asked Chatterton to meet him at the *Seeker*. The men walked upstairs to the boat's wheelhouse, where Nagle locked the door and related Skeets's story to his friend. What could be at that site? Nagle proposed a plan. He and Chatterton would organise a trip to the site. Each would recruit six top divers, guys who could survive a 200-foot plunge into the unknown. Each diver would pay $100 to cover fuel and expenses. There would be no promises.

The trip was booked for the beginning of September, 1991. Nagle and Chatterton called every good diver they knew. Nearly all of them refused the invitation, but Nagle and Chatterton kept calling. And finally, their lists exhausted, they found their twelfth diver.

Just after midnight on September 2, 1991, Nagle, Chatterton and the twelve divers who had signed up for the exploratory trip stuffed the *Seeker* with tanks, masks and bundles of other gear. They faced a six-hour ride to Skeets's numbers. Some grabbed a bunk and went to sleep. Others caught up on one another's lives and laughed about the folly of paying to chase a pile of rocks. At 1 a.m., the *Seeker* was ready. A few minutes later, she was nose up into the Atlantic.

DEEP-SHIPWRECK DIVING is among the world's most dangerous sports. It bears only passing resemblance to its cousin, the resort-area single-tank scuba-diving familiar to the general public. In the United States, of the ten million certified scuba divers, it is likely that only a few hundred dive deep for shipwrecks. To those few, it is not a matter of if they will taste death, only of whether they'll swallow. If a deep-wreck diver stays in the sport long enough, he will very likely either watch another diver die, or die himself.

A deep-shipwreck diver breathing air confronts two primary dangers. First, at depths greater than about sixty-six feet, his judgment and motor skills can become impaired, a condition known as nitrogen narcosis. As he descends farther, the effects of narcosis become more pronounced. Beyond 100 feet, he can be significantly handicapped, yet he must perform feats and make decisions upon which his life depends.

Second, should something go wrong, he cannot simply swim to the surface. A diver who has spent time in deep water must ascend gradually, stopping at predetermined intervals to allow his body to readjust to decreasing pressures. He must do this even if he believes himself to be suffocating or dying. Panicked divers who bolt for 'sunshine and seagulls' risk a case of decompression sickness, or the 'bends'. Severe bends can kill a person.

Narcosis and decompression sickness are both conditions born of pressure. At sea level, atmospheric pressure is roughly equal to the pressure inside the human body. Throwing Frisbees on the beach we are at one atmosphere of pressure, or 14.7 pounds per square inch. The air we breathe at sea level, which is composed of 21 per cent oxygen and 79 per cent nitrogen, also enters our lungs at a pressure of one atmosphere. The oxygen nourishes our blood and tissue. The nitrogen is inert and doesn't do much of anything.

Things change in water. Every thirty-three feet below the surface, the pressure increases by one atmosphere. A scuba diver chasing sea horses at thirty-three feet is at two atmospheres, or twice the pressure he experienced at the surface. He barely feels it, but something is going on in the air he breathes from his tanks. While that air is still made up of 21 per cent oxygen and 79 per cent nitrogen, there are now twice as many of each of those molecules in every lungful of air he breathes. At three atmospheres, there are three times as many oxygen and nitrogen molecules in his lungful of air, and so on.

As the diver breathes under water, the extra nitrogen molecules being taken into his lungs dissolve into the bloodstream and travel into his flesh, joints, brain, spine—everywhere. The longer and deeper a diver stays under water, the more nitrogen accumulates in those tissues.

At a depth of around three atmospheres, or sixty-six feet, that accumulated nitrogen begins to have a narcotic effect on most divers. That is nitrogen narcosis. Some compare the effects of narcosis to alcohol intoxication. Symptoms are relatively mild at shallower depths—judgment skews, motor skills dull, emotions heighten. As a diver descends farther, the effects intensify. At 130 feet, or about five atmospheres, some divers struggle to complete simple tasks, such as tying a knot. As a diver descends to 170 or 180 feet, he might begin to hallucinate, until lobsters begin beckoning him by name. Below 200 feet, tiny problems—a missing knife, a bit of silt—can be perceived as unfolding catastrophes and snowball into panic. Serious problems—a depleting air tank or the loss of the anchor line—can appear as niggling annoyances.

If the diver ascends slowly, atmospheric pressure decreases gradually and the accumulated nitrogen passes out of his body tissues in the form of microscopic bubbles. The same effect can be observed by slowly opening a soda bottle: if you gradually reduce the pressure inside the bottle, the bubbles stay small. The size of the bubbles is key. Only when nitrogen bubbles are microscopically small inside a diver can they travel efficiently through his bloodstream and back to his lungs, where they can be discharged through normal respiration. This is what a diver wants.

When a diver ascends quickly, however, the surrounding atmospheric pressure drops rapidly. That causes the accumulated nitrogen in his tissues to form massive quantities of large bubbles, just as when you rapidly unscrew the cap of a soda bottle and large bubbles erupt violently from the bottle's mouth. When large nitrogen bubbles form outside the bloodstream, they can press on tissues, blocking circulation. If this happens in the joints or near the nerves, the result will be agonising pain that might last weeks or even a lifetime. If it happens in the spinal cord or the brain, the blockage can cause paralysis or a fatal stroke. If too many large bubbles make their way back to the lungs, the lungs will shut down.

To guarantee that he ascends slowly, keeping nitrogen bubbles microscopically small, the diver pauses at predetermined depths to allow these bubbles to work their way out of his system. These pauses are known as decompression, or 'deco', stops and have been optimally calculated by scientists. A diver who spends twenty-five minutes at 200 feet might spend an hour working his way back to the surface. Longer and deeper dives mean more decompression. That is why shipwreck divers don't spend hours working under water; the decompression time for a two-hour dive might be as long as nine hours.

Equipment is the deep-wreck diver's soul mate. It grants him passage into an off-limits world, but should any of it fail, he will find trouble. He carries several thousand dollars' worth of gear: strobe lights, flashlights, crowbar, knives, regulators, compass, mesh goody bag for artefacts, clips, gauges, writing slate, waterproof marker, laminated decompression tables, stopwatch, weight belt. Then he packs back-ups for some of this gear. He shuns the casual diver's wet suit for the warmer dry suit. He carries two air tanks, not one.

When a charter boat nears its destination, the captain uses his navigation equipment to put the vessel 'on the numbers', or as close to the wreck as possible. His mates grab hold of the anchor. A dive boat's anchor is a steel grapple with four or five long teeth. It is attached first to about fifteen feet of chain, then to hundreds of feet of three-quarter-inch nylon line. When the captain gives the order, the mates will drop this grapple, hoping that it lands on and snags the shipwreck.

The anchor line is the diver's umbilical cord, the means by which he makes his way to the shipwreck and, more important, finds his way back. A diver cannot simply jump off the boat and expect to land on the wreck. Even in those rare cases when bottom visibility is pristine, say forty feet, a free-descending diver who lands forty-five feet away from the wreck still won't see it. Only by descending along the anchor line can the diver find his wreck.

The trip back up the anchor line is even more critical. If a diver cannot locate the anchor line, he will be forced to ascend and decompress from wherever he happens to find himself. He will find it more difficult to maintain the precise depths necessary for proper decompression. And without an anchor line to clutch, he will be moved about by currents. A free-floating diver who decompresses for an hour in a current of just two knots—about two miles per hour—will surface more than two miles from the boat. At that distance, he will probably never see the boat, and the boat will probably never see him.

The grapple has to be secured because currents shift under water, and grapples can move and come undone. This is the work of the mates, who dive down to the wreck and 'tie in'. Once the tie-in is complete, the mates release several white Styrofoam drinking cups, which rise to the surface to signal that the anchor line is secure. When word of the cup sighting reaches the divers, they put on their equipment. Soon the geared-up diver's 350-pound footsteps and hunched posture make him a neoprene Sasquatch.

Once in the water, the diver taps valves on his dry suit to bleed a bit of air, making himself slightly negatively buoyant. When he reaches the anchor line, he vents a little more air. Now he slowly begins to sink.

Typically, it will take the diver between two and four minutes to reach a wreck lying at a depth of 200 feet. He is virtually weightless as he drops— an astronaut beneath the sea. He hears two primary sounds: the hiss of his regulator on his inhalation and the booming gurgles of his bubbles on his exhalation. Together they are the metronome of his adventure.

The diver sinks to 190 feet. Now he stands face to face with the ship-wreck, crooked, cracked and broken. Covered in plant life, only a ship's most basic shapes make sense—a propeller, a rudder, a porthole.

The diver has perhaps twenty-five minutes to work the wreck before he must begin his ascent. Most divers stay outside the wreck. They come to touch the ship, search for loose artefacts, or snap photographs. The spirit of the ship, however, lies inside. Shipwreck interiors can be terrifying places, spaces in which order has fractured. Hallways dead-end abruptly. Fallen ceilings block stairways. Rooms in which ladies played bridge are now upside down or sideways. Dangers come camouflaged in every crevice.

Once a diver has exited the shipwreck, he begins the journey back to the boat. He cannot relax now. The trip to the surface is rife with its own perils, each of them capable of striking down even the best man. On a deep-wreck dive, no one is ever truly safe until he is back on the deck of the dive boat.

A Shape of Power

The *Seeker* had twenty minutes behind her when the last embers of Jersey Shore nightlife snuffed out under the grey-black horizon. Nagle and Chatterton worked in the wheelhouse, while the remaining divers slept in the salon below. They were Dick Shoe, Kip Cochran, Steve Feldman, Paul Skibinski, Ron Ostrowski, Doug Roberts, Lloyd Garrick, Kevin Brennan, John Hildemann, John Yurga, Mark McMahon and Steve Lombardo.

Some of these men had arrived in pairs and planned to dive together: Shoe with Cochran, Feldman with Skibinski, Ostrowski with Roberts, McMahon with Yurga. The others preferred to dive solo. Around sunrise, loran read-outs showed the boat a half-mile from the target site. Nagle cut the autopilot, throttled back the twin diesels, and swivelled to face the bottom finder. In the salon, divers began to wake up.

Nagle nudged the boat closer to the numbers. A shape appeared on the bottom finder's electronic display.

'There's something on the numbers,' Nagle said to Chatterton.

'Yeah, I see it,' Chatterton replied. 'It looks like a ship on its side.'

'It also looks like it's deeper than two hundred feet. I'm going to make a couple of passes over it to get a better look.'

Nagle cut the *Seeker*'s wheel hard to port, pulling the boat around for a second pass, then a third and a fourth. All the while, he watched the mass at the ocean bottom morph in and out of the bottom finder's screen. Brennan, Yurga and Hildemann climbed the ladder and entered the wheelhouse.

'What do we got, Bill?' Yurga asked.

'This is deeper than I was expecting,' Nagle told them. 'And whatever it is, it's lying low. It might be a two-hundred-and-thirty-foot dive.'

Chatterton was capable of diving to 230 feet. He and Nagle devised a plan. Brennan and Hildemann would throw the hook. Chatterton would splash and check out whatever was on the bottom. If it looked worth diving and the depth was reasonable, he would tie in the anchor line. If it was some crappy barge or if the depth really was 260 feet, he would trip loose the hook, return to the surface, and call off the dive.

Chatterton began to suit up while Nagle attempted to hook the wreck. When the anchor caught, Nagle cut the boat's engines.

'Give me six minutes,' Chatterton told Nagle. 'That'll give me time to look around. If the thing is no good or too deep, I'm gonna pop two cups. If you see two cups, that means you should take up the grapple, and I'll come up with it. But if I send up one cup, that means it's worth diving and it's not too deep. You see one cup, take in the slack, because I'm already tied in.'

Chatterton walked to the edge of the boat, placed his regulator in his mouth, pulled his mask over his face, and checked his watch: six minutes. He then knelt on the rail and fell sideways into the ocean. He swam just below the surface to the anchor line. The current began swirling and ripping, so that Chatterton found himself forcing himself down two-handed in a fight to keep from being blown from the rope.

In normal seas, such a descent might have taken two minutes. Five minutes after he splashed, Chatterton was still fighting. As his watch clicked six minutes, he landed on a mass of metal near the sand. White particulate matter flew horizontally past his eyes in the swirling, dark green water, a sideways white Christmas in September. In the poor five-foot visibility, he could see only specks of rust on the metal and, above him, a rounded railing and a soft corner of some kind—an oddly streamlined shape, he thought. Chatterton checked his depth gauge: 218 feet. The sand below him looked to be at 230 feet. He scanned for a high point to tie into and noticed what looked to be a strut at about 210 feet. Chatterton tripped loose the grapple, swam to the strut, and tied the grapple and its fifteen feet of chain until the hook was secure. He took one white Styrofoam cup from his goody bag and released it. This dive was a go.

Aboard the *Seeker*, the crew at the bow scanned the waves.

'He blew one cup!' Yurga yelled. 'We're going diving!'

Chatterton would probably spend twenty minutes on the bottom, meaning he would owe an hour of decompression. No one made a move for his equipment. Everyone waited for Chatterton.

At the ocean's bottom, Chatterton clipped a strobe light to the anchor line's chain. Sideways white particles rushed through the green-black ocean panorama, limiting Chatterton's visibility. In his headlight beam, Chatterton could make out the general shape of a ship's hull. But this hull seemed to him to have a soft roll to it. At 205 feet, he reached the top of the wreck and began to pull himself forward against the current. A few seconds later, Chatterton hauled himself to an area overgrown with bent and rusted pipes. Beneath this broken equipment, bolted to the wreck, lay four undamaged cylinders, each perhaps six feet in length.

Those are pipes, Chatterton thought. This is a pipe barge. Damn, this is probably a tanker or sludge barge.

He continued along the top of the wreck. Moments later, he spotted a hatch. He stopped. Barges did not have hatches like this. He swam closer, and pushed his head inside the hatch. The interior of the mass lit white under his headlight. This was a room. Visibility was excellent in this enclosed space protected from ocean particulates. Against one of the walls lay a shape. Chatterton stayed motionless and took it in. This shape, he thought, is unlike any other shape in the world.

Chatterton's heart pounded. Was he seeing things?

Fins. Propeller. Cigar body. A shape from scary books and terrifying movies. A shape of power. A torpedo.

Chatterton began a dialogue with himself.

'I'm narced,' he told himself. 'I'm at two hundred and twenty feet. I'm exhausted from fighting the current. I could be seeing things.'

'You are on top of a submarine,' he replied.

'There are no submarines near this part of the ocean. I have studied books. There are no submarines here. This is impossible.'

'You are on top of a submarine. There is no other shape like that torpedo. Remember those rolled edges you saw on the hull? Submarine. You have just discovered a submarine. This is the holy grail.'

Chatterton pulled his head out of the hatch. He knew that submarines fired torpedoes from both ends. That meant he was near either the bow or the stern. The current moved in the direction the torpedo pointed. If he let go and drifted with the current, he would quickly arrive at one end of the wreck. As he released his grip, the current awoke and flung him past the anchor line, slingshotting him towards the end of the wreck. Instinctively, he thrust out a glove. Something solid hit his hand. Chatterton caught hold of a bent piece of metal at the tip of the wreck. Beyond that metal, there was only ocean and sand. He breathed deeply and steadied himself. The end of the wreck was before him.

Submarine bows were blunted and angled downwards, while the sterns were streamlined horizontally. This was the bow. And there was no mistaking the ship's vintage. This submarine had come from World War II. Chatterton knew from his books that there were no American submarines in this area. For a moment, he dared not think it. But it was undeniable. 'I'm holding on to a U-boat,' Chatterton said out loud. 'I'm holding on to a World War II German U-boat.'

By now, Chatterton had reached the end of his twenty-minute bottom time. He swam back to the strobe light he had clipped to the anchor line. As he swam, he watched the hull's rolled edges unfold below him, beautiful curves engineered for stealth.

Chatterton made his first decompression stop at sixty feet. The catalogue of submarines he had studied over the years emerged as a dossier before him. Some were hundreds of miles to the north, others hundreds of miles south. None was anywhere near here. Could there be a crew on board? Could this be a U-boat with a crew on board that no one in the world knew about but him? Too fantastic. And what was it doing in New Jersey waters?

Chatterton ascended to forty feet and began his second hang. Topside, the divers watched Chatterton's bubbles as they gurgled to the surface.

'The suspense is killing me,' Kevin Brennan told the other divers. 'I gotta do something.'

Within minutes, Brennan had flipped over the *Seeker*'s side. Seconds later, he reached Chatterton. Brennan startled him with a tap on the shoulder, then put his palms up and shrugged his shoulders, the universal 'What's up?' signal. Chatterton removed a writing slate and waterproof marker from his goody bag, then scrawled a single word. It said, 'SUB'.

For a moment, Brennan could not move. Then he began to scream through his regulator. The words came out as if spoken from behind two pillows. 'Are you kidding, John? Are you sure? Really?'

Chatterton nodded.

Brennan shot back up the anchor line, bobbed on the surface, and yanked the regulator from his mouth.

'Yo, Bill! Bill!' he called to Nagle, who was in the wheelhouse. 'Yo! Bill! Check this out: John says it's a submarine!'

Nagle did not need to hear anything else. He ran down the wheelhouse stairs and gathered the remaining divers. 'Chatterton says it's a sub.'

Until this point, many of the divers had held deep reservations about exploring a new wreck at 230 feet. The word 'sub' vaporised those concerns. The divers rushed to gear up. Only Nagle, whose alcoholism had degraded his physical condition, remained behind. On the anchor line, Brennan stuffed the regulator back into his mouth and headed down, pumping a pair of 'Way to go!' fists as he passed Chatterton. Several minutes later, as Chatterton ascended to his twenty-foot stop, the other eleven divers dropped past him in an express parade to the virgin wreck.

When Chatterton finished decompressing, he climbed the aluminium ladder at the *Seeker*'s stern. Nagle hung on the back rail until Chatterton had removed his mask. Nagle wanted to say something momentous, because this was the day men like him and Chatterton dreamed of. Instead, the two men simply looked at each other. 'I hear we did good,' Nagle finally said.

'Yeah, Bill,' Chatterton said. 'We did good.'

As Nagle helped Chatterton undress, the other divers began their exploration of the wreck 230 feet below. Ostrowski and Roberts studied the outline of the wreck and the flatness of its topside decking. Both pegged it for a submarine. The duo swam slowly along the top of the wreck. They soon reached a hole in the top of the steel hull that looked to have been blown violently inwards. They stuck their heads inside, and their lights brought to life a zoo of broken pipes, machinery, valves and switches. Neither dared enter. This room might contain answers, but it also held a hundred ways to kill the overeager diver.

Shoe and Cochran took in the wreck's cigar shape and considered its level of deterioration. Each had experience diving World War II ships, and this wreck looked to be worn in just the same ways. Skibinski and Feldman ventured forty feet from the wreck to obtain a wider view, a bold decision at this depth and visibility. They looked at each other and nodded: a submarine. They swam back towards the strobe they had clipped to the anchor line.

McMahon and Yurga remained atop the wreck. Yurga spotted flooding vents along the hull, the centrepiece of a submarine's diving system. A minute later, Yurga beheld the angled hatch that Chatterton had seen. He pushed his head and light inside. He, too, saw the tail fins and propeller of the most notorious sea weapon ever built. The men yearned to see more, but each had agreed topside that at this depth, their first priority would be to stay near the anchor line and therefore stay alive.

Brennan, the first to arrive after Chatterton, inched forward in the current until he came to what he recognised was the bow of the sub. He allowed himself to drift farther forward until he was twenty feet in front of the wreck, then turned round to face the bow. I can't believe this, he thought. I know this is a U-boat. I know this thing is German. Look at it! It's coming right at me, like in the opening scene in *Das Boot*.

Between 1939 and 1945, Germany assembled a force of 1,167 U-boats. Of those 1,167 U-boats, 757 were sunk, captured, bombed in home ports, or disabled by accident or collision. Of the 859 U-boats that left base for front-line patrol, 648 were sunk or captured while operating at sea. Some were sunk by enemy vessels and aircraft that could not confirm the kills, others by mines, still others by mechanical or human failure. Because most U-boats died beneath the water's surface, as many as sixty-five disappeared without explanation.

When the divers began to surface and board the *Seeker*, they rushed out of their gear and into debate. Each of them already had a theory. It could be *U-550*, a U-boat supposedly sunk in the far North Atlantic but never recovered. It could *not* be the American *S-5*; numerous divers had searched for and researched that sub for years and were certain it lay near Maryland. The crew could have escaped—a hatch looked to be open, though it was hard to tell. Something violent might have happened to the submarine.

Then Yurga joined in. He had stopped, by chance, at a naval bookstore the day before to pick up some light reading for the trip. His choice: *The U-boat: The Evolution and Technical History of German Submarines*. When he produced the book, the divers crowded over his shoulder to compare their memories to the book's detailed schematic diagrams. As the divers continued their discussion, Chatterton and Nagle climbed into the wheelhouse. The crew pulled the anchor. Nagle set a course back for Brielle. Then he and Chatterton began a private discussion.

This was a historic dive, they agreed, but discovery was only half the job. The other half, the everything half, lay in identification. Were they simply to announce that they had found a submarine, what would that really tell anyone? But to announce the identity of the submarine you discovered, to give the nameless a name—that is when a man rewrites history.

Nagle and Chatterton believed it would take just another dive or two to pull a positive piece of identification from the wreck: a tag, a builder's plaque, a diary—something. Until then, there was sound reason not to utter a word of the discovery to anyone. A virgin sub, especially a U-boat, would attract the attention of rival divers everywhere. The gravest threat came from a single source: Bielenda.

In 1991, the eastern seaboard featured only a handful of big-name dive charter boats. The *Seeker* was one of them. Another was the Long Island-based *Wahoo*, a fifty-five-foot fibreglass hull captained by fifty-five-year-old Steve Bielenda, a barrel-chested, cherubic-faced man. From the moment Nagle entered the charter business in the mid-1980s, he and Bielenda seemed to despise each other. By 1991, the Bielenda–Nagle feud had become notorious.

Nagle was certain that if word leaked of the U-boat discovery, Bielenda would head straight for it, and his goals would be threefold and deadly: identify the wreck; raid the artefacts; take the credit.

'The *Seeker* is booked for the next two weeks,' Nagle told Chatterton. 'Let's come back on the 21st, a Saturday. We invite only the guys on this trip. We make a pact. Nobody on the boat breathes a word to anyone. This is our submarine.'

'I'm with you,' Chatterton said.

Chatterton called the divers together. 'This is a huge dive,' he said. 'But finding it isn't enough. We need to identify it. We identify it, and we rewrite history. Bill and I have made a decision. We're coming back on September

21st. It's a private trip—only you guys are invited. But we gotta keep this thing secret. Word gets out, and we'll have two hundred guys crawling all over our asses out here.'

Chatterton paused for a moment. No one made a sound. He asked the men to swear an oath of secrecy. One by one, the divers spoke. Every man agreed. This was their submarine.

The *Seeker* glided back towards Brielle on a cushion of hope and possibility. Six hours later, at about 9 p.m., Nagle eased the boat into its slip again and the divers gathered their gear.

One diver, Steve Feldman, stayed behind, waiting for Chatterton to emerge from the wheelhouse. Of the fourteen men aboard, Feldman was the newest to the sport, with about ten years of experience. As Chatterton made his way down to the back deck, Feldman stopped him.

'John, I want to thank you,' he said. 'This trip has been so cool. And it's important; it's really important. I can't wait until we return. This is like a dream come true.'

'It is for me, too, pal,' Chatterton said.

THE *SEEKER*'S SECRET lasted nearly two full hours. Around midnight, Kevin Brennan dialled his close friend, Richie Kohler, a fellow Brooklynite.

At twenty-nine, Kohler was already one of the eastern seaboard's most accomplished deep-wreck divers. He was also a passionate amateur historian with a keen interest in all things German. To Brennan, it would have been disloyal to keep such news from his friend. Kohler, in fact, would have been invited on the *Seeker* trip but for a history with Bielenda that virtually guaranteed he would not have been welcome.

The phone rang in Kohler's bedroom.

'Richie, wake up. It's Kevin. We found something really good.'

'What'd you find? What time is it?'

'That's the thing, Richie—I can't tell you what we found.'

Kohler's wife rolled over and glared. He took the phone into the kitchen. 'Look, Kevin, you can't call here at midnight, tell me you found something great, then expect me to go back to sleep. Let's have it.'

'I can't, man. Take a guess. If you guess right, I won't say no.'

So Kohler plopped down at the kitchen table and guessed. Is it a passenger liner? No. A barge? No. The guessing continued for another five minutes. Kohler rose and paced the room. Then it came to him. A U-boat.

'You found a U-boat?'

'We did.'

Kohler sat back down. 'It's gotta be the *Spikefish*!' Kohler finally exclaimed, referring to the World War II American submarine sunk in the 1960s for target practice.

'No, Richie! I was in front of it, looking up, and I could hear the music from *Das Boot*.'

'I'm calling Bill Nagle,' Kohler said. 'I gotta be on the next trip.'

'No! No! Don't do that, Richie! You can't say anything.'

Kohler finally agreed to keep the secret.

The same evening, Nagle hit the bottle in celebration of the discovery. With each sip, the notion of keeping such a secret seemed selfish, even criminal. He called Danny Crowell, a mate on the *Seeker* who, because of a business obligation, had been unable to make the trip. 'We found a U-boat,' he slurred. 'Don't tell a soul.'

The next morning, as John Yurga punched in at the dive shop where he worked, he received a call from Joe 'Captain Zero' Terzuoli, a friendly dive-boat captain. 'Yurga, hey, it's Zero. How was your trip?'

'Oh, it wasn't too bad. It was a rock pile.'

'Oh, well, you took your shot,' Zero said.

Five minutes later, the phone rang again. Yurga answered.

'This is Zero! I just talked to Ralphie, who talked to Danny Crowell, who says Bill Nagle told him it was a U-boat!'

Yurga's stomach pounded. He hung up and raced to dial Nagle before Zero could do it. 'Bill, this is Yurga. Did you open your mouth?'

'That fucking Danny Crowell!' Nagle exploded. 'I told him not to tell!'

Soon, word of Nagle's indiscretion reached Chatterton. He suggested that Nagle make several outlandish claims until no one believed any bit of it. Nagle mumbled that he would try.

TWO WEEKS was an agonising wait for divers so alive with mystery. Many did the next best thing to diving—they hit the books. Their strategy: find any submarines recorded sunk anywhere near where the mystery wreck lay. Two U-boats leapt from the pages.

In April 1944, Allied forces sank *U-550* at a location of 40° 09′ N latitude and 69° 44′ W longitude, about 100 miles north of the mystery wreck's general location. To most of the divers, the 100-mile discrepancy might be explainable. Perhaps *U-550*'s sinking location was recorded imprecisely; perhaps *U-550* had only been wounded and then limped under water to the mystery wreck site before sinking. She became the divers' odds-on favourite.

Close behind was *U-521*, which had been sunk in June 1943 in Virginia waters, about 120 miles south of the mystery wreck. As with *U-550*, the divers considered such a discrepancy to be explainable. Nagle was convinced that the submarine they had discovered was either *U-550* or *U-521*. He phoned Chatterton and asked him to drop by the *Seeker* after work.

Around dusk, Chatterton pulled into the parking lot. Nagle was on the *Seeker*'s deck, standing watch over a pile of research papers.

'John, come on board. You gotta see this,' Nagle called to Chatterton.

For the next hour, Nagle walked Chatterton through the sinkings of *U-550* and *U-521*. With each detail, Chatterton became more convinced that neither U-boat was the mystery sub. When Nagle finished, Chatterton said, 'It's not either of those U-boats. Bill, look at the reported sinking location for *U-550*. It's a hundred miles from our location. That is a huge distance—'

'The Allies must have got the location wrong,' Nagle interrupted. 'It was the heat of battle. Someone made a mistake.'

'Didn't happen, Bill. You've got three destroyers there. Are you telling me that three separate warships made three separate but identical mistakes?'

'Well then, our wreck must be *U-521*,' Nagle said.

'It's not the *521* either,' Chatterton said. 'Again, we're talking about a United States Navy ship relatively close to the coast. Are we supposed to believe that the navy can't tell if they're off Baltimore or Brielle?'

'OK, wiseass! Which U-boat is it, then?'

'I don't know. But I'm pretty sure it's neither one of those.'

A few days later, Chatterton decided to take a trip. Chicago's Museum of Science and Industry was the permanent home of *U-505*, a Type IXC U-boat captured by the Allies off Africa in 1944. It was open to the public.

'I want to walk through the submarine and feel it,' Chatterton told his wife, Kathy. 'I want to go inside it and absorb things.'

Chatterton arrived at O'Hare Airport on Wednesday, September 18. Only three days remained until the *Seeker*'s return to the wreck site. He took a taxi to the museum and followed signs to the U-boat. He stood in line alongside restless schoolchildren on field trips, vaguely interested retirees, and a few military buffs. Then he calculated how many times he might repeat this tour before his flight left for New Jersey.

John Chatterton

In ways, it amazed Chatterton that he was still alive to visit museums. He had lived a life of startling decisions, many of which he'd known could kill him. Now that he was forty years old, married, and ideally employed, his past sometimes seemed to belong to someone else.

After leaving high school he had joined the army. He told his father he didn't know where he was going, just that he had to go, that he had to see for himself. In January 1970 the army assigned Private Chatterton to the neurosurgical ward of the 249th General Hospital in Asaka, Japan. He was eighteen. The ward existed for a single purpose: to treat the horrors of the Vietnam war. Chatterton bathed patients, applied their dressings, turned them in bed as they tried to recover from damage done by cruel weapons. Many of the patients were Chatterton's age.

He liked his work—it was emotional and important. He was seeing the world. He was out of harm's way. But as he watched the parade of ruined lives delivered to the neuro ward, he began to ask questions that would not go away: What caused people to do this to one another? How is this happening to these guys? Chatterton began telling friends that he might request a transfer to Vietnam. Their response was unanimous: 'Are you crazy?' But Chatterton requested the transfer. In June 1970, he was on an airplane to South Vietnam.

Chatterton was assigned to the 4th Battalion 31st Infantry of the Americal Division. When he landed, he was told to report to the battalion aid station on a firebase near the Laotian border, a place called LZ West. He reached the firebase late that morning.

Around noon, a telephone rang on the base. A man answered, said nothing for a moment, then mumbled, 'Shit,' into the receiver. Soon everyone on the base began scrambling. An administrative officer called to Chatterton, 'Get your gear! A medic in the field just got killed getting off a helicopter. You're taking his place.' Chatterton stood and waited as men grabbed weapons and gear and zigzagged around him. He did not know what to do. A minute later, a smallish man with scruffy brown hair grabbed his arm and told him, 'Listen, I'm a medic, too. I'll get you ready to go out there.' The medic looked old, at least twenty-four. He introduced himself as 'Mouse'.

Mouse led Chatterton to a bunker on the firebase and offered to show him the ropes while he waited for the helicopter to arrive. Mouse stuffed Chatterton's aid bag with the field medic's tools—malaria pills, tetracycline, morphine, IV, tape, scissors, field dressings—and for the next two hours explained the jungle way to use them all.

A helicopter arrived. Someone shouted, 'Let's go!' Chatterton grabbed his helmet, then climbed into the chopper and the machine lifted away.

The helicopter released Chatterton and several boxes of supplies in the jungle, then disappeared back into the sky. He heard rustling behind a patch of trees, and turned to see a dozen men emerging from the jungle, men with filthy faces, long hair and scraggly beards. To Chatterton, it appeared as if a California motorcycle gang had materialised in Vietnam. As they came nearer, it seemed to Chatterton that each soldier carried the same expression: the look of a man who could no longer be surprised.

No one said a word to Chatterton. As the men finished packing the supplies, one of them grunted, 'Let's go.' They were on the move to a new location. The group walked into the jungle. Chatterton walked with them.

An hour into the jungle, shots rang out. The platoon hit the ground. Bullets polka-dotted the dirt around them. Chatterton believed his heart was going to explode. Minutes later, the men resumed walking.

The platoon spent the evening under a sweltering moon. While the others slept, Chatterton lay awake. The next day, as the temperature broke 100 degrees, the platoon arrived on the outskirts of an abandoned village. Reports indicated enemy soldiers in the vicinity.

The men in the platoon were heavily armed and none more so than John 'Ace' Lacko, a twenty-eight-year-old whom Chatterton had pegged as the platoon's top dog. Lacko, six foot two and 220 pounds, was completing his third tour, an old-timer by Vietnam standards.

The platoon came to a dried-up rice paddy that looked to provide easy passage through the otherwise hilly terrain. They entered the open area, scanning the hillside for the enemy. About fifty yards into the clearing, Lacko stepped up onto a rock to get a better view of the surroundings. Shots rang out from a hillside forward left. Five rounds tore through Lacko's left hip and travelled clear through to his right hip. Stunned, he placed his gear on the ground and lay down, partially camouflaging himself in the two-foot-high grass. Blood began flowing from his wounds.

The rest of the platoon turned back and took cover near the opening to the field behind a ten-foot pile of dirt and rocks. Someone yelled, 'Ace is hit! Medic! Medic!' Chatterton and another medic crawled forward. Lacko was in the open, a clear target.

The platoon's other medic, Chatterton's superior, hugged close to the protective cover. 'I'm not going out there,' he told Chatterton.

'I'll get him,' Chatterton said.

The platoon went silent. No one was more surprised than Chatterton. He began to remove his gear, all except for the small aid bag. The platoon took position to provide cover fire. Chatterton's vision narrowed and the jungle sounds compressed, until the only impressions in his world were his own heaving breaths and pounding heart. Now, as he readied himself to make the naked run to Lacko, he thought to himself, I'm going to find out what I am.

Chatterton sprinted into the open. A barrage of gunfire rang from the hillside far left. Bullets sprayed dirt around him, but he kept running. He could see Lacko lying in the grass. Chatterton expected to be killed, but a blur of a feeling kept him from turning back, and that feeling was that he did not want to go through life knowing that he had given up. A second later, he slid into the grass next to Lacko.

'I was lying there, and the numbness and shock were setting in,' Lacko recalled. 'And I see this new guy, and he's coming with everything he's got.'

Chatterton took cover in the grass beside Lacko. Bullets tore up the ground around them. Chatterton looked for arterial damage but there was none. Lacko could be moved. Now Chatterton had to get him back to the protection of the dirt wall, a distance of fifty yards. The wounded soldier outweighed him by fifty pounds.

Chatterton sat on the ground behind Lacko and took his arms. He began to drag Lacko backwards, all the while waiting for a bullet to strike him. Two minutes later, they were halfway to the dirt wall. By then, the platoon had pinpointed the source of the enemy fire and was beating back the attack. Soon the men were ten feet from the wall, then five feet, then behind it. Soldiers rushed to them. Moments later, two American Cobra attack helicopters swooped in and unleashed hellfire on the enemy hillside. A medevac chopper followed the Cobras in and airlifted Lacko to a hospital.

As the chopper disappeared, Chatterton collapsed to the ground. He was dehydrated and exhausted. He scarcely knew where he was. But he could see that something had changed in the men. They rubbed his shoulders. They smiled at him. They called him 'Doc'.

In the days following Lacko's shooting, Chatterton volunteered for every patrol available to the platoon. Something was rumbling inside him. He could not imagine turning away from the first thing in his life at which he had been special. Every day for the next two weeks, the men took fire. Chatterton always went to get the wounded guy. And he always went the same way: he just up and hauled ass, all six foot two of him, to hell with enemy gunfire. Soon enough, Doc had developed a reputation.

As weeks turned to months and Chatterton continued to distinguish himself, he studied himself and others in action, watched soldiers live and die and show courage and break down, all to divine further insight into the right way to live. Gradually, he distilled certain principles that seemed to him indisputable truths. As he neared the end of his six-month field obligation, he had come to believe these things:

– If an undertaking was easy, someone else already would have done it.
– If you follow in another's footsteps, you miss the problems really worth solving.
– Excellence is born of preparation, dedication, focus and tenacity; compromise on any of these, and you become average.
– Every so often, life presents a great moment of decision, an intersection at which a man must decide to stop or go; a person lives with these decisions for ever.
– Examine everything; not all is as it seems or as people tell you.
– It is easiest to live with a decision if it is based on an earnest sense of right and wrong.
– The guy who gets killed is often the guy who got nervous.
– The worst possible decision is to give up.

IN JUNE 1971, after completing his twelve-month tour, Chatterton returned home to begin a two-week leave before returning to Vietnam for a voluntary six-month extension. His mother was stunned at the sight of him. Her son would not sit in a chair or sleep on a bed but would exist only on the floor. When she asked him to speak, he said nothing for a while, then sobbed and told her about men missing the backs of their heads and screaming for their mothers, about the first time he'd killed someone, about seeing the worst things a person could see. He went quiet again after that.

His mother called a family friend with military clout. Chatterton never made it back to Vietnam. He was reassigned to the dispensary at Fort Hamilton in Brooklyn and developed a bad attitude. The army referred him to a psychiatrist, where he pretended to be what they wanted him to be until they certified him as healthy. For two years, he punched the clock, feeling angry and confused, wondering about his future, until he had completed his four-year obligation to the army.

Chatterton spent the years from 1973 to 1978 trying to find a niche. After his father died of a heart attack in 1976 at the age of forty-eight, Chatterton moved to New Jersey and started a construction business in the town of Cape May. None of this work afforded him the feeling of excellence he had realised in Vietnam, a feeling missing from his life since he'd returned to the States.

In the spring of 1978, Chatterton walked to the Cape May docks and approached an acquaintance for a job on a local scallop-fishing boat. A day later, he was at sea. Chatterton took to scallop fishing from the start, and for two years earned a handsome living and learned the sea as a scallop fisherman. He often vowed to go scuba diving, but his intense and unpredictable work schedule prevented it.

In 1980 Chatterton met Kathy Caster, a co-owner of a dockside restaurant in Cape May. While many women Chatterton knew had locked onto safe and predictable paths, Kathy's life had been creative and open-ended. She enjoyed active sports and the outdoors, and respected that Chatterton made his living on the seas. He was twenty-nine years old and was nowhere close to finding himself. When Chatterton told her he wasn't sure where he was going in life, she told him she believed in him.

Kathy and Chatterton moved in together. He bought her a .380 pistol to keep for protection while he was out at sea. At the shooting range, he admired her facility with a gun; she had never fired a weapon before, but the bull's-eyes on the targets kept exploding. This was his kind of girl.

The couple had lived together for less than a year when, in 1981, the bottom fell out of the scallop market and Chatterton's earnings plummeted. Kathy's restaurant had closed, leaving the couple financially strained. He and Kathy discussed the future. His GI Bill benefits expired in a year, so if he intended to go back to school, he needed to do it now.

Chatterton enrolled at a school in Camden which offered classes in commercial diving. He'd been in class just a few minutes before he concluded that this was indeed his calling. The instructor said commercial divers made a career of one-of-a-kind jobs, improvising and solving problems on the spot, working in hostile and rapidly changing environments.

After graduation from the four-month course, Chatterton signed on with a commercial diving outfit that worked in New York Harbor. In his first month, he made fifty dives, each unique in its challenge. In a single week, he might be asked to demolish underwater concrete or install pile wrap or weld a rusted support beam. He told Kathy, 'This job was made for me.'

By 1985, Chatterton had moved to Hackensack, New Jersey, and was earning an excellent salary as a commercial diver. He dedicated much of his free time to scuba diving, especially at one site where two small shipwrecks lay a few hundred feet offshore. The wrecks made Chatterton want to see more. He dropped in at a dive shop to enquire about other nearby shipwrecks. A clerk nodded towards a pile of fliers announcing the shop's charter schedule. Listed under trips for August was the *Andrea Doria*.

'The *Doria* is Mount Everest, buddy,' the clerk told him. 'It's only for the best. Guys die on the *Doria*. Start with something smaller.'

Chatterton signed up for charters to modest inshore wrecks. Each trip fascinated him for the history he envisioned attached to the ship. He returned from these dives so enthusiastic that Kathy signed up for diving lessons. Together, they explored dozens of nearby shipwrecks, and Kathy could have been content diving these wrecks. But Chatterton decided to work towards his scuba instructor's certificate to prepare to dive the *Doria*.

Late in the summer of 1985, a dive-shop owner suggested that Chatterton join some of the shop's more experienced divers aboard the *Seeker*, a charter boat owned and run by Bill Nagle, one of the sport's legends.

Nagle hardly grunted towards Chatterton on their first trips together, but Chatterton drank in the captain. 'What kind of man,' Nagle would growl, 'says that something's impossible? What kind of man doesn't go look?' Chatterton signed up for every *Seeker* trip available.

In 1987, Chatterton proposed to Kathy. Since he had bought her a pistol for home protection, Kathy had transformed her affinity for the weapon into a competitive shooting career. She travelled across the country to matches, and was on her way to owning several national records. The couple married on a diving trip to Key West.

A few months later, Chatterton earned his scuba instructor's certificate. He now felt ready to challenge the *Andrea Doria*. Nagle was running a five-day marathon to the wreck, for which Chatterton signed up. The trip produced several museum-quality artefacts. The *Doria* was now in Chatterton's blood.

For the next three years, Chatterton owned the *Doria*. He penetrated into third class, second class, the first-class galley—all ground-breaking achievements. He gained a reputation as one of the best shipwreck divers on the East Coast. One day Nagle paid him the highest compliment by saying, 'When you die, no one will ever find your body.'

As Nagle spiralled deeper into alcoholism, Chatterton managed much of the charter business so that the *Seeker* could remain viable. By 1991, Nagle's drinking had made it impossible for him to dive. Still, at night on the *Seeker* while customers slept, Chatterton and Nagle spoke about exploration, and about how beautiful it would be to find something new and important, something no one knew was there.

Crazy Deep

C hatterton stepped inside *U-505*, the U-boat on display at Chicago's Museum of Science and Industry. In every direction, fantastical mechanisms jutted from the walls and ceilings in a forest of technology. The roomiest spots stretched barely four feet wide and six feet tall. To pass into some sections, a crewman would have had to shimmy headfirst through a circular steel door. No one, including the commander, had a bunk that looked long enough to accommodate his body.

The audio tour in Chatterton's headphones told about life aboard a U-boat. Crewmen slept in three shifts on the ship's tiny bunks. In the forward torpedo room, the U-boat's largest compartment, perhaps two dozen men slept, worked and ate atop canned goods, containers of sausages, and up to six live torpedoes. In icy seas, overhead pipes dripped with condensation; often, the only escape from the chill was in the diesel motor room, where gargantuan twin engines pounded, creating 100-plus-degree temperatures.

Chatterton moved slowly with the audio tour, making careful mental notes. He studied the composition of shelves, components, gauges and floors. He craned his neck round machinery, looking for anything—a tag, a builder's plaque, a diary—inscribed with the U-boat's number so that he might search for the same in New Jersey. When a guide asked him to move along, he exited the U-boat and got back in line for another turn. He got in line six more times.

At O'Hare, Chatterton bought a yellow legal pad, a pen and a pink high-lighter and began sketching *U-505*. He marked in pink the places that might surrender identification tags or other useful artefacts. As he boarded the air-plane back to New Jersey, he thought, I accomplished what I came here for. I got a sense, a feeling, an impression of a U-boat.

THE RETURN TRIP to the mystery submarine was scheduled for Saturday, September 21, 1991. The crew and passenger list remained the same but for one addition and one subtraction: Ron Ostrowski had a family obligation and could not attend; Danny Crowell, a boat captain and long-time *Seeker* crewman who had missed the first trip, joined the roster.

Some divers, like Doug Roberts and Kevin Brennan, counted down the days by safety-checking their gear and fine-tuning their set-ups. Others, like Kip Cochran, Paul Skibinski and John Yurga, continued to research U-boat construction and lore, hoping for some nugget of insight that might steer them towards solving the mystery. Everyone savoured the build-up. Wreck divers spent careers dreaming of the chance to write history. These men were just three days away. Perhaps no one was more excited than forty-four-year-old Steve Feldman, a top props man at CBS's television studios and the diver who had thanked Chatterton at the end of the discovery trip.

The *Seeker* pushed away from its Brielle dock at around 1 a.m. The night was calm and made for sleeping, but everyone stayed awake for this ride. Six hours later, the *Seeker* reached its destination. The men geared up. Chatterton would splash first and tie in, then go about his dive. While the other divers intended to pick a spot and search for a tag or other piece of identification, Chatterton planned to swim the wreck, orientating himself according to his Chicago memories. Only when he understood a wreck did he believe he could formulate a plan to approach it.

Chatterton moved down the anchor line. Visibility was decent, about twenty feet. As he neared the bottom, he could see that the grapple had hooked into a metal mass lying beside the submarine in the sand. Its rectan-gular shape was unmistakable—this mass was the conning tower, the obser-vation post that was supposed to be atop the submarine. The submarine was shaped as in the photo books and lay intact except for a gaping hole in its side, perhaps fifteen feet high and thirty feet across.

He swam to the top of the wreck and then turned left, studying the boat's topography. A picture of the submarine began coming together in

Chatterton's mind. At the bow end of the wreck, he reversed course and swam the other way. He nearly reached the stern before his dive timer ordered him back for his ascent. He had got what he'd come for—knowledge. He could save exploration for his second dive.

As Chatterton made his way up the anchor line, the next divers reached the wreck. Paul Skibinski and Steve Feldman got inside the hole near the fallen conning tower and began searching the debris. Skibinski found a foot-long tubular piece of equipment he believed might be inscribed with a serial number. For the next several minutes, both he and Feldman dug in earnest, enthralled by the magnitude of promising debris. But both men had sworn to start up the anchor line after just fourteen minutes, no matter how tempting the exploration. When Skibinski's watch read thirteen minutes, he tapped Feldman on the shoulder and pointed up. Feldman nodded OK. Skibinski headed for the anchor line.

As Skibinski ascended, he glanced down for Feldman, who appeared to be examining something on the wreck. 'He better stop digging and get his ass up here,' Skibinski grumbled through his regulator before ascending another few feet. He looked down again, and this time, he noticed that there were no bubbles coming from Feldman's regulator. Narcosis started to hum in the background of his mind. Something's not right, Skibinski thought. He dropped down the anchor line to his friend.

Skibinski grabbed Feldman and turned him round. Feldman's regulator fell from his mouth. His eyes were not blinking. Skibinski looked deeper into his friend's mask, but Feldman just kept staring back, he would not blink, *a man had to blink, goddamn it, please blink, Steve*. Nothing. Skibinski tried to replace the regulator in Feldman's mouth, but the mouth just hung open. Skibinski's head pounded and he breathed harder, which made the needle on his air supply drop. He wrapped his left arm around Feldman. He would carry Feldman with him to the surface. Sometimes unconscious divers snapped out of it with ascent. Still negatively buoyant, Feldman was lead in Skibinski's arm. Skibinski pulled with all he had, gulping air as he one-armed himself and his friend up the anchor line. With each pull, Skibinski grew wearier and sucked more air. He made it to 160 feet. Then he saw Kevin Brennan and Doug Roberts, above him coming down.

Skibinski released the anchor line for just a moment. Instantly, he and Feldman began to drift away in the current. Skibinski, knowing that he was burning air and could get lost at sea in a matter of seconds, began kicking furiously to regain the anchor line, thrashing against the current until he could no longer maintain a grip on his friend. He let go of Feldman. The limp diver began sinking rapidly.

Instinctively, Roberts bolted for the body, but Feldman kept sinking. Roberts knew that by leaving the anchor line and chasing this diver, he could get lost himself. But he could not allow another man to drop into the abyss. At around 200 feet, Roberts caught hold of Feldman's harness, but the leaden diver was so heavy that both men continued to plummet towards the sand. Roberts pumped his own suit full of air, but that did not arrest the duo's plummet. Both divers hit bottom together. Roberts looked into Feldman's face. He saw no life. He could not see the wreck. He could not see the anchor line. There was only sand in every direction.

As Roberts sat on the bottom alongside Feldman, a panicked Skibinski regained the anchor line at about 160 feet. His eyes turned giant, and he rushed towards Brennan, making the slashing-across-throat motion that indicates a diver is out of air. Brennan reached for his back-up regulator and offered it to the thrashing Skibinski. Skibinski took it and started to gulp Brennan's reserve. Brennan began to ascend with Skibinski, stopping with him to do brief decompression stops, all the while thinking, I gotta go get Doug. At around thirty feet, Brennan passed Skibinski off to another diver and bolted for the bottom to search for Roberts.

Sitting in the sand with Feldman at ocean's bottom, Doug Roberts checked his gauges; he had burnt sixty per cent of his air supply struggling with Feldman. If he stayed much longer, he would incur a decompression obligation beyond his remaining air. Feldman's body lay next to him in the sand, mouth and eyes agape. Roberts thought, If I don't get out of here fast, there will be two of us dead on the bottom.

Roberts tied a line to Feldman. But his motor skills were blunted, and he could not make a good knot. Finally, he secured the line and began his ascent. At 100 feet, the first trickles of light began to penetrate the ocean around him, and Roberts saw a miracle. Somehow, he had been blown back to the *Seeker*'s anchor line, a huge long shot. He attached the thin nylon rope leading to Feldman to the anchor line, then improvised a decompression stop. Brennan reached him moments later. The two of them made their way to the surface.

Brennan climbed aboard the *Seeker* first. Chatterton and Nagle saw him coming up the ladder. 'There's a problem,' Brennan said, pulling off his mask. 'There's a guy dead on the wreck. I think it's Feldman.'

Chatterton called to Steve Lombardo, a physician, who had yet to splash, and asked him to stand by. Nagle rushed down from the wheelhouse. A few minutes later, Skibinski climbed the ladder. As he reached the top rung, he pulled off his face mask and began sobbing, 'He's dead! He's dead!' Then he pitched forward and fell face-first onto the *Seeker*'s deck. Chatterton, Nagle and Lombardo rushed to the mumbling diver. Chatterton removed the diver's hood. Skibinski was covered in vomit.

'Paul, listen to me,' Chatterton said. 'Did you do your deco?'

'I don't know . . .'

'You must answer me,' Chatterton said. 'Did you do your deco?'

Skibinski managed to nod confirmation that he had decompressed.

Roberts surfaced. 'Feldman's down there! You gotta go get him!' he yelled.

Chatterton noticed blood on Roberts's face. His medic instincts took over. 'Let me look in your mask,' he ordered. 'You might have embolised.'

Nagle took the mask. It was full of blood. Chatterton looked into Roberts's mouth and nose. The bleeding had stopped. 'I think he busted a blood vessel,' Chatterton said. 'There's no embolism. Give him oxygen.'

As he breathed oxygen and settled down, Roberts confirmed that Feldman had been without a regulator for close to thirty minutes, that he had tied Feldman to the line from his reel, and that the reel was now tied to the anchor line at about 100 feet. Chatterton gathered Nagle and Danny Crowell. 'We have to get everyone back on the boat and make sure everyone's OK. Then Danny and I will go get the body.'

Crowell nodded. He and Chatterton would have to wait until they had off-gassed enough nitrogen from their first dives to return to the water.

Two hours later, Chatterton and Crowell went to get Feldman. At around 100 feet, they found Roberts's line. Chatterton descended to retrieve the body. He reached the bottom. Connected to the line were Feldman's mask and snorkel, but no body.

Chatterton knew what had happened: in the tunnel vision of narcosis, Roberts had tied the line to Feldman's head instead of to his harness or tanks. As the current had tumbled Feldman across the sand, the line had slipped and come free. Feldman was still somewhere on the ocean bottom. Chatterton and Crowell, however, were out of time. They returned to the boat and gathered the other divers. 'Listen,' Chatterton said, 'we gotta go down and try to find this guy. He was negatively buoyant, so we know he's not floating on the surface somewhere. He's in the sand. I don't know that we can find him. But we gotta look. We gotta do sand sweeps.'

Wreck diving offers few more dangerous propositions than the sand sweep. A diver ties a line from his penetration reel to the wreck, then backs up in the direction of the current. When he reaches a distance of, say, twenty feet, he walks a 180-degree arc in the sand, searching. If the search is fruitless, the diver lets out more line, backs up farther, and sweeps a bigger arc. The diver's life depends on his line. If he loses the line, he is gone.

Chatterton asked for volunteers. John Hildemann and Mark McMahon stepped forward. Hildemann would go first. McMahon would follow.

At the bottom, Hildemann attached a strobe to the anchor line. Visibility was now perhaps thirty feet. The current blasted past his face. He paid out some line. He walked his arc and scanned the ocean floor. In every direction, he was alone. He found broken pieces of wood but nothing else.

McMahon was next. He tied his line to the top of the wreck, then backed up slowly, allowing forty feet of line to unspool from his reel. When the line went taut, he began sweeping. Nothing. He let out another twenty-five feet. Wherever he looked, McMahon saw only dirty green water. He let out another twenty-five feet. A crab popped out of the sand and spoke to him.

'Keep coming, Mark,' the crab said. 'Keep coming, man.' McMahon was startled. More crabs popped out of the sand. They all waved their claws at him. Each of them spoke perfect English. 'Over here, Mark, over here,' they said. McMahon took a deep breath. He started talking to himself. 'I gotta get outta here,' he said. 'When a crab talks, it's time to go home.'

Back on board, McMahon told the divers that he, too, had come up empty. By now, Feldman could have drifted five miles from the boat. Dusk was approaching. It was a terrible thing to leave a diver behind, and it would be crushing for his family. But Chatterton and Nagle had reached a limit. They agreed to head back to shore.

Nagle radioed the Coast Guard and reported a dead diver. It was 4 p.m.—five hours since he had first heard that Feldman had died. When the Coast Guard asked why he had not called sooner, Nagle told them he had been busy organising the underwater searches. When they asked him for the accident location, he gave them rough coordinates, within a few square miles of the site. That would keep claim jumpers, especially Bielenda, away from what rightfully belonged to the *Seeker*.

The Coast Guard ordered Nagle to Manasquan, New Jersey, where they would meet the *Seeker* at the pier. The five-hour ride was melancholy and quiet. Some divers speculated as to what had caused the accident, the consensus being that Feldman had succumbed to deep-water blackout, a not-uncommon condition of sudden unconsciousness that afflicted divers for reasons science still did not understand.

The *Seeker* arrived at the US Coast Guard Station in Manasquan Inlet at about 10 p.m. Each man was taken inside and asked to write an account of the incident, then released. Driving home that night, Skibinski thought back to a conversation he'd had with Feldman the night before. They had been discussing the trip, especially how happy they were for the opportunity. Out of nowhere, Feldman had said, 'I want to die diving, because I love it so much.'

BRENNAN RETURNED HOME after midnight. After his girlfriend went to sleep, he called Richie Kohler. 'Richie, man, it's Kevin. Something terrible happened.' Brennan could choke out only the most basic details. 'I gotta go, Richie. I'll call you tomorrow and tell you the whole story.'

Kohler hung up the phone. He felt bad for the dead diver. But he had just one thought as he climbed into bed: he had to replace Feldman on the next trip.

Brennan called back the next day and told Kohler the whole story. At the end, Kohler spoke frankly. 'Kevin, you gotta get me on the next trip.'

'I know, Richie. I'll talk to Bill today.'

Brennan pitched Kohler that afternoon. To Nagle, the idea was perfect. Kohler was smart, tough and relentless, one of the best. He had steeped himself in World War II history and knew German lore and artefacts. Ordinarily, Kohler would have been included from the start. But there were issues. Kohler had dived with Steve Bielenda. And Chatterton disliked Kohler. He was a member of the infamous Atlantic Wreck Divers, a hard-core dive gang that raised hell on the boats they chartered. They were fearless and first-rate wreck divers, Chatterton would give them that, but he despised their overriding lust for tonnage, a collective instinct to take every last piece of crap from a wreck. Nagle could forgive Kohler. Kohler had had a nasty falling-out with Bielenda and had sworn off him for ever. This dive was big and Nagle needed the best divers. He told Brennan to give Kohler the green light.

Word of Feldman's death ricocheted through the wreck-diving community. Divers everywhere now knew that the *Seeker* had discovered a submarine. As the working week began, Nagle's phone rang off the hook with requests from divers to join the team. He invited two of these divers along: Brad Sheard, an aerospace engineer and underwater photographer, and Steve McDougal, a state trooper. They would replace Lloyd Garrick, who took some time off diving shortly after the incident, and Dick Shoe, who vowed never to return to something so dangerous as this submarine. Nagle planned a return trip to the wreck for September 29, just eight days after the Feldman incident. Kohler arrived at the dock at around 10 p.m. dressed in full gang colours—denim jacket, with its skull-and-crossbones patch and *Atlantic Wreck Divers* logo.

Chatterton, already aboard and joking with another diver, turned away from his conversation and took a step towards the dock where Kohler stood. A half-dozen conversations around the boat faded to a hush. Each man shot his convictions into the other's stare. Kohler's shoulders twitched, just enough to give life to the *Atlantic Wreck Divers* patch on his back. Chatterton hated the jacket and took another step forward. Ordinarily, either of them might have pressed the plunger then. Tonight, however, neither moved farther. Feldman was just eight days dead and still missing. Chatterton returned to packing his gear, and Kohler stepped onto the *Seeker*.

THE NEXT DAY, Chatterton splashed first and tied in the grapple. His plan was trademark: shoot video, forgo artefacts, return with knowledge. He swam into the gaping hole in the submarine's side and turned his camera in all directions, careful to record the way in which the mechanical chaos splaying from the boat's wounds might catch and trap a diver. He then backed out and swam over the wreck. When his time ran out, he returned to the anchor line and began his ascent.

Kohler and Brennan followed. Immediately, Kohler recognised the wreck for a submarine. He and Brennan swam aft and above the ship until they reached an open hatch. Submarine hatches were supposed to be closed. Kohler shone his light inside. A ladder led downwards into darkness.

Someone had to have opened that hatch, Kohler thought.

Soon Kohler and Brennan began their ascent to the surface. Once aboard the *Seeker*, all the divers discussed their findings. No one, it turned out, had recovered anything meaningful.

Around noon, Chatterton dressed for his second dive. Brennan, slightly bent and achy in his joints from his dive, packed his gear away and called it a day. Kohler geared up and would make his second dive alone. He and Chatterton splashed within minutes of each other.

This time, Chatterton intended to penetrate the submarine. He swam towards the fallen conning tower, which lay beside the submarine. A single pipe connected the fallen tower to the body of the submarine. From diagrams he had seen, Chatterton recognised the pipe as one of the ship's two periscopes. He drifted inside the conning tower, where the periscope's other end remained in its protective metal housing. Chatterton recalled having seen a builder's plaque attached to the periscope housing in photographs of *U-505*. He searched for the plaque but found nothing.

He exited the conning tower and now faced the submarine's gaping hole. He swam inside and then through a small circular hatch. He finger-walked forward, meticulously avoiding the forest of jagged metal and traumatised electrical cables projecting from walls and ceiling. The water inside the submarine was still, the particulates scarce and hovering. The submarine's ribs, intact and visible, arched across the curved ceiling.

Chatterton continued forward, moving left through one rectangular doorway and right through another, until he came to an area filled with elbow-shaped pipes and cracked metal flooring. Something tugged at his memory of the sub in the Chicago museum. There might be a cabinet here, he thought. He swam left and shone his light. He stopped moving and allowed his eyes to adjust. A cabinet shape appeared before him as if from a vapour. The rims of bowls and plates seemed to protrude from the cabinet. He swam forward and reached for the china. Two bowls came loose. He brought them to his face. The fronts were white with green rims. On the backs, engraved in black, was the year 1942. Above that marking were the eagle and the swastika, the symbol of Hitler's Third Reich.

At the same time, Kohler was completing his second dive. He had swum to the open hatch inside the U-boat's hole, but by this time, Chatterton had disturbed the visibility enough so that Kohler did not dare enter. Instead, he ventured inside the conning tower and found a piece of speaker tube, the kind a crewman would talk into, but it revealed no writing. He stuffed it in his goody bag and began his ascent.

Chatterton checked his watch and saw that it was time to go. He was exuberant as he ascended. He would give Nagle one of these bowls. The look on the captain's face would be priceless.

For nearly an hour, both Chatterton and Kohler ascended and decompressed. At thirty feet, Chatterton caught up to Kohler and settled just below him. Kohler angled his head sideways to steal a glimpse at Chatterton's bag. Kohler could not contain himself. He released the anchor line and drifted down to Chatterton. The unmistakable bone white of china seemed to light the ocean around Chatterton. Kohler's face flushed, and his heart pounded. There was history in Chatterton's bag; he could smell it. He reached for the bag.

Chatterton snatched the bag away and turned to block Kohler. Their eyes locked. Neither moved for what seemed like minutes. But as Chatterton searched Kohler's eyes, he could not find anything sinister in them. The man was just flat-out excited to see the china. Chatterton pushed the bag forward. Through the mesh, Kohler could see the eagle and swastika, and he erupted, screaming through his regulator, 'You did it! I can't believe this!' For a minute, he danced like a child, twirling and kicking and punching Chatterton in the arm. Now there was no doubt: the divers had discovered a German U-boat.

Chatterton did his best to block Kohler's celebration punches as the two ascended to their next stop. On board the *Seeker*, Nagle held the bowls and could barely talk. The other divers slapped Chatterton's back and snapped photos of him holding the bowls.

As the *Seeker* steamed home, Chatterton and Kohler found themselves sitting together. The trip had overwhelmed Kohler. It had brought together, in a single day, his passions for naval history, submarines, exploration and artefacts. For a while, he and Chatterton discussed the U-boat. 'You know, this was the most exciting dive of my life,' Kohler told Chatterton. 'The whole thing was once in a lifetime. But the part I liked best was the time we spent in the water just looking at those dishes. For a while, you and I were the only people in the world who knew this was a U-boat. The only two in the world.'

Chatterton nodded. He understood what Kohler meant. He could tell that Kohler was not talking about diving now; he was talking about life, and he thought it would not be a bad thing to get to know this man better.

Richie Kohler

If ever a person had been born to dive a virgin U-boat, that person was Richie Kohler. His father, Richard, was of German descent while his mother, Frances, had her roots in Sicily. The Kohlers lived in a close-knit Italian and Jewish neighbourhood in Brooklyn. Both parents aimed to instil their sense of culture in their three children, and especially in Richie. As the Kohlers raised him, they noticed that something unusual was going on with their boy. He read voraciously, but not the kiddy stuff typical of first graders. Instead, he studied *National Geographic*, war histories, particularly German history, and anything concerning outer space.

As the owner of a glass business, Richie's father worked long hours, but he made certain to spend time with his children on weekends. If Richie wanted to be with his dad, however, he would have to do so on his dad's terms, which meant on the boat. Richie's father loved to fish and often they fished shipwrecks. While they watched their poles, Kohler told his son that row after row of wrecks lay beneath them courtesy of the German U-boats. 'Can you believe that, Richie?' his father asked. 'The Germans came right here. Look, you can see the Verrazano Bridge. That's how close the U-boats came.'

One year, as the boating season drew to a close, Richie's father decided to learn scuba. At home, Kohler allowed Richie to assemble and disassemble his tank and regulator. He threw the equipment to the bottom of the family's above-ground back-yard pool, then told Richie to swim down, assemble it, and begin breathing.

When Richie was eleven, his father finally took him diving in the dock where the boat was kept. The New York water was dotted with Styrofoam cups and cigarettes, but Richie could hardly believe the beauty beneath the surface—horseshoe crabs crawled by, minnows darted, and a jellyfish drifted past on the current. He had penetrated another realm.

By the time Richie turned twelve, his parents had separated. One night in 1975 Frances took her three children to Florida where she eventually set up home near her mother's house. Richie did the rest of his growing up in Florida. At the age of fifteen, he and a friend signed up for scuba classes and earned their junior certification. After that, they dived constantly, spearing fish and even tangling with sharks. Richie thrived on the feeling of independence that came with spearfishing.

At high school he pulled A's and B's, but during his junior year started drifting to the rowdy crowd. Richie and four football teammates decided to pull a prank on some seniors by setting their gym clothes on fire through the metal grates in their lockers. The school pressed charges. In court, the judge told the boys that if they stayed out of trouble, the record would be expunged. After that, Richie kept clean.

As the year wore on, the boy began to think about his future. An idea took shape in his mind. He could join the navy. In that way, he could live on the water, travel the globe, and maybe work aboard a submarine. Late in

Richie's junior year, a US Navy recruiter visited his high school. The man told Richie there were officer-training programmes available to the highest scorers on the Armed Services Aptitude Test. Those programmes guaranteed training in a recruit's area of choice, including submarines. Richie signed up for the test and scored at the ninety-eighth per centile. The navy said they would love to have him. Richie and his mother signed the papers.

After graduating from high school, Richie and several dozen other new recruits were taken by bus to a Florida naval air station for induction. The recruits were sworn in. Richie was a member of the United States Navy.

Later that day, an officer called Richie into a room and asked him to sit down. The officer explained that they had found a record of Richie's high-school arson incident. The navy had no intention of allowing anyone connected to arson to serve on board a navy ship. A few hours later, Richie was on the street, disorientated and heartbroken. He had been a member of the United States Navy for a day. He wandered around for the next few days, taking stock of his life, and decided to move back to New York to work for his father.

For three years, Kohler worked long hours to build the mirror division of his father's company. Not once did he touch his dive gear. One day he was called to a window-repair job at a scuba shop on eastern Long Island. While working, he noticed a photograph of a diver on a shipwreck. Kohler asked the shop owner, a man named Ed Murphy, about the photo.

'That's the *Andrea Doria*,' Murphy said.

Kohler had read books about the *Andrea Doria*. This was not the kind of wreck Kohler had seen in Florida. The *Doria* looked like a Hollywood shipwreck, with intact rooms and echoes of life and tragedy.

'I want to dive that,' Kohler blurted out.

'Oh, no, no, no,' Murphy scolded. 'The *Doria* is something you work up to. It's only for the best divers. But I got a group of customers going out this weekend to a wreck called the USS *San Diego*. It's a World War I cruiser lying in the sand at a hundred and ten feet. You can come along.'

That weekend, Kohler set sail for the *San Diego*. When the dive boat reached the wreck site, he began to gear up. The other divers sniggered and coughed. Kohler had no gloves, no hood, no boots—just a wet suit that did not even cover his arms.

A minute into the dive, Kohler was shivering. The green-grey water was no more than fifty degrees. When he reached the wreck, he realised it was upside down, or a 'turtle'. He swam along the side and finally found a compartment open to the ocean. Kohler had no training in digging or excavation. He just stuffed his hand into the silt and came out with dozens of bullets. Amazing. His body began to shake from the cold. He checked his watch—he had been down only five minutes. He began his ascent lest he die of exposure. On the way up, he stared at the bullets. The ammunition had travelled directly from World War I into his hands. He was hooked.

After that, Kohler began to buy proper Northeast wreck-diving gear. He signed up for all the dive shop's charters. Diving was back in his bloodstream. On one *San Diego* dive, he squeezed through a rotted hole into a room black with oil. In zero visibility, he filled his green mesh bags with china, lanterns, telescopes and bugles, then divvied up the bounty to colleagues topside. The dive earned him notice in enthusiast magazines.

One day, Murphy told Kohler about a group of divers that he believed to be Kohler's kindred spirits. They were fearsome, Murphy said, in their appetite for artefacts and their reputation for hard living. But they were also among the best divers on the eastern seaboard. 'They dive crazy deep, Kohler,' Murphy said. 'They go places no one else goes. They're your kind.'

Murphy invited the gang on one of the dive shop's charters. Kohler signed up, too. Murphy made the introductions. The group of six men each had at least ten years of deep-wreck diving experience. They were loud and rowdy aboard the boat, but on the shipwreck they were transformed. Kohler watched as the gang melded into a single entity, flashing hand signals and lining up for what was obviously a plan. He felt he could watch these men work for ever.

The gang did not like outsiders, but they liked Kohler. Over the next year, they threw an education into Kohler which a diver could not purchase for any price. The men stripped Kohler of his civilian equipment and outfitted him in the gear of the great wreck diver. Then they stripped him of old thinking. They pushed him to study deck plans and photographs to determine a wreck's meatiest locations; divers who dug blindly never bagged up like a man with knowledge. They preached a group ethos whereby the gang worked together and shared the spoils. Kohler took in every word.

One day on the way back from a dive, the divers' discussion turned to solidarity. If the gang could add members and organise themselves, they could charter their own boats, saving money and dictating destinations. One by one, the men on the trip said, 'I'm in.' The gang would need an official name. Someone suggested 'Atlantic Wreck Divers'. Perfect. How about matching denim jackets with skull-and-crossbones patches? Beer flowed. Oaths of loyalty were sworn. The Atlantic Wreck Divers had been born.

Around the time Kohler became an Atlantic Wreck Diver, he heard through the grapevine that his father was dating Richie's ex-girlfriend. He confronted his father, who admitted it was true. Richie was devastated. That day, he removed his possessions from the basement at Fox Glass. It would be years before he would see his father again. Now he had to find work. A glass salesman tipped him to a company paying top dollar and looking for someone with his experience. Four months later, he was the company's foreman.

Over the next two years, Kohler worked hard and provided a vision for the company. The owner rewarded the effort by making Kohler a partner. Life was good again. During summers, he committed to the Atlantic Wreck Divers.

Around this time, Kohler met Felicia Becker, a pretty sales clerk for one of his customers. She understood his passion for diving. They married in the fall of 1989, and shortly after the wedding, Felicia became pregnant. One night that year, Kohler stopped for dinner at a restaurant in Brooklyn. He was alone. As he sat at the bar, he felt a slap on his back. It was his father. The two had neither seen nor spoken to each other in five years. The elder Kohler asked if he could sit down. Richie told him he could. 'You're going to be a grandfather,' Richie said. His father did not even know his son had married. Richie and his father spent hours catching up. Neither man mentioned Richie's old girlfriend. His father proposed that they become business partners and open their own glass company in New Jersey, and Richie accepted.

In 1990, Kohler and Felicia celebrated the arrival of their first child, a son. Kohler worked gruelling hours, then devoted his free time to Atlantic Wreck Divers. Often the vessel the gang had chartered was the *Wahoo*, Steve Bielenda's boat.

For a while, Kohler had no problem using the *Wahoo*, but eventually he clashed with Bielenda. Now Kohler needed a new boat to get to the *Doria*. He had dived several times with Nagle on the *Seeker* and had long admired Nagle. Kohler signed up for several *Seeker* charters in 1990 and 1991. Though Chatterton was practically running Nagle's business by then, he and Kohler never found themselves together aboard the boat.

In the fall of 1991, Kohler heard word of the virgin U-boat discovery. The news stopped his life. For days, he was a blur of longing and desire, distracted from family and friends. Then Brennan called and said, 'You're in,' and the words lifted Kohler back across the thousands of pages he had read about World War II, and he knew that he had to be part of this U-boat.

Horenburg's Knife

The swastikas on the dishes Chatterton recovered from the U-boat reached through time and gripped his imagination. A person could spend a lifetime studying Nazis and U-boats, and, in the end, it was all just information. The dishes were heavy. The swastika's angled arms rubbed rough against a person's fingertips. No one had touched this china since the U-boat fell. The dishes had travelled from Hitler's Third Reich directly to Chatterton's living room.

Ordinarily, the *Seeker* would have been back to the submarine the next week—the men were sure that with another dive or two, the U-boat would surrender her name—but it was now hurricane season. Landlocked, Nagle renewed his vow to get sober and work his body back into diving shape for next season. Chatterton returned to his research. If he could not penetrate the wreck from the ocean, he would try to get inside it through history.

Chatterton was not the only man engaged in serious investigation. From his home in New Providence, New Jersey, Kohler barrel-rolled into his collection of U-boat books, devouring titles past midnight even when his glass company demanded that he be fresh before dawn.

The divers had put in dozens of hours of research, and one fact screamed above all the rest: no U-boat had ever been recorded sunk within 100 miles of the wreck site. To Chatterton, it seemed as if his research was moving backwards. Then he hit upon an idea: Why not put out news of the U-boat discovery to the world? Surely there were historians or experts who knew the wreck's identity. The *Seeker* would still enjoy the glory and fame of discovery, and Bielenda and others would be precluded from claim-jumping the wreck, and the mystery would be solved through the *Seeker*'s research. Chatterton pitched Nagle on writing a press release. Nagle loved the idea.

Chatterton mailed the release with Nagle's phone number to all the media outlets he knew on the 10th of October. A day passed without a reply. Then a few days. Several days later, Nagle's phone rang. He referred the call to Chatterton. It was from a reporter at the Newark *Star-Ledger*. The man sounded uninterested.

'So, you supposedly found some mysterious U-boat, huh?'

Chatterton said that he had. The reporter asked more questions. By the end of the conversation, the reporter asked if he might visit Chatterton's home. A day later, he was there taking notes and handling the china. He said he thought the story might be good enough to run on page one.

The next morning, Chatterton walked to the end of his driveway and picked up the *Star-Ledger*. At the bottom was a headline: *U-boat Wreck Found Off Point Pleasant*. Alongside the story was a photo of Nagle and Chatterton inspecting the dishes. The *Star-Ledger* story unleashed a media frenzy. That evening, Nagle's and Chatterton's phones rang nonstop with interview requests from radio, television and print reporters. CNN sent a crew.

Chatterton's phone now rang relentlessly. His mailbox overflowed. Many of the contacts came from people who claimed to know the identity of the U-boat or the explanation for its sinking. Sons and grandchildren swore that loved ones had sunk a U-boat on a secret mission that the government refused to acknowledge. Others claimed to have classified U-boat information.

Early on, Chatterton received a letter from the German embassy in Washington, DC. It was written by Dieter Leonhard, a captain in the German navy. The letter began cordially, acknowledging Chatterton's discovery and offering assistance in researching the wreck. Further down the page, however, Leonhard made plain Germany's position:

> The Federal Republic of Germany retains ownership of the submarines, regardless of the present position of the wreck. Sunken German warships are principally defined to be 'tombs of a seaman's grave'. Diving and exploring the wreck is therefore not permitted. To keep a wreck a tomb, the FRG prohibits any violation to a World War II submarine and will enforce this condition through legal means.

Chatterton called Leonhard and told him that he had received the letter and would be grateful for assistance with documents and research. Leonhard said he would be happy to help. Chatterton then popped his big question.

'Do you know the identity of the wreck?'

Leonhard said that the German government often relied on a man named Horst Bredow at the U-boat Archive in Cuxhaven-Altenbruch, Germany, as a repository for such information. He offered Chatterton the contact information. Then Leonhard reiterated what he had written in the letter—that Germany did not permit diving on sunken U-boats.

'I'm going to be honest with you,' Chatterton said. 'I want to be respectful.

My goal is to identify the wreck, to put a name on the tombstone. I'm going to continue diving it until that happens.'

'You understand our position, Mr Chatterton. We do not want divers descending on this U-boat and scattering any human remains,' Leonhard said. 'We cannot and will not allow that.'

'I understand that, and I don't intend to allow it to happen,' Chatterton said. 'You have my word on the matter.'

By now, Chatterton understood Leonhard's position. The man could not formally grant a diver permission to explore a war grave. He sensed, however, that Leonhard would not make official trouble for him so long as he treated the wreck with respect.

About a week after the first U-boat story appeared, Chatterton had several promising leads. One of the first came from Harry Cooper, the president of a group based in Florida 'dedicated to preserving the history of the *U-Bootwaffe*,' as their motto read. Cooper sounded eccentric, but the man asked questions no one yet had: Does your wreck have saddle tanks? Does your wreck have two stern torpedo tubes or only one? The answers could easily be gleaned while diving, Cooper explained, and would reveal much about the U-boat's type and the year it might have sailed. Chatterton resolved to inspect the wreck for that information on the next dive and report back to Cooper with the answers.

Chatterton also drove to the Naval Weapons Station Earle in Monmouth County, New Jersey, and showed a videotape of the wreck to experts there. They arrived at this consensus: the damage to the U-boat's control room looked to be caused by explosion rather than by collision; the explosion most likely occurred from outside the submarine; and the damage was likely caused by a force far greater than a depth charge.

'We can't be certain,' one of the men said. 'But if we had to guess, we would guess it was damaged by a direct torpedo hit.'

Driving home, Chatterton turned the idea over in his mind. Who would have fired such a torpedo? An account of an American submarine that had sunk a U-boat would have made every history book on the subject, yet there had been no such incident anywhere close to the wreck site. Could another U-boat have mistakenly sunk a friend? One thing was certain: the idea that a U-boat had limped from some other location with such an injury seemed far-fetched. To Chatterton, whatever had blown up that U-boat had done it at just the place in the ocean where the divers had found it.

The *Star-Ledger* story was barely a week old, and already Chatterton had gathered reams of information from sources great and small. The best, however, were still to come. One piece of information emerged at a meeting at Nagle's house attended by Nagle, Chatterton and Major Gregory Weidenfeld, a Civil Air Patrol historian who had contacted Nagle. The CAP were a group of civilian pilots organised in 1941 to fly small, privately owned airplanes to help defend coastal shipping. Weidenfeld explained that over the course of the war, the CAP had detected more than 150 subs and had dropped depth charges on several of them.

'We sank two U-boats,' Weidenfeld said. 'But we never got credit.'

'I've read about those incidents,' Chatterton said. 'You guys believe the navy didn't want to credit civilians.'

'That's right,' Weidenfeld said. 'The navy didn't want to acknowledge it, because it would have terrified the public to think that average civilians were needed to fight the U-boats and that the U-boats were coming so close to our shores. Anyway, one of the kills was off the Florida coast. The other was in New Jersey.'

Chatterton got out his pen. Weidenfeld told the story: 'On July 11, 1942, two of our pilots in a Grumman Widgeon spotted a U-boat about forty miles off the coast just north of Atlantic City. The guys chased the U-boat for four hours, until it began to rise to periscope depth. When it finally surfaced, they dropped a three-hundred-and-twenty-five-pound depth charge, and the bomb exploded. They could see an oil slick streaking on the surface where the sub had been. They dropped the other depth charge right into the oil slick. It was a kill, absolutely. The pilots are both dead now. But I've been working for years to get my guys credit for this. I think you found their U-boat.'

Weidenfeld had provided an exact date and a location only about twenty-five miles from the wreck site. If Chatterton could find a list of U-boats lost in American waters in July 1942 he might find a way to explain its movement to the wreck site and solve the mystery. He thanked Weidenfeld and promised to do all he could to resolve the question.

AT AROUND THE SAME TIME, a phone call came in from a collector of Nazi memorabilia. 'I correspond with a lot of U-boat commanders,' the man told Chatterton. 'One of them is Karl-Friedrich Merten, the eighth-most-successful U-boat ace of World War II. He read your story in a German newspaper and has some information to share with you, if you'd provide your address.'

'Absolutely,' Chatterton replied.

Over the next few weeks, letters arrived from Germany. In them, Merten thanked Chatterton and the divers for their efforts. He also told a singular tale. His colleague Hannes Weingärtner had also been a U-boat commander and, like Merten, had been promoted to training flotilla commander, a prestigious land-based position. Weingärtner, however, still had battle in his blood and, at the advanced age of thirty-five, walked away from the desk and back down through the hatch of a U-boat. His assignment: to take *U-851*, a Type IXD2, or 'U-cruiser', U-boat designed for the longest-range patrols, to the Indian Ocean to carry supplies to Far East German bases and deliver cargo to the Japanese navy. The assignment, Merten speculated, might not have been what Weingärtner had in mind. He believed Weingärtner to have been 'a submariner of the first hour', meaning that the man's instincts to aggressively hunt and kill enemy ships had never withered.

Merten reasoned that the tameness of Weingärtner's assignment might have prompted his colleague to head towards New York. 'I myself am pretty sure that the wreck you have found will be that of *U-851*,' Merten wrote.

AS CHATTERTON CONTINUED to field the rush of phone calls and letters, he got word that Bielenda had secured the exact location of the U-boat wreck site, and was planning to hit the wreck any day. Worst of all, the numbers were said to have come from Nagle.

The plan, as Chatterton heard it, was this: Bielenda had organised a mission to the wreck site to recover Feldman's body. Another captain had offered his boat for the trip; Bielenda was to supply the divers, who would search the area for the corpse. Chatterton doubted that Bielenda or the others would make even a perfunctory search for the body. He called Nagle at home.

'Ah shit, John. I gave up the numbers,' Nagle admitted.

The way Nagle explained it, he had received a late-night phone call from another dive-boat captain and long-time friend. Nagle had been drinking. The captain had announced that he had three sets of numbers and knew one of them to be the U-boat's location. Nagle listened as the captain recited the numbers. The captain was right—one of the sets was correct. Nagle suspected that Bielenda had wrung the general location from his Coast Guard cronies, then had asked this captain to check his voluminous book of numbers for anything close. Now the captain was leaning on him to reveal the exact location. In his stupor, still guilty over Feldman's death and the

Seeker's inability to bring the diver home, Nagle mumbled something about location number two 'possibly' being correct.

A few days later, Bielenda and several divers made the trip. Some of the divers did, in fact, make a good-faith search for Feldman. Others just dived the wreck. No one saw a corpse but many went home that night with an overriding impression: This wreck is going to eat people.

ON A MONDAY in early November, the skies bathed New Jersey in sunlight. The sight rejuvenated Nagle, and he called Chatterton.

'We can make it to the U-boat one more time,' Nagle said. 'We can identify this thing Wednesday. Are you in or out?'

'Have I ever been out?' Chatterton asked.

Nagle and Chatterton made phone calls. The trip was planned for November 6, 1991. Since Feldman's death, a pair of the divers from the original trip had decided not to tempt the U-boat again. Everyone else was in. Two empty bunks remained. Nagle called some legends. Tom Packer and Steve Gatto were perhaps the most formidable deep-wreck diving team in the region. They told Nagle they were coming to identify the U-boat.

The divers gathered on the *Seeker* near midnight. Memories of Feldman still arched over the boat. Lying in their bunks at opposite ends of the salon, Chatterton and Kohler mentally rehearsed their dive plans. Chatterton would use his first dive for two purposes. First, he would follow the advice of Harry Cooper and inspect the submarine for saddle tanks, the externally affixed compartments primarily used for fuel in Type VII U-boats. If he had time, he would also look to see if the submarine contained two stern torpedo tubes. Cooper had suggested that a U-boat so configured was most likely one of the larger Type IX models, while the Type VIIs contained just a single stern torpedo tube. For his part, Kohler had the eagle and swastika in his crosshairs. He was going straight for the dishes.

Chatterton dressed early the next morning. He, Packer and Gatto would set the hook, then dive the wreck first. They would enjoy pristine visibility but would create silt clouds for subsequent divers, making artefact recovery more difficult. Kohler got wind of the plan. He stormed the stairs to the wheelhouse, where Chatterton was shooting the breeze with Nagle.

'Bill, what the hell is going on with this guy?' Kohler asked, pointing to Chatterton.

'What's wrong, Richie?' Nagle asked.

'The visibility. I'm going forward for dishes. He went first last time. Let me go first today.'

'John's going to videotape,' Nagle said. 'He needs clean water to shoot in.'

'Why does he automatically splash first? He eats all the good visibility while the rest of us get silt. Where's our fair shot?'

'John's going first,' Nagle said. 'There's plenty of room on the U-boat, Richie. Go somewhere else on your first dive.'

Kohler shook his head and returned to the deck. He hated Nagle's decision but would respect the word of a captain on his own boat.

The water was calm when Chatterton, Packer and Gatto splashed. They tied in to the wreck just above the damaged control room, then parted ways. Chatterton swam along the side of the submarine, searching for the saddle tanks. He saw none. This was good evidence that the submarine was not a Type VII—the most common of the World War II U-boats. He would inspect the stern later; to swim that distance now would consume valuable dive time. Instead, he would enter the wreck in the control room below him and videotape his push towards the forward torpedo room.

The control room, for all its devastation, looked like home to Chatterton. He had studied videotapes of his last dives, memorising formations and openings, and he saw order in the chaos. He glided between dangling cables through the control room, pointing his camera in every direction, until he passed the commander's quarters on the port side and the sound and radio rooms to the starboard. He moved past the galley to the officers' quarters, where he had found the dishes. Now it was time to push to the forward torpedo room, the U-boat's forwardmost compartment.

Video camera raised high, Chatterton inched ahead. A wooden partition materialised before him—the path to the torpedo room was blocked by a fallen piece of cabinetry. Chatterton swam closer. He allowed the water around him to still. Slowly, he raised his right arm to shoulder level and opened his palm, then held the position motionless, as if he were a python about to strike at prey. When everything in the compartment settled, he raised his right arm to shoulder level, opened his palm and thrust his arm forward, crashing his hand into the partition. The wood exploded, spitting a cloud of debris about the room. When some of the visibility returned, Chatterton could see the circular hatch leading to the torpedo room at the front end of the U-boat. He moved forward.

Now he hovered in the noncommissioned officers' quarters, the place where crewmen like the navigator, chief machinist and senior radioman slept. He scanned the debris and sediment on the floor area for the familiar white of china. He saw something white. He moved closer, until the white became a round shape with eye sockets and cheekbones and an upper jaw. This was a skull. Chatterton stopped. Beside the skull lay a long bone, perhaps a forearm or shin, and beside it several smaller bones. If men had attempted to flee this U-boat, at least some of them had never made it out alive.

Now Chatterton faced a decision. Pockets, boots and other personal effects were the likeliest places to find a wristwatch or a wallet inscribed with a crewman's name. But if he searched for personal effects, however carefully, he might disturb the human remains, and he was not willing to do that. This was a war grave, and whatever the politics or justness of a country's cause, a soldier deserved respect in death. He also understood that he might someday have to answer to a family about the bones before him, and he was unwilling to say that he had shuffled those remains in order to identify a shipwreck and maybe gain himself a little glory.

Chatterton kicked his fins and moved forward. A moment later, the forward torpedo room took shape in the distance. Chatterton swam into the compartment. Two torpedoes lay poised and pointed forward. Only the top two of the room's four torpedo tubes were visible; the other pair lay underneath several feet of silt and debris. Chatterton knew from research that the torpedo-tube hatches were sometimes marked by identifying tags. He also recalled that the torpedo men often wrote the names of girlfriends and wives on the outside of the hatches. He swam forward and searched for such evidence, but any trace of a tag or writing on the hatches had been eaten away by time and sea water. Chatterton panned his camera round the room in slow motion, capturing as much detail as possible.

The postscript to Chatterton's entrance was a swirling black silt that reduced visibility to zero. To leave the wreck, he would have to follow a map that existed solely in his brain. Chatterton exited through the control room, swam towards the flashing strobe he had clipped to the anchor line, and began a ninety-minute ascent to the surface.

Still steaming over Chatterton's dibs on the U-boat's forward section, Kohler decided to explore aft instead. Remembering an area of damage on top of the wreck's stern, he wondered if he might gain entrance to an unexplored section there. His instincts were excellent. The damaged area had been blasted open by some external force, and it left enough room for a courageous diver to drop in. As Kohler settled into the wreck, he detected the outline of two adjacent torpedo tubes in the haze of his white light. At once he understood where he was and the implication of his discovery: this was the aft torpedo room inside what was definitely a Type IX U-boat, the kind built for patrols of long range and duration. Though Chatterton had intended to inspect the stern torpedo tubes himself, Kohler had beaten him to it. In just a half-hour, the two divers had answered the two most important technical questions about the mystery U-boat.

Kohler shone his lights about the room. Under some fallen debris, he found a metal tag and an escape lung, the combination life vest and breathing apparatus used by crewmen to escape a submerged U-boat. Kohler's pulse raced. These were just the kinds of items that often bore identifying marks. But any writing that might have been embossed on the tag had been eaten away by nature. The lung came up blank as well. Kohler packed the items in his goody bag and began swimming aft to get a closer look at the torpedo tubes.

Kohler never got to the tubes. During his swim, a white object came into view. It was a femur. Kohler went cold. He had never seen bones on a wreck before. Kohler backed away several inches, and in his movement, the silt swirled and buried the bone as quickly as it had been revealed. He decided it was time to return to the *Seeker*.

CHATTERTON WAS THE FIRST to return to the water for his second dive a few hours later. His goal was to search the area around the galley and the noncommissioned officers' quarters for cabinets that might contain the ship's logbook or other written materials.

Chatterton had little trouble reaching his target area. He began digging, feeling around for cabinet shapes. He found none, but he did run his hand along a smaller object he took to be a box. A moment later, he unearthed the item from beneath a pile of silt. It appeared to be a silverware drawer, about eleven inches by eight inches, with sections for knives, spoons and forks. A gelatinous black mud had cocooned the drawer and sealed its contents. Chatterton saw the outline of spoons in one of the sections. He nestled the drawer into his bag and turned back for the anchor line. Perhaps there might be a date stamped on one of the utensils inside.

Not long after Chatterton had departed the sub, Kohler entered. He navigated through the last remnants of Chatterton's haze and into the noncommissioned officers' quarters. He poked through sediment and debris and found a four-inch-tall cologne bottle imprinted with a German word, *Glockengasse*, which he took to be a brand name. But he had not come for cologne; he had come for dishes. He resumed his search in earnest, running his hand through silt and sediment the way a child works a sandbox. He found nothing. He dug farther. As he cleared some debris, he came upon what he could only describe to himself as a boneyard. 'I'm standing in a mass grave,' he told himself. 'I need to leave now.' He packed the cologne bottle in his bag, then turned round and manoeuvred back out of the U-boat.

Up near the surface, Chatterton clipped his goody bag to a line attached to the boat—he dared not climb the *Seeker*'s ladder in bouncy seas holding such delicate bounty. On board, he undressed and dried, then fished his bag from the ocean. Divers gathered to inspect the haul. Chatterton took the silverware drawer from his bag and reached into the gelatine. A methane smell of rotten eggs and petroleum burst from the artefact.

The first items out were silver-plated forks, stacked one atop another. The forks had been consumed so fully by electrolysis that all that remained was the rice-paper-thin shape of the fork. Nagle stepped forward. He had seen this kind of artefact before and understood that the slightest jolt could cause it to crumble into powder. He reached forward, took the forks, and, without breathing, separated each from the others and laid them on the table. Each of the forks was stamped on the underside of its handle with the eagle and swastika. Nagle moved them around delicately, searching for any other identifying mark. When he found none, he backed away and began breathing again.

Next out of the drawer came several stainless-steel spoons. They bore no marks. That left only one section of the silverware drawer: the knives. Chatterton looked closely. Only one utensil appeared to be in that section, a knife with a stainless-steel blade and wood handle. He fished into the remaining gelatine and pulled out the knife.

The knife was covered in mud. Chatterton dunked it in a bucket of fresh water and began rubbing the handle between his thumb and forefinger to remove the dirt. As the mud flaked away, he began to feel the imprint of letters beneath his thumb. He dunked again and rubbed harder. Carved into the knife's handle, was a name: Horenburg.

For several seconds, no one moved. Finally, Brad Sheard stepped forward and clapped Chatterton on the back. 'Well, that's it, man,' Sheard said. 'You've identified the U-boat. All you have to do is find crewman Horenburg. Congratulations.'

'This might be the best artefact I've taken from any wreck,' Chatterton told the divers. 'This guy actually carved his name into the knife. It's not like a tag that was made in a factory. This is like a personal message.' By this time, Kohler had climbed aboard the boat. He and the other divers took turns inspecting the knife and congratulating Chatterton, each of them gracious but also disappointed that he had not been the one to identify the wreck.

AS THE *SEEKER* steamed back to shore, Chatterton came and sat beside Kohler. For a while, neither spoke. 'Richie,' Chatterton finally said, 'I don't need to be the first one to splash every time. If you don't mind setting the hook, you're welcome to go first next time. But remember, tying in is a gamble. If you run into trouble, you can blow your whole dive while you fix things.'

Kohler said, 'I respect you. I just want a fair shot.'

Again, neither spoke for a few minutes. Then Kohler began to tell Chatterton that the U-boat meant more to him than the chance to load up on Nazi artefacts. He explained that he had been buying and reading books like a man possessed since his first trip to the wreck; that while he was eager to recover artefacts from this U-boat, he also found himself capti-vated by the history of the U-boat war and the men who had fought it. To Chatterton, these were not the typical leanings of an Atlantic Wreck Diver.

'Listen,' Chatterton said, 'I got a lot of calls and letters after the media got hold of this story. I think you might find some of them interesting.'

For the next three hours, Chatterton regaled Kohler with news of the last few weeks. Kohler gulped the information and asked endless questions. As night fell and the *Seeker* made its way into the inlet near Brielle, Chatterton asked Kohler for his address.

'You going to send me something?' Kohler asked.

'I'd like to send you the videotape I shot today, and some others,' Chatterton said. 'You have to promise me that you won't show them to anyone or let them out of your hands. I think they can help you navigate the wreck. I'm going to trust you with this.'

'Thanks, man,' Kohler said, jotting down his address. 'You have my word.'

That night, Chatterton took the knife he had discovered and placed it on his desk. The name Horenburg looked as clearly carved as the day the crew-man had inscribed it. 'Who were you?' Chatterton asked as he gazed at the knife. 'Just another day or two,' he said to himself. 'Just another day or two and I'll have the answer to the mystery of the U-boat.'

Nothing at That Location

The morning after Chatterton recovered the knife, he set out to find Horenburg. To this end, he wrote a letter detailing his discovery and mailed it to Karl-Friedrich Merten, the U-boat ace in Germany; Charlie Grutzemacher, curator of the International Submarine Document Centre in Deisenhofen, Germany; and Horst Bredow, founder of the U-boat Archive in Cuxhaven-Altenbruch, each of whom he believed could trace Horenburg and thereby identify the mystery U-boat.

For his part, Kohler continued to rampage through historical texts, learning the patrols of America-bound U-boats. In these pursuits—Chatterton with the knife, Kohler with the books—each was answering to more than a mystery. Each believed that once the U-boat was identified, he had a responsibility to the families of the fallen soldiers and to history to explain why the U-boat was in American waters, and how it had met its end.

Just after Christmas, Chatterton received replies from Merten, Bredow and Grutzemacher. Each of them had reached the same conclusion: there had been only one Horenburg in the German navy—Martin Horenburg, a *Funkmeister*, or senior radioman, in the U-boat service. His last patrol had been aboard *U-869*, a U-boat sunk by Allied forces off Africa in 1945. That U-boat's entire crew had been killed in the attack. It was the only patrol *U-869* had ever made. It had happened 3,650 miles from the mystery wreck site.

Perhaps there had been another Horenburg his sources had overlooked. Chatterton had heard about a U-boat memorial in Germany inscribed with the names of U-boat veterans killed in action. If he travelled to Germany, he could inspect that memorial, visit the U-boat museum, and look at Bredow's archive himself. He checked his calendar. March would be a good month.

Chatterton invited Yurga and Kohler to accompany him to Germany. Yurga accepted. Kohler, who ran his own business, could not free himself for the week-long expedition. But the invitation moved him. 'I'll keep my end going here,' Kohler told Chatterton.

As the March trip approached, Chatterton received a telephone call. An elderly gentleman introduced himself as Gordon Vaeth, a former intelligence officer for the Atlantic Fleet airships during World War II—the blimp squadrons. He had read of the divers' discovery and asked about any research Chatterton had undertaken. Chatterton told him.

'If you'd like to come to Washington, I would be happy to introduce you to the heads of the Naval Historical Center,' Vaeth said. 'Maybe they can help you find what you're looking for.' Chatterton could scarcely believe his good fortune. Vaeth had been on the spot for antisubmarine warfare—in intelligence, no less. And he had connections at the NHC. If anyone knew the answer to the mystery, it had to be the American government.

A few days later, Chatterton made the four-hour drive to Washington, DC. He was due to meet Vaeth at the Naval Historical Center at 10 a.m. He arrived early and made his way to the NHC building. Inside, a snowy-haired man in a tweed jacket introduced himself as Gordon Vaeth.

Vaeth outlined his plan for the visit. He would introduce Chatterton to Bernard Cavalcante, the head of operational archives and a world-renowned U-boat expert, and to Dr Dean Allard, the director of the centre.

Vaeth then escorted Chatterton into Cavalcante's office. Cavalcante, a slightly built, middle-aged man in a checked sports jacket, emerged from an adjacent room. He greeted the men warmly but with a cocked eyebrow, as if to say, 'Oh, jeez, another U-boat nut in my office.'

The men sat down, and Vaeth asked Chatterton to tell his story.

Chatterton was direct and economical. He and other divers had discovered a World War II U-boat about sixty miles off the New Jersey coast. They had recovered artefacts proving as much, yet had not been able to identify the submarine. The divers had shot videotapes, a compilation of which he had brought along.

For a moment, there was only silence. Cavalcante looked to Vaeth, then to Chatterton. 'We are the United States Navy, sir,' Cavalcante said. 'We know a good bit about what lies in the ocean. We have an accounting of shipwrecks off the East Coast. We track this for military reasons—not for historical reasons, not for researchers or . . . if you'll excuse me, for divers. We have this list here. But I cannot show it to you. I'm sorry.'

Chatterton's heart sank. 'Mr Cavalcante, I don't have to see the list,' Chatterton said. 'I'm just interested in this particular wreck at this particular location. Putting a name on this grave is the right thing to do for the families, and it's the right thing to do for history. There are dozens of dead sailors down there, and no one seems to know who they are or why they are there.'

Cavalcante nodded slightly. 'Well, I suppose I can look it up,' he said.

'But you cannot have any photocopies of the information, and you cannot take any photographs with you.'

'That's fine. Thank you,' Chatterton replied. He wrote down the U-boat's latitude and longitude and handed them to Cavalcante, who excused himself and disappeared into a fortress of documents. Vaeth grinned and gave Chatterton a nod that said, 'Nice going.' The answer was moments away.

Several minutes later, Cavalcante returned, a massive binder under his arm. He looked at Chatterton with that cocked eyebrow again.

'Are you sure about that location?' he asked.

'Positive,' Chatterton replied. 'We've been there three times.'

'Well, we do not have anything at that location. Let's take the videotape to Dr Allard and watch it together. He has to see this. I have to tell you, Mr Chatterton, we hear from a lot of people who believe they've discovered a U-boat. It's almost always nothing. But this is just fascinating.'

Cavalcante ushered Vaeth and Chatterton into a stately office. The men were greeted by a middle-aged man with wavy pepper-and-salt hair, a bow tie and a tweed jacket. The man introduced himself as Dr Dean Allard, director of the centre. Cavalcante launched into the story. Mr Chatterton, he said, had found a U-boat off the New Jersey coast: location definite, vintage definite, casualties definite, videotape available.

Cavalcante paused a bit for effect. 'Here's the thing, Dr Allard,' he continued. 'I've checked the books. There's nothing there.'

Allard nodded slowly. As Cavalcante prepared the videotape, Allard called William Dudley, his second-in-command, into his office. Soon the five men viewed scenes of Chatterton moving about the conning tower, then into the torpedo room. Various murmurs—'Fascinating,' 'Unbelievable,' 'Astonishing'—wafted through the office until the tape had finished.

'I can't believe there's a World War II German U-boat out there and we don't know anything about it,' Allard said. 'Mr Chatterton, if I can get a navy ship and divers to go to your location, would you be willing to work with the navy to identify this U-boat?'

It took Chatterton a moment to process the magnitude of the offer. Allard was offering the resources of the United States Navy to solve his mystery. He could only utter, 'Definitely!'

Dudley stepped forward. 'Dr Allard, I'm sorry. We can't do that,' he said. 'As you know, the US has filed a complaint against France in international court over the Confederate ship *Alabama*. The heart of that case is that the

French are diving on an American warship we argue has protection for being a war grave. We can't at the same time be diving a German war grave in America.'

'Well, you're right, Bill,' Allard said. He turned to Chatterton. 'I'm disappointed. But if we can't actively go out there and help you with the diving, Mr Chatterton, we can still provide you with whatever you need in terms of research assistance here.'

Vaeth and Cavalcante then showed Chatterton to the archives, where they introduced him to Kathleen Lloyd, an archivist who would assist him. Chatterton thanked Cavalcante, then disappeared with Lloyd and Vaeth into a research area. There, Lloyd told Chatterton about four critical research tools available to him. Each struck Chatterton as a revelation. They were:

– Antisubmarine Warfare (ASW) incident reports: a daily chronology of underwater contact between Allied forces and enemy vessels
– Eastern Sea Frontier War Diaries (ESFWD): a daily chronology of interesting activity or observations made by Allied personnel
– BdU KTBs: a daily summary written by German U-boat Control (BdU) detailing U-boat activity around the world
– Individual U-boat files: dossiers of US Navy-compiled information on specific U-boats

Lloyd suggested that Chatterton begin by searching the ASW incident reports, checking for any Allied underwater engagements in the area of the mystery wreck site. If he found any, he could request detailed files about those incidents. She brought him the first boxes labelled 1942. (The US entered World War II in December 1941.) Vaeth wished him luck, and left.

Chatterton sat down and opened the first box of 1942 ASW incident reports. He began at January 1 and skimmed the page for latitudes and longitudes within a fifteen-mile radius of the wreck site.

Several hours later, he finished with 1942. He had scanned more than a thousand incidents. None of them had occurred within a fifteen-mile radius of where the mystery U-boat lay. He was due home that night. He called his wife and told her he would be staying another two days. The next morning, he was first in line at the archives, asking for '1943'.

Chatterton made his way through every incident report for the entire war. Not a single Allied force had engaged a submarine within a fifteen-mile radius of the wreck site.

TWO WEEKS LATER, Chatterton and Yurga landed in Germany. The divers bought a large bouquet of flowers, then headed to the U-boat Memorial in Möltenort, near the port city of Kiel. Here, listed on eighty-nine bronze plaques, were the names of the 30,000 U-boat crewmen killed in action in World War II, each according to the submarine on which he died. Freezing rain needled into the divers' necks. For three hours, the men traced their fingers down plaques to the letter H, in search of Horenburg. They could find only one—Martin Horenburg, the *Funkmeister* who had perished with his crew on *U-869* off Africa, just as the experts had said.

That night, Chatterton placed a call to Merten. He knew that Merten had recently taken ill, but he hoped the eighty-six-year-old U-boat commander might be well enough to receive visitors. A young person answered the phone and apologised: Herr Merten could welcome no visitors; the once-great U-boat ace did not wish anyone to see him in such a weakened condition.

That left Bredow's U-boat Archive in Cuxhaven-Altenbruch. By this time, Chatterton had come to understand more about this unusual private repository. A U-boat veteran, Bredow had converted his own home into the archive, cramming files, photos, records and mementos next to his kitchen and beside his appliances. The operation had come to be viewed by the German government and by historians as the country's premier U-boat archive.

Chatterton and Yurga rang the doorbell as the clock struck 9 a.m. A short, balding, bespectacled sixty-eight-year-old man with a white beard opened the door. Above Bredow's shoulder, they could see filing cabinets standing sentry over the house, artefacts in glass cases, and dozens of framed photographs of U-boat crewmen.

'All the answers you are seeking are here. You need go no other place!' Bredow exclaimed, spreading his arms. 'But first, before I give you the answer, I shall show you the archives.'

For the next ninety minutes, Bredow took the divers through every room in the house. Finally, Bredow sat behind a desk and asked the divers to sit across from him. He took a typewritten scrap of paper from inside a drawer and pushed the paper across the table, face down.

'Here is your answer,' Bredow said.

Chatterton's hands shook as he received it. He turned over the paper. On it, Bredow had typed the names of seven U-boats. Chatterton went numb. This was a list of U-boats lost off the American East Coast, a list available in public-library books. These were the U-boats the divers had eliminated first.

Chatterton took a deep breath. 'There are problems with all these boats, sir,' he said. 'It cannot be any of these.'

'It must be one of those boats. Your location must be wrong.'

'No, sir,' Chatterton said. 'The location we gave you is very accurate. We have returned to it many times.'

Bredow's forehead furrowed. 'You can look through my files if you like,' he said. 'I do not know what else to say.' With little left to do, Chatterton and Yurga began to copy crew lists of every Type IX U-boat sent to America's eastern seaboard. Two hours later, they had done all they could.

In the hotel that night, Chatterton bought a postcard for Kohler. On it, he wrote, 'We know more than they do. We must go back to the wreck.'

AFTER CHATTERTON returned to the States, he phoned Yurga and Kohler and called a meeting at his house. It took Kohler all of eight minutes to reach Chatterton's place. The two had lived five miles from each other for years and had never known it. In Chatterton's living room, Chatterton and Yurga briefed Kohler on the Germany trip.

'I gotta say, this is a mystery like you read in a book,' Kohler said afterwards. 'A U-boat comes to our doorstep in New Jersey. It sinks with maybe sixty guys on board, and no one—no government or navy or historian—has a clue that it's even here.'

Chatterton recounted his research in DC. 'I went through the entire war, page by page,' he said. 'Not a single thing happened anywhere near our wreck site during the entire war. Nothing.'

Kohler paced the room. 'You know the stories you read about how the Nazis tried to smuggle gold out of Germany at the end of the war? Or even the stories about how Hitler fled in a U-boat as Berlin fell? Well, think about it. If our U-boat was used for something like that, there wouldn't be any record, would there?'

'Whoa! Whoa! Whoa!' Chatterton and Yurga called out from the couch. 'Are you saying Hitler might be on our U-boat?'

'What I am saying is that we need to start conceiving of scenarios that might explain why no one in the world has a clue that this U-boat and these dead crewmen are in New Jersey. If we don't consider every possibility, the answer might slip right past us.'

Chatterton, who had returned from Germany deflated, basked in the innocence and single-mindedness of Kohler's resolve. Kohler stood his ground and kept his eyes locked on Chatterton's, nodding ever so slightly, as if to say, 'We can do this.' Chatterton found himself nodding back.

'OK, it's about scenarios,' Chatterton said. He reminded the divers that two theories remained strong. First, that the U-boat had been sunk by the Civil Air Patrol on July 11, 1942. Second, that the wreck was *U-851*, the submarine Merten believed his maverick friend had taken to New York in violation of orders. Two months remained until dive season began. The divers would use that time to return to DC and research these theories.

A FEW DAYS after the caucus at his house, Chatterton returned to the NHC in Washington. On his first visit, he had searched the historical records for any activity that might have occurred within fifteen miles of the wreck site. He had come up empty. This time, he would expand that search to a thirty-mile radius, then to a sixty-mile radius. The research lasted four days. He found nothing. Not a single event had been recorded within sixty miles of the wreck site.

On his next trip, made with Yurga, Chatterton turned his attention to the Civil Air Patrol theory. He posited a basic question: Had Germany sent any U-boats to the American East Coast during early July 1942, when the CAP claimed to have sunk one off New Jersey? The answer would lie in the BdU KTBs, the diaries kept by German U-boat headquarters. Chatterton requested those diaries from the research room.

Bingo. Several U-boats, it turned out, had been hunting in American waters then. According to the diaries, all but two of those U-boats, *U-157* and *U-158*, had returned safely to Germany. Both *U-157* and *U-158* were Type IXs, just like the U-boat the divers had found. Chatterton requested the attack reports associated with the sinkings of *U-157* and *U-158*.

According to the navy, *U-157* had been sunk northeast of Havana on June 13, 1942, by a US Coast Guard cutter, killing all fifty-two men on board. The incident had happened nearly 2,000 miles from the divers' wreck site. The attack report was ironclad. *U-157* was not the mystery U-boat.

He next checked the attack report for *U-158*. That proved more interesting. On June 30, 1942, an American amphibious airplane spotted *U-158* off Bermuda, with perhaps fifteen of its crew suntanning on deck. As the submarine crash-dived, the pilot dropped two depth charges, one of which lodged inside the U-boat's conning tower—a nearly impossible bull's-eye. As the U-boat submerged, the bomb detonated and, according to the report, destroyed the submarine. There was just one witness—the attacking airplane—and no debris had been spotted or recovered. That left the possibility that *U-158* had not been sunk where it had been attacked. Chatterton copied the documents and placed them in an envelope marked *RICHIE*. Kohler would be the perfect man to investigate the last days of *U-158*.

ARMED WITH THE ATTACK REPORT for the sinking of *U-158*, Kohler set out for Washington to do his own research. Rather than duplicate Chatterton's work at the NHC, Kohler went instead to the National Archives and Records Administration, storehouse for the majority of America's most important records, including many naval documents. He had learned that many of the captured German records resided with the National Archives.

At the sign-in desks in various research rooms, Kohler requested information on *U-158*. Staff members brought stacks of files and boxes of microfilm. Much of the information was in German. He kept at it, copying reconstructed logs from *U-158*'s doomed mission and diaries from its earlier patrols in hopes of seeing into the mind of Erwin Rostin, its commander.

A few nights later, Kohler called a meeting at Chatterton's house. With Chatterton and Yurga settled on the couch, he wove a singular tale from his research. On June 30, 1942, as they knew, an American amphibious airplane patrolling off Bermuda had dropped a depth charge directly into the conning tower of *U-158*. According to the pilot, when the U-boat dived to escape, the bomb detonated and sank the submarine, killing everyone aboard.

'But what if,' Kohler asked, '*U-158* is only injured? Or she escaped damage completely? Let's say her conning tower is damaged, but she still is able to move. What would she do? I say Commander Rostin thought to himself, "I'm within striking range of New York City. I'm going to New York to sink American ships with my deck guns." He gets as far as New Jersey when the Civil Air Patrol spots him and lets him have it. Now *U-158* is really wounded. She hobbles forty miles before the conning tower finally separates and she sinks—right at our wreck site. The Civil Air Patrol never gets credit, because the first airplane claimed the kill.

'I'm going to tell you about that commander,' Kohler went on. 'His name was Erwin Rostin. A few months before this, on his first war patrol, he sank four ships. On this patrol, the guy sank thirteen ships. Rostin is so unstoppable, they award him the Knight's Cross by radio while the U-boat is still at sea! Rostin is not limping home, no way. He's only a thousand miles from New York. He's still got enemies to kill.'

It was Chatterton's turn to speak. He acknowledged that Kohler had made an intriguing case for the wreck being *U-158*. Now it was time for him to make the case for the wreck being *U-851*, the boat commanded by Merten's colleague Weingärtner.

'Merten knows his man,' Chatterton said, 'and he is convinced that he came to New York. That's why there's no record of *U-851* in our wreck area—the boat was ordered to the Indian Ocean. Weingärtner disobeyed the orders. When he disappears, Germany presumes he sank where they'd sent him.'

Now it was Yurga's turn. He specialised in the technical end. 'We've got two favourites,' he said. 'It sure looks like it's gotta be one or the other. I know how to settle it. According to my research, *U-158* was built with a deck gun. But some Type IXs were not. Next time we hit the water, we look for evidence of a deck gun. If our U-boat was built without one, it can't be *U-158*. Period.

'Now, as to *U-851*. It was a Type IXD2, a special model they called a U-cruiser. U-cruisers were about thirty feet longer than typical Type IXs. All we need to do is drag a tape measure across the wreck. If it's two hundred and eighty-seven feet, it's a U-cruiser. If it's shorter, it ain't *U-851*.'

The divers shook hands and called it a night.

A Heavy Toll

The season's first trip to the U-boat was scheduled for May 24, 1992. By now, the divers had taken to calling the wreck *U-Who*, but no one expected the mystery to last much longer. Especially Chatterton. Between research trips to Washington, he had messed with voodoo.

For decades, scuba divers had breathed good old-fashioned air from their tanks. In recent months, however, a group of cutting-edge warm-water divers had ditched air in favour of a mixture of oxygen, helium and nitrogen known as 'trimix'. As Chatterton heard it, trimix offered a fantasyland of advantages: sharpened motor skills, longer bottom times, shorter decompression times, reduced risk of oxygen toxicity and deep-water blackout, and elimination of narcosis.

Imagine working the U-boat without the pounding, narrowing fear of narcosis, and being able to do it longer, better and safer than ever. When a Florida diver offered a trimix workshop in New Jersey, Chatterton and Yurga rushed to sign up.

Kohler, however, stayed away. He believed that if something sounded too good to be true, it was. Chatterton and Yurga attended anyway. Attendees received a binder with photocopied articles and tables. The principle behind using trimix—known as technical diving—struck Chatterton as sound. By replacing some nitrogen with helium, you could diminish your risk of nitrogen build-up, the culprit for so much of what goes wrong in air dives. The benefits were said to be quantum leaps in safety and productivity.

But there were downsides. First, there were no technical diving classes or certification agencies; a diver experimenting with this new art was on his own. Second, divers could make just one dive per day, not two as was customary, because the intricacies of off-gassing helium while topside were not fully understood. Third, because divers breathed a separate gas, called 'nitrox', during decompression, they had to add nitrox tanks to their rigs, thereby carrying more gear. Fourth, northeastern dive shops did not stock trimix; if a diver wanted the stuff, he had to mix it himself. Finally, there existed almost no dive tables to instruct a technical diver on how long to decompress. It would be a matter of improvisation and experimentation.

Chatterton was willing to pioneer. In January 1992, he and Yurga set out to mix their own gas. For weeks, they mixed gases in Chatterton's garage. Soon they were expert at preparing the mixture of 17 per cent oxygen, 30 per cent helium, and 53 per cent nitrogen that they hoped would revolutionise their diving. They purchased dive tables, then used imagination and daring to extrapolate those tables so that they might make two dives in a single day. They purchased new and larger scuba tanks.

In February, while the divers were brewing their own trimix, word arrived from the Coast Guard: a fishing boat about 100 miles off Atlantic City had pulled up a human body dressed in a diver's dry suit. The Coast Guard identified the corpse as Steve Feldman. His body had been recovered perhaps five miles from the U-boat. He had been missing since September.

When the weather warmed, Chatterton and Yurga took the new rigs with their newfangled gas and splashed in a Pennsylvania quarry, adjusting buoyancy and learning to breathe the magic gas. In the quarry's shallows, their minds remained crystal clear, their coordination precise. The bottom of the Atlantic, however, would be another matter.

On the evening of May 23, 1992, the divers gathered at the *Seeker* for the season's first trip to the *U-Who*. Everyone asked trimix questions of Chatterton and Yurga. Kohler was among the last to show.

A few minutes later, Nagle emerged. Few had seen the *Seeker*'s owner since the end of last season, when he had vowed to quit drinking and work himself into diving shape. It took a moment for the divers to process the sight. Nagle's skin was spotted with jaundice, his hair greasy, his body like a rumpled suit on a wire hanger. He had brought along no dive gear.

In the wheelhouse, Nagle and Chatterton took turns steering. Chatterton updated Nagle on the latest developments on the two favourites, *U-158* and *U-851*, and how Danny Crowell and Yurga planned to measure the wreck and search for evidence of a deck gun, two simple tests that would pronounce on these original theories. Nagle stared straight ahead. For several minutes, he said nothing.

'The *Seeker* is bigger than me,' Nagle said finally. 'Diving is bigger than me. The *Seeker* will go on long after I'm gone.'

Chatterton said nothing. Ocean mist spattered the windshield. Nagle continued to steer a course for the *U-Who*.

The divers woke the next morning to a glorious day. The sun shone, and the ocean was glass. Chatterton and Kohler began dressing. They had decided weeks before to dive together and now rehearsed their plans. Chatterton knew from his research that torpedo-tube hatches were supposed to contain on their faces a tag bearing the U-boat's number. On his first dive, Chatterton would slither into the forward torpedo room, videotaping his navigation for study topside. On the second dive, he would return, penetrate to the end of the torpedo room, and remove the tags from the hatches. With any luck, the tags would reveal the wreck's identity. The plan was classic Chatterton: tape, study and return. For his part, Kohler planned to explore the stern, searching the aft torpedo room for torpedo-tube hatch tags and any other useful artefacts. Measuring the wreck would be left to Crowell. Yurga would search for evidence of a deck gun.

Chatterton and Kohler splashed just after sunrise. Neither had seen the Atlantic so still and limpid. Chatterton's trimix flowed into his lungs and brain, as theory had promised, keeping his thinking sharp and the enemy narcosis at bay. At 100 feet, in this miraculous visibility, they could see the submarine end to end. But for the mortal wound to its side, it looked ready for war. The divers descended to the wreck and secured the grapple. Kohler watched Chatterton for signs of delirium or other symptoms that might occur when one dabbles in the black art. Chatterton smiled and gave him the OK. The divers went their separate ways.

Chatterton made his way into the control room, through the commander's quarters, and into the noncommissioned officers' quarters. Again he saw piles of human remains. This time, after a winter's research, he felt a connection to the bones, as if he were returning to the home of a family he had known. He felt as if the men might not mind his efforts to find their names.

Chatterton corkscrewed himself through more obstructions, dodging hanging wire and jagged metal until he arrived at the forward torpedo room. He videotaped the inside of the room. After a few minutes of filming, he turned back, made his way out of the wreck, and ascended to the surface.

At the stern, Kohler worked into the aft torpedo room and began to search for artefacts. He spent twenty minutes searching but found nothing. Once back on board the *Seeker*, he and Chatterton compared notes. Each had been in the water for about ninety minutes. Chatterton's trimix, however, had enabled him to stay on the wreck for thirty minutes, while Kohler had stayed only twenty-two before needing to decompress.

By this time, Crowell was preparing to splash and measure the wreck, and Yurga was dressed and ready to dive for evidence of a deck gun. Yurga had brought along a customer from the dive shop where he worked, a physician named Lew Kohl, who had also outfitted himself to breathe trimix.

'You sure about him?' Chatterton whispered to Yurga.

'He's used trimix on some shallower dives this year. He says he's ready. And I'll be diving with him,' Yurga replied.

Kohl adjusted his mask, bit down on his regulator, and flopped sideways off the gunwale. Chatterton and Kohler could not believe what happened next. Rather than bob to the surface, as most divers do after the splash, Kohl plummeted like an anchor towards the ocean bottom. The topside divers knew at once what had happened: Kohl had not adjusted the buoyancy for his new trimix equipment. He had become what divers called a 'dirt dart'.

The furious increase in water pressure squeezed the dirt dart's suit into a second skin. Rapid compression would cause his regulator to free-flow, explode his sinuses and blood vessels, burst his eardrums, and induce vomiting and vertigo. And that was before he hit the bottom. But Chatterton could see that Kohl was still breathing—he could see his bubbles.

'Look at his bubbles. He's wandering around looking for the wreck, which means he's alive,' Chatterton said. 'Yurga, I'm going to give you a line. Follow his bubbles and go get him. Richie and I cannot get back in the water now.'

Yurga splashed. But as he spiralled downwards round Kohl's bubbles, Kohl managed to drop his weight belt. Now positively buoyant, he began to ascend. At 150 feet, however, he ran out of gas—nothing was coming from his regulator. At that point, he lost interest in proper dive protocol. Kohl decided to rocket towards sunshine. Seconds later, he broke the surface.

'Now he's a Polaris missile!' Kohler shouted. 'He's gonna be bent for sure if he lives.'

Kohl began flailing and thrashing on the surface. But he was not vomiting or trembling, evidence to Chatterton that he had not yet been seriously bent. 'He's only been in the water maybe ten minutes,' Chatterton yelled. 'He's got a chance.'

Tom Packer and Steve Gatto dived into the ocean, dragged him up the ladder, and put him on the dressing table. 'Get me a stethoscope and the crash kit,' Chatterton ordered. Kohler cut off Kohl's dry suit. He took Kohl's vital signs and began recording dive information doctors would later need. As he made notes, he asked, 'Lew, are you in pain? Lew, can you hear me?'

Kohl could not respond. Chatterton told Nagle to call the Coast Guard rescue chopper. He shoved aspirins down Kohl's throat, forced him to drink massive amounts of water to reduce the gas volume in his blood, and put an oxygen mask over his face. He used the stethoscope to listen for the gurgling of an embolism in Kohl's blood vessels. A minute later, Kohl began to come round, almost as if he had been reanimated in a mad doctor's laboratory.

The divers continued to comfort Kohl and keep him stable on oxygen and water. With each minute, Kohl seemed healthier. Several minutes passed. Nagle poked his head from the wheelhouse and announced that a Coast Guard chopper was en route.

'Ah, jeez, I'm really sorry, guys,' Kohl said. 'Everyone's trip is on me. I pick up the tab for everyone.'

Chatterton smiled and allowed another diver to stay with Kohl for a while. He then moved to the back of the *Seeker* to help Yurga climb aboard. Nagle cut the anchor line and headed to meet the Coast Guard helicopter. Kohl continued to improve. The chopper took him away. He would suffer joint pain as a result of the bends but would recover fully. The divers had lost the most perfect day any of them had ever seen. The season, however, was young.

NAGLE BOOKED the next *U-Who* trip for June 9, 1992. Dr Kohl had had enough of the U-boat for one lifetime. He was replaced by two divers unlike any Chatterton and Kohler had known before.

Chris Rouse, thirty-nine, and Chrissy Rouse, twenty-two, were father and son, though with their identical wiry builds and Mediterranean features, the men were often mistaken for brothers. They smiled a lot. They argued even more. The Rouses bickered incessantly, flinging insults at each other at the slightest provocation. Chatterton and Kohler watched in amazement. Yet the Rouses were excellent technical divers. When they hit water, they remained absolutely loyal, each willing to sacrifice himself for the good of the other. When Nagle had invited the Rouses to join the *U-Who* expedition, Chrissy vowed to solve the mystery.

'They're more than talented and capable enough to do it,' Chatterton told Kohler. 'They may be the ones who get this done.'

The weather for the June trip was not nearly as perfect as it had been in May, but the divers' plans remained the same: Chatterton would search the forward torpedo tubes for numbered tags; Kohler would hunt for identifying artefacts; Crowell would measure the wreck; Yurga would determine if the *U-Who* had been built with a deck gun. As for the Rouses, they would penetrate the wreck and begin to learn the U-boat.

As before, Chatterton and Kohler dived together and set the hook. This time, Kohler swam forward with Chatterton, his eyes scanning the areas where crewmen kept records and personal belongings. Chatterton moved into the torpedo room, and up against the torpedo-tube hatches. He saw a white, tag-shaped patch of encrustation on the hatch. He grabbed his knife and prised the blade under the encrustation. White flakes fell away, revealing the perfect outline of a tag. Except no tag remained. Corrosion had eaten away the metal. Chatterton's heart sank. He inspected the other three torpedo-tube hatches. Same story.

Just behind Chatterton, Kohler was having better luck. While in the non-commissioned officers' quarters, he discovered a closetful of boots and shoes, still lined up neatly, just as the crewmen had left them. He took one of the boots, believing a crewman might have written his name inside.

While Chatterton and Kohler decompressed, Crowell and Yurga set about their missions. To measure the wreck, Crowell attached one end of a surveyor's tape measure to the U-boat's bow, then swam aft, allowing the tape to unspool from its reel as he moved. He had affixed a tag to the tape at the

250-foot mark, the length of the typical Type IX. If this U-boat was any longer than that, it would be powerful evidence that the wreck was *U-851*.

Crowell allowed the line to unspool slowly as he began his journey along the wreck's top. Line spun free of the reel. As the tip of the U-boat came into view, the reel hiccupped. Crowell looked down. His marker had come up. The wreck was about 250 feet long. U-cruisers were 287 feet long. This could not be *U-851*.

While Crowell prepared to ascend, Yurga settled in just forward of the control room. He knew exactly where to look for the deck-gun mount, a feature of *U-158*. Yurga crab-walked along the top of the wreck. He surveyed the relevant area. The evidence was plain as day: this U-boat had been built without a deck-gun mount. This wreck could not be *U-158*. In the course of twenty minutes, the divers' two leading theories had been sunk.

The men regrouped topside. Each seemed more shell-shocked than the next. A winter of research had come to naught. They halfheartedly inspected the inside of the boot Kohler had recovered. Befitting the day, it contained no information. The Rouses surfaced. Neither father nor son had found much of significance. Chatterton and Kohler made another dive but found little. As the boat headed back to Brielle, the divers knew that summer was upon them, meaning that Nagle would begin running the *Seeker* to the *Andrea Doria*, his money trips. None of them knew when the boat might again be available to take them to the *U-Who*.

THE DAY AFTER returning from the *U-Who*, Chatterton wrote a letter to Karl-Friedrich Merten. He explained that divers had measured the wreck and determined that it could not be *U-851*. Merten wrote back expressing gratitude for Chatterton's efforts. Chatterton did not phone Major Gregory Weidenfeld of the Civil Air Patrol; though the divers had ruled out *U-158*, they still allowed that the wreck might have fallen to the CAP.

For the next three months, Nagle ran to the *Doria*, and even when he had an open date for the *U-Who*, the weather interfered. Chatterton still could not believe that the sub's torpedo-tube hatch tags, which he had thought were made of resilient brass, had been eaten away. He tracked down an elderly U-boat veteran in South Carolina who had also built U-boats in Germany's naval yards. The man explained that as brass had become scarce, tags had been made of leftover materials, a metal stew that could not survive long in the marine environment.

'One other thing, if I might,' the old U-boat man said.

'Of course. What is it?' Chatterton asked.

'Thank you for what you are doing. Thank you for caring about those boys down there. They don't have anyone else.'

It took three months for the *Seeker* to set sail again for the *U-Who*. In September, the divers had to make the most of their opportunity. The weather would be unpredictable come fall. Optimism aboard the boat was muted this time. Chatterton and Kohler had exhausted their leading theories. Their disappointment, however, did not extend to the Rouses.

'I'm going to identify the wreck,' the junior Rouse told Chatterton. 'I'm going to be the one to do it.'

As before, Chatterton and Kohler splashed together and tied in the anchor. This time, Chatterton swam towards the stern and dropped into the blown-out deck section that led to the aft torpedo room. His research had revealed that this room contained an auxiliary steering station possibly marked by a brass tag. But when he began to look round, he saw a boot, then a life jacket, then several skulls, and other remains. Chatterton turned and swam out.

Kohler, in the meantime, had chosen to explore forward. As he entered the NCO's quarters, he spotted the cuff of a dark blue shirt that appeared to have spilt from a cabinet. Since it lay far from the human remains in the compartment, Kohler felt comfortable tugging at the shirt. Black silt billowed from the cuff. When the cloud cleared, he saw an arm bone in the sleeve. He let go of the shirt and apologised aloud, saying, 'I'm so sorry. I had no idea.'

Chatterton and Kohler's second dive was equally unproductive. The Rouses, however, had better luck. In the galley, Chrissy had discovered a canvas-like fabric imprinted with German writing.

'I don't know what the words mean,' Chrissy later told Chatterton and the other divers topside. 'All I know is, I gotta dig the thing out. It's stuck in there. But it looks important. I think I can get it on the next trip.'

IN EARLY OCTOBER 1992, Nagle booked the *Seeker* for the season's final journey to the *U-Who*. It would be a two-day venture.

The day before the trip, Nagle called Chatterton and begged off.

'I just don't feel like it,' Nagle grunted.

'Bill, this could be the time. We need you,' Chatterton said.

'Don't you get it?' Nagle exploded. 'After I'm dead, nothing matters!'

Chatterton had seen this transformation building all summer. Nagle had begun the season reflectively, taking comfort in the idea that even if he were unable to sober up and rebuild himself for diving, the *Seeker*'s legacy would outlive him. Now sicker than ever, a failure at countless rehabs, he could not bring himself to take his own boat to one of the biggest dives ever.

'You and Danny take the boat,' Nagle said. 'Go without me.'

On the night of October 10, the divers gathered at the *Seeker*'s Brielle dock. No one had to ask why Nagle was not in the wheelhouse.

While the other divers tied down their gear, the Rouses began their bickering. This time their argument was more serious than usual. Neither father nor son could afford trimix for the trip so they would be forced to breathe air—a saving of a few hundred dollars.

The next morning, Chatterton and Kohler splashed first. While Kohler explored the NCO's quarters, Chatterton returned to the forward torpedo room in search of more tags. On the way out, he spotted a bent piece of aluminium about the size of a tabloid newspaper lying amid a pile of wreckage. Ordinarily, he would have ignored such junk. This day, something urged him to pluck it from the garbage and drop it into his bag.

Topside, Chatterton emptied his bag. The aluminium piece, splotched with marine growth, clanged onto the dressing table. Yurga walked over to inspect it. Chatterton opened the bent metal as if it were a magazine. Engraved on the inside were technical diagrams—a schematic illustrating the mechanical operations of some part of the U-boat. Chatterton grabbed a rag from a bucket of fresh water and wiped it across the artefact. The sea growth lifted easily, revealing small German inscriptions along the tattered bottom edge. Chatterton pulled the schematic towards his face. He read, 'Bauart IXC,' and 'Deschimag, Bremen.'

'Hold everything,' Yurga said. 'Deschimag-Bremen was one of the German U-boat construction yards. That means this wreck was a Type IXC built at Deschimag-Bremen. There couldn't have been more than a few dozen Type IXs built there during the entire war. This is huge for our research.'

That evening over dinner, as the *Seeker* rocked in the waves while anchored to the U-boat, the Rouses admired the schematic and told Chatterton about their day. They had nearly excavated the piece of canvas covered in German printing and believed they might be a dive away from bringing it topside. Optimism echoed off the salon walls. In a single day, a season of dead ends had transformed itself. But that night, as men slept aboard the *Seeker*, the ocean turned the vessel into a bathtub toy, tossing some divers from their bunks. The forecast had changed for the worse. At 6.30 a.m., Chatterton walked down to the salon and roused the divers.

'It's getting nasty out there,' Chatterton said. 'Anyone thinking of diving best get going now. After that, we're pulling the hook and going home.'

'You diving, John?' someone asked.

'Not on a day like this,' Chatterton said.

Of the fourteen divers on the trip, just six moved from their bunks to gear up. Kohler was first to roll into the ocean. The dive team of Tom Packer and Steve Gatto followed, as did New Jersey State Trooper Steve McDougal. The Rouses also rolled out of bed.

'I'm not diving, forget it,' Chrissy said. 'Too rough out there.'

'If you can't dive these conditions, you got no business being out here,' Chris said. 'I can't believe you're my son. You're an embarrassment!'

'OK, you old crow,' Chrissy said. 'We'll go diving.'

For a moment, Chris said nothing. Then he said, 'That's OK. I was just jerking your chain. It really is too rough. Let's pass.'

'Too rough? Maybe too rough for you, you old geezer,' Chrissy said, taking the offensive. 'If you're too soft to go diving, I'll go myself. You stay here with the women.'

'You're not going without me,' Chris said. 'If you go, we both go.' The Rouses continued bickering as they decided what to have for breakfast, whether to shave, how long their dive should last.

As the Rouses geared up, they reviewed their plan. Chrissy would return to the galley to free the piece of canvas. Chris would wait outside the wreck, his lights a beacon for his son's exit. Chrissy would work for twenty minutes before exiting the wreck.

Chrissy went over the gunwale; his father followed. It took just a minute or two before the team hit the wreck and made their way to the opening gouged in the control-room area. There, Chrissy unfastened the two small stage bottles he would breathe from on his ascent and laid them on the U-boat's deck. Next, he clipped one end of a nylon line to the torn-open entrance of the U-boat and slithered into the wreck, allowing the line to unspool from a reel attached to his harness. This way, even if the visibility dropped to zero or he became lost or disorientated, he could follow the line out of the U-boat and back to his father.

The pillowcase-sized piece of canvas Chrissy had worked on for so long still lay buried under a floor-to-ceiling cabinet made of heavy-gauge steel. Chrissy could not hope to move the massive cabinet. To free the artefact, he would have to dig beneath the cabinet into the rotting debris until enough space had been cleared to pull the canvas out. For perhaps fifteen minutes, Chrissy burrowed with his hands, creating a silt tornado. The canvas began to loosen. Chrissy pulled harder. Maybe seconds remained in the dive. Chrissy pulled again. The steel cabinet, deprived of its bottom support, began to collapse, hurtling several hundred pounds of steel atop Chrissy's head and burying his face in the hole he had dug. Chrissy tried to move. Nothing happened. He was trapped.

As the gravity of his situation sludged into Chrissy's consciousness, the feral dog that is narcosis set upon him, with full fangs bared. His head throbbed. His mind narrowed. He believed, more certainly than he knew his name, that a monster was on top of him. Outside, Chris checked his watch and saw that his son was overdue. He swam into the wreck.

Chris reached his son and began working to free him from the trap. Chrissy struggled to climb out but only burnt faster through his remaining air and deepened his narcosis. Finally, after several minutes, Chrissy came free. He checked his watch. It read thirty minutes. He and his father were ten minutes over on their time.

Ordinarily, the Rouses would have followed Chrissy's nylon line out of the wreck and to the tanks they needed to breathe from to make their ascent. But in Chrissy's struggle to free himself, the line had become tangled round the canvas until it was a morass of knots. He and his father swam in the direction of the control room and managed to exit the submarine through a crack between its skin and bulkhead. The tanks and the anchor line were now in front of the divers and just forty feet away. All the Rouses had to do was swim aft, locate the bottles, and begin their ascent. In the struggle, however, Chrissy had become disorientated. He swam towards the bow, away from the tanks and anchor line. His father followed.

The Rouses searched frantically for their tanks. Chris, who had dropped only one of his stage bottles outside the wreck, gave the remaining one to Chrissy. A minute passed, and the Rouses kept searching, but they were now 150 feet from their stage bottles, and their narcosis was spiralling deeper by the second. They searched for another five minutes. Chrissy checked his watch. He had been under water for forty minutes. The Rouses were now twenty minutes over their dive time. Their required decompression, originally sixty minutes, had now expanded to two and a half hours. Neither had enough air to breathe for that long.

Chrissy, terrified at losing his stage bottles, made a decision that divers spend a lifetime dreading—to bolt for the surface. His father shot up after him. Nagle had a saying about divers who rocketed to the surface after so long down deep. 'They're already dead,' he would say. 'They just don't know it yet.'

The Rouses missiled towards the surface. At about 100 feet, they intersected a miracle. Somehow, in their explosive ascent, they spotted the anchor line, swam to it, and held on. Now they had a chance. They could fashion a decompression from their remaining air, then switch to the oxygen tank the *Seeker* dangled at twenty feet for emergencies.

Chrissy switched from his main tanks to the stage bottle his father had given him. He sucked from the new tank and gagged—the mouthpiece had torn and was delivering water, not air. That was enough for Chrissy. He switched back to the main tanks on his back and bolted for the surface. Again, his father followed.

In the *Seeker*'s wheelhouse, Chatterton, Kohler and Crowell saw two divers pop to the surface about 100 feet in front of the boat. They had come up an hour ahead of schedule.

Chatterton said, 'This ain't good.'

Chatterton and Kohler tore down the wheelhouse steps and onto the *Seeker*'s bow. Chatterton raised his arm and put his fingertips on his head, the universal 'Are you OK?' signal to divers. Neither man responded. Six-foot waves threw the divers closer to the boat. Chatterton and Kohler looked into the men's faces. Both father and son had the wide, rapidly blinking eyes of the newly condemned.

'Swim to the boat!' Chatterton yelled.

Chrissy moved his arms and inched closer to the *Seeker*. Chris also tried to swim, but he flopped sideways and half kicked like a sick goldfish.

'Chrissy! Did you come straight to the surface?' Chatterton yelled.

'Yes,' Chrissy said.

Chatterton grabbed two throw lines to fling to the Rouses. The *Seeker* rose and fell on the raging waves like a carnival ride. Each of the Rouses managed to grab a rope. Chatterton and Kohler pulled the divers along the side of the boat.

'Mayday! Mayday! Mayday!' Crowell called into the radio microphone. 'This is the vessel *Seeker*. Requesting immediate helicopter evacuation. We have injured divers.' The Brooklyn Coast Guard station responded. They were sending a chopper.

Chatterton, Kohler and other divers continued to tow the Rouses towards the back of the boat as the *Seeker*'s bow rose and fell with thunderous booms. Chris came nearest the ladder. Chatterton rushed towards him.

'Chris, get up the ladder!' Chatterton yelled.

'Take Chrissy first,' Chris grunted.

Chatterton began to insist but stopped himself when he looked into Chris's widened eyes. In them, he saw only fear and knowing, the kind of knowing that occurs when one's fate is certain and moments away.

'OK, Chrissy, come up!' Chatterton yelled to the younger Rouse, who was holding on to a line about ten feet behind his father. The divers pulled Chrissy to the ladder. He screamed in pain.

'I can't move my legs!' Chrissy yelled. 'It hurts so bad!'

Chatterton knew that serious decompression bends were already upon the divers. He and Kohler straddled the gunwale on either side of the ladder and put their arms under Chrissy, grabbing the underside of his tanks for leverage. The *Seeker* rose and fell with nature's onrushing tantrum. Between wave impacts, they managed to lug Chrissy up the ladder until he thudded onto the deck.

'Get him onto the dressing table!' Chatterton ordered. Kohler and others dragged Chrissy to the table and began cutting off his gear. Barb Lander, a nurse by profession and the only woman on board, force-fed Chrissy aspirin and water and put an oxygen mask over his face. She cradled his head.

'You're OK, Chrissy,' she said. 'You're on the *Seeker* now.'

'I can't move my legs!' Chrissy yelled. 'I'm burning! A monster pinned me! I was trapped!'

At the ladder, Chatterton turned his attention to Chris.

'Chris! Come on, you're next. You can do it!'

'I'm not going to make it,' Chris said. 'Tell Sue I'm sorry.'

Chris's head flopped into the water. Chatterton and Kohler, both dressed in street clothes, leapt into the freezing ocean. Chatterton lunged for Chris's head and lifted it into the air. 'Get me a knife!' Chatterton yelled. 'I gotta cut his rig off!'

Kohler pointed to a knife sheathed on Chris's shoulder. Chatterton grabbed it and slashed at the diver's harness until Chris's rig fell away. Chatterton then muscled Chris into a fireman's carry and brought him up the ladder, straining to hang on as the *Seeker* heaved and exploded into the ocean. Kohler looked inside Chris's mask. Chris only stared straight ahead. The men dragged him onto the *Seeker*'s deck. Chatterton began CPR on the elder Rouse.

Chris did not respond to Chatterton's efforts. His skin began to turn blue. Kohler murmured, 'Come on, Chris. Don't let go.'

Chatterton kept relentlessly at his CPR, but with each compression, he felt increasing resistance, evidence that Chris's blood was turning to foam and clotting in his body. After five minutes, Chris's heart stopped and his skin turned from blue to coal grey. Chatterton knew that he was dead. He kept pumping anyway. You did not give up on a human being just because he was dead.

'My father! How is my father?' Chrissy asked from the dressing table.

Kohler and Lander looked towards Chatterton as he pumped away on Chris's lifeless body. They knew Chris had died.

'John's with your father,' Kohler told him. 'He's gonna be fine. Can you tell me what happened?'

Chrissy went calm and for a moment spoke with a crystalline mind. He told Kohler that something had fallen and pinned him inside the wreck, that his father had come in and freed him, and that, while they were ascending, he had run out of air. Then Chrissy spiralled back into delirium.

'Please shoot me!' Chrissy begged. 'It hurts so bad. Someone find a gun and shoot me. Please kill me. Dad! Dad!'

For the next ninety minutes, Chatterton and others continued CPR on Chris's dead body. Crowell, who had cut the anchor line, headed thirty degrees into the wind as instructed by the Coast Guard.

On the horizon, the divers could see the orange-and-white Coast Guard chopper speeding towards them. All but Chatterton, Kohler and Lander ran into the salon to stay out of its way. The chopper settled to a hover just over the *Seeker*'s bow and strained to hold its position in the roiling winds. From the side door, a muscular search-and-rescue swimmer dressed in a DayGlo-orange dry suit, goggles and fins jumped feet-first towards the ocean. As he surfaced, he threw a medical bag onto the *Seeker*'s deck and climbed aboard the boat. He strode directly to Chatterton.

'You're a little slow on those chest compressions,' the swimmer said from behind rounded goggles. 'It should be one-two . . . one-two . . .'

'I've been doing CPR on this guy for ninety minutes,' Chatterton answered, still pushing into Chris's chest. 'He's dead.'

The swimmer pivoted and looked at Chrissy, who still had colour in his face and was writhing in pain. 'OK, we're going to take both these guys— one at a time,' the swimmer said.

'Listen to me,' Chatterton said. 'This guy is dead. Forget the old man.'

'That's not the way we do it,' the swimmer said.

'Taking the old man will cost you twenty minutes,' Chatterton said. 'Take the son and rush him to a recompression chamber as fast as possible. The time you waste with the father might cost the kid his life.'

'We take them both. One at a time,' the swimmer said.

The swimmer radioed to the chopper. A moment later, a metal stretcher was being lowered by cable towards the *Seeker*. The swimmer pulled the basket towards Chrissy, who was now bundled in a blanket, still screaming for his legs, and placed him inside. Soon, the helicopter was heaving Chrissy into the sky.

'Look, I'm begging you,' Chatterton told the swimmer. 'Leave now. The kid's life depends on this.'

'Not possible,' the swimmer said.

The basket came back down for Chris. It took twenty minutes to load Chris onto the chopper. After both Rouses were aboard, the helicopter lowered the basket a final time for the swimmer. The jet engines screamed as the chopper swooped away and raced towards the recompression chamber at Jacobi Medical Center in the Bronx.

One by one, the divers made their way from the salon and towards Chatterton. Each thanked him or hugged him. Everyone knew that Chris was dead. Everyone believed Chrissy would make it. The trip back to Brielle was sombre but hopeful.

That evening, Barb Lander called Chatterton at home.

'Chrissy didn't make it,' she said. 'He died in the chamber.'

Chatterton put down the receiver. In thirty-six years, there had been several thousand dives on the *Andrea Doria*, the most dangerous of all shipwrecks. Six people had died. In just over a year, the *U-Who* had claimed three lives. Chatterton walked into his office. For months, he had come here to gaze at the Horenburg knife and ask, 'What happened to you?' This time, he sat for hours, not asking much of anything.

History Mauled

Shortly after the Rouses died, Chatterton and Kohler set out for the *U-Who* to retrieve the fallen divers' equipment. Inside the wreck's galley, Chatterton shot footage of the fallen cabinet. The tangled line Chrissy had relied on for navigation had been twisted round the piece of canvas he had worked to excavate. In the now-pristine visibility, Chatterton recognised this canvas as part of a life raft. Its German writing gave instructions for use.

At home, Chatterton and Kohler returned to the business of research. Now armed with the information from the schematic Chatterton had found, they tore into their reference books in search of Type IXC U-boats built at Germany's Deschimag-Bremen shipyard. Fifty-two such U-boats, it turned out, had never returned from patrol. That list of fifty-two, the divers agreed, could easily be narrowed. Over rib eyes at Scotty's Steakhouse, a popular nearby restaurant, they agreed on two exclusionary guidelines: Eliminate any U-boat in which crewmen survived the sinking—if there were survivors, the U-boat's identity would be known. And eliminate any U-boat built with a deck gun—the divers had already determined that the *U-Who* had been built without a deck gun.

Chatterton and Kohler set out for Washington to begin the elimination process. Reference books indicated that there had been survivors on twenty-two of the fifty-two U-boats on their list. That left thirty U-boats to consider. Of these, ten had been built with deck guns. The list was now down to twenty possible U-boats. Neither man could remember having been so excited. This was original research. This was exploration.

Back in New Jersey, the divers went to Scotty's again and began to brainstorm. They needed additional exclusionary criteria to narrow the list. They quickly settled on a plan. They would return to the BdU KTBs—the German war diaries—to inspect where U-boat headquarters had ordered and plotted each of the remaining U-boats on their list. Any submarine the Germans believed to be operating more than a few hundred miles from the US East Coast would be eliminated from the list. After all, the Germans would know better than anyone where their U-boats were patrolling.

THE DIVERS RETURNED to Washington and blitzed the U-boat Control diaries. According to the German records, eighteen of the twenty U-boats on the divers' list had been ordered to areas so distant from New Jersey as to be unworthy of consideration.

That left two U-boats: U-857 and U-879. According to the diaries, each of these submarines had been ordered to attack targets of opportunity on the American East Coast. As the divers read further, they came upon a bombshell: both of these submarines had been docked in Norway in early 1945—the same place and much the same date as Horenburg's boat, *U-869*.

'That could explain the knife!' Kohler said.

'Exactly,' Chatterton said. 'Maybe Horenburg lent the knife to a guy on the U-boat next to his. Maybe he lost it, and it ended up on a nearby boat. Any way you look at it, the knife now makes sense. One of these two submarines has got to be the *U-Who*. It's either U-857 or U-879. We're down to two U-boats.'

The divers consulted their history books. According to these texts, *U-857* had been sunk off Boston by the USS *Gustafson*, while *U-879* had been destroyed off Cape Hatteras, North Carolina, by the USS *Buckley* and USS *Reuben James*. That seemed to leave no chance that the mystery wreck was either *U-857* or *U-879*.

'Let's do this,' Chatterton said. 'Let's check the files for the sinking of these two subs, Let's see for ourselves what the navy says about how these two U-boats were killed.'

'Are you saying these two U-boats might not have been sunk where the history books say they were?' Kohler asked.

'I'm saying we have to check,' Chatterton said. 'I'm getting the feeling we have to check everything.'

The divers looked first at navy files for the sinking of the *U-857* off Boston, which gave this account: While patrolling Cape Cod on April 5, 1945, *U-857* fired a torpedo at the American tanker *Atlantic States*, wounding but not sinking her. American warships were dispatched to the area to hunt and kill *U-857*. Two days later, one of those warships, the destroyer USS *Gustafson*, obtained a sonar contact on an underwater object near Boston. She fired several Hedgehog bombs into the ocean towards the contact. Crewmen reported hearing an explosion shortly thereafter and then smelling oil.

And that was it. No evidence of a U-boat had floated to the surface. No blobs of oil had been spotted on the surface. Navy assessors who analysed the *Gustafson*'s attack had written the following conclusion:

> It is considered that although a submarine, known to have been in this area, may have been lost, it was not lost as a result of this attack. It is therefore recommended that this incident be assessed 'E—probably slightly damaged.

'Wait a minute,' Kohler said. 'The grade on this attack report says B—probably sunk.'

'Yeah, but look here,' Chatterton said, pointing to the report. 'The original grade of "E" is crossed out. Someone changed it to a "B".'

The divers knew what the alteration meant.

'The postwar assessors upgraded this report!' Kohler said.

Chatterton and Kohler had only recently learned about the postwar assessors. As navy investigators, it was the assessors' task after the war to make a final report on the fate of all U-boats. In most cases, the evidence was clearcut and the assessors' job simple. In rarer instances, when a U-boat could not be accounted for, the assessors stretched for an explanation. They were loath to leave question marks in the history books.

'That must have been what happened here,' Chatterton said. 'The *Gustafson* never sank *U-857*. The U-boat survived, continued past Boston, then sank somewhere else. After the war, the assessors needed an explanation for the loss of *U-857*. So they looked at this really dubious attack by the *Gustafson* and said, 'Let's upgrade it from an "E" to a "B".'

'Well, if the *Gustafson* didn't sink *U-857* off Boston,' Kohler finally asked, 'what happened to that submarine?'

'We gotta figure that out for ourselves,' Chatterton said.

An hour later, they had their answer. According to German diaries, *U-857* had been ordered to proceed south along the American East Coast. She had last attacked a ship off Cape Cod. That meant New Jersey lay 200 miles away—to the south. Neither Chatterton nor Kohler could move. Here was a U-boat that fitted every criterion they had established, had possibly been docked beside Horenburg's sub, had very likely survived the *Gustafson*, and was believed by the Germans to be on her way towards New Jersey.

'I think we've got our U-boat,' Kohler said.

The divers, however, still had to inspect the box of files for *U-879*. Again, they found history mauled. Over the last half-century, various assessors had ascribed three fates to *U-879*: they first pronounced her lost without a trace, then sunk off Halifax in Canadian waters, then sunk off Cape Hatteras, North Carolina. As the divers studied further, they recognised that the current assessment by German naval historian Axel Niestlé—that *U-879* had been sunk off Cape Hatteras—was correct. But the lesson was stark and by now familiar: written history was fallible. As they left Washington for New Jersey that night, Chatterton and Kohler each marvelled at how easy it was to get an incomplete picture of the world if one relied solely on experts.

NOW ARMED with abundant evidence that their wreck was *U-857*, Chatterton and Kohler determined to use the rest of the 1992–93 off-season to complete the proof. Chatterton placed a classified ad in *Proceedings* magazine, a publication of the US Naval Institute, seeking information on the sinking of *U-857* by the USS *Gustafson*. Several *Gustafson* crewmen, now in their seventies, replied to the ad. Chatterton interviewed them about the day they attacked the U-boat off Boston. None could offer any more evidence of the sinking today than they had in 1945. They had fired Hedgehogs and smelt oil. And that was it.

For his part, Kohler set out in search of the grand master of U-boat knowledge. For decades, Robert Coppock had been caretaker to Britain's U-boat records, including captured German records, and he still worked for the Ministry of Defence in London. According to an archivist Kohler had met, no one had a more comprehensive understanding of U-boat records than did Coppock. Kohler called London the next day.

An English-accented woman answered the telephone. 'Great Scotland Yard. Can I help you?'

Kohler believed he had misdialled. 'I must have the wrong number. I was trying to reach Mr Robert Coppock at the Ministry of Defence.'

'One moment, and I'll connect you to Mr Coppock,' the woman said.

Coppock took the call and Kohler introduced himself.

'Ah, yes, the diver from New Jersey,' Coppock said. 'I know of you, sir. I have been following your adventure with great interest.'

Coppock asked detailed questions of Kohler about the divers' research, about the *U-Who*, about Horenburg. When Coppock asked if the divers had fashioned any theories, Kohler laid out the case for *U-857*.

Coppock listened intently, then agreed that Kohler had made a persuasive argument for *U-857* as the New Jersey wreck. He asked if Kohler would like him to consult his records and sources. Kohler replied, 'Yes, sir. I'd be grateful for that. Thank you very much.'

Then Kohler called Chatterton. 'John, I talked to Coppock.'

'What'd he say?' Chatterton asked.

'I laid out the case for *U-857*. He said it sounded "persuasive". He really liked it. He's going to look into it on his end.'

Shortly after Kohler spoke to Coppock, the divers contacted Horst Bredow and Charlie Grutzemacher in Germany and made the case for *U-857*. Each of the archivists pulled out his own records, asked a few questions, then agreed: the *U-Who* almost certainly was *U-857*. Kohler redialled Scotland Yard to follow up with Coppock. Coppock told Kohler that he had consulted records and considered further the divers' theory. As before, he believed it likely that the divers had discovered *U-857*.

As the early months of 1993 wore on, Chatterton and Kohler continued to meet for steaks at Scotty's Steakhouse. They no longer speculated, however, about the *U-Who*'s identity. Instead, they began to imagine how the U-boat had met its end. All evidence pointed in one direction: the U-boat had been destroyed by a torpedo.

But whose torpedo? If an Allied sub had fired on the U-boat, there would have been a record of the incident. If another U-boat had fired and inadvertently hit the sub, that, too, would have been recorded. Could one of the U-boat's own torpedoes have exploded accidentally from within? Impossible, as the blast damage showed a strike from outside the sub. That seemed to leave a single explanation. The divers had read about occasions in which a torpedo's steering system malfunctioned, causing the weapon to reverse direction in the water and head back towards its own submarine. Those derelict torpedoes were called 'circle-runners'.

'Imagine you're Rudolf Premauer, commander of *U-857*,' Kohler said to Chatterton one night at Scotty's. 'You've made it all the way from Norway to the United States, and now you're a few miles from Manhattan. You spot a target in the distance. You order your men to their battle stations, climb into the conning tower, and raise the attack periscope. You give the order, "Fire torpedo!" The torpedo flies out of the tube. Everyone's waiting for an explosion. Nothing happens. Then the radioman says, "Circle-runner! Our torpedo is bearing down on us!" Premauer orders the sub to crash-dive; it's their only hope. They give it everything they've got. Too late. The torpedo hits.'

'And that explains why there's no incident report,' Chatterton said.

THE DIVERS still had two months before the start of the new dive season, time enough to learn about the last year of the U-boat war. By 1993, Kohler had built a collection of U-boat books worthy of a university library. Now he spread those books on his living-room floor and divided them in half. He would lend Chatterton one pile for study and keep the other. Between them, they held in their hands the story of the men who'd waged the final campaign of the U-boat war, the men who lay dead in their wreck.

Chatterton and Kohler found hundreds of pages soaked in blood. By the war's end, more than 30,000 U-boat men out of a force of about 55,000 had been killed. No branch of a modern nation's armed forces had ever sustained such casualties and kept fighting. A U-boat sent to war in early 1945, as *U-857* had been, stood only a 50 per cent chance of returning from its patrol. A crewman's life expectancy in that period was barely sixty days. Those ordered to American or Canadian waters almost never came back.

By nearly every account, the late-war U-boat man had not just fought through the final hours of the war, but had done so nobly and bravely, all the while knowing the odds against his survival.

In October 1940, at the peak of what German submariners called the 'Happy Time', U-boats sank sixty-six ships while losing only one of their own. The U-boats enjoyed a second 'Happy Time' in early 1942 with Operation Drumbeat, a surprise attack on American ships off the US East Coast. In that offensive, U-boats pushed up against American shores so close that crewmen could watch automobiles drive the parkways, and tune in American radio stations. Five months later, just a few U-boats had sunk nearly 600 ships in American waters at a cost of just six of their own, the worst defeat ever suffered by the US Navy.

The Americans, however, did not remain vulnerable for long. The navy began running convoys, an ancient maritime strategy whereby armed escort vessels protected groups of boats sailing together. Now when a U-boat fired on an Allied ship, the convoy escorts would be there to spot, chase and kill it. As convoys increased, sinkings by U-boats dropped to near nothing.

Scientists joined the war effort from US laboratories and universities. One of their most potent weapons was radar. Even in total darkness, radar-equipped airplanes and ships could detect a surfaced submarine at great distances. The underwater environment presented its own perils. An Allied ship that suspected there was a submerged U-boat in its vicinity could use sonar—the broadcast of sound waves—to sniff it out. Once sonar echoed off the submarine's metallic form, a U-boat was tagged for death.

U-boats relied on radio to communicate with German headquarters. Allied brains pounced on the dependence. They developed a radio detection system known as 'Huff-Duff' (for HF/DF, or high-frequency direction finding) that allowed Allied ships at sea to fix the position of U-boats. Now a submarine using its radio was announcing its location to the enemy.

Perhaps the deadliest Allied breakthrough came in the form of code breaking. Since the war's beginning, the German military had encrypted its communications through a cipher machine known as 'Enigma'. A boxy, typewriter-like device capable of millions of character combinations, Enigma was believed by the German High Command to be invincible, the strongest code ever created. Allied code breakers estimated the odds against cracking Enigma to be impossibly high, but they tried anyway. With the help of a captured Enigma machine and key documents, teams of Allied cryptographers and mathematicians at Bletchley Park, outside London, spent months attacking Enigma, even building the world's first programmable computer to aid in the effort. With the help of covert intelligence, they cracked it, and by 1943, the Allies were using intercepted Enigma messages to direct hunter-killer groups to unsuspecting U-boats.

By spring 1943, the fangs of Allied technology had encircled the U-boats, leaving no safe areas in the ocean. The 'Happy Time' had yielded to *Sauergurkenzeit*, or 'Sour-Pickle Time'. The hunters of the early war had now become the hunted.

A Missed Signal

The first U-boat trip of 1993 was scheduled for May 31, Memorial Day. As Chatterton and Kohler drove to the *Seeker*'s dock, neither could remember having felt so content. Chatterton had made every important discovery inside the wreck. He had been relentless in his research until his thinking had produced a solution even the world's great U-boat minds did not dispute.

Kohler felt a similar satisfaction. Two years earlier, he had been a ferocious tonnage king and Atlantic Wreck Divers hellraiser. But as he'd come to know the U-boat and feel its crew, and as he'd done original research that had corrected written history, he'd come to feel himself not just a diver but an explorer. Things had changed so much, in fact, that Kohler had dedicated part of his off-season to converting to trimix. He had seen Chatterton's and Yurga's diving transformed by the benefits offered by the new gas.

The parking lot at Brielle looked emptier than usual to all the arriving divers, though none found himself surprised. If Feldman's death had started the *U-Who*'s reputation as a deathtrap, the Rouses' demise had cemented it. Divers capable of this depth wanted to live. Most said 'No, thanks' to the *U-Who*.

On board the *Seeker*, the divers shook hands and compared off-season notes. Near midnight, a skeleton wobbled from the Horrible Inn towards the *Seeker*. No one spoke as the figure drew closer.

'That's Bill,' someone whispered.

Nagle's face was yellow from jaundice and splotched with purple bruises. His hair was oily and his T-shirt grimy. He weighed perhaps 120 pounds. Under his arm he carried the cowboys-and-Indians sleeping-bag he had used since boyhood, the one he'd brought along when he had taken the bell off the *Andrea Doria* in the days when he ruled the world. As the boat left the dock that night, everyone gave thanks that Chatterton and Danny Crowell—two capable and sober captains—were also on hand.

As the *Seeker* steamed for the *U-Who*, the divers made a final review of their strategies. Packer and Gatto would penetrate the diesel motor room. Until now, the diesel motor room had been inaccessible, its entrance blocked by massive air-intake ductwork that had fallen from the upper casement of the submarine. Packer and Gatto, however, had prepared to remove the obstruction, even if it required using a rope and several lift bags. By gaining entry to the diesel motor room, the divers would also have a clear shot into the adjoining electric motor room, the only other remaining compartment inaccessible to divers.

Chatterton's plan was simpler. He would return to the wreck's forward section—the radio room, commander's quarters and officers' quarters.

'This is a matter of seeing,' he told Yurga. 'This is a matter of looking at a big pile of garbage until one little thing in the pile starts to look a little different than the rest. I'm looking for a glimmer of order in the chaos. If I just stay quiet and look long enough, I think I'll see something.'

Kohler's plan was similar. Like Chatterton, he believed important items would be located in the forward part of the wreck, where the crewmen had slept and stored their personal effects. Unlike Chatterton, however, he was willing to dig, trusting his hands to become his eyes in the silt clouds raised by his activity.

The morning sun was a brilliant alarm clock. As they had the previous season, Chatterton and Kohler splashed together. At the bottom, the two divers wriggled inside the wreck and swam forward. Kohler penetrated farthest, landing in the noncommissioned officers' quarters. Chatterton settled into the commander's quarters and began to go still.

As minutes passed and he stayed locked on the scene, specks of order began to dance in and out of the chaos. That shape is not random, Chatterton thought as he reached forward into the pile of rubble. He pulled out a pristine leather boot. That speck of metal is smoother than the rest, he considered, as he pushed his hand into another wreckage heap. He pulled out a signal flare. That brown is not from nature, he speculated as he fidgeted his hand into a mound of splintered wood. He pulled out a crewman's escape lung, complete with oxygen tank, breathing apparatus and vest.

In twenty minutes, Chatterton had salvaged three prime artefacts he had overlooked on earlier dives to these forward rooms. As he made his way back up to the *Seeker*, he found himself unusually proud. In detecting beauty camouflaged in wreckage, he had done the very thing that had made Nagle great, and it had always been his dream to dive like Bill Nagle. When Chatterton climbed aboard, Nagle came over to inspect the artefacts.

Kohler followed Chatterton onto the boat. He had recovered only some pieces of a coffeepot, so he rushed to the dive table to join in the inspection of Chatterton's finds. The divers placed the leather boot, the flare and the escape lung in a bucket of fresh water. Nagle removed the boot first. The divers crowded in, looking for a name. The boot was barren.

Next, Nagle pulled the shotgun-shell-shaped flare from the bucket. He rubbed it in soft, genie-lamp circles. German writing appeared in answer— a manufacturer's name and the flare's gauge size.

Only the escape lung remained. It consisted of a brownish rubberised canvas life vest, a black rubber tube, an orange rubber mouthpiece and a Thermos-sized aluminium oxygen cylinder. The oxygen bottle was dented and bent out of alignment. Nagle wiped at the apparatus. Mud fell away. A tiny eagle and swastika materialised.

'Is there a name written anywhere?' Kohler asked.

Nagle wiped some more. 'No name,' he said.

Chatterton's hopes evaporated. 'Zero for three,' he said. 'This wreck is one tough s.o.b.' He took the escape lung and placed it in his cooler. 'May as well take it home, clean it, and let it dry,' he told Yurga.

At the ladder, Packer and Gatto surfaced with promising news. The fallen ductwork that had blocked the diesel motor room had disappeared during the off-season, a gift from a winter storm. Inside, the team had seen several pieces of equipment, any one of which might be engraved with the U-boat's number. Another dive, and they would have time to begin inspection.

'How much of the diesel motor room did you see?' Kohler asked.

'Not much,' Packer said. 'We only got about ten feet inside. There's another obstruction that blocks the rest of the way. You still can't reach the electric motor room. But I think we got in far enough to hit it big.'

Rough seas and plummeting visibility cut short the second dives. As Nagle pulled up anchor and coaxed the boat to life, many of the divers fantasised aloud about the wonders Packer and Gatto would yank from the diesel motor room when next they got the chance.

Chatterton returned home from the dive near midnight. He unpacked his gear quietly, careful not to wake his wife. When only the cooler remained, he fished out the escape lung and walked it into his garage. Shelves everywhere held the overflow of shipwreck artefacts from his house, making the garage a museum. He found a spot for the battered lung alongside several years' bounty from the *Andrea Doria*.

A few days later, Chatterton went to his garage to check on the escape lung. He stood dumbfounded at the door. Broken china lay strewn across the floor. Shattered glass had been shrapnelled against the walls and ceiling. 'Someone blew up my garage,' Chatterton said. 'Someone came in here with a bomb.'

Virtually nothing on the garage shelves had survived. In the rubble, he spotted a metallic silver shape. He picked it up. This was the escape lung's oxygen bottle, but it was no longer cylindrical and closed. Now it was flattened, like a toothpaste tube sliced open.

'Goddamn,' Chatterton said. 'The oxygen bottle exploded. The thing was still live. The escape lung blew up my garage.'

Chatterton looked more closely at the flattened cylinder. The explosion had blasted away a half-century's encrustation, the part that could not be removed with simple wiping. Chatterton pulled it close to his face. Stamped onto the flattened metal was a bit of writing, which read, '15.4.44'.

Chatterton knew right away what the numbers meant. He ran into his house and called Kohler.

'Richie, man, the oxygen bottle blew up my garage,' he said.

'What?'

'The escape lung. Remember the oxygen bottle? It was still charged. I let it dry in my garage. The corrosion must have caused it to blow. All my *Doria* stuff in the garage is destroyed. My garage is like a war zone. But listen to this: the explosion produced a clue. The bottle has a date on it—fifteen-dot-four-dot-forty-four. That's European for April 15, 1944. That's the hydrostatic test date, the date the bottle was examined and certified to be good.'

'That means our U-boat sailed after April 15, 1944,' Kohler said.

'Exactly.'

Then, Chatterton called Major Gregory Weidenfeld, the Civil Air Patrol historian who had dedicated himself to proving that two everyday civilians in a private plane had sunk a U-boat off New Jersey in 1942.

'Listen, Greg,' Chatterton said, 'we found a hydrostatic test date that proves the wreck sailed sometime after April 15, 1944. That excludes the chance that this is your U-boat. I'm really sorry.'

'Thank you, John,' Weidenfeld said. 'That means there's another U-boat out there you'll have to find.'

A few days later, Chatterton received word that his friend the U-boat ace Karl-Friedrich Merten had died at the age of eighty-seven. Chatterton knew that Merten's passing, together with his own goodbye to Weidenfeld, meant that a chapter in the divers' quest had closed.

WEATHER AND SCHEDULING prevented the *Seeker* from returning to the *U-Who* until July 31, two months after the season's first trip. Chatterton and Kohler splashed and headed towards the sub's forward compartments. As before, Chatterton studied the debris field. In the commander's quarters, lying in plain view, he spotted a pair of binoculars. He placed them in his bag. If the pair had belonged to the commander, perhaps his name lay inscribed underneath the muck. The remainder of Chatterton's search produced little.

Kohler continued to dig in the noncommissioned officers' quarters. In a silt pile, he spotted what appeared to be a bowl and brought it to his mask for inspection. It took just a moment for Kohler to realise he was holding a skull. A year earlier, he might have panicked. Today, he held it and said,

'I'm going to do my best to figure out your name. Your families should know where you are.'

Topside, Chatterton and Kohler washed the binoculars. The apparatus was unmarked. Now they could do no more than await the arrival of Packer and Gatto, who had gone to work inside the diesel motor room. An hour later, that team climbed the ladder. Packer's goody bag bulged. He opened the mesh container and removed a pressure gauge the size of a dinner plate. Etched on the gauge's aluminium face were the eagle and swastika. The rest of the face, however, contained only generic words and numerals.

Ripping currents made short work of most second dives. Chatterton made a short entry in his logbook. It read, 'Where to next?'

The *Seeker* made four trips to the U-boat over the next six weeks. Packer and Gatto gathered beautiful and interesting artefacts from inside the diesel motor room: a gauge panel, tags, even a telegraph—the instrument used to signal orders like full ahead and dive. All the marks were generic; none identified the wreck. Further access into the compartment was blocked by a massive steel pipe that lay angled in the narrow walkway between the two diesel engines. Kohler recognised this pipe as an escape trunk, a vertical tunnel with an interior ladder through which crewmen could flee a sinking U-boat. The loss did not seem severe—if the items Packer and Gatto had thus far recovered revealed nothing about the U-boat's identity, it was unlikely that the remainder of these technical rooms held the answer.

Chatterton and Kohler devoted their dives to the U-boat's forward section. They recovered various artefacts—bowls, cups, shoes, gauges—not a bit of which contained identification. Chatterton pulled a gem from the wreck—a surgeon's kit—a collection of stainless-steel medical instruments complete with instructional diagrams. None of it revealed the wreck's identity.

Riding back to Brielle that night, Chatterton told Kohler that he had begun the dive season with a ferocious optimism, certain that his hard work, preparation and instinct would pay off in a positive identification of the wreck. Now, four months and six trips later, he worried for the first time that a greenhorn diver would climb the *Seeker*'s ladder with an identification tag stuck to his fin, becoming the accidental but official discoverer of the *U-Who*'s name.

'It's not that I care about who gets the credit,' he told Kohler. 'It's that it would mean my approach hadn't worked.'

'Listen, John, we can do it,' Kohler said. 'I'm with you. I believe in what we're doing. You tell me what you need and I'm there. We ain't quitting.'

It was then that Chatterton fully understood what Kohler had meant to the project. He was a first-rate diver and a passionate researcher. But deeper than that, he was a believer, and Chatterton knew that this was the most important thing, that in a quest in which men were asked to really know themselves, an unflinching belief in the possible survived all.

Chatterton shook Kohler's hand. 'We ain't quitting,' he said.

In October, Bill Nagle was rushed by his girlfriend to the hospital, bleeding from the throat. Years of alcohol abuse had caused him to develop oesophageal varices—varicose veins in his throat—which had ruptured. Doctors hurried him to surgery and cauterised the damage. In the recovery room, they told him, 'You came within fifteen minutes of bleeding to death. If you continue to consume alcohol, we might not be able to save you next time.'

Nagle's girlfriend broke up with him while he was still in the hospital. She could not bear to watch him kill himself. A few weeks later, Nagle checked himself out of the hospital. That night, after consuming nearly a full bottle of vodka, he bled to death from the throat. Bill Nagle, one of the greatest shipwreck divers of all time, was dead at forty-one.

THREE DIVE SEASONS had passed since the *U-Who*'s discovery. Though certain that the wreck was *U-857*, Chatterton and Kohler were no closer to proving it than they had been in 1991.

As winter claimed New Jersey, Chatterton noticed fraying round the edges of his marriage. While he had worked to master the *U-Who*, Kathy had become one of the finest women pistol shooters in the world. Discordant schedules squeezed the couple's time together, and diverging interests made that time awkward.

At Kohler's home five miles away, Kohler and his wife, Felicia, had argued for more than a year over his availability to her, their two small children and Felicia's ten-year-old daughter from a previous relationship. She understood the necessary evil that was Kohler's glass business—the company was growing and required constant attention. She had less patience, however, for Kohler's use of his free time. He spent nearly every day of the year working the *U-Who*—diving it, researching it, meeting with Chatterton, whisking off to Washington. Felicia told him, 'If you gave up diving, our marriage would improve.' Around Christmas 1993, he and Felicia separated. She moved with the children to Long Island, and he took a bachelor pad on the northeastern tip of the Jersey Shore. He insisted on having his kids every weekend.

For a month or two, Kohler revelled in his new-found freedom. He dated, danced at nightclubs, and read his U-boat books. But he missed his children. Weekend visits were not enough. He entertained notions of reconciliation with Felicia, but believed she would not consider it unless he agreed to abandon diving. As February 1994 froze the beaches near his apartment, he became convinced that something would have to change.

In late February, Chatterton received a letter from Robert Coppock at the Ministry of Defence in London. Standing in his bathrobe and holding a cup of coffee, Chatterton began to read:

U-869 . . . was [originally] bound for the US East Coast [and] allocated a patrol area about 110 miles south-east of New York.

Chatterton went numb. U-869 was Horenburg's boat. It was supposed to have been ordered to Gibraltar.

U-869 . . . may not have received a [new] signal ordering her to Gibraltar . . . In view of atmospheric conditions . . . it is certainly possible that Control's [new] signal ordering U-869 to the Gibraltar area was not received by the boat . . .

Chatterton rushed to the phone and called Kohler.

'Richie, we just got an unbelievable letter from Coppock. He dropped an atomic bomb. You won't believe it—'

'Slow down!' Kohler said. 'What's it say?'

'It says this: U-869, Horenburg's boat, the one all the history books say was sunk off Gibraltar, was originally ordered to New York. And not just to New York, but just south of New York, right to our wreck site! It says that headquarters later changed those orders to Gibraltar. But get this, Richie, and I quote, "It is certainly possible that Control's signal ordering U-869 to the Gibraltar area was not received by the boat."'

'This is unbelievable. I'm stunned.'

'Richie, can you conference-call Coppock from your office? We have to ask him to explain where he got this information.'

A moment later, the phone rang at Great Scotland Yard. Coppock told the divers that his information had been gleaned from reading intercepted radio messages between U-869 and U-boat Control in Germany. The messages and their interpretations by American code breakers, he said, could be found in Washington, DC.

Chatterton and Kohler had seen radio intercepts before but had never inspected those relating to *U-869*, a boat conclusively recorded as having been sunk off Gibraltar.

'I'm going to DC tomorrow to investigate,' Chatterton said.

Kohler wanted to join Chatterton, but he could not free up the time from his business. Instead, Chatterton took Barb Lander, who had long been diving the *U-Who* and who had shown keen interest in its history.

Chatterton and Lander started at the National Archives, where they requested U-boat intelligence summaries starting on December 8, 1944— the day *U-869* had departed for war.

The divers scanned the US Navy's intelligence summaries. They found a report dated January 3, 1945. Navy intelligence had intercepted radio messages between *U-869* and Control. The code breakers wrote:

A U/Boat (*U-869*) now estimated in the central North Atlantic has been ordered to head for a point about 70 miles southeast of the New York approaches.

Chatterton could scarcely believe what he was reading—that would have put *U-869* directly on the wreck site. He pressed further. In a report dated January 17, 1945, navy intelligence wrote:

The U/Boat heading for the New York approaches, *U-869* (Neuerburg), is presently estimated about 180 miles SSE of Flemish Cap . . . She is expected to arrive in the New York area at the beginning of February.

Chatterton checked the crew list, one of several dozen Chatterton had copied at the U-boat Archive in Germany. Neuerburg was *U-869*'s commander. He kept reading. In a January 25 report, navy eavesdroppers detected a communication problem between *U-869* and Control:

One U/Boat may be south of Newfoundland heading for New York approaches, although her location is uncertain due to a mix up in orders and Control assumes she is heading for Gibraltar . . . [But] based on the signals she received, it appears likely that *U-869* is continuing towards her original heading off New York.

'I can't believe it,' Chatterton told Lander. 'They were ordered right to our wreck site. Control changed the orders to send the U-boat to Gibraltar. But it looks like *U-869* never got those new orders. She just kept heading for New York.'

Still unresolved, however, was the matter of *U-869*'s reported sinking off Gibraltar by two ships, the USS *Fowler* and the French patrol craft *L'Indiscret*. Every history book had it recorded that way. Chatterton and Lander raced to the Naval Historical Center and requested attack reports for the sinking of *U-869*. Minutes later, they were looking at butchered history.

On February 28, 1945, the American destroyer escort USS *Fowler* picked up a sonar contact southwest of Gibraltar. The *Fowler* fired a pattern of thirteen depth charges. Two explosions followed, and debris of an 'unknown identity was spotted on the surface. The *Fowler* fired another pattern of depth charges. When the smoke cleared, crewmen dragged a towel through the debris, which 'had the appearance of lumps and balls of heavy oil sludge, but no samples were recovered.' The destroyer searched the area for further evidence of damage. It found none.

Hours later, *L'Indiscret* attacked a sonar contact in the same area, which 'caused a large black object to break surface and immediately sink.' The boat could not identify the object and spotted no debris.

Navy intelligence graded each of the attacks 'G—no damage'.

But as he read the reports, Chatterton could see that postwar assessors soon changed the grade from 'G' to 'B—probably sunk'.

'I've seen this before,' Chatterton said. 'The postwar assessors have no clue about intercepted radio messages, so they don't know *U-869* went to New York. They check the German records. The Germans believed *U-869* went to Gibraltar. When she doesn't come home, the Germans presume her lost off Gibraltar. Then the postwar assessors see these attacks near Gibraltar. They attach the attacks to *U-869*, change the grade from G to B, and that settles it.'

Chatterton ran to the payphone. He told Kohler that the history books were wrong.

'We found *U-869*,' Kohler said. 'We found Horenburg, didn't we?'

'Horenburg was there the whole time,' Chatterton said. 'Think about it, Richie. If there were radio problems between *U-869* and Control, Horenburg would have been front and centre. He was the senior radioman. Horenburg must have been there for it all.'

None of Us Is Coming Back

Bremen, Germany, January 1944

In the chill morning of a new year, as ruins smouldered in Berlin from fresh British bombings, hundreds of young German men made their way to the seaport town of Bremen to begin naval training. Fifty of these men were told they would be the crew of a new submarine that would be commissioned as *U-869*. They were young—average age twenty-one, with twenty-two teenagers—and were worlds away from the crews of 1939, when the U-Bootwaffe selected only the elite.

Among the most experienced men assigned to *U-869* was twenty-two-year-old Herbert Guschewski, a radio operator and veteran of three war patrols, all with *U-602*. Guschewski counted himself lucky to be alive. He had been ordered off *U-602* because his services were needed elsewhere. *U-602* set sail for the Mediterranean. It never returned.

As Guschewski unpacked that evening in Bremen, he heard a knock at his door. When he opened it, a handsome man with wavy brown hair and dark eyes asked if he might come inside. The man introduced himself as Martin Horenburg, the *Funkmeister*, or senior radioman, assigned to *U-869*. He told Guschewski that he was looking forward to working with him. Guschewski shook Horenburg's hand, but his heart sank. He had expected to be the crew's most senior radio operator. But Horenburg ranked higher. The men spoke briefly before wishing each other good night.

It would be a few days before the crew was officially assembled. In the meantime, several men assigned to *U-869*, including Guschewski and Horenburg, hopped a cable car to the Deschimag shipyard in hopes of glimpsing their U-boat. A guard inside the gates directed them to a dock.

And there she was. Her cigar-shaped hull grooved into the water at bow and stern, she appeared an eyebrow of the sea, raised for a moment to observe the curious. She was painted overcast grey, the most impossible colour to see when the world changed from light to dark or dark to light, the times when U-boats were deadliest. For a moment, Guschewski stood awestruck before the machine. This is a great boat, he thought.

Commissioning was scheduled for January 26, 1944. On that day, those assigned to *U-869* dressed in formal navy uniforms and made their way to the submarine's dock. It was the first time the men had come together as a crew. An officer took attendance. All the while, the crew cast their eyes to the side, where a tall, handsome man with black hair and penetrating dark eyes was observing the proceedings. They knew this man to be their commander. The men had grown up in a country wallpapered with images of the invincible U-boat commander. Here, in the form of twenty-seven-year-old commander Helmuth Neuerburg, that image had come to life.

The men climbed aboard the submarine and fell into rows of three on the deck. Commander Neuerburg looked over his men. By now, the men knew this to be Neuerburg's maiden command. Neuerburg's speech was short and in proper German, his voice military and exact. But it took no more than these words for even a U-boat veteran like Guschewski to think, There is great courage and competence in this man. You do not go against this man.

After Neuerburg spoke, he gave the order to raise the ship's ensign. When the flag reached the top, Neuerburg saluted it not with the Nazi *heil* but, rather, in traditional military style.

'The boat is commissioned,' Neuerburg announced.

Onboard training began after *U-869*'s commissioning. As the men shimmied through the sub's three deck hatches, they found themselves in a technological wonderland. Swarms of instruments, gauges, dials, tubing and wiring forested every centimetre of the boat. Everywhere, the boat smelt of fresh paint and oil and promise. The men spent the next several days loading the submarine and becoming accustomed to U-boat protocol. In a matter of days, a bond began to form between crewmen, each of whom likely sensed what Admiral Karl Dönitz had written years before: a U-boat crew was a *Schicksalsgemeinschaft*—a community bound by fate.

From the start, the crew studied Neuerburg. Whatever the task, he remained cool and restrained, the picture of military discipline. Even as news of Germany's worsening fate trickled into Bremen, Neuerburg betrayed no fear or hesitation. Instead, he spoke of duty, and he acted and stood and moved as if it were his guiding principle.

HELMUTH NEUERBURG had joined the marines in 1936 when he was nineteen years old. Upon graduation, he began pilot training as part of the naval air arm. By 1940, he was an officer flying North Sea reconnaissance missions near England. For the next three years, he continued to fly, to train pilots, and to earn excellent reviews. But if Helmuth's military career looked to be the National Socialist ideal, his heart and mind told a different story.

While Helmuth did not dare speak against the Nazi regime publicly—an officer could be executed for such a crime—he had no such reservation when speaking to his older brother, Friedhelm, who served in one of the army's Panzer divisions. During visits, he told Friedhelm that he believed the Nazis to be authoring the downfall of Germany.

'What you are saying is very dangerous!' Friedhelm warned. 'Please, be careful with what you say.'

In 1941, Helmuth married Erna Maas. Bright, beautiful and energetic, Erna was also passionately antimilitary. The two loved each other deeply. At home, Helmuth collected American jazz records, a music form forbidden by the Nazis, and tuned to enemy BBC radio for news of the war, another wartime offence. One morning, he heard a BBC report of America's entry into the war.

'We have lost this war already,' he told Erna.

In 1943, Neuerburg and others were offered a choice: they could remain with the Luftwaffe or join the U-boats. Those who stayed with the air force would go into combat immediately; those who transferred to submarines might spend a year or more in training before going to battle. Neuerburg was now father to a two-year-old son and a one-year-old daughter. He chose the U-boats, and spent the next twenty-one months in training, using his leave to see his son, Jürgen and infant daughter, Jutta. Just before *U-869*'s commissioning, he spoke to Friedhelm. He looked his brother in the eye and said, 'I'm not coming back.'

CLASSROOM INSTRUCTION complete, the U-boat loaded with food and supplies, the crew of *U-869* pushed out of Bremen in late January 1944 and steered to the Baltic Sea for several months of training. The men used February to get to know their jobs and one another. In the radio room, Guschewski and Horenburg groomed two radiomen, one of whom was eighteen years old, the other nineteen.

While Neuerburg commanded respect and even a measure of fear, his first officer, twenty-one-year-old Siegfried Brandt, was growing beloved by the crew. In many ways, Brandt was Neuerburg's opposite. He was small, perhaps five foot seven, with warm eyes and a voice flecked with humour. He always seemed to be smiling. In a U-boat culture that shunned personal relationships between officers and crewmen, Brandt seemed most in his element among the enlisted men. But he undertook his duties with a palpable gravity. If the commander died or became incapacitated, the first officer would assume command. In his work, Brandt demanded an unrelenting excellence of himself, and he asked the same of the crew.

EVEN BEFORE he joined the marines, young Siegfried Brandt of Zinten, East Prussia, was known in his town as an *'aufrechter Mensch'*—a genuinely good person. 'Siggi', as he was called, had been raised as an observant Protestant, the eldest of three brothers born to parents open to the world of new ideas and different people. The family believed strongly in their religion, which stood starkly opposed to the Nazi faith in the Thousand-Year Reich.

After high school, Siggi volunteered for the navy. In 1941, he began his naval officer training. During his visits home, Siggi's youngest brother, Hans-Georg, heard Siggi making jokes about 'Adolf'—sarcastic snips about how Hitler 'knows everything'. Even at eleven, Hans-Georg knew that his brother neither liked nor trusted Hitler.

For a time, Siggi served aboard a minesweeper. Twice he saw battle action. When naval brass asked for volunteers for the U-boat service, the young Brandt raised his hand.

In February 1943, Brandt's submarine, *U-108*, was bombed by British airplanes in the Atlantic. Crippled, the sub made it safely back to port. Around October of that year, Brandt was made first officer of *U-869*. He met the boat's commander, Helmuth Neuerburg, and its chief engineer, Ludwig Kessler. During training, Brandt was the consummate professional, dutybound and willing to die for Germany. During visits home, however, thirteen-year-old Hans-Georg heard his brother call the U-boat an 'iron coffin'.

THE *U-869* CREW continued its training into spring 1944, anxious for the first of several tests by inspectors near the Polish fishing peninsula of Hel. *U-869* would go through testing five times between March and October. Each time, Neuerburg performed excellently, controlling his boat and firing his torpedoes with a marksman's precision. In emergency dive training, the crew was quick and nimble, a single organism of unified reflexes built from relentless training and a sober understanding of the odds they faced. Like the famed U-boat aces, Neuerburg stayed cool no matter how threatening the moment. His crew grew to respect him even more.

Despite their growing proficiency, the men remained realists. Most knew that the Allies owned antisubmarine technology for which the German navy had no answer. None, however, dared speak openly of his fears.

One day, as Neuerburg boarded *U-869*, the crew gave him the Nazi *heil* salute in place of their usual military salute. A recent assassination attempt on Hitler had resulted in a new governmental order: military officers were now to use the *heil* salute. Neuerburg tore into the crew, telling them that the *heil* was not to be used aboard his boat. Some crewmen tried to explain about the new order. Neuerburg told them he did not care.

If Neuerburg seemed difficult to read, an incident in Hel only furthered the enigma. As the crew prepared to spend the night, Neuerburg announced that they would walk to a special barracks set in the thick woods of the peninsula. Inside, Neuerburg served a good, strong beer and asked the men to gather their chairs in a circle. Inside the circle, he took a guitar, sat down, and began playing beautifully. Neuerburg motioned for the men to join him in singing lightly patriotic songs. None questioned his motives. They could see by the way he sang that the music came from his heart.

One of the crewmen who very likely sang along that night was nineteen-year-old torpedoman Franz Nedel. Nedel nurtured two loyalties as he trained with *U-869*. The first was to Hitler and the Nazi Party. The second was to his fiancée, Gisela Engelmann, who despised the Nazis as much as her beloved Franz admired them.

Nedel and Gisela had met in 1940 while she was attending a Hitler Youth programme in the countryside and he was pursuing an apprenticeship as a butcher. He was fifteen, she fourteen. He delighted in her freethinking and fiery personality. She adored his intellect, his compassion and his belly laugh. Inside a week, they were boyfriend and girlfriend. He called her Gila; she called him Frenza. They knew they would spend their lives together.

The couple was inseparable. Nedel's gentle nature, however, seemed at odds with one of his passions: he was fascinated by U-boats and was determined to enlist in the submarine service when the day came for him to join the military.

Gila begged him to reconsider. 'These are swimming coffins,' she told him. 'Get on a battleship or a cruiser.'

'No, Gila,' he replied time and again. 'I want the U-boat.'

Gila told him she understood. She had a shakier grasp, however, on Nedel's political beliefs. The Nazis had imprisoned his father, a butcher, for holding anti-Hitler beliefs. Nedel loved his father, yet he found himself sympathetic to Hitler and the Third Reich. Gila's father also had been arrested. For months, he had delivered food and supplies to a Jewish family hiding in a nearby basement. He was arrested and sent to the Dachau concentration camp.

Still, Gila loved Nedel deeply. As Nedel entered naval training in 1943, the couple became engaged. 'When the war ends,' he promised, 'we will have our life.'

Less than a year later, Nedel was aboard *U-869*. He told Gila that he admired Commander Neuerburg and trusted the sub's crew with his life. 'When we're out at sea, all we have is each other,' he said.

THAT SUMMER, First Officer Brandt took a short leave to visit his family. He played with his thirteen-year-old brother, Hans-Georg, then enjoyed his mother's cooking. As the evening settled, he and his father went into the study and closed the door. Hans-Georg pressed his ear against the keyhole.

'I am taking a pistol with me on *U-869*'s patrol,' Brandt told his father. 'I will not wait until the end should something happen.'

Hans-Georg's heart pounded. What did his brother mean?

A short time later, Brandt invited Hans-Georg and his mother to visit the U-boat in Pillau, where it was stationed. Hans-Georg could barely contain himself. At the harbour, Brandt picked up his mother and brother in a small boat and took them to a back port where the warships were docked. As the boat approached, Hans-Georg picked out *U-869* right away, a massive sculpture of grey fighting technology, brand-new, proud and invincible.

Brandt invited Hans-Georg to board the U-boat, meanwhile apologising to his mother—Commander Neuerburg did not permit women on his submarine, as he considered their presence aboard bad luck. If she would not mind waiting, he would give Hans-Georg a tour. Hans-Georg's heart pounded. This is the greatest moment in my life, he thought to himself.

When the brothers reached the deck, Hans-Georg saw a man dressed in shorts, lying on his back, sunning himself. The man saw the Brandts and rose. Hans-Georg bowed, as was proper for a young man of the day. The man shook Hans-Georg's hand.

'Commander Neuerburg, this is my brother Hans-Georg,' Brandt said. 'With your permission, I would like to show him the boat.'

'Of course,' Neuerburg said.

The Brandts climbed through the conning tower down a smooth, freshly painted metal ladder. Brandt showed his brother the diesel engines, the electric motors, the radio room, the torpedoes. Everything smelt of oil. Brandt pointed Hans-Georg to his bunk. A moment later, Hans-Georg was sitting on his brother's bed.

No one, he thought, has a brother like mine.

ON AUGUST 30, 1944, *U-869* was docked at the U-boat flotilla base at Stettin. Already, much of the town lay ruined from Allied bombing. That night, the crewmen were woken in their barracks by the sound of air-raid sirens. When Guschewski heard antiaircraft fire from German ships, he leapt from his bed and rushed towards an underground bunker. Bombs exploded. The crewmen waited inside the bunker. When it was safe to emerge, the men surveyed the area. Craters lay where their barracks had stood. No one said anything, but Guschewski could read their thoughts. Each of them was thinking, The war is lost. Why isn't there peace?

Autumn gave the crew a reprieve from the searing summer temperatures, which could reach 110 degrees inside the U-boat. It would now be just a matter of weeks before the boat was assigned a war patrol.

In late November, Brandt sent a letter to his family. It read:

By the time you receive my letter I will already have started my journey. I wish Hans-Georg a happy birthday. I hope to be back home for his confirmation. I also wish you a blessed and healthy Christmas and New Year. Christmas is a family celebration; even if this time it is only in my thoughts. By thinking of each other we can remember how nice it used to be.

As Brandt wrote his letters and *U-869* prepared for its maiden war patrol, Neuerburg made a final visit home. Upon returning home, he always removed his uniform and changed into civilian clothes in order to turn back into a '*Mensch*'—a human being. He never discussed the upcoming mission with his wife, Erna, except to say that *U-869* was manned by a fine crew. The couple added entries to their 'Baby Daybook', a diary they kept for Jürgen and Jutta. His final entry, written to Jürgen before *U-869* left on patrol, concluded this way:

Soon, Daddy will have to go out to sea with his U-boat, and our most ardent hope is that we will all see each other again soon, in good health and in peaceful times. Then hopefully you will again wait for me with Mummy and Jutta and cry out in a happy voice: 'Mummy, there comes Daddy!' May this time not be very far away. May a protecting hand keep you, my dear ones, from terrible things, protect and shield you till a sunny and carefree time reunites us again.

With much love,
Daddy

U-869 was scheduled to depart for war around December 1, 1944. As Neuerburg said goodbye to his family, Erna noticed that he had left something behind.

'You have forgotten your gold pocket watch, Helmuth,' she said. 'Take it with you.'

'No,' he said. 'You keep it and count the minutes until I return home.'

At around the same time, torpedoman Franz Nedel and a group of his *U-869* comrades travelled to his parents' house for a farewell party. His fiancée, Gila, threw her arms round him. His mother went to the kitchen to serve food and drink. Ordinarily, Nedel and his friends already would have been talking and singing and enjoying their free time. Instead, they sat in the living room, still in uniform, and stared straight ahead, saying nothing. Gila's smile slowly faded away at the sight. She looked at the men. One of them began crying, then another, then all of them.

'What is wrong?' Gila asked, rushing to Nedel's side.

For a moment the men could do nothing but cry. Nedel said nothing. Finally one of the other men spoke.

'None of us is coming back,' he said.

'What do you mean?' Gila asked. 'Of course you're coming back.'

'No, we're not coming back,' said another.

The next morning, the men rode the train with Gila and Nedel's mother back to *U-869*'s dock. Gila did not let go of Nedel's hand during the hours-long trip. No one mentioned the events of the previous night. *U-869* was to leave on its war patrol that day.

Gila saw *U-869* for the first time—a magnificent and proud machine in which her future lay.

Gila and Nedel's mother stood near the boat. The men lined up in rows on the U-boat's deck as a four-man band made its way to the dock and played a melancholy German folk song. The U-boat began to move away from its dock. Nedel and the other crewmen stayed on the deck and waved. A few minutes later, the U-boat disappeared into the overcast horizon.

The U-Boat Is Our Moment

Since 1991, Chatterton and Kohler had believed in history. Every book, expert and document listed *U-869* as sunk off Gibraltar. Now, two and a half years later, the intercepted radio messages between *U-869* and U-boat Control virtually proved that the New Jersey U-boat was *U-869*. The divers dug deep into their filing cabinets for *U-869*'s crew roster. Kohler, who understood the German rank and position abbreviations, called Chatterton and read him the basics.

'There are fifty-six crewmen listed,' Kohler said. 'A guy named Neuerburg was the commander. He was born in 1917, which would have made him twenty-seven years old. The first officer was . . . let's see . . . Brandt, Siegfried Brandt; he was only twenty-two. Here's our friend Horenburg, the *Funkmeister*, aged twenty-five.'

'How young did they go?' Chatterton asked.

Kohler did some computations. 'There are twenty-four teenagers. The youngest was Otto Brizius. When *U-869* left on war patrol, he was seventeen.'

'We've been swimming past these guys and bumping into their bones for three seasons and never had a clue who they were,' Chatterton said. 'Now we know their names.'

Word of the radio intercepts flashed through the U-boat community. To many experts, the mystery of the New Jersey U-boat was now solved. But Chatterton and Kohler were not prepared to close the book. The wreck still had not su rrendered evidence that conclusively proved her identity. They would return to the wreck. Their fellow divers recoiled at the idea. Three men had died diving the boat. 'You guys know it's *U-869*,' their colleagues protested. 'No one's disputing it. You rewrote history. Why risk your lives?'

We need to know for ourselves, they answered. We need proof.

As the Atlantic warmed, Kohler's longing for his family deepened. He had never fully appreciated the depth of pleasure he took in full-time fatherhood, nor the importance of that role to his self-image. For years, he had considered himself a diver. Now, as his children began to know a new life in their new home, Kohler realised that he considered himself a father most of all. 'I can't live without my kids,' he told himself.

Kohler began to contemplate the impossible. He called Chatterton. They met at Scotty's, and Kohler told Chatterton that any reconciliation with Felicia would require him to give up diving. 'It's for my family,' he said. 'If I have to give up diving to save my family, I'll do it.'

'That's great, Richie,' Chatterton said, his face reddening. 'You're on the verge of putting the final pieces of the U-boat puzzle together, and you're going to walk away.'

For a minute, neither man spoke.

'I love my kids,' Kohler said finally. 'They're already learning to live without me. I gotta really think this through.'

A short time later, Kohler called Felicia. He told her he wanted his family back. She gave him two ultimatums. First, he would have to join her for marriage counselling. Second, he would have to give up diving.

He told Chatterton the news that night at Scotty's. Kohler had never seen his friend so disgusted.

A month later, Kohler and his family reconciled and rented a house in suburban Middletown, New Jersey. At his office, he packed his U-boat work into a filing cabinet and locked the drawer. That day, Kohler began his new life as an ex-diver.

CHATTERTON'S FIRST TRIP to the *U-Who* in 1994 was booked for the first weekend in July. He had spent months wrestling with a single question: Where do I go next on the wreck? On the eve of the dive, he still had no answer. The trip was as Chatterton expected. He rolled off the boat without a plan. He swam the wreck without priorities. He told Yurga, 'Without a vision, I'm wasting my time.'

As if to exact revenge against the *U-Who*, Chatterton turned his creative fury to the hunt for other shipwrecks. In July 1994 alone, he discovered and identified the tanker *Norness*—the first ship sunk by a U-boat on the American side of the Atlantic during World War II—and discovered the *Sebastian*—a World War I-era passenger liner sunk by fire and storm eight miles east of the *Andrea Doria*.

While Chatterton made these discoveries, Kohler undertook a dry-docked life in suburbia. He tiptoed around Felicia and screwed up enthusiasm for family grocery trips. He bought his-and-her bicycles. Occasionally, he would slip. On a calm and sunny Sunday, he might remark, 'I bet the ocean's like glass for those guys today.'

'I don't want to hear that!' Felicia would say, glaring. 'You're dreaming about diving? Don't you want to be with us?'

'Of course I do,' Kohler would say. Then he would recite his silent mantra: It's for the kids. I love my family. It's for the kids.

Kohler expected the onset of autumn to provide some respite from his longings. Instead, he found himself thinking about the *U-Who*'s crewmen. As winter crawled over New Jersey, these thoughts became an obligation. More than ever he believed that he owed these men a duty, that they must not lie in an anonymous grave with their fate unknown to their loved ones. Kohler watched the snow fall outside his rented home. For years, snow had meant that Kohler was just a few months from returning to the ocean. This year, he felt like he had never been farther from himself, and the snow seemed as if it would keep falling for ever.

By early 1995, Kohler was white-knuckling his marriage just to keep it breathing. He had entered marriage counselling and locked away his dive gear. Still, things grew worse. In the early spring, he wrote Felicia a twelve-page letter, took off his wedding band, then moved onto his friend's floor in Levittown, Pennsylvania.

For a few months, Kohler took custody of his kids every weekend. Then, in July 1995, Kohler took over full custody of the children. He was ecstatic. He called a real-estate agent and requested a home in the best school district within a twenty-five-mile radius of his Trenton, New Jersey, shop. Two weeks later, he and his children moved to a town house in Yardley, Pennsylvania. He hired an au pair and registered his kids in school.

On the other side of New Jersey, bad weather limited Chatterton to just a single *U-Who* trip. As in 1994, he dived the submarine without a plan and came up empty. Stonewalled by the U-boat, he threw his creative muscle into the quest he had started the year before—the discovery of historic, previously undiscovered shipwrecks. One such wreck was the SS *Carolina*, a passenger liner sunk by a U-boat during World War I. Some began to call him the greatest wreck diver in the world. Yet he sank further into despair.

For the first time in his career, Chatterton heard the clock tick. He was forty-four years old, an elder statesman in a sport that wore down athletes half his age. Other divers no longer wanted to explore the *U-Who*. If Chatterton broke bones in a car accident or developed cancer, the submarine would very likely never be fully identified.

Chatterton was at a loss as to what to do next. In his darkest moments, he wondered about quitting. The fantasy always felt good for a minute, but it always ended with Chatterton thinking, It's what a person does at the moment of his greatest struggle that shows him who he really is. Some people never get that moment. The *U-Who* is my moment.

When he thought that, Chatterton would snap out of his brush with quitting, sit down at his desk in front of Horenburg's knife, and start drawing sketches of the places on the *U-Who* he planned to go next.

Now separated from Felicia, Kohler began to receive invitations to go diving. The first came from Chatterton. Kohler told him what he would tell all his friends that season: 'I can't dive. I physically and mentally can't do it. My head's not in it. I'll die.'

As the 1995 dive season wound down, Kohler continued as a full-time father and businessman. In September, he went to the Hudson City Savings Bank to do a glass job. There, he met a pretty thirty-year-old blue-eyed blonde who complained of a problem door. When Kohler deduced that part of the problem was that the woman, Valentina Marks, had been kicking the door with her high heels, he took a liking to her. He asked her to dinner. It went well. He asked her to dinner again. It was the real thing.

Kohler told her about the *U-Who*, and she asked to know more, especially about the fallen crewmen. Tina was of German descent. Even before Kohler confessed it, she knew he felt an obligation to these men.

In late 1995, Kohler received the same phone call he had placed two years earlier. It was from Chatterton. His marriage was in trouble. They met at Scotty's. Chatterton's situation was different from Kohler's. There had been no suggestion that Chatterton give up diving. The couple had simply grown apart.

'Maybe the worst part,' he told Kohler, 'is that the U-boat is hanging over me. It's with me at work and home. I'm not who I used to be. I'm not as friendly. I'm not as happy.'

'John, you just had one of the greatest diving years in history,' Kohler said. 'How can you be unhappy at a time like this?'

'The U-boat is different,' he said. 'The U-boat is our moment.'

For several minutes, neither man said anything. Finally, Chatterton spoke. 'You coming back, Richie?'

'I just don't know,' Kohler said. 'It's been a very long time.'

Kohler spent the winter of 1995–96 contemplating a future with Tina. His life had stabilised, his kids were happy, and his business was growing.

Then spring began to dab warmth into the air, and Tina said it would be a shame if a man turned his back on his passion. So Kohler walked to the phone and dialled. Chatterton answered.

'John, it's Richie,' he said. 'I'm back.'

They met at Scotty's, and began work on a plan. They would force their way into the electric motor room, the only unexplored compartment on the *U-Who*. That room and part of the adjoining diesel motor room remained blocked by a steel escape trunk. For years, the divers had figured the trunk to be unmovable. Now they vowed to move the trunk at whatever cost.

The plan took shape like this: Chatterton and Kohler would rig a three-ton chain fall to the escape trunk that blocked the diesel motor room. The chain fall, a heavy-duty, ratchet-driven hoist, was powerful enough to pull a car from a ditch. Divers almost never risked a dangerous move like this. Chatterton and Kohler discussed the possibilities. They decided to proceed.

Chatterton borrowed a chain fall from the commercial diving outfit for which he worked. The divers booked several trips. Time and again, however, inclement weather forced them to stay onshore. The entire 1996 season passed. If this audacious plan was to happen, it would have to wait until 1997.

The winter passed slowly. Chatterton's marriage continued to fossilise. His wife had taken a new job, further reducing their time together. They entered counselling. It didn't work. In May 1997, as the dive season began, the couple hired a divorce lawyer.

As New Jersey's charter-boat captains put their boats back in the water for the dive season, Chatterton and Kohler reviewed a book by Henry Keatts on wreck diving. In one chapter, they came across photographs of several tags that had been recovered from *U-853*, a World War II U-boat of the same type as the *U-Who*, located near Block Island, Rhode Island. Most of the tags contained no meaningful writing. One of them, however, stunned the divers. It read, '*U-853*'. Chatterton and Kohler had recovered dozens of tags from the *U-Who*. None of them was marked with anything like this kind of identifying information.

Kohler called Keatts, whom the divers knew casually.

'Hank, in your book there's a photo of a bunch of tags from *U-853*. Where on the submarine did those tags come from?'

'I'm not sure,' Keatts said.

'Where are the tags now? Who has the one that says *U-853*?'

'I think Billy Palmer pulled that tag.'

'Thank you very much,' Kohler said.

Billy Palmer was a hard-living, cigar-chomping, fiftyish captain who ran a small dive boat, *Thunderfish*, near Block Island. He was also a first-rate wreck diver. Kohler found Palmer's Connecticut home phone number and placed a call.

'You still have those tags from the *853*?' Kohler asked.

'I got buckets of tags,' Palmer said.

'You remember where you got the one that says *U-853*?'

'It's been a long time, Richie. My memory's a little cloudy.'

Kohler asked if he and Chatterton might drive up for a visit. Palmer told him he'd be happy to see them.

A day later, the divers knocked on Palmer's door. Palmer gave them a guided tour of his artefact-filled house. The divers were itching to see the tags. Palmer took his time. Finally he escorted them to his basement.

He lifted the glass on a display case. Inside were at least fifty tags. One of them was stamped '*U-853*.' The divers sat dumbstruck.

'Can you tell us where on the wreck you found this one?' Kohler asked.

'It was on a wooden spare-parts box, a little bigger than a shoebox,' Palmer said.

'In what room?' Chatterton asked.

'It was in the electric motor room.'

The divers nearly leapt from their chairs.

'The spare-parts boxes had to be labelled with the U-boat's number,' Palmer explained. 'That way, if a part was used during a mission, they could send the box to the warehouse, have it refilled, and the warehouse would know which U-boat to return it to.'

Chatterton and Kohler sat frozen. Of all the places on the *U-Who*, the electric motor room was the only one that remained inaccessible. Now more than ever it was imperative that they move the massive steel escape trunk. They stood up and thanked Palmer.

The divers booked a trip to the *U-Who* for June 1, 1997. Chatterton brought the three-ton chain fall and an aluminium support beam. The plan would be executed in two stages. On the first dive, Kohler would take precise measurements of the escape trunk. He and Chatterton would then rig the chain fall to the trunk and pull it out on the second dive. If all went well, they would have unfettered access to both motor rooms.

The weather and current waved a gentle welcome to the divers.

Chatterton glided down the anchor line and tied the anchor into the wreck. Kohler followed, swimming through the gaping wound in the control room and heading aft. Just inside the diesel motor room, he came face to face with the escape trunk, a massive steel tube that lay fallen at a thirty-degree angle between the two giant diesel engines built on either side of the room. Wire splayed like Einstein's hair from all parts of the trunk. Kohler moved in slowly. Though he was supposed to measure the obstruction, he instead removed a crowbar strapped to his tank and nudged it between the trunk and the engine. He surveyed his surroundings, taking stock of how he might escape if the trunk fell. He pushed on the crowbar. The trunk rocked, billowing silt clouds into the compartment and causing wires to rattlesnake towards Kohler's face mask.

He moved the crowbar again. The trunk rocked in reply. If the trunk fell on him, it would pin him or crush him, and Chatterton—who was working forward in the sub—would never hear him scream. Kohler placed one hand under the lip of the trunk, the other on an engine block for purchase. He spread and planted his feet Sumo wrestler-style on the steel beams that supported the engines, praying that he would not slip. Then he reached inside himself for every muscle he had ever used. He lifted the trunk six inches off the ground. The metal ground against the steel engine blocks.

'Don't fall backwards,' Kohler told the trunk. 'Don't bury me here.'

He lifted harder. The trunk rose farther off the floor, and for a moment, Kohler held it aloft. The floor creaked. His arms burned. He stepped backwards. Now he released the trunk, allowing it to plummet downwards. As it fell, Kohler thrust the trunk away from him. It hit the floor and crashed to the left, raising storms of dark oily silt and sounding thunder off the U-boat's steel walls. Kohler held his breath and looked down. He was not trapped. He could see nothing, but he knew he had moved the unmovable. The obstruction to the electric motor room had been felled.

Kohler would have liked nothing more than to swim between the diesel engines and into the electric motor room. But he was winded, and the visibility had dropped to zero. He and Chatterton would have to wait until the day's second dive to move in.

Topside, Kohler told Chatterton the story. 'I muscled it. It's moved. We're in.'

Chatterton shook his head. 'We brought a three-ton chain fall to do that work. And you muscled it?'

Around noon, Chatterton and Kohler re-entered the ocean carrying lift bags and goody bags for the spare-parts boxes they hoped to recover. A minute later, they were inside the *U-Who*. The silt had cleared inside the diesel motor room, leaving a clear view aft. The divers could scarcely believe what they saw. Just a few feet past the escape trunk Kohler had moved lay another obstruction, this one a huge, crescent-shaped steel fuel tank, about twelve feet long and very heavy. It lay wedged diagonally between the diesel engines, with just a whisper of space between its top and the room's ceiling. The divers knew that even a three-ton chain fall could not move this mass. The electric motor room was still a million miles away.

Back on board the dive boat, they undressed in silence. For an hour during the ride back to Brielle, neither man said a word. Then, as the sun set over the horizon, Chatterton turned to Kohler. 'I have a plan,' he said. For the next five minutes, he described a vision, a three-dimensional epiphany, for moving past the fallen fuel tank and into the electric motor room. After he finished, Kohler looked him in the eye.

'You'll die,' Kohler said.

'I'm going to do it,' Chatterton said. 'But I can't do it without you.'

'I won't be part of that. I won't watch you die.'

'I'm going to do it,' Chatterton said. 'This is our last chance, Richie. I know I'm going to do it. And I need you with me.'

Circle-Runner

Kristiansand, Norway, December 4, 1944

A week and a half after leaving Germany, Commander Neuerburg and *U-869* arrived in the southern Norwegian port town of Kristiansand, where they took on fuel and supplies. Brimming with provisions, the U-boat could now wage war anywhere in the Atlantic. Neuerburg's first assignment was to crawl northwards along the Norwegian coast, then break into the open Atlantic via the Iceland-Faeroes gap. He would receive further orders—war orders—when the submarine reached the open seas.

For three weeks, the U-boat crawled along Norway's coast and then onwards into the Atlantic. On December 29, Control radioed its next order:

U-869 was to head for naval grid CA 53, the centre of which was about 110 miles southeast of New York. Neuerburg had been issued perhaps the most prestigious assignment a U-boat could receive: *U-869* had been sent to wage war against America.

The U-boat pushed westwards. Protocol required Neuerburg to radio a report to Control once *U-869* broke into the open Atlantic. Control had expected such a report no later than December 29. None was received. On December 30, Control requested a passage report. Again, it received none. On January 1, 1945, Control requested a position report from *U-869*, this time in strong language. It received no reply. Now Control was worried. For the next several days, Control demanded position reports from *U-869*.

By January 6, Control was very likely mourning for U-869. In almost every case in which a U-boat was five days late in reporting to Control, that U-boat was lost. But that day, in a broadcast that must have seemed a miracle inside Control, *U-869* radioed her position. Even as Control officials celebrated, they scratched their heads: *U-869* was about 600 miles southwest of Iceland. She should have been farther southwest.

It was then that Control most likely realised that Neuerburg had made a bold decision. Rather than use the Iceland-Faeroes gap, the most direct route from Norway into the Atlantic, he had diverted north, making a loop over Iceland before heading southwestwards through the Denmark Strait. The Denmark Strait was less heavily patrolled by Allied antisubmarine airplanes and ships. Though a commander was allowed such discretion, Control never liked the move; every day spent in transit was a day away from the war.

What no one knew—not Neuerburg, his crew, or Control—was that Allied code breakers had intercepted *U-869*'s broadcast and now knew where the U-boat was.

Neuerburg's decision to use the circuitous Denmark Strait sent Control strategists scrambling. Going the long way meant that it would cost the boat 100 days to stay perhaps fourteen days off New York, an unacceptable ratio. Control requested a fuel-status report. Again, it received no reply. As Neuerburg had showed himself willing to use the radio, Control probably blamed atmospheric conditions for the lack of communication. Control radioed a new order to Neuerburg: *U-869* was to change course and head to Gibraltar, to patrol the African coast. By rerouting the submarine, Control could expect a longer patrol from *U-869*.

Control would not have expected *U-869* to acknowledge receipt of this order; it would have been too dangerous for Neuerburg to use his radio simply to confirm the directive. Control therefore presumed Neuerburg had received the order and began plotting *U-869* to Gibraltar, calculating that the submarine should arrive there around February 1. Had Neuerburg received the order, he would have followed it—while a commander had discretion in choosing his routes, he had no such option when receiving a direct order. It is virtually certain that *U-869* never received the new order.

The Allies, however, were receiving almost everything. On January 17, their intelligence wrote:

The U/Boat heading for the New York approaches, *U-869* (Neuerburg) . . . is expected to arrive in the New York area at the beginning of February.

On January 25, American intelligence pegged the situation:

One U/Boat may be south of Newfoundland heading for New York approaches, although her location is uncertain due to a mix-up in orders and Control assumes she is heading for Gibraltar.

Then, in the chillingly matter-of-fact language of war, American intelligence announced its plans for *U-869*: 'The *CORE* [a US aircraft carrier] will begin sweeping for this U/Boat.' The Americans would be sending a hunterkiller group to destroy *U-869*. They knew where the submarine was going.

U-869 VERY LIKELY approached American coastal waters in early February. From that moment, Neuerburg would have kept the submarine submerged full-time. By now, the American hunter-killer group had begun its search for *U-869*. Neuerburg, who knew well the Allies' ability to stalk a U-boat, must have navigated with extreme stealth. The hunter-killer group found only empty sea.

Finally, *U-869* was in American waters and bearing down on the New York approaches. Neuerburg's targets would be whatever enemy vessels he could find. Perhaps a day passed, perhaps several days. Then, Neuerburg must have spotted an enemy ship. He would have ordered his men to their battle stations. From now on, every order would have been whispered.

As *U-869* crept forward at a speed of perhaps two knots, the crew very likely heard the sound of water outside the submarine, the hum of the electric engines, and perhaps even the faint revolutions of the enemy target's propellers in the distance. All else would have been quiet. Now *U-869* was ready to attack. Neuerburg kept the periscope raised. The men remained at their battle stations. Seconds later, Neuerburg whispered this kind of order. 'Tube one ready—fire.'

An Audacious Plan

Chatterton's final plan for the *U-Who* was audacious. He would swim into the diesel motor room with just a single tank on his back, not the customary two. He would then remove that tank, hold it in front of him—much as a child holds a kickboard when learning to swim—and push it through the narrow opening between the fallen fuel tank and the U-boat's ceiling. Once on the other side, he would reattach the tank to his back and swim into the adjoining electric motor room, where he hoped to find identifying tags attached to boxes of spare parts. After recovering the bounty, he would swim back into the diesel motor room, pass the bounty over the top to Kohler, again remove his tank, and slither back out the way he had come in.

'Forget it,' Kohler said by phone on the evening Chatterton revealed the plan in full detail. 'That is the single most insane plan I have ever heard. I'm not watching you die.'

'We can't stop now,' Chatterton said. 'I have a plan. This is why I dive, Richie. This is the art.'

'I'm bailing on this, John. I'm out.'

For three days, Chatterton and Kohler did not speak. Kohler envisioned the dive from a thousand angles, and it always ended up the same—with Chatterton slumped over, drowned or pinned under some piece of fallen steel, Kohler helpless to move through the crack to save him. But he also found himself imagining another scene, one from his first dive to the *U-Who*. While hanging under water, he had been overcome with joy at the sight of Chatterton's mesh bag filled with china and had reached instinctively to take a closer look. For a moment, there had been a stand-off. Then Chatterton had offered his bag to Kohler.

Kohler called Chatterton. 'John, I'm scared to death for you,' he said. 'But we're partners.'

'We are partners, Richie,' Chatterton replied. 'Let's do this.'

THE FIRST ATTEMPT was scheduled for August 17, 1997. Chatterton spent the weeks leading up to the mission rehearsing his moves—a combination of mime and ballerina practising for a recital in which a single misstep could mean death. By this time, his divorce was nearly final. In 1991, when he'd discovered the *U-Who*, he had believed his marriage would last for ever. Now Kathy did not even know of this daring plan for the U-boat.

On August 17, Chatterton, Kohler, and five other top wreck divers boarded the *Seeker* and set sail for the *U-Who*. In the morning, Chatterton reviewed his plan with Kohler. He would use the first dive as a trial run to investigate the accessibility of the electric motor room and learn the layout of the compartment. Kohler would hover near the top of the fallen fuel-tank obstruction, shining his flashlight as a beacon and waiting to take any artefacts Chatterton might pass through.

A few minutes later, Chatterton and Kohler were in the water. In total, Chatterton carried three gas tanks—the one he would breathe inside the electric motor room, plus two stage bottles for his trip down to the wreck and back. As the divers reached the *U-Who*, Chatterton placed his stage bottles on top of the wreck and began breathing from his primary tank.

The divers swam towards the fallen fuel tank that blocked much of the diesel motor room. Chatterton removed the tank from his back and held it in front of him. He kicked his fins and began gliding forward. A few seconds later, he pushed his tank through the gap and then sardined through himself. On the other side of the diesel motor room, he slung the tank onto his back. He began to explore.

The path to the electric motor room was clear. Chatterton swam to the hatch that led into the compartment and passed through it. He had ten minutes of gas remaining. He would use it to become accustomed to leaving these compartments. He swam back up to the fallen fuel tank in the diesel motor room and again removed his tank. A few seconds later, he pushed the tank and himself back through the opening near the ceiling and landed on the other side. From there, he reattached the tank, glided to where his stage bottles lay atop the wreck, and switched regulators. He now had plenty of gas with which to do his decompression. Kohler shook his head in amazement. Chatterton had made a near-perfect trial run.

Bad weather blew out the day's second dive. The next trip was scheduled for August 24. The plan would be the same as on the first trip, with a single exception: Kohler would pass Chatterton a video camera once he got past the obstruction. Chatterton would thus be able to videotape the compartments for future study.

As before, Chatterton's tank manoeuvring was seamless. The video camera he had taken from Kohler, however, would not work. Frustrated, he swam to the top of the compartment to hand it back through the gap to Kohler. By now, however, he had reaffixed the tank to his back, and he found that the equipment made him slightly too bulky to reach the gap. Chatterton spotted a massive steel beam near the ceiling, a piece he could use to pull himself closer to Kohler. He grabbed the beam and pulled. The steel shook for a moment, then gave way, crashing into Chatterton's lap and hurling him against one of the diesel engines. His heart pounded. He ordered himself to control his breathing. Then he slowly reached to remove the steel from his lap. Its weight was enormous, at least 200 pounds out of water. Still, he managed to begin lifting it. His breathing rate increased. His gas supply dropped. He lifted harder. The beam moved just an inch before stopping cold. Chatterton was trapped.

Panic is how guys die, he thought. Collect yourself.

Kohler looked into the gap. Silt had billowed everywhere. He could see nothing. He presumed Chatterton was going about his dive.

Chatterton's gas gauge crept downwards.

This thing got onto me, he thought. It's just a matter of figuring the way it landed on me, then reversing the process. Stay calm.

Chatterton used his mind's eye to replay the collapse of the beam. For five minutes, he gently tried to push the steel in the opposite direction. The object would not move. Another five minutes passed.

With just a few minutes of gas remaining, Chatterton again reached to move the beam. He pushed up and felt one end clank free. He pushed on the other end. The beam collapsed forward and pivoted away from his lap. Chatterton then pushed himself off the diesel engine and swam swiftly towards the gap near the ceiling. His gauge needle dipped into red. He removed his tank and pushed it through, then kicked his fins and wriggled out of the compartment. Kohler moved to join his partner, but he backed off when he saw Chatterton head directly for the tanks he had left on top of the wreck.

A moment later, Chatterton had switched to one of his stage bottles. He had exited the diesel motor room with less than a minute of air remaining.

Topside, Chatterton told the story. Kohler turned white. He'd had no idea that Chatterton had experienced any trouble. 'Forget it,' Kohler said. 'This is too dangerous.'

'Let's get that video camera working,' Chatterton said, reaching inside a cooler for a soda. 'I'll want to shoot lots of film on my second dive today.'

Kohler walked away. 'Crazy bastard,' he muttered.

A few hours later, Chatterton was back inside the diesel motor room, Kohler hovering outside, waiting. This time, the camera worked. Chatterton moved through the hatch that led into the electric motor room. Silt exploded in clouds around him. He pointed the camera to where his research indicated the spare-parts boxes and their identifying tags should be—the camera could always see better than the human eye under water. Then Chatterton exited the electric motor room and swam back up to Kohler and passed him the camera. He removed his tank and made his way out of the diesel motor room. He had not recovered any artefacts. He had almost lost his life on the first dive. But now he had video. Topside, he thanked Kohler for his support.

'Next trip, I haul the boxes. I feel it. The next trip is the one.'

THE NEXT CHARTER to the *U-Who* was scheduled for a week later, on August 31. Chatterton spent the intervening days studying the videotape he had shot. In one of the spots, he saw what appeared to be a stack of three or four boxes. Now he really knew the next dive would be the one.

At home, Kohler went to war with himself. He knew that the electric motor room was jungled in the worst, most ravenous scream of wires, tubes, jagged metal and silt. He also knew Chatterton's heart. His friend would breathe his tank dry on Sunday before he would exit without his answer. Kohler decided to quit. Yet whenever he picked up the phone, he ended up putting the receiver back. There might be one scenario worse than watching his friend die in the wreck. The worst scenario would be to allow his friend to die while he stayed home and waited for the news.

ON SATURDAY EVENING, August 30, 1997, the *Seeker* jockeyed away from her dock and pointed towards the *U-Who*. Chatterton and Kohler spoke little.

The next morning's weather was perfect and calm. Over a bowl of cereal, Chatterton asked Kohler if he was ready to receive the spare-parts boxes he expected to recover and pass over the top of the fallen fuel tank. Kohler nodded. An hour later, they were on the wreck. Chatterton took off his tank, extended it in front of him, and moved through the crack between the obstruction and the ceiling. Kohler turned on his flashlight and lifted it to the space, a beacon for Chatterton's return.

Visibility was good inside the diesel motor room. Chatterton reattached his tank and glided into the electric motor room. The scene was just as his video-tape had depicted it. He looked to the right. There, stacked in a freestanding pyramid, were four boxes of spare parts, each fused to the next by decades of marine encrustation. The smallest was slightly larger than a shoebox.

Chatterton inched towards the boxes. Lying at a thirty-degree angle against the top box was what appeared to be a five-foot-tall section of broken pipe. Chatterton pushed gently against the boxes. The pipe was wedged against them and nothing moved. He turned back and exited the compart-ment. He now understood he would have to take drastic action.

Topside, Chatterton briefed Kohler. 'The boxes are fused together and pinned down by this huge pipe,' Chatterton said. 'But those are the boxes, Richie. If there are identifying tags on this wreck, they're on those boxes. I'm taking a short-handled sledgehammer down there. The boxes are mine.'

Slinging a sledgehammer at 230 feet was perhaps the best way for a diver to blow through his gas supply. Kohler did not bother to object. Chatterton was being directed from somewhere deeper than good advice.

Chatterton and Kohler splashed four hours later. Chatterton moved swiftly into the electric motor room. The compartment remained brown and cloudy from his earlier dive, but he could still see the boxes and the pipe through the silt. He would use the sledgehammer to knock the pipe loose, then prise the boxes free from each other with a crowbar.

Chatterton crept to within two feet of the pipe. He spread his hands wide across the sledgehammer's handle—using the tool in the water required a different technique from on land, one in which the diver pushed from the chest rather than swung with the arms. He anchored his left knee in front of the boxes and his right foot across the aisle on solid machinery. Then he thrust the sledgehammer's head into the section of pipe. The compartment thundered with the impact as pieces of encrustation flew from the pipe and hailstormed the room in rust. Chatterton stayed motionless. When the pieces settled to the bottom, he stood, amazed at the sight. The pipe had not moved. And the pipe was not a pipe. Naked and shiny without its encrustation, the object flashed its true identity. This was a five-foot-tall pressurised oxygen tank. This was the colossal big brother to the miniature version that had destroyed Chatterton's garage. It was a miracle it had not just exploded.

I need to make a decision, Chatterton said to himself.

He flashed through his options. They numbered exactly two: He could turn and leave the compartment. Or he could take another swing at the giant oxygen tank. If the thing blows, Chatterton thought, I'll be dead and in a billion pieces. If I leave now, I can leave in one piece.

He stepped forward and found purchase with his feet.

It's what a person does at the moment of his greatest struggle that shows him who he really is.

He lifted the sledgehammer against his chest.

Some people never get that moment.

He breathed deeper than he had ever breathed.

The U-Who *is my moment.*

The sledgehammer bashed into the tank. The room thundered. Silt flew everywhere. Chatterton waited for the sound of a million sticks of dynamite. He heard only the whoosh of his bubbles leaving his regulator and the clank of falling metal. He peered through the silt. The tank had dropped away from the boxes. He was alive.

Chatterton moved towards the boxes, pulled the smallest one free, and stuffed it into his mesh bag. He checked his watch—he had five minutes remaining. He swam out of the electric motor room and up towards Kohler's flashlight beam. Though the box was heavy, he managed to hoist it through the gap to Kohler, who passed it to another diver to take to the surface and inspect for tags. By all rights, Chatterton should have exited the diesel motor room then, while he still had three minutes of time remaining. He could not. It was possible that the first box did not contain a tag. He needed to retrieve another box. Chatterton turned round.

A minute later, Chatterton found the second box. This one, however, was even heavier than the first and could not be picked up and swum to Kohler. Instead, Chatterton began to roll it end over end out of the electric motor room. The visibility dropped to zero. He pushed the box farther, huffing and puffing just to move it another foot. He pressed his watch against his face mask. He could make out only the outline of his timer. He had already stayed longer than planned. He abandoned the box.

I've gotta get my ass out of here, he thought.

Chatterton swam to the top of the electric motor room so that he could use the ceiling topography to feel his way out of the pitch-black compartment. His navigation was perfect, delivering him to the hatchway that led to the diesel motor room. He was now just a few kicks away from Kohler. He swam forward. Suddenly, his head jerked back. A wire noose had caught round his neck. Chatterton was being strangled.

The equipment on his back had become tangled on dangling electrical cables. He was now fully sewn into the wreck. Chatterton knew he did not have time to relax and reverse the process, as was necessary in such a predicament. He would have to fight. From his waiting post, Kohler checked his watch. Chatterton was not just late. He was crazy late.

Chatterton pulled at the wire noose round his throat and managed to muscle it off his neck. His breathing quickened even more. He reached up and clawed at the cables that had snared his equipment. Nothing gave. He could not move. He tore harder at the restraints. They would not loosen. He pulled at them with all he had. Finally, they dropped away. Now free, he dug hard for Kohler, knowing that the slightest additional entanglement would kill him. A moment later, he was there. All that remained was for Chatterton to remove his tank and swim through the gap. He took a breath as he reached for the tank. Only the tiniest trickle of gas came through the regulator. Chatterton knew this sensation. He was a breath away from going empty.

Chatterton ripped off his tank and shoved it through the crack near the ceiling, then lunged through the space himself. As he reached the other side, he inhaled, but nothing came from his tank. He was entirely out of gas. Chatterton spat the regulator from his mouth. His only remaining hope lay in reaching his stage bottles, a swim of at least fifty feet. He dared not risk buddy-breathing with Kohler, as even a slight delay or mix-up in communications could be deadly. Chatterton, his mouth now totally exposed to the ocean, kicked with force and equanimity. He had seen guys die flailing. He was near death. He would not flail.

Chatterton torpedoed out of the diesel motor room and up towards the top of the wreck. Kohler, stunned by the sight of his friend without a regulator, gave chase behind him. Chatterton's lungs screamed as his stage bottles came into sight. Every cell in his body shrieked for oxygen and pulled at his jaws to breathe. He clenched his mouth shut. He reached the stage bottles. In a single motion, he grabbed a regulator from one of the bottles, stuck it in his mouth, and turned the valve. Fresh gas flooded into his lungs. Chatterton had come down to his final breath.

A few seconds later, Kohler arrived at his side. The divers began their long decompression hang. For nearly two hours, Chatterton thought of the terrible risks he had taken during the dive. He had long since forgotten the spare-parts box he had recovered, which Kohler had passed to another diver for tag inspection topside.

Near the end of their decompressions, Chatterton and Kohler saw another diver swim down the anchor line. He handed Chatterton a slate just like the one on which Chatterton had written 'SUB' during the discovery trip six years earlier. This time, however, the slate said something different. This time, it read: 'The *U-Who* now has a name—it is *U-869*. Congratulations.'

In his younger days, Kohler might have jumped for joy and slapped Chatterton on the back. Chatterton might have pumped his fists in triumph. Today, they looked into each other's eyes. Then each extended his hand. The divers shook. Today, they had found something important. Today, they had their answers.

Epilogue

C hatterton and Kohler identified *U-869* in 1997. To this day, mysteries remain. Why did *U-869* continue to New York after being rerouted to Gibraltar? How did *U-869* meet her end? How did the crew die?

The answers to these questions will probably never be known. It is possible, however, to construct a most-likely-case scenario. That scenario looks like this:

The cataclysmic damage to *U-869*'s control room was almost certainly caused by a strike from a circle-runner—one of the U-boat's own torpedoes. Based on damage to the wreck, the circle-runner most likely impacted just below the conning tower, in the centre of the sub. Steel doors were blown open. So strong was the blast that it bowed the steel hatch leading into the diesel motor room and blew the hatch off the torpedo-loading tube in the forward torpedo room. The force of the explosion was easily strong enough to blow open the overhead hatches—hatches Chatterton and Kohler once speculated had been opened by crewmen attempting to escape the sinking sub.

It probably took the U-boat less than thirty seconds to fill with water. The submarine would have sunk to the ocean bottom in less than a minute. If anyone had survived the explosion and somehow made it out of the boat and to the surface, he very likely would not have lasted more than an hour in the icy waters. The enemy target ship, now as far as ten minutes away, its own engines running, wind and water lapping at its sides, would almost certainly have never heard or seen a thing.

THE SEEKER, the dive boat conceived and built by Nagle and used to discover and dive the U-Who, continues to run charters with its current owner, Danny Crowell. Crowell rarely runs to U-869.

In November 2000, Chatterton was diagnosed with metastasised squamous cell carcinoma of the tonsil, possibly a result of his exposure to Agent Orange in Vietnam. He was back diving shipwrecks by May of the next year.

Chatterton and Kathy had divorced in 1997, less than a month after he had identified U-869. In January 2002, Chatterton married Carla Madrigal, his girlfriend of three years. The couple moved to a beachfront home on the New Jersey shore. In September 2002, Chatterton quit commercial diving after a twenty-year career to pursue a history degree at Kean University in New Jersey. After graduation, he hopes to teach high school or college history. Chatterton and Kohler remain close friends and still dine together at Scotty's. By May 2003, Chatterton's cancer was in remission.

Chatterton's involvement with U-869 largely ended the day he identified the wreck. Unlike Kohler, he felt no pressing obligation to find the crewmen's families or to deliver news of their loved ones' fates. 'I cared about those things,' he says. 'But they were in Richie's heart. There was no one in the world who should have done that besides Richie.'

The first person Kohler had called after he and Chatterton had identified U-869 was Tina Marks, his girlfriend. She had believed in him. The couple grew closer. She became pregnant. Tina, however, was being harassed by a former boyfriend. One day in 1998, when Tina was eight months pregnant with Kohler's child, the man showed up at her door, shot her with a 9-mm pistol, then shot himself. In a moment, Kohler's love and future had disappeared.

As it had for years, diving served as his salvation. In 1999, Kohler became co-head of a British–American expedition to identify previously discovered World War I and World War II U-boats sunk in the English

Channel. In the autumn of that year, Kohler opened a second branch of Fox Glass, in Baltimore. His son, Richie, and daughter, Nikki, who continue to live with him, became honour-roll students.

Kohler's involvement with *U-869* entered a new phase after he and Chatterton had identified the wreck. In 1997, he set out to find the crewmen's families. He found contact information for Barbara Bowling, the half sister of seventeen-year-old Otto Brizius, the youngest of *U-869*'s crewmen. He also found Martin Horenburg's daughter.

Bowling, it turned out, had been living for nearly twenty years in Maryland. She and Otto shared the same father, a man who had spoken lovingly of Otto since Barbara had been a baby. Bowling had grown up admiring this brother she had never known, always believing he lay at the ocean's bottom off Gibraltar. A fluent German speaker, Bowling agreed to help Kohler with his further search for family members.

Horenburg's daughter was less eager to speak to Kohler. Her mother had remarried after *U-869*'s loss, and her stepfather had raised her as his own. Out of respect to this man, she preferred not to pursue contact with Kohler. Through an intermediary, she expressed gratitude to the divers and supplied them with several photos of her father. Chatterton took the knife off his desktop—a knife that had spoken to him for seven years—carefully packed the artefact, and drove it to the post office. A week later, the knife belonged to Martin Horenburg's daughter.

For a time, Kohler found himself frustrated in his efforts to locate more families. He focused on his personal life and began dating Carrie Bassetti, an executive for a New Jersey pharmaceutical company and the woman who would later become his wife. But by 2001, he had secured excellent contacts with crewmen's families. He booked a trip to Germany.

Just before leaving for Europe, Kohler chartered a boat and took Bowling and her family to the wreck site. There, he read a short memorial he had written, then splashed into the ocean and affixed a wreath and ribbons to *U-869*.

On New Year's Day, 2002, accompanied by Bowling as his translator, Kohler landed in Hamburg. Kohler's first appointment was with Hans-Georg Brandt, First Officer Siegfried Brandt's younger brother. Now seventy-one years old, Hans-Georg waited nervously at his son's home for Kohler's arrival, eager to see the face of one of the divers who had risked his life to find Siggi. Kohler knocked. Hans-Georg opened the door.

For six hours, Hans-Georg remembered his brother, a brother he loved today as much as he had at thirteen, when Siggi showed him the secrets of his U-boat. The conversation was emotional and painful at times. At the day's end, Hans-Georg thanked Kohler.

'I brought you something,' Kohler said. He reached into his briefcase. A moment later, he produced a metal schematic he had recovered from *U-869*'s electric motor room. 'You were probably in this room when you visited your brother.'

Hans-Georg took the schematic and stared at the metal. For several minutes, he could not break his gaze from the artefact. 'I can't believe it,' he said. 'I will save this for ever.'

The next morning, Kohler and Bowling drove several miles outside Hamburg to meet with a sixty-year-old surgeon. The man, thin, tall and handsome, welcomed them into his home. He introduced himself as Jürgen Neuerburg, the son of *U-869*'s commander, Helmuth Neuerburg.

Jürgen could produce no memories of his father, as he'd been just three years old when *U-869* was lost. But he remembered well his mother's stories, and for hours he shared these stories with Kohler, showing dozens of photographs and diary entries.

'Since I was a child, I believed my father had been lost off Gibraltar,' Jürgen said. 'When I learned that divers had found the boat off the coast of New Jersey, I was very surprised. But in the end, it did not change how I felt. I suspect it might have been a shock for my mother, after so many years of believing the official version of events. For this reason, I'm happy she never found out about it. She loved him dearly. She never remarried.'

Kohler asked Jürgen if his father had siblings. Indeed, his father had an older brother, Friedhelm. Kohler asked if Jürgen might have a telephone number for Friedhelm. Jürgen gave him the number.

That night at the hotel, Kohler and Bowling dialled the number. An elderly woman answered. Bowling introduced herself as the sister of one of *U-869*'s crewmen. The woman said she would be happy to bring her husband to the phone.

For the next hour, eighty-six-year-old Friedhelm Neuerburg remembered his brother, Helmuth. 'When I close my eyes and picture my brother today,' Friedhelm said, 'I see him doing his duty. I think he had a premonition that he wasn't coming back. He did his duty.'

In the morning, Kohler and Bowling drove from Hamburg to Berlin. The next day, they took the Berlin subway to the home of an elderly woman. On a mantelpiece in the living room were framed photos of her children and one of a young, handsome man from World War II. The woman introduced herself as Gisela Engelmann. The man in the photo, she said, was her fiancé, Franz Nedel, one of *U-869*'s torpedomen.

'My two husbands knew about Franz, of course,' she said. 'When I would speak of Franz to my children, they would roll their eyes and say, "Mother, you've told us this story a hundred and fifty times already."'

As with the Brandts, Engelmann was left to wonder about her loved one's fate long after the war's end. It was not until October 1947 that she received official word that *U-869* had been declared a total loss.

'I missed him every day of my life,' she told Kohler.

Kohler had one more appointment before flying back to New Jersey. He and Bowling flew to Munich, rented a car, and drove west through miles of breathtaking, snow-covered rural countryside. Kohler exited at the small town of Memmingen.

Kohler manoeuvred down narrow side streets until he arrived at one of the town's most ancient homes. He rang the doorbell. A minute later, a handsome and dignified eighty-year-old gentleman opened the door. Dressed in a blue suit and red tie, his cotton-white hair combed perfectly, he looked as if he had been expecting his visitor for years.

'I am Herbert Guschewski,' the man said. 'I was the radioman aboard *U-869*. Please, welcome to my home.'

In his living room, surrounded by his family, Guschewski told Kohler the story of how he had survived *U-869*. On a November morning in 1944, just days before *U-869* was to leave for war, Guschewski became dizzy and collapsed, unconscious. Onlookers rushed him to the hospital, where he remained in a coma with a high fever for three days. When he came to, the doctors told him he had contracted pneumonia and pleurisy. Though *U-869* was to depart in hours, he would be forced to remain in intensive care. He was also told he had visitors.

His hospital door opened. Standing before him, holding chocolate and flowers, was Commander Neuerburg. Behind him were First Officer Brandt and Chief Engineer Kessler. And behind them were many of the U-boat's crew. Neuerburg approached Guschewski.

'You'll be all right, my friend,' Neuerburg said.

Brandt stepped forward and took Guschewski's hand.

'Get well, friend,' he said, smiling.

'It finally came time to say goodbye,' Guschewski told Kohler. 'I had the feeling that we would not see each other again. When I looked into the eyes of some of my comrades, I could see they thought the same.'

Kohler stayed for two days. Guschewski spoke for hours about Neuerburg, Brandt, Kessler and the other men he knew from *U-869*. He told Kohler that he missed his friends.

'It is horrible for me to see the way the boat lies broken in the ocean,' Guschewski said. 'For more than fifty years, I remembered it as new and strong, and I was part of it. Now I look at the film and pictures and see the remains of my comrades . . . It is very difficult and sad for me to think of it this way.

'I believe in God and an afterlife. It would be wonderful to be reunited with my friends, to see them again, and to see them continue in peace, not in war, not in a time when so many young lives were lost for no reason. I would like to see them like that.'

Finally, Kohler and Guschewski rose and shook hands. Kohler's flight to New Jersey departed in just a few hours. As Kohler reached for his coat, Guschewski made a request. 'Might it be possible to send me something from the boat?' he asked. 'Anything would do. Anything I could touch.'

'I would be happy to,' Kohler said. 'I will send you something the moment I return home.'

'That would mean very much to me,' Guschewski said. He waved goodbye to Kohler and closed the door.

As Kohler walked towards his car, he felt the bands of his obligation loosen. No one should lie anonymous at the bottom of the ocean. A family needs to know where their loved one lies.

It had grown colder outside since Kohler had arrived. He reached for his car keys. Guschewski pushed open his front door and walked into the winter. He moved towards Kohler and put his arms round the diver.

'Thank you for caring,' Guschewski said. 'Thank you for coming here.'

SHADOW DIVERS

Left page: 1 The *Seeker* was built for a single purpose: to take scuba divers to the most dangerous shipwrecks in the Atlantic Ocean. **2** Richie Kohler after bagging up on the mystery U-boat wreck. **3** A dish recovered by John Chatterton, marked with the eagle and swastika, dated 1942. **4** John Chatterton (left) and Richie Kohler. **5** Richie Kohler, 'tonnage king' and Atlantic Wreck Diver.

Right page: 6 The U-boat's periscope. **7** Horenburg's knife. **8** One of the U-boat's steel hatches. **9** The lost crew of *U-869*, in a photograph taken after commissioning on January 26, 1944. **10**. Chatterton and Kohler in the summer of 1996.